To Byron,

I hope you enjoy my story.

Best regards,

Jerry

Westfest, 2007

Join other readers on our website's
Reader's Forum and tell me what
you think about my story?
www.smultron-pub.com

European Invasion-Battle Timeline

IRELAND

GREAT BRITAIN

London · Amsterdam

Eisenhower

Atlantic Ocean

English Channel (June 1944)

BELGIUM

Invasion of Normandy
(D-Day, 6 June 1944)

Montgomery
(Aug. 1944-May 1945)

Paris · Bradley
(Aug. 1944-
May 1945)

FRANCE

Vichy ·

Lyons ·

Patch
(Aug.-Sept. 1944)

PORTUGAL

Madrid ⊕

SPAIN

Pyrenees

ANDORRA

From Great Britain

Gibraltar
(Great Britain)

Ryder
(Nov. 1942)

Alexander
(Nov. 1942-May 1943)

(Nov. 1942)

SPANISH MOROCCO

Mazagan · Port Lyautey

·lanca ·

Oran

Fredendall

Algiers

ALGERIA

Bône ·

MOROCCO

First edition, 2007

Published by:

Smultron Publications
715-664-8130
www.smultron-pub.com

Dedication

This work is dedicated to emigrants, no matter when, or from where they originated, for having the courage to be different and to venture into a new land, a new culture and a new langage.

And to the men and women who have participated in any war, in order to quell the aggression of those who would bully a population into submission to their selfish wills. Courage is the most important value one can hold. It gives a person the ability to step forward, as a minority of one and be the first to say no, in the face of adversity. *My Enemy's Child* touches on a few of those persons, on both sides of a conflict.

ISBN 978-0-9789854-0-0

My Enemy's Child

G. R. Revelle

Acknowledgments:

In researching the historical facts, in order to make the work as accurate as my own, limited knowledge would permit, I resorted to researching several "actual" accounts on the world-wide-web. But to really prove the knowledge, I also interviewed actual (live) combatants from the era and had the good fortune to have the bomber scenes, in particular, vetted by two former RAF Bomber Command members, veterans of The Era. And courtesy of the US Army Air Corps, later to become the USAF, I was also channeled important navigation fact from the time, from American and British veterans of many bombing runs.

Special thanks are warmly extended to the following:

Everyone who offered continued encouragement and helped to proof the manuscript copies.

In June of 2002 I interviewed (the now, late) Mr. Howard W. Roemer in his home in Eau Claire, Wisconsin. Serving in the U.S. Army Air Corps, *Mighty Eighth Air Force*, Bombardier – Class 43-8, 94th Bomb Group – B17, Howard was stationed in England, at Bury Saint Edmonds and flew many daylight bombing missions over Europe in B17s, as a bombardier, for which he received the Distinguished Flying Cross. Although the aircraft type was not the same (as in this work) and American missions were flown in daylight, rather than night-time (as with the RAF), I found some of his experiences in B17s similar to the accounts of British airmen and found Howard's interview extremely helpful. Information gleaned from this conversation offered insight into my further questions of other combatants.

As an instrument pilot myself, I had structured my questions well in advance of the interview, to hopefully touch on areas of flying an airplane (fully-loaded bomber), not normally depicted in novels of this sort. Of particular interest to me and possibly ponderous to the casual reader, were the mechanics of flight preparations—pre-flight/post-flight briefings, debriefings, engineering and ground crew duties and the like.

Just the task of getting an aircraft, fully-loaded with 100 octane gasoline and a ton or so of high explosives, off the ground, was an accomplishment. But preparing for a flight into the heart of Europe, in the dark of night and then getting back again safely on the ground before daylight, considering the climate in England—must have been really touch-and-go. Though some radio direction equipment was available on the ground, the pilots had nothing to compare with today's modern navigation/guidance equipment: NDBs, VORs or ILS systems. GPS, of course, was unthinkable, as we know it today (non-pilots, please excuse the acronyms).

As a result of my different approach to questions, the place Howard had to go in his memory, for the answers, brought to light entirely new recollections. Mrs. Roamer, hearing his new reminiscences from where she'd adjourned in the kitchen, soon joined us at the dining room table, saying: "these are stories I've never heard before. And as Howard's recall reached back over 60 years, she and I sat, mesmerized. Unfortunately, Howard has passed away since the interview and will not be able to see the fruit borne partially from his reminisces.

And to a couple of Englishman I have never met: Mr. Dave Sanderson, current keeper of the "Night Flyer" the official newsletter of the 96 Squadron Association for the RAF and Charles H Pinion, who takes care of *Avro Lancaster Heavy Bomber* Website.

Dave Sanderson kindly picked up a query of mine from the web site he care-takes for the *96 Squadron Association RAF*, for which I owe him a very big thank you. Engrossed in writing about fighter squadron combat during the early stages of the novel, I was seeking specific information about Britain's Spitfire and Hurricane fighters, their specific flying times-in-air—fuel consumption, ammunition availability, etc..

It was from Dave I learned the true (*attributed*) meaning of a term I once though had to do with sporting events: "the whole nine yards," which, according to Dave, is accounted to mean the exact length of the full ammunition belt for a machine gun in the British Spitfire fighter. Does a pilot give the enemy merely a burst of fire, or *the whole, nine yards*, in continuous fire? The *Spit* would exhaust its nine yards of ammunition in about 12 seconds continuously firing, 1200 rounds per minute, at 60 rounds per minute (RPM) per gun. The term supposedly was coined in the Pacific Theater.

Once Dave learned I was also in need of navigational methodology of the era—I was working on the bombing runs by then—he again rose to the occasion, querying friends and voluntarily researching information about the subject for me. Dave funneled many articles my way, covering the specifics of methods and equipment used by the RAF for night flying and bombing runs, for fighters and bombers, which differed in both complexity and problems from the American's daylight sorties. Without Dave's kind, accurate assistance, this volume would have taken far longer to write and could easily have lacked whatever exactness I've been able to attain.

When I needed technical specifics about the Avro Lancaster bomber, Charles H Pinion provided extensive information about the Lanc's hydraulic system, operating and controlling the undercarriage (landing gear) and flaps. His offering gave me a wider understanding of the ship's flaps and hydraulic systems.

It was through Dave Sanderson that I was able to query another *Brit* and former *Hurrybird* and *Spit* pilot, Mike Isherwood-Bennet. Mike provided additional information, through Dave. Before Mike was finished, he asked Dave to request that I "ring-up" an American aviator acquaintance of his living in Colorado. The American turned out to be none other than Wilson "Bill" V. Edwards, Major (Ret.), who served in the American Eagle Squadron in England during the war.

I eagerly complied by calling Bill; but he wasn't home at the time, though I later learned why. Here is a veteran of the second war who by 2003 must have been getting on in age. So where was he when I'd called? Out giving aerial acrobatics instruction to some young pilots (probably in their 60s). I did reach Bill eventually and he agreed to help me with my project, asking for the draft of the novel to date, with post-it notes marking the areas I was concerned about. He said he'd go through it and also pass it around to anyone else "...still alive by the time," he'd finished, for another look.

Bill read it as promised and passed along a wealth of technical terminology about aerial combat, for which I'm very grateful; thanks Bill!

Maj. Wilson V. Edwards, FO
336th Fighter Squadron
Squadron 133
American Eagle Squadron

To further insure accuracy in the combat flying and bombing sequences, I was fortunate in 2003 to have a British business associate, living in the south of England near The Solent. Sharing flying interests as fellow pilots, he and I had flown and worked together in both America and England, in our respective Beech aircraft, both of us at the time owning our own *Sundowners*, on either side of the Atlantic.

It was a rainy day when we trudged the soggy moor among the bristly gorse and shin-high heather around the New Forest. Near Bournemoth, in the south of England, he pointed out the eroded, weed-grown cement foundations, bristling with rusted bolts from long-removed emplacements of forgotten military apparatus. According to my guide these were remnants of one of the "bouncing bomb" test areas used by the "Dam Busters" team, endeavoring to prove their theories in the early stages of that rather now-famous tactical bombing development. To destroy many *Nazi* controlled dams in Europe, the British perfected a technique to fly over a targeted lake dam at a given height, drop and bounce a rotating, cylindrical bomb onto the water's surface. This delivery method caused the cylinder to bounce several times, until it finally slowed, striking the top of the dam...somewhat like hitting a fence before sinking and exploding deep underwater and rupturing the concrete dam. Certainly, this was one of England's many innovative applications of trigonometry and physics...landing a bouncing projectile against the vulnerable base of several hydroelectric power dams.

When I later learned both my British guide's father and father-in-law were former RAF Bomber Command pilots in the war over Europe, I quickly enlisted his help to tap those two sources of knowledge and experience in order to vet some of the bomber flying scenes in this work.

I was able to get a draft manuscript to these two gentlemen, to "give the book a read," in an effort to further warrant the details of bomber flying at night (the RAF bombed at night and the USAF, by day). Needless to say, I got far more than I'd bargained for, as they quickly pointed out many significant differences between how the British bomber pilots conducted their missions, versus we Americans. Regarding statistics, terminology, etc., there were some significant differences. I was fortunate, indeed, for without their aid, these sequences would not have been nearly as historically and technically correct.

When I asked for the specifics of the gentlemen's credentials regarding their military service, in order to honor them here, they both preferred I not use their ranks, nor would they proffer information about their assorted military decorations, deeming it sufficient to simply supply their names and having been a part of RAF Bomber Command. I list them alphabetically, below:

Mr. Thomas "Tom" Addis, RAF Bomber Command
Mr. Peter Ward-Hunt, RAF Bomber Command

Luckily, "Tom" Addis and I shared a few precious moments together over a gin 'n tonic in the summer of 2004. He'd brought along his original WW-II Bomber Command logbook which began with his first flight. We poured over this in the living room of his son's home in Ferndown. This was, long after I'd completed the second draft of this work. At that meeting I learned Tom actually participated in the "Battle of the Barges" scene, which I'd already related in this work. The information I'd originally drawn from was based on other articles and written accounts. So it was a pleasure to hear the story from a real participant and quite a coincidence, I thought at the time. I was saddened to learn before the publication of this work that Tom Addis had joined so many other veterans in death.

Mr. Ward-Hunt had previously served in the same squadron as Capt. Guy Gibson. Most of the credit for the "dam buster" project's success are attributed the Capt. Gibson. Mr. Ward-Hunt had transferred out of his command, prior to the dam buster endeavor. Known as the "Bouncing Bomb", the raids eventually resulted in the filming of an early, semi-fictional (black and white) movie. Several television documentaries and more recently, a British postal stamp, have since commemorated the event. The photo upon which the postage stamp (British) was based came from a snapshot taken prior to the dam busting adventure and included Peter Ward-Hunt, who was still in the "Gibson" group at the time.

Thank you one and all for you kind assistance and generosity, so willingly offered; I know your efforts made this book more readable and certainly lent confidence that my story was as accurate as I could possibly make it, for the time and the eventual readers.

Our Writers Group

And last but certainly not least, to Sharon and Bob, able companions in our writing enclave, now well over fifteen years old. Our twice monthly get-togethers to discuss ongoing and past projects proved the value of trusted, writing friends who unselfishly serve as sounding boards to ideas, themes and dialog, speaking up fearlessly to criticize, or praise, each other's endeavors. Let us hope our invention of the exercise, *real-time writing* will inspire other writer's groups to experiment as we do, in order to prosper in their own creative endeavors and that their work will be heard with well-meant criticism and they, too, will grow from the experience, as I have.

1

CHAPTER

A June Wedding and Old Memories

America, 1960

Robert Johnson ducked into the shade behind the faded brick church in the Midwestern town where he'd grown up. It was a hot, clear June Sunday…ideal for the wedding. A tuxedo jacket was crooked over his shoulder on one finger. Ancient red gum trees shaded the old graveyard. Mindful of getting rust on his trousers he edged through the squeaky, iron gate. No one would notice him idling among the tilted tombstones.

His second appearance at the church in two hours, he'd driven his adopted daughter Kate over earlier, with a car-full of "necessary items." As a lifelong bachelor, learning about children proved a never-ending experience, from little girls to grown women, as his Kate grew from a child of three, to a woman of twenty-two years.

An hour earlier he'd struggled up the narrow church stairway carrying her bridal grown safely enclosed in a crackling, plastic envelope. She followed with a make-up case and who knew what else, in a brown grocery bag.

"Got everything Honey," he asked, pausing at the half-open dressing room door, after grinning at the shrieks from her curler-adorned attendants, when she'd opened the door without knocking.

"Honestly…!" she remarked, frowning at her entourage before turning back to her father.

"Thanks Daddy…I think so…I'll call you if we forgot something."

"OK…. Guess I'll be off then Kate?"

But he didn't move. They stood looking at one another

for a few seconds. Finally she put an arm on his arm.

"Don't you go an' get dirty now Daddy...once you're changed into your tux."

"Don't worry Honey." he bent, kissing her forehead, "I won't."

"'N' don't dawdle either, Daddy. We don't want you bein' late for my wedding."

"Quit worrying Sweets...I wouldn't miss this day for anything."

They both knew this was their last moments together with her as a single woman...as his little girl. Waving to her as the door closed he turned and thumped down the groaning steps. The church smelled of polishing oil, soap and fresh flowers.

He'd gone home to the very empty house. It almost startled him it was so still without her. He almost expected to hear "...that you, Daddy...?" come from the kitchen.

He crossed directly to the hall closet and removed a garment bag. By the table, he took out a tuxedo and hung it on the open bathroom door. He stood looking at it for a moment and then glanced at the clock on the table. It was too early to dress.

Finally in bored frustration, he plodded into the front room and turned on the radio. After dialing past a few of the many sermons in progress, he abruptly flicked off the set and crossed to the window facing the front yard, where he stared out on the empty street, looking for something to occupy himself with.

The lawn was freshly cut. He glanced over at his empty car in the driveway. The car was clean...he washed it the day before The windows were up. It's gonna get hot in there, he thought, but didn't want to brave the heat again to roll them down.

He stepped closer to the window, drawing aside the translucent sheer. Glancing at the flowerbeds along the driveway, he thought about pulling out a couple of weeds he could see peeking from the iris. But he'd showered already.

He turned, finally, returning to the hallway where he grabbed the tux hanger and went to his bedroom and began slowly undressing. Standing in front of the bureau's mirror, buttoning the stiff shirt, he was trying to remember the last time he'd worn a tuxedo.

But he couldn't. Maybe chaperoning one of Kate's high school dances, he thought? He slipped on the sharply-creased trousers.

I remember the first time, though: England, 1939—a party at uh...some hotel, in the south...he struggled to fold the starched French cuffs on the long, shirt sleeves. It had been a real party and also his introduction to the world of espionage.

"Not so many zippers, snaps and elastic then." He mumbled around a cuff link held between his lips. He watched his hands in the mirror as he struggled to push through one of his father's old silver cufflinks. Finishing the second link he began struggling with the cumberbun.

After some moments he was satisfied. Picking up the jacket, he slipped it on and buttoned the center button before turning sideways to the mirror. He dropped his arms momentarily, pulled down each shirt sleeve again and dropped his arms again. He pivoted slightly in front of the mirror, admiring the trim figure he still cut.

"Quarter inch of cuff..." he said aloud, curled fingertips even with the jacket bottom. "Good fit..." he said, nodding to the graying head that stared back at him.

Stiff with starched cotton and new-pressed wool, he walked through the house and out to the front porch.

"Better get the dry cleaner smell out of this though..." he said to the screen door.

Outside, he removed the jacket, draped it across the back of a metal lawn chair and sat down in the flanking porch swing, hanging empty from chains suspended from the ceiling. So often he and Kate had sat here on the warm summer evenings, talking. In later years, she'd preferred to sit alone...with boyfriends. But he'd wait and after the boy had gone home, he'd join her and they would discuss their respective days or evenings. Usually, she'd eventually get around to telling him about the boy and how the date had gone. These were nice evenings of togetherness draped in the heavy summer smell of the flowers she'd kept blooming around the house and yard since she was a young girl, after her step-grandma had died.

Flexing his knees, he set the chains to squeaking rhythmically. Mockingbirds in the mulberry tree were arguing with an absent cat. He soon relaxed with the rhythm of the swing. This wedding's going to change me back to a single-person family—something I haven't been since...since I was...what, twenty-five, he thought?

"God, the time went fast," he said toward the screen wire. "She really grew up so fast."

Lost in the past for a bit, he fidgeted absently with a cuff link, rolling it idly between thumb and forefinger as he rocked rhythmically and watched the street as the occasional car passed. Returning from church, he suspected, glancing at his wristwatch. Each car was either filled with a family, a couple, or a single occupant—single old men or single old ladies.

Bachelors, widowers...old maids or widows, he thought. For some reason the sight of them disturbed him, probably knowing he was destined to join them in the distant future. He turned his thoughts away, preferring to follow the reflection the cuff link flashed on the ceiling as he idly turned it with his other hand. He no longer glanced up at the sound of a passing car but occupied himself with focusing the reflection on assorted targets on the ceiling before growing bored again.

"It's gettin' hot," he commented to the morning glories after he hit every target of any size on the ceiling. Already well up the trellis, the mixture of blue and red blooms were folded inward in daytime slumber, reclining against the rusty screen in the bright, midday heat.

"Widowers—and widows," he said aloud, thinking again of the passing cars.

"That'll be me, soon enough, one car, one driver...'til I'm too old to drive," he laughed aloud at himself suddenly beginning to feel sorry for himself.

"To hell with that thinking...." He stood up abruptly, pushing out of the swing. Grabbing the tux jacket he kicked open the screen door and tripped down the front steps toward the car.

"There'll always be somebody to talk to over at the church," he said stepping lightly over the iris. He opened the car door and recoiled momentarily from the blast of hot air that greeted him. He rolled down the front windows before starting the car. Putting it in gear and backing out the drive, he had another idea as he reversed gears, If I go 'round back of the church...to the tombstones, I can check on the old folks graves. "Plenty of family there to talk to."

There were no cars remaining from the morning service and the wedding arrivals hadn't started coming yet—just the wedding party, he guessed and the church volunteers: cooks, food servers and such. Parking in the shade beneath the ancient trees he got out and crossed the narrow street. Glancing over his shoulder, he didn't believe anyone saw him dawdling along the side of the red brick building as he headed toward the cemetery gate.

Despite the shade in the graveyard, he draped his tuxedo jacket over the cast-iron fence that enclosed his great-grandfather's plot. Hands in pockets he began to wander around, stopping momentarily to glance at the assortment of stone shapes, reading the names and dates for the hundredth time. Most of the stones were afflicted with a frilly, mossy growth which, on some, nearly obliterated the hand-cut inscriptions in the soft limestone. Time had had its way with the grainy monoliths. Several markers dated from the mid-eighteen hundreds.

"Before then," he'd remembered his father saying, "...our people were in Illinois—Tennessee, North Carolina. And way back...*England.*"

One stone he always saved for last. It was his mother's. It had a poem carved in Swedish text, just below her name. Below and to the side of the words, a stem with leaves and bluebells—flowers. He'd fussed over the design with the monument company's manager...giving him special instructions to get the queer, Swedish letters just right in the inscription, with the extra dots and rings over some of the letters. The date of death was scarcely fifteen years ago. It'd turned out pretty nice. Kate liked it too, though she was only a little girl at the time.

He knew the Sunday before Kate had put a fruit jar-full of wildflowers on the grave. The water was long gone and the flowers now stiff and brittle looking. This was going to be a hot summer, he thought. When this shindig's over, I'll have more time...next week, maybe. I'll pick more flowers and bring them out...while she's off...honey-moonin'. Maybe get some of the irises if they're still coming along.

"Won't have anything else to do," he spoke to his mother's stone. "Nothin' at all, Mom." It was turning out to be a sort of bittersweet day. He couldn't shake the note of depression over losing his daughter.

He gathered the waterless jar and spent flowers and strolled back toward the gate. Leaning over the boundary fence, he shook the dry stems into the tall grass of the hay field. The sound of an arriving car made him look up and then glance at his watch. Tentative organ sounds wafted around the corner...a little early practice warm-up, he thought...still plenty of time.

"That'd be Betty-Lou, the preacher's wife." Setting the jar beside the fence, he turned back toward the plot: "Still some time yet."

Sauntereing over to retrieve his jacket he considered again the importance of the day. They'd spoken often about the *someday*...when her prince charming would finally come. Ever since he'd brought her back from Europe. The tale had begun with fairy tale books, he guessed. First, it was the prince charming stories and then—when Kate was a gawky-looking, eleven or twelve year-old, hc'd had to reassure her of her hidden beauty again and again, that...someday, her prince would truly come.

He'd assured himself privately, that the beauty of her mother...which he knew lay just beneath the awkward movements and gangly body, would one day, burst forth. He'd read Kate the ugly duckling stories...the little homely duck that turned into a glorious swan. Then...when she'd finally started to fill out, losing her ungainly appearance, the crisis of a little acne had to be worked through.

Well, *he'd* finally come, her prince...not long after she'd bloomed gloriously with her late mother's beauty. And the prince didn't have far to travel, living just across town. Strange, Robert never thought it would be quite like this, though. He really felt like he was losing the most important thing in his life...since her mother.

"I'll sure miss her...just home from college a year and now, gettin' married..." he said to the draped jacket as he deftly plucked it from the fence. "Knew it was comin'...of course. Ronnie will make her a good husband...good stock and good kin for us. She needs a family around her. Now the folks are gone..." he stared at the stones within the fence.

"She needs more than just me. It's time...there'll be grandkids soon enough…probably."

He tried to conjure a feeling for what that might be like but gave up, wondering whether he'd have the energy for them by the time they arrived. With a final glance at his mother's stone he started for the front of the church, sorting out the right sleeve of the jacket as he walked.

With one arm in the jacket, the sound of an approaching aircraft made him stop, cock an ear and listen. He lifted his free arm up against the bright sunshine. The sound came from high over the trees. He pulled his arm from the jacket and staggering around the lawn, trying to locate the airplane, staring through the foliage before finally spying the speck just below the towering cumulus. He stepped back into the shadow holding up the jacket in one arm against the glare watching the fast-approaching aircraft. After a moment, he spoke again:

"It's a biplane."

He smiled, recognizing the pair of wings and stubby-shape, as it worked it's way toward him.

"An old Stearman—1930s…" he squinted, "…from the beginning of the last war…crop dusted in one like that, before I went over…" he trailed off still grinning upward. Soon he smiled shaking his head in wonder at the old memories.

As the aircraft drew closer the nose suddenly turned upward and he heard the radial engine's labored roar from the steep climb. Spellbound, he watched as it's nose dropped suddenly and the brightly-colored aircraft began gaining airspeed in a shallow dive. On and on it came, until the pilot hauled back the stick and the aircraft climbed again…up, up, *up*… its flight slowing. Just beneath the scattered clouds, it seemed ready to stop in mid-air—pointing straight up, ready to stall and tumble backwards. But the skillful pilot nursed it on over the top, doing a perfect hammerhead stall and turn before the plane plunged downward again, engine screaming. Robert had twisted and turned his body in sympathy to the imagined control efforts of the pilot.

"He's really good," Robert said, again, grinning despite himself.

The wedding was momentarily forgotten.

"He's sure havin' some fun…."

He reached up, shading his eyes, grinning again as the radial engine roared, carrying the plane into another steep dive as it picked up airspeed, leveled, then started another climb. Up, up—up he went, gaining altitude but again losing airspeed in the climb. The nose dropped again and down he came, picking up airspeed...before, quickly—up, upside down and then completely over, this time, in a full loop, coming out smoothly in level flight, going in the opposite direction...all this to the screaming cylinders of the vintage engine.

Robert leaned against the iron pickets of the fence, oblivious to the increasing traffic on the other side of the church. He could feel every tug and pull of the pilot's seat harness and visualize the ever-rolling horizon in his imagination and he tasted the smell of exhaust and oil washing past the open cockpit from the prop's slipstream. The pilot was executing every maneuver by the book-—like a drill and Robert was right up there with him.

"Precision...that's what he's going for," he noted. "Precision counts...save your life in combat. Aircraft were unforgiving, like the sea. Make a mistake and if the other guy's waiting...you buy it—it's his job, just like it's yours...to get him first."

He strolled beside the fence, following the plane's meandering just beneath the cloud bottoms, now heading further toward the south. Robert was transported back to another time...another place, lost in memories of greater risks and greater rewards. He no longer saw the Stearman climb and fall, turn, roll and loop against the blue sunlight, spattered by high, cumulous cloud. He saw a *Foch Wolf,* or a *Messerschmitt,* suddenly appearing from out of the sun. And diving, kicking his imaginary rudder pedals hard, he'd fall off and try to loose the attacking German aircraft that still sometimes haunted his nightly dreams.

A horn sounded behind him then and he reluctantly turned from the spectacle, inserted his other arm in the tux's sleeve and started for the church.

"Those were other times..." he said and buttoned the jacket as he hastening around the church, "...long, gone times."

England, 1940 — The Solent

The squadron was coming up through heavy cumulous, breaking out into a brilliant blue sky. Hurricane fighters were well spread out as we continued to climb southeastward above the heavy cloud, 6000 feet over *The Channel*. I banked in a climbing turn and saw Foster's kite pop out of the stuff off my right wing. Instead of continuing the climb to altitude, he immediately dropped his nose, picked up airspeed and bored on, just above the cloud, corkscrewing forward, breaking in and out of the puffy tops and making a grand show of it all for the *newbies*. A trail of swirling cloud followed his Hurricane for a while, painting white powder against the color of his kite. The red of the circular target on his ship's side in bright contrast. He finally broke off after a few rotations and continued his climb out with the rest of the squadron.

God, I thought, too tired to waste energy getting angry. *Why* does he do that—ignoring the regs about acrobatics? It only encourages the green pilots to misbehave and get themselves in trouble. *Hurrybirds*...they'd taken to calling the Hurricanes by that name.

And we were in a hurry—without a doubt we were; Hitler had made certain of that. I could hardly remember when I'd slept for six hours straight. But—last evening, we had, collapsing after two, earlier missions. And we were still exhausted.

Ignoring Foster's juvenile antics I dipped my left wing, glancing at the balance of the squadron, all nearly up and through the stuff, now. I began silently to count the bulky fighters as they approached my own Hurricane, slowly closing in and forming up for combat. We'd gotten word of an inbound German bomber flight and were on our way to intercept.

I knew why Foster did it...he'd already lived longer than any of us and simply no longer cared. This was what...his sixth...maybe his seventh Hurricane, since joining Fighter Command? He was in the squadron when I took command and that was over a year ago. I wondered whether he even remembered how many aircraft had been shot out from around him. The odds were squeezing him. He knew it and I knew it, too, as the second longest time in squadron pilot, myself. We were both overdue. Foster'd taken to saying he'd soon use up all the Hurricanes in the RAF and start on the Spits, before he finally bought it, he reckoned.

Glancing around again, I could see everyone was finally up to altitude and had begun forming in close. As they grouped in front of my *kite* I maintained the steady climbing course southeastward toward intercept altitude. I noted the altimeter and reluctantly began fitting my oxygen mask, having put it off as long as I dared. We continued droning upward, closing the formation tighter and tighter as we went into the hunt. It wouldn't be long. GIC[1] had given us an estimated time to encounter the approaching bombers...not long at all, I thought, glancing at my wristwatch.

By strict order we'd maintained radio silence since taking off from Group 11, RAF Hornbeam. From time to time, we could hear pilot chatter from other fellows in the thick of it elsewhere. I suspected they were somewhere to westward...maybe around The Lizard. Their chatter was pretty faint and faded completely from time to time. My eyes did the unconscious flying panel scan, noting the gauge readings without consciously seeing them. The *kite* was functioning perfectly.

Closing the group at last, we were now in the tight, protective flight formation we would maintain until we sighted enemy aircraft, or were ourselves sighted. Ten minutes passed...any time now, I thought—Jerry'l show. Earlier, on the ground, the approaching German bombers had been reported just as we were enjoying our tea, disturbing the squadron breakfast and taking us away from our well-earned rest. I was still unconsciously sucking bits of toast and marmalade from my back teeth, confined now by my rubber oxygen mask. They'd have fighter cover, I thought...we could bank on that—the heavy bombers.

We flew on. I didn't usually doubt GIC, but we should've encountered aircraft by now. I didn't appreciate having so much time to think...and we were using precious fuel. I liked getting in and getting out as soon as the Hurricane's cartridge caches were depleted. Then, turn for home, land, refuel, rearm and go up again, if there were still bombers threatening—and there usually were.

Waiting. This was the hardest time. The time when I began

to sweat—always, just before we sighted the approaching aircraft. Inside my mask I could feel the condensing dampness begin to run past my nose. It was like the signal that alerted my other senses, making the rubber inside the mask smell differently. With each quickening breath, the odor grew stronger. Was it the smell of fear—my fear? Hell...I knew it was. I'd even started getting goose bumps. And then, *the trembles*—as I secretly called them, would begin. Lately, I had taken to having a very bad case of nerves. Were the situations reversed and I knew any one of my pilots was similarly afflicted, I'd ground any of the Group in an instant. *Sauce for the goose*...I mused.

At first I'd thought nothing of the minor trembling of my extremities, laughing sardonically to myself—but not mentioning it to anyone. The *Old Man* at 24—I was that scared. Maybe he couldn't handle it any more, they might think. My nerves had grown much worse, of late. In fact, they'd gotten bad enough that I didn't even want to admit it to myself. I could feel the twitching beginning in my finger. It was the shakes and I knew it.

Absently, I tweaked the burn mixture control, cracking it a little, watching the EGT gauge rise, indicating the exhaust manifold temperature was rising on the engine...giving it a slightly leaner fuel burn. Just before I let my left hand fall back atop my thigh, I noticed the slight trembling of the glove's fingertips. I watched my hand...willed it to stop. But it didn't.

Glancing out the perspex canopy, I saw Green staring at me from off my port-side wing. He made a futile gesture with his left arm as if to say: "...where are they?" I shook my head and shrugged inside my sheepskin, pointing to my eyes and then the headphones nestled in my goggle cap. I hadn't seen or heard anything I signaled.

After another five minutes I began hearing *Jerry* conversation in my headphones. There were still no visible bombers approaching toward our side of The Channel. Radio range for our TR9Ds[2] was around 35—40 miles at this altitude. I was also watching for advance fighters we knew would be covering the Heinkel bombers, heading north. This was our chance to have a piece of them before they crossed The Solent on their way up to Derbyshire and Yorkshire in the north and the valuable industrial targets they would find, along with a little flak from us.

I glanced around our group of *kites*. As far to each side as I could see, everyone was maintaining tight formation. We continued steering one-zero-five, the course *Control* said we should intercept them on. Looking out across the wing, each aircraft rose and fell slowly, moved in and out, but generally were maintaining altitude well as a tight group. The RAF had mostly given up formation flight for small squadrons of our sort but I liked the discipline it brought to the group, when we had the time to take it on. The men grumbled, but I knew the value of piloting skills; everything helped and it just might keep one of them alive longer. I felt it also brought us some of the closeness we might not be able to obtain on the ground, eye-to-eye, so to speak——our airborne family. We'd had so many losses and replacements, there wasn't enough time to knit...become close. In addition, it just possibly added self-discipline.

I glanced across at Ashcraft, our newest addition. I was surprised he was doing as well as he was and only his second combat mission at that. He'd done badly on the first—not unusual, damn near taking off Roberts' horizontal stabilizer when he failed to throttle back enough. Now Roberts was laying for him. So I'd tucked Ashcraft up front with me, hopefully out of harm's way. Hemmed in as he was, he couldn't run into anyone in front and anyone behind him could slack off their own RPM, should he begin to slow his Hurricane for some reason...unless it was Roberts.

We continued under radio silence, boring on for another five minutes, possibly toward the source of the Jerry radio chatter. I went over the aircraft ground prep again in my head: fueling, arming, checking the engine, the guns—undercarriage...I'd gone over the fueling routine so many times with the ground crew to insure they were following my standing orders for maximum fuel. I'd felt reassured, as I watched them tip up the kites by the tail-plane to top off the tanks, holding the ass-end up high, to warrant every drop of fuel was added in the air gap at the top of the tanks. If the ships remained reclining on their tail wheels—a portion of the slanted fuel tanks wouldn't be filled. This way they'd have maximum range, just over two hours in the air, with normal maneuvers. Far more fuel than we ever had ammunition for, if we encountered *Jerry*.

I'd come up with the boys again today because so many

were still green and unproven. In this flight alone, we had four near *virgins*, counting Ashcraft—pilots who'd never seen combat before this week. In times like these I always tried to stay above the action and call the targets, shout warnings and generally sweat for them all, young and old alike, all the while trying to keep my own backside intact. I felt it'd saved many a new pilot for a while, anyway. More than once I'd offered advance warning of a pending bushwhack from behind.

No more than five minutes passed before Baxter broke radio silence:

"There they go, Cap—whole *gaggle* at four o'clock—low! We missed 'em!"

Sure enough, there were the bombers below and to the right. We'd nearly flown past two, large formations.

"Right...let's get 'em boys."

As a group, we began turning toward them. Peering closer at the approaching aircraft, I was confused. As we drew closer there was no mistaking the familiar *swastika* and cross. They weren't the old familiar *Heinkels* though...some different bomber type. Their *Stuka* fighter cover must be out ahead of them, behind and to the west of us now. That meant they'd soon be back, now that we'd been sighted. But it would give us some time alone with these helpless, pregnant mothers, possibly take a few down, first.

"Flight one 'n two, go for 'em. You greenhorns—Red-1 'n Red 3—try 'n get under 'em—but stay away from the gunners. Flights three, four and five—take the ass-end of the south bunch."

Watching the approaching formation, I finally realized these bombers must be the Ju 88s we'd been briefed on earlier. We'd not seen this *Junkers* type before today.

"If those are the new *Junkers,* they're suppose to be vulnerable from behind, lads...but watch it—'til you know for sure."

"We won't go in the back door—without ringing their bell first," someone shouted in the radio.

Then they were well on their way, peeling off to do their own hunting, live or die on their own now. I climbed up and held back for a bit to see what shaped up in the skirmish behind the bombers, keeping my eyes open for *Stukas*. There were more heavy bombers coming from the east. Another *gaggle* to the southeast also—there'd be fighters too, somewhere...soon!

Then, their *Stuka* escorts came on fast, returning from the west after having over flown us. I turned to follow my first flight, coming up under the action, already underway and just in time to strafe an inbound *Stuka* on the way. I didn't see any smoke or pieces come away as we quickly met and flashed past each other. I tromped left rudder and dove, trying to get under yet another. As I came around I caught a burst from someone I couldn't see. I'd hoped it was a Stuka, but there was no telling with so many trigger-happy kids up this time. And it wouldn't be the first time I'd caught friendly fire.

But nothing seemed to come off me as I held the Hurricane in the dive. Then, as I came on, rolling up and around I saw Ashcraft above and ahead of me, closing on a *Stuka* from behind—really behind. It looked like he was going to get in the back seat with the rear gunner.

"Red-3—*Ashcraft*—you damn fool...." I held the mike button, shouting into my mask, "...get below 'im. He's gonna' cut you in two if you get on top."

But Ashcraft wasn't listening. He was frozen with some sort of green pilot fixation, on the German in front of him, prime meat for the sharp-eyed rear gunner, who I could see sitting, facing backward. I wondered why he wasn't firing the *Stuka's* guns. After a second I realized why Ashcraft was still alive. The gunner was slumped forward, beneath the long, perspex canopy. His head lolled against the clear plastic, smearing blood at each roll of the aircraft, as the pilot swerved from side to side, trying to shake off Ashcraft. The *Stuka's* canopy was pocked and shattered from several bursts. But that close, Ashcraft couldn't hit a bull in the ass....

"Ashcraft, back off—you're too close. You're guns 'er firin' over him...."

But he didn't hear me. I was afraid he was going to over-fly the *Stuka* and fall on top of him, get his belly cut up from its prop. But he didn't. I saw his machine gun fire turn to tracer, indicating only a couple seconds more ammunition remained. He flew right up the guy's ass and started chewing away the horizontal stabilizer with his own prop. In a matter of seconds his prop would begin parting company with the shaft.

The *Stuka* pilot had little choice, becoming unstable immediately. Shuddering, it suddenly fell forward into a steep dive then began tumbling over and over, now completely out of control without most of its stabilizer and rudder. Having lost the ability to level off, the German pilot was attempting to fly the *Stuka* with only the ailerons—but failing miserably. Ashcraft continued following him. Part of the *Stuka's* rudder'd come off and went over Ashcraft's kite, I noticed as both of them disappeared below us.

"Christ, Ashcraft, turn back and head toward home," Jergens shouted as he passed. "You'll never make it on that prop—you'll be closer when you finally ditch...*hurry!*"

Coming around again I saw Ashcraft finally break off, seeming to come out of his daze, at last.

"Try for a landfall around Dover and bail out," I shouted. "Ashcraft—you're not gonna make it...."

I didn't have time to nursemaid him further; just then I caught a burst from a passing fighter—barely missing me. I kicked right rudder and fell off on the wing to see who was around. I spotted a *Stuka* just as he flamed and lost a wing. Good job—somebody.

I kicked the rudder again and hauled the stick, rolling completely around to see if someone was under me—and there was. But one of our guys was on him from behind and the *Stuka* broke off firing at me to maneuver away. Everyone seemed to have their own *Stuka* at the moment, so I decided to have a go at the bombers. I came up fast under one of the larger ships to a full complement of fire from guns in her under-nose. There didn't seem to be any belly turret or waist gunners though the nose gunner could fire aft somewhat. I approached with caution and he soon picked me up, began firing tracer just behind me, until I was out of his pivot reach. I came up and over then and started working on him from behind. I was on the inside, between the two formations so the others couldn't easily get at me without danger of hitting the second group. With only nose gunners the German bombers were definitely under-armed. I soon had one smoking heavily in the starboard engine. I didn't need to kill him completely; time and distance would take care of that and he'd ditch before he got over France or Holland. I let him have one more burst into the vicinity of the crew cockpit and peeled off to turn my attention on another nearer the edge of the formation.

Same strategy—keep the bomber between his companions

and me. This continued with all of us either fighting off or attacking *Stukas* or *Junkers*, until I finally shot out my ammunition and broke it off. As it was, I'd gone on a little too long. I turned for the coast, pressing the microphone switch.

"Johnson here—goin' home—watch your fuel gents…we've been up a while."

I took a last glance at the remaining bombers continuing to ply their way northward. I'd seen at least two of them going down in smoke and one *Stuka* fighter.

"Leave 'em for Duxford to have a go. I'm empty—headin' in—good luck."

"Me too…" someone else shouted. A BBC broadcast had begun to lap over into our frequency and I began to hear bits of the news reading mixed among the Jerry's chatter.

"Who's missing?" I asked.

Ploughman responded first: "I'm already at the coast, Sir…I took a bit in the starboard wing but it looks like it's holding.

This went on with Foster, the oldest time in squadron, going first. "Spencer got it. Saw him go in—no chute."

There was a pause. Spencer would have called next and we waited that short interval for him, as if he might come on after all. But he didn't and the third pilot came in: "Culgary—confirming Spencer went in, Sir. I'm done too."

"Right," I answered absently, wondering what Ashcraft had done.

Homeward bound we didn't see him in the water, finally striking landfall ourselves, a little east of Dover. We met several more outgoing squadrons of Spits and Hurricanes sent from some where west of Bournemouth, or further north, possibly…close enough to have a piece of what remained of the bomber group as they continued northward with their bomb load.

When we got on the ground, we'd lost four, not counting Ashcraft. Later we got a call during debriefing that he'd landed in a potato field just west of Eastborne Cross and he was OK, taking a train back to the aerodrome.

"Can't wait to go up again," the messenger reported. I shook my head; maybe he'd make a pilot after all, for a while anyway.

So the war went...go up with the call. Scrambling the fighters; then try to get home again in two pieces: you and the airplane...refuel, rearm, a swig of water, a pee 'n a puff 'n off you go again. Weather was always a problem. Sometimes we would get over The Channel and we couldn't find the *Jerrys*—not for love or money. We'd sometimes lose one of our own green pilots because of the weather. They'd get in the stuff and become disoriented, lose it, turn upside down—sideways and come roaring down, unable to right the spinning Hurricane. Maybe they'd recover before they hit the water. Sometimes, the ceiling was so low they'd never even see the water; that fast and that thick, it was. The fog would snake in across The Channel from France and it would all look the same: water and cloud. If they couldn't use their instruments competently, they'd buy it. The new guys never had enough time in their machines, before they were given over to me—just not enough time. Wasn't really fair to them: sink or swim, that's what it was...sink or swim. And most of them were sinking. And it was bothering me...bothering me a lot.

In those days everyone had a war story—how they'd joined up. They always eventually got around to tell about it. Some had been conscripted, some had already been in and some joined first. I never felt my story was particularly special, but others did, mostly because I was an American. When I told them I was an American crop duster with a Swedish mother and that I'd gone to England to "join up", they first told me I was crazy, that I should have gone to Sweden and hid out.

But later, they said they were only kidding. In America, most folks didn't even know where Sweden was...thought they yodeled over there. I told them, no—that was Alabama. That always got a chuckle. From the first, I hadn't wanted to be in the Swedish military, especially when I learned they'd again declared for neutrality. For a while, I'd thought of going to Canada, but it was easier this way: the Brits. They talked funny, overcooked their food—even by Scandinavian standards, but in the end they were OK, for the most part. Many of 'em still hadn't gotten over the fact that they were no longer a world empire and were loosing their ass to the *Jerrys*. But I'd learned to admire their quiet courage. They accepted me gladly, enjoying the strangeness of having a Yank around and then even more so when I continued to rise in command, not that it gave them a sense of security: a Yank up there running things. But, as my time in squadron grew...and grew, that changed: "Must be special if we still 'ave 'im," they thought...bit of all right, 'e is...can't be killed...'n he'll teach us that...staying alive."

Little did they know how little time I had to teach them and then, how to convey luck? Thinking back, I suppose it was a little unusual, what I'd done. Having both Swedish and American citizenship and joining the RAF. I'd learned to fly early, as a kid, with an uncle who had a crop-dusting busines in The States: Missouri and Arkansas. "Killin' weevils..." Uncle Jesse would echo whenever anyone asked why, or what he sprayed, roaring over the cotton plants and under the power lines. Back and forth he would go. Hour after hour—day after day, we flew converted biplanes over the upper delta country, along both banks of the Mississippi River valley; thousands and thousands of acres of cotton ground. When I went away to college, Uncle Jesse'd only had one plane. I came back from graduating in English at the university and had no idea what I wanted to do. So I'd started flying his plane on Sundays for the fun of it, then on "paying" jobs, to spell him and then I guess I was hooked, for a while anyway.

Once he saw I could fly his Stearman as well as he could, Uncle Jesse bought another and rebuilt it to spray cotton. Soon we were keeping a crew busy hauling weevil juice and gasoline to two airplanes. If it wasn't too windy, we flew twelve-hour days...except Sundays. Then I'd wash a week's worth of dirt away, borrow Jesse's Ford and prowl the small, river towns, looking for girls Most were in church, or with their families, so it was mostly just a long Sunday drive. Jesse stayed at home with his family and now and then, I'd eat Sunday dinner with them, out of boredom.

The first of September, 1939 Hitler went into Poland. It was *the* news, even in southeast Missouri.

"Cotton's big—'n gonna' get bigger now," My Uncle Jesse and employer had said. When I later told him I was leaving to go to war, he tried to talk me out of it.

"We ain't in it yet—'n hits this big. What 'ill it be after we get in?"

Of course he was right, but I'd had my fill of cotton rows after two years. I'd become bored dodging high-lines and cotton gins, the tallest things around that part of the country, barring the odd cypress tree. There'd be one old tree standing for some reason, there among the fields, sometimes in a fence row. Strange, how they did that—the farmers. They'd leave a single, big tree in the middle of all that cotton—plowing, cultivating and spraying around it, year after year, decade after decade.

They'd cut all the other trees—the forests—in my grandfather's time—when they cleared that part of the Mississippi River valley. One time, they must have been part of some big swamp timber, but now—just those odd cypress snags sticking up there in the middle of nowhere..."lookin' for lightnin', Uncle Jessy would say.

They were very dangerous. You always had to remember they were there, as you crisscrossed the cotton or bean fields—or they'd get you in the monotony of the pattern. Forget—bank and turn—there one would be, just waiting to break off a wing and kill you. They always seemed to turn up when you didn't expect them.

Later in England, over The Channel, I'd found the *Luftwaffe* pilots like that. Forget, get careless for a second—there they'd be. One—maybe two of them on your tail. Get you in a crossfire and that'd be it. Those old cypress snags taught me a good lesson. Always be aware, I'd drummed into the *newbies*, hour after hour.

"Situational awareness...speed and altitude. All will be your friends," I'd told them, "...but forget, get careless...you're dead."

I was fortunate; already an experienced pilot well when I came over...way-long before most in my RAF squadron. It was near second nature to step first, into the trainers and then the fighters. What the early British fighters...like the Hurricanes...lacked in speed against the Germans, I could make up in out-guessing, or out-maneuvering. My buddies hadn't yet acquired those skills, so they died early and they died often, trying to learn before they were killed.

I'd had to start in RAF Coastal Command, after trying for Bomber Command. They soon found out I'd flown the crop dusters and moved me into Fighter Command, instead, lickety-split. I still preferred Bomber Command but that eventually seemed out of the question. I'd been promoted rapidly, right off, rising up and up:

Squadron Leader—then Wing Commander and finally, Group Captain and always trying to get me to take over a training op, which I'd been trying to get out of for some time.

It was almost unfair, the way the promotions kept coming. Other pilots just kept dying ahead of me. Many of them were far brighter, certainly better educated and even better suited for leadership duty. And they probably even would have wanted to be Group Captain, but they couldn't fly as well, or were unlucky—careless, or both...and they died. My previous flying skills helped keep me alive, but they seemed poor qualifications for a job: "your mates couldn't outlive you." I constantly wanted to somehow make up for their deaths in those days, mainly killing *Jerrys*. I thought I could ease my conscience in that way. But I'd not yet lived that long, watching them die...hadn't had enough of fighting. Eventually I figured it out: I wasn't gaining; no matter how many flaming *swastikas* went under me, it wasn't making the difference that made a difference, in my head.

Despite my rank, I didn't spend any more time pushing paper than I had to. Relegated it totally to clerical, made decisions and flew with the pilots, where I was most effective...and I had competent under-staff. I thought, if I hung up there with them, yelling at them long and loud enough, maybe...just maybe, some of my experience would help them live a little longer. And maybe, they'd just make it through this thing. Then, it wasn't long before Command tried something again: sending me off to command a fighter training school.

Teach 'em," they'd said; "that'll make the difference you want."

But I didn't want to teach any of them at that level. The last thing I wanted to do was nurse another bunch of first-time plowboys. Trade in the plow handle for a fighter's stick. It was already bad enough when they arrived at Squadron, already trained, supposedly.

Now, keeping twenty percent of them alive for a month was my goal. I didn't usually make it and they kept dying. I got out of that assignment after two months of debating it with Command. I knew I could be more effective flying with them, but High Wycombe didn't want to give up. They wouldn't leave a good thing be.

Then, again in the spring of 1941, somebody in High Wycombe, got interested in changing my life. Seems they heard about my Swedish heritage, or at least that's what I thought. They weren't particularly interested in my American side. One day in the middle of the week, we got a visit from the Air Marshal for our sector of the RAF. It started with a call from my immediate superior, Air Vice Marshal Charles Barrett-Alcott's office—my immediate superior and personal friend. "*Marsh*" I'd taken to calling him since his last promotion. Not in public of course..."never do..." he would've said.

Earlier, I'd told him why the nickname: "You Brits have these long titles—double-barreled names and all that. Marsh...that's what I'll call you: *Marsh*."

He didn't' mind. We'd come up rapidly together through the ranks. Near neck-and-neck, though I'd never be able to keep pace—make the same grade, being American...a *foreigner*. There was no real RAF rule against it, just an unwritten *British* thing.

"Not done, you know...old boy..." I could almost hear them say, in High Wycombe.

That morning I was about to take off, going up for recognizance cover with one wing of the squadron, when *Marsh* had rung up. I was looking forward to taking up one of the new Spitfires—we'd begun changing over to Spits by then. I still had my helmet in my right hand when I took the receiver with the other hand. Of course I didn't call him *Marsh* in public.

"Air-Vice Marshal—*hello*...how kind of you to ring—I was just about to step out..." A little sarcasm wouldn't hurt.

Through the control room's window, I watched the squadron gunning their engines; the dust and grass were flying against the side of the building as they revved up the Spit's...the props a mere blur. I had to put a palm over my other ear to hear him.

Marsh spoke steadily, telling me exactly what I didn't want to hear at the moment: "...and drop whatever you're doing and get changed...something special—come for tea, Robert."

After listening impatiently, I stammered: "But...Air Vice Marshal...can't it wait until later today?"

My voice was irritable. Certainly not any way to address Air Vice Marshal Barrett-Alcott over the company phone. I was frustrated at my annoyance and lack of self-control. And I'd probably embarrassed both of us. But I knew the Air Vice Marshal well, even though he was my CO. Surprise and frustration had prompted my short reply when he'd butted in. When had I developed this short temper, I wondered as I shut up and listened, wincing at his retort to my own stupidity.

"It bloody well can't wait..." he recounted. Knowing Marsh, he was collecting his temper. I winced inwardly, imagining him composing himself to reply to me. "One doesn't keep the Air Marshal waiting. *Immediately*, please, Group Captain Johnson...*immediately*, if not *sooner!*"

He seemed to take a breath before going on: "My house, by the way...this is not for clerical staff's ears. Just knock...Millie'l let you in. Plan to stay for tea—casual uniform's O.K. Might as well be comfortable and won't attract any attention; don't know how long it will take."

So the Air Vice Marshal was down from High Wycombe. I wondered what could bring him this close to operations.

"May I ask what this is all about?" My annoyance was obvious in my tone, but mostly for losing my temper. What was wrong with me, I thought, this isn't like me.

"You may, but you'll learn little from me Group Captain...especially over the telephone."

"But..."

"Millie will let you in, Robert...*now....!*" Then he added a little kindlier: "...please, Robert, don't be difficult. Most of the lads can survive one mission without you."

"Yes—Sir," I offered, humbly. We were good friends, but this was one I apparently wasn't going to get out of. I put one finger on the hook then released it and phoned my exec and told him to tag along with the wing...that I'd be busy. Then I hung up, returned to my quarters and immediately began shedding my flying kit.

It took only ten minutes and I was biking to the Air Vice Marshal's.

At my second knock the door opened, revealing a pert Millie in a ruffled apron. She was my favorite officer's wife. Actually, I was madly in love with her, as was every man in the squadron who had the good fortune to fall beneath one of her smiles. Marsh knew it and loved her the more for the hearts she captured. She was related to The Crown somehow, but you'd never know it…distant cousin of a cousin, or something. She was so very pleasant and helpful to all the new officers—and there were many of us at first. And she especially liked Americans, she'd said, further capturing my fealty.

She was the one who broke the news to the wives of the married pilots—when they'd bought it. Thank God, I didn't have to do that. Writing the parent's letters home was bad enough.

Leaning casually against the doorframe she smiled up at me as if we both had all the time in the world.

"And don't you look particularly dashing this morning, Group Captain Johnson. Too bad you have to waste that trouser crease on the likes of them," she tilted her head pertly toward the hallway, playing the tart, "we could go out and do the town, we could."

She mimed a Cockney accent and I melted under her feminine attention. I could only smile as she placed hands on hips, turned sideways in the doorway, posing, one leg turned coyly, magazine style. This forced me go through into the foyer ahead of her. Catching up to me in the hallway, in her perfect public school accent she said: "I must dash down cellar for some brandy for lunch, Robert…can you find your own way? They're in the library now with tea."

"Oh—yes, certainly Mrs. Alcott …thank you."

She smiled. "Millie…Robert…" she said, "*Millie*…please?"

Yes, certainly…*Millie.*"

She smiled a thank you and turned down the hallway as I stood, staring after her. She suddenly spun around, as if she'd forgotten something and caught me admiring the sight of her rump bounding pertly beneath the cotton dress. She smiled, a regular coquette.

"Oh *Robert*…?

"Yes…?" I replied toward the toes of my shoes, embarrassed, but smiling to myself, having been caught.

"I'm afraid I've just remembered—I'm in a bit of a pickle…"

I didn't look up, still somewhat embarrased.

'Robert…*look at me, please.*"

I did.

"You see," she continued, smiling demurely, "we have dinner guests coming Saturday evening and I'm one male short. Would you mind terribly, Robert...be my odd man *in*? I could really use your help...for a—a tenth...I believe it is."

I hesitated, trying to think on my feet. I didn't feel like socializing at these affairs.

"Odd lady coming, you see. You'll be the fill-in if you're willin'..." he paused at her silly rhyme, "...I *can* promise you, Robert—*she's pretty...?*"

I still had no excuse as she went on.

"And you're simply brilliant with making the ladies feel at ease...that ever-so-charming American southern accent of yours."

I was wavering.

"This lady's a particular problem. She doesn't get out in *mixed* company very much—a bit shy you see...reclusive almost."

I didn't answer, changing my mind again. I'd been to Millie's and Marsh's parties, before. They were the usual crowd, other officers, local clergy, city and Shire officials, the odd foreign delegate who might be in the area. They were boring. I much preferred a beer with the mates in the officer's mess. But Millie didn't give up easily; she began walking back toward me, feigning a slinky gate.

"Won't you please help me out?"

I was still embarrased that she'd caught me staring at her bum. Fearful of what she might do or say next, I stammered a reply.

"Yeah...sure...I'll help out Mrs....*Millie.*"

I hadn't been able to think. God, what was I getting myself into, again. An evening of trying to make small talk with a wallflower. She was looking at me as if I was about to reconsider

"Yes..." I said again but not with as much conviction.

"Good," she said, brightening again, nodding. "It's settled—you are a dear one, you are Robert."

She stood there a couple of seconds like she might say something else, but I straightened and she smiled again.

"Thanks loads, Robert," she added seriously, tipping her head pertly. You make things so...*easy.*"

Turning away she walked down the hall and vanished around the corner into the pantry. I wondered what she meant, as I watched her disappear. I waited a moment before following her, half way down the hall, where I stopped at the library door and straightening my trousers, shirt and tie. I cleared my throat, stepped up and knocked twice on the door, opened it and entered.

Air Marshal Claxton and the Air Vice Marshal were standing beside the open windows. They were holding up a large photograph transparency toward the window's light, their heads nearly touching as they peered up, through the sheet of celluloid. The Air Marshal glanced over as I entered and he held up his pipe.

"Be just a moment, Group Captain Johnson...in fact, come over—you might want to take a look at this." As I strode across the room, Air Marshal Claxon stepped around the Air Vice Marshal...Marsh, to offer his hand: "Nice to see you again Group Captain—thanks for coming on such short notice—Air Vice Marshal's told me the importance you place on your group's missions. I appreciate it."

Turning and pointing, he said: "I believe this..." he nodded, indicating the large, monochrome film Marsh was holding, "...this was taken last weekend."

I leaned closer; the two had now returned to peering up at the aerial photo in Marsh's hand. "This area," Marsh said, circling an area with the bit of his pipe, "represents some alterations in terrain that was done rather recently. We expect there are some factories there...he outlined another general area...with false roofs—structures. All meant to deceive the recognizance boys and the photo interpreters, of course, but they've caught it here."

I looked at the areas he pointed out with his pipe stem. "How do you know that, Sir?"

"Oh—sorry...same film..." he rummaged around on the desk beside him, "...taken the previous week shows a significantly different layout. Too big...," he held up the second film for me to look at, but had to rotate it so it would be the same, "...'n too large to be put up that quickly, if it were a real factory building. Can only be a deception. We don't know why they would bother—changing it like that. What good would it do to decoy their stuff, other than waste gunpowder destroying it. They're trying to draw our fire away from something else. We wouldn't have noticed it but one of the photo guys used to live nearby and he always checks the photos from that area to see if his old house got it in one of the raids. He happened to notice this."

"Hmmm..." I said aloud, not knowing what to make of it and wondering what it had to do with the real reason for having me here "...interesting though." I added, hoping to encourage them to fill me in.

"Well..." the Air Marshal said, "...that's not why we asked you around this morning, Group Captain. Although it's fun to try to figure out what the *Jerrys*'r doing with these things," he nodded to the photos, "I never get it right. The photo and hush-hush gents—always come back to me with the real answers—after a couple of weekdays and I am always a mile off. Never fails." he added chuckling.

If that wasn't the reason I was there, I wondered what was coming next as I crossed the room with the two men and took a seat on the leather divan proffered by the Air Marshal.

"Tea...?" Marsh asked, carrying a laden, wooden tray over from the sideboard. I could see Millie'd been busy.

"Yes, thanks I said as he handed a cup and saucer to my companion; "...milk only, please," I responded at his questioning look, as he held a little, silver spoon poised over the cup before adding condiments. "Thank you, Sir," I said taking the cup from him. I waited while he took his place in the armchair across from us.

"S'pose you're wondering why we've gotten you out of your duty today, Robert," the Air Marshal began, stirring his tea vigorously. He paused, waiting for my answer. At my nod, he smiled cunningly.

"Yes...thought so...well—I can warrant it's not to try to ship you off to run another flight training school..." he glanced at Marsh. "I never did figure out whose idea that was, anyway.

Marsh looked at the ceiling as he stirred his own tea. I could see the muscles in his jaw clenching slightly as he surpressed a snicker.

The Air Marshal turned toward me, cocking one heavy leg up on the divan, groaning with the effort.

"Group Captain, this is important—*quite important*.... That is all I want to say about it and I only will say it once."

I nodded, still confused, replying: "Yes Sir?"

"You have a particularly interesting background. It isn't as if we've been trying to find another job for you...all this time, you know? It's simply, an officer with your talents can be more useful to England and the war effort in other, *better*, ways, than queuing up, mission-after-mission, to kill himself, against all odds, over The Channel...in a Spitfire."

He paused for emphasis. And apparently satisfied he'd made his point, went on: "We would like to put you into Special Branch and use that talent...and second *language* of yours—you do speak Swedish, I understand...?"

"Yes Sir—a rather old fashioned variety."

"Yes, good, I thought your dossier stated that," he waved his hand toward a file folder lying partially covered beneath the tea tray.

"Any others?"

"Well, I had German in college, but I've forgotten most of it."

"No matter...but it might come in handily, though; have to brush it up a bit—just to be sure. You see young man...there's an opportunity in Scandinavia—all over Europe for that matter, to exercise your God-given intelligence, your Swedish...*all* your language skills actually and possibly to fly airplanes at the same time—if that's what you wish to continue to do?"

He paused again, awaiting the nod I eventually gave him, over the steam of my yet un-tasted cup.

"Anyway, we require more information about so much that's happening in Scandinavia...the *neutrality* status of the Swedes and how they're interacting with the *Jerrys* and the other Axis powers, industry wise, intelligence—all of that sort of thing."

He hesitated, again for emphasis. I thought, wondering if I should say thank you for the compliment, but decided against it as being possibly vain. He went on, anyway, before I could decide.

"This sort of information now comes to us from many sources: the Norwegians—since they capitulated, gotten themselves damn well organized—the *Mil Org³* people, particularly...and they're now getting us some good information through the Danes and the Swedes, about them, after losing a few people at first. The Swedes don't say much, themselves. Play it pretty close to the chest. Have to— *Jerry'l* be down their throats too. People there are with us, most of the government's pro-*Nazi* though. They're on the same tightrope together. We get a lot more from the Danes and there are some of our own people coming and going who bring back tidbits now and then, too." He paused to watch Marsh light his pipe. "What we really need is someone who is *vanilla*. Someone like you Group Captain...someone who could move around Scandinavia—Europe in general—a neutral. A neutral who isn't *really* neutral but was clean enough to appear to be and wouldn't be suspected of anything, assuming nothing untoward was done."

He mused for another moment. "*You*, Robert...you could do that. Given your Swedish passport...your languages and you look as much Swedish as you do—*anything...*" he said, smiling, "...but you also have the knowledge, the intelligence and the skills to pull it off, we believe, with a little help from our chaps, here and there. Get in there, become established, get to know the right people; using a front we have created, travel Scandinavia and The Continent picking up and delivering information for us. While you work as an airline pilot, you would be most valuable to us and the overall war effort."

He paused again, picking up his cup; then, waving away Marsh's offer to refill it for him, he stood up and carried it over to the tray. "What sort of little cakes..." he mumbled, lifting up the corner of a linen towel that covered a square basket, no doubt containing several goodies from Millie.

But Marsh interrupted my momentary lapse as I considered what had been said. "So...what do you think, Robert? What is your first impression? Sound like something that might work for you? Please be frank."

"Undoubtedly, Sir. But whether I'm your man...well, that's another matter. I've never done anything like this before, you understand. I can't even get away with self deception without someone pointing it out to me."

Marsh chuckled, "Air Marshal—would you mind passing those cakes over while there are any still remaining."

"Harumph..." he replied choosing another pastry before handing the plate across.

"Air Marshal..." I said, picking up one of the little white pastries before handing the tray on to Marsh, "...the Air Vice Marshal mentioned my *cover* I believe you said…and a *front*…what exactly is that—*those?*"

Marsh was at that moment trying to corral one of the cakes, which had broken apart in his hand as he was taking a bite. He gestured to the Air Vice Marshal who…after a glance at his subordinate, quickly took up my question.

"Your cover would be as an operative commercial airline pilot for the Swedish airline *ABA*…know them?"

"Yes, I believe I've hear of them."

"As a Swedish pilot based wherever *we* send you, you will be our agent-at large…as an illegal, in most countries, *foreign* agent. You're a Group Captain, rank-wise; we will discharge you from the British Royal Air Corps. You'll take on the rank of Captain for *ABA*. But it doesn't really matter much, unless you have someone or something to command. Rank, that is. It seems the war has gotten to the Swedes, too, like everyone else's and brought them up short handed."

"Bloody well off making munitions for the *Nazis*, aren't they," the Air Marshal quipped, rolling his eyes as he chewed. "And sending them raw materials by the shipload, too."

I waited to see if there was any response to his outburst. When there wasn't, I asked my question.

"I see, I said, wanting to stick to the subject. "How do I go about slipping into this roll, Sir? Are the…is the Swedish government aware?"

"All taken care of. You just go to Stockholm, take a cab to your apartment. Enjoy a good night's sleep and go to your flight office the next morning; you'll be expected. You *are* an early riser… aren't you?"

"Yes Sir."

"Thought so…you're an early riser and like to go in the aerodrome before staff. That's when you get most of the work done—pre-flight…all that. Several have resigned in the civilian flying game in Sweden. Took better paying positions when things got *busy* after *Jerry* came to Norway in forty. Right after Quisling organized his *Regiment Nordland*[3]. Many of them are our people—*your* staff, but Swedish nationals, citizenship-wise. They can do anything for you except your job. They're prepared to fill you in should you accept, or *the candidate*, whenever we find him, on the full breadth of his duties; *training*, if you will. We will do some of it in London and elsewhere; then, whoever goes, it's off to Stockholm and then—the world. Who knows? This *position* will get you into places we can't get into. Give you contacts with who knows—people we wouldn't easily be able to meet, otherwise. We have some people we're running there in Norway; you'd be working with any one of them."

Though Marsh had more or less asked for an answer, when I didn't reply immediately, they glanced at one another, both respecting my momentary silence, seeming to understand I needed more time.

"Think about it for a bit, Robert," Marsh said nodding to the Air Marshal, more or less signaling that that part of the interview was over. They stood up, crossed to the sideboard and refilled their cups, took another pastry apiece and went back to the file containing the photos they'd been examining when I came into the room. Soon they were muttering quietly to themselves out of my hearing.

I sipped my cold tea in silence rolling over in my mind, whether I would tell them, immediately, or make it look like I'd considered it for a while, given it more lengthy consideration before turning them down. I felt I wanted nothing to do with leaving the wing at the moment. But, pondering the recent fears I'd been experiencing in combat, I hesitated, considering that problem: how long would I have before I was discovered...or they killed me? I would have to deal with them—somehow. Maybe it needed more thought. I decided being too thoughtful might not be too good, either, giving them the impression I might be thinking of accepting. I sat for another moment in silence and as I didn't want to give them any hint of what I was really thinking, I stood up.

Their conversation had now gone to the air war and presently they drew me in again, but not saying anything further about the question they'd posed. We spoke of several other war-related items. They didn't seem to want to press me further and after some time the conversation eventually lapsed. It was clear to them I wasn't going to proffer any hint of commitment at this meeting. Finally, they looked at each other, nodded as if to indicate that was that.

"So...why not think about it a little longer, Group Captain? Get back us."

"When do you require an answer, Sirs," I said, addressing the Air Marshal.

"Well, ideally right away, of course, but considering the gravity of the situation—what about Monday before lunch. I'm staying the weekend and will leave right after I hear from you Group Captain, regardless of your decision.

"Very good," I rose, "thank you Sirs, you will have my answer as you requested, before Monday, lunch." I saluted smartly.

They both nodded and I as I turned to leave the room, the Air Vice Marshal added: "If you want to talk about it over the weekend—anytime, just let us know Robert."

"Thank you...good day..." I replied, opened the door and walked into the hallway. It was empty. On my way out the front, there were no sounds from elsewhere within the house, but I'd already forgotten about Millie and her party.

CHAPTER
2

Indecision

After leaving the two officers, I spent the balance of the day being a royal pain in the ass to most of the squadron who'd had to remain on the ground. Until the wing returned, I'd had them doing spit and polish stuff, before I finally became so agitated and nervous with my own behavior, I retired to my quarters to consider my new options and more importantly, in order to give the men some peace. I couldn't imagine how I would ever be able to take the assignment High Wycombe were offering, even if I'd wanted to. And I still felt I definitely didn't, in my worsening emotional state.

As I lay on my bunk, I reflected on the year past, considering that for six months I hadn't taken any of my accumulated leave. I'd spent nearly every day on mission work, either flying with, or accompanying the new men as a trainer, whenever possible. I felt if I could drum anything into them, it might save their life. I'd delegated the majority of the deskwork to clerical. Flying from the ground, as I'd been forced to do today, taught me that possibly there was a reason Command had been trying to reassign me. I wondered if there were some outward signs that I'd been unknowingly exhibiting. I intended to speak to Marsh about it, when I dared. The trembling of my hands...continued, but disappeared the moment we were in combat. Maybe Command saw something which, until today, I'd been unaware of. Maybe I *was* cracking up. It really made me think as I lay there.

So—given what I'd just surmised about myself—or thought I'd learned, I pondered: would I be able to handle the posting they offered? It was certainly food for thought. The other fact, my behavior today, certainly had to be dealt with. Finally, I decided to put myself on sick call on the following morning assuming there were no desperate measures requiring my being on duty. Flight Lieutenant Foster, my number two, could handle my normal duties. Even take over the command, I reasoned, thinking about the Air Marshal's offer again; could I handle it? *Ever*—let alone now. Or did I need some time off—something I didn't wish to even consider...admitting my worsening condition—*to resign?*

The following day, Friday, I did as promised. It wasn't easy. The staff wondered what was up. I'm ill, I told them—upset stomach, all that—don't want to vomit in the oxygen mask. As I walked around glancing at this and that around the ships, the crews looked askance at me. It was like they were waiting for an explosion, like the day before; one that never happened, but they didn't know that—how close I'd come. I was right about myself; it was tough.

That evening I remembered the coming evening and the Air Vice Marshal's dinner party. What had I gotten myself into? Being on sick leave, I could easily continue the charade, feigning continued illness. But I truly enjoyed Marsh and his wife Millie. Her parties weren't always boring, she saw to that, taking the time and care to charm every single one of her guests...so that took care of that. Unless I truly became ill, I would attend as promised.

However, back to the assignment. I wondered if I really *needed* something like this now—a diversion? Whether or not I could perform? I definitely had to take some time away from the combat pace I'd set for myself...that was evident. I'd begun to dig the hole they would bury me in. Thinking about it, I frightened myself.

I managed to get through the end of the day. It was Friday and I stopped to have a soft drink in the officer's mess before I hit the hay. I felt taking a beer would look suspicious Most of the men were talking about the day's mission, so I had little more to do than stand by and listen politely. I was certain they hadn't noticed any change in me; I suppose it wasn't that apparent. The day had gone well other than the apparent loss of crew and ships.

For the coming Sunday I'd had long-standing plans to go fishing. It had been a while—last summer, since I'd wet a line. After I finished my soda at the mess I bought a round and quickly left before anyone could return the favor. I wanted to get home to bed, hoping I would be able to sleep and if not, get some serious thinking done.

The following morning, after early breakfast in the mess with the men, I sat one out in the briefing room. Another officer, Flight Lieutenant Carlisle, went through the weather, the target and the plan, before the boys went up on a planned mission, for a change—to fly cover for some Bomber Command mine laying operations. When the briefing was completed, I wished them luck as they trickled out to their ships, joking. I stood with flight operations officer Reggie Allisson and watched them go up then.

"It is always a pleasure to see you blokes go up—from down here," Reggie mumbled around his pipe stem. The Spits 'r different, somehow. Hurricanes were all right. But, somehow—didn't have the romance these Spits 've got. Must be their *lines*—like the female body?"

"Oh…I don't know…as for romance…" I mumbled, going on about long hours of being shot at in a tight seat and such. Regg asked: "How you doing, by the way. Chaps said you have a touch of something?"

I was still officially on sick leave so no one really thought much about it. A Spit was revving up as he locked one wheel brake in a taxiing turn in front of us. The engine's roar was deafening. I made a wry face, tapped my stomach and gave a wing-wagging gesture with my hand, indicating I was still a bit queasy. Regg nodded as we turned our backs to the blast of the prop that carried all sorts of debris past us. Once he'd taxied past we watched in silence as the ships got off one by one. I was contemplating my quandary.

Another day though, unless I reported to hospital, someone would begin to wonder. I would either have to go back to work with the group, or take the new position. I'd avoided mentioning the meeting with the Air Marshal, but finally said something to Regg. He and Marsh must be holing up somewhere, because Regg didn't even know the Air Marshal was on the aerodrome. He'd raised his eyebrows inquiringly when I made mention of it earlier.

"Really..." he said, removing the pipe in surprise. Another Spit was further out in the field rolling up to take off. "...what 'd you think those two are up to?" He spoke as the pipe went back in, cutting off his next speech.

I shrugged my shoulders as the Spit went to full throttle; it wasn't unusual for the chain of command not to know what was going on. After all, there's a war on. After the Spit had become airborne, Regg mumbled.

"Must be something big?"

Staring at the empty field where the ships had stood, I didn't comment. How many would be parked here again tonight? A question I always asked and never got right, always guestimating low. We stood a while longer before I walked away, having planted the seed of suspense to torment Regg. I'd not wanted to enter into any discussion about my meeting and then have to deliberately lie to Reggie. I thought a great deal of him, though I loved tormenting him. Gave Reggie something to think about for the day, anyway, I thought as I returned to my quarters to prepare my fishing kit for the following day. I knew that task would occupy me.

Fishing season was open for pike and I knew a quiet mill pond in the New Forest [4] where I'd heard some of the locals in a pub describe the fish they'd occasionally caught there. I'd asked the local town Mayor about it and he'd given me directions. Some time previously, I'd been to London and on an impulse, had purchased some tackle, consisting of a very springy, magnesium casting rod and a beautifully-made reel with a level wind mechanism to keep the line evenly wound on the spool.

I'd reasoned a rod like that wasn't likely to be made again until after the war, due to the dearness of magnesium for aircraft and I'd bought it on impulse.

Was it really last year already? I found it hard to believe...and I hadn't wet a line since that first week. Time had flown since I'd last used the equipment in...August, wasn't it...of last year. After that day's fishing, I'd carefully unwound the wet, cotton line off the reel, onto the floor to dry. And then that evening, I rewound it again. Cotton line had a tendency to decay if one didn't dry it quickly and completely and that was best done off the reel. This line had to last the duration of the war, so I planned to care for it properly.

After I'd returned to my quarters, I decided I'd better peel off a few layers from the reel to check its breaking strength, before chancing losing a big fish, tomorrow. I'd already lain out and arranged my small kit of tackle. I regretted the absence of a landing net, but felt I could be extra careful if I got any large fish on the line.

Sitting on my bunk, I took the chrome-plated reel from the box and unwound several coils of the black, braided line on the floorboards. I paused now and then, yanking the line smartly in order to test it—but I couldn't part it. Finally I reasoned it would be OK for about any fish I might hook in England.

One-by-one I selected each of my five lures, laying them out on my little table, checking the treble-hooks for sharpness and firm attachment to each plug. I'd purchased five lures at the London sporting shop of a department store. I was totally unfamiliar with the lure selections. They were totally alien to anything I had used in America. Every fisherman has his favorites and I remembered pondering the selections carefully, as the older, female clerk looked on, unable even to comment. I didn't even know what sort of fish there were in England at the time and didn't know whether I would be going after top-feeders, or what. The woman clerk had apologized for her lack of knowledge of the hobby.

"Of course," she'd said, "the regular clerk worked in the department five years, before going off to war, like everyone else."

She'd worked in millenary for fifteen years and could give me excellent assistance, she said, with any yard-goods selection—but alas, not with fishing paraphernalia.

"And there aren't very many men going fishing anymore, anyway..." she'd said, "...the war, you know."

Of the small assortment of lures I inspected and finally came to choose, three were shiny metal...spoon-shaped affairs, with paint on one side and a single treble hook attached to their bottom ends. The other two were wooden, painted green with yellow and black stripes and spots. In the store I'd reasoned they were meant to imitate a frog lying on the surface of the water, since they floated. After casting a lure of this sort onto the water, one waited thirty seconds or so without disturbing it and then twitched the rod end, reeling in the lure just a bit. This went on until a fish either struck the lure or the lure was entirely retrieved. One repeated this until either catching a fish, or growing tired of the entire process. These "top-water" lures required far more patience than the others, but when a fish struck, it was often spectacular, especially if it were a larger fish. They often hit the lure with such force, they'd knock the lure into the air. As a boy of twelve or so, I was taught to use them by my father.

"After casting it, leave it about the length of time it takes to take out and light a cigarette..." he had always told me. I hadn't smoked at the time, but recalled going through the motions with my hands, just to try to get the delay correct. But it was almost too much for a boy—the long pause between twitching and retrieving the top-running lures. I'd preferred the deeper-running baits; it gave me more to do—the casting and reeling in coming more often.

Among the other lures, one wooden one had a shovel-shaped, blade attached at the front, where the line connected. This affair made the lure dive deep below the surface as it was retrieved. The remaining lure had a painted, lead head with a long "hula" style skirt around the bottom half, made from thin, black strips of rubber; the skirt draped downward, disguising the tenacious treble hook beneath (as if the fish knew the difference). Each of the three, barbed hooks had thin wire guards over each prong, made from springy, music wire; these wires helped prevent the hook from catching in rushes or lily pads, but didn't stop the fish from biting hard enough to be caught.

One could cast the lure directly into the weeds where the big fish lay in hiding and twitch and snake the lure down through the water, in among the excellent covering weeds. Small fish hid there among the stems and blades, attracting the larger prey-fish—the ones I was after. This was already my favorite lure although I had yet to try it. I had great plans for the lure, especially after I'd seen the condition of that mill pond. The upper end of the flowage tapered into the small river among a crowd of lily pads. That's where I hoped to find a pike lurking, Sunday.

I considered skipping lunch entirely, but on second thought, decided to stop at the mess and pick through anything they had left over. It turned out to be bread and cheese with a glass of milk, which was fine since I'd little exercise that day anyway. Nor had I undergone the emotional stress of a normal morning's flight. I thought about the pending supper at Marsh and Millie's that evening. It would be more than adequate, once we sat down to it and I wanted to save my appetite.

I went to the laundry and picked up the uniforms I'd dropped off earlier in the week. I'd checked to insure I had a fresh shirt for the dinner party. The remainder of the afternoon I spent in my office, going through some of the paperwork, including several hand-written letters to the parents of two of our recently-lost pilots. No matter how many we'd given up, the letters remained a struggle to write. And at the rate we were losing flyers a CO didn't get an opportunity to get to know the boys well enough to compose something really personal.

In one way it was better—easier. The emotion of losing a friend was removed. But with every letter, I wondered whether a superior officer would one day write one about me. Because of this I felt a stronger sense of dedication to get the letters right, so I tried to put as much comfort into each of the correspondences as I could, mentioning all the usual things about *bravery, duty—above and beyond.* All that did little to make the task easier. I always feared the letters sounded shallow and I was always relieved when I'd finished the task.

In a way, the letters somehow felt like a bit of a lie. In actuality, I was writing a letter for the wing—each Sector. They were all giving the *above and beyond*—we all were in this war, doing our damndest.

Before midmorning the flights began returning, straggling in, one by one, as they'd departed. I watched them for a while and eventually Reggie stuck his head to say there would be no letters written home from this mission.

"Two ships been badly shot up—Caulder's and McGuire's, but they made it to the coast and pasture landings, both. They've already been picked up and will be returning by train."

I thanked Reg as he closed the door. I finished my afternoon early and returned to my quarters, after leaving word that I would be at the Air Vice Marshal's for the evening, if I was needed for anything. I knew they'd call Flight Lieutenant Foster, first.

Late that afternoon I laid out the dress uniform on the bed before I bathed. I wanted to make certain everything was ship-shape. It'd been so long since I'd worn it, I had to go through the mental list to check the polish and pressing on the wool. I didn't have a full-time orderly as would another officer of my rank. I relished my privacy and used the optional service only when I absolutely needed it.

Everything looked OK on the uniform and after a slow bath I dressed carefully, glancing in the small mirror. The visage staring back at me seemed correct enough, though a bit too slender. I put away my shaving kit and dirty socks, then picked up my hat. After another quick glance in the mirror, I opened the door to leave. Just before I closed the door, I glanced at the fishing kit standing ready for the morning in the corner. It looked very good to me.

I couldn't help smiling to myself in anticipation as I crossed the yard. I'd decided to walk; the exercise would put me in better mood for the meal and I could think about tomorrow's fishing. I planned to take the bus in the morning if I couldn't wrangle a jeep. It would require a couple of transfers, but I didn't mind that much. It would involve standing on the corner of the highway, waiting for the connecting coach to appear. It would just take longer. They weren't running many busses, trying to conserve fuel for the war.

A couple of hours of daylight remained as I walked along the sidewalk and cut across the parade ground toward the CO's residence. Along the way I returned the salutes of several airmen before coming to the married officers quarters. Marsh and Millie lived just off station on the edge in a sort of compound area, in a very old house, one that must have been repossessed when they built the aerodrome during the last war, probably around 1909 or 1910. The house went back much farther. Architecturally, it appeared to be Jacobean, possibly even earlier, with some remodeling probably covering it's real history. Whether it truly dated from that period was anyone's guess, but it looked the part—and well, too. It was formidable, built completely of stone, of course, proportioned sufficiently small so as not to appear grotesque or out of balance with the garden or surrounding houses. Whoever designed the structure knew his business.

I'd always admired the residence and its surrounding garden and as I walked up on the building in the late afternoon light, I did so again. I could hear music coming from behind the stone garden walls as I approached the front along the meandering path. The house was quaint in that way. None of the past occupants had altered the approach, so you came upon it, sitting there behind its wall, in the midst of a sort of exterior front garden. It gave the grounds the appearance of deep country, with its winding path leading to the front entrance—a garden within a garden.

Rounding the last corner several parked staff cars and bicycles dispelled that vision. There was even a contingent of armed enlisted men in full bandoleers. That surprised me. Each man had a pistol and carried the new Stenguns—automatic weapons, slung ready, over their shoulders. They were positioned at strategic points along the front hedge. I thought, the Air Marshal really travels equipped...and well-guarded. As I went through the gate, one of the guards approached me, but Millie was just seeing someone in at the front door then.

She gave me a quick wave, saying to the guard: "He's all right—he can come through..." and disappeared inside with the couple, only to reappear again as I reached the door. She was wearing a lime-green dress with puffy sleeves. It was formally-casual, if there was such a thing. She had her hair done up in a tight bun, pulled tightly atop her head, rather than in the back like an older woman might. As I came closer she smiled broadly, disarming me immediately. As others approached, I didn't have time to do much more than comment about the armed guards, inclining my head back to one side.

"Well...being awfully careful, aren't we?" I said.

"Hello Robert..." she replied, standing on tiptoes to give me a kiss on the cheek, "...am I relieved to see you. The Air Vice Marshal said you'd been under the weather and might not show. I knew you wouldn't leave me hanging, if you didn't have to...so you must be feeling better...?" She said, placing her arm in mine and turning us toward the door, either not having heard my remark about the soldiers, or ignoring it.

"It was nothing—bit of upset stomach...that's all Mrs.—*Millie*. I took it easy and I'm nearly good as new. I do look forward to dinner, too...got anything good? I've been fasting you know."

"Oh good—I'm glad to hear that. My guests are often so proper, you know? They don't really tuck in—it's as if they're afraid to eat…know what I mean? But you—you and your appetite will be a welcome diversion…encourages the others," she said smiling again.

I opened my mouth to reply about not wanting to seem a glutton, but she cut me off.

"What are we having…hmmm…?" she tipped her head back slightly, laid one finger beside her nose and closing her eyes in feigned concentration, then continued: "Cook's done a haunch of beef, sauces—you know, the usual—potatoes of course. Some *veg*…two kinds I hope, and a nice trifle for dessert…we've even got *coffee* and whipped cream to go with your Cognac and cigars, later…how's *that* sound, Robert?"

We'd passed through the hallway, completely traversing the house and had now exited into the rear garden.

"That should take the edge off it," I replied, joking. To my delight, we continued down the steps and along the rear garden path, Millie still clinging lightly but needlessly to my arm.

"Certainly sounds delicious," I said to keep her diverted as we approached the assemblage of guests.

"I believe you know everyone Group Captain Johnson, except…" she glanced around, as I did. She seeming to be searching for someone, obviously who wasn't there.

"Lose someone Millie…?" I thought of a skinny spinster with thick glasses.

"Yes…I did. Your dinner partner…she seems to have gotten away. But never mind, I'll find her and bring her 'round again. Just help yourself to a drink, meanwhile…gin 'n tonic, isn't it? You know where they are," she indicated a trolley with a wave of her hand, put on a pensive look and set off in search of my missing dinner partner. Secretly, I hoped it would be a while before she found her.

Left to myself, I went to fix a drink while she rather bewilderedly wandered off toward the house, seeking my wall-flower.

I ambled over to the little wheeled drink caddy, which bore several bottles of liquor, ice and some seltzer. There was lemon for my gin 'n tonic wedged between a small cup of sugar (which must have been as difficult to obtain as the coffee) and a little pitcher of cream. I mixed and tested my drink with a sip before ambling over to Marsh to pay my respects. He was standing with the Air Marshal and the Mayor of the local community, whom I had met before to discuss fishing. He'd invited me to speak to the town council once and we'd gotten to know one another a little. He was also a fisherman and had been the one who told me about the millpond.

"Ah—Group Captain, glad to see you could make it, after all," Marsh beamed, putting one hand on my shoulder.

"Good evening Sirs—Charles," I greeted the Mayor, "thank you for inviting me Sir. Yes, better...it was really nothing. Just a bit of nervous stomach, I guess. Everything's fit now."

"Nervous stomach," Marsh intoned. "You? Not hardly...must've been a *royal* bug—got you down." He glanced at the Air Marshal and the Mayor, "...man's a total workhorse. Never takes time off...leave? If we had an army full of the likes of him, we'd have already beaten Hitler."

The Air Marshal smiled wryly. "Got to watch that Group Captain Johnson—all work and no play...know what they say about Jack?"

"Oh, he can play, too—let me tell you," Marsh beamed, winking at me.

I was getting nervous with all this talk about me.

"Why one time...."

I interrupted him. "Speaking of playing, Mayor..." I said addressing Charlie "...tomorrow morning, bright and early, I plan to beguile the wily pike at that mill pond you showed me in the New Forest. Got my fishing kit standing ready in my quarters. How do you think I'll do?"

At the word fishing, the Air Marshal's ears came up.

"*Pike*—you're going fishing...tomorrow...*where?*"

Midway into sipping my drink, I held out a hand toward the Mayor to let him respond for me, satisfied I'd gotten *Marsh* off my back.

Eager to join in, the Mayor replied enthusiastically: "There's a millpond 'bout three quarters of an hour north of here in *The Forest*. Chock-full of pike, it was, years past. Since this started everyone's gone off and no one's fishing 'em at all. Must be as long as your leg—the small ones. I put the Group Captain onto 'em after he told me some of his American fishing stories—knew they'd suit his fancy. Told him we could equal pike that size in a bet." Turning to me, he said: "What'd you plan to carry for lures?"

Marsh excused himself: "Someone Millie wants me to speak to...be right back," he said, to the Air Marshal, who didn't even hear him. His mind was on fishing and he was hanging on the Mayor's words. Marsh winked at me inclining his head as he turned away.

"I have a small lure assortment...a couple of painted and shiny, metal spoons, top-runners and one deep-diving bait...with a grass skirt made from white rubber. One of the top runners has a weed-less get-up configured. See how that does in the lily pads on the upstream end of the millpond."

"That should do the trick," the Mayor beamed, proud of my selection and his being the instigator of the trip.

The Air Marshal was bubbling over: "*By God*—I *would* enjoy a day with you, Group Captain—bit o' fishing...just what I need, *what*," he chuckled, rubbing his beefy hands together in anticipation.

"Oh really?" My heart sank. "Well, Air Marshal—please join me, by all means." I would have my transport licked if he decided to come along, though. I really didn't relish a companion.

"Love to m' boy, but too much to do—too much to do. Heavy's the head...wearing the crown—you know? Figuratively."

"Yes Sir, I can only imagine, but there's plenty of room—it's a big pond and we could take a picnic lunch...I plan to?"

"Who's going on a picnic..." Millie said, from slightly behind me. I turned to see she'd returned and was standing beside a very striking young woman, also in evening dress. This woman resembled a fashion plate from somewhere...a magazine picture I couldn't remember. She was stunning.

"If there's a picnic going on during this war, I would like to be a part of it. Do I ever need a break. All this entertaining." She put an arm around the Air Marshal.

I stepped aside to widen the space of the circle to make room for the new arrivals. I smiled at the woman who returned it brightly.

"Group Captain Johnson was making me envy his day-trip

tomorrow, Millie. He's going fishing, of *all* things...isn't that a wonderful way to spend a morning, considering the times? A day away from *this*..." he gestured in the air with his half-full whisky "...to beguile a pike—maybe even *eat* him, too, in the end."

Everyone waited expectantly. I wondered whether he would accept my invitation.

"However, I fear I can't be a part of it, though the Group Captain's generous invitation *is* tempting...I find I must remain and hold the attention of your husband for yet another day, Millie. There's a picnic in the offing, too and I'd jump at it if I were you young people. Metro said the morrow's warranted to be a fine day—unfortunately for our chaps in the air. Stick out like a sore thumb when they go over tomorrow, aye Group Captain?"

My mouth was open to speak.

"Air Marshal," Millie interrupted, "we don't talk about *business* at *my* parties, remember? At least not in mixed company, so please reserve your comments about the weather to...to *fishing* and picnics," she said, smiling round and squeezing my arm and making my heart thrill again.

"Point well taken, Millie," he responded. "Unfortunately, I must find your husband again and fix something I just thought of...the weather you know...before your fine dinner ruins both my appetite and my memory. Will you all please excuse me?" He bowed slightly, nodding to Millie's companion as if he knew her and turning, strode across the garden.

Millie turned back toward me, taking a step backward and bringing her companion around to face me "Robert—Group Captain Johnson—I'd like you to meet a new friend of ours and a house guest for a while—Birgitta...this is Robert—Group Captain Johnson."

The woman smiled and slowly extended her hand to me. "How do you do, Group Captain Johnson. Millie has spoken very highly of your exploits."

"It is a pleasure to meet you—Ma'am..."

"Oh—he *is* American, Millie..." she chuckled, "...I've never been called Ma'am, before—how...*enchanting*," she said, smiling first at Millie then toward me.

"I told you Birgitta...you won't find much Swede in him—at least that shows, anyway, but there's lots of American sticking out all over."

"You—you are Swedish?" Birgitta asked me.

"Yes—no, well, Mother was Swedish—I'm American, but I carry both passports. I grew up in America—in the mid-south. That's why you got a Ma'am before. I'm sorry if it…"

"Oh, please, do not apologize—I find it most charming. I have met few Americans in my life and then only the stuffy, diplomatic ones. None of them ever called me *Ma'am*. I liked it."

Millie interrupted us. "You two—duty calls and I must be off. Will you be all right for a while? Dinner's not for another forty-five minutes so help yourselves to some *hors 'd oeuvres*." She scurried across the garden in the direction of a young girl with an apron and carrying a tray.

Millie'd only introduced the woman by her first name.

"Miss…" I stammered.

"Please, just call me Birgitta."

"Thank you, Birgitta. Then you must call me Robert. I'm sorry, may I get you a drink? I was confused that Millie didn't mention your last name…"

"Oh…do not concern yourself, but that is normal. It is rather complicated and hard to pronounce, you see…a foreign sounding name."

"Oh. Is it English—one of those double-barreled names, like…Smith-Grosvenor, or something?"

"Yes—or something," she laughed, still not saying what it was, which I found curious.

"You come from London?" I asked, trying to guess her accent.

"What makes you think that, Group Captain…*Robert?*"

"Your accent. It's—it's not local—South-of-Englandish…*nor* is it London. It's…it's hard to tell, actually? Somehow, it almost sounds—*foreign.* No offense, please, I should have said it's *exotic*, that's a better choice of words."

"Oh that is nice: *exotic*…I do like that Robert. But I'm afraid it is far from that, you see. But you have a good ear. I *am not* British…*Jag kommer från Norge*…" she said in perfect Swedish: "I come from Norway".

I believe my mouth must have opened and closed; I was

rather taken aback.

"I did surprise you, did I not? Please—are you...*upset...?*"
She reached forward, taking my upper arm as if to comfort me if I
was offended.

"Why—no. Only...Millie didn't tell me...it's a pleasant
surprise, Birgitta. And a total one."

"I am pleased I did not offend you. I see you speak Swedish—or, at least understand it enough to understand my Norwegian-
Swedish?"

"Yes, a little of both, actually. Mostly what I speak is from
the last century. The emigrant generation, you know. But I've picked
up enough of the new Swedish to get by. I often surprise some of
the Swedes I meet...my old words do. Some of them don't even
know what I'm referring to. I believe they assume I am a farmer or
something."

"How interesting...I studied languages in school. I wanted
to take up our old, local dialects—*mål*—do you not call them that?
But I didn't have the time; and there are so many of them, of course.
Old *Norsk* and *Svenska* and especially the older post-Viking dialects,
they are supposed to be quite similar."

"A lot from the Viking's words, I'm told, came into English.
That's always been an interest of mine. But—as with you, I didn't
pursue it."

"So what brings you to Britain's war, Robert. As a Group
Captain, you must have been in the service quite a while...to attain
such a high rank...and remain so...*young?*"

"No, not really. I..." I started to say, I'd outlived all my
potential competition, but instead, I said: "I've been lucky, I guess
the right place at the right time, you might say."

"Really...how do you come to...being an American...be in
the British military and as an officer, at that?"

"Like some other Americans, I came over early to join up;
before it is really going for us. A lot of Americans also went to
Canada to join, as you may know."

"Yes, I have heard about that. Very brave of you all."

"Thanks, but I don't think bravery figured into it much, at
least in the beginning. More—*naivete* I think. After I got into air
combat, I found out what bravery was—or the absence of it—being

scared, but I believe I'm violating Millie's rule of talking shop."

"I'm certain Group Captain, if you fly those airplanes in combat, you're certainly not without bravery."

I didn't know what to say, not wishing to continue on the subject of the war, but I didn't know where else to go with it. Fortunately, the young woman with the apron had traded her tray for a dinner gong and had come through the back door and was now vigorously banging it with a little cloth-covered hammer, saying: "dinner—please come to dinner now. Dinner is being served...."

Birgitta glanced around searching for a place to put her glass. "Here, let me take that for you," I said, taking the glass and walking over to the little caddy. There was a tray beneath the trolley, where I put both glasses. But, when I straightened and looked round, she was gone. I looked over the heads of those going through the doorway, but didn't see her. I was momentarily disappointed, then, wondering where she'd disappeared to so quickly. Then I saw her immediately behind me, down the garden path, bending over a brilliant rose bush. I caught up with her just as she straightened, exhaling deeply.

"What a fragrance," she beamed. "Whenever I think of the war—all this," she gestured around the air, "I can smell a fragrant bloom such as this and know nature is beyond the mere folly of man, able to produce extraordinary beauty of sight and smell, despite the environment. After we are finished with our petty quarrels, she will again be foremost in our minds."

"The garden *is* lovely," I said, impressed with her sensitivity. "It's one of Millie's prides." This lady's forthright manner was disarming, I thought, wondering where she'd come from to be at this party. And she was a real beauty, too, but different somehow. Regal beauty—not merely pretty, or cute, like Millie. Birgitta had a certain bearing about her. Yet, she was common enough and fun to be with; she laughed like a young girl. But thinking about it I realized my heart was still safe with Millie. There could be no romantic leanings with Birgitta, though I was really enjoying her refreshing manner and company.

"Listen to dreary, old me," she said. "I've been around *them* too long," she gestured toward the wealth of graying heads entering the house ahead of us. "Perhaps I should have another glass of wine before we go in—improve my attitude...."

"I can get a glass....":

"No, thank you. I'm merely being silly, Robert. There will no doubt be ample alcohol at the Air Vice Marshal's table—or, do you know?"

"Yes, I've eaten...*dined* here before. Millie does a nice job."

By that time we were up the steps and turning into the dining room. Millie was already directing couples to their chairs. Marsh was already seated at the head. The Air Marshal sat three chairs to his left. I assumed Millie would be somewhere there, but she directed Birgitta to his right hand, instead. I helped her with her chair, surprised she was seated there instead of the Air Marshal, whom I thought would have been highest ranking guest and occupy the right hand of the host.

"Robert—sit right there *please*—beside Birgitta...yes, that's correct. Agnetha...no—not there dear. Two to your right...there where it says Agnetha. Yes, that's it...."

She continued barking orders efficiently until we were all seated. I ended up with Millie seated directly across the table from me, which pleased me. I'd be able to look into her green eyes throughout dinner. Birgitta was seated on my left; the best of both worlds. Millie had the Air Marshal on her right and there was the Mayor's wife between him and her husband. So it went, around the table.

As we began arranging our napkins in our laps, Millie picked up a small, brass bell and gave it a shake. It tinkled brightly, sounding rather strange, somehow, in the formal atmosphere of an elegant dinner party. Oddly, it reminded me of the bells the women put on goats in rural Sweden, where my relations were from—Dalarna, in the *fäbod*. My mother'd occasionally taken me there as a child.

"Why are you smiling Robert?" Birgitta asked in a hushed tone, glancing at me below lowered lids.

"Oh, nothing. It was that sound—the bell. It reminded me of someplace, that's all."

"Another dinner party?"

"No, not at all. To the contrary—far from it."

"So who...?"

"My great-grandmother's farm, actually...it sounded like her goat's bell."

"*Goat's* bell...?" She laughed out loud, smiling at me.

"Yes...they put them on some of the goats, in the forest—in Sweden. My grandmother...."

"Yes—that is true in Norway also," she interrupted, "we do the same...when we let the animals run free."

"Where, in Norway?"

"I come..."

"What are you two conspiring about?" Millie chirped, leaning forward across the table. "Not talking shop, is he Birgitta? Better not be, Robert."

"No—we were talking about goats," Birgitta replied, smiling mischievously.

"*Goats*, the Air Marshal said, guffawing. *Lord Mayor!*" he leaned forward and peered down the table, "they're talking about us over at this end...*goats.* Ha!" he exclaimed, shaking his head and slapping the tablecloth lightly. "Thought they bloody be talking about something else." He was muttering and I never heard him finish the sentence since he bent back over his soup.

And so it went through the soup course. The Air Marshal had had his measure of grog, although he didn't quite become obnoxious. He did remain rather spirited, laughing and teasing Millie about the cut of her gown, among other subjects. For a while I chatted with the woman on my right, who seemed a bit out of place, despite the status of her husband's office; he was someone in the local shire government. I felt a little sorry for her; she wasn't able to hold up much of her end in the conversation. Then her seat-mate on the other side, a local manufacturer, got to discussing cats with her. They were soon off on a subject I found excruciatingly boring. I was happy to give her up and turn back to Birgitta who'd been mixing with Millie and Marsh.

I was content to just take my time with the food and wine, happy I'd not overeaten at lunch. We were in the fish course when I heard the Air Marshal laughing and then Millie chided him again about talking shop.

"Air Marshal, I simply won't have it—not at dinner. We

can't get away from it during the day, so I don't wish to discuss the war at dinner—even if your are sympathetic to the Norwegian predicament." I hadn't been following the discussion so had no idea what they were on.

"But Millie! I *wasn't* talking shop, I tell you. I was discussing philosophy—*history*, if you will. We're living it—*right*, Princess!" he said, turning to Birgitta.

I was surprised by his usage of *that* word and wondered at his being rather childishly familiar with her. Maybe he'd known her long enough to use an endearment like that, but I doubted it. It seemed out of place, that form of endearment. She didn't seem to take offense, or remark about his comment. No one else seemed to take notice, either, but Millie frowned: "Sir...you *were* discussing the *Nazi* invasion of Norway...oh—now see, you have me doing it, too."

"I was only sympathizing with the Princess' family, having to rush off like that and come to England on such short notice and now, probably having to rush off again and live in America."

"Can't really say it was short notice Air Marshal," the Air Vice Marshal spoke up, winking at Birgitta. "Hitler announced his intentions long ago."

Millie protested again, flustered and seeming to lose her own war about breaking the rules of discussion and speak of the war.

"Of course he did. But he couldn't let Norway walk that thin line of neutrality, as he's done in Sweden. And besides, they didn't have the iron ore or the ball bearings."

"*Has* Sweden?" someone down-table chimed in. "Hitler *isn't* yet finished with Sweden."

"Well...anyway," it was the Air Marshal again, "you can hardly call England exiled. Not like Elba—*Napoleon*...you know."

"But it isn't her *home*, Air Marshal," Millie again. "Being forced, against your will, to go—*abide* anywhere—anywhere that isn't your home, away from your subjects, *is exile*."

They *were* talking about Birgitta. He had called her *Princess* three times. And still, no one took any special notice. They'd also said "subjects," so she must be; I think my mouth stood open in wonder.

When I turned to Birgitta, she met my glance evenly. Then, with an embarrassed smile playing about her mouth, she said quietly, placing her hand on my arm.

"They did not tell you, did they?"

"I'm not quite so sure about what they didn't tell me?"

"I am truly sorry," she glanced at Millie. "You see..." she bent, speaking quietly again. The two officers were trying to out-talk each other and took no notice. "...Millie didn't want to tell you right away." Birgitta seemed to lose her line of reason. "She wanted me to tell you later, after we had grown to know one another somewhat."

"For God's sake, why?" I hesitated to ask. "Certainly not...potential *romance?*"

"Oh, no. It has something to do with..." she glanced to my right. No one paid us any attention from that quarter; it was still cats, as far as I could tell.

"With what they've offered you, earlier. The new *posting?*" She almost whispered it.

"You know about *that?*" I whispered back, leaning toward her.

"I—we are a part of it...my family are."

"The king...and queen...*of Norway,*" I whispered?

She put a finger to her lips, glancing sideways. "My parents...*yes,* at least the whole family, while they're still here...in England. We are a small country and very few responsible people have gotten out *yet,* since the *Nazi* invasion. More come all the time; but for now, we must make do with what we have. Yes, my father is active, as am I."

I was flabbergasted and could only look at her. Finally, I said: "I suppose everyone tells you they've never met a real princess before?"

"No, actually, they do not. Most people do not know who we are, when they see us. We do not actually get out into the public that often, either. The *Nazis* would kill my father...and mother, my other siblings...all of us for that matter, in an instant, if they could find us. We must keep moving. Especially those of us here in England."

"Well now, this explains all the armed soldiers out front. I'd wondered...a bit much, even for a Air Marshal."

"You mean the soldier guards? Yes, unfortunately, it is a

necessity. Even in Britain."

Millie had been listening by that time. "I've had the worst time with those guards, Robert. They continually become tangled with the roses. I've asked them to stay on the paths, but no...they must peek and pry in every nook and cranny. They expect *Nazis* to be hiding under every garden stone—along with *your* two's *trolls*," she added with a conspiratorial wink.

I grinned then: "I'm certain, Millie, especially now that I know the reason for their being here, that they can't leave any potentially suspicious person, or *troll*, unchallenged...for the safety of— well, everyone here who might get in the way of any potential assassination targets."

"Of course you're right, Robert. Birgitta is a treasure to us and we're so pleased to have her here."

"You are so kind, Millie...to have me."

"What a *morose* subject you are discussing," I quipped to Millie. "Let's talk about something more cheerful...like the war."

"Thanks, Robert. I guess I deserved that."

"Not really, Millie; just teasing."

"I know dear, but your point is well taken.

Most of us had finished our desserts by then. Millie stood, putting her napkin on the table beside her plate. "It seems everyone is finished...?" she glanced up and down the table and then addressed the lot of us as a group. "I think it's time for the gentlemen to retire to the library for the three "C's," coffee, cognac and cigars, or, cigarettes, if that is your choice. Ladies...we are left to our own resources, if you will follow me."

There was a scrape of chairs as we all pushed back and tossed our napkins on the table. I helped the princess with her chair, now having a new respect for her position. "I'm not much for smoking, Birgitta; want to have a stroll in the garden?"

"Yes—thank you. I would enjoy that...we could discuss your inclination...*you know?*" She whispered, bending toward me.

"You mean, my decision—the Air Marshal?"

"Exactly. Do you mind? I know you promised them you would let them know by Monday, was it? But I have a specific interest in getting on with it."

"Yes, I did tell them that. I must admit, now that I know

you...your family—government are involved, I'd like to hear your side of it, if you don't mind?"

We were down the front steps and soon walking along one of the paths. I noticed one of the guards had broken off and was following us at a discrete distance. He'd un-slung his automatic rifle

"I would like my personal chance to influence your decision, Robert. Thank you."

"Really—you're that serious, are you?"

"Absolutely committed. I have seen your dossier. I know rather a lot about you. That is why I asked to be invited here—to meet you, personally and if you were willing, to attempt to give you a sense of the need my country has for men...*people* like yourself. We are—*have*, recruited many women as well."

"What did you learn from my file...my dossier? I'd like to see it," I said curiously.

"Oh," she smiled, "all sort of things. I know how old you are—only a year older than I...and, you've never married...you come from a...how do you say it...a country life—background?"

"Rural background we might say; but, yes, country...the same thing."

"And...?"

"Excuse me, Birgitta..." I interrupted her. "Why...why this personal stuff? I would have thought you'd be most interested in how many Hurricanes or Spits I've cracked up or my personal impact on Hitler's *Luftwaffe*."

"We have already been assured of those—I hate to call them skills: *talents?* But given those, we still needed to feel assured you would have the other personal qualities of someone working with us should have."

"And how do I measure up, if you don't mind my asking...so far?"

"Superbly...that *is* why I am here. We feel we are made for each other, figuratively speaking—the Norwegian need and you to supply it."

I frowned at her remark, not that I didn't enjoy flattery, when it was well meant. But I didn't feel *superb* at the moment, after my recent battle of nerves. I'd also had enough of people talking about me, that evening. I was quiet for a moment as I considered what

Birgitta had related.

"You're frowning, Robert. Have I offended you by speaking so plainly? I am sorry if I have."

"Well, no, not really. It's just—recently, I haven't felt I deserved much—much of that."

"I see—I suppose we all go through that: good days, bad days. In the end they all even out. Robert?" she'd stopped along the path, turned and put her hand on my forearm. "I wish to put all my cards on the table. Is that the expression?"

I smiled at the Americanism, which made her frown.

"We play cards in Norway? You know what I mean. Anyway, your talents do not need to be elaborated upon. You have outlived almost all the fighter pilots in the RAF, flying fighters in combat. You and *we* know, it is only a matter of time...the odds? You will *buy it* Robert; it will happen—it should have happened before now—you know it, too."

She paused as if to let me consider her extremely frank remarks. I merely nodded.

"Yes—you are an exceptional pilot they say, but the odds, Robert...we do not wish to sacrifice you to a mathematical formula. Your talents are honed; your skills perfect. Your background: the language, your looks..."

I frowned then.

"Yes—well, there is a woman involved in our plans...." At my frown again, she quickly added: "...but not me, Robert. I hope you are not disappointed now?"

"No. It's that, we are going so fast here."

"I know Robert and I am sorry, but we must. I am speaking as plainly as I can. My country—Norway, needs you. Never mind you're part Swedish—God, some of my ancestors would roll over in their graves at the thought of having to depend on a Swede [6] for anything for the Norwegian Crown." She chuckled, shaking her head slowly.

"Yes, I know. It even exists a bit in America—the rivalry."

"Really? Who would have thought it would follow the emigrants? But to continue, there is a situation where we desperately need someone, as I said—with your talents, to assist us. I'm sorry I can not say anything more—until you agree to grant our request.

Your superiors want you for one matter, shall we call it and I, for another: something personal, but concerning a great deal of my countrymen—*countrywomen*."

"Well, it has certainly gotten interesting, Birgitta. I never thought I would meet a princess, or be useful to a country—directly." I thought for another moment. "And you say there is *another* woman involved?"

"Yes, I did say that and there is."

"Is she pretty?"

Birgitta smiled brightly, turning back along the path.

"Yes—she is very pretty; even beautiful, I am told...and quite bright, also, they say."

"As pretty as you..." I said, hoping I wasn't being impertinent.

Birgitta actually blushed and for an instant I got a glimpse of the real young woman beneath the sometimes-regal visage.

"I—I am afraid I can not be the judge of that, Robert—and thank you...I believe you really meant it."

"Birgitta, believe me, I did." She smiled and squeezed my arm above the elbow.

We walked along the meandering path, turning where it entered the far end of the rear garden. There was another soldier who, seeing us, melded into the undergrowth so we could pass unrestricted and undisturbed.

"I just don't know, Birgitta." I didn't want to give her false hope. "Before we spoke—based on my conversation with the Air Vice Marshal and the Air Marshal, I was prepared to turn them down."

"I feared that might happen, Robert, after hearing a synopsis of the planned presentation that was to be made to you. That is why Millie arranged for me to be here. I—in advance, I asked her to invite me, knowing you would be attending. My small experience has proven to me already...career officers—line officers...they do not make the best public relations persons. An instance like the one we have discussed required that, I felt. And that is why I wished to make my appeal personally. I felt you had the sensitivity, in addition to all the *physical* attributes, to carry out our request."

"It is my turn to thank you, Birgitta and I do: thanks for the confidence. I'm still not sure I deserve it. And I would still like to *fish* on it."

"I am sorry Robert…did you say *fish* on it?"

"Yes fish," I nodded, "tomorrow, I'm going fishing…in the New Forest, for…pike—*gädda* they say in Swedish; I don't know the Norwegian."

"Really," she laughed out loud, bending and glancing at the tips of her toes poking from beneath the gown. "Are they large ones…these English *gädda?*"

"I certainly hope so. That's what *all* fishermen wish for." She stared at her inter-linked fingers for a second before answering.

"My grandfather, when I was a child, he would to take me *lax—salmon* fishing. It was very enjoyable, even for me as a girl. He would have a picnic lunch packed for us. And…when it was time, after he had fished for a while and he suspected I was hungry, we would both sit beside the stream eating and drinking in the sunshine—all sorts of delicious things we had brought along. He drank some things which I could not, of course, beer and spirits, probably. But, it was such great fun. I wish…how I wish…I could do it again—just one more time. But he has died some years ago and now there is the war."

"I'm sorry, I said."

She smiled and nodded slightly.

"Then it's set?"

She had re-clasped her hands in front of her as we strolled, interlacing her fingers. "Set…what is set?" she laughed twisting toward me.

"Fishing with me tomorrow…why not come along? I'm sure the food's not up the caliber your grandfather got up, but…?"

"I meant, after the war Robert. Grandfather is dead and I fear I could not repeat the same feeling. It would not be the same again…*now*. With the war…but thank you just the same," she smiled and waved casually to a guard who momentarily appeared in front of us along the path.

"Why not—get them…" I nodded toward the guard, "…to exchange their Stenguns for fishing rods for a day?"

"Do not be ridiculous, Robert. It is not that."

"Then what is it? Another…fisherman; do I have a rival? Is there previous rendezvous? Break it—spur of the moment…come have some fun...*forget* the war for a day."

"Oh Robert—you are impossibly immature I believe—*it* is with the King and Queen—my father and mother...we have plans. We are having luncheon together tomorrow."

"Oh—sorry, I didn't mean to be impertinent."

"It is all right, Robert; there is no need to apologize. It is nothing special. We make a habit of lunching together Sundays, if we can. You see, they are parents...like your parents? Concerned, caring and right now, very busy with the war and trying to get our country back from the Nazis."

"I understand. But you'll miss your only chance to convince me."

"Oh—damn!" she said quietly, "I hadn't thought of that. In that case, Robert; I *accept.*"

"You do?" Just like that? What about your parents?"

"I will be excused."

"You will postpone your meal...for me?"

"Yes. When do we leave? What should I wear? Must I bring a—a fly rod?"

I suddenly liked the idea and I realized how very much I'd come to *like* her, in such a short time. Not in a womanish, romantic sort of way; she was just a good sport and working hard at something she really believed in, but was quite ill-equipped to handle properly because of her position. I laughed at her nervous excitement.

"No, unless you truly intend to fish. I don't believe a fly rod will do you much good. The salmon, or trout season isn't open at the moment, either, I don't believe. You must also acquire a license, if you are going to fish. Otherwise, you could get arrested and have to explain that to your father and mother—probably King George, too, since they're technically *his* fish."

Birgitta laughed and took my arm. "Just tell me what I have to bring, Robert and when to be ready—all of us," she said, gesturing toward the guard who had since vanished, "...at least a dozen of those go everywhere with me."

"God...ok, how will *we* get there then...I hadn't planned on...*bearers.* A bicycle is now probably out of the question. It will look like a convoy of schoolboys—with machine guns."

"We can take the staff vehicles I have at my disposal. What about...if we pick *you* up...at your quarters?"

I shook my head. "Better make it the crossroads to Evershley."

"All right, I'll inform the soldier's commander. At what time, Robert?"

"How about seven?

"In the morning...*so early?*"

"Fish won't wait for pretty girls."

She blushed again. "*Robert....*"

"Seriously, Birgitta. I'll bring lunch for us. Can they take care of themselves?"

"Of course. They're His Majesty's—*British Majesties*—finest troops. Just give me an idea how long we will be away."

I thought for a second. "Oh—fishing—lunch—clean the fish—more fishing—dinner—a *movie....*"

"Oh, you are hopeless," she laughed openly, her head back, slightly. I had a feeling she hadn't done that for some time.

"We should be home in time for tea," I said, meaning it."

"Wonderful! I will inform the men. I really must be going now, Robert. Thank you! We shall see you at seven." She squeezed my arm again, a habit of hers. Must be her way of touching her subjects, I reasoned. She dashed up the back stairs disappearing inside. I saw two of her guards walking briskly around one end of the garden, headed for her car, I supposed.

Back in the house, Millie cornered me as soon as she could separate herself from her other guests.

"Robert—are you upset with me that I didn't tell you?"

"Certainly not, Millie, I was just surprised, that's all. And...I guess I don't understand why you did it—when everyone else seemed to know Birgitta was a Norwegian princess."

"I wanted you to be at ease with her when she approached you. I thought you could easily become acquainted with her without any pre-conceived notions—*knowledge* that might cause you to put up some reserve, put her off you...and vice-versa."

"Oh?" I didn't know what else to say. "I guess it worked. She's a lot of fun. I enjoyed the evening, Millie. Thanks for inviting me."

"You are most welcome, Robert."

She stood waiting as if she expected something else.

"Do you...is there any chance...will she have a chance to present her case?"

"Before I come to a decision about the Air Marshal's offer?"

"Yes, that's what I meant."

"I should think so, Millie."

"Oh," she said hastily, "then I can arrange another meeting—you two...?"

"No, need—we're going fishing in the morning. She can work on me all she wants to then."

"*Fishing*? Oh, *Robert*! You can't take a princess...*fishing*?" She shook her head in disbelief.

"Sure I can. The Air Marshal will eat his heart out when he hears what he turned down. I only hope we catch some nice pike. Then he'll really be envious."

"Oh, Robert." She shook her head, laughing.

Before I could respond, my superiors joined us. The Air Vice Marshal walked over and put his arm around my shoulder.

"Well, Group Captain," he said, smiling, "you've certainly been busy this evening," giving a knowing lift to his eyebrows. "Any questions?"

"No, Sir, none. I might tomorrow, but not this evening."

"Well, just ask...just ask, my boy. How about another drink?"

"No thank you, I must be going. Early...fishing, tomorrow, remember?"

"Oh—yes...that. Damn me—wish I could accompany you."

I bid him a quick good night before he figured out a way. Then I sought out my hosts and feigning the need to prepare my fishing kit, I also bid them goodbye and left the party as quickly as I could.

CHAPTER

3

Fishing

Home from the party and back in my quarters, I did a lot of emotional sorting out, so to speak. I made a small pot of coffee from my private stash and then took the cup and lay down on my bunk, crossed my legs and put my hands behind my head, in order to contemplate the week's events. First of all, I'd come to the realization that flying combat missions had me close to cracking up and that I probably would, soon, if I continued in Spits. A valid and convincing footnote to that given was the probability that it could easily cost the life of others, depending upon me to do my part, at the time.

Second, I'd been offered a new posting which, though it would take me away from flying Spits—my only true love and also commanding the squadron and keeping others safe, *countering* the previous, favorable argument The position would still have me flying, but something far larger, multi-engined, slower passenger aircraft. Also, passengers...another area I had no experience with. No doubt Squadron had some plans to update my skills, there. This was the part of the puzzle they had held back on in the morning meeting.

Thirdly, I'd actually met a real princess and I'd found her a surprisingly nice person. More than that, she was enjoyable and was to be a part—I wasn't sure how much—of this new posting.

I considered that for a while before I finally decided that she

71

must have really brought herself away from the things a princess normally did, whatever that was. To become deeply involved in the war effort, after being expelled from one's own country, was something an ordinary person might do. However, for someone of royalty—it now seemed an exceptional effort; especially, a young woman. Somewhere, I'd gotten the idea that kings and people of that sort usually ran away from such endeavors.

The coffee cleared my head and I was glad I'd saved it for something special. I took the last sip, even drinking the sludge in the bottom of the cup. I wonder if I can get coffee in Sweden? As an international airline pilot in Sweden, I should be able to bring in about anything into the country I wanted and take it out, too. I rinsed my cup and undressed for bed. I made sure all my fishing clothing was lain out. It was nothing special; just a worn out and faded version of the same uniform I wore every day. The one exception, was a beige, coconut-palm hat I'd bought up in London, on a whim. It took away a bit of the military, I thought, turning off the single bulb beside my bed.

I'd decided to ride a bicycle to the rendezvous point to avoid questions. It was cold when I strapped on my gear and swung a leg over the seat and there was fog. If the squadron was up, they'd had to take off in near zero-zero weather. No fun to return and land in, if it didn't clear enough to see the ground by then. They might have to put down elsewhere and wait until it lifted. Maybe go to the station at Debney.

I pedaled across the parade ground to the base kitchen to see if there was anything to eat. I found an airman washing up. I thought the Princess' boys might not be able to shift too well for themselves and decided to bring extra sandwiches. When I inquired, he said he'd gladly fix me up enough kit for a dozen men. Later, it presented a problem with my bike, but between the airman and I, we got all of it secured without breaking my fishing outfit and I was soon off on a wobbly start for the crossroads.

I hadn't banked on all that extra weight and despite the fact there were only gentle grades here and there, I was bushed when I finally coasted in between a pair of commandos who appeared out of the fog. They were facing me with their Stenguns in readiness. Seeing my rank when I dismounted, they both saluted.

Birgitta came out of the mist just then and climbed over a stile. She'd evidently been roaming in the dew-wet pasture. She wore muddy *wellies*, army drill pants and a light straw hat with a long blue ribbon, which completely broke the mood of her county squires lady's dress trousers.

"You are late, Robert," she said taking off her hat and watching as I unloaded my gear, "and I can see why, too. What do you have in those sacks?" She was peering curiously at my loaded bicycle, which resembled a pack burrow.

"A picnic for twelve," I joked.

"Oh—really...*honestly*...?" she asked, when I nodded. A young lieutenant jumped from the cab of one of the trucks; he appeared to be in charge. Birgitta turned as he approached.

"Your lot are fortunate, Lieutenant—the Group Captain's fixed you lunch."

The lieutenant, saluted me and then smiled and nodded toward another of the trucks that was parked across the intersection. Glancing around, I reckoned there must be no more than ten soldiers. There would be extra lunch.

"This is Group Captain Johnson..." Birgitta introduced me to the tall, young man, Lieutenant Stone. "The Lieutenant forgot the men's lunch, so you will be in high favor today, Group Captain."

Lieutenant Stone shook my hand: "Sir, if you would let me take your bicycle...and lunch...*lunches*, we can put them in the back of one of the lorries. You should also take a seat and ride up front with Her Majesty."

I nodded and stepped aside, letting him take my bike and wheel it toward the rear of the truck where another of the guards, slung his Stengun and disappeared around the truck with it. I followed the princess up to the third truck in line, where she started to climb up.

"Second one, Mum," the lieutenant said, gesturing with his arm toward the rear of our convoy of four trucks.

"Oh—I forgot. Sorry," she said and we began walking back to the next truck.

73

"What was that all about?" I asked, following her up the short truck's ladder. Sliding behind on the left side, I squeezed into the seat next to her and slammed the door. She was in the middle between the driver and me.

"At each stop, I must change vehicles. That way, if we have been *targeted* from a previous stop, they will make the mistake of thinking me still in the same vehicle I started out in."

"Oh, not bad thinking; have you seen anyone suspicious yet?" I had to keep from smiling, though I knew the threat was real.

"So far—so good, but then…I've not been watching. That's up to the lieutenant and his men."

"Four-to-one…" I said, smiling to myself, "…the odds."

"Yes, not such bad odds. When my parents travel, there are often many different vehicles in the entourage, but that's not very often.

The trucks had started moving by then, not going very fast because of the fog. We probably resembled a small training convoy. As we came to a straightaway, I was surprised when the curtain covering what I thought was a window in the rear of our cab slid open and the lieutenant's face appeared.

"Driver—now, take the lead…perhaps you will be so kind as to direct us to the…destination, Sir," he glanced at me.

I felt a little silly about the whole thing by this time. All these men…and a princess; I only just wanted to go fishing and was beginning to regret my impromptu invitation. We swung onto the opposite side of the tarmac and began to accelerate, quickly passing the other three trucks on the right.

It was too noisy in the cab for general conversation and I had to shout instructions to the driver from time to time, warning him of the turnings and gesturing direction my left hand. The princess was comfortably nestled between the driver and my right side. Occasionally, our thighs touched as the truck bounced and swayed along the narrow road; not an entirely unpleasant sensation, I realized. After three-quarters of an hour's driving in silence, I raised a hand to warn the driver.

"The village of Bexley Green is just ahead," I shouted, gesturing forward. "Take the second turning to the left after the pub…the Green Lion and then the first left right after. Go slow for the turn. It becomes a dirt track at that point."

The driver nodded and continued ahead. Within five minutes we approached Bexley Green. It was a very small villiage and
like all, old English towns had kept its narrow streets. As we slowed
to pass through the main square, my side of the truck nearly touched
the colorful flower boxes filled with red-blooming geraniums, hanging beneath nearly every window.

I noticed a trapped bicyclist closely hugging a wall as we
passed. We didn't stop for the intersection and a couple of pedestrians glanced angrily in our direction. In the rear view mirror I saw the
bicyclist glance back after our last truck passed to see if it was finally
safe to venture onto the road once again.

Slowing only slightly as we turned onto the graveled road,
we worked our way out of the village and eventually approached a
large curve that I remembered came before the second to last turn.
Suddenly the driver braked hard. There was an old truck crossways
in the road, completely blocking the passage.

"Take to the field and carry on 'round 'im!" the lieutenant
shouted from the window behind us. "Put on more speed!"

I turned, glancing through the back window to see him directing two soldiers to leap from the rear of our truck. Turning
toward Birgitta as we hit the soft earth along the shoulder of the
road, I reached across in front of her, grabbing the seat back between the driver and her. She was pinned safely behind my outstretched arm and my body just as the truck lurched over a plow
furrow, so hard, I hit my head on the back of the cab.

The driver was wrestling the steering wheel while down-
shifting to keep the lumbering monster from overturning, or becoming mired as we bounced past. We'd slammed and bounced off the
gravel, into the field and then back on the road again. Birgitta careened between my chest and the arm I'd locked onto the seat back.
The motion was so violent, the driver was forced to slow, momentarily.

"Don't stop...carry on!" the lieutenant shouted, his head
and shoulders again in the opening. Back on the gravel, I let go of
the seat back and Birgitta glanced up at me, fright on her face. Her
lips moved, but I couldn't make out what she said. I assumed it was
a thank you.

I glanced in the side mirror again and saw that all the trucks had safely bypassed the blockade, if in fact, that was what it was. One of the trucks had stopped and I could see our soldiers spreading out alongside it, Stenguns in readiness. There were also more soldiers standing along the shoulder. The soldiers from our truck had also leaped out and were taking defensive positions around our vehicle, front and rear.

"What do you think, Lieutenant?" Birgitta glance over her shoulder. "Could it have been...you know?"

"Difficult to determine...but we shan't take any chances. The Sergeant Major will report soon. Meanwhile...*driver*, hold up, but keep your engine ticking over. We'll remain here and await the report. If firing breaks out, put the truck in gear and move away post haste."

To me he said, "Sir...where does this road go if we keep going straight ahead?"

"To London, if you go far enough. But if we take the turning then, as we planned, it ends at the mill pond. We have only to go another quarter mile to the final turn. If you have extra arms, Lieutenant, I'll gladly take one."

No sooner had I spoken than he handed me his Wembley revolver, butt first. I examined it for cartridges in the cylinder; it was full. Birgitta watched me. I was glad the lieutenant didn't expect me to use one of the Stenguns; I'd never even held one.

"I hate those," she said quietly, gesturing with a nod of her head. The driver glanced sideways. Even though the truck's engine was at idle, we both heard her. "Every since...since the *Nazis* came. Before, the entire palace hunted during the season—I grew up around firearms...hunting. But now...these only remind me of what one is capable of—their misuse."

Before I could respond, the lieutenant spoke through the opening: "Hello—something's happening back there."

I glanced in the mirror and watched the Sergeant Major double-timing it up the road toward our truck. He came up behind and the lieutenant went back to the tailgate. After a minute's conversation, the lieutenant turned and crouch-walked back toward us and I saw the soldier trotting back toward the lone truck, still halted between us and the suspect vehicle.

The lieutenant's head came through the opening: "Seems to be all-right. The truck is legitimate—local farmer; got a load of grain of some sort. Said he'd forgotten his wallet to pay the miller that would grind the grain—where we're going. Tried to turn around, killed the motor and wasn't able to start it. Sergeant Major said the float was stuck in the carburetor. Precious gasoline pouring out and the farmer fit to be tied with the waste. Told them to push him around so he's not blocking traffic, but nothing else and to be careful. He'll have to get it fixed, himself, somehow. We can move on in a minute. I don't wish to take any chances."

After a few minutes the other truck started up the road toward us.

"All right, driver, carry on. Follow the Air Commodore's instructions for the proper turnings."

It wasn't far. We soon slowed and tipped off the pavement onto the rutted, dirt road that led to the mill and pond. "Ideal place for an ambush," I commented over my shoulder to the lieutenant. I still held his revolver. But nothing appeared in the half-mile drive and we were soon unloading men and fishing equipment beside the millpond.

"Appears your bicycle took a bit of a knock-about, Sir, when we took to the field, the lieutenant said. "Lunch's seems OK though, according to the men."

"Thank God for *that*," Birgitta said, smiling. "I am certain they would have fought even harder for the lunch." We all laughed at that, happy for the relief of some humor.

"Robert," she asked, "how do we go about this?"

"Maybe we should ask the lieutenant, I said."

"Where did you plan to uh...fish, Sir? Perhaps we should have a contingency plan...just in case."

"Up-stream—that's in the main body of water—work our way along the shoreline. We might go below the mill wheel later and fish the river there where the water's fast. But that would probably be after lunch if we do."

"Just go ahead as you would, Sir. My men and I will set up a parameter. We won't get close enough to be much of a bother. But if I call loudly, return immediately to the protection of the trucks, or to where ever I direct you verbally, or with hand signals. You'd better hang onto the sidearm, too."

"Easy enough," I said and began gathering up my fishing gear.

"Jones—cross the stream at the mill there; go with him, Bendix and Mc Laughlin, have a quick look around the mill and then come back here. Jones, set up a post on the other side of the dam after taking a look around the forest, there."

I turned to Birgitta who was watching this as if it was normal set up for her day. "Ok, Birgitta—let's do it." She followed me over to the lunch packs. I rummaged in one of them and came up with a thermos bottle and an extra cup. There was another paper bag I had pre-marked as our sandwiches. We gathered up the rod and my little tackle box.

"Here, you carry the lunch and I'll take the tackle."

We started up the path. None of the soldiers followed, but I knew they would and wouldn't be too far behind. I assumed there was at least one guard scouting the pond's shore ahead of us. I could hear the machinery running inside the mill and a small dust cloud drifted from the down-wind side. I wondered when and if our stranded farmer would arrive with his grain to be milled.

"This is pleasant, Robert. Thanks for asking me along."

"You're welcome and yes, isn't it."

"I do not want to ruin this beautiful day, but is there a spe-cial time when I am permitted to *talk shop*, as Millie might put it?"

"Oh...you'll know the right time, Birgitta. I trust you."

"But...? I do not want to ruin your pleasure—your fish-ing."

"You won't."

"But if...."

"Just use your judgement, Birgitta—look!" I pointed to ripples where a fish had just rolled over. "Did you see that one jump? Let's stop here," I said and put down my box and began to run the cotton line through the guides of my casting rod. Birgitta had placed the small pack containing the lunch on the grass bank and begun to watch me.

"I have never seen this type of fishing before Robert. My father uses a fly cast with a much smaller...thing on the end. I do not know how to say it in English: *flug?*"

"Fly—that's right. But this is called a plug...*lure.* We use flies—*flug*, also, but this is different. These lures are meant to imitate a small fish, frog, or, sometimes, even a mouse."

"Pike eat *mice*...Oh..." she continued to watch as I tied on one of my new, top-water lures. Since I'd just seen the fish surface, I thought they might be feeding on top of the water. I approached the shore, drew back, glancing behind me to be sure Birgitta wasn't within range of the rod-tip and the sharp hooks on the lure. I didn't want to hook a princess. I flung the lure, trying to control the line with my thumb pressing on the speeding spool, as line left the protesting reel. The reel handles spun in a blur for a moment and suddenly stopped with a jerk of the rod.

"Damn..." I muttered, not yet accustomed to the equipment.

"What...?"

"Nothing. I just got a backlash." I'd have to get accustomed to this new reel, I could see. As I untangled the birds-nest of tangled line in the reel spool, ripples spread concentrically from the lure, barely fifteen feet into the pond.

"Do you normally fish so close to shore, Robert? I believe my father cast his *flug*...his *flies* further into the water."

Repressing an urge to utter something nasty, instead, I replied. "Normally I do too. But this is new equipment—I must get used to the feel of it—grow accustomed...." I muttered the last words as she smiled behind her hand. I finished untangling the line by stripping it from the reel onto the grass. I reeled in the slack line, tightening it up until, finally, the lure twitched slightly. I waited a moment, concentrating on the rings growing outward from the lure. The words of my father returned and silently I gauged the time with an imaginary cigarette. When the rings reached the shore's edge, I twitched the rod tip again. The lure advanced toward me half a foot, making a loud "pop" sound.

"Why do you start and then stop returning it? Do you not want to throw—*cast* it again?"

"Yes—this is a slowly-fished lure. It must be brought in slowly. If I rush it..."

Just then there was the sound of smacking water and the

lure disappeared in a boil of water. I raised the rod quickly, tightening the line and gave the rod a big jerk. I felt solid fish on the end.

"Oh Robert!" Birgitta shrieked "...something has taken it under! Is it a fish?"

"Yeah—and a big one, too." I could feel the pull as the fish made its first run, diving deep. "I think it's a pike," I said over my shoulder.

"How can you be sure...did you see it?"

"No, just the swirl of the water and the strong pull. It's big and now...it's diving deep. That is the way pike behave when they're hooked."

The fish made another run. I let him go, controlling the pressure on the line coming from the reel's spool with my thumb until it began to burn from the friction. His automatic weapon momentarily forgotten, one of the guards had stopped to watch from across the pond. I deftly changed hands with the rod, sticking my aching thumb in my mouth. After a moment of continuous running, the fish began slowing from the steady pressure I was exerting. I switched hands again and slowly began to crank the reel handle. The pressure increased again and the taunt line made a "V" in the water toward the middle of the pond. And then the fish exploded from the water, coming high out, arching, seeming to dance on the surface for an instant. Silver spray flew in all directions in the sunlight. Just before the long, slender form fell back into the water, I noted the variegated green, silver and black, vertical stripes along the side of a very large pike.

"He must be over a yard long," I said to Birgitta, glancing over my shoulder.

She stood open mouthed, holding her hat in both hands, watching in wonder.

"Yes..." she said.

I patiently reeled against the steady pull of the fish. It now struggled less after the jump, making a couple of short runs before it tired and then let me lead him toward the shore. I was careful, though and sure enough, fearful of the moving forms it saw looming over it through the dimness of the water, as soon as I got it pulled close in, the fish bolted. I gave him his head and it took out some line from the reel. I kept a steady pressure on the spool with my thumb. When it slowed, I turned the pike again and it didn't take much to bring it back; it was tired now.

I carefully slid the fish into a shallow, sandy inlet in the bank. Running one's hands inside the gills of a pike will lead to torn fingers, when you try to remove them again. Using extreme care I stooped over, grabbing the fish behind the head. It was well-hooked and the sharp hooks on the dangling lure were dangerous should the fish flop or suddenly shake its head.

Birgitta was now leaning over me. "Robert, it looks terrible—such sharp teeth and so many! Be very careful. This is not like the salmon we have at home—*oh*!" She started, as the fish flopped wildly on it's tail.

Working carefully, I soon had the lure unhooked and then inserted a thin rope stringer through the pike's lower lip, leaving the gills free to breathe, so the fish could stay alive and fresh in the water until we were ready to leave. I was taking this one back—to eat, I thought, as I tied the other end of the rope to a tree limb and as evidence. I regretted I didn't own a camera.

I rinsed my hands after letting the long fish drop safely back into the water. As I removed the last of the slime from my hands, a satisfactory tugging on the rope convinced me the fish would remain alive and fresh until we were ready to leave later in the day.

"I need a rest after that one, Birgitta. Care to share a little coffee from the thermos?"

"Oh, yes. Gladly." She glanced around and pointed toward a large log a little further along the shore. "How about that tree?"

"Great," I said, picking up my tackle box. I noticed both the closest guards had been watching me land the fish were now chatting and laughing. Everyone was in the picnic mood.

Birgitta and I sat down on the log, each finding a limb crotch where we could sit and lean back on a branch arm for comfort. She'd poured us each a half-cup of steaming coffee.

"I hope you don't mind black coffee," I said.

"No, I am flexible." She leaned back, finding a comfortable fit with her part of the tree. There was a slight breeze. She'd taken off her straw hat and was smiling upward toward the sky and the morning sun was full on her face.

"If I didn't know better, I would say you looked like a common shop girl who is as happy as a princess," I chuckled.

"Thank you Sir, I am...except...."

"Always an exception?" What's your's this morning, Birgitta? I'm about perfect, having just landed the largest fish I ever caught in my whole life."

"That sounds like my entrance line: 'how to recruit a spy'—surely the timing couldn't be more perfect, Robert, how about it? What can I say to convince you of the importance of the endeavor?"

"Actually, Birgitta, I'd already decided to accept the Air Marshal's—and *your*, offer."

"You had! Why—you *cad*—why did you ask me to go fishing with you then?"

"Oh—I don't know. Maybe I was just lonesome; I hadn't decided yet, anyway, then. And of course, I'd never met a princess, as I said. And I liked you, too, if you don't mind saying, Birgitta. In fact, do you mind if I am a bit personal?"

"Well, that depends. How personal?"

"I guess, not that personal. I wanted to say you seemed, yesterday in the garden, a little overwhelmed by this whole thing; a person swimming in an awfully large sea."

"That is probably more accurate an observation, Robert, than I would like to admit."

"I didn't want it to sound like a criticism, Birgitta. What I also wanted to say is that I thought...though you were breathing hard, you were swimming quite well, in that sea. I felt a little sorry for you—please don't take offense. It isn't meant that way: pity. I thought you might profit from a day's fishing—getting away from it all. You seemed very earnest to recruit me for this new job, whatever it is? And had taken the time from your family to do it. So, I thought we might as well use it."

"Well, Robert, what can I answer to that? Thank you for the...I believe there was a complement in there somewhere...the *swimming*? I am enjoying myself. In fact, really for the first time since this whole thing started. This is the first real time I've taken time away to do something, but really, done nothing...but fish...watch you fish and enjoy the sheer nothingness of it."

"That's nice to hear, Birgitta. I'm glad."

We sat for a while silently sipping our coffee. Birgitta seemed truly happy now.

"You now look the cat that got the cream."

"Feel like it too," she answered. "And I believe it was a mouse...the cat got."

"Ummmm," I was in no mood to argue. We sat a little longer, saying nothing.

"Robert?"

"Yup?"

"Promise you will meet me again...after they get this...operation going, and keep me up to date. I'm beginning to have personal doubts, now that I have...*recruited* you. I am considering the risk of stage two. I would feel terrible if—well, if something bad happened?"

"So would I, Princess...you don't know how badly. But it could happen to me tomorrow, in a Spit...slip and fall in the bath...anything. One never knows when it's coming."

"Certainly, there is always that."

"To tell you the truth, Birgitta, I've had some self-doubt about my present capabilities, stemming from long before this offer of...new employment."

"What do you mean?"

I hesitated, wondering whether I should let her know the current state of my nerves.

"Or, is this something...you would prefer not to speak about?"

"No, it's not that...I can talk about it—in fact, since you are making the investment in me, I probably should speak of it." I paused, reconsidering my decision to let the cat out of the bag. "You see, lately my courage seems to be suffering a little. The signs are making themselves known—signs, if I saw them in another pilot, I might ground him for...a medical."

"I see. Is this something I should be concerned about?"

"I'm not sure. It is those signs that concern me. Whether or not they will continue to manifest themselves...make themselves...apparent," I clarified at her puzzled look, "in this new assignment. I don't know what the level of stress will be, or whether that is actually what is bringing on the behavior."

"Your file did state, Robert, that you were beginning to show *signs* of normal combat fatigue. We selected you as our optimum candidate, despite that...those indications, since they were not emphasized. I believe it was pointed out to me those *man-e-fest-a-shons...*" she struggled with the pronunciation, "...were perfectly normal. But, should your current duties continue, with you pushing yourself and your command...as I have been told you were, you would probably get careless...make a mistake. Generally, lose the luck we hear so much about with fighter pilots. Despite that...we still want you, Robert."

"Thanks for the confidence, Birgitta. I'll try to live up to it...with emphasis on the word, *live*."

"Good. And you will stay in contact as it goes along?"

"Of course. Once a princess is met, the heart is captured...forever."

"Now you are being silly again."

"That's what the day is for, *Ma'am*, being silly."

She looked serious for a few seconds: "Robert, have you ever been to Germany...that part of Europe?"

"No, never."

"Scandinavia—*my country*, Norway, in particular?"

"No, not there either. Only Sweden."

"There is something happening in Germany, Robert...something which has spread into every country where the Nazis are holding control. It is called *Lebensborn*. Do you know what that word means?"

Nope, but it sounds German...maybe *life-birth—born to life*...something like that. I'm afraid my high school German's not good enough, Birgitta."

"Paraphrasing, it means spring of life, or life-spring, I think. It is this *project* that I want you to work on for me, Robert. Your superiors have something else in mind for you, which will take precedence, but this is my personal project, Robert. I want to learn enough about this plague's progress in my country to help me to stop it."

She was frowning very seriously.

"But we can talk about that later, anyway. What is next on this glorious day's agenda Robert?"

How about some more fishing before lunch? Then we can try it a little below the falls, under the waterwheel. You can dangle your toes in the water—act the proper shop girl, while I see if I can top my record over there with an even bigger pike."

We got up and walked a little further up the shore of the millpond. The willows were hanging into the edge of the water. The surface was floating with water lily pads, well into the state of blooming.

"Oh, Robert, are they not beautiful? Is this not a beautiful place?"

"Yes and I'll bet there is a big one lying in there somewhere, too, that's what it looks like to me," I said and began rummaging for my new, weedless lure."

"I was not thinking of fish...I thought the scene more resembled a French Impressionist canvas...perhaps, *Monet*," she laughed?

I chuckled as I tied on the lure, not really hearing her. "The difference is not princess and pauper—more woman and man."

"Yes, I agree. Insurmountable obstacles...both in attitude and make-up."

"Well, not insurmountable; there's a work-around for everything. That's what marriage is all about, I believe."

"I suppose you are right—I will give you that one, having no experience in the matter. What about you, Robert, have you ever been married?"

"Nope."

"My, that sounds awfully emphatic. Is there an attitude in there."

"I hope not...just never been asked...*yet*. How about you, *Princess?*"

"No—never."

She seemed to ponder the thought as I stepped closer to the shore, swung and landed a perfect cast into the midst of the pads. The lure hit with a splat, square on one of the floating pads. I frowned and twitched the rod's tip as the shiny lure slid off easily into the water and began to sink.

"Perfect," I said quietly to myself and began to retrieve the bait, cranking the reel steadily and twitching the rod now and then.

"I was asked, though—once," Birgitta finally offered whimsically, from behind me.

"Yes...?" I was only half listening, concentrating on the lure's retrieval. I really liked the action of this lure and so far, it hadn't become hooked on anything. I imagined it weaving its way among the long stems of the lotus leaves. In a world of my own, I imagined the clear depths beneath the floating pads and a long pike suddenly charging—open-mouthed, grasping the lure before turning hard to flee with his prize, pulling the end of my rod down suddenly.

"Um—huh..." Birgitta said to herself. I glanced around quickly. She was smiling, face turned upward into the sun again, "...and he was a prince, also, though a rather insignificant one."

"Really?" I answered, surprised, but still concentrating on my retrieval. "I suppose he would have to be wouldn't he?" The lure was out now, unscathed and dripping as I prepared to cast it further up-shore. I turned more toward Birgitta, causing her to take a precautionary step backward.

"Yes—a prince...but he was not a fairy tale prince. Far from it in fact. He was more like the prince that turned into a frog, instead of the opposite, like in the children's stories? He was..." she stopped speaking and looked at me in the way women did when you were doing something important and still trying to pay attention to their conversation.

"Yes, go on," I said quickly, trying to keep the conversation going, "I'm listening...."

"Well...."

I interrupted, "Not being a prince myself, I'm out of the running anyway, Birgitta, so I'd like to know what, or who, you've been turning down? Promise not to tell."

She almost giggled. "We were very young. Perhaps, fifteen years, when he proposed. He was from one of the Balkan monarchies—to the southeast. They were an *old* family of culture...but quite poor, I now understand. I will not say from where, but very small by any standard and a third son in line, at that. He was very coarse and ugly, actually...lots of pimples and he had an annoying habit of sniffing all the time and—excuse me for saying it, wiping his nose on the backs of his hands in a nervous fashion. And if I remember correctly, I do not believe he washed often, either."

"Heavens...how horrible..." I cast far out into the pads again. I quite enjoyed the action of this lure, but was beginning to become disappointed that I hadn't had another strike yet.

"Yes...so I declined his proposal. He and his parents were at our home on a state visit and I believe they were 'trying us out' so to speak. I told my mother, after, how horrible he was. She agreed and that was the last we heard from him. His country has been overrun now, too—by the Russians; and though I found him repulsive, I sometimes wonder how he is coping...whether he is in hiding, or in service, fighting? We have heard nothing from their family since...all this began."

I wasn't listening: "I think we should move a little further upstream, Birgitta. I'm not doing very well here. Grab the lunch, will you?"

"Oh—certainly," she said stooping and idly picking up the parcels. We walked a few paces along the shore. Birgitta was pulling the seeds from the stray stems of grass along the narrow path. "Tell me Robert...why have you not yet married?"

I drew back and threw the lure so it would fall along the outer edge of some reeds, running out on a spit of sand. Should be plenty of small fish hiding in there and a submerged hunter along the outside edge, I thought. "I haven't been asked yet, Birgitta. Even the ugly, pimply-faced girls didn't seem to want me enough to pop the question."

She chuckled. "Oh come now, Robert...you can do better than that. Surely there were girls...in university? You are *somewhat* handsome..." she smiled just before bending her head so I couldn't see her face when I glanced around. "Did you not have any affairs of the heart, there?"

"Well, when I think about it, there were a couple of girls."

I brought the lure up to within six inches of the rod's tip and threw it again, further to the left this time.

"There must be another one in here somewhere, even a smaller one," I said, absently.

"That was university—what about since then...do you have a lady-friend...*now?*"

"Nope—had my heart set on a princess, but...well, you know...."

"*Robert*, please be serious."

I was ready to give up for lunch. Maybe the fish would be

biting below the spillway of the mill. "All right, Birgitta—what was the question again?" I carried the knapsack over to the remains of a fallen tree and took out a wool blanket with "RAF" embroidered in one corner in red thread.

Birgitta took the cups, thermos and one of the sacks while I unfolded and flung the blanket over the grass, spreading it smoothly.

"Have you no female friends...currently, Robert?"

We sat down with our backs to the log. "Oh, I already answered that question. No, no one. I haven't been out with a woman since..." I had to think "...since before I left The States." She filled one of the cups partially and handed it across to me.

"Oh? May I ask, is that not a long time?"

"Nearly two years."

We began to open our sacks. I noticed one of the guards had begun distributing the lunch bags to the other soldiers. The two by the dam were comparing each other's contents and laughing. One of them put his aside and continued patrolling the perimeter while the other leaned, still in readiness, against a tree by the mill.

"Have you no interest in...English or, European women, Robert?"

"No. I mean, I have no *disinterest* I guess, but I just haven't seemed...to take the time. Women—are women."

"I do not know about that, Robert. We Norwegian women—we like to think we are somewhat special."

We chuckled about that, unwrapping the wax paper binding the thick-sliced bread.

"Am I being too personal, Robert?" she asked, with a puzzled look at the sandwich she'd just bitten into, as if she wondered what it was made from.

"Not at all. You're just asking questions out of curiosity...right? No one has really had any interest in me in a long time. I guess, myself included, for that matter." She lifted one of the bread slices and examined the contents. I hoped she liked Spam. "I haven't had time, Birgitta, really, to tell the truth. That's the only reason. I guess I would like to escape to London for a week or two with a special someone, but *the someone* hasn't come along and I wouldn't be able to spare the time away from the group even if she had. And now—there's this new assignment."

We sat eating and looking out over the millpond. Here and there a fish jumped, but I found I'd somehow lost interest. The war had come back and all the deprivations, which went with it: lack of time, overwork, relationships out the window, or the absences of opportunity to even create one. Maybe it was just ranking officers, as I thought about it. The enlisted men seemed to be having a grand time in the pubs.

"Birgitta...you must be suffering the same pangs...loneliness, wanting to meet a special someone...*prince?* How do you cope with all those natural emotions, if I may be so bold to ask? The same way as I?"

"If you mean overwork, yes, exactly. You will have to admit that princes are not hiding around every street corner the same way other eligible men might be. Moreover, there were not that many royal families left in Europe, even before the war. Now...my chances of dying a thwarted spinster have increased significantly."

"Maybe you'll just have to break the tradition...marry a regular guy, that is."

"Maybe I *will* have to, at that Robert. Do I detect an offer in there somewhere?"

"Gosh yes, if you think you'd like to spend the rest of your life watching me fish? Because that's exactly what I expect to do after this is over: fish. I don't want to ever hear the sound of gunfire again."

She laughed out loud, continuing to play the game: "In that case...do you mind if I think about it, Robert? I must say it's the best offer I've ever had, *counting* the pimply-princely proposal. I noticed one of the guards glance over and smile, looking pleased that at least someone was having some semblance of normal fun. Maybe they spent quite a bit of time with the Princess. My guess was that she didn't laugh that much. We were quiet for a while, sipping from our cups and finishing the last of the sandwiches. Finally Birgitta looked at her hands, squirmed and looked up at me, her hands neatly folded in her lap.

What about it, Robert?"

"Marriage...?"

"Of course not—you know what I mean. When will you begin...leave commanding your fighter Command...start working

89

for us? Have you thought about it?"

"There hasn't been that much time, Birgitta. After all, I just said yes."

"I know…but…we are in a hurry, my parents and I."

"Yes…I've decided to get on with the posting as soon as possible. My second in command is more than capable to step in."

"That is good news." She reached across the blanket and squeezed my arm. "I can not tell you how grateful I…*we* will be, Robert."

"All in the line of duty, I believe, Birgitta."

We finished our sandwiches, more or less in silence and the day continued to drone along like the summer bees that visited the wild blooms all around. We smiled at each other now and then, watched the pristine day pass, with her guards appearing and disappearing in different places around the small lake each time a farm vehicle approached the mill. Eventually, I poured us both some more coffee and we had a bar of candy. After another two hours we packed up our wax paper wads, folded the blanket and I whistled to the guards.

I walked over to the water's edge. As it surged slightly with the fish's attempts to pull free, I reached down and untied the line. "I really hate doing this," I said, drawing in the rope and releasing the beautiful fish. "Now I won't have any proof that I ever caught it." We watched the pike slowly sink and then with a flick of its tail, it was gone, master of the pond once again.

"Certainly you do, Robert. I will be your witness anytime you wish it, for the rest of our lives."

We both chuckled as we gathered the remainder of our stuff. In another ten minutes, we were back at the trucks, where two guards had remained, ever vigilant. They seemed happy to see us. Bored, I'd supposed, or eager to leave. Take their charge out of harms way.

We drove back to the crossroads where the truck had been stalled, passing quickly through the town again . Though we went with speedy caution, the lazy villiage was mostly deserted, offering no outward sign of threat.

They dropped me at he crossroads, along with my now-lighter bicycle. I thanked the lieutenant for his services and he saluted, smiling, taking my place in the front beside Birgitta. But before they pulled away, Birgitta stopped the driver and motioned for me come back. I jumped on the running board as the lieutenant stepped out and stood beside the open door.

"We shall be in contact, Robert...within the week," she said. Leaning around the door, she stretched forward, putting a hand on my arm, kissed my cheek and then whispered above the truck's idling engine: "I hope you find your own princess, soon, Robert. She will be very fortunate when you do."

I smiled and squeezed her extended hand before jumping back from the truck. Taking his seat once again, the lieutenant slammed the door and nodded to the driver. I backed away watching them pull back out onto the tarmac and grind their way through the gears back toward...London? I supposed it could be somewhere else, but who knew where they would spend the night. That was the idea. Keep any would-be assassins guessing.

My bicycle was hard to pedal. I thought about the day's conversation with Birgitta. It's about time I began getting more exercise, I thought as my legs began to ache. Finding my own princess also began to sound like a good idea.

I'd really enjoyed the day with Birgitta. The fact that she was off limits, from a romantic stance, made the day easier. Both of us had probably been freer with our conversation because of it. I wondered about this subject she spoke of: *Lebensborn*. I made a mental note to look it up when I got back to station. Then I thought about Birgitta some more. She was a great young woman. Somewhere, there was a lucky, prince-to-be, I hoped, for her sake, realizing that all of a sudden, I found the idea of the company of women desirable.

CHAPTER
4

The Move

I lived up to my word to wrap up my affairs in England quickly. The Monday following my fishing excursion with Birgitta, thinking I would be heading for Norway straight away, I formally accepted the Air Marshal's tendered assignment, in writing, as requested. The Princess had completely disappeared from sight, as probably planned. We'd promised to stay in contact so I assumed she would take care of that, somehow, since I had no idea how to reach her.

They sent me to High Wycombe, The War Offices, in London. First, I had to have a new identity as I began one of the many clerical sessions I would be put through.

"Can't be tracing you back, you know..." I was told by a cute young interviewer. At the day's end I had my new identity. I was handed paperwork warranting that I'd been Alex Andersson...forever. It was obvious I'd have a job of it, memorizing the information about my new, old history. Most of my American/Scandinavian heritage remained unchanged.

I was surprised to learn I'd be remaining in England for some while, yet. There was much preparation and planning in store for me as I met and worked with a series of experts in every field, from explosives to hand-to-hand combat. I'd figured at worst, that I'd have to wrestle an intoxicated airline passenger, or an overstuffed suitcase.

They processed my discharge paperwork from the RAF, but Command didn't sign them; this was a precaution in case I was captured (or killed) in some of the bombing runs I would eventually be making over the occupied area of France or Holland. I doubted I would be able to get all the way to Germany before they turned me loose in Scandinavia.

I was transferred to a bomber group at RAF Coningsby where I quickly became familiar with multi-engine aircraft operation, including a refresher course in navigation, since many of the aircraft required both skills and didn't provide sufficient crew for both. If I was to find my way around Scandinavia and Northern Europe, I knew I could use all the help I could get, so I paid particular attention.

This duty was to continue for nearly three months. I believe I flew every multi-engine aircraft Great Britain ever manufactured and a couple by Germany. We went up to work with two, different aircraft at first. I started in the Blenheim-class, depending upon how it was configured, as either a bomber or fighter. They carried a normal crew of three and could carry a bomb load up to around 22,000 feet.

After I got the hang of the Blenheims, we switched to Whitleys. This aircraft normally carried five crewmen with a ceiling altitude of near 18,000 feet. In my Scandinavian assignment I would probably be flying a German-built *Junkers* JU 52 or JU F13, twin and single engine, corrugated fuselage aircraft. Seeing photos of them during training, I was reminded of a sheet of barn roofing metal blown away by a tornado. But both aircraft had good reputations for reliability and endurance on the Arctic routes, for ABA, the airline. That fact gave me some comfort. It was a while before I got time in one, though.

Nearing the end of my training in August of 1940, we flew a couple of final missions: low level bombing runs of German barges being amassed on the other side of the channel, ostensibly for a German invasion. *Jerry* was getting ready to ferry troops and equipment to England and we poured everything we had into discouraging this, buying time.

Finally, before my "graduation" from the first form, I moved into one of the newer bombers, an Avro Manchester. I spent three weeks practicing takeoffs and landings and we even did some high altitude and low level bombing practice. At least three of us always went up together to practice formation flying. This was like flying a hangar in itself after the Hurricanes. We wouldn't need this skill for night flying, as it was too dangerous, a hard learned fact. Instead, we'd string out and follow each other's tails. The Manchesters were slow, cumbersome, but rock steady when carrying thousands of pounds of ballast, simulating bombs. Then we finally went for the real stuff.

That day began with the fateful flashlight in my face; it was 04:30. Breakfast was in half an hour and flight briefing at 06:00. We knew the probable target but didn't know exactly what part of the French coast we would be hitting that day.

Walking to the morning mess, I didn't have the usual butterfly stomach of most of the crew. I would be flying in the right seat to a young Lieutenant named Ames. I had more hours in crop dusters than he had total time in any aircraft, but he knew the Manchester better than I and I was there to learn. So I did my best to keep my mind open and my mouth shut.

I'd either flown too many missions in Hurricanes and Spits, or I was too stupid to know how vulnerable we were going to be. I wondered if the shakes would return again, sometime. So far, so good.

The morning was dawning through a terrible fog. It was near zero-zero visibility on the ground and not a probable morning for a mission. It was sure to be scrubbed, I remarked, around a mouthful of eggs, nodding to Ames who was sitting beside me, coldly staring at his own untouched breakfast.

Less than an hour later we headed for the briefing room. There was a blackout entrance manned by two MPs, checking I.D. s. Only officers were permitted entrance; enlisted men had their own special briefing. The information fed to us was too important to trust to anyone who didn't need the information, especially if they were captured.

We entered a long room with an aisle up the center flanked by folding wooden chairs, eight deep on either side. Many of the crew were already seated. Many had probably skipped breakfast. Some were talking in groups, or leaning over the backs of their chairs, one arm over the chair back of their neighbor. Others were sitting alone, silently staring at the curtain covering the briefing board behind the stage at the front of the room. Yet, others appeared to be dozing, sitting arms-crossed, head forward, chin nearly touching chest, waiting for the briefing to begin. I'd been in enough fighter briefings that I could smell and feel the tangible fear in the room. It was the one thing I understood. Each of us handled fear differently.

Our crew took seats near the middle of the room, chatted a little with our seat-mates and then waited in silence for the briefer-officers to arrive. Sitting there, I thought of the many new skills I'd learned and those I'd been able to pass along from my days in fighters: keeping a condom over the mike in the oxygen mask to keep it clear of moisture and ice, when flying at high altitude. Or, continually squeezing the mask to retard ice formation and then shaking out the ice that did form. Some crewmen even carried a spare mask. On the long runs, when we'd accompanied bombers, we pissed in a condom, tied a knot at the top and pitched out, "personal bombs," our gift to the enemy and a gesture we could safely perform at altitude with impunity, to some degree. When you had to go, you had to go. Fighter flights were short enough so we could almost always go, in between sorties.

Finally, the doors at the back of the room burst open and to the shout of "*Attention,*" we sprung to our feet as the uniformed "ground-pounders" strode up the aisle to give us our words of doom. They quickly read the roll call with every commander answering for his crew. Then the curtain of doom, covering the map, was withdrawn and we saw the outline of the north coast of France. The silence was always broken by moans at this point when we saw the target.

It was the turn of the security officer, who now gave us the daily once-over, telling us what personal items to carry on the mission and what not to carry. We were ordered not to discuss the mission with anyone, before or after it began, even if it ended up being scrubbed. We were cautioned to remain inside the briefing room through the entire duration of the briefing. When he had finished, he stepped aside and the intelligence officer took over.

"We will be working the north coast again today, gentlemen. Every effective hit is a strike for British cities and the lives of our citizenry—so I urge you to use the utmost care to adhere to your training and the mission's objective. Every bomb counts. Every shell fired at the assaulting fighters counts for the final summation. Solution…? Defeat *Jerry.*"

He paused for a moment, glancing around the room to add emphasis to his comment, before continuing.

"The targets are well defended from the ground and from the air. Enemy fighters can be expected in great numbers and they will be aggressive. They are well-trained. Ground fire from flak will undoubtedly be heavy and well aimed. It will be effective, you will be hit and we will lose aircraft and personnel." Another pause to let that ominous remark sink in. "Their ground gunners are getting better. Our losses due to flak are mounting with every mission, so expect the worst en-route to the IP (initial point).

Because this is coastal bombing you can only expect from five to seven minutes of flak before most of the targets. On the way in, you must maintain both true course and altitude—*at all cost! Fokkers* and *109s* are going to be aggressively attacking your ships, most likely in a head-on manner, attempting to get *you* to flinch first. But you must not…no matter that they look as if they will fly straight through your cockpit."

"Earlier this week, one of the Yank missions took a head on…the ship flying lead was knocked out with all of crew lost. *Lead* is the number one target of the *Luftwaffe* pilots. If your *lead* ship is knocked out it is easy for the entire formation to go amuck and it becomes easy pickings for enemy fighters, for about two minutes, until you can close up once again and maintain fire cover."

"Again Gentlemen—you must stay your course and your altitude, remaining in formation at all cost. Should the ship in front of you get hit and drop out, immediately close into his position, as you've been trained in order to maintain the formation. The formation is your savior. The formation is nearly invincible and it will protect you more than your own single firepower will protect you. In the final run to IP, absolutely no evasive action on your parts can take place. You must fly straight and you must fly level—on to the target, guided by your navigators and bomb-aimers. They own your ship during those final moments before bombs gone."

Another pause and then he went on in a quieter voice. "In

the unfortunate event you should fall from formation..." he glanced around the room, "...you know the procedure. Get out of the way if you can—turn out and attempt to come home immediately...if you can. Stragglers will be very vulnerable, as you know. Bring into play the procedures for air-sea rescue you've been trained for and do your best to come back to your families and friends here. We need you to do your job again until you are no longer able to do it...for whatever reason." He stood looking at each of us for a bit and then turned and joined the others at the side of the platform. Then the weather officer rose from his chair and took the floor.

"Well...that was cheerful news, wasn't it chaps." The entire room groaned as one man. "The other *good* news is...weather's expected to lift by the time you're in your aircraft, so you should be able to get away right on schedule. There's a front coming through, as I speak, from Scotland and you can expect visibility to improve to around five hundred feet by take off. Tops will be around fifteen hundred. There may be another layer with ceilings at ten thousand, enroute. You may get up in that stuff on the way but since this will be low level running, you'll either fly out of the stuff or come down to approach altitude before getting into it. Get home before dark, though, because there's a warm front moving in from the Bay of Biscay by late afternoon...heavy cloud and rain. We'll be socked in again, solid, before midnight tonight and you'll have to wait around until morning if you don't hurry home." No one laughed so he sat down again.

The Major took over this time and outlined the targets for the various crews. Because there were several, it took a little longer than if we were hitting a single city in several waves. When it was finished, we rose again, standing at attention, very tense, as they left the room. We dispersed into small groups to bemoan our fate before finally departing.

Some of the crew went to the chaplains, some to the toilet and some directly to the ship. I did the latter two, catching a ride with a truck to our Manchester.

As second pilot, I had to wait for the pilot before getting the dope on the ship from our ground crew chief. I did my own walk around, though, looking for anything suspicious. When I returned, Ames still had not shown up and while we were waiting, I chatted with the flight engineer, navigator and air bomber. The remainder of the crews soon trickled in and ours began supervising the loading of the ammunition for our defensive guns. The bombs were already in their places.

And then our pilot, Lieutenant Ames, looking white and worried, stepped out of a passing truck; it had slowed only long enough for him to grab his gear, before speeding off to the next ship. I assumed Ames'd had a rather long visit to the latrine by the look of him; I could remember the feeling. We went over the ship with the mechanics and then climbed up into the cockpit and began our preflight check.

Seemingly, in no time the green flare was up and we began cranking the engines and taxing into positions for takeoff. Between the roar of the engines and the screeching of brakes as we pivoted and turned to the flares and lights, my excitement grew.

True to the weatherman's word, the ground fog was lifting by the time we were ready to taxi into position for departure. We had runway enough for a safe zero-zero takeoff, but wouldn't have to, after all. We stood planted on the asphalt taxiway, rocking from side to side, standing on the wheel brake pedals, locked hard against the strong pull of the propellers, which threatened to sweep our ship into the one waiting in line in front of us.

We watched as ship after airship taxied, turned and sped down the strip. And finally, it was our turn. Ames came off the brakes, hitched himself forward toward the yoke. We'd already advanced throttles to full and were holding the ship back with her wheel brakes. Then he let go and we went down the runway, faster and faster until Ames pulled the yoke toward his chest. We seemed to hang onto the tarmac for a while, but then as the gear came up, the ship lifted ever so slowly and pointed skyward for the climb-out and form-up for the channel crossing.

Our take-off went smoothly. We were forming up at a climb rate of about four hundred feet per minute, heading southwest for France. Soon we were up to twelve thousand feet without oxygen. The cloud had completely disappeared and within minutes we were able to see blue skies all the way to the French coast, ahead and to the left. The *con* trails from the engines stretched all the way back to England, painting a sure path for any patrolling German fighters to find us.

We were flying a thirty six plane group with nine planes to the squadron. Lieutenant Ames nervously told me this was the first time we'd ever grouped that way. The usual complement, he said, was four squadrons of seven planes each. He seemed to be having trouble with the formation.

Lieutenant Ames had given the order on take off that we weren't to use the intercom, unless there are fighters coming in. I thought that odd, since it was my experience that to and from the target it was the custom among all the crews to continuously chatter back and forth on the plane's interphone, kidding or making wise cracks at each other. Now we had to be real quiet and only use the interphone to answer the periodic oxygen check to insure everyone was receiving oxygen and were alert at their post. I wondered whether the chatter distracted him from flying the ship.

Then the signal came to descend for final formation into smaller groups to make our runs down the beaches.

The intercom came to life: "fighters at ten o'clock...lots of them." The *Luftwaffe* were waiting for us. Soon the approaching fighters opened up. I saw flashes of light winking at us in the distance. Then a canopy of cannon shells and aerial mines began exploding in our face. The sound of the fighter's 20mm cannon shells rattled through the fuselage of our Manchester. I glanced at the gauges, checking the vital information of the ship's hydraulic, electrical and fuel systems.

The big bomber then began to shake with the recoil of our own gunner's firing, answering fire and having their way with the German fighters. They seemed to be all around us. The rattle of our own guns could be heard above the roar of our engines. The intercom grew alive with the excited chatter of the crew who, in their release of tension had completely forgotten Ames' standing orders.

In the first attempt to reform, the fourth ship in formation to the left of lead made an awkward move just as a greasy brown flak burst struck below it. It climbed suddenly, veering to the right and raising its left wing. The number four prop parted company with it's shaft and neatly sheared the fuselage right at the waist door.

The stricken ship's tail went whizzing past us, over our wing, tumbling in the air, its skin flapping. In all other aspects, it was intact. The rest of the now stricken ship began a slow, rolling dive. Then, a human form tumbled from the gaping cross-section. A lone chute opened and the crewman went past, again, just missing our left wingtip. The balance of the formation had to quickly adjust to avoid striking the largest part of the ship as it disappeared below us. I couldn't tell whether anyone else got out.

Then I heard a welcome sound: "Hurrybirds incoming— help is on the way, boys." Truly then, four Hurricanes swept past in rolling pursuit of German fighters, slowly closing the distance on the retreating planes.

Our descent was ongoing; no one had slowed from the fighter onslaught and we were now on the final run, following the ships in front of us, maintaining the formation, holding our position, flying straight and level—holding the appropriate altitudes. I could already see the devastation beginning ahead of us from the bombs already released. There were fiery explosions of flak all around us and on the ground, mushrooming black and gray-brown clouds interspersed with geysers in the water from misses as the bombs smacked the sea harmlessly. Some bombs were falling on the beach sand, but the earlier hits were sending mushrooms of cloud higher and higher in the air.

Our turn would come soon enough. The flak had now begun in earnest and the ship heaved, pitched and rattled from the shell explosions and flying shrapnel. Flak literally paved the sky ahead of us. It was as if one could get out and walk upon the dark brownish red clouds. I'd never encountered flak like this flying fighters. At first it was a marvel to watch; but I knew, not a marvel to be the target of. It resembled lightning flashing in the sunlight. As they began to explode nearer the ship, each burst made a squeaky-gritty noise and the smell of exploded cordite permeated the ship, even with our oxygen masks on. With each burst, it was as if someone were striking the ship with a horrendous, hard pillow, all the while keeping time to the bursts.

Suddenly there came a feeling that something inside the ship had exploded...a tremendous jolt. I was completely stunned for an instant and was very slow to comprehend what was happening around me. Though I thought we had been hit, my body's fear had pumped something into my blood—slowed my world down and every incident was going by at such a slow rate I could nearly step out of myself and walk around me, examining the situation touching the moment. I remember seeing the bomb-aimer's feet and legs, in front and below me, suddenly lifted into the air with the impact of the shell and then fall again. I imagined the look of surprise that must have been on his face. Pilot Ames had not yet recovered from the hit, which must have been directly outside the port side of the aircraft.

Eventually, I got some of my senses back and pulled hard on the yoke as I realized we'd started to dive. The resistance I felt was from the Ames lifeless body slumped over the control yoke. His flight suit was smoking and there was blood on the ceiling. The Perspex windows beside him were shattered though mostly, still intact. Where I could see through the blood, I knew there were holes, open to the sky. The flying panel had also been spattered and the throttles were covered, which I learned, when I grabbed for the handles and my gloved hand slipped off.

The engineer came forward to help pull Ame's corpse out of the seat as I struggled to bring the ship back up to altitude. I didn't know how much height we'd lost during the time directly after the impact of the flak burst. We'd no doubt nearly taken it dead on and lost quite a bit of altitude. We were in danger of losing our position in the group forma-tion. However, now I was afraid of pulling up again directly into the path of a ship behind us, closing up into our previous position, as was the drill. If there were already someone pulled up in our place, I'd come up under his wings or belly. I was also afraid of straggling, getting the ship beneath a descending load of bombs from one of our ships above.

I shouted into the intercom to the mid-upper turret gunner: "Top—I want to climb back up into formation—is there still room—or are they now on top of us?"

"There's room Sir...take it slow and they'll see us coming up. I'll watch out. Damn...!"

I heard the turret gun go off then, as he let go at a passing fighter. I'd shoved the throttles all the way forward and began to slowly haul back the yoke. I stared at the vertical climb indicator dial; the needle began to indicate positive and soon showed a climb rate of about 100 feet per minute. Holding this attitude, in no time the rest of the formation had descended sufficiently to come down to our level, as we climbed back up, taking our place in the stream once again. We'd regained our position and were again following them in for the run.

Then we approached the target and I turned the ship over to the bomb aimer and followed his verbal signals, until our own bomb load was dropped. With each release of a bomb, the ship jerked slightly upward, trying to climb as it shed the explosive weight burden.

Then in no time we were turning right, away from France, back toward the North Sea and around—home to England once more.

When we got back to base and went over the ship we realized a 20mm shell had gone just behind number five bulkhead and nearly shattered the control cables. Yet another 20-mm shell had exploded near the bomb bay and torn two holes about a foot in diameter. It apparently had happened before bombs gone. Why it didn't explode the bombs, none of us knew, but it gave everyone something to think about on the ride back across the tarmac to the debriefing room. We followed the ambulance carrying Ame's body.

CHAPTER
5

A New Life

There was a good deal of damage done in those bomb runs—what they later, jokingly called the *Battle of the Barges*. And seemingly before it even began, I was free of the flying school stuff, with military airplanes, anyway. I felt like a *90 day wonder*[8] all over again and they officially (though secretly) discharged me from the RAF. I turned in all my kit, uniforms, shoes—everything, for it was truly the real thing. I would now be a civilian pilot with a Swedish passport.

My training really began in earnest. I was at it again. A fortnight of twelve-hour days finished every evening with me carrying away homework to my quarters in order to be well prepared for the one-student classes I was put through by a series of instructors. I was only permitted to know their first names. Usually, I had one instructor in the morning and another in the afternoon. I learned, or refreshed myself in topo-map interpretation and commercial weather forecast charts. A cipher expert also introduced me to a little simple code writing. The latter was nothing that would fool an expert but would probably delay any German line officer on the ground, sufficiently, for me to "choose alternate means," the meaning of which I was never informed.

A series of *drop boxes* were set up for me and I memorized the locations in various cities—mostly in Scandinavia: Stockholm, Oslo, Bergen, Copenhagen and Helsinki. Others were also situated in major cities in Europe, most of which were currently *Nazi* occupied countries. I had a written list I had to memorize, but must destroy before I graduated. The list wouldn't be collected, the instructor told me; it was up to me to commit the addresses and specific locations totally to memory. I'd best keep refreshing the list every day or so, he cautioned, lest I forget and be unable to collect valuable information from any contact I cared to have use of.

From time to time they would use these contacts, if needbe, failing all other normal means of written communication, the primary one of which was to be my supervisor at *ABA*. Should the list not be destroyed, they said and found...it could compromise the whole mission and cost all the contacts and me, our lives. I should bear in mind, they said, other contacts had me as a contact name on their hopefully, now-destroyed lists. The importance of the lists' destruction was not lost on me.

I asked whether other spies like myself would be using the same drop boxes and was told mine were unique to me, but would be monitored by my specific contact. Should the mission fail, another person would replace me and with a completely different set of drop locations. A comforting thought.

Then came the portion of the training I had somewhat been eager for: that which would involve the *Nazi* counter spy, my contact in Scandinavia. I wasn't given any name, description or background. I was only told at this point that this person was being "used" by MI5, thinking the information provided was valuable, war-critical secrets. Something about the regularity of the *Nazi* spy's information was a signal for our people to carry out the next part of the operation, explained to me in short order in the following fashion:

ABA's flights often carried *Nazi* spies or high-level, government officials, even military officers of importance. This practice would increase as the Finnish and Swedish contacts, especially the latter, encouraged the practice and made it more convenient with specific routing. Usually these *Third Reich* officials would carry diplomatic pouches. Our "contacts" in *ABA* had established a certified courier service, via our *ABA* flights, which, eventually permitted carrying the pouches without the expense and bother of the couriers having to accompany them. In those instances, a member of my aircrew trained in micro-photography would be able to open the pouches and photograph the contents. Afterward, *my people* would return the documents to the pouch and secure them in such a way there was no evidence they had been invaded and of course, all without the knowledge of the *Nazis*.

I found the method they'd devised, of getting into the pouches undetected, rather unique. The beautiful hand-tooled, leather bags contained a tamper-proof, padlock with an intricate safeguard, especially designed to forestall picking, even by the best expert. Our people didn't even try to figure out a method to get around these locks. They found candidates highly skilled in the art of harness making and re-trained them to be photographers, far easier than turn about. After a month's schooling, they were able to open the skillfully-sewn, hand stitching without visible damage, remove and photograph the contents, then carefully stitch them together again without damage to the leather, using the finest running harness stitch. This all occurred within the duration of the flight; I marveled at their speed and skill, all within the limited lighting of a small area in the freezing cabin. They had several tools, threads, waxes and abrasive methods they used to disguise their rework, each tailored to suit the individual age and condition of the particular pouch on that flight.

I had only, I was told, to supervise the overall operation and keep the airplane airborne. The crew of that particular flight would be aware of the mission, so to speak and would all be trained similar to me in their special skills. I would receive notification of the special passengers, or materials by *ABA*'s flight manifest number, which would always contain a telltale, seven-digit number. Normal flights would have a "B" inserted as the second digit of the flight number. The *special flights* would have the "B" moved to the next to the last digit and would always be followed by a "7". I thought that simple enough, but later learned the code would prove a nuisance to us since it would be changed constantly, often without sufficient notice. But finally I graduated, tore up my list of drop locations, having already committed them to memory and was, I felt, willing and able to go on assignment.

MI5 never knew where there were unfriendly eyes and ears so the eradication of all traces of my previous military life had to be complete, they informed me. There could be no trace of any past connection lingering, or otherwise, to my former life in the RAF. Another expert in spy craft even went through my remaining personal items to insure nothing remained of my past history which might tip off anyone that I'd never been anything other than a Swedish airline pilot. They even planted a couple of items, both Swedish and American to substantiate my actual background, pre-RAF.

I had a week's leave coming before the official assignment to Finland and the *ABA* schedule of flights commenced. I didn't know what to do with that much furlough, knowing no one in England who wasn't connected with my *previous* life, with whom, of course, I could not communicate—should even avoid at all costs. As I was mulling over my options, I received a surprise telegram at my hotel on the south coast.

```
CAPT. ALEX ANDERSSON--C/O DORMY
HOTEL-FERNDOWN--HUNGRY FOR FISH-STOP-NO
TIME TO PICNIC AND CATCH THEM-STOP-CON-
SIDER ATTENDING FRIDAY EVENING AT ROYAL
BATH  HOTEL-STOP-FORMAL  RECEPTION-AT
19:00-STOP-BLACK TIE-STOP-THE FISH ARE
ON ME-STOP-REGARDS BIRGITTA-STOP
```

I read Birgitta's telegram a couple of times through and decided it might really be more of a demand than a request. Seeing my *new* name still took some getting used to. I considered it for a bit and then found a snag: I didn't own a tuxedo. I had to think about that, but finally, I telephoned my new, local contact, explained that I needed to purchase formal-wear and didn't have much time, or money.

"Thought you were off for a week's holiday," the unknown voice chided, "...planning on a bit 'o partying are you?"

"So did I...but I got a...*request*..." I said, not wanting to say anything further over the telephone, "...probably an invitation I shouldn't refuse."

He seemed to understand and after listening to the details. "Stand by a moment will you," he said. The line went silent but for static.

It was Thursday. After keeping me on the line for a few moments, he picked up the telephone again.

"Thank you for waiting, Sir. You can go up to London—

Threadneedle Street—number 23, Ascot Press. They'll fit you out and you can carry it all away the same day. Arrive on the early train—depart later—when it's finished. There is no charge. We have an...an account there," he had added before I thought to ask.

The following day I did as instructed, coming up from the underground before 09:30. And they were in fact expecting me. The little tailoring shop had me measured in half an hour, gave me a seat in a beautifully plush waiting room, complete with magazines, tea, cakes and a nice older woman who stepped in now and again to see if I needed anything. I spent the morning reading and had the first trial fitting before noon.

I went to lunch down the street, spending some of the cash Operations had left in an envelope for me with the taylors and I was back for a second fitting by 13:30. I had a final look-over at 15:30 and was carrying my new monkey suit, two shirts, shoes, ties, gloves and a new overcoat onto the train at Victoria Station by 16:15. The train back to the south coast was very crowded but everyone seemed to accept it. Many women and men were in uniform.

With time to spare, from my hotel in Ferndown, I hailed a cab to take me to the Royal Bath, in Bournemouth. I'd not been issued an automobile and hadn't quite gotten used this new life yet, but decided I liked the luxury of it so far. This would be good practice for my newly acquired identity. Hopefully, I'd spent enough time learning and mastering the ability to adopt, to accommodate unexpected situations—think on my feet.

The Royal Bath was a monstrous affair with tall, castle-like turrets at either end of the building's entrance. It was situated on the seaside, within a long stone's throw of the bathing beach

And of course it was filled with servicemen from every service branch. I arrived early and after determining where the reception was being held, went into one of the bars and ordered a Carlsburg, as I was still a bit early. I thought that appropriate considering my new role. No Carlsburg...so I settled for a local brew and after sipping once from the tall glass, glanced around the room. From my vantage point on the wooden stool there appeared to be lots of officers in uniform and a scattering of enlisted men drinking and talking. A few lucky ones were with girls, in and out of uniform; but mostly it was just servicemen.

I turned back to the bar and was admiring the cut of my new jacket in the back mirror when I saw the Air Marshal stroll in. He glanced around; our eyes met in the mirror. Obviously startled, he offered only the slightest flick of the eyes in recognition, turned on his heel and left.

Well, that was unexpected, I thought. As per my training I wasn't to know anyone from my previous life. If they acknowledged me first; then, I was advised to try to play along and get away from them as soon as possible without arousing anyone's curiosity.

I nursed my beer for another half-hour before downing it, then walked out of the bar. It was getting pretty noisy as more soldiers come in with girls. Now and then there was a shriek of laughter. It was a woman's heaven, their being outnumbered five to one with very attentive, male admirers.

I turned a few corners and ambled down the hallway where the concierge had directed me. I was soon brought up short by two military policemen standing on either side of double doors. They were checking IDs and I didn't have anything but my Swedish pilot's operation certificate and passport. So I thought I'd try walking in. I didn't get far; as I approached, they both glanced at me, then at my hands. Seeing I wasn't carrying any invitation...why hadn't they sent me one? Another test of my mettle, possibly? Both men stepped sideways, blocking the door.

"Excuse me—Sir!" one of the two Royal Marines put a re-straining hand on my shoulder. "Sorry, Sir. This is a private party—invitation only."

"I *know* that, Sergeant, that's why I'm wearing these clothes." I thought I'd try a bluff. "I wasn't...they didn't send me an invitation, you see.. It was last minute...by telephone."

One of the two glanced at the other: "By telephone, you say?"

"That's right...telephone." I pulled in a little then catching myself feeling indignant with these enlisted men. No need treating them like the officer I had been...they were just doing their jobs.

The taller of the two smiled at me, then glanced at his companion.

"Check the list Al...what's your name, Sir."

"Andersson—Alex...Alex Andersson," I repeated having

slipped again, offering my name in the military fashion, last-first, instead of the way a civilian might. The corporal consulted a list for a moment. Apparently there were a number of persons who didn't have formally issued invitations.

"Right—'ere's an Andersson. Where d' you work, Sir?"

"Work?"

"Yeah...your job...you know, for a livin'."

"Oh, of course, I'm sorry...*ABA Aer—o—transport*—the Scandinavian airline. I pilot for them...flying out of Stockholm, Helsinki...?" I'd momentarily drawn a blank. He must be thinking I was a little thick for a pilot.

"That's 'im, Albert—says here..." he struggled with the word, "...Air—O—transport..."

The taller soldier nodded: "Thank you Sir...go right in, Captain Andersson."

"Thank you Corporal." I walked between them as they stepped aside. There was a short hallway. I turned a corner and stepped into a large room full of men and women in formal dress, similar to my own. There were about half of them in uniforms. Most had drinks in their hands; not wishing to look out of place—mostly, I was nervous, I strolled toward the bar. As I passed through the crowd I didn't see a single person I recognized. After thinking about it, I realized that was a positive; I didn't want to try to fend off an acquaintance, trying to explain away my new name.

There were a lot of dress uniforms, mostly navy officers. It wasn't unusual since we were so close to Portsmouth and the Brit's naval headquarters. I saw the odd RAF uniform from Costal Command, didn't recognize any of the men inside them, to my relief. I was just contemplating the beer and ale selections when someone called out my *new* name.

"*Captain* Alex Andersson!"

I tuned in the direction of the unfamiliar voice. A red-haired civilian about my own age leaned casually against one the giant support columns in the ball room. He carelessly held a half-finished glass of white wine in one hand and a cigarette in the other. He appeared to have just stepped out of an up-scale magazine ad for men's clothing. His hair was combed back, slicked down, twenties-style and he wore his tuxedo with the casual carelessness of someone born to wearing one.

"Yes…I am Alex Andersson and…who might you be?"

"My name's Clyde—Clyde Whittwell. Actually, Whittwell's the surname…*last name*.…"

"I know what a surname is, Mr. Whittwell. How, if I may ask, do you know me—*my surname*? Have we met before, somewhere?" I was frightened he knew me from Command and I was going to have to get away from him. Yet…he'd used my new, my spy name.

"Sure, Alex…I've flown with you many times on *ABA Aerotransport* flights: Stockholm, Helsinki—Oslo. Remember now?"

He winked and straightening, stepped across the carpeting toward me, adding the wine glass from his right hand to his cigarette hand as he came to meet me.

"You couldn't have forgotten so soon?" He extended his hand. "We're great chaps, Alex…*buddies*, you might say. Moreover, I felt sorry for you, always having to stay up in London on your stopovers, so I invited you down to the coast for this party. Picking up your tab at the Dormy, too, since your *Kronor* don't spend so well down here, I might add."

I didn't know what to expect when I came here, but *he* certainly wasn't it. He knew my role and was playing it to the hilt.

"Oh…why—of course, Clyde, how could I forget my manners? So nice to be here…the party. Thanks for the invite." My stammered reply was hardly up to his debonair demeanor.

"Oh…" he replied, grinning and waving off my feigned gratitude, "think nothing of it, *please*. Glad you could make it. How were the trains, by the way? Can be frightfully busy nowadays…so many servicemen…*and women*, traveling.

Then he turned and extended his arm in a broad gesture, indicating the buffet. "Up to some food…*some chow*? Shall we step over and gather a plate of *hors d'oeuvres*?"

He dropped the cigarette in his glass and set it down on a sideboard. I found his habit of trying to Americanize his speech to try to help my understanding rather annoying.

"Oh—I say…*Whyyyyy…not*…old chap!" I said, aping his public school affectation on the "I's" in my best British accent.

"Oh…I say…" he chuckled and dug me in the ribs, "…rather guess I deserved that, didn't I? Shall we begin again?"

"Sure, why not...no offense intended."

"None taken," he replied, smiling an rubbing his hands to-gether in a conspiratorial fashion. "The story is..." he glanced around, lowering his head and not to be overheard, though there wasn't another soul within twenty feet, "...story is we're acquainted through your work...as air *Kaptain.*"

I bent near him, partially to participate in the exaggerated charade and partly in order to hear him, for he'd also lowered his voice.

"I travel a good deal, you see: business, charity do's, that sort of thing—and we've made friends as a result of being together so much in the air?"

I nodded.

"We've become fast friends. I'm a Peer, you see and...not to put too fine a point on it, I can afford to...shall we say, *sponsor* these little endeavors." He flourished his arm to indicate the party in progress. "I'm to be your contact in the south of England, Alex and elsewhere, when and if you need help, instruction...all that. Any-thing I can do to help."

As he spoke he'd picked up a plate and begun working his way down the table. We'd stopped before a beautifully-lain platter of cold meats. Some of the classes weren't suffering, I saw, as I followed his example, filling one of the fine China plates for myself. In addition to the bar set up across the room, there was wine, cham-pagne and beer at the end of the food table. I noticed a caddy with an assortment of liquor bottles and a soda siphon to one side.

"Who's sponsoring this anyway, Clyde...paying for it all?"

"We are, as I said."

We—you mean *you*...your family?"

"Well, no...not exactly. We—us, our family—*yours and mine?*" He stressed the last part so I finally realized the intelligence organization must be paying for it.

"And why would *we* do this, Clyde?"

"We're...*trawling,* you might say, Alex."

"Trawling? Fishing? Sorry, Clyde, you've lost me."

With overbearing patience he took my arm. "We hold one of these..." he waved his fork around the air, indicating the room in general, "…every now and then—ask everyone who is anyone and see who else wrangles invitations and shows up."

"I see. Exactly who *else* are we expecting to show up?"

"*Nazi* spies, of course."

"Oh—!" I was completely taken aback. "And have any…shown up yet?"

"Yes…actually, one just did." He had lowered his head slightly over his plate and frowned as if he didn't wish to be seen with me.

I turned, scanning the room in the direction he had been facing but he'd turned around by then and I couldn't determine who, or what he'd seen. I glanced over my shoulder; I didn't see anyone who resembled what I thought of as a spy.

"Needent look over there Old Boy."

"Where is he, Clyde?"

He was now preoccupied in a different direction, staring over the heads of our nearest guests.

"Sorry *Chapie*…but got to go off for a minute…tail him you know. But first, let me introduce you around a bit."

He'd put down his plate and quickly took my arm and began leading me across the room, plate in one hand, champagne pipe in the other. Before we stopped he had another cigarette dangling from the right corner of his mouth like a gangster in an American movie. We drew up before two ladies and an man in uniform,. They seemed to have been in deep conversation. The uniform was Royal Navy; the women had their backs to me, however they looked attractive, from the back. One was brunette, shorter and the other, a taller blonde with long hair drawn up tightly in a bun at the back of her hair. The brunette seemed slightly familiar. I set my plate and the glass on a tray stand, already well filled with half full cocktail glasses.

Clyde confronted the threesome and as he put an arm around the nearest lady, smiled and spoke to her. The brunette turned and planted a sisterly kiss on Clyde's proffered cheek. I was surprised when she turned toward me, to see it was my fisherman Princess, Birgitta. I took a deep breath and prepared myself *not* to appear as if I knew her. I assumed that was my role, during the introduction and I was sure would follow it to the letter of my training.

The other woman had also now turned at Clyde's approach

and smiled at the kiss he was receiving. Glancing over, she stared directly at me...actually, for such a long time, I wondered if she suspected something by my mere appearance. She was spectacular to look at and her directness I found quite disarming.

I stepped up beside Clyde as he was being introduced to the blond woman and the officer, wondering whether she and the naval officer were also part of *our* game. That vantage afforded an even better look at the blond woman. In profile she was smiling broadly as Clyde, no doubt, flattered her. She had extremely striking looks. I'd especially noticed her bright, blue eyes and high cheekbones. I wondered if she was Norwegian, too; possibly even Birgitta's sister? Had she said she had siblings? I couldn't recal

Clyde pivoted expansively around toward me, putting a hand on my shoulder. I was shocked when he began speaking Swedish.

"Here he comes, at last. Ladies, may I present my very good friend and...sometimes I feel, *personal* pilot, Alex Andersson of *ABA Aerotransport*—Scandinavia's only remaining airline, I believe. The *Kaptain* and I fly together so often we've become rather chummy. *Kaptain* Andersson, may I present *Fru* Birgitta Olsson, *citizen* of the world and *Fru* Greta Stopff, Director of Culture for the Norwegian something-or-other-ministry...sorry, *Fru* Stopff—I have such a poor memory when it comes to ministerial titles."

The ladies inclined their heads slightly and smiled. But the blonde extended her hand.

"How do you do...*Fru* Olsson—*Fru* Stopff. It's so nice to meet you."

"Oh—and Commander Jarvis—Royal Navy," Clyde added almost as an afterthought, with a further flourish.

"How do you do?" He extended his hand, smiling.

"Commander..."

"Actually," the officer said, stepping backward, "I must speak to someone who's just come in. Please excuse me...it was a pleasure to see you all again...and nice to meet you *Kaptain* Andersson."

"Here, Jarvis..." Clyde switched to English as he hastily put out his cigarette, "...let me walk with you. I was just going out for a bit, myself."

But then he turned back, having thought twice: "Ladies—

please look after *Kaptain* Andersson for me...he's unaccustomed to the rich food and drink they have at these things. He has to fly again on Monday and I want him if fine fettle...since I'm going along." We watched him link arms with the navy commander and saunter across the carpet toward the entrance.

All the while I watched these goings-on in silence, trying to smile and hopefully hide my fear. I didn't know how to break the ice with Birgitta so it might appear as if we'd never met and she wasn't offering to take the first step.

"Uh...*Fru* Olsson..." I began, recalling the difficulty I'd had the first time we met, "where do *you* know Clyde from?"

She turned toward me and smiled: "I met him at The Ministry; I am a...worker there. Gosh..." she said, putting her fingertips to her lips and opening her eyes wide, "I almost said what I do. That is forbidden you know...now there's a war."

"Yes, but it doesn't apply to me, being a civilian and a citizen of another country...neutral country at that."

The striking blond woman spoke for the first time since the introduction. Her voice was smooth, confident and controlled. She had a fairly heavy accent. "*Kaptain* Andersson, do you often fly to other countries from Scandinavia...and Europe?"

"Yes, regularly. There's some discussion our airline may begin terminating some of the flights due to a decline in passengers...and in the dangerous areas, we've lost a couple of machines because of the war. But, I have an offer from *Finnair* for an immediate position...along nearly the same routes, should that happen." I was telling the truth, since this problem had developed right in the middle of my training. The Swedes were considering terminating their airline until the war was over.

She had a strong, deep voice, like a singer, possibly and she looked so directly into my eyes as we spoke, almost as if gauging my every response. Her beauty was enchanting and she seemed to have no compunction or embarrassment, about being so direct, even having just met me. I found the openness almost like seeing into her soul—so open and somewhat disarming.

"Do you know any of the pilots who flew the Norwegian Royal Family, *Kaptain* Andersson?" *Fräulein* Stopff inquired, innocently. I felt my heart jump into my throat; could she have guessed who Birgitta really was.

"Yes—one of them...Eriksson, was it...? Luckily, I'd run into him in one of the *ABA* training runs and recalled his name.

"Yes, that is correct—that is his name. He told our Chief Cultural Minister he thinks he will be retiring soon."

"Really? He isn't that old."

"No, but he said he didn't like the risk involved—not to himself, but in flying The Royal Family around in the middle of a war. He feels they should go somewhere safe and remain there...like *Amerika* or Canada."

"Good for him. He's probably correct, no doubt; they should not be traveling in these times," I turned my glance at Birgitta. I sensed she was about to contribute something.

"Try to tell the King, that, from what I hear" she said smiling demurely. "According to the London papers, he is very busy and does not wish to waste time with special train cars and automobiles, which are so slow...and possibly dangerous," she said looking directly at me. I recalled our fright with the stalled truck the morning of our fishing. "And now that the Queen is in America, too. He must have plenty of time on his hands."

Fru Stopff commented instead: "No doubt these are the duties of ministers, princesses and monarchs...these matters of war. Loved-ones must be absent. What would their country do if something were to happen to the monarchy?"

She had turned and directed her question to the Princess of Norway. Did she know—*somehow?*

"We Norwegians would continue with the assigned order as has been our history, but I doubt we have anything to worry about. It is merely a matter of time before the Americans come in, I believe. Then the Axis powers will find they have awakened the sleeping giant."

"Do you really believe the *Reich* will eventually confront America?"

"Of course. Evil knows no restraint. They will do something—sooner, or later, I am certain." I wondered whether she was taunting *Fru* Stopff? Birgitta spoke with such confidence I feared she was over playing her hand. I thought I'd better change the subject.

"*Fru* Stopff, do you reside in England?"

"Oh no, I am just here for a conference about setting up cultural events. I have been spending most of my time in Norway, actually, doing music and dramatic production coordination there for the government."

"It must be difficult?" Birgitta said, turning again to the other woman. If I didn't know her I would never have been able to hear the thin veil of ice in her voice. "With the war going on there—the occupation. I did not think there *was* a government remaining in Norway."

Fru Stopff seemed not to notice. "Fortunately, it is not difficult. The fighting, as you probably know *Fru* Olsson, is completely finished...well, nearly. One needn't fear being harmed now in most places in the cities. Possibly in the north, far into the countryside, one should still be careful, but elsewhere...no. The Norwegians offered hardly any resistance to the occupation forces."

The young Commander returned just as an orchestra struck up the first waltz. The Big Band sound had reached Britain's shores. We stood there tapping our toes to the orchestra and watched the first of the dancers join the floor. I didn't know the name of the tune, but I remembered hearing it in The States before I'd come over. We watched the dancers warm up. Then Commander Jarvis invited *Fru* Stopff for a dance and the two of them disappeared into the crowd. I was immediately jealous of him.

"How am I doing?" I asked Birgitta from the side of my mouth, visibly letting down my guard.

"Perfectly, Alex. One would never know either of you were agents."

"*Either* of us...you mean...*the Commander?*"

"Of course, but not only him. Guess again."

I thought for a second. "The woman...*Fru...?*"

"Yes," she interrupted me, "the woman, *Fru* Stopff—actually *Fräulein* Stopff, is a spy of sorts, also...in Norway."

Oh—that's nice, I thought. "Are we to work...*together?*" I relished the thought, suddenly remembering those eyes, my jealousy temporarily forgotten.

"Yes—in a way, but of course she is not to know you are a British agent."

"Oh...why not—if we both to work together anyway?"

"She is a part of the program I mentioned to you...when we fished: *Lebensborn*? Remember?"

I hardly knew what to say. Any preconceived, romantic evenings with this striking woman, had I even been daring to think of them, went out the door in a flash.

"Yes, I remember, but a *Nazi*?" was all I could utter.

"Careful Alex, your eyes just gave you away...practice your self control."

"It's a good thing they had left us alone," I said quietly. I'd totally lost my composure.

"A *Nazi*?" I repeated, this time more quietly, "How—how do you know?" I almost said, how can anyone so beautiful be a *Nazi*.

"She is also a high-ranking officer in the *Waffen-SS*. She bears the civilian rank of *SS-Hauptsturmfuhrer*, a Captain. Anyway, we have ways. We feed her bits of information, at affairs of this sort and that sort..." she waved one hand slightly. And she also feeds us small tidbits of information, in return, some harmless—some more valuable than she knows. Clyde hopes to use her in the future when her confidence in us is higher. Of course, she will not be able to come to England again, probably.

I pondered what she had related. I was disappointed, no doubt about it. "Sounds awfully complicated. And she isn't to know I am an agent...for anyone?"

"Are you someone else's agent, Alex?"

"Well, no, I guess not? *Of course not!* But how am I to work for—with her—them, *whoever...*?"

"We help you in your role, as you know. But first, we wish to build her trust in you and then, eventually, further gather her trust and confidence. Soon she will begin to see your sympathetic nature and potential benefit to the Norwegian *Nazi* Party, as a pilot; then we believe she will attempt to persuade you to work with them—we believe she will attempt to do that within the year."

"Then...?"

"Then we will provide information for you to give out, harmless things, but information they will come to find valuable. This is all in addition to the diplomatic cases, of course."

She had begun to walk slowly toward the eating area, again.

I turned and followed. "What will she try to persuade me to do—
something...?"

"Of that, we are yet uncertain, Alex. Her cover is a thinly-
disguised propaganda effort. It is unfortunately a very, very serious
project. Have you heard of Vidkun Quisling[4]?"

"No...*yes*—a Norwegian somebody...I'm not sure."

"Quisling is the leader of *Nasjonal Samling* [5]...the Norwegian National Socialist Party. This organization met with such resistance in conquered Norway, the Germans have begun to push him
aside and have appointed their own man, a *Nazi* named Josef Ter-
boven; he has reorganized it all. They now use the nationalistic
nature of folk culture—music, dance, costume...to gain the confidence of the local population, especially the young women and girls.
That is where *Fru* Stopff comes in, with her specialty in folk studies.
Their efforts are most often in rural areas. She coordinates festivals
and the Norwegian *Nazi* Party recruits converts at the same time.
But they do not have a good deal of success. You see, Alex, Norwegians and other Scandinavians are strongly nationalistic and very much
despise what the *Nazis* have done, for the most part."

"I can certainly understand that. Invade your country."

"Furthermore..." she ignored my limpid humor, "...*Fru*
Greta is also a key player in this despicable project—*Lebensborn*.
We will fill you in later about this. *That* project is mine and my
mother's—the Queen's, primary concern at the moment, simultaneously with winning the war and driving the *Nazis* from our country. They are taking control of many young Norwegian women with
false promises, merely to—to, *breed* children for them-—we discussed this earlier."

"Yes, but not in detail, Birgitta."

"Do not worry; we will discuss it more, later. At first, we
believe, you must simply try to get to know *Fru* Stopff—Greta,
better...and vice-versa. Clyde also has plans for you both. We are
not so certain as to how you must set about doing that. Clyde does
not wish to give you a co-assignment yet; he fears some curiosity by
her superiors and an investigation on their part if you become too
active. We must think of something else, or let her initiate the over-
ture. Please, if you have any ideas as the adventure progresses, do
not hesitate to speak up."

She looked around to insure we weren't being overheard.

"Do you have any questions—for now Rob...*Alex?*" She frowned.

I didn't feel quite so badly after she'd also slipped and nearly called me Robert. "No, not yet; I've not had time to really consider it. Give me a couple of weeks—a month, if you can. Meanwhile, do you think you can somehow keep me apprised of her location? She said she travels. Better yet, if you could let me know where she's likely to be in a couple of days in advance. Then, at first, at least, I might be able to arrange to *accidentally* bump into her sometime, since I'll be all over Scandinavia with the airlines."

"I envy you that, Alex—traveling freely in my country..." her voice trailed off for a moment. "But...that *is* a good idea. I believe we could try to keep you updated. It might take a few days to set it up though and get it functioning. We would probably do it through the normal *airline* communication channels. I will think of something—coordinate it with Clyde. It should be easy to organize some pretense and we could arrange to have it convenient to contact her, in the incidence we would provide her with information. And it could be coincidental to your arrival in town. We will think of something, Alex."

"Yes, but what about Clyde...how does he fit into this?"

"I am not certain yet, myself. But I know he is trying to convince Greta into believing he is himself a *Nazi* spy—but for the British."

"Here we go again...."

"He has probably told her you might be a *Nazi* spy, yourself, working in Sweden."

"Oh...no...I don't think I will ever get this straight, Birgitta. And I doubt he'll be able to get away with making anyone believe that."

The dancers were returning and we had to stop talking. Birgitta nodded to signify all was set. She squeezed my arm and whispered: "It is merely a case of misinformation, confusion."

I was certainly that...confused.

"Strange way of waltzing...I must say, *Fru* Stopff. You say all the Scandinavians dance that way?" The British officer was shaking his head and laughing. "Thanks for the lesson, though."

"Yes. It is not only the *vals*—waltz, I believe you say. It is different. All of the national dances of Scandinavia are. They even differ somewhat between Norway and Sweden—Denmark—Finland…the waltz is nearly the same though, but is more in a straight line, as you saw and felt, unlike the Austrian—Vienna version or your *waltz*. That version is more swinging side to side as you move and turn. The Swedes, on the other hand…" she glanced at me and smiled, "they turn all the time in their *vals*. The Norwegians…not so much, but they do a little more up and down on the toes, without so much turning."

"There's another." Clyde said from behind us. He'd just returned, unnoticed. The musicians began again. I thought this one was by the Dorsey brothers. Clyde leaned toward me and from the side of his mouth: "Why not take her out and see if she can teach you anything, Alex. *Fru* Olsson and I can sit this one out."

I took what I thought was a strong hint that I should take a more active part and stood up.

"Would you like to dance, *Fru* Stopff?" I asked, putting down my glass, turning and bowing slightly.

"Yes, thank you *Kaptain*, I would. And I promise, I will not be a teacher, despite what the Commander says."

"Oh, I won't mind. I'm sure I can use the instruction; it's been an awfully long time since I did a real *vals*."

We moved out onto the floor, waited for a space between couples and caught the timing and soon were flowing around the floor in a counterclockwise direction, avoiding the other dancers who were dancing the more conventional Vienna style. Greta smiled up at me. As close as we were, I wondered if she felt or heard my heart going flip-flop. After a couple of turns I didn't know where to look. She was so close and wearing a low-cut, sleeveless gown and the cleavage leaped up at me when I first glanced down. Between that chasm—and her eyes…I tried to look elsewhere, but realized that that was impolite; I had to communicate.

I finally settled on her eyes and then her right ear. It was so delicate and there were several wisps of blonde hair, which had escaped the confines of her coiffure, that floated with us around the floor. Oh—she felt so light in my arms, sensing my every move. I finally became brave then and tried a couple of continuous turns, which didn't turn out as badly as I suspected they might.

"Possibly it is about time for some instruction," I joked after she smiled beautifully, nodding her head.

"No—no," she protested, earnestly, "you are doing very well, *Kaptain*. Possibly if you relaxed just a little more though? You are holding my hand...somewhat tight."

"Oh...sorry." I relaxed my grip. "Relaxing's a little easier said than done," I smiled down at her.

I thought I was going to have to deal with matching wits with this woman—as an inexperienced spy, not having to control my sexual urges.

We remained on the floor for a second dance and before it ended, I found I was losing my heart and didn't really know what to do about it. *Fru Stopff* was sociable, witty, bright and a tremendous dancer...how could she be an enemy agent?

I'd have to ask Clyde to take me out of this one, I thought, looking again into that direct stare of hers. It wouldn't do to become emotionally involved in this job. Yet, the thought of calling it off, just when I'd met her, went counter to my emotions, overriding the good sense of good conscience.

After another turn or two, Greta remarked: "You do not really need any practice *Kaptain*. You are a very smooth dancer. I feel so comfortable...in your arms," she added a smile to punctuate her earnestly declared belief. "You must have had a good deal of practice."

She was serious and again when I turned my head away from her ear, she'd be looking directly into my eyes, then at my mouth and then into my eyes again.

"That's very nice of you to say, *Fru* Stopff." I wondered if I'd blushed. We turned smoothly at the corner of the floor, to emphasize my regained skills. She was most disarming.

"No...I am serious, you are *very good*. I would like to recruit you into our little touring group when you are nearby, but I know as an American pilot, you have other, more important things to do."

My senses suddenly screamed caution; what did she already know about me beyond what she might have learned at the party in England?

"I'd very much enjoy dancing with you again sometime, *Fru*. But I must correct your assumption: I am *not* an *American* pilot. I am *Swedish* and the airline is Scandinavian: *ABA*? I only share the dual parentage: Swedish and American. I've never flown an American warplane...*honest*."

"I am sorry; I did not mean any offense *Kaptain*. But...tell me, do you favor the American or the Swedish side of your ancestry, or, do you mind my asking?"

"No, it's a fair question, *considering*...probably, the Swedish. It is far more interesting...culturally and historically." I'd hoped I was giving her the answers she wanted which would increase her trust.

"Yes, I agree. But surely, you will admit, there is some real fascination for the American culture from the standpoint of we...*Europeans*. It seems so...so carefree and gay—sooo...rich, monetarily, though somewhat wicked...if you do not mind my observation...though, I have never visited that country?"

"No, not at all. I suppose it's about like any culture and your observation sounds fair enough."

"And tell me, *Kaptain*, how has America been able to succeed—all the different nationalities and cultures from around the world—how can such different people get along together and prosper in that way?"

"I'm hardly an economist, *Fru* Stopff, but America has been fortunate in that they have had a great deal of natural resources to exploit, from the beginning—a couple hundred years ago. Once the government took the land from the indigenous inhabitants—the Indians, the farmland was nearly free of charge for the emigrants. Because there was always something around that needed doing and plenty of money to be made in doing it, the emigrants, from all nationalities, probably felt it was more beneficial to get along and work together so both could make a profit, thinking it was better than fighting. So...they pretty much learned to cooperate. They needed each other's unique, individual skills, if their own individual endeavors were going to prosper."

"Like in Europe?"

"Well...yes—no...not like Europe. There are too many people in Europe and not enough free wealth—easily available to anyone. The economy has also been in a shambles, like *Amerika's* and now...now—well, there's the war."

"What do you think of the war, *Kaptain* Andersson?"

"I think it makes it damn inconvenient to fly a passenger airline."

She smiled. "Do you believe Sweden will be...will get into it?"

"I'm not sure. I certainly hope we can remain neutral. The government blows hot and cold. The people's sympathies lie...have lain, in the past, historically, with Germany. But in the last half century, they've gravitated more toward the new order."

"America...the new order?"

"Well, not necessarily America. But the large emigrant population that went to America and other places in the world in the last century, have brought back ideas and a new way of thinking. Of course, travel and communication...they also make a difference." I was concerned about this conversation and was becoming fearful Greta was going to trap me away from my "neutrality."

"It is suddenly tiring—this war," she said, surprising me with her candor; but then, she *was* an agent for the Nazis. It was probably meant to disarm me.

"Yes, it is that...tiring."

"Let us discuss something else then, *Kaptain* Andersson.

We took a couple of turns with neither speaking. Finally, she tilted back her head and smiled: "Family...do you have a family, *Kaptain*...a wife...children?

"No—none of those; my mother is alive and I have uncles and cousins in Sweden and in America, although I haven't seen the American relations for some time. It wasn't a lie I was telling her. "What about you, *Fru* Stopff? Are you married...any children, yourself?"

She hesitated so long, I was beginning to wonder if she would answer at all. We'd made several turns and I'd had to concentrate for a moment on traffic on the floor.

"I am not married, *Kaptain* Andersson," she finally answered, quietly, giving me a somewhat sad smile. I now felt uncomfortable by both her hesitation and that smile.

"Oh, I see...I didn't mean to be nosey...pry...."

"No, that is all right. I know it was merely curiosity. Anyway, I started it—did I not? It is just…I have a daughter you see and because of the war now, I do not get to see her…as often as I would like to, so it makes me somewhat sad."

"That is unfortunate. Yes, I suppose you are busy. Do you travel a good deal?"

"Yes, but that is not why I do not see her. She does not live with me."

"Oh…I see," I said. I wondered what the intention of this conversation was, but said nothing further, letting her take it where she would. We danced a while longer without her speaking; I finally ventured:

"She lives with your husband?"

She looked up, serious now. "No, with someone…a foster family—in Germany."

I thought about that statement for a while. Before I could respond, the dance ended and we strolled through the scattering crowd toward where we'd left Birgitta and Clyde, neither of whom were anywhere to be seen.

"Shall we grab this table, *Fru* Stopff?" A couple had just gotten up ready to leave.

"Yes, possibly we should. Who knows where they have gone." She glanced around. "I suppose we should await them here."

By this time, I'd run out of small talk and wished for Clyde or Birgitta to return and rescue me. We sat speechless watching the couples dance.

"*Kaptain* Andersson, did you learn the old ways of dancing in America—the *gammaldans?*"

"In the Swedish community, where my grandparents came from…in America; there was no dancing permitted."

"Really? I thought all Americans loved music and dancing."

"Most probably do, *Fru* Stopff, but my great-grandparents emigrated for religious reasons. They were instrumental in the foundation of a free church in Sweden, sort of chased out and then did the same in northern America, after they emigrated. The Lutheran clergy sort of *encouraged* them to leave Sweden. So many of them emigrated…also for reasons of poverty, understand. But to better address your question, I've spent time in both countries, but learned the *gammaldans* in Sweden."

She nodded, seeming unconcerned now that I'd responded.
"Would you like another drink or some more food, *Fru* Stopff?"

"No thank you, but help yourself, I will wait for the others."

"I'm fine for now. We can see what the others are planning
when they return."

We watched the dancers for a bit as a tango began. "That is
what the Finns like," *Fru* Stopff said, off-handedly.

"What's that?"

"The *Tango*. They very much like to dance and play *Tango*."

"Really...I didn't know that. I thought Tango was...South
American, or Spanish, not Finnish?"

"No, not necessarily, there seem to be two different types
danced, in both areas."

We sat for a while longer; I didn't know the Tango and if she
did she apparently wasn't willing to take on a student, tonight. I thought
I'd try some different inroads and decided on the subject of her child.

"Your child, *Fru* Stopff...do you mind my asking how old
she is?"

She looked up, interested. "No...she is a little over three
years."

"Oh...." I had to think of what to say next; I couldn't imagine
leaving a child that young. It was all coming too fast for me. I was too
new to this spy game to separate my own feelings from the obvious
suffering of others, especially someone so beautiful. I couldn't think of
how a spy would respond so I just acted myself: concerned.

"Couldn't you somehow arrange for her...*caretakers* to bring
her here to see you—to Norway, I mean?" The look that crossed her
face was an answer in itself. She smiled a bittersweet smile and looked
directly into my eyes again. It was unbelievably disarming; there was
pain behind that smile.

"They are...they are unable, *Kaptain* Andersson, to travel
such distances during the war...it is really a long story and I do not
wish to bore you with my problems."

"No, that's OK—I don't want to pry, either. I'm sorry if it
made you sad."

She shook her head and gave a gesture of dismissal.

"No, it is all right. You may ask."

"What do you plan to do then *Fru* Stopff…about getting to see your daughter?"

"Oh, I will wait to see how fast the war progresses. It is difficult to say. She…*Sophia*, is safe with her foster parents, I think. There is little more I can do at this time. A long story, as I said."

"I hope it is only the poor communication."

"Yes, I also."

Fru Stopff had been fidgeting and now glanced around, probably looking for the missing couple. By now, I'd decided they'd abandoned us so I could get my wings so to speak in the spy world. She glanced at her wristwatch.

"*Kaptain* Andersson…I really must be going. Would you mind saying my good-byes to *Fru* Olsson and Lord Whittwell."

"No, not at all. Can I…see you somewhere? Do you have a ride?"

"No, thank you. I'll take a taxi. I leave again on the ferry tomorrow…for Norway."

I began to wish I were also going to be on the ferry. She finally stood up and turned toward me, extending her hand.

"*Kaptain* Andersson, it was so nice to meet you…" almost hesitantly, she added: "I know we will probably meet again. I look forward to…to that. And thank you for the dance. I quite enjoyed it."

"You are most welcome *Fru* Stopff. I also look forward to meeting you again. If you are going anywhere…flying…telephone the airline office in Oslo, or wire Helsinki. Let me know through them…possibly we can meet…have lunch—dinner…another dance, even?"

"I will do that, *Kaptain* Andersson…thank you again and good by."

We shook hands again—a quick, single shake and a slight curtsey on her part. Old world, I thought. Her hand was firm and warm. I hung around for another half-hour waiting for the others. I had a beer and some of the snacks from the buffet and sat watching the remaining crowd. There was no telling when I'd encounter another spread like this one and I might as well make the best of it. When *Fru* Stopff left, the party sort of ended for me anyway. Those were *some* blue eyes.

CHAPTER

6

We Meet Again

Birgitta was true to her word in that, through *ABA*, she'd keep me pretty well up to date on Greta Stopff's activities. It wasn't long before our paths crossed again, with a little manipulation on *ABA*'s and my part, from Helsinki.

In a planned meeting, I'd *arranged* a flight with an overnight layover in Bergen. There had been some weather coming across Sweden, moving toward the Baltic, but we got in ok. My *contacts* had informed me we were to be staying in the same hotel. *Fräulein* Stopff, or the cultural organization she represented, was hosting an exhibition in the local war veteran's hall. It was somehow connected with a district folk festival, a celebration of sorts, which had been going on for a few days. The group Greta worked with was scheduled to perform dances the evening of my arrival.

In the lobby of our hotel a placard mentioned there had been teaching dance sessions, earlier in the day, for both dancing and *Hardanger* fiddle playing.

I don't know who was around to take the lessons, with the war on—children, possibly. At the front desk I got directions to the hall. Once I realized it was only a few blocks from the hotel, I decided to walk. It was brisk, a cold front having moved through as our flight was arriving; it would be a bitter night, no doubt about it. I quickened my step. Even with the northwest wind behind me, it still got beneath my fleece-lined flight jacket. I was happy for the long underwear and wool trousers.

Inside the hall, I hung my coat in the rack and looked around for the bar. Just then the music started and a gaily-dressed group of dancers marched onto the floor. Because she was so tall Greta's blonde head immediately stood out from the dancers. As much as I was prepared for the sight of her, my first glance drew an intake of breath at her beauty.

As she executed a turn with her partner, decked out as she was, seeing Greta made my knees weak. It wasn't only her clothing. She was wearing very colorful Norwegian folk *bunad*,[8] not unlike the other couples, but she carried herself far better; her turns and the walking part of the *Røros pols* [9] dance they were performing, was smoother. There was this—*sophistication* about her demeanor, as if she really did something more important in life that required a more artful bearing and she was carrying the poise through, even in her dancing.

There were several musicians on the slightly elevated stage area: most played violins, one stroked a bass fiddle and there were a couple with accordions and a mandolin. I could see an assortment of other instruments on the floor, behind the group. With the exception of three younger women, the remainder were old men. The dance finished as I watched, but they started a second tune. I continued watching from near the entrance to the bar, lost in the beauty of her execution. She seemed to be in a world of her own, though she smiled frequently at her shorter dance partner.

When the musicians began playing a waltz I gradually moved closer. And by the second waltz, I was watching from the closer proximity of the bar. It was a really small, four person affair that really served more as a place for the two waitresses to lean while the barman hurried to draw and place drinks on their waiting trays. Unable to hear me for the music, I pointed and he nodded and drew a tall stein of the beer from the pump I'd indicated and put it on the bar. He took my money and made change.

From the caustic way she'd been treating him, I suspected one of the waitresses was the barman's girlfriend or spouse. While they waited for their drinks the servers stood watching the dancers, leaning back with both elbows on the bar.

As the piece finished, the dance group seemed to be taking a break after they'd taken a nice round of applause. The music began again, but without the dancers performing. They were milling around beside the musicians; some remained sitting on the slightly-raised bandstand while others disappeared toward the door.

As soon as the musicians began the next tune, couples from the crowd of spectators started to take the floor and were soon dancing the straight and level waltz of Scandinavia. It was easy to pick out the locals from the invaders...the Germans and Austrians stuck out, even though they weren't wearing their uniforms. Swedes, in particular, weren't supposed to enjoy the dance—strong Lutheran churching——the Norwegians, they had a little more fun and had put some bounce to their step. But the invaders...their dance style was completely different.

I pushed away from the bar, having finished my beer and started working my way toward the idle dancers, winding my way between the couples as they danced their way around the wooden floor. I wanted it to appear to be a complete coincidence that we were meeting. Greta was standing beside the musicians discussing something with her dance partner. I dodged between a fast-moving couple and stepped up beside them. She was listening to what her partner was saying. I waited, not wanting to interrupt. Looking at *Fräulein* Stopff's colorful *bunad* I could see it was exceptional, nearly covered in embroidery. But then she had to play the *Norwegian* role in her department's recruiting efforts and using the folk traditions was one of the many tools of the *Nazis*.

Her companion was younger than she, as were the village males now also dancing. Younger female Norwegians were mostly working on farms, in the factories, supervised by Germans. In the case of the males, they'd *disappeared* into the Norwegian Resistance or across the border into Sweden. And some had just disappeared completely. Looking at her companion, I surmised he was a *Nazi* propagandist.

The couple didn't take notice of me. I waited another minute to see whether they were engaged in a particularly intent conversation. I didn't want to break in on a quarrel, as I'd planned to ask her to dance with me...as an icebreaker.

The music was loud and she was forced to lean forward,

bending toward the young man and away from me. He was earnestly speaking about some topic, waving his hands and gesturing. During this she stood more as if she were enduring, than listening. Her body language said she was becoming somewhat annoyed.

I eased around in front of her and a little closer, while trying to appear nonchalant. She saw me, smiled slightly, but then went right back to listening. Taken aback, I hesitated, watching to see whether she might interrupt him. She didn't seem to be having any success and looked even more annoyed as he paused to take a breath. My chance, I thought and stepped up, held out my left hand without glancing at her partner and asked her to dance.

"*Skall vi vals?*" I said in Swedish.

I didn't know any *Norsk* but knew the two languages were close enough. The young man cleared his throat loudly in annoyance. From the corner of my eye I could imagine him glaring up at me. But I didn't bother to turn and meet his gaze. He glanced toward Greta, as if to see what her reaction would be.

Without hesitation she took the bait, putting a hand on his shoulder: "*Tack*," she said turning to me and taking my hand. Before he could interrupt I led her onto the floor, leaving him standing by himself.

"*Tack för räddning mig...*" thanks for the rescue...she said in Swedish.

We paused a moment to find an opening between the dancers and as she put her arm on my shoulder, we swung smoothly onto the floor.

"I'm sorry," she said in Swedish, "I know we have met and I even remember where, but I don't remember your name...you are an—no—*the American aviator.* Right?"

Was she testing me, I wondered?

"Alex...*Anderssson*, at your service," I answered, "yes, a *Swedish* airline pilot. We met at the Royal Bath—Bournemoth...a party? About two months ago?"

Either she was faking it or my string of hints finally jogged her poor memory.

"Yes I remember. I am so sorry to forget your name though...I meet so many people you see."

"Thank you *Fru—Fräulein* Stopff, for the dance."

"You did not forget my name?" She smiled a little impishly.

"I certainly did not."

We continued around the floor with the next tune. It took a moment for me to get the three-step of the waltz right—but not her. After working half way around the floor admiring her ear again, I finally dared to look directly in her eyes again. She peered right back openly, smiling slightly. Curiosity played about her lips as she looked at me in that way she had.

"*Ni ar det Amerikansk—från Står Brittania...?*" she asked me, thinking I was living in Great Britain.

"*Nej*, I'm from Sweden, but I had an American father."

She nodded. "*Ja...*"

"Remember now?"

"Umhuh...your accent sounded more—British? What brings you to Norway...*Kaptain* Andersson...with war—so new to us? Have you come to fight, or just fly?"

"Fight? Oh, no, I'm a civilian pilot—Swedish neutral—remember...*ABA Aerotransport?* Actually; I'm here on a stopover, on my way back to Helsinki."

We paused a moment in the dance to avoid a floundering couple ahead of us, then started again; she smiled at the couple as we danced around them.

"Does your airline company make a lot of business with Norwegian companies?" She seemed interested in small talk and interrupted me before I could answer. "Has the war been good for business?"

"Yes, Norwegian, British, Swedish—even German companies,, they all use us. But we have had to alter our routes to accommodate the war, certainly." I wanted to change the subject.

"You dance very well...*Fräulein* Stopff. I hadn't realized how well, watching you from the bar—before your performance ended."

She smiled and nodded her gratitude.

"Not that I didn't expect otherwise, since our last meeting...and dance. Do you dance with this group frequently?"

I remembered from my briefing by Birgitta and Clyde that

Fräulein Stopff was the director of the Norwegian *Nazi* Folk Society. He'd said they toured Scandinavia promoting cultural events, sort of a headliner—an opener for various agencies. The ultimate goal was to improve the image of the Norwegian *Nazi* Party and encourage young Norwegian girls and women to travel to Germany for the program he didn't know much about called *Lebensborn*. Clyde has said it was one of Himmler's pet projects and Birgitta had said it was her mother's, the Queen's, first choice for eradication in Norway.

Fräulein Stopff brought me back to my question.

"Yes, *Kaptain* Andersson, but not always; I'm the director of the cultural portion of the agency. The small budget dictates I also be a working manager. So I often times take the part of one of the dancers, sometimes only to substitute if someone is ill, at other times, just because I love to dance."

"It shows—your love of dance, I mean," I said as the music ended. "Would you care for a drink—or do you have to perform again?"

"Thank you, but I must join my companions again for one more performance before the dinner break. Then we are done for the evening. If you are remaining, I will be happy to accept your offer, after? It should not be long."

"Sure, I'll hang around—*say*, better yet...I haven't yet eaten," inclining my head toward the dining room, "wouldn't you join me later for that drink and dinner, too?"

She looked toward the room and glanced back at the forming dancers.

"Oh—there is no need. I did not mean to hint..."

"Oh, I know that. We've met again—sort of by accident...and I don't have anything else to do for the evening?"

She nodded: "Well...no....

"I know no one in the city and I thought possibly we could get to know one another better. Two ships in the night, so to speak?"

She pondered the question, looking intently at me again. I wondered whether she was trying to see whether she could trust me, as it seemed her habit...this direct, deep staring, almost into one's soul. I felt a sort of tingle...a tingle I'd not felt in so long I couldn't remember when it had last crept up the back of my neck like that. It felt good. God…I thought. I'm hooked. What'll I do? I should turn myself in to Clyde. Take myself off this mission. But I knew I wouldn't.

"Yes—yes, I would be delighted to have a drink and dinner," she said, smiling and taking my hand in a gesture of parting. Meanwhile, please feel free to watch us perform if you have not yet seen enough."

"OK, I will, right after I fix it for dinner for two. Maybe I'll learn something new in Scandinavian dance."

"Oh—I doubt that you will, but please enjoy yourself. Since there is a shortage of young men in Norway, you will probably find another woman to converse with—or to dance with, even." She smiled mischievously: "I'll not be too long."

I remained long enough to watch them begin their performance. It started as a large ring, with all joining hands and in a fluid motion round and round, until they broke up to form into three rings of four dancers each, two women—two men. The tune was a *schottische*. Greta was correct about the number of young women, as there were a goodly number of potential recruits in the audience for the breeding program. Many of the young women were actively laughing and talking with the young German soldiers, no doubt the *bait*.

I avoided the crowd and the inviting smiles of the unoccupied women. I didn't need someone else complicating the evening just as the opportunity to get to know *Fräulein* Stopff was offering itself.

As I had begun this evening, I thought to myself watching the whirl of color on the dance floor, I'd sort of dreaded it. It'd been a long, tough week, flying, with terrible weather every day. All the landings had been made difficult with the ice and it was taxing on the whole crew. So after I'd bathed and changed to come out for this evening, knowing it would be more work, I had a minor sense of dread, preferring rather to remain in my room and just make a night of it, reading.

But after the short conversation and dance with *Fräulein* Stopff, I was now eagerly anticipating the remainder of the evening—not so much the challenge of growing the assignment, but to be able to spend a couple of hours staring into those beautiful, blue eyes.

I finally broke off watching the dancers and made my way for the bar again. The man was busier than ever. "Can you arrange a meal for two—when the dancers finish?"

"You can go in and do it yourself," he indicated the restaurant entrance with a nod, pulling the handles on two glasses of beer, simultaneously. "The meals are provided by a different family than the bar."

I thanked him and did, walking into the nearly-empty dining room. It was still early and the hostess reassured me that there would be no problem for a table this evening, as long as we came immediately after the dance finished.

"Do not wait too long," she said. "I can not reserve it for you with so many here who will also expect to dine."

I returned to the hall and stood at the edge of the crowd watching the performances. The dancers made a few more rounds. I marveled at their skill. The younger man—the one Greta had been in such an intense conversation with at the bar, seemed to be her partner in each of the couple's dances. He was a good dancer too, but I could tell that his skill had long ago been mastered and the challenge of the dance appeared to be gone for him—he danced in utter boredom, taking little pride in his skill or the beauty of the dance. His performance was the worse for it, unlike his beautiful partner; he didn't give the impression by his demeanor that he was enjoying it. Greta simply shone, smiling brilliantly all the while they danced. I wondered possibly whether she had upset him in some way; there was something bothering him.

The set finally ended and the dancers trooped over to the small stage where an aged master of ceremonies thanked them for their wonderful performance. *Fräulein* Stopff was given some flowers by her partner, which brought another round of applause and after curtseying twice, she left the stage. I held up an arm so she could find me in the crowd.

Her partner took the podium immediately, loosened his vest and shirt and while rolling up his sleeves, he began giving what sounded like something which would work itself into quite a speech.

Greta was making her way in my direction but was being stopped by every other person wanting to shake her hand. She took her time and smiled and nodded while receiving their complements for their performances. Finally, she made it to my side, raised her eyebrows and smiled up at me, taking my hand.

"All in a day's work, *Kaptain*...still wish to buy my dinner? I must warn you, I'm famished." My heart skipped a beat.

"Yes...but do you mind if I listen to him for a moment?"

"No...certainly not, if you wish.."

Her companion was really getting warmed up; he drew our attention for a moment as he was so loud. He was speaking about the glory of the *Third Reich*, of Norway, Quisling and of course, old Adolph. I listened as attentively as I could. The language was just similar enough to Swedish that I could get the gist of what he was saying. Of course I wasn't buying a word of it, but pretended to be interested. I thought from time to time that my companion glanced up at my profile to determine whether I was intent, or merely being nice. I tried to fool her and take in enough of the, by now ranting, in case she decided to test me with a quiz later.

Then I felt her tugging my sleeve and looked down; she inclined her head in the direction of the dining room and raised her eyebrows. Then, standing on tiptoe, she reached up toward me with one, cupped hand and for an instant, I thought she was going to kiss me; I felt my face and ears go hot. But instead she tipped her head sideways and laying her hand gently on my shoulder, spoke directly in my ear.

"If we are to have any food, we should go in now, *Kaptain*, or we will have to wait a long time."

Her breath was hot on my neck and I could feel the gentleness of her fingertips on my chest. I nodded vigorously, took her arm and we began to work our way through the smoke and crowd toward the double French doors of the attached restaurant.

Between stretched and pleated white curtains, I could already see a few diners through the closed glass. Greta seemed a little tense as we negotiated the crowded hallway by the dining room entrance. I wondered what was wrong, wondering whether I'd unknowingly done something to offend her. We stopped before the open doors and waited for someone to come and seat us. I looked down at her somewhat rigid stature and she glanced up, with a fierce expression, surprising me. Then she smiled a little bitterly, putting her hand on my forearm.

"Sorry..." she said, taking my arm.

"Did I...say something?

"No...certainly not. *He* did," she gestured backward with her head. "I'm sorry, but I'm afraid my personal feelings are show-ing. You see," she said, inclining her head again back toward the ballroom, "I've had more than enough of him for today...for a long time, actually."

A waitress beckoned from the middle of the dining room, indicating a table with her other arm. We started toward her and she nodded, satisfied we'd seat ourselves and turned back to disappear through the double, swinging doors. As I held her chair, Greta nod-ded toward the dance area again, taking up her napkin.

"He has been quite a problem today. I just need to cool off a little. She gave the starched napkin a brisk shake to one side. "I don't mean to bring my personal troubles with me to dinner, but just as we left—did you hear him? He began *again* with the young girls...we had an agreement, he and I."

"No—I didn't catch it, but don't worry about complaining if you're upset by him.

I'm a good listener," I pulled my chair closer. "Anything particular...want to complain about...is he your...boyfriend?"

"No—certainly not...that thought *would* ruin our evening," she smiled brilliantly. "It's just he...he is a young man who thinks he God's gift to Adolph Hitler." I couldn't help laughing silently, trying to disguise my amusement behind my napkin, but I was shaking a little, laughing.

"It is not a matter of humor," she said, looking seriously at me as I put the napkin in my lap.

"*Sorry*—I thought you were joking."

She didn't have an opportunity to respond as the hostess arrived, asking us if we were there for a meal, or merely a drink. I held up the menu: "We'd like to eat—*and* have a drink. Please give us a little more time to decide for the meal but we probably will order a drink now."

We did. Greta had white wine and I ordered beer.

"Fine, Sir. I will return shortly," our server responded. "Take your time."

Fräulein Stopff picked up her menu sort of shaking her head.

"As I was saying, I didn't mean to take my problems out with you...about Herman, but...ohhhh, I get so angry with him!"

"Think nothing of it, *Fräulein.*"

"I would like to explain...if I may: Herman is burning with idolatry for the *Führer, if* you hadn't yet noticed."

"I thought he seemed to be getting a little overheated for just a dance...a little too serious, is he?"

"Correct—he always does. But today—*tonight,* he tells me he wants me to become an advocate also."

"Advocate?"

"Yes—to help him deceive the young girls——Norwegian women, to get them to...to be in our project. I prefer to do it by persuasion...touting its merits."

I played dumb. "I'm sorry, I don't understand. Your *project...?*"

Get them away from their families to have babies with our soldiers!"

"Oh...at home?"

"No—no...we take them to special places we have put in place, away from their own houses. There are other girls like them. They feel at home—they have companions their own age, doing the same thing."

"That's...like kidnapping them, isn't it—nearly—and a violation of the...of the Geneva Convention, or something?"

"I'm not certain about the other countries' rules, but I know that I wish to have no part in it in Herman's way. To persuade them—with songs and dance—to join, that is one thing...if they are willing. But to trick them, or worse, to force them? *No, absolutely not!* I'll have none of it."

She was really growing rather animated again.

"I can't say that I blame you. I know there's a war on but...."

"Oh—let us speak of other matters, *Kaptain* Andersson. Enough of this war...I'm sick of it—*really!*"

"Would you mind...then, calling me Alex...instead of *Kaptain* Andersson?"

"No...of course not...if you will call me *Greta, without* the fräulein, please?"

"It's a deal...*Greta.*" We nodded binding our agreement,

then turned to our menus.

The waitress returned with our drinks.

"Thank you," I said, taking my beer. "We'll probably be another five minutes with the menus."

She nodded, leaving Greta and I to concentrate on the selections. We were hungry and mulled over the limited choices. Greta finally chose creamed herring and potatoes. I debated over pigs feet and boiled potatoes. We discussed the choices and determined there must be a German chef in the kitchen, based on the menu offerings. I changed my mind and ordered baked codfish and potatoes. When our waitress returned I ordered another glass of beer to be served with my dinner.

"I've just realized how badly I've behaved, Alex, possibly I've gotten too hungry." She reached over and touched my hand across the table. "Like a child...I apologize again for my bad mood. I'm completely well now, again—you see?" To prove it she flashed me a smile. That made my knees weak—and I was sitting down.

"No need to apologize, so long as I wasn't the guy you were angry with. Besides... *Greta*, you become more attractive when you're angry."

"*Oh* really...do I detect a complement mixed in there? In that instance then, thank you, Sir."

"Possibly," I said returning her smile. I was beginning to enjoy her company again. "There was one meant—disguised as it probably was. You're most welcome, Madame."

We chuckled then began chatting small talk for a half hour, waiting for the food. The server came with both hands full of plates. With some help from us she was soon rid of her burden as we spread them around the table.

"I will bring some bread when I return," she said.

I began to cut the potatoes beneath the thick coating of gravy from the Codfish, which was more creamed than baked. We both tasted our fish.

The basket of bread arrived, wrapped in a linen towel. There was no butter at all, of course. I broke one of the pieces and dipped into my fish gravy with the tip of my table knife and smeared the end of the bread. Tasting it, I smiled when I saw Greta had stopped and was watching me expectantly.

"Possibly not the best etiquette," I said, "but it's better than no butter?"

"I'll try it, too," she said. "I really miss having butter." She tasted her own bread and frowned a little. She cut off a piece of the herring, tasting it and frowned again. "It is very salty, Alex. Would you mind if I had some beer, too?"

"Sure. I'll go ask the waitress."

"Thank you."

I found her talking to the bartender in the other room and I made my request. She told me she would bring it directly.

"It's coming," I reported, back at the table, sitting down. "Want some of mine, meanwhile?"

"No. I have some water, thank you. I really do like the herring but this is a little too salty."

"I can ask them to take it back?"

"No. I will eat it. It's normal for Norway."

The beer appeared and Greta took a grateful sip. "That tastes good."

We got into our meals then, not speaking for a while. But I eventually opened the conversation again.

"What do you do...exactly, Greta? Besides dance, I mean. What's your job, here?"

"I work for the Norwegian *German* Government, of course. The *Reich*—a division of the *SS Waffen*," she said nonchalantly without glancing up from the fish she was de-boning.

"It is the...the Cultural Improvement section, I guess you might term it." She looked up, slowly chewing. After a couple seconds she asked: "Why do you ask, Alex? Interested in abandoning your neutrality status as a Swede—I hope not, for the Allied side?"

"No thanks. I'll stick to my Swedish side; it's safer." I took some of the bread and tore it apart. "I just didn't think the *Reich* was so strong on cultural events."

"The *Reich* is very interested in culture, Alex. Why...Germany, since the war, has been very careful to preserve and collect priceless art objects from all over Europe, before the deserting peasant soldiers can steal, or destroy it, as they flee the *Wehrmacht*. In fact, there are some who say the war is really about nothing but culture—the differing cultures of each nation."

I thought of the stories I'd heard of the *Nazi* plundering of many Old Master's works in museums around Europe, especially the *Louvre* in Paris, but said nothing. I wanted Greta to feel comfortable with me, so I encouraged her to continue to talk.

"How can any war be about culture? Do you mean cultural differences?"

"No—that's not what I mean..." she paused, finishing her beer with the last of the fish and returning to her wine.

I waited. She held up the glass, cupping it in both hands before resuming.

"It's about individual cultures—*separate* cultures, good cultures and bad ones...not-so-good cultures. Cultures which can be improved—improved by *other* cultures."

"Still don't follow you Greta, but keep talking."

She frowned having to concentrate to make her point. "Well...you see, we Germans...we feel our culture—our *race* is..." she reached across the table with one hand, clasping my wrist and smiled, "...like the Scandinavian race, rather superior to many others in Europe and the world. We want to foster that superiority among the other *lesser* cultures to *improve* and help them *grow*. It's really—eventually, for our—*their* own betterment."

I'd almost winced.

"By making war on them...?" I couldn't help myself and regretted the momentary loss of control. But she didn't seem to notice.

"Well *no*, not really. But...sometimes, maybe...it *is* necessary to conquer a culture in order to educate them—make them see their...their *shortcomings*. Just look at what Rome did for Europe and The British Isles."

I thought of the forced labor camps we'd heard rumors of in the eastern Europe; rumors in Poland, Romania being emptied of Jews, Gypsies—other minorities, dying by the hundreds. But I kept my mouth shut and an interested expression on my face, nodding from time to time to continue to encourage her, loving the sight and sound of her voice, while hating the words she was declaring so earnestly. Finally, I could remain silent no longer.

"I'm afraid I can't condone conquering a people, making

war, just to impose one's culture upon them; it's... *inhumane*, among other things. Wouldn't a mono-culture—a singular world culture be extremely boring?"

"Yes, it would, at first," she sipped her wine, "but think about it. That superior culture would diversify—break up into smaller, individual—*special* cultures, which would eventually be diverse and individual—but far more superior than the ones they replaced. And, eventually, they would take on the traits of the superior, *conquering* culture and meld it with their own...improving it."

"But to make war—kill innocent people in the process, Greta—I—I can't really condone that for any reason."

"Do you really—*disbelieve* it?" She seemed to be genuinely considering the doubt I'd expressed.

"Absolutely. To fight—*kill* a people *to better* them...idiotic...absolutely idiotic! I'm sorry for my directness."

"I understand...don't worry, I am not taking this discussion personally. I know you Swedes are known for your pacifist nature. But the question of the unfortunate death resulting from this cultural improvement...I did not expressly mean *to kill them* to improve them—I meant to take the control of their society away from them and show them the light of a far *better* society and...."

In spite of myself, I interrupted her: "Show them the light? Religious orders have been doing that for years, as an excuse to persecute those who didn't believe in the same color god *they* believed in. Witch burning in Europe and America were common under exactly that guise—to *improve* the population. And there have been no end of other examples." I stopped just short of blurting out the current *Nazi* Party's growing record was one of the worst in history.

"Alex, that is possibly your Swedish neutrality showing."

"No it isn't! And it isn't the American side, *either*. It's...all of them—everything... world view, maybe."

"I see I've made you angry and I am sorry Alex. Let's change the subject. Don't pay attention to my commitment and vehemence. They take control of my reason and my manners sometimes. I can become rather rude company, somewhat like my overheated companion, tonight—after the dancing, *eh?*

I said nothing for a moment. She had angered me; partly

because of the *Nazi* line she was repeating—I thought she seemed too intelligent for that. And the other, because if I was going to be involved with Clyde's hocus-pocus game, I'd have to gain better control of my emotions and I certainly hadn't demonstrated that tonight. She continued to try to persuade me.

"But surely Alex, I don't believe in killing *anyone* in order to impose one's culture upon another people, simply because they don't believe as we do. I believe each people—culture—race...has its own particular beauty and should be preserved. Preserved, not imposed upon, or depressed."

"That's completely different, Greta." It seemed like an olive branch.

"And I don't mean to imply cultures and races shouldn't mix; I meant to say, it would be a shame if the blond, blue-eyed Aryan race we are attempting to preserve—*to improve*, were to vanish into another culture or race. An Oriental should always look like an Oriental, but that is not to say they could not intermarry and mix the races. Just...just *not everyone*. Or, it would become a mix up of some completely new and different race. Do you see what I mean?"

"I believe I do. It's quite a bit different from what you originally said."

"I'm sorry, I didn't make myself very clear. I believe there is beauty in the individuality of the races and because I am one, I believe ours—*Aryan*, is the best."

"It seems the *Third Reich*, as it is imagined and being carried out, wishes to go further with *their* preference for we of Aryan lineage. They are killing innocent people, I am told, in Poland and other places in the East—all in the guise of improving them. What good are they *improved*, if they're dead?"

"Yes...I've heard that rumor, too, Alex, but I don't believe it's true. I think it's nothing but Allied propaganda—fostered by the Allies—*specifically*, the Americans and British, to discredit we Germans. I can hardly conceive of huge refugee camps to murder people; not in a civilized society like ours. Imagine, Alex...the culture that produced Beethoven, Bach and Mozart."

I could feel my blood pressure had peaked again during the short exchange. I'd lost control again, of both my temper and my heart this evening. I was a failure on both parts in light of my first covert assignment. Greta had also become quiet, possibly also sensing the soured tract the conversation had taken. She sat idly looking at her hands folded over the glass. Her meal was finished and only a little wine swirled within the glass.

"Greta, I'm afraid I lost control of my emotions and I was rude to you. I apologize."

She looked up and smiled rather melancholy in my direction.

"Yes...perhaps we both did get a little excited. I believe you touched upon an area I myself have questioned from time to time, but not dared ask myself about. And your discovery and revelation of it in me angered me somewhat. Anger at myself—not you Alex and I, too, apologize."

We sat quietly, having finished our meals. The music had begun again in the ballroom. Once, while we were deep in conversation, I'd seen her partner appear through the curtained doors. He'd seen us at our table, stared for a moment and then turned on his heel. Greta, her back to the door, didn't see him and I didn't acknowledge his appearance.

Greta had folded her hands on her lap and sat staring down at them. The part in her hair was perfect. Each side was braided and wound in the Swiss/German peasant girl style one might have seen in the movies of Hansel and Gretl. I thought I'd better act now or never.

"Would you like to go for a walk, Greta, or do you think it is too cold outside?"

She looked up, expectation and excitement changing the somber countenance.

"No...and yes! If you let me return to my room and add another sweater over my costume, I'd love to take a walk."

We got up and as I was paying the woman, Greta thanked me and said she would only be ten minutes in her room.

"OK...I'll grab an extra sweater too and meet you in the lobby in five minutes."

I'd put on my sweater when I remembered a knit hat I'd also packed; I stuck that in my coat pocket before returning to the tiny lobby.

Out on the street we strolled for a while without saying much, our breaths mixing as we gradually picked up and held a fast walking pace. It was cold after sitting in the restaurant and we both had our hands in our pockets. After nearly a block Greta moved closer and linked her left arm in mine and blowing a cloud of fresh breath, smiled up at me, waving at it with her free hand as if to demonstrate the coldness of the night.

Another few minutes walking in silence and I resolved that I owed her something further. Mind and heart pulling from two directions.

"I guess we talked our way into an impasse back there in the dining room, Greta?"

"We do seem to have talked ourselves out of conversation, didn't we. But, no need to worry. It's quite natural...we both have our convictions. Even though we come from similar worlds, yours—Sweden...has...questions without answers, where mine—Germany, has conviction with purpose. We were once closer as countries and may still be, in the hearts of the people, but by Her continued neutrality, Sweden has taken a step away from Germany. Though it may not be in the direction of The Allies, it is an estrangement, nonetheless."

I didn't comment.

"But, surely there's no need for us to do the same, Alex."

I didn't reply with the words I was thinking: that question was conviction and neutrality was action.

"I agree," I finally said, bowing to duty rather than conviction and we walked on into the dimness of the cold evening.

CHAPTER
7

The Confession

For another three-quarters of an hour, we circled the area in and around the square of the city, in ever increasing blocks. Finally, we grew both cold and fatigued and returned at last to the hotel without having spoken again about the war. I suppose, like me, Greta was cautious—fearful of another argument arising over our obvious dissimilarities of opinion. The few comments made were restricted to the architectural facade of an occasional building we passed.

Though we had walked at a brisk pace, I was cold as we entered the lobby again. The heat felt good and I quickly loosened the buttons on my jacket to let the room's warmth get at my body. Greta did the same, struggling to shed her heavy coat. I helped her free her arms and then folded the coat neatly over one arm as she watched, then I handed it back.

"You are kind, Alex; thank you."

She turned, glancing toward the elevator. I gestured with one arm and let her start across the lobby before falling in step beside her and into the small elevator. I leaned past her and pressed the lever. The brass behemoth rattled a little behind the wall and groaned and we could hear the cables passing through the pulleys, bringing us the car. After a few seconds, the doors parted slightly, closed again, then slowly opened again.

We watched the agonizingly slow process until they gaped and finally, Greta stepped into the car; I followed, turned, leaned forward to see to my floor selection, but then remembered my manners:

"Your floor, Greta?"

"It is seven, please," she said glancing up at the long, brass arrow now pointing all the way to the left on the arc of floor numbers.

"Seven it is," I said needing two stabs with my thumb to get the light to glow behind the button. I then pressed eight, my floor. The car began gathering what might be called speed. We could feel the floor vibrating along the car's upward flight. At each floor, there was the click of something against the car's bottom as we rose. As we neared the sixth floor the car groaned to a stop and the doors slid open effortlessly.

We stood staring at the vacant hallway without moving. A tall, cylindrical pottery ashtray stood beneath a picture of some sheep in a meadow. There was a cigarette smoldering in the ashtray. I reached for the *close door* button and pressed it. Nothing happened. We glanced at each other and smiled. I was about to press it again when the doors suddenly slid shut. I stepped back again, folding my arms as the car began another groaning climb to the next floor, then lurched to a jumpy stop, as we saw when the doors opened a crack, we were about a foot short of being level with the floor. The car stood, unmoving, with the doors remaining partially open. I looked at Greta and we both frowned at the inconvenience of the machine. Impatient, she leaned forward before I could…intending to press the *open door* button, when the doors lurched open another couple of inches. I stepped forward and pulled the one on my side, while she did the same for hers, until finally, she was able to escape through the narrow opening, jumping up as if the car might plunge to the bottom at any second. A thought I must admit, I'd been having, myself.

In the hallway she turned to face me. I leaned sideways, still propping the doors open with my shoulder. Our faces were equal in height. She switched the coat from right to left arm and extended her hand awkwardly into the opening.

"Thank you again, Alex. This was a very exciting ending to

what could have been a very boring evening."

"You mean the...your dance partner's lecture or the elevator ride?"

"Exactly—both, but mostly the nice dinner and walk you took me on. And I have heard it all before—*him*. Thank you again Alex, for the evening...and your company. I hope we can meet again somewhere like this. Wasn't it a nice coincidence?"

"Yes, it was fortunate. I'd like to see you again, Greta. Is there somewhere I could contact you? I guess I don't even know where...here in Norway, that you live."

"Oh...yes, please..." she glanced backward along the hallway. "If you don't mind waiting...she glanced at the stranded car. Or, you can come in for a moment and I will write it down—my address? You can write me if you are coming...back again."

I let go of the doors and half stepped, half leaped free of them and into the hallway foyer. As if eager to be rid of me, the car groaned loudly; then the doors closed with a bang.

We laughed at the inconvenience of the apparatus, as I followed her down the hall to her room. I waited as she turned the key, swung the door and I followed her into a mirror image of my own room. She flung her coat on the bed, crossed to the nightstand, sat down and began removing writing materials from a traveling writing satchel.

I remained standing just inside the doorway. She unscrewed her fountain pen cap and began scrawling away on the note-paper. Finishing, she lifted the paper by one corner and waved it back and forth a few times in mid-air as she stood up.

"Now it is your turn," she said, standing up and holding out the fountain pen, indicating the chair.

I took a seat and wrote out my own address in Bergen, c/o ABA, since I didn't know how long I'd be there. I didn't want to miss any correspondence from her.

"I'm unsure of how long I'll be reachable a this address, but they'll forward any messages within the *ABA* system. It may be delayed a few days, but I'll eventually receive anything you send me, Greta."

I finished then, stood up and turned toward the door, handing her my address as we crossed the room. She read it as we walked.

"Your hand writing is very old fashioned, Alex—your "A", it is just like my grandfather wrote his "A's. I think it's very nice, for a man."

"I suppose I got it from my mother's side—artistic."

"Curious, isn't it," she said smiling up at me and holding out her own address sheet.

"Here..." she said, opening the door and extending her hand with the slip of paper.

"I'm seldom there at that address, but if you wrote me...or telegraphed in advance...I know it is expensive...you could possibly reach me sooner. I'd enjoy meeting again—for dinner or something. But I must insist, if there's a next time, I will pay."

"Thank you Greta," I said, folding the note and putting it in my pocket. "I'll take you up on that offer, hopefully soon, now that I know where to reach you."

"I enjoyed our conversations Alex, despite our dispute over...politics and I sincerely look forward to another. Perhaps we can find some more common ground?" She held out her right hand to shake mine. "Thank you again. Good night."

"Good night, Greta. Thank you...I enjoyed myself, too."

I turned toward the elevator as her door closed quietly behind me. I walked toward the elevator, thought for a moment and then strolled to the "stairway" sign and opened the stairwell access door beneath it. It would probably be easier I thought and began tripping gleefully up the stairs.

It was nearly another three months—early May, before I had an opportunity to see Greta again. I'd decided not to take any chances on missing her. Spending Clyde's—our money, I sent her a telegram, asking her if she was busy the following weekend—that I would be in town for three days, arriving on the Friday. Of course, the three days were planned on my part to coincide with a long weekend holiday.

Luckily, she responded the next day. She'd be around for the entire week and that I was welcome. She even recommended a close hotel, if I hadn't made previous reservations, she said. I spent some more money, telegraphing the hotel and secured a room.

Just before noon on the following Friday, I carried my week-ender into the little hotel a few blocks from Oslo's downtown. Walking in the summer morning sunshine was glorious. The taxi I'd gotten at the aerodrome had dropped me in the harbor area at my request. ABA's dispatcher had shown me a map of the city and the hotel's location.

The taxi driver was an old man and wanted to chat along the way. He learned immediately that I was Swedish and then began questioning me about my loyalties to "...your brothers in Norway" and whether I thought Sweden would enter the war and on which side. I attempted to be non-committal. He was very open in speaking his mind about the *Nazi* invasion and their continued occupation of his country. He even went so far as to say that if he were a little younger—he must have been over eighty—he would himself, take up arms, learn to drive a tank or maybe even an airplane...to fight.

"You know the English have come with their fighter planes—in broad daylight this spring? Attacked the *Gestapo* headquarters...right here in Oslo!" He turned around in the seat and waved a hand behind us, nearly striking a parked truck in the process. "Right on a spring day, it was...they came roaring in at low level. Made my day for me, it did...for the whole month. They came and defied the bastards," he turned again to gesture. "Several little bombers they were. Kept turning and diving again and again until they'd emptied all their bombs. Killed some Norwegians in a restaurant next door to that rat's den...but it was worth it. I was sitting right down the street near your hotel here and they came over as they turned to go back. I got out and cheered them, lot of people were doing that. *Bastards!*"

Is my hotel near here?"

"Oh, yes, just...less than a mile."

"Why don't you let me out here then. I can use the exercise..."

He didn't think twice, but drew the old Volvo over to the left side of the street, stopping right there. But he wouldn't stop talking, even as I gathered my jacket and bag and opened the door.

"And there is something you Swedes need to know." He slid across the seat with some effort, pausing in mid-sentence. Sticking

149

his head and shoulders out the window, he entreated:

"You tell them—the people back at home...they'd better come in the war on the side of the Allies and help their Norwegian brothers...or, well, they'll have to live with us to their west, for a long time...an *awfully long* time."

I got out, slammed my door and walked around to where he was hanging out the open window. I paid him but he wouldn't accept a tip, insisting on making the exact change.

"Come into the war and fight with us..." he said looking at me through tilted glasses, "...we want your *anger*—not your *Kronor*."

I'd turned and was walking along the side of the road. After I'd gotten about twenty feet away, I turned and waved. He was still gesturing and talking from his window, but I was no longer able to make out what it was that he was saying, though I could easily guess the gist of it.

After ten minutes walk I'd forgotten the old man, as it was such a nice day. Along the streets the foliage was bright green against the summer sunlight. Despite the gloom of Occupation, bordering shops and house's balconies sported baskets of early-blooming flowers. Spring bulbs had sprouted from the boulevards and their so long-treasured blooms were at last opening to the spring sunlight, beckoning the insect world to a feast of nectar and pollen.

Hardly a breeze was stirring in the unusually warm, early days of summer. I walked briskly up the hill, from the harbor-side. The exercise felt good. I'd had an easy flight over from Stockholm. We were early to arrive and I felt...*expectant* and anxious to see those beautiful blue eyes again. I had a very good feeling about the weekend.

"*Herr* Andersson...?"

I turned back to the front desk clerk where I'd just checked in.

"Yes?"

"I am most sorry, I almost have forgotten...a young woman left a letter for you earlier today—I have nearly neglected to give it to you."

He reached beneath the front desk as he spoke and brought out a long envelope.

"Again, Sir, my apologies."

"No—no, it's OK…no harm done."

As I climbed the three flights of steps I wondered what message the envelope contained. Of course it *was* from Greta. The handwriting on the envelope was crisp and elevated—tall, thin, not rounded the way most women's handwriting.

Upstairs, after putting my bag on the bed and hanging up my few articles of clothing in a small wardrobe beside the sink, I tore it open.

> Hej Alex,
>
> Velkommen till Norge! I hope you had a good journey. I am barely five minutes walk away. Just exit the front door of your hotel, turn left, walk two blocks, turn left again onto Griegsvagen, go half way up the block (sorry for the hill climb!) and knock on number 87. I have the whole house and that includes the rear garden. If you arrive in time, we shall have a light lunch.
>
> Greta Stophff

I didn't hear her tread in the hallway, after my knock. Suddenly, she was there, smiling beautifully through the light veil of the yellow-flowered curtains. She leaned back, tilting her head to one side and smiled as she opened the door.

"Welcome, Alex. You are just in time for lunch. I hope you're hungry." She extended her hand.

"Thank you Greta…I am."

I reached for her hand, thinking to shake it. But as I did,

she drew me close, leaned forward and kissed me lightly on the cheek. I was a little taken aback. Before I could recover, she was leading me down the hallway into the center of the house. She wore a light blue and green dress with puffy sleeves.

"Yes...I'm hungry," I stammered.

"That's good. We'll eat right away."

From the hallway I could see all the way through and out the back windows of what turned out to be the dining room, where there was a table covered with a linen cloth and many pieces of china, freshly polished and waiting for two diners. Greta hadn't relinquished my hand as she lead me along—through the dining room and into the adjoining kitchen, also bright, crisp and filled with a great smell as soon as we walked in.

"Do you mind sitting at the kitchen while I finish preparing our lunch? I'll only be a minute."

"Oh, no...not at all. I prefer it if I can watch, or even help with something. It smells wonderful, Greta...thank you for inviting me, by the way. This is really special after flying day and night. I don't know when I had home cooking last."

"Oh—thanks, but I can finish. I'm happy you could come...would you like a glass of beer while you wait?"

"Sure, that'd be nice. I'm allowed to drink alcohol, now that I won't be flying for a couple days."

"Good. One glass of beer coming right up—literally, up. I must go to the cellar to fetch the bottles, you see. I'll only be a moment. Please, make yourself comfortable."

She turned a corner and disappeared, so I got up and walked to one of the casement windows, drew aside the curtain and glanced around the small back garden. There was a table with four painted chairs tipped forward against it. Flowers, in a colorful vase centered on the table added a blaze of color and femininity; budded daffodils and tulips nodding here and there among the various shrubs and trees emphasized spring. The grass, what of it there was, had been neatly trimmed. There was a curving, brick-lined path leading off around a shrub and out of sight. I heard a door close quietly.

"I told you it would not take any time," she said, emerging again. "I will just get us a glass. Maybe you should pour for both of us?"

"Certainly." I took the two bottles. She handed me two glasses from an overhead cupboard.

"I'll just finish cutting the bread and we can go sit down. I have made a fish casserole...*sorry.*" She smiled coyly.

"Sorry...why?"

"Because you fed me fish the last time we ate together; herring, remember?"

"Oh, yes...I'd forgotten. But that doesn't matter."

"Let us hope my fish will not be so salty. And I actually have some butter for our bread this time!" she added, excitedly.

That reminded me that I had brought a tin of black market coffee.

"Oh...Greta, that reminds me. I have some coffee for our...for after." I'd almost said dessert and didn't know if there was to be any.

"Coffee? Wonderful! Alex, it is so precious now...I can not remember when I last had coffee to drink. I made a little cake for us. It will be perfect with coffee...just like old times, before the war."

She had the towel-covered basket in one hand; reaching up with her free hand she turned my face and gave me another kiss on the cheek.

"Thank you for being such a thoughtful guest. Shall we eat now? Sit down again...here. I'll go back for the fish. It's quite hot so be careful. Please...."

I blushed from the kiss and tried to hide my confusion and pleasure when I sat down by fussing with my napkin. Then she took the seat opposite and we began to share the meal.

True to her wish, the fish was superb...and the bread, the potatoes. I had three helpings. Greta beamed each time I glanced at the casserole dish, pushing it toward me again. It had been a long time since I had enjoyed home cooking and Greta did an excellent job, especially, given the food shortages of the war.

We were enjoying our second cup of coffee in her sitting room. As I devoured my portion of the cake, she seemed to savor every sip of the strong coffee. We were well fed and relaxed. I was also extraordinarily happy to be free of work and with an attractive woman.

I'd noticed a photograph of Greta and a young, female child on the sideboard. I hadn't bolstered my curiosities' courage until she was pouring the second cup of coffee back in the kitchenette.

"Do you mind if I ask a personal question, Greta?" I asked from the joining hallway where I waited to carry the tray with the coffee things.

"No...what is it?"

"In your..." I waved my arm toward the door to the sitting room, "...sideboard—on it, you have a photo?"

"Yes—with a child...what about it?"

"I was wondering who it is."

"It is my niece, Inga."

"Oh..." I said, relieved.

"Yes, Alex, my niece...not Sophia whom I told you of—my natural child...remember, I once told you she lives with foster parents in Germany?"

"Yes—I'm sorry, I didn't mean to pry."

"You wanted to know if I was married, I think, that was the real reason for the question?"

"We already had this conversation, to some degree—at the party at the Royal Bath, but yes, I wondered."

"I am not. I had no husband when I had Sophia and I still have no husband. Nor have I seen or heard from my child since I bore her—over four years ago. You see, Alex, I mislead you somewhat at the party. It might have been...what, wishful thinking? Who knows? I—I'm sorry—I lied about it."

I looked at her, trying to determine her mood, her attitude, but said nothing.

"Are you shocked, Alex?"

"No, I'm not shocked. I was just curious. I didn't want to pry into your affairs."

"Does it change what you...how you look at me...?"

"No, of course not." She'd brought the pot to pour coffee for both of us. "But...why did you lie?"

"Why don't we take our coffee and move to the rear garden. I'd like to answer your question out there. It's a little more pleasant and I want to tell you a story. It is rather long and to some

degree, painful for me to speak of, but I would wish to tell you sooner or later. I would not consider *not* telling you, considering...well,
the war and how we find ourselves fitting into it."

I didn't know what she meant by that, but stood up and
helped her gather the china onto a tray, to which she'd added two
more slices of the small pastry. I took up the tray and she opened
and then closed doors behind us, letting me go ahead to the table.
It was now a fine afternoon and the sun was high. Late as it was, the
dew still lay heavily upon the chairs and table. Greta frowned and
removed the cloth she'd placed over the pastries and began to wipe
off each chair seat.

"When I was about twenty years old," she began speaking
as she turned and examined the chairs, "...I realized the situation in
Germany—the deep depression in which Germany was caught up...I
realized I must change my life.

She paused as if she was thinking.

"I had nearly completed my university studies and was extremely poor. My parents were both dead...and I wanted— needed
moral reinforcement in my life from some quarter. The *Nazi* party
was there, eager and willing to offer it. Previously, I had joined and
then left, several youth organizations, dissatisfied. Most of them
were filled with enthusiastic students, *burning* with a passion to change
the world; unfortunately they couldn't think for themselves and most
of them bored me to tears.

I soon became caught up in this program begun by *Reichs-
fuehrer-SS Himmler—das Lebensborn*...a special project. Have I
told you about all this before?"

"No, not much. You mentioned it in...Bergen, when we
dined," I wanted to hear it again in the event I would learn something that might further Birgitta's cause.

She nodded, continuing. "It is a program meant to encourage and facilitate the furtherance of the Aryan race, especially for
Germany but eventually, the world. The program encourages German women...and other Nordic—Aryan-like women, to...to *mate*
with *Aryan* men of similar characteristics and produce a pure proge-
ny for the *Fatherland.*"

She paused and looked at me, undoubtedly to gauge my

reaction.

"I see...but, what about Sophia? Was she...did you...?"

"I gave birth to Sophia while I participated in the early part of *Lebensborn.*"

"Where is she now then...you mentioned Germany?" I hadn't seen any children's photos previously.

"Yes, *Lebensborn*, at least in the early stage, sometimes mandated that most all children born from the program would be immediately removed from their birth mothers and given out to foster parents to rear under the auspices of the program's directors. This insures they become the best Germans for the *Fatherland* since they are the finest example that can be found. Neither the birth mother nor the new parents know the location of the other. This is in order to guarantee a healthy example of the German—the *Aryan* race...a product—a future citizen of the new *Reich.*"

"I'm not quite sure I understand, is this program a sort of match-making program...to introduce the correct people to marry...to have children?"

"Introduce? Yes. Have children? Yes. But marry? No...just breed good Germans...by approved *SS* fathers, no less."

"Oh," I said somewhat taken aback. I'd have thought from what I knew of Greta, she would have been smarter than to become involved with such a scheme. As if she could read my mind, she went on.

"I'd fallen in love with an officer—a handsome young *SS* officer. I was very young—so was Johan...it was natural for us to progress toward the program. Neither had played any significant part in anything like it up to this point, but it was easy to be accepted. We just enrolled. They wished to get the program well-started and were only too eager to welcome us. It was far more difficult to get out, however. If I hadn't become involved in my present program, which is similar, I do not know what I would be doing...excuse me, please."

As she finished speaking she sort of shook her head and picked up the little pot and hurried into the house to refill it a second time. I waited and listened to the silence of the garden. I could hear some machinery down near the harbor but couldn't make out what it was.

Greta returned, sat back down and poured another coffee for us. She didn't say anything for a while, just sat there staring into her empty cup. Finally she looked up and there were tears in her eyes.

"I'm not a very good *Nazi*, you see...I miss her terribly, my little Sophia."

I was surprised at her emotion and very strongly resisted an impulse to take her in my arms; instead, I reached over and laid a hand on her forearm.

"No doubt. Who wouldn't? When did...when was the last time you saw her?"

"When she was *born*—in *Steinhöring*, they took her away—immediately. It was the...the rules, *then*. I only had a glance, but I have thought of nothing else since. I know it is wrong to feel this way. The program's dictates are correct and should be obeyed. It is best for mother and child. But it's so difficult. I never had a child before. I didn't know I would love her so much—long for her. Even though I hardly saw her. They have changed it—the program now permits the children to remain there for a longer time—even up to a year...with their mothers. But it was...is too late for me."

I stared into my coffee cup. I felt terribly sorry for her; it was obvious she was suffering.

"I should think that would be even more difficult to bear...parting after that length of time."

Dabbing at her tears, she nodded her agreement.

"There's nothing you can do, then? You couldn't just go to work in a factory there—a hospital and somehow, get her back?"

She shook her head.

"Why not?"

"Guilt, I suppose. I worked in the program—*believed* in the program...Sophia isn't her real name of course. Since they took her, I've heard nothing. I know nothing about her—her name, what she likes to eat, if she smiles a great deal...nothing. I couldn't keep thinking of her as "her" so I gave her the name of my grandmother: Sophia. And now...I couldn't get her back, even if I wasn't involved in this program. It's too late."

She'd begun to cry openly as she spoke. Not sobbing or sniffing. Just sitting there calmly weeping. I didn't say anything for a moment, trying to consider this quandary of hers...and mine. She trembled a little with the emotion of the moment. I stood up and came around the table to her, looked down smiling as understandingly as I could and patted her shoulder gently. I held her other hand.

"But...I thought you'd have known—before hand, Greta...that they'd take away Sophia. Didn't you...?"

"Oh...I *knew* all right...but that makes little difference to a childless young woman. And then afterward, to one who has just borne Sophia—motherhood, you might term it—a mother's instinct changes things."

I stood taking all this in.

"Do you think me crazy, Alex, to feel this way? A silly, emotional woman?"

"It certainly doesn't sound crazy, or silly, to me. Sounds like your feelings are quite normal. I believe the program...*Lebensborn*...is what's crazy. I'm sorry to say it, Greta, but I truly do."

"You can not say that without knowing everything it fosters Alex and understanding it—the good it will eventually do. Imagine, a purity of race, breeding out genetic illnesses, ugliness—*stupidity.* It *can* be done with selective breeding. Despair and sadness? They can be virtually eliminated in only three or four generations."

I didn't want to debate that program with her at the moment. Nevertheless, I couldn't resist plunging ahead.

"But the price, Greta; is it worth the price, now that you've paid it...Germany? The tide is turning and not in Germany's favor."

"The price? It didn't sound so high in the beginning, Alex. Still, even now, I weigh it sometimes: perfect children, good looking, strong, tall—superior in all aspects—intelligence?"

She began to wring her hands.

"But afterwards...and these young girls? I don't know how long it can continue. Surely they, too, will begin to long for *their* offspring as I now do mine. If only there were some way? A way to reunite us all."

I'd sat back down and reaching across the table, covered her hand with mine. I didn't tell her what I was thinking, about heritage...that I was one of those...a product of an imperfect union:

a Swedish mother and an ancestral line on my father's side like a stray dog.

"What can you do about it Greta?"

"Nothing," she said, without looking up.

"Nothing...nothing at all? That seems strange."

I suspected she was probably correct, knowing the mad dreams the *Nazis* harbored. The rumors of the growing numbers of extermination camps had eventually proven true, though some, even in the Swedish government, still denied their existence, or simply turned a blind eye, continuing to look upon Germany and The *Reich*, favorably.

What she said next didn't necessarily come as a total surprise as Clyde's group had briefed me on her work subject.

"The underlying goal of my cultural program here in Norway—sometimes Denmark—and Sweden if need be, is to make the acquaintance of young women...at the dances and to "export" these young girls back to Germany, to breed children for The *Reich*. First and foremost, they must be girls who have strong Aryan physical characteristics, which, in these countries mostly goes without saying. They are virtually perfect sources for our material."

She stopped talking then and didn't look up for a bit. When she did, she looked surprised.

"Material—I called them *material*, didn't I? I begin to sound like Herman. But, to breed as I bred...more good Germans for *The Reich*. It sounds rather sterile and heartless doesn't it, saying it here in my home...with you. Strange...in retrospect it didn't sound so in Germany when I was younger. We have also now expanded this program, I understand, into the rest of Eastern Europe, Poland in particular. There, we remove the children...those bearing these specific *characteristics* and give them to foster parents in Germany, too. For the most part they tell me they come from orphanages, or from situations of poverty, so we are in a sense, rescuing them. But in certain other instances, we take them from good homes—happy homes."

When I didn't comment, she glanced up. Her eyes were red.

"Are you surprised Alex, about these things and that I am a part of them...contributing to the furtherance of this thing—of such a program?"

"You mentioned...your dancing partner, in Bergen...but, yes—yes, I'm surprised...very much so."

And I was. Apparently neither Clyde nor Birgitta quite realized the extent of the program, I didn't believe much of it at the time. This thing wasn't taking place only in Norway, it was happening on a much larger scale, over the whole of Nazi occupied Europe from the sound of it.

"I thought as much. Did you know we have nearly three hundred employees here in Norway, alone? We have physicians who help us by referring unwed, Norwegian mothers to us. We have hospitals—clinics, safe, warm, healthy places where the young girls can come—move in and be comfortable during their confinement, until they have their babies. German soldiers father many of the children, anyway...already situated here for the occupation. Why—there are around four hundred thousand German soldiers in Norway, alone, I think. Many of the children come through prostitution, of course. The women have no other way to live. Although it is discouraged, it is inevitable as in all wartime situations of this sort with so many troops away from their wives and girlfriends. We take these children, willingly, if they are suitable."

I waited for her to go on, glancing across at her slumped in her chair, half leaning, staring into the window of the house, one arm up with her elbow against the table top, her head in her hand.

She was fidgeting with her other hand in her lap, looking down at it. When she didn't speak again, I did, asking the question I hoped she had already asked herself many times.

"And if they aren't, Greta, aren't...*suitable?*"

She sat up a little straighter and grasped her hands tightly together, interlocking her fingers and then staring at them for a moment.

"That is one of the many, growing questions which trouble me, Alex." She glanced up then. "What happens when they are not."

Then, it was after another pause she said:

"There are certainly some...some are not going to be blonde—blue-eyed. It is obvious even at such a young age. I know they take them away then. Where they go—that is what troubles me; I can not learn where they take them."

"You mean...they, they just...*disappear?*"

"Exactly that: they disappear. They tell me they are in or-phanages, but where, I ask."

"They *have* to go somewhere...they're *infants, children.* Someone must take them—adopt them?"

"I hope so, Alex. Oh—how I hope so. She visibly straight-ened then, attempting to pull herself together. "But look what a mess I have made of your little holiday. I invite you to visit and I tell you the most depressing story and then I cry on your shoulder. What a terrible hostess I am...can you ever forgive me?"

"Well...you're not that, exactly...you have a right to wor-ry...."

Greta remained silent and I didn't know what else to say, so I changed the subject. During the conversation, I'd wondered whether she was planning to marry that *Johan*...German guy, she'd men-tioned, but had hesitated, wondering if the topic would be as trou-bling to her as the subject of children.

"Where is...Johan, now? You said that he wasn't your hus-band?"

That seemed to rouse her.

"No," she glanced up at me smiling slightly, putting her hand on top of the one I had left on the table, "we never married. He is still a soldier, stationed somewhere on the eastern front...the Russians, you know."

It was very bad on the eastern front. I didn't know whether Greta knew how bad. "Do you hear any news from him, regularly?" I asked as normally as I could.

"From time to time, I've gotten letters. They're always two or more weeks old. Each time I read about a battle in the newspa-pers, I wonder about him...and worry, not knowing where he is in relation to the fighting, if he's safe—well."

"When was the last time you two were...able to see each other—to be together?"

"It was almost two years ago, in Berlin; he received a week-end furlough, had a friend send me a telegram and we...met. I wasn't working here then. I was...in Germany, another location."

"Do you write him...often?" I seemed to wish to torture

myself to no end.

"Yes, nearly every week."

"Have you ever had any of your letters to him, returned by the post?"

"No, I haven't." She looked uncomfortable and I suspected she had and was lying to me.

"Then I should believe he is still alive," I said, as cheerfully as I could muster, "...well enough anyway, to receive his mail."

"I haven't heard from him for over two months. But, yes...you have a good point. I hadn't considered that aspect, Alex."

I was in this far, so...I thought I might as well get completely wet.

"Do you plan to marry...after the war?"

"I suppose I have thought about it, but not a good deal. Things have been so uncertain...since this all began. It had always been our intention to."

"It has? Well then...I wish you both lots of luck." I glanced across and smiled a smile I didn't really feel at the moment.

"Thank you Alex, you are kind to listen."

She'd taken my arm with her other hand and she now squeezed it, looking up at me again with those bottomless, blue eyes. The dappled sunlight played across her face, softly filtering through the leaves of the birch we sat beneath. It was then that I knew how very much I'd come to love her. And looking directly into that dazzling but now somewhat sad smile, I squeezed her hand and wished it wasn't true.

CHAPTER
8

News From The Front

Months later I was on base in Helsinki playing catch-up on paperwork—both *ABA*'s and Clyde's. When I examined the little pigeon-hole where our company mail was stuffed, to my surprise there was a short communication from Greta in my drop. I'd hoped, now that she was back in Oslo for a little while, Greta and I could meet again and possibly have dinner or something involving entertainment. I'd heard nothing from her after our sad, weekend meeting. We'd finished lunch that day—I helped her with the dishes; we had gone for a walk around the town. Surprisingly, she knew a good deal about the culture of the community, though she was German. But she'd said because her position involved so much cultural material, it necessitated that she become very aware of the local culture, wherever she worked in Scandinavia. Then I bought her dinner at the *Fleur d'lis*, a French restaurant serving the same creamed herring and potatoes as its Norwegian counterparts of other names, around the harbor. There were few diners; most seemed to be ships officers, the establishment being a cut above the seaman's fair-serving of most eating establishments in that area.

The next day...Sunday, we had breakfast at her house. We savored my black-market coffee along with her fresh-baked scones, covered over with some homemade strawberry jam she had somehow found the time to make during the previous summer. It was a late breakfast. Afterward, we decided to skip lunch in exchange for a stroll along the stone quay that wove in and out of the old harbor. Some areas were difficult to approach because of the ongoing military operations under the occupation. Skirting those that we had to, we still saw many sights and were able to maintain a good conversation, which gave me a greater understanding of who…at least, I thought Greta was and the same for her, I assumed. We didn't speak about her work or her child again.

Around three o'clock I received a hug and a peck on the cheek and said good by on her step; I took a cab to *ABA*'s operations office at the airport. My *Fokker* and crew were fueled and waiting for the passengers to board. After a walk-around of the ship I climbed in and while the passengers carried their baggage aboard, we went through the check list in the cockpit. Then we were off for Stockholm, with a couple of short stops in between. The following day I penned a hasty thank you for the weekend note, posted it and that was the last I'd heard from Greta—until today's note.

So when I saw the hand-addressed envelope, which had again come to me through *ABA*, my heart beat a little faster. I hung onto it until lunch when I was finally able to huddle over it, having closed the door to my little cubby-hole office inside the hangar. I huddled against the small electric fire that served to heat each cubicle in the breezy steel building. Winter had arrived early in Scandinavia this year.

> *Kära Alex,*
>
> *Do you remember when I told you about Johan and you reassured me of his well being? I am sorry to bother you about this, but you seem to be the only person who showed interest and cared enough to inquire about Johans well-being. Please excuse me for this request, but I wonder if you expect to be in my city anytime in the*

near future? If you are, you would very much welcome in my home again. Matters have devel— oped which make me fear for the worst and I value your advice. Please reply to the usual address.

Respectfully,
G.

I wondered what had happened to prompt the note and how I might be able to help. My caution flags went up at her request for a meeting. I thought I'd better run it past Clyde and immediately began to make up the appropriate dispatch to be posted to him, in code, sent with the evening's transmissions. There was ample time since my next run to Oslo wasn't until the following week. Clyde responded promptly and I had his reply two days later...and he was in a humorous mood:

Matey...

If the note's purpose does not seem out of the ordinary—just a woman asking for comfort—best pull out all the stops and give her what she appears to want— post haste, I know I would. If you see no reason you shouldn't take a day or two and learn the reason for her distress, I certainly don't; but do keep me posted Old Boy.

C.

I sent off a telegram to Greta that same day letting her know I would arrive the following Monday. I'd packed extra clothing in my flight kit, not knowing what lay in store. Again, I learned how very special *ABA*'s scheduling personnel were. I knew, on the frequent occasions when I threw one of these: "...I have to be in Oslo on Tuesday morning...and I don't know if I'll be returning the following day..." requests—they never complained. They did roll their eyes—but they always came through for me with a scheduled flight that seemed to make sense and dispatch pouches to keep us occupied enroute.

On Tuesday we touched down onto an ice-coated runway with a strong crosswind. An early fall had blown winter down from the North Atlantic during the night. I'd gotten up once around three a.m. and telephoned the weather advisors, checking to insure we would be able to depart the following morning. They reported then that it could be touch and go the following morning for a departure to western Norway.

But later, when I checked in at flight operations well before daylight, we got a clear ticket for weather. Our flight was able to depart right on time. We only had two passengers, due, I assumed, to the hastily-arranged schedule. A stand-in pilot had also been assigned to take the plane back since I would be remaining the weekend. I told him I was visiting a sick friend. There were ample Norwegian and German dispatch pouches to offset the unscheduled cost expenditure of the extra flight. And that's what Clyde wanted; they were to be dealt with sometime before the agent picked them up in Oslo.

The flight was uneventful. I saw the last of the two passengers and crew safely out of the aircraft and into the small terminal and then helped the ground crew secure the parking wheel chocks and tie-downs. Inside the *ABA* office the agent placed the dispatch pouches under lock and key, safe until a member of *Gestapo* staff would collect them.

By the time the female *ABA* agent handed me my own inter-operations dispatches, I was ready to telephone for a taxi to take me to the same hotel as last time. Clipped to the large, brown *ABA* envelope was a small, white one; "*Kaptain Andersson, Personal*" was neatly penned on the front. There was no return address. I thanked the agent and strolled to one side of the small office as I opened the larger envelope, then folded it shut again. Just as I suspected, it dealt with normal *ABA* operations paperwork which could be dealt with on the return flight, three days hence.

The second envelope was from Greta. It was short, informing me I could take a taxi directly to her house and let myself in. She said there was no need to spend money on a hotel and she'd taken the liberty to cancel my reservation. She had plenty of room, she said. After all, she added, I was there at her request. She'd prefaced the note with a statement that she might not be at home when I arrived because of her job commitment, but that the key was beneath the door mat and that I should let myself in anyway and make a cup of tea.

I stood in the warmth of the freight office contemplating the turn of events. If the meeting she requested only lasted a day, I would have to move back to the hotel, anyway and wondered whether I should stop by the hotel to insure the availability of rooms. I crossed to the operations desk and requested the agent telephone for a taxi.

Within ten minutes an ancient Volvo sat sputtering outside the entrance, huffing steamy exhaust into the wind. I thanked the agent, telling her I wouldn't see her for a couple of days but would telephone to check in, in the event there were orders for me.

I stared through the steamy cab window, blurred somewhat now after I'd swiped it with my coat sleeve. The landscape was the same as the previous summer, though it now appeared to be in a different city. Everything had changed. During the summer, the season had been festive. Shop doors were thrown open and all around there had been bright sunshine and warmth, blooming flowers and greenery. Today, the streets were shut. The few pedestrians were bundled against the damp winter wind. Everything was rectangular—angular and mono-colored...gray. Windows, doors and building silhouettes against the low-lying, Scandinavian daylight had half-tone, gray-sepia shadows. The little snow and ice which had come with the night didn't sufficiently cover the landscape to turn the scene completely into a winterscape. Here and there, small piles of snow were collected against a sidewalk, a building, or a fence, merely touching up the fall season with winter's hint.

Bending to pay the cab driver, I glanced toward Greta's house; it even looked different. Beside the door, there was an old crock stuffed with tall birch limbs; brittle golden leaves of summer clung to the thin twigs, dried now for want of warmth and water. For color, pine boughs had been added around the edges. This was the best the season could offer for decoration until Christmas—*Jul*, which would bring more pine boughs and colorful berries, at best.

I knocked on the heavy door and waited before bending and rolling back the floor mat. The long, brass key greeted me with promise of warmth inside. I had to remove one glove in order to pick it up. The brass ring on the end felt cold in my hands as I rolled the key over twice. From within the mortise I heard the double lock mechanism roll the second time, amplified by the solid wood door. I withdrew the key and leaned on the door handle, swinging the door wide and stepped inside.

It wasn't very warm. I was surprised, but it wasn't entirely unpleasant either, mostly because it was Greta's house and already again, I loved being there, even in her absence. I put my bag down and thought about calling out in case she hadn't heard my knock. But the key beneath the mat answered the unasked question. I slipped out of my sheepskin jacket, flight boots and in wool-clad stocking feet, walked along the polished hardwood hallway, through the dining room, crossing into the bright kitchen. In the center of the dinette table, beneath a red, wooden *Dala* horse, there was another note:

Kära Alex
There is soup in the kettle for you.
To heat it you must make a fire in
the stove. Do you know how to
do that? Surely you know about
fires?

If you become cold, there is an—
other fire in the tile stove in the

parlor. It will need some at-
tending if it is not to go out. Do
you mind? Of course not. I
hope to be home by the late after-
noon. Please, Alex, be at home
in my house. Take a nap or go
for a walk.

Kramar,
Greta

As I scanned the note I glanced up at the little kitchen cook stove and the pile of split birch in the box on the floor. The note still in my hand, I stepped over and lifted the cover of the copper kettle. The soup appeared to be vegetable, with some sort of meat; I could see lots of white beans, too. It was definitely cold and would need heating. I hadn't been hungry until I smelled it. I pondered waiting for Greta to come home. No doubt she'd also be hungry in…what would it be, maybe two hours.

I read the note again and decided I'd better start the fires. I opened the kitchen stove lid to cold wood ashes. I glanced around for something…kindling, to start the fire. There was a small bundle of newspapers rolled up beside the wood box. I withdrew several of the sheets and confirmed the old date. Tearing and wadding the papers I dropped them atop the cold ashes of the black stove and began adding the small pieces of split birch kindling-thin, on top of the crushed paper.

There was a tin matchbox holder hanging on a nail on the wall, half full of wooden matches. I pulled one out, but on second thought retrieved another and bent to the stove again, frowning and squinting into the dark little firebox.

A butterfly damper in the shiney pipe lead into the chimney and I turned it wide open. Another small, draft door hinged directly beneath the firebox. I tipped it outward, providing the inlet for the air the stove would need to make the smoke go up the chimney and not into the room.

I struck one of the matches, breaking off half the end. It fell, blazing brightly, onto the clean, kitchen floorboards. I muttered to myself and grabbed the flaming stub and threw it back onto the firebox, slightly burning my fingers in the process.

I stood with my finger in my mouth and watched the match flare momentarily against a piece of birch, flicker and go out. I bent over the firebox with another poised to strike, struck it and held it steady for a moment before poking it under the paper. It caught and as I moved the match further along, more paper flared. I dropped the match and closed the lid with a self-satisfied smirk. The wood was nearly dry enough to start without papers. Now, for the parlor stove.

Confident with my first success, I grabbed a few more papers and sticks of kindling. Before I left the kitchen I cracked the cook stove door and seeing the leaping flames, closed it with bolstered confidence and walked into the parlor to take on the tall, ceramic-tile-covered heater. I'd seen similar home heating stoves in Sweden.

For its size—running from floor to ceiling, this stove had a surprisingly small door, though the firebox was considerably larger than my kitchen challenge. After a couple of tries, I got the kindling ablaze. I took notice again of the unusual dryness of the birch wood, thinking it must be stored somewhere where it was dry, probably under cover. I knew I'd need more wood before Greta returned and decided to bring some in from wherever she kept it sheltered.

First I hurried back to the kitchen and added larger pieces of wood from the box on the floor; this should heat our soup. I closed the bottom draft door and turned the pipe damper closed slightly. Then I repositioned the soup kettle over the round lid, directly over the fire. I was tempted to taste it, but didn't.

I returned to the parlor stove and added larger pieces of wood, nearly the last from the box and went to the front door to get my flight boots, ready to fetch more wood . I walked back through to the kitchen door dragging the brightly-colored, braided runner over to a chair so the boots wouldn't drip on the polished wood floor while I pulled on the boots.

Outside, I finished buttoning my coat, turning up the collar around my ears as I glanced around for a woodpile. Thinking back to last summer's visit didn't bring any particular memories of any woodpiles. Where would it be, I wondered as I walked further out into the yard, finally stopping beneath the tree where we'd had our pleasant breakfast coffee. I stood musing for a moment, the wood temporarily forgotten as I recalled what Greta had said sitting there in the freshness of spring and her ardent convictions of the right of the *Nazi*'s aggression.

Shaking my head, partially because of the recollection and partly because of my frustration over the wood's source, I renewed my search. Turning a full circle and seeing nothing, I decided to search the small garden shed; it had to hold the wood supply; there was nowhere else.

But there were only some simple garden tools, neatly hanging on one wall. There was a wood-handled grass cutter sitting on its rusty, cast iron wheels. In one corner several clay pots—the bottom one broken neatly in half, stood leaning, ready to fall. Another corner contained some woven baskets tipped upside-down. I went back outside, completely stumped, latching the door. I walked to each side of the house, thinking there might be a stack along one, or the other sides. I even peeked into the front yard least I'd missed it when I arrived. At least, I'm keeping warm I thought.

Where could it be? Everything was neatly trimmed, covered, or tied up. A pile of wood couldn't hide in such a space. Nothing. I gave up and returned to the house to get warm. I took off my boots on the rug in the kitchen, where the copper soup pot was now beginning to make noises like the stove might be doing its job at last.

Maybe she's out of wood, I wondered as I twisted the pipe draft open, closed the bottom one, opened the firebox side door and poked in two more sticks of birch. I closed and opened the drafts again but a little less on the lower draft shutter. This was turning into work. There was plenty of kitchen stove wood for my soup, at least. I vowed to look for the coffeepot, hoping for more success, but only after I'd again tended to the parlor stove. I'd brought another couple of tins of coffee along for Greta.

My search for a coffeepot bore as little fruit as the woodpile; I finally decided it must be the small, copper kettle hanging on the wall beside the window. Removing it and lifting the lid, I thought

I could smell the faint odor of coffee. Who knows when it was last used? I filled it half-full with water and set it on the cook-stove beside the soup.

I went to the parlor's tile stove again and put in two more pieces of the larger chunk wood from the box. There were four pieces left. At this rate, they wouldn't last more than an hour or so; by then the house would give up the cold and just start to come up to a living temperature.

Where *was* that wood stored, I wondered, returning to the front door where I'd retrieved the coffee from my bag? Back in the kitchen, I put it on the small countertop, retrieved the copper pot, added a couple more of inches of water and set it back on the stove. Some water dripped from the pot and sizzled on the hot stovetop beside the soup kettle, which was now making even friendlier noises.

Now to open the tin...I crossed to the counter and opened two drawers before I found the can opener and then soon had the lid off the coffee. It smelled really great.

That done, I didn't know what to do until the water boiled; the absence of wood still bothered me. I sat down at the table but didn't feel like sitting still, so I got up and began opening doors. After the fourth still revealed nothing, I crossed back by the chimney, near an inside wall. I opened a large cupboard door and there it was, a dumbwaiter affair of some sort, stacked high with birch wood that came up from the cellar. Suspended from a large pulley on the other side and disappearing through a rectangle of the same size, a rope hung down into the basement.

Peering down into the dimness, by shielding my eyes I could see an identical box affair suspended above the floor, but instead of wood, it held two, large bricks. On a shelf in the cupboard, three or four more bricks were stacked alongside the wood box. At last the mystery was solved. The wood had been carried into the basement for dry storage. One simply went downstairs, filled up one of the empty boxes suspended on the rope and hauled it up. If bricks were in the other box, the load was evenly counterbalanced. One could add, or take away wood and bricks to suit. Not bad, I thought. Saved a lot of the mess; I recalled my mother sweeping up after I'd carried in an arm load of wood. But then, I thought, that was also partially me being careless. If we'd had this in my boyhood home, I'll bet there'd been more than one ride to and from the cellar on that platform. Staring at it now, I thought I could nearly fit on it now, in a pinch. Shaking my head...too old for that, Alex.

Some of the wood was the larger, chunk-style for the tile heater. The balance was more thinly split for the cook stove, or for kindling. I began removing chunk wood for the heater; the other box immediately started to descend slowly, raising my box containing the wood. I grabbed the rope, pulled it back down and thought for a moment about my predicament; how *did* it work? Then I reached over, taking a brick, I placed it in the box. The load's balance stabilized. That was it...once the wood had been replaced with bricks, the box remained balanced and went down easy. In the cellar, the bricks were removed and replaced with wood and the process was reversed—counterweights.

Satisfied now that I'd finally located the missing firewood, I took the larger chunk wood into the parlor and returned to unload the smaller wood, adding the last brick before closing the little closet door. I decided not to worry about adding more of the wood in the cellar.

Satisfied with myself, I returned to my flight bag and extracted the paperwork I'd been postponing all week and reluctantly carried it to the kitchen table and began to fill in the appropriate forms to appease the bureaucracy. That was where I was when I heard Greta at the door an hour later.

CHAPTER 9

The Revelation

"Al--ex...are you here?"

My heart leaped with excitement and I stood up dropping the papers beside me.

"Yes—in the kitchen—coming."

She appeared in the hallway door.

"No need...is that *really* coffee I smell—how can that be?" She smiled broadly, shaking her head as she crossed the kitchen and put a hand on my shoulder and kissed the cheek I presented.

"I hope you've been able to entertain yourself?"

"Oh, no problem...I've been catching up on my paperwork."

Leaning over the pot, she finished removing one arm from the sleeve of her coat and lifted the coffee lid. "Ummmmm..." she said turning to me "...that smells good," and pulled her other arm free. "I'm sorry to get you all the way over here and then not be here when you arrived."

"Oh, I'm doing very well by myself," I said taking her hand. As if she'd changed her mind, she pulled me lightly toward her and leaned forward kissed my cheek again lightly, thrilling me to my toes.

"That coffee smell has made me irresponsible, I am afraid...sit down and let me get you something to make you comfortable."

I recovered quickly from the second kiss. "Don't worry about it. I'm just happy to be here again. I miss the summer warmth, though."

"Don't all of us? But you seem to have figured out my heating. It is beautifully toasty...I am so accustomed to coming home to a cold house. It hardly warms up by the time I am ready to go to bed." She smiled and lifted the lid on the soup.

"Alex, don't you like the soup?"

"Oh yes...or at least it smelled wonderful, but I got so caught up in the fires and then my paperwork it got so late, I decided to wait for you and just had a cup of coffee, instead."

"Oh—it's unfortunate I'm so late; are you hungry?"

"Yes, I'd be lying if I told you I wasn't starving."

"Then we'll eat right away, Alex. I've managed to buy some things from the market, though there's not much to choose from these days. I have a chicken from a farmer, but possibly we should save that until tomorrow...it will take too long to prepare tonight. We can roast it. What would you think of some bread, butter and cheese...again from the farmer...to eat with the soup? Will that hold you until breakfast?"

"Sounds like a feast."

"Oh—and I also have some wine," she said with a smile, withdrawing a bottle of Red Bordeaux from the cupboard. "And...she said, smiling mischievously, I purchased a bottle of Danish *aquavit* a month ago. I believe it is homemade, but it is good, nonetheless."

She held the cupboard door open.

"What do you say to an appetizer?"

"Sounds perfect...what can I do to help? Better start by removing these papers," I realized I'd taken over the area around the table.

"Oh they are all right for a little while yet...but when you finish you may set the table. I'll bring you a tablecloth—the eating things are here..." she patted the counter above a drawer, "...so I'll slice the bread."

I removed the papers before shaking out the same tablecloth she'd used last summer, spreading it smoothly on the table. Greta was singing lightly to herself. The soup pot continued to rumble. I was happily expectant.

"Here," she said, placing a couple of crockery bowls on

the end of the counter. "Use those. I'll get some glasses. Do you wish to have water also Alex?"

"No thanks...*aquavit* for the toast and then Bordeaux."

I placed the bowls and silverware across one corner of the table. By then Greta handed me two, tall wine glasses, intricately shaped and cut with a floral pattern.

"Wow—those are certainly nice glasses. Were they in your family?"

"Thanks," she said. "No, they're Venetian, I believe. I bought them in Paris a little while ago."

I'd almost said 'those are romantic', but caught myself. Paris, she'd said...who else but the *enemy* could go to occupied Paris and buy Venetian crystal. I wondered then whether she would add candles.

"Would you open the wine, please Alex? Please be at home—the cork extractor is there on the little rack—yes, there. In fact, you should taste it also, while I tend to this cheese."

She rattled some dishes as I grabbed the corkscrew and began to work on the bottle. It was only a moment and I had the cork out, inspected, smelled it and then tasted the wine, pouring an inch in one of the glasses. It was delicious and even with the small taste, I felt it plunge into my legs. It was my empty stomach.

Less than five minutes later the meal was ready. I realized I'd really enjoyed the little things we'd done together getting the meal ready. She'd teased me, laughing and joking about my bread slicing skill.

"Our bread came already sliced from the store, in America," I teased back.

"I'm sorry Alex...I don't own my own slicer."

"Oh—you baked the bread yourself?"

"Yes, sometimes, when I have time, I do. I enjoy baking...and cooking, too."

I nearly blurted: 'you'd make someone a good wife,' but instead, I said:

"Those are handy talents."

She smiled, "Here, Alex, it is ready now—let us eat while we can still stand up. You must be famished."

"Pretty soon I'd need a steadying hand from someone."

We sat down then and unfolded the colorful little napkins.
Greta began ladling soup for both of us, handing me a bowl half
filled and steaming.

"Ummm...that smells really good," I mumbled as she repeatedly dipped the long ladle into the pot.

"Please, don't stand on formality—take some bread and
butter it while I do this. I'll soon catch up...and pour the wine,
please."

I did and when both glasses were half full, she already had
her own bread ready.

There was a quick toast and we sang her wine praises before diving into the soup.

Apparently Greta was hungry too. We ate mostly in silence
until I was ready for my second bowl. She'd been keeping an eye on
the level of my bowl and just as the spoon struck bottom she reached
for it.

"Let me give you more Alex."

"Thanks, it's really tasty...and the bread. I think I've had
three slices."

"Thank you. There is plenty, so please...help yourself."

I was spreading butter on a fourth slice when she placed my
bowl back in front of me. I'd been thinking as we ate, I'd never really
interacted with a woman like this; family-like, eating, partnering in
the meal preparation. I realized I quite enjoyed it. It was probably
not a lot unlike what it would be like being married to her. Of course
then there would be every meal, keeping house, sleeping together
and...sex. I glanced at her bent head then. I wondered what it
would be like...sex with her. She certainly was beautiful, had a gor-
geous body. She seemed kind and gentle, but I wondered whether
she'd be aggressive...or, would she be shy—embarrassed? Maybe
she'd be adventurously—aggressive?

"Oh Alex—do you know what I've done?"

She abruptly stood up, one hand to her cheek, looking rather
mischievous. She was flushed from the wine and from the fire I'd
built, obviously, with too much wood. She turned and hurried back
to the cupboard.

"I've forgotten the *aquavit*," she said, bending to retrieve the bottle from beneath the counter. Her backside bobbed as she struggled, hanging from the countertop on one hand to steady herself, peering into the cupboard's depths as she attempted to locate the bottle with her other hand. I could hear muffled sounds as she commented on its whereabouts. Backing out again, she said, "It is not there. I thought I put it there. *Ohhhh*...I hate it when this happens to me. I've forgotten where...*oh*! Now I remember. I put it in the top cupboard, behind the boxes. I have to hide it from the landlord." Here she glanced at me and giggled a little bit. "He sometimes comes in to inspect the *plumbing*...when I am not here."

She strode over to the table and grabbed her chair by the back and slid it across to the cupboard to use as a stool.

"Can't I get it for you, Greta?"

"No...I'll just be a second...."

She'd climbed on the chair and put one knee on the countertop, swinging the door wide.

"I know it is here...somewhere."

I stood up, a little concerned at the way she was weaving around.

"Are you sure I can't help?"

"No...I've put it up here, I—I know it...but it's moved to the back. I can just feel it with my fingers...*ohhhhh*, damn!"

I heard a slight noise.

"I've tipped it over now."

In her struggle, she'd began to tip sideways, too, as much from her impatience as the wine. When I heard the bottle bang and roll, I walked closer to the counter, stopping beside her chair. The cupboard door she was hanging onto slowly pivoted outward, with Greta coming along with it. As I reached for her, it swung her outward, away from the cupboard. She fell into my waiting arms.

"*Ohhh*...!" she said again, throwing one arm around my neck. I'd sort of scooped her body up, midair, one of my arms beneath her thighs and the other in the small of her back.

"What...oh, Alex, look at us...what have I done...so clumsy."

Our faces were only a couple of inches apart. She became

very quiet in my arms. Her whimsical mood reflected in a smile playing about the corners of her mouth. But I'd never seen her more appealing as I looked directly in her eyes. Her lips parted slightly and I could see her teeth. She seemed as if she was about to speak, but before she had the chance and totally without thinking, I leaned forward and placed my lips on her mouth.

She started momentarily, uttered a slight sound of surprise which turned to a slight moan of pleasure. She tilted her head, seeming to relax in my arms and she began to return my kiss. Another soft sigh escaped her. We remained like that as she gently returned my kiss.

Greta was holding on to my neck with both arms and began to grow rather heavy. I started to hitch her up a little higher, when she leaned back and put her palm against my chest.

"You had better put me on the floor Alex."

"OK," I said, not hiding my reluctance. "But I'll get the bottle for you." I let her down and she smiled at me and stepped aside.

I climbed up onto the chair. Even with our height difference it wasn't easy for me to move the box aside and retrieve the bottle. As I reached, straining upward into the cupboard, Greta placed her palm against my thigh to steady me.

"Here," I said, turning with the bottle in one hand, "I have it." I handed it down to her, nearly falling in my excitement. She took the bottle.

"I'll get the glasses. We can have at least a taste before we finish our soup, which I suppose it is cold now, too."

"It should be all right, yet," I said returning to my chair, "I'm going to have a little more cheese…and bread with the drink. Do you want more—I can slice it while you pour?"

"Please—yes, a small piece of each." She returned to the table with the bottle of clear liquor and two, little, round glasses. She put them on the table and poured them full.

"Have you had *aquavit* recently, Alex?"

"No, it's been a while. When I'm flying, I don't like to take the stronger spirits."

"Are you flying…tomorrow?" she asked coyly looking in my eyes and smiling.

"No...remember?"

"Good. Can you stay tomorrow night too?"

"Well—I assumed you'd planned...well, to—to have our...you wanted to talk...and then I'd go to the hotel...I didn't wish to impose."

Greta interrupted me.

"Think nothing of it. You are staying. Consider it done—a...a payment for having to listen to me tonight."

She was holding her glass and looking at me silently, but her eyes—her eyes said so much.

"Shall we have another toast?" she finally said after I picked up my own glass not knowing, or not wishing, to break her silence.

"Certainly." I raised my glass and held it toward hers. "To—to the weekend," I said, clicking my glass to hers and then taking a sip. Our eyes met and I saw the faintest hint of a question before she averted them again with a smile toward the table. She picked up her spoon and began to eat. I followed its movement to her mouth. She was still smiling over her bowl. We finished our meal and decided to postpone another glass of the *aquavit* and have it with our coffee, instead.

Later, doing the dishes with Greta, I could really feel the effect of the two liquors. I wasn't accustomed to drinking much, especially since I'd been flying and between that and my body's fatigue, saying I was pretty relaxed was an understatement.

I noticed Greta behaved with a new carefree abandon that I'd not seen on the previous occasions we'd met and I must say, I didn't find it unpleasant. Some spies we were, I thought, getting drunk and giggling together over the dirty dishes. She was prattling away about something. I wasn't listening too closely, thinking instead about the sight of her behind as she'd probed the cupboard for the missing bottle. As I was drying a small plate I was imagining her lying naked...on a bed. I wasn't accustomed to straight alcohol. After a moment I noticed she'd stopped speaking.

"You OK, Greta?"

"Oh...Yes, I'm fine Alex."

She sounded so serious.

"I was thinking, just now. You see, I feel embarrassed about not telling you why I asked you to come such a long way—just to talk."

"You needn't feel that way, Greta; you sort of intimated that it was about Johan."

"Pardon me...*intim?*"

"You said you had news of Johan."

"Yes, thank you—I am—I mean I did. You see, you don't really know the whole...situation, Alex. I—I didn't tell you the whole truth, the last time we were together."

"I'm listening, Greta." And this time, I was. We'd finished the dishes by then and she'd closed the cupboard doors and was standing in front of the sink, facing me, folding and unfolding the damp, linen towel.

"Let us take our coffee to the parlor...and I will tell you about it—about Johan."

We dried our hands and she opened a cookie jar and one by one, began stacking up a plateful of something bristling oatmeal. She handed one to me to try.

"Ummm..." was all I could say, wondering where she'd gotten enough sugar to make cookies.

She smiled, handing me the plate. "Please take these in; I will follow with our coffee."

"OK," I mumbled, "are you sure you can manage?"

"Certainly—go, make yourself comfortable. I will be in shortly."

When I opened the door to the parlor, the room was like an oven. "Ohhh..." I groaned, turning back toward the kitchen. "It is very warm in here..." But she didn't hear. I went inside and put the cookies on the coffee table beside the settee and glanced at the closed draperies, contemplating opening the window. We certainly wouldn't be very comfortable in the room as it was.

"Oh—" Greta stood in the doorway, recoiling, cups in one hand and a small pot in the other. You certainly mastered the stove, Alex."

"Overmastered, you might say. Shouldn't we open a window or something, Greta?"

"Just let me put these down, first. The trick with these old tile stoves, Alex, is knowing when to stop putting wood in them. You see, they have this lag time which follows the firing. It takes the stove a while to catch up to the last fire you have built. Alex...I think you kept going?"

"Yes, no doubt about it; it did."

"Well, no matter..." she sat down on the settee, unbuttoned the top button on her blouse, curled her legs up beneath her and patted the other end for me to also sit. "It will not go to waste."

"Uh—should I open a window first?"

"If we open the blinds with the lights on the blackout police will come. We could...and turn off the lights first, if you would like?"

"Seems like a lot of work. Let's try it first." I opened a button on my shirt and sat down beside her.

"OK.

I didn't know what to do so I leaned forward and took another of the cookies, biting off a piece. There were some dried fruit pieces inside—not exactly raisins, but something.

"Ummm...these are good."

"I baked them a couple of days ago. The flavor improves with age, don't you think so?" She seemed to be stalling.

"Don't see how they could get any better." I'd put one leg on the edge of the coffee table. Greta had leaned forward and taken her coffee cup and saucer onto her lap and now sat stirring the brew, still without yet having tasted it.

"Aren't you going to try the coffee, Greta? I braved a whole cadre of black market police to sneak the tins into the country."

"Oh, certainly," she brought the cup to her lips and sipped. "It's delicious, Alex. Thanks for bringing it. You know you could sell it for a lot of money."

"And have the police after me?"

"I doubt anyone would report it...they'd be too happy to taste coffee again."

"I suppose—and the evidence would disappear rather quickly." I paused again, still waiting for her to speak about what had drawn me there.

"Alex...."

"Uh-huh?"

"As much as I think about—Johan...I feel more and more silly for asking you all the way over here just for you to hear me tell you I have been receiving my letters back—returned from his unit."

I didn't remark, feeling she wasn't finished.

"For some time— even when we last talked, I'd already had two come back to me then." She looked down at her cup. "So I was being untruthful to you and that bothered me, especially after you'd shown me such concern for my well-being. I don't like being dishonest. But I didn't wish to trouble you, either."

I listened, thinking and feeling rather guilty myself, for thinking about her naked backside, five minutes before. What did she want from me?

"Was there anything that accompanied them? Any letters...from someone else? Something to explain their return?"

"No, only my unopened letters. They were all stamped on the front...saying the person they were addressed to, was not available at that headquarters command."

"What did you do?"

"I did nothing...at least at first."

"And then?"

"Then I wrote the commandant."

"What did you learn?" It was like pulling teeth.

"That Johan had been transferred further north—somewhere in Russia. And I only learned that by pulling some strings in Berlin."

I thought about that revelation, wondering how high the strings went.

"Did you receive a satisfactory answer—or any further information?"

"Yes, but not about Johan, at least immediately. They were able to furnish the names and addresses of Johan's parents in Austria. I had always known he came from Austria, but I never really learned where. He may have told me, at one time or the other, but I probably just wasn't paying attention." She sighed and smiled at me. "Our minds were on other matters, then."

She glanced toward me with another winsome smile. I nodded and smiled back, wanting her to keep going now that she'd begun, thinking we were getting somewhere, at last. I was feeling jealous of Johan after that smile.

"I'd tried to write them before but I only guessed at the

address and the letter came back. Now, I wrote another, the adderss of his parents."

"Yes...and...did they know where he was?" I took another cookie.

"I didn't hear anything for over a month. I'd begun inquires elsewhere—trying to learn his whereabouts, when a letter arrived from his mother. She'd been contacted by *Gestapo* investigators and learned of *my* interest in her son from them. She knew I wasn't a part of them—the *Gestapo*, knowing I was merely the woman Johan had told her about. The woman with whom he had had a *Lebensborn* child."

"So he'd told them about you...and the child?"

She nodded, taking a sip from her cup before she leaned forward and placed her nearly full cup back on the table. She folded her hands in her lap, bowed her head and just stared at her hands for a while, turning her fingers round and round as if she were inspecting them. It was becoming rather agonizing, though I wasn't quite certain why. I reached across and put my hand on hers.

"What else did her letter say, Greta?"

"She said...*she wrote* that the *Gestapo* had questioned both herself and her husband...and that then...they'd taken her husband away, in September. She's been trying, unsuccessfully, to learn his whereabouts. She thinks he is...is in jail."

Greta choked as she spoke. I could see she was becoming very agitated. I didn't understand any of this. There was a missing piece to a puzzle and I wasn't certain whether I was going to find it.

"Did she write anything else?"

There was such a long silence after my question, I wondered whether she was going to answer at all. Finally, she did:

"Yes...she—she wrote me that her son had been taken from his regiment and shot as a Jewish spy—over nine months ago. Her husband was a Jew."

I know my jaw dropped, I was so surprised. I didn't know if I'd really heard her correctly. She was speaking so deliberately though, measuring every word—I had to ask again.

"Her son...Johan—*your* Johan? She was writing about him?"

"Yes, my...Johan."

"Oh Greta, I am so sorry." I moved closer to her and took

her hands.

"When did this happen—when did you learn about this?"

"I received her letter in June—late June."

"But...why...?" I had almost asked her why she hadn't contacted me, but then why should she? She hardly knew me. Certainly Greta had relatives, back in Germany, people who could offer comfort.

"Did you—*tell* anyone, talk to anyone about this...*family?*"

"No...I don't' have any...well, one aunt—in Berlin, but she has her own family."

"But Greta...it must have been intolerable...the grief. I wish that I'd known. Now I feel so badly. Someone..." I trailed off, not knowing what more to say.

"My parents have both been gone for many years...I have the aunt in Berlin, as I said...she is all. And...I didn't dare speak to anyone at my job about it. I was afraid for Sophia...afraid for myself. She was silent for a moment, then she looked up. I could tell—she was about to cry.

"It *was* terrible, Alex, but in an absent sort of way. Johan and I had not even seen each other in nearly two years. I'd long since reconciled myself to the idea—he's gone. I did that, I guess, long ago."

I waited. I stared at her bowed head and watched as tears welled in the corners of her eyes. Then, a single tear slid from her cheek and fell atop my hand. I squeezed her hands but said nothing further.

"Johan's father was a Jew...his mother was Austrian."

It was difficult for her to retain her composure. All I could do was to squeeze her hands.

"When being Jewish came to be a problem in the *Reich* we didn't know what to do. At first we thought nothing of it, but in a little while, we knew it could be nothing but a serious matter. She glanced up, smiling sadly.

"Johan was an officer by then. He was well respected; he'd proven himself in battle. There was no question of his loyalty. Meanwhile, they continued the purges, always watching, always listening, seeking anything—anyone who might be even slightly Jewish."

"Did his superiors ever speak to Johan...then, personally,

or to you?"

"No, no one ever suspected it. I didn't even know at first...until he told me. Then, we didn't dare to tell anyone. Even our best friends in the program didn't know. It was too dangerous."

I thought about what she'd said. Her shoulders were quivering slightly as she silently wept; her hands remained tucked neatly in her lap.

"Greta, was there no one, during this time, to...to comfort you?"

She took a deep breath and looked me in the face. I wanted to cry out from the expression of pain I saw in her face. Then she totally collapsed, bending forward as if holding her stomach. I slid over the cushion and took her in my arms. She leaned her head on my shoulder placing a hand against my chest and sobbed deep, deep sobs. I'd never been this close to anyone suffering to this extent, especially a woman who I felt so strongly about. I held her gently while feeling guilty for simultaneously glorying in the closeness and the trust she'd shown me in her grief.

We sat for several moments as she cried herself empty of grief. Twice, after I thought she had no remaining tears, she would seemingly think of the event again and renew her weeping. It was as if she was weeping for past sorrows, a collection of remorse, doubts, mistrusts and betrayals, stored and now allowed at last to escape in a rush of tears. I was thankful—so thankful, to be able to play the part of comfort giver.

After half an hour Greta calmed, seeming to relax in my arms; I believed she had fallen asleep. After a few more moments she sat up, glancing around. I'd given her my handkerchief when she first began crying. It was a wilted mass of white in her fist. She blew her nose once more and glanced at me.

"Oh—I must be a sight. Excuse me for a moment while I go and wash my face, Alex—oh, do you wish more coffee?"

"Sure, but I'll get it myself. Can I get you some, too?"

"Oh, that would be nice," she said, standing. "Why not pour us a little more of the *aquavit*. I think I need something to brace me up a little."

She reached across, placing her palm against my cheek.

"I must wash my face...I bet I look terrible." She stood. "I am sorry for doing this to you, Alex."

"Please Greta. I'm happy to be able to be of any help. Go...wash your face...I'll take care of these things."

As she disappeared I gathered our cups and returned them to the kitchen. She'd hardly touched her coffee. I'd finished mine. Standing there, I contemplated pouring her cold cup-full down the drain, then thinking how precious it was, stepped over to the cook stove and carefully poured it back into the small coffee pot. I crossed to the counter with the empty *aquavit* glasses, refilled them and put the collection back on the tray. It may have cooled down a little in the house. I was rebuttoning the button on my shirt as Greta returned.

She'd changed her dress to a cotton or linen frock with a long blue ribbon woven in and out the full length along the row of buttons of the front. Her face, though red and somewhat puffy, appeared fresh-scrubbed and she was smiling weakly.

"I feel much better for that, Alex. Thanks again for the shoulder."

"You're welcome."

She gave me a weak smile, then glanced around, looking for the *aquavit* glasses. "Have you gotten our coffee cups?"

"Yes and already filled them. I was just going to take in the tray."

"Here, let me help." She took one of the cups and linked her arm in mine, pulling me to her slightly and at the same time, leaning her head against my shoulder. I picked up the tray and walked awkwardly toward the parlor. Greta didn't move her head or remove her arm. We arrived at the settee and I put the tray on the table and we sat down again.

"Alex...?"

I looked up as she reached for her glass.

"Yes...?"

She held her glass up as in a toast.

"During dinner we toasted to the conversation we were about to have. I know you had no idea at the time you offered the toast, what the conversation was going to entail."

"No, I didn't—or I wouldn't have made such a toast."

"I knew that..." she patted my hand "...anyway, now I'd

like to offer a new toast, a toast to a finish of that conversation and
that part of my life. We don't need any more depressing discussions.
I appreciate the comfort you've offered by being a good listener.
You don't know how relieved I feel. I was carrying the burden of
Johan's death for over a year. I think I knew—secretly, in my heart,
he was probably dead; even before the letters began to return,
unopened. What I didn't suspect was that he'd died at the hands of
our own people, instead of in battle. So...I have had my mourning
period and now I have had my grief, as I said. Let there be an end to
it and let's toast toward that end and...*the future?*"

With that, she smiled, holding up her glass. "I really needed this evening, Alex...*bottoms up*, I think you say?"

And with that she tilted her glass. I did the same, fearing
the consequences. Greta leaned forward and placed her glass on
the little table with a loud crack, leaned back on the high back of the
settee and closed her eyes.

"Umm..." the sound she made was sort of sensual, strong
like the purring of a large cat, or a powerful engine. I did the same—
but to disguise the burning in my throat from the *aquavit*, a raging
tongue of fire. I didn't *need* any more of it and I *knew* it. I was
becoming rather drunk, but I no longer cared so much. The evening
had taken on a life of its' own.

Greta leaned her head on the settee back, feeling the liquors effect also. She glanced over at me and smiled a conceding,
rather assuring smile. This appeared to be a Greta I had not yet
seen. Was it the liquor, or was she really taking an interest in me at
last. She sort of sized me up as if for the first time. Her eyes caught
my glass on the table.

"More *aquavit*, Alex?"

"*Oh—no*, really...I've had my limit and then some."

"I also...in fact, I'm becoming somewhat intoxicated, Alex."

I didn't respond, not wishing to break the spell. I nodded
and smiled back, my hands in my lap. She screwed up her face in a
question.

"Is it a wake we were having...for the long-dead Johan?
Tonight was some sort of culmination. Maybe I've felt the need to
confess to you, Alex—there are no real friends...here—I've made
none and you showed genuine concern, empathy, as I told you. I

needed to speak it, speak his death out loud to make it real at last to me. It hurt one more time in doing it. But it doesn't hurt much any more. Maybe it is nearly over—the difficult part of my mourning."

She glanced at me—as if for confirmation. Her countenance was surprisingly open, bare—almost raw, she was so unguarded. Then she reached over and took my hand. My racing heart gained on itself.

"You've long had an interest in me—more than just our relationship with our work, is that not true Alex?"

"Yes, yes I have."

"And I have talked endlessly of Johan whenever we have been together—I am even doing it again—now, yes?"

I said nothing, only smiled again. I was uncertain whether it was because I was too drunk to respond lucidly, or whether there was no need.

"You've listened—heard me talk about my whole life, my relationship with Johan, my daughter...and you haven't complained. Oh, Alex, why have I been so cruel to you?"

She leaned toward me then and placed her palm against my cheek in a gentle caress, my signal to sober up or do my best to respond properly.

I did, turning toward her, I put my arm across the back of the sofa and leaned around in front of her and as her eyes closed and her lips parted slightly, I kissed her gently.

She reclined, turning slowly toward me and at the same time responding strongly. Surprising even myself, I put my right hand on her breast and pressed gently. She started slightly, then after a few seconds shuddered slightly. Her arm slowly circled my back moving up my shoulder to my neck.

We kissed long, sensuous kisses for a couple of moments and I took my hand off her breast and felt for the front buttons on her dress. She cooperated by leaning forward slightly as I struggled with fumbling fingers. Frustrated, I finally used both hands and soon had her dress open. She was perspiring slightly and her chest was heaving. We were both still overheaded somewhat from the stove, but even more so now from our mounting passion fueled with abandon brought on by the liquor. I gently slipped her dress from her shoulders and reached behind for the clasp of her brassiere. It proved little difficulty after the small buttons.

I reached beneath the loose garment with both hands. We hadn't once broken apart from our kiss. Finally she moaned slightly and twisted away. I thought at first I was being repulsed—that she was having afterthoughts. But she smiled quickly and slipped down the sleeves of the dress and extracted the brassiere in two fluid motions, flinging it with abandon into the dimness.

She raised both her arms and circled the back of my neck with hands, interlacing her fingers, all the while, smiling at me. We weren't close enough to kiss. As she raised her arms, her breasts rose as if beckoned upward, the nipples jauntily pointing, hardening and invitingly relaxed in their new freedom. I took one mound in each hand, cupping them, feeling the weight, the firmness of each. It had been years since I'd touched a woman.

I let my fingers play over their surface lightly until I again felt the stiffening of each nipple as I rolled each in turn, between my fingers, playing with them with firm but gentle pressure.

Greta had closed her eyes, moaning slightly. As we kissed she'd quickly taken on a different aspect in her passion, now giving way to an exotic air of abandon, almost...sanguine relaxation. I marveled that each of her emotions evoked a completely different and even lovelier countenance. I leaned forward, about to encircle her left nipple with my lips. She put a hand on my chest, gently pushing me away.

"Alex—wait... let us go up to my bed. It is far too warm in here. If you want to get your bag, I'll be right back. I just want to lock up...all right? Can you wait?" She rose and on her way, picked up the cups and glasses.

"Yeah—sure, OK. I'll get it." I followed her out, smoothing my trousers on the way to the hallway to fetch my bag. As I grabbed it I heard her in the end of the hallway.

"Alex, would you please bolt the front door before you come up...I've done the back?"

"OK," I dropped the bag and walked back up the hall. In the dimness I found and then pushed the heavy bolt's handle toward its bracket, having to lean hard on the door before I felt the bolt slip home into the casing.

Back in the kitchen, Greta was drying her hands on a towel.

"I just closed the drafts on the stoves for the night. Do you think you will want more coffee—or liquor?"

"I really don't believe so." I waited as she walked toward me. She stopped, leaned forward and rising slightly on stocking feet, kissed me gently. "Come..." and taking my hand led me quickly up the dark stairs. It was dark as soon as we entered the stairway. "Can you manage the stairs in the darkness, Alex?"

"Yes, just don't turn too quickly or you might lose me."

I was feeling along the wall with my free hand. We walked past two doors on my left before finally entering a third doorway on the right.

"Stand here for a moment, Alex. I wish to inspect the blackout curtains before turning on the light."

There was a rustling sound in the darkness and after a moment I felt her beside me again, a click and a single, orange lamp glowed on a bedside table. The bed was covered with a hand made spread of some sort with a blanket folded neatly and draped across the end. I was now beginning to feel the cold of the upstairs, after the overheated parlor.

"Brrrrrr..." it's much colder up here after the inferno, below."

"Yes, the tile stove goes up through the house's, center but I forgot to open the bedroom doors so it will be cold until the heat comes in from the hallway. But..." she turned and took my hand, "...you can warm us up, can you not, Alex?"

Her dress was still around her waist on one side. In the cold of the room her nipples had come alive and were pointing up. Her brassiere she'd slung over one shoulder and her dress barely covered her nakedness below the waist.

"Yes, I believe I can do that."

She smiled and turned away, walking around to the other side of the bed. She had began removing clothing as she crossed the room.

"Please turn off the lamp when you have finished undressing, Alex...*brrrrrrrr...*!"

CHAPTER
10

The Loving

I awoke in the darkness thinking of the night of passion we'd had. Twice we'd awakened and made love. It wasn't wild lovemaking, but gentle, patient and slow—deliberate. The love-making of well-matched participants. Greta was an eager—a hungry lover, but not inconsiderate. Without a great deal of sexual experience, I followed her lead, matching her signals, gestures, urges and each time finishing in a clasping climax of passion, falling asleep nearly instantly and within an hour or so—I never knew how long, only to renew our struggle of pleasure again. I was only too happy to sate her hunger each time, match and even exceed it.

It was almost...I thought...as if she were trying to *love* Johan from her life, through me. I could have been jealous and for an instant, I was. But, of a dead man? I felt it was better to be the vehicle of his exorcism than the victim. I knew, somehow, she must rid herself of the grief and if I eventually stood a chance to be the new vessel of her affection, there would be plenty of her love remaining by the time he was at last obscured.

In the coming dawn, I lay quietly with the bedclothes beneath my chin. I couldn't see my breath as I exhaled but I knew it was cold enough, had there been more light. I tried to imagine the time of day, hidden behind the blackout curtains. My body clock seldom failed me. I reckoned it to be around eight thirty or nine.

Greta hadn't yet stirred. I thought about getting up and making coffee, but decided against disturbing her and just lay savoring the feeling of our thighs and hips against each other. The flannel bed sheets were only slightly cool against my skin. Sometime in the night, Greta had pulled more heavy quilts over us and we now lay beneath several inches of wool, goose down, or both. The tile stove, so far away down the hall, must have lost all its bluster. My nose was cold.

Then Greta started stirring slightly. Her movement began with her feet, then her left calf tentatively reached across the chasm to my own. She stiffened—stretching—arching her back in a long yawn and thrusting bare arms into the darkness. As she relaxed again, she turned toward me and began nuzzling my neck. Her nose was also cold as she turned toward me, reaching across my chest with one arm and sliding one long leg across my thighs.

"How did you rest?" I asked, hoarsely.

"Ummmm," she mumbled into my neck, "I died—literally...each time.

She chuckled and nuzzled my neck.

"Ummmm...how could I have been so tired? I haven't slept like that since...since I don't know when.

I didn't reply, savoring the attention.

"Alex?" She raised her arm and stroked my cheek. "I seem to have been awakened a couple of times?" She snickered hoarsely. "Apart from that—which does not count by the way, if anyone is keeping score." She moved her fingers along my cheek to my nose with her forefinger, laughed again. "Your nose is cold, too. What sort of a Swede are you—where is that *Viking* blood, I ask you?"

"Down in my feet, I believe." I turned toward her, reaching over, drawing her closer. "And with a little in the middle."

She chuckled, reaching forward. "A bit more than a little, I think."

Later, we savored boiled eggs Greta had found somewhere, along with fresh-stuffed sausage. I pasted some of her strawberry jam on a second thick slice of her bread. The first slice I'd washed down with coffee.

"You know, Greta, I feel somewhat guilty drinking up your coffee. We should save it."

"Nonsense. It tastes better with you across the table, Alex."

"Thanks, but we should save it, nonetheless."

She wrinkled her nose at me in a teasing way, trying and failing, to make an ugly face. She was so beautiful, even when she tried to appear unattractive, her features wouldn't permit it.

"Maybe you can bring me another packet sometime...*soon?*"

"Oh...that could be arranged I think."

It'd taken a half-hour to get the stoves going again and now, after another hour, the rooms were only just beginning to get somewhat comfortable.

"What shall we do today, Greta?"

She smiled a wry smile, grasped her chin like an old man and cocking her head upward, glanced about the ceiling as if the answer lay there.

"Hummm...we could have a nap—*later?*"

I laughed despite myself.

"Yes, there's always that. Isn't there something we can do, somewhere we can go—see something?"

We did. We walked all around the city. It was cold but we both bundled up, donning long underwear and we walked for miles, talking and laughing...at one point we even joined some children in a snowball fight. Each of us taking an opposing side, excited the children and spurred them on with renewed passion as we quickly became the prime targets for the children. After being pelted a dozen or more times we finally broke it off and retreated before a chorus of arching snowballs and gleefully screeching children.

We found a restaurant near the harbor with real tea and sat in the dining room for an hour, warming up, drinking tea and eating little cakes suffering for lack of sugar in them. Greta had become quiet and had a far away look about her as she cupped her tea in both hands, staring across the room.

"In *Amerika* we have a saying, Greta: a penny for your thoughts."

She smiled. "I am sorry, Alex. Yes, we too. But, do you

know what I'm worried about now?"

I reached across the little table and took her hand. "What are you worried about?"

"My child." She looked up then and almost smiled. "I hadn't thought about it until just now. If they sought out Johan—because he was Jewish, will they also look for Sophia, with the same tainted blood? I have had some suspicion of this, after...after some thing I have heard at my job."

I didn't comment, having struggled with the same thought myself. She was probably right, if they were as ruthless as she indicated. I'd hated to think about it and had avoided the question.

"How would they go about it...finding her, I mean...and then—what *would* they do?"

"Oh Alex, they won't have any problem finding her—it was they who placed her with the adopting family in the first place. They can just go there—go to the place...wherever it is and then they can take her, if they want to."

"I see...you're probably right, of course, Greta."

"As for what they will do...I can not even bear to think about it, Alex. I'm afraid—afraid they'll take Sophia the way they took Johan's father."

We didn't speak much about it, depressing as it was, but I could tell, it was gnawing on Greta. We finally walked back to the house and after shedding our clothing we made love before dinner. Then we prepared our last meal together, before I flew out with the incoming crew on the following morning.

We sat up listening to the radio that evening, sitting in the darkened parlor, the tile stove safely banked and the blackout curtains tightly in place. Listening in the darkness, the only light coming from the orange glow of the radio's dial, we became lost in the local program from Radio Norway. It was a live broadcast of *Peer Gynt* and as we listened to the masterwork of Greig, I thought of the play by Hendrik Ibsen, after which Edvard Greig had written the music. With closed eyes I was taken back to a college classroom in The States, where I'd studied literature, reading Ibsen, Strindberg, Kierkegaard— all Scandinavian authors. I could never have imagined I would one day be remembering them while reclining in a woman's arms, in the city of Oslo, Norway, during a second world war.

I don't believe we said ten words to each other after dinner. When the music was over, there was an interview with the orchestra conductor. It was in Norwegian but was full of Nazi propaganda, Greta said, because the broadcast was sponsored or controlled by her own organization, bringing culture and propaganda to the Norwegian people. So we turned off the radio and went up to bed. We made love only twice that evening: once when we retired and again, sometime during the night. And Greta cried in my arms, for a time after the second lovemaking. I knew she was worried about her child. We lay in each other's arms, thinking separate thoughts, until we both fell asleep.

The next morning, there was a false cheerfulness about the kitchen. Before I put on my coat I gave her instructions about *ABA*'s plans for my schedule, as best I knew them.

"I'll be moving to Bergen, Greta —but not before the first of the year. You'll be able to reach me there at *ABA*'s office, anytime after January first. I wrote out the information for her and she made gentle fun again of my old fashioned handwriting.

As I left her in the hallway, I told her not to worry about her daughter—that she'd probably been absorbed so well into the adopted parent's family, no one would be able to find her...even if they did try to look. I didn't know what else to say since there was nothing I could do about it. Both of us knew that wasn't true.

And that's how we parted. Tears were blinding her and too emotional to speak, she merely nodded when we kissed goodbye, trying to smile through them, putting on a good front. I left her there with a long kiss and closed the outside door and swung out onto the sidewalk, wondering what we were going to do. For I was now certain...*we* had become an *us* and it thrilled my heart. I wanted to marry her sometime, I thought and the sooner the better.

Finally, I figure the others had left me completely to my own resources so I got my coat at the coat check and left, smiling to myself, thinking I'd not done too badly on my second, or was it third encounter with the enemy.

CHAPTER
11

Greta and the Surprise Inquiry

I was tired after returning to Oslo. I wanted to sleep late but had too many things waiting for me at my office in the culture promotion center. As I was hanging up my new dance costume, my director's office girl stopped beside me.

"Oh, there you are Greta... *Herr* Strauser would like to see you in his office when you are finished unpacking."

"Thank you, Helga, please tell him I'll be right there."

I finished putting away my things and stopped by my office to pick up a pen and paper before going to the meeting. *Herr* Strauser and I seldom had the occasion for any encounters. His duties were more involved in interacting with German Command and coordinating our programs with my boss, so it was a surprise that he wanted to see me. He would occasionally be in a meeting with my manager, Herman, that I would be called into. But usually, I'd only meet with Herman... *Little Caesar,* I secretly called him, because he was quite short and had somewhat of a Napoleon complex. He hated anyone taller than himself.

"Please have a seat *Fräulein* Stopff," he waved a chubby hand toward the chair beside the window that looked out on the street. "I am sorry to bother you so early on a Monday morning and after such a long journey, too. But...I wished to speak with you before you went anywhere, again. As you are our most frequent traveler I felt it best to catch you early."

"Thank you for your concern, *Herr* Strauser, I only just returned last evening and I really have no immediate plans to travel again this week. So, if you would rather...."

"No—no...I have the time...and the need..." he hesitated a moment as if he wanted to say more. "Well, now that I have caught you...anyway, so to speak," he chuckled and raised is eyebrows suggestively. "I wished to speak about a matter of which I know absolutely nothing. Since it could possibly concern someone you know, I thought you might shed some light upon it, *Fräulein*. You see, it seems someone in Berlin has been making inquiries about you and your work, especially during the period before we became *guests* of the Norwegians.

I waited for him to continue, but he didn't go on. "Yes...*Herr* Strauser, *and*...?"

He cleared his throat, sat up straighter and shuffled some papers on his desk before leaning back in his chair.

"The inquiries were not official, *Fräulein*; however, anytime that I hear the Berlin *SS* are sniffing around, anywhere...well, I become interested, as you may well understand."

He looked over his glasses to see if I understood.

"Certainly, Herr Strauser, that is understandable, but...do you know why they were asking and what their questions concerned? Did they speak with you by telephone, write...?"

"None of these, *Fräulein,* the information came to me through a...a source—*friend*, in Berlin. Friends look after friends, you see."

I was afraid *Herr* Strauser was insinuating that he wished to become my friend. When I said nothing, he continued, again, all business this time.

"My friend has noticed that a project is being instituted to locate a former wife, or girlfriend of a *Kaptain*, now on the Russian Front. It seems the *Kaptain* is...has been found to be...*a Jew.*"

Again, he paused for any response I might have. "A Jew, *Herr* Strauser...*a Jew*—serving in the German infantry...*and* a *Kaptain*? It sounds...rather improbable?"

"Yes, a Jew, improbable or not *Fräulein*. I have nothing

particularly against Jews as Jews…but this particular Jew—*Kaptain* Johan…something-or-other, was apparently involved in a very early *project* of *Reichsmarschall* Himmler and some young German woman, which resulted in a child being born and subsequently adopted out. Apparently the *Reichsmarschall* has somehow learned of this error in…*race* and he is most concerned that the error be…*erased*, shall we say. Anyway, for some reason, your name was mentioned, *Fräulein*. It is none of my business, but I thought I should make you aware of it in case you had the necessity to…to do anything."

He straightened his chair and stood up, indicating the interview was over. I stood up also and followed him to the closed door.

"Thank you *Herr* Strauser. It is a very interesting story. I wonder why they were mentioning my name. I certainly do not know the *Reichsmarschall*. So…it must have been a different *Fräulein* Stopff."

"Well…yes, *Fräulein*…you know best. I just do not wish to have the Berlin *SS* in my business, if you know what I mean."

"Certainly, Herr Strauser…nor do I."

I'd opened the door to leave, when he called me back.

"*Fräulein*…I wish to tell you that I receive good reports from Herman on the progress you have been making…your endeavors with our Norwegian hosts."

"Thank you, *Herr* Strauser, we certainly do try. Good Day."

"Good Day, *Fräulein* Stopff."

I tried to walk calmly back to my office. This news was frightening. *Herr* Strauser was taking a great chance in revealing it and even before I'd reached my office door, I decided I should try to contact Johan's parents as soon as possible and warn them. I didn't know Johan was a Jew. Not that it made any difference to me. But now he was definitely in danger. How would I be able to contact him. He wasn't answering my letters as it was. And the child; *Herr* Strauser had referred to her as a mistake—an error that needed to be *erased*. What did he mean? Certainly not…to kill the child…my Sophia.

After closing my office door I sat down at my desk, took out a plain piece of paper and wrote a letter to Johan's parents in Germany, explaining what I had just heard from *Herr* Strauser and already knew with my past experience with Johan. I was unsure how much his parents knew of me, or even that Johan had fathered a child, who had been adopted to someone, somewhere. I explained that if there was Jewish blood in the family, they, and the child were in danger.

I didn't dare to inquire further of *Herr* Strauser; he had already done enough, just passing along the information he'd heard. What did *Herr* Strauser mean by "erasing the mistake?" Did he mean covering up the paperwork, or, could he mean killing my child? I was very quickly becoming frightened and concerned.

CHAPTER
12

The Note

Nearly three weeks later there was a short letter from Greta in my Bergen drop, transferred from ABA through the locals. I'd hoped now that she was back in Oslo for a little while, we could meet for the weekend and possibly have dinner and then do the town, or at least do our best, considering it was wartime.

As I'd been trained, I didn't open the envelope until I'd walked another half hour along the canal, insuring several times that I wasn't being followed. I eventually settled into a table with a hot brandy at an outdoor café. My back to the restaurant wall, I greedily scanned the single page as I sipped the steaming cup the waiter put on the saucer.

Greta had left Oslo again. She'd be gone for a while, she said. I was immediately disappointed, reading on. She hadn't remained in town as we'd planned, because of earlier fears...but she didn't disclose what sort of fears. I wondered then, whether she was suspecting she was herself in danger, possibly being watched. But that would be rather sudden and a surprise to me I mused, reading on.

She'd gotten word about her daughter, Sophia...that was great news! But I still couldn't quite understand why she'd left Oslo. I wondered from whom she'd gotten word of Sophia. Coming to the end of the note, still without understanding it, I re-read the mes-

sage, looking for some clue to offer an idea—some hidden meaning. Strange, too, Greta's note sounded rather...*desperate*, leaving as she did without much notice, all of which I also found unusual.

Sipping my drink I sat back after reading the letter a third
time. Looking up from the table to consider the letter's contents, I
ran my eyes along the old facades fronting the canal, copper and tile
roofs intermittently shadowed by the steaming chimney pots, quoin-
ing on the building corners, tall, narrow windows, black in the
cloudless afternoon. There was nothing in the letter I could fathom, absolutely nothing.

It just didn't make sense. It *did*...it almost sounded...*frantic*,
to some extent. I didn't think she'd known anything at all about the
whereabouts of her little girl, but now this; she'd learned, somehow.
I was concerned for her. I began to wonder then whether she could
have returned to Germany; she had to, I reasoned, if the trip was
about her seeing her daughter. She'd told me she always assumed
the girl was adopted to some family in Germany. Silently, I wished
her luck, and a quick, safe return. I was swallowing my feeling of
disappointment and frustration. It never dawned on me she could
be in any danger, returning as she was, to her own homeland.

Saddened and concerned, I found a telephone and called
Aerotransport's office; did they have any flights out of Bergen that
needed a pilot? My holiday had been canceled, I said. Yes...they
did. So I caught a cab and was in the air in less than two hours
taking charge of an empty plane. The letter's contents remained in
my thoughts, nagging at me. I continued to think about her on and
off the rest of the day.

I was able to put it in the back of my mind, when I landed
after a long, weather-ridden flight to Helsinki. I looked forward to
food and rest, but I still had to go into the office and discuss the
coming week's flight planning. It was during flights like these that I
longed for the days of bright, clear weather we usually had in The
States. Scandinavia seldom enjoyed cloudless winter skies; it was
always a mixture of freezing rain, snow, or sleet to contend with, not
to mention the endless fog.

All of which made for murderous flying weather, especially
from western Dalarna, across Varmland, in Sweden, westward into

Norway. There the mountains got up well into the clouds, forcing aircraft, hoping to fly free of cloud, with no choice but to go up into it to avoid the rising terrain of the approaching mountains. But once the airplane went into the cloud, it must eventually come out. The "where" one came out and the "what" was immediately in front of one's aircraft during descent, was critical and very often deadly. If the clouds went down nearly to the surface, planes would crash before they found the runway, or a safe alternative to land. All this, that is, if an icing airframe didn't take the aircraft down, instead, as it descended through the moisture of the clouds.

During the *ABA* briefing the following day, I learned we were to have a welcome day off, followed by a special flight from Helsinki to Stockholm and Oslo, where we would spend another night. The following morning, we would gather fresh passengers and hopefully, a special set of German dispatches, and proceed on to Copenhagen and then direct to London. There'd be a day's layover in London, to rest for the repeat of the return. I had immediate hopes for a short holiday in England, but without the thought of someone like Greta sharing it with me, it left me with a hollow feeling. I didn't know how long we would remain in England once we reached London. I would also be away from any drops Greta would have had access to, so the chance for communication with her was lost during that time, a thought I didn't relish, either. I was concerned for her, not knowing whether she had returned to Germany or was somewhere on an assignment in Scandinavia.

We were off the field at Helsinki well before dawn the next morning . The flight to Oslo was totally uneventful. But right after departure from Oslo, our JU-52, began developing some rather elevated exhaust manifold temperatures on the port-side engine. We were about forty-five minutes out when Per, the ever-worrisome flight mechanic nudged me, inclining his head toward the instrument panel. As I leaned closer, he tapped on the glass dial of one of his gauges, shaking his head mournfully. I glanced at the needles behind their circle of glass and then at the dial for the starboard engine. Fortunately it remained in normal temperature range. We still had one, fully-functioning engine on the Junkers. I nodded to Per and shouted for him to keep an eye on it and the oil pressure, too, I indicated by tapping the face of that gauge. I turned my attention back to maintaining the aircraft's altitude and heading.

From the look of the cloud ahead we would have to begin letting down soon for Copenhagen; thank God there were no mountains to contend with below; merely ocean. I could let all the way down to the water if need be as long as we could see the field to land. I trimmed the Junker's elevators to a pitch that would gradually let us down, as we progressed along the south coast of Norway toward Denmark.

Investigating the cause of the abnormal temperature reading caused a delay in Copenhagen. The local mechanic along with Per removed the port engine's cowling, a task that always inspires passengers who watch and wonder and then question. I answered their questions as best I could without knowing the cause of the problem while the others began a closer inspection to determine whether they could find the culprit. While I addressed the concerns of our passengers in the waiting area inside the aerodrome, the mechanics performed what turned out to be a fruitless search. Our weather luck didn't change either as I watched even heavier weather moving in as we remained on the ground.

We were still on the ground after two more hours and a half, not due to the engine, but waiting for some local icing conditions to subside. Then we had news of some "late materials" arrival, in the form of more diplomatic bags from the occupying *Reich* command, so we waited for them.

By the time we were finally off the ground and an hour enroute to London, the gauge again began to creep slowly upward, until it was indicating elevated-operating temperatures again. Damn, I thought. What is it? Per had been watching right along with me and shrugged his shoulders and held both palms up to indicate hoplesness.

I considered returning to Copenhagen, or continuing on toward the British Isles. Our *leathersmiths* were by this time, well into removing the bottom stitching on some of the pouches. After considering the alternatives, with Per, who thought it was simply a malfunctioning gauge, I called Axel forward and advised him to fire up his set and radio Copenhagen that we were changing course. We turned due west in order to cross the North Sea by the most direct route and pick up the northeast coast of Scotland. This manoeuver would add flight time, but I wanted to get the aircraft over land as soon as possible in the instance we had to put the *Junkers* down. A plowed field was far better than a cold, North Atlantic Ocean, any day.

Once we had visual on the coast, I altered course and turned the aircraft directly toward Edinburgh. I'd debated whether to cut to the southeast, picking up the German coast, instead. There were more airfields and friendlier skies that direction, but it was farther. If I did, we'd have to turn west again, flying across Holland, Belgium, northern France—up that way, into the south of England and finally, London. In either event, I was afraid of Allied aircraft mistaking the *Junkers* for a *Jerry* bomber and letting go a few bursts at us. Despite our obvious commercial markings I could see a green Spit pilot shooting first and looking at the civilian airline markings later. ABA had lost its share of machines to friendly fire from both sides.

I didn't know what else to do. Still concerned about the elevated temperature, I throttled the failing engine back somewhat, letting the other, starboard engine take the major pull and drag us forward. Our airspeed quickly decreased as a result. The weather had improved, so there was little danger now of getting caught in something hazardous, weather-wise. The ship was a bit more difficult to hold on course, however, because of the uneven pull, despite the trimming I'd done to try to improve it.

The fact that we were also flying in a southerly direction added to our overall slow-down. The weather folks indicated there was a warm front moving north across Great Britain from Spain and the Bay of Biscay. Beside fighting a headwind, this development could possibly exacerbate our troublesome engine: warmer weather—warmer manifold temperatures.

Per kept a constant eye on the little dial, tapping his forefinger on the glass from time to time, hoping against hope that it was a gauge malfunction. But it wasn't. Several hours later as we approached the north coast of Scotland we began to lose oil pressure on the engine.

We struck the coast of Scotland at the Firth of Pentland where I turned the *Junkers* south again, following the coastline toward Moray Firth, before cutting across and turning due south toward Edinburgh. The engine's temperature continued to climb slowly. Axel radioed ahead to London, advising them we were coming in from the north with a bum engine. I debated putting the *Junkers* down at Edinburgh but it continued to limp along, seemingly without getting any worse. We plowed onward, crossing the marker near Edinburgh, the city totally dark below us in the blackout. We passed over The Pennines, which I could no longer see in the darkness and headed on south for Yorkshire.

Much later, we were crossing near industrial Manchester, west of Halifax; both were also invisible in the blackout. But we soon spotted a small glow on the horizon to the southwest. *Jerry'd* been busy there from the look of it and got by some of the southern defenses with their bombers. We talked about the glow as we slowly flew abreast and then put it behind us, reckoning they were hitting Sheffield's steel and other factories with incendiaries.

From my time in Fighter Command I grew more and more concerned our German built aircraft was going to be mistaken for a stray German bomber, returning home from a raid in the north of England, or Scotland. I surmised that returning German aircraft normally swung more eastward and went out over the sea, down past the Straight of Dover and home from there…but I wasn't certain. So I saw that Axel kept busy on the radio, calling ahead and letting everyone know who we were, where we were and where we were going. I asked him to ask them to advise fighter command, too, just in case.

Of course no one answered our calls, fearing triangulation by the *Jerrys* for targeting on *their* radio signal. Our signal didn't matter, since we were moving and also we were neutral—though I didn't know how much that mattered anyway. I kept reminding myself, whenever I got on edge. I still worried mostly about a trigger-happy Hurricane or Spit pilot.

The dales of Yorkshire and Derbyshire would be passing silently below us, though we were unable to see their beauty. The engine grew no worse. At Luton we began to let down for the permissible approach to London, well within the corridor for *friendlies*, in-bound for London without bombs. With a southerly wind, approach and landing would be straight into the field.

We touched down at quarter to three in the morning with a sigh of relief. London had been hit again during the night. We flew around the glow of the burning city, remaining within the passage limits and dropped the *Junkers* on the field with two bounces, waking any passengers brave enough to sleep through the approach.

There were no terminal personnel at the field. We were not expected at this time of morning, or even at all. After dealing with the passengers—I was able to get them most into cabs headed to their destinations, or to the station to connect to their trains. This took me nearly two hours. When I finally finished, I curled up on a bench in the *ABA* office and slept until a clerk surprised us both at eight in the morning. I felt terrible and looked it. Red-eyes and fatigue stared back when I peered into the mirror in the tiny washroom; the face staring back in the glass affirmed my disheveled condition. I blinked at my reflection in the cloudy glass. I was so tired...I wondered whether I really wanted to continue to do this...*job*, not that I had much choice. Glancing at the lines in my face, I thought to myself: better than a snowy foxhole, buddy—*far* better.

Outside in the office area, I learned from the clerk that we could expected our return orders from Helsinki in the next day or so. I told him about the bum engine, which would now change all their arrangements. I asked him what we could do about it there in London, if anything. He wasn't sure himself and wanted to contact headquarters, which he said was regulations. It didn't sound as if anything was going to happen very soon, at any rate. I asked him to relay my doubts to *ABA* and advise them that it was my recommendation, they should definitely not attempt to return with the airplane and relief crew, before having the engine repaired, or replaced.

He said he would let them know. *KLM* had a skeleton mechanic crew usually checking out our birds, when in London. He felt he could find someone. I told him I'd be at *The Lennox*, sleeping, so not to call me until the following day, which was Thursday, unless it was an emergency. I caught a ride to the tube station, jumped a train into Victoria Station, London and a double-decker bus to the hotel.

Much of the city appeared quite normal; other sections we passed through were nearly impassable from the previous night's bombing. Smoke and the stench of crumbled, old building stone permeated the bus as we passed blocked-off sections. I wanted to have a quick sandwich and a glass of beer in the hotel restaurant, but of course it was shut tight. So I ran a bath, toweled myself dry afterwards and collapsed on the single bed.

Starvation woke me at 3:00 PM.. I dressed, preparing to go down to eat. I knew I'd have to settle for tea, again, as the restaurant wouldn't be eager to deal with an between meals order. I felt I deserved this little holiday and I intended to enjoy myself, despite the ongoing war and the absence of Greta. A lot of sleep was on my schedule.

The phone on the little nightstand jingled; I suspected it was the desk clerk with a call from ABA and picked it up.

"Hello Old Boy...welcome to London."

"Clyde? How'd you know I'd come in?"

"Oh, I do get around somewhat, don't you know. What do you have on today, Mate? Have you slept enough? I waited hoping you would get some *shut-eye.*"

There was a significant pause while he savored the American movie westernism...he just couldn't help himself.

"I didn't have anything on, Clyde, but something to eat and back to bed. Why, what did you have in mind?" I'd begun to see my impromptu holiday eroding.

"Oh...nothing in particular, Chappie, but how 'bout a cup of tea to think about it?"

"Sure...why not, too early for a drink. Where?"

"Why not in your hotel's tea rooms?"

"OK, but I have to get something to eat, not just tea 'n crumpets. I haven't eaten since...Copenhagen, maybe...can't remember. I'm starved."

"Fine by me."

"Ok, what time? I'm not going to wait for you, you know."

"Don't expect you to old chap...let's say...two minutes. Give you time to comb your hair, change your shirt...all that."

"Two minutes—are you *that* close?"

"Oh, yes. I'm in the bloody lobby right now and I've already read the newspaper twice waiting for you to get up. So don't be too long. I'm also hungry. I shall see you soon, Alex."

He rang off, leaving me wondering again at his unpredictability. Shaking my head as I changed my shirt I considered how he could know what was on my mind?

As I walked down the narrow hallway toward the lobby, I wondered whether Birgitta, or even Greta, somehow figured in it and whether he was aware that Greta had left Norway as I surmised. And I meant to ask him, too, but soon forgot it; for the coming events began to take place with such rapidity I became hard pressed to keep up.

Clyde stood up smiling and folding his newspaper as I entered the lobby. As usual, he was dressed impeccably, this time in a bulky Harris tweed jacket, rumpled wool trousers and a jaunty tie to complement the ensemble. Smiling broadly he strode toward me, changing the ever-present cigarette to his left hand.

"Greetings, Old Boy..." he chirped jovially, extending his hand, "...don't know whether to say good morning—or good afternoon. You certainly keep irregular hours."

Ever the joker, he was grinning all the while.

"If you'd had the flight we had *Chap*," I mocked his accent "...you'd *still* be in bed."

"No doubt Old Boy, no doubt it at all. I don't *do*...those things well you know."

He extended his arm toward the double French doors and we began walking side by side along the paneled hallway toward the restaurant.

"I'm not at all good at the *manly* things, Alex...bravery—valor, all that...never my thing, you see. Born coward my father always said...born coward, this boy."

Clyde had apparently made the arrangements in advance as we were immediately taken in hand and led toward the rear of the very expansive dining space. The ancient waiter guided us toward the brightly-lit, window-side of the room. It was very nice; pretty-patterned tablecloths and flowers were on every table, far different from dark Scandinavia. Here we were, peacefully surrounded by the bored normality of the English war, in winter. Greta would like this room, I thought, momentarily loosing Clyde's conversation.

We'd followed the rigid back, weaving between the tables

and were soon seated. The stoic waiter handed me one of the menus. But before he'd crossed to Clyde's side of the table, Clyde put in his oar: "Could you bring us a pot of coffee and some pastries and butter while we decide?"

"Of course Sir..." the waiter didn't blink.

Glancing at me, Clyde hesitated "...or, did you already decide?"

I hadn't yet opened the menu, nor did I need to:

"Yup, I'll have the full English...if its not too late, or maybe two?" I was ready to eat the kitchen out of their stock of food.

"No Sir, never too late to serve the customer's wishes...and you, Lord Whittwell," he said bowing to Clyde slightly, "are you also prepared to place your order?

Clyde looked annoyed and fidgeted, having to decide too quickly.

"Oh—well...why not, make it two...there's a good man."

The waiter bowed again slightly. Clyde waited until the waiter picked up my menu and left before breaking the silence again, winking as the man left:

"Where was I? Ah yes...horses, hunting, fast cars...more my thing...women, too."

The waiter had neglected to pick up Clyde's menu and he'd opened it and paged through it idly as he spoke.

"There you are...quail eggs and toast."

"That's what you're having now?"

"No...no, of course not...merely making a point Old Boy, I never liked participating in the shoot...killing innocent things like that seemed...wrong somehow."

"Sorry, Clyde, but I liked hunting. It was a way of life where I grew up and I enjoyed eating what we shot, too. The faster it flew or ran, the more we enjoyed the skill of the hunt."

He grimaced at that, but didn't reply for a moment. Then he folded his menu.

"Now—fast women, why...they're another story. Father had his comments about them also, not that he should have spoken down to me about *that* subject...rather the pot calling the kettle...*if* you get my drift," another wink. "Mum died when I was a child and there was an endless troop of them marching through the house as I was coming up. Father called them my Aunties."

He seemed lost in thought for a second, then chuckled:

"My *real* aunts, however...had other names for them."

The waiter had seated us behind a tall potted palm. We could see into the main dining room but couldn't be seen from the street, or even easily, from within the room itself, not that there were that many guests.

"There was this chamber maid...I was mostly away at school then. She taunted me, the sassy little lass. But when I came home...wanted to play as much as I. Oddly...wasn't a gold digger, either...or anything like that. Just liked...well, 'nuf said.

He seemed reluctant to broach the subject of his invitation to our late breakfast and lapsed once again back into contemplative silence. After a moment of staring out the window at the passers-by, I brought him back.

"Where do *they* get coffee, Clyde? I have a devil of a time getting any for...friends. By the way, what do you want me to call you, anyway?" I asked, remembering his many pseudonyms or code names, none of which had gotten by our waiter.

"Oh, anything will do *Buddy*," he said, turning on the Americanisms again.

I thought I'd dig him a little.

"I noticed the waiter knew you. Want *me* to call you *Lord* Whittwell?"

"If it pleases you, Alex, you may...but I rather prefer the hush-hush thing. It's jolly fun...don't you agree?"

"I find it confusing, in and out of these roles. It's far easier when I'm working. I know what to expect and the names remain the same."

"Do it enough—long enough and you won't even realize you're doing it."

I thought about that. "It'll never become second nature to me, Clyde...especially when I'm surprised. I'll mess up, I'm afraid...not fast enough on my feet."

"Oh, I doubt it Old Boy; in a pinch, you'll come through. Why...I was in France last month...chap—German sergeant, actually, came up behind me—surprised me, you know?"

I couldn't believe what he'd said. "You were in France?

German soldier...?"

"Yes, France—the Germans are everywhere in France, don't you know...anyway, where was I? Oh...yes, anyway, he wasn't supposed to be *there*, you see. I was with this French farmer...one of ours he was, middle of the night. *Dark*...it was and this German sergeant comes up, grabs me by the shoulder, 'n asks me in perfectly good butcher shop German, what the hell I'm doing out that time of night, so near their radio command center. Of course, we'd been searching for their radio command center and *he* didn't know that *I* didn't know it was the radio command center that we just happened to be looking for, but had gotten lost in the dark. He still had his hand on my shoulder, having spun me around rather suddenly, holding his bloody machine pistol in the other. You know—surprised me completely. I was wearing the farmer's, brother's clothes, so I'd look like one of the locals—belonged, if you know what I mean. Smelled that way, to, if you get my...*drift*."

I didn't bite at his windy pun and again there was the poignant pause as he waited. I waved a hand impatiently, eager for him to get on with the story.

"But, wouldn't you know it, instead of responding in German, or even English, up came my French, just like it was supposed to. Told him I was just a stupid butcher's son like him and I couldn't speak *proper* German. Also told him I didn't own a radio so I couldn't hear it was a radio transmitter to know I shouldn't be near it. He probably didn't understand a word I'd said to him. But he shouted at us then and turning up his nose, pushed me away...down the road he shoved me, with a kick in the breeches for good measure...must have felt we were comrades, even though he didn't understand my farm-French. I'd gotten down to his level without giving a forethought—right off, too. That was the secret, Alex. Second nature, you see...after a while."

The waiter arrived then carrying a tray with a pot of coffee and two cups, saucers, sugar, cream pitcher and spoons and began methodically to assemble each together in front of us, before finally pouring. As soon as the waiter left, I prodded Clyde.

"France, huh. Thought you said you were a coward, Clyde."

"Oh I am, Old Boy, frightfully so. I was bloody scared to

death the whole week I was over there...and it was so bloody cold. I much prefer France in the summer—*holidays...Coat 'd Azure*—warm sun, great painting light, you know? But now...."

"What did you do with the German, Clyde?"

"Oh..." he chuckled, wagging his head mischievously, "...can't talk about that, Mate—*hush-hush*, don't you know," he said, casting a confidential glance from side to side and then a knowing smile in my direction, laying his forefinger against the side of his nose.

"You are a marvel, Clyde—a marvel," I chuckled, shaking my head.

"Not at all my friend. Duty you know...God and country."

He emptied what appeared to be half the sugar bowl in his coffee and poured just a touch of cream in his cup, handing the pitcher to me. He remembered, somehow, that I took cream but not sugar. As we stirred our coffees, I tried again.

"How'd you know I was in London, Clyde?"

"Heard it on the wireless."

"Yeah, sure."

"*I did*, old boy, *I did*. So did half of Europe, for that matter."

"What do you mean, the BBC?"

"Of course not...who do you think you are—on the BBC? Your radio operator was shouting it constantly down the whole length of Scotland and England, as you came down. Something about engine problems..." he chuckled, fidgeting again with his napkin this time. "Was that the bit of sticky stuff you mentioned earlier?"

"Oh, now I know what you mean. Yeah, exhaust manifold temperatures through the roof...lean burning starboard side. Fried half the valves, no doubt. But the Germans build damn good aeroplanes, so we made it in."

"That they certainly do, among other things. By the way, speaking of well built things, how is it with our mutual acquaintance? The dancer from the *Deutschland?*"

"Who...Greta?"

"The same."

"She's disappeared." He raised his eyebrows but remained silent, waiting for my report.

"I thought you might know where she went, Clyde. I got a note in my drop just before coming down."

"Not a clue Old Boy—which drop?"

"Gothenburg...just off the airfield."

"Hummm," he thought for a couple of seconds. "Nothing happening in that end of the boat that I know of, but I'll look into it. Any hint what it's about?"

"Yes, I believe so. Nothing official—Greta has a child...you know?"

"Yes—you told us...a little girl, wasn't it?"

"Yes. She's worried about her daughter. For some reason, I believe she went to check into it, whatever and wherever *it* is."

"Oh...personal stuff. Where would she go then, Germany?"

"Yes, to the best of my knowledge."

"There is no husband I presume...*boyfriend?*"

"Yes—no...it's complicated."

I told Clyde a little of what I knew about the situation with *Lebensborn* and Johan now being dead, or so she thought, anyway.

"Well that is interesting and a bloody shame. Terrible things happening over there...Jews, Gypsies, Black People...terrible!"

We sat in silence for a while.

"Seems a silly goose, doesn't she...running off to Norway—away from her daughter? We've heard about the "L" project of course, for some time. Far as we can tell, just another bit of silly nonsense from Himmler. Believe that chap's batty, you know Alex...absolutely mad. But it is serious, silly nonsense, nonetheless."

"I'll take your word for it, Clyde." I didn't want to talk about Greta for fear he'd catch onto how I'd come to think of her. He seemed to have a second sense, because he stared at me for a good bit but didn't say anything more.

"Why'd you want to meet me anyway, Clyde? I'd think you'd be off pursuing those fast women you mentioned, just back from behind enemy lines as you are."

"Oh, I've already done that...and doing it again, tonight. Want to join us? She'll find a nice friend...?"

"I don't think so, Clyde. I believe your friends are out of my class and I don't want to cramp your style anyway."

"Oh...never fear for that Alex...never fear for that. I do all right in that area, as I mentioned…not like…*war*. Ghastly stuff— *war*."

"Yes you did, mention it, I believe. You didn't say, why the get-together—us, *here…today?*"

"You're here for a few days, right—your engine-whatever?"

"Yes, probably—now. I was set for barely a two-day lay over and a *holiday*…but now, with this engine…who knows? Could be a week or more. Why?"

"We thought you could do with a little excitement for a change…engine over-temperatures aside. Hadn't planned on that bit of excitement. Thought to give you a bit of our own, or rather, the Air Marshal did. Actually—rather need you Alex."

"Well, I planned to take a couple days vacation—*holiday*," I corrected myself, "but there's nowhere to go—with this war. There's war on in all the warm places, or hadn't you heard and I don't crave any of the behind-the-lines stuff. You can have that, Clyde, coward or not."

"Oh, I'd heard—I'd heard…but this is different. You see, there's a big thing on…" he glanced over his shoulder toward the kitchen and then behind us "…boys want to really show the *Bosch*."

He looked as serious as I'd ever seen him. "Big air raid— thousand of mothers dropping eggs in the *Deutschemark*. Factory Morale of the citizens, never mind the military. The tide's turned in Europe since you went away, Alex. We now pretty-much own the skies over The Channel and we'll soon own the real estate again in Europe, too. They've got more birds than chaps like you to fly them. The Air Marshal—over my objections, mind you—thought you might enjoy trying your hand again, particularly in this one, since he heard this morning that you were back in town. Historical, it will be…make you famous, all that…you know. Largest air raid in history. I think you're too valuable to risk, but he runs this ship. What do you say, Mate…told him I'd *ask* you?"

He drained his coffee and poured more for both of us and then began ladling off the sugar. Rationing must have been hard on him. I thought as I watched him satisfying his sweet tooth.

"What do I have to do, Clyde?"

"Drive a Lancaster over Germany in the middle of the night, evade what's left of the *Luftwaffe*, get the hell shot out of you by flak, drop a bunch of bombs and get shot up again by flack and fighters on the way home—that's about all, I believe."

There went another R & R, I thought. But then, I couldn't go fishing and I knew hardly anyone in England. Greta was somewhere else.

"I don't know, Clyde. I thought I'd take off a few days...'n I don't know how to drive a Lancaster."

"Course you don't have to go old boy; they'll understand—flying all the time with one engine as you do—having four, all functioning...that'd no doubt be boring."

I ignored his sarcasm. Certainly don't need the excitement, I thought.

"You flew a couple Lancs in training for the Junkers, didn't you?"

"Yeah."

"Well...little training...couple of hops, good as new again. Up to snuff?"

"I don't know, Clyde."

"Well, as I said, the Air Marshal just thought you'd enjoy the change of scenery. We're against it; you are a valuable asset to us. Quite valuable, but your coming—driving a bomber, will put a good deal of munitions into Germany, right where they don't want them. But...."

"But...?"

"I don't agree, as I've said. I feel you're more valuable doing what you're doing...and remaining alive. I feel this...*thing*, is a needless risk of asset—sorry for the term. The Air Marshal—well, he said you'd go and we were to give you the *opportunity*."

I pondered the thought of getting shot at again and shuddered inwardly. Yet, there was excitement in the thought, some temptation and sudden adrenaline. Maybe because it would be in a Lancaster and dropping bombs: my lifelong dream. I'd always been interested in what the boys did in Bomber Command.

"Oh, all right. I'll do it....where's it going to be...?"

The waiter showed up then with another tray completely covered with our breakfasts. Clyde smiled sadly and moved his cup and saucer.

"Oh that looks lovely, doesn't it?"

The waiter tipped out a tray stand and carefully lowered his burden onto it. Lifting lids with a large white napkin, he served our warm plates. He'd brought another pot of coffee and drained our pot, replacing it with the fresh one. He also brought another cream pitcher and sugar bowl. Apparently he knew Lord Whittwell.

"Will there be anything else, gentlemen?"

I shook my head. "No...this looks quite nice, thanks."

"We will let you know, Albert" Clyde said, nodding a dismissal to the waiter as if he did it every meal, which he probably did. I expected they had servants at his father's houses.

After the waiter was out of earshot, Clyde began elaborating on the planned mission over Germany, while he sliced one end off a sausage.

"Can't actually tell you that much, Old Boy...don't even know myself. Out of my realm of 'need to know', if you know what I mean."

He held up for inspection the taunt-skinned sausage morsel he'd speared on the end of his fork, then popped it in his mouth soundly. I wondered if anything was really out of his realm.

"Then, I can assume it will be in enemy territory...all those bombs...someone will tell me where to drop them?"

"Oh I do hope so old chap. Frightfully messy if they didn't. Make even more history, wouldn't it...bad stuff. Happens you know, though? Happens sometime. Yes—yes..." he mumbled, shaking his head as he chewed vigorously, "...wrong kind of history."

"Ok..." I broke my egg yolks with a piece of sausage on the end of my fork and dipped in, holding a piece of toast ready in my other hand, "...if I can't know where, how about when and what do I need to do? I've never really flown loaded Lancasters, you know."

Clyde had sorted through the cold toast slices and was soon smearing bright orange marmalade around a piece, already dripping butter.

"The day after tomorrow—afternoon—late briefing. Unfortunately, could meet my doll and her friend during that time. I ask you, why must they get up so early and work so late in these military operations? Could as easy do them in the middle of the day, when everyone's awake, working...ready? I shall never understand that...anyway, Command Center—you know where it is. At the gate, there'll be a pass waiting for you. Report to the briefing room. I'll be there with some of those togs you blokes wear...wool-skins, you know. They'll furnish charts, maps, whatever...of that sort of thing—aircraft, too. Don't be late, or it's my bum the Air Marshal will go for."

I nodded, chewing. The food tasted good to me. If I closed my mind, looking across the cheery decor and ignored the uniforms passing on the other side of the gauze curtains, I could almost convince myself there was not a war on.

"Now," Clyde started up again, about tonight and my, uh...*friend*...are you *certain*...Old Boy? Her friend has a—a...shall we say, a reputation..."

CHAPTER

13

Visitors

Since I'd been with Alex, I felt much better about my future. He was really a dream come true, representing something I didn't have from Johan, or any other man I'd known: stability. He was also extremely bright, kind, generous and understanding. For God's sake, how could someone like him...almost an enemy, say he loved me and then truly...attempt to help me?

Nevertheless, without fail, I'd been waking in the middle of the night, thinking again of what *Herr* Strauser had warned me about...the *SS* prying into my past.

As I told Alex, the letter from Johan's mother was short and direct. Her husband had been taken away by the *SS*, who had come, she said, as thieves in the darkness. She was now alone, she'd written and had thought she was without anyone in the world but Johan, until my letter arrived, for which, she thanked me. But it was no use, she'd written. Her most fervent inquiries had yielded nothing from the authorities as to the whereabouts of her husband. They were, she wrote, as fearful of the *SS* as she.

No, she'd also written, she was not aware of our child, or of me. Let alone any relationships her son had had. Could it be true...did I have some proof of this? Where was the supposed grandchild? She looked forward to meeting me sometime, she wrote. She hoped I would bring our child to visit. What was her name? She had asked.

I debated whether I should write her back and tell her that her son was now also dead and her granddaughter's life was probably in jeopardy.

I'd returned from one of my trips into the country—in the Trondheim area—just this evening, having been called back by Herman. He said the Director—*Herr* Strauser, wished to call an important staff meeting for the following morning, early. It was very important, he'd said when he telephoned my hotel in Trondheim; I should take the first train he stressed. Unusually polite, I'd thought after hanging up. Could Herman be turning over a new leaf, I wondered.

Of course with such short notice I was unable to purchase a ticket, so I had to use my priority credentials and have someone else put off the train so I could get a seat. I disliked having to do that but my superior had more or less demanded that I return. What could be that important, I wondered, about a staff meeting. I had never been recalled before. My suspicions mounted; Herman was too polite, for him.

I'd gotten home without any delays but didn't have much to heat at my house. By early evening I'd grown cold and wanted to get some water starting to heat. I had planned to eat some bread and cheese before going to bed. I went to the cellar to pile more firewood on my closet trolley so it would be ready again in the morning.

I had recently installed a gas ring so I could now prepare faster meals. I was heating water for tea and was just about to start the fires in the stoves when someone knocked on my front door. I looked at the kitchen clock. It was nearly nine...who would that be this time of night, I wondered, grabbing my torch.

Opening the front door I looked into the beady eyes of a tall man in civilian clothing. He shielded his eyes from the stabbing beam of my torch. He didn't remove his hat when I appeared, nor did he greet me, which meant he also had no manners. I immediately distrusted him. Behind him, there stood an army officer and a sergeant in uniform. I noticed the *Waffen SS* emblem on the offic-

er's uniform collar and suspected immediately why I had been recalled that day.

"*Frau* Stopff?" the civilian asked me, as if he already knew
who I was.

"I am *Fräulein* Stopff."

"*Fräulein*...we would like to come inside, please...I am *Herr*
Swartz and this is *Waffen-SS-Sturmbannfuhrer* Hestberger, who has
come from Oslo to ask you some questions."

Even before I had an opportunity to respond, he'd stepped
in front of me but stopped in the foyer, turning to wait for me and the
others. The *Sturmbannfuhrer*, who was quite obese, came next,
suggesting by holding out his hand, palm outmost, that I should step
in and follow *Herr* Swartz. I doubted it was his manners that prompted
such behavior; more that he did not wish to offer me the opportunity
to escape. He turned to the Sergeant.

"Go to the rear door and remain on guard outside, Sergeant. We will call out if you are needed. Remain at your post until
summoned."

The Sergeant saluted smartly and *Herr* Swartz closed the
door, motioning again that I should precede him into the house.

I walked into the parlor, turned on the lights. It was cold in
the room.

"You are just in time, gentlemen. I have been fortunate
enough to have *acquired* some coffee. Will you have time for
coffee...gentlemen?"

SS-Sturmbannfuhrer Hestberger replied. "You have cof-
fee? How...well, *yes*...we *will* have coffee...but first, *Fräulein* Stopff,
I would like to ask you about your relationship with a Jew named
Johan..."

"*Götterdämmerung!*" It is very cold in this room, *Fräulein*..."
he was interrupted by *Herr* Swartz, "is there no warmer room in the
house where we can talk?" Both men glanced around as if to find
one.

"I have only just returned from Trondheim...," I almost said,
as you are aware, "...and I have not yet started the fires."

"Then do so, by all means," *Herr* Swartz replied. "Our
questions can wait for the fire...and the coffee. Where, may I ask,
did you obtain coffee in these times, *Fräulein?*

"A Swedish man I met in my work gave it to me. I have been saving it for a special occasion, *Herr* Swartz."

"Hah—those damn Swedes…always conniving, working the black market…taking profits from the war—just like the Swiss."

"The water is just about hot on the gas ring, Gentlemen. Let me add the coffee and then I will build a fire in the stove."

"Yes, *Fräulein*, do that."

I started toward the kitchen and the officer groaned, lifted his bulk, rising to follow. I stopped.

"I do not need any assistance, thank you Sir."

"I am sure you do not, *Fräulein*, but I would prefer you were not out of our sight. You might be thinking of…*disappearing*, before you have an opportunity to answer some questions. Fraternizing with a Jew and a spy…they are both capital crimes against the *Reich*…I am certain you are aware of the punishment for either of these."

I said nothing, but walked directly into the kitchen and got out the remainder of the coffee Alex had left for our next get-together. I also took out some of the buns I'd baked the day before going to Trondheim and arranged them on a plate. They were a little stale. I took out a separate plate and a larger coffee mug for the Sergeant. My mind was racing. They would have come alone, had they planned only to question me, I thought. The Sergeant guarding the back porch door was to be my escort when we left I guessed, if they took me away. I could sense it. Somehow, they have linked me to Johan. Because we participated early in *Lebensborn* and with Johan being a Jew, our child was a blight that suddenly appeared in *Herr* Himmler's pet project…and it must be *erased*, my superior, *Herr* Strauser had said. I shuddered. The Sergeant, *Herr* Swartz and the *Sturmbann-fuhrer* were here to do that to me, too, now that Johan had been removed. Had they already killed my daughter, I wondered? I must find out. Somehow, I must learn the truth before deciding what to do. Maybe they plan to kill me…here, in my house.

"That looks very tasty, *Fräulein*, have you any other black market goodies to serve?" my fat companion inquired, greedily.

"Uhhh…no, I do not…Yes…yes I do…I have some chocolates."

"Chocolates! *You have*…ummmm, where are they? Get

them out, too, by all means."

"The box has already been opened...I'm afraid and I don't know whether I have enough for..." I inclined my head in the direction of the parlor and *Herr* Swartz and lowered my voice,"...everyone."

I'd finished lighting the kindling in the cook stove as we spoke. I took some more wood from the closet. I would have to get more firewood for the heater in the parlor, I thought...if they let me stay that long. I must think—*plan.*

"Well, if there is only enough for one...I will have them then. He can content himself with a—stale bun, he said," nibbling on the corner of one of the rolls. He followed me over to the stove and watched as I added the larger pieces of wood. The water had begun to boil so I took down the coffee tin and spooned a generous amount of the beans into the grinder.

"Would you like to grind this while I take the cups into the next room," I said, handing him the grinder. He was confused for a moment, but then took it while I picked up the tray of cups and saucers.

Fetching the wood had given me a plan. Putting down the tray again, I went to the cupboard and took out a full box of Swiss chocolates. I carried it over to the table where the *Sturmbannfuhrer* was grinding the coffee.

"I see the chocolate box is still unopened. I made a mistake...there will be enough to share with *Herr* Swartz, after all."

He looked disappointed, as I removed the wrapping and the cover and the odor of sweet chocolate mixed with the smell of freshly ground coffee. One could almost see the *Sturmbannfuhrer* salivating with greed.

"Here..." I offered him a sample. He switched hands with the bun, but paused, hand over the box, unable to make a selection. I took the box away again, before he'd made a selection and removed one for myself to taste.

"Ummmmm...delicious."

"Wait...I didn't....even..."

"Here..." I held the box out again. "Better get a couple pieces...while they last.

Without hesitating this time, he snatched the whole box from me and immediately stuffed two of the pieces in his mouth. I picked up the coffee grinder and poured the contents of the little drawer into the boiling water, removed the pot from the gas ring and set it on the counter beside the sink, for the grounds to steep and settle.

"I'll take the buns in now, *Sturmbannfuhrer.*" He'd put the box of candy back on the table and was chewing, both cheeks stuffed.

"Do you wish more, or should I take the box in, now?"

Unable to speak, he picked up the box again, shaking his head and gesturing with his other hand for me to go.

I picked up the plate of buns and started for the parlor. I must get out of here now, regardless of whether they have killed my child yet, or not. They may execute me, even if they have not yet killed her. If they have not yet harmed her, I must find her and get to her before they can carry out the inevitable. But...I am dead, one way or the other. If I can save her life first...

"Here you are, *Herr* Swartz. The coffee is about ready. I've also some buns here and also...I've found a box of Swiss chocolates?"

He looked at me and smiled behind the little eyes. "This will not help, you know, *Fräulein*...all this special food. You know we believe you to be guilty of fraternization, to say the least and we must ask these questions and then..." his voice trailed off behind another smile.

"And then you will do your duty, *Herr* Swartz, *correct?*"

"Of course, one must do...what one must do."

"Tell me, *Herr* Swartz, were you the one who...*took care* of Johan, my...*lover.*"

"Of course not, *Fräulein*, I do not go anywhere near the Russian front...that was someone else—infantry possibly." He spat the word as if they were underlings.

"Ah...you prefer to remain in...*comfortable*, Norway, safe from the dangerous area of war."

"Insult will certainly not help you either, *Fräulein*...it can only harm you cause."

"*My cause?* My cause has nothing to do with this madness, *Herr* Swartz. I suppose it was you...also wishing to remain *safe*, who erased—excuse me, took care of Johan's and my little mistake...in safe, Germany?"

"No it was not, *Fräulein*...that task has not yet been undertaken, but as soon as I can arrange it, I will look into it and see that it is, personally, you can rest assured of that."

I picked up one of the cups from the tray, pretending to polish a nonexistent spot on it.

My mind was made up then—my plan. The final bolt was shot. I let the cup fall onto the wood floor, where it broke into pieces.

"*Oh, shisen*!" I said under my breath, "I have just bought this set, too." I bent and began to gather up the pieces. "I'll bring another cup...with the coffee, Herr Swartz."

I returned to the kitchen to find the *Sturmbannfuhrer* still stuffing chocolates.

"Guess what, *Herr* Swartz has told me he has a passion for chocolate...especially Swiss chocolates. I must take the box in now."

I picked it up and paused in front of the glutton, standing there like a frustrated child about to lose his treats. He stared greedily at the box in my hand.

"I suppose *Herr* Swartz will devour these...would you not prefer to come in now and *help* him to eat the remaining pieces?

I started for the parlor with him close behind. Herr Swartz looked up, a half-eaten roll in his hand.

"Ah—the Swiss chocolates...my favorite." I put the box beside the plate of rolls as he put down the roll he'd been eating.

"I'll bring the coffee now, then start the fire," I said, returning to the kitchen.

I stooped in front of the sink and opening the door removed a small can from the rear of the cupboard, stood up and quietly placed it on the counter. From the drawer I quickly removed a large spoon and used the handle to pry off the can's cover. Glancing over my shoulder, I reversed the spoon and walked over to the coffeepot. I tipped the can and began spooning the white powder into the steaming coffee. I thought four would be enough but not so much they could taste the poison, but as an afterthought, added another heaping spoonfull.

I replaced the can cover and returned it beneath the cupboard. I had just stood up again when the *Sturmbannfuhrer* returned, a roll in each hand.

"Is the coffee ready, *Fräulein?* It really smells good."

"Just now, it is ready...but, would you give this to the Sergeant, first?"

I was still stirring the pot but quickly began pouring a cup for him and nervously placed it on the plate, beside the buns. I had almost been caught with the arsenic can.

"My hands are full, *Fräulein*, open the door and give it to him, yourself.."

I unlocked the back door, took the plate, opened the door and walked across the small porch. The young Sergeant stood just outside on the step.

"I thought you would like this, Sergeant...the others are having theirs in the parlor. It is *real* coffee! They said to tell you it would be another half hour...before they were ready...all right?"

"*Danka, Fräulein*," he said, his voice shaking with the cold. "*Real* coffee?"

"Yes, *really.* Will this be enough for now, Sergeant? I'll bring more in a few minutes when I can get away, but drink this first. Oh...you'd better hurry, though...they will drink it all before you have time for another cup."

I went back through the kitchen door and turning the latch as I closed it, again, locked it.

The officer had finished one roll and was waiting. "There...he was cold," I said, "...the Sergeant."

The *Sturmbannfuhrer* only nodded, "Ja—ja..."

"Shall we take in your coffee, now?"

He followed me into the parlor and I carefullly poured two cups full.

"Oh, I have forgotten. I broke one of the cups," I said, setting the pot down on the tray. The *Sturmbannfuhrer* was at the chocolates, again. I noticed half the rolls were missing and nearly all the chocolates had disappeared.

"I'll get another cup for myself and return." I picked up the pot again and stood in front of them. "Perhaps, I should offer the Sergeant another cup full. I have given him a large mug so he can have enough to keep him warm...outside."

"No—leave the pot! Forget the Sergeant... he has had enough already; just get your cup and come right back....and, do you have milk? Bring it too, if you do."

I smiled bitterly, returning the pot to the tray and walked back to the kitchen, took another cup from the cupboard. I had no milk for them. Back in the parlor, I sat down, poured half a cup and pretended to drink. I broke a roll in half and nibbled it. The two men, both with mouths full, were chewing rapidly and drinking greedily, each trying to be certain to get his share.

"I'll go to fetch some wood. Will one of you help me make a fire in the stove? I am very cold."

Herr Swartz, his mouth full with another bite from the bun, merely waved his roll that I should go, nodding his head and sipping the hot coffee with the other hand.

I walked back to the kitchen, waited a few seconds to see they were not following. Picking up my suitcase, still packed from my Trondheim trip I went to the closet where the empty wood trolley was waiting. I carefully opened the door, placed my suitcase on the platform, made certain the little hand brake was locked and squatting very low, duck-walked onto the platform and sat on my suitcase. I leaned in and slowly closed the closet door from inside the shaft leading to the basement.

It was very dark. The only light came from the kitchen, peeking through the cracks around the closet door. I reached up with both hands and slowly moved the handle on the brake mechanism that released its grip on the pulley ropes. I felt the platform lurch and then begin moving downward in little jerks. The pulley squeaked and I felt the platform, loaded with a counterbalance of bricks, pass me in the darkness on its way up. Then I felt a firm thump as I landed on the basement floor. I locked the brake lever again, took a careful step onto the cellar floor to check that it would hold the bricks, suspended high above my head in the kitchen closet. It held. I stooped in the darkness, felt for my suitcase handle and began working my way through the obstacles in the basement, over to the wall, then the doorway and the stair that lead to the exterior door, invisible from either of the two house entrances. In less than a minute from entering the kitchen closet, I was on the street.

The *SS* staff car parked near the front of my little house was a nine-passenger Mercedes. I considered whether to follow my original plan and proceed directly to the city and try to catch a train. Hesitantly, I tip-toed to the driver's side window and peeked inside. There was no one in the driver's seat, or in the back seats. I opened the door and got behind the wheel, feeling for an ignition key. It was there; how trusting. Who in Norway would dare to steal an official *SS* staff vehicle, a crime probably punishable by death? I stepped back onto the street, snatched my valise and put it in the passenger seat.

I started the engine, engaged the clutch, shifted it into first gear and pulled away.

"I would..." I said aloud, grinning madly in the darkness "...Greta Stopff would...she will do *anything* now—anything to save her Sophia."

CHAPTER

CHAPTER
14

The Air Raid—A view from above

I'd gone shopping that afternoon after Clyde left me in a taxi, hoping to pick up some toiletries and other items unavailable in Scandinavia. I was tired by that time and I retired early after eating alone in the hotel's dining room. I enjoyed dining in the midst of wartime Britain again. The comings and goings of the mostly service officers, with wives or girlfriends was entertaining enough, that I remained over the dessert and coffee with an extra brandy, just to listen and watch the goings-on.

I slept well that night, rising early the following morning to meet a staff car, arranged by Clyde. It carried me out to the station where I'd previously trained in one of the newer Lancaster bombers, prior to beginning the ABA venture.

Later, suited up and briefed, I went through the checklist with a competent and experienced pilot who seemed to be overly admirable of my long time in Fighter Command.

"And you're still alive," he remarked, shaking his head. "After all those missions. Remarkable."

"Luck," I'd replied, "I pinch myself each morning to prove it."

We talked a bit about the differences in Lancs and Manchesters; I didn't mention the German aircraft I'd flown, not wanting to let him in on the ABA venture. We then took the single Lancaster up for a couple of hours of in-air maneuvers, takeoffs and landings. There were no problems. I was duly cautioned that the bomb load would significantly reduce the lift-off capabilities of the ship, but that there was plenty of runway to handle it. I remembered that from my earlier barge battles over the coast of France, but that was a daylight raid

Overall, everything went well. That afternoon, I walked around the city. I badly needed and got the exercise and it helped sooth my pre-flight jitters. That evening I had another dreamless sleep, taking another brisk walk the next morning after a hearty breakfast. After the staff car returned me to the Lennox by early afternoon and I just lay around, trying to get some sleep for the long, all-night run to come. I wasn't that fatigued and the jitters were still with me. I probably slept an hour thanks to the earlier exercise and fresh air. I got up, bathed and dressed in a flight officer's uniform they'd provided, since I only had *ABA* uniforms.

As I came out of the elevator into the lobby, the hotel porter stopped me as I passed the front desk.

"Captain Andersson, you have a dispatch that arrived, Sir." He handed me an envelope. "It was delivered earlier this morning. I hope it wasn't too important…you'd said you didn't wish to be disturbed?"

I noticed the *ABA* insignia in the corner. I thanked him, thinking it must be travel orders for the return flight. I didn't bother with it and tucked it in my trouser pocket. The day before, they'd sent word the alternate mechanics and a new engine was being ferried down from Stockholm. Repairs would likely be completed for a trial flight in a week.

I'll read it later, I thought to myself and promptly forgot the envelope, my mind on the coming mission. Just then the staff car drew up beneath the hotel portico: give it a read in the plane, I thought, again, if I have time.

At the station again, I changed with my crew. As I donned my flying kit I folded the ABA envelope and stuffed it into the thigh pocket of my sheepskin flight pants; then we headed for the briefing. The flight briefing room was crowded. Pilot officers occupied every chair and stood in every inch of space along the walls and in the rear of the room, by the time the briefing finally began. We were told up-front that there were several, simultaneous briefings for officers and crews due to the size of the mission. We had a ceremonial intro by the Air Marshal and before he turned it over, he had a few words for the group:

"You chaps are no doubt aware that big things are happening and for the success of this operation...absolute secrecy is necessary. Most every one of you knows one another, but you can't know everyone. But won't you please take a good look at the other crewmen around the room...look over your mates to each side."

We all did. I got a couple of glances but wasn't challenged

"Do you see anyone in this room you think should not be in attendance? Please don't hesitate to speak up...he could be a *Jerry* spy."

Several crewmen looked queerly at their mates, as if they were about to turn them in...but no one spoke up. After a moment the Air Marshal smiled and stepped back: "Thank you...carry on," he said stepping back and turning the next phase over to another officer briefer who proved to be an no-nonsense Air Vice Marshal. Without a word, he drew aside the large curtain that had been covering the map for the night's mission. We saw a large map of northwestern Europe and England.

"Gentlemen...your target tonight will be Köln—in northwestern Germany."

There followed a chorus of groans and mumbled comments about inept fighter cover, heavy flak and fuel. The Air Marshal ignored the buzz of voices, pausing for five seconds, before plunging right into the detailed briefing, swinging his stick around the map.

After he'd finished outlining the mission, he called for questions. There were many from the regular pilots. I surmised by the nature of some of the inquiries that many of the men had little experience flying cross-country, let alone at night. It seemed there would be a lot of us and it wouldn't be an easy run with the headwind we would be battling en route. I began to understand why they'd asked me to fly one of the lead airplanes. Experienced pilots, let alone bomber pilots, were spread very thin in England.

"Were any of them easy..." someone in ranks echoed behind me about an earlier remark by a green pilot officer.

The experienced pilots knew the strong headwind, slowing our ground speed, meant an easier job for the enemy anti-aircraft gunners. We'd be sitting ducks for the flak coming up from the AA guns on the ground, especially with a full moon: "...silhouetted geese," someone said. We should all pray for cloud, I thought...I'd already been doing it.

Command, thanks to Clyde, had asked for me to "ride along" and steady 3-Group. They'd recently lost their leading pilot officer and crew. Eighty percent of the group had less than five missions. Command felt it might lend a lot of confidence to the boys to have an old Hurricane and Spit driver at the controls of one of their *Lancs*.

I wasn't so sure; I wondered if it might not be more intimidating. Of course, my true identity wasn't to be revealed and I wondered afterwards, why no one beside Clyde considered the risk I'd be subjected to and measure it against what they had me doing in Scandinavia. Had /been in command, in retrospect, I wouldn't have sent me—or even permitted any investment of like personnel to accompany the flight, thinking it would jeopardize Birgitta's mission. I was beginning to have second thoughts, about the wisdom of the higher-ups in Bomber Command and MI-5, by that time. The risk far outweighed the potential gain, in my opinion. Too late...I thought—too late as the briefing continued.

I'd been advised that near the end of the briefing they would introduce me as Group Captain Andersson. They finally got around to it and asked me to stand. I got up and then sat right down again and listened, embarrassed, while he related a bit about my total time in Fighter Command. "Watch him Mates, in case he tries to turn out one your Lancs onto the tail of a Jerry 109. He'll have the wings off her before he's through."

That got a big laugh and everyone strained to see where I was sitting.

""He's a proven pilot, Lads and he's eager to see if he can have as much fun in a bomber as a kite, so...let's see if we can give him a real show tonight." That got some applause from the crews.

"Anyway...he knows what he's up to and will take 3-Group straight down the throat of the Köln target...let's welcome him to Bomber Command. Another round of applause followed. I wasn't above giving them their chance a publicity promotion to cheer the boys on. God knew few enough would be returning in the morning.

Our ship'd been assigned the radio code identifier of "A-for-apple" and were to be part of 3-Group, Squadron 2. I familiarized myself with the rank and file once more in my head: Squadrons were part of Groups, which were part of a Command. Bomber Command comprised several Groups: 1-Group, 5-Group and so on and 3-Group comprised several squadrons.

My second officer was a flight engineer by training. He was new to bombers and flying in general. After listening to some of his questions, I had serious concerns about his experience. He was a pilot understudy and had been trained somewhat in Manchesters. I wondered whether he might be incapable of maintaining the string formation we would be holding, in the darkness.

If the flak got heavy—if we were hit and I was injured or killed, I seriously doubted his ability to bring the ship home, without another ship to follow. I had other things to worry about, though I didn't appreciate a pilot trainee as my flight engineer, given my own low time in bombers. But I supposed they had no one experienced to share.

The briefing concluded at last and there was time for chapel, or whatever else we wished to do before heading out. I went outside and hitched a ride out to the flight line in order to check out my Lanc.

All of us in 3-Group were manning Avro Lancasters—four-engined, all-metal bombers—but actually, redesigned Manchesters. These ships were new to Bomber Command and as of yet not fully proven. My chief mechanic, after I introduced myself and admitted some familiarity with the earlier design of the ships, informed me that so far they'd been great performers, but he cautioned me:

"Keep an eye on the engines...Rolls-Royce Vultures...they're newly-fitted and an unproven design. They're newer than the ships and have already become troublesome to the ground crew fitters. Little things, mostly, but still—we've lost a few: just seized up from loss of oil pressure."

"Thanks...that's nice information to know...*now.*"

I walked around the ship with the chief fitter. My observer

and the second pilot-to-be, the *newbie* Ajax, accompanied us. We finished the inspections and separated, my second and I ready to do our own flight check. I asked him for the checklist, but he didn't have it, so I told him to go get one and then made him hold it, reading off the items as I checked them out on the walk-round of the ship. It'd been embarrassing for him, in front of the others, but it was unforgivable and I would have grounded any other crew member for the infraction had I been in full-time command of a bomber flight.

Once inside the Lanc, he sat in the folding, flight engineer's seat to my right. Ajax was as green as summer grass. He was a newly qualified flight engineer...just barely and, supposedly, pilot as well. He was very nervous and couldn't seem to keep his mind on the checklist as we'd circled the aircraft, earlier.

The inspection should have been the other way around—him doing the inspecting; but I didn't trust him. As we'd gone around, him reading from the checklist, I inspected additional areas and items—not even on the list, which I suspected, could cause us problems. I laid it down to fighter pilots instinct. Better safe than sorry.

I'd had to leave the armaments and bombs to Forbes, our bomb-aimer and the other fitters on the ground, who knew something of them. I could see some bombs were the delayed acid fuse types, with their characteristic propellers mounted on the rear, behind the tail fins. Once the bombs left the bombay and began falling, these propellers would begin to spin from the air speeding past and would eventually spin completely off during their descent to target, only then, safely away from the aircraft, were their acid fuses armed for a delayed explosion. After striking and burying themselves deep in the ground, some fuses were set for to explode up to 140 hours later. These 1000 pounders, packed with high explosive and/or incendiary, wrought terror in the hearts of German repair workers at factories. Set as they were with variable, long delay fuses, they would suddenly explode without warning, hours or days after they'd been dropped. Once the factory workers learned of this practice, German authorities were hard pressed to get workers or clean-up personnel into a bomb-damaged factory. In total, tonight our Lanc's bomb load was around 14,000 lbs.

Aside from Ajax the remainder of the six crewmembers seemed competent enough. So in the early evening light they joined us in the aircraft, taking their individual places. Everyone began the final check off with me reading the list:

"OK gentlemen...and I use the term broadly, by the odor on your breaths this evening...ready to check out our systems. Wireless operator, wireless OK?"

"Wireless OK, Cap."

"Oxygen OK...?"

"Oxygen's OK, Sir."

And so it went as we checked off the assorted flight systems. Finally, I shouted through my little side window to the fitter standing by on the ground:

"OK to start engines?"

"OK for starting up Cap."

"All right...stand clear, starting starboard side."

I set the switch. "Contact!"

The starter whirred and groaned as the prop slowly rotated, kicked a few times before the engine caught with a roar. The prop turned into a blur and blew gray exhaust back in a steady stream. The engine began leveling off smoothly as we adjusted the air/fuel mixture and the smoke cleared.

Then the same for the port side engine, until it and eventually, all four engines were ticking over smoothly. As the engines warmed I adjusted the pitch control, exercised the flaps, then set the directional gyro to match the magnetic compass. Once that was completed I finished running up each engine, checking the magnetos on both sides. Another glance round and I finally signed the logbook, handed it down to the fitter below. Before I closed my window and waved the wheel chocks away I waved away the stepladder and Ajax saw the hatch cover secure.

The navigator Phillips was seated directly behind me at a small table, facing the port side. Forbes, the bomb-aimer, was lying forward in his Perspex bubble, checking his precious bombsight, prior to assuming the sitting position for operation of the nose machine gun, when we neared fighter territory.

Glancing out the cockpit I noticed the other crews seemed to be ahead of us in their pre-flights. Still a bit unfamiliar with the new aircraft and crew, I'd taken my time. Ajax was fussing and talking too much. I finally told him if he didn't slow down and pay closer attention, he'd kill an aircraft crew some day and himself along with them.

That comment seemed to sober him and after a while he relaxed somewhat. I think he sort of left it in my hands at that point. If I were training him, I wouldn't have let that stand. But, as it was, I wasn't planning to fly another mission with him anyway, or anyone else. I didn't care beyond the fact that I'd probably make a report in the debriefing, recommending that he be grounded until he could prove his rank. I wanted to come back alive and it went without saying, that any potential crew of his would too. Besides, I had plans with Greta.

The aircraft in front of us began revving up and was soon waddling onto the tarmac. Clamping his starboard-side wheel brake, he swung the massive bomber around in a ninety-degree pivot, following the others toward the marshaling point marked by the dim runway lights. We soon followed, starting and stopping the aircraft to position it until it was our turn at the runway.

Finally, we pivoted sharply and faced into the wind at the end of the runway. I was holding both foot brakes with the rudder pedals while maintaining some revs on the engines, keeping them hot and clean. Ready to go, we sat staring toward the windows of the control office, waiting for our takeoff clearance.

After thirty seconds, a green light blinded at us in the dusk. I spoke into the interphone:

"Stand by now…we're taking off."

I eased the throttles up to full and felt the ship pulling on the locked wheels. Once the revs were up, I relaxed my feet on the pedals. The aircraft shuddered and began lumbering forward along the tarmac, pointing into the wind for takeoff. As our ground speed slowly increased the dim runway lights flicked past, faster and faster on each side. When I felt free movement on the control wheel, I pulled back, gradually bringing her off the ground. When the wheels lost contact, I eased the control forward again to let her gather herself for the climb out as I pulled up the undercarriage control lever and the indicator lights cycled from green, to red then locked and went out. She hung there for a moment as our airspeed slowly increased and I brought pressure back on the control again and we slowly began to climb into the darkness.

The night before I'd had a little over three hours time flying practice in this same Lanc. The controls felt about the same, even with the additional weight of full bomb bays, crew and small arms ammunition. Her climb speed indicated the added weight, however and I didn't want to be fooled by her feel now and stall her on climb out. It was now nearly totally dark, though I could still see some glow on the horizon. It had also begun to rain as we'd lifted off in the sunset. We were well up before reaching the end of the field, which impressed me. I'd expected the ship would use most of the runway, loaded as she was and considering the low barometric pressure. I watched the attitude indicator on the panel to insure we maintained a shallow climb, until I finally felt it was safe to let Ajax take over.

"She's all yours, Ajax."

He seemed surprised and pleased as he leaned forward, taking over the yoke on his side. I sat back and alternately watched him and the instruments, as he held the climb and we moved ever higher, gaining altitude along with the rest of our winged armada.

She continued to climb with ease, if not haste, not seeming to lug, labor, wallow, or weave about too much. All four engines hummed as smoothly as seemed possible, with Ajax on the throttle handles, trying to synchronize the engines. He was playing them more like a four-instrument orchestra, actually. But he wasn't harming anything, as he learned, so I left him alone to it, continuing to climb the ship on course.

I stayed on task, passing on cautions and instructions from time to time, for mixture settings and engine syncronization. I helped him trim the aircraft when necessary, knowing I'd be stepping in again when we had to throttle back at cruising altitude. I didn't want to give him anything other than confidence from this flight, in case he had to bring the ship home, if something happened to me. Leave someone else to his instruction, later, I reasoned, if he lives long enough. I'm only here for this one run. A greenhorn wasn't going to kill me in an airplane over Belgium or Germany.

Over The Channel, we climbed steadily through the cloud. At each radio beacon we turned 180 degrees, back on our selves, again and again, as we continued climbing to the assembly altitude. Even before we were above the cloud we spotted the assembly flare, already let go by the higher, circling, lead ship. When we finally broke out, we turned slowly toward it, joining the gigantic circle of bombers forming up in the moonlight, high above the coast, over The Channel.

Before we got too close to our wing-mates, I advised the gunners to test fire their guns into the sea. Presently, our ship rattled and shook with the simultaneous firing, as they let go, proving the operability of our defensive armaments.

"Pity the fighter that comes against us tonight," I said into the interphone.

As the first ships came together at altitude and lined up in proper formation, one after the other, we turned southeasterly toward Germany. We must cross the Channel just above the northern French coast and high above the antiaircraft gun emplacements. Above those, and out of gun range, only German night fighters could threaten us.

I saw a squadron of American P51 Mustangs squaring up with the lead group. They carried wing pod tanks, offering them added fuel to enable them to reach the target along with us. They would afford us much fire cover for as long as they had fuel and ammunition.

Minding Ajax at the controls kept me busy until we were eventually lined up in single-file formation with our own flock and turning out on a course which would put us behind the groups already neatly tightened up in line and on their way. I assisted Ajax in trimming the throttles, mixture and generally telling him what he needed to know, finally breaking my vow against giving him instruction.

It wasn't until we were well away from the English coast that I remembered the brown envelope I'd put in my pocket; I wondered for a while as we droned south easterly, what the new orders from *ABA* entailed. Had they also decided to supply a replacement aircraft, with skeleton crew to be ferried back, in addition to a replacement engine? I glanced at the instruments and then over both wings of the aircraft. All seemed well. We rose and sank slowly in time with the other bombers, ahead and behind us, like ships sailing a gently rolling sea. Their engine exhausts burned bluish-orange under the flame arrestors, in the fading light of evening. Each aircraft had three, hooded lights mounted to each wing, with another three atop the fuselage. So long as the formation was lined up, airplane after airplane, you could keep the ship in front of you in sight. Each of the engine exhaust's glow pipes had flame arrestors to avoid being seen from the ground. These lights were only visible to a following ship, looking forward, toward the rear quarter of the preceding ship. If one wasn't flying close enough it was easy to lose sight of the ship in front of ou. Close meant a hundred feet...not much more. German fighters would try to follow bombers home on the darkest nights, getting into the pattern, beneath the bombers and attempt to shoot them down. In the earlier briefing, several ship's crews voiced concern they would attempt to do that to us, tonight.

Cloud was thick below the altitude of 20,000 feet, near maximum for the Lanc with our fuel and bomb load. The sun, just sinking below the horizon behind us, somewhat illuminated the backs of the ships ahead. On the ground, it would already be dark

We droned on for another hour. I spoke to Ajax from time to time and kept up a lively chatter with the crew. I cajoled them about the loneliness of piloting a Spit and that flying Lancs was just like a holiday with the family, so many people around to talk to.

"We'll be havin' tea 'n cucumber sandwiches over Belgium, Cap," one of the crew quipped.

"What? Not a whiskey?" I retorted.

"Savin' that for when we get back, Cap.

The bandying went on that way for a time; I hoped it might break the tension of them being unfamiliar with me and give them some confidence that I was willing and able to do my part, if they did theirs when we got in the stuff.

Even Ajax seemed to relax a little more as there came less and less to do now that we were at altitude. "Just keep it from running into anyone," I told him. "Simple, just stay between your wing mates and don't release the bomb load on top of anyone below when the time comes."

Finally, simply out of boredom, I extracted the brown envelope from my flight suit pocket and tore open the end, pulling out the contents. It was another envelope, which surprised me. I turned it over feeling it and then holding it close to the dim light of the dash. It bore a hand-written address—to me, at *ABA*'s office in Copenhagen. There was a German stamp in the corner, with a picture of Adolph Hitler's profile staring out my ship's window. In the dimness of the cockpit's red, night lighting, I squinted at the handwriting, finally realizing that it was from Greta. My heart jumped. I glanced at the ship ahead of us, then across at all four engines and turned back to scan the instruments, then back to the letter.

Someone had sent it through to me in *the* company mail. How'd they think of that, I wondered beginning to tear open the back flap...Clyde? I hesitated, pondering whether it would be wise to read it before the mission was even well-begun, let alone, finished. I didn't need any distractions right now. I glanced again at the aircraft ahead, then the instruments. I thought about it for another five minutes as we droned on into the headwind. I was soundlessly slapping the envelope against the thigh of my flight pants. What if I buy it on this run, I thought? Never know what she'd written. We continued on until finally, over Belgium, I tore off one end of the envelope, thinking it was probably cheerful news and would only uplift my spirits. Another instrument scan and glance at the ship ahead.

It was only a single page, written in Greta's small, neat hand, difficult to make out in the dimness. I glanced at the address again, recognizing her neat script: "*Herr* Alex Andersson" it said. "Personal." Ajax glanced over at me as I leaned forward tipping the page up so it would catch the red glow of the night instrument lighting.

"Watch the ships, Ajax," I said into my oxygen mask? "I've something here I must read."

Ajax sat upright quickly and a bit stiffly and took a new hold on the window frame.

"Got the course?" I asked, leaning over and touching the paper on the clip board strapped to his left thigh.

"Yes...yes Sir. I have the course, Sir."

"Good man...keep an eye on the our mates ahead."

I leaned back and watched him for a bit, just long enough to give him a little confidence but not so long as to give him the impression I didn't trust his piloting. He was driving, so to speak, now. He didn't appear as if he'd relaxed too much. Finally, I turned again to the letter. I held the page close, leaning forward again. It wasn't a long letter. I glanced ahead once more at the *companions* and then I began to read:

Min Kära Vän

I have only a moment to let you know what I am about. I have learned my little S. is indeed in trouble. I have been told by my superior that someone in the SS is looking into the parentage of my little S. Also, I have now seen a name on a list here in N. which routinely itemizes the products of Lebensborn in which one of the other of the parents is later proven unsuitable. It is a maintenance list. An adoptive could be placed on the list for assorted reasons, including finding contaminated heritage. A finding of this sort will result in the agency interven— ing and retrieving the problem child in order to ensure continued un contamination of the race.

I was shocked to find my own name and that of the father on this last list; further investigation revealed S. had been added, as well. The father of S. was dis— covered, you know, Kära, who that is. This means S. is indi—

241

gible to remain in the program
and is going to be removed, the
document states, to the east, most
likely I fear.

I have come to the decision that I
must find her immediately, Kära
Alex and bring her back to N. It
is *absolutely* *essential*. I have no
idea yet where she is living, but a
friend knows the whereabouts of
documents which disclose the names
of the adopted parents of products
and to where they have been adopted.
I should have a room at the Re—
ichland in Köln, by the time you
receive this letter, as I am well on
my way when I seal this note and
post to you as you may see a date
over the postage stamp. Keep safe
my darling and I shall try to do
the same. Once I have more in—
formation I will try to send you
another dispatch by the same means,
before I set out to wherever the
trail leads.

Wish me luck and Gods speed. I
shall find the dear thing and bring
her to the place she has always
meant to be: her mothers arms.
If I have difficulties, I will con—
tact you by this same means. I
do so wish you could be close to

me right now dearest.
All my love,
G

I'd looked up from the note three times, checking the position with the mates in front and the course on the DG. Ajax seemed to be alert and swiveling his neck in his perpetual scan. I stared forward through the Perspex windscreen into the darkness ahead, highlighted only by the exhaust glow from the engines on the ships in front. I was trying very hard to calm my hammering heart.

Köln—she'd written *Köln*. "*...I should have a room at the Reichland in Köln....*"

I reread the page again, my mind racing. We were on our way to Köln...*tonight's* bombing target. I frantically turned over the envelope, holding it close to the light. There wasn't a legible postmark date on Greta's envelope or the one from *ABA*. So I could only guess when she might have arrived and whether she could still be there. If she'd been successful, she'd probably already have left Köln to locate her daughter's whereabouts. If she had to search in the city itself, how long would she have had to remain in Köln? I tried to think. I supposed it depended on whether the search had been immediately successful...German bureaucracy...that was usually efficient. Possibly, she got in and got out and was now nearer her daughter, than Köln. When did she leave Norway, I wondered? When did she send the letter to *ABA*? Was she still there now...*where*, now?

The ship continued on course; we rose and fell in the wake of the ships ahead, our wings rocking slightly and Ajax appeared to be still somewhat tense, looking across each wing and fixating on the DG. I imagined his knuckles would be white beneath the sheepskin of his flight gloves. I glanced out the Perspex on both sides, then ahead. The glow of the ship's lights ahead was dimly visible. I thought about it—the power, the living, breathing creatures inside, huddled in sheep's wool from the earth below, barely able to keep the warmth contained, breathing our air from bottles. How silly, actually...war and what we go through to fight them. Turning to look out at the port wing, I watched the light blue blur of the two props for a moment, trying to calm my screaming nerves. If Greta were really in Köln, would she hear the raid warning sirens? Did they have air raid warnings? Would I, this evening, kill the woman I loved?

I shuddered at this thought. Ajax was squirming. He was having trouble holding our altitude and course in the buffeting wind and prop wash flung back from the ships preceding us. Watching him out of the corner of my eye made me want to slap him. He shouldn't be here. They shouldn't have sent someone so inept up here in second command of a bomber. He might never be capable of commanding a ship in combat. Crew lives would depend on him.

We continued rising and falling within the formation, turning slightly from side to side as Ajax learned to fly. I knew what the crew of the ship behind us was probably shouting through the panes of their own cockpit, when our airspeed slowed and they got too close for comfort. We maintained radio silence.

Without expressing any emotion, I casually spoke into the mask.

"Relax a while Ajax—I'll take 'er again."

"I'm doin' OK?"

I crammed the envelope back in the leg pocket.

"Sure, you are. But why don't you grab a portable oxygen bottle and go back and check the load...see how the mates are making out? If I need you again before you're finished, I'll shout."

"Right...Sir," he said, unstrapping his harness and standing before removing his mask hose and interphone connection, he said. "It's OK Sir...we're still on course." He struggled to untangle himself from his oxygen hose.

Glancing away, toward our companions in the dim moonlight, I replied, "Yes, I see that, Ajax. Good work." He turned and reconnected his oxygen mask to the carry-around tank. Crouching low, he disappeared along the catwalk toward the rear of the ship.

"Don't be too long....," I yelled, around my mask, "...we'll be picking up flak anytime now. The border shouldn't be too far ahead." But he couldn't hear me, by then.

Back in my mask, I said. "Phillips...what does it look like?" turning around slightly in my seat to glance at our navigator, who should have some idea of the time to target.

"We're over Belgium now Cap...have been for a half hour—forty five minutes. German frontier *innn...*" he hesitated, "...another half hour or so, then another forty—fifty minutes, depending on this headwind...to target. This east wind...it's a bugger, Sir...still."

"Thanks, Phillips. Keep me posted on the winds after we're over the border and update the ETA from time to time, too, will you?"

"Right, Sir."

"Oh...and Phillips...our current ground speed...any idea?"

"Not lately, Sir. I checked when we struck the coast...about an hour ago.

We were making a little better than 170 knots, more or less, probably less, as we close on the weather front."

"Airspeed...is this right?" I asked looking at my instruments in disbelief.

"'Bout 210, Sir...at the most...?"

"Yeah...*good God*, Phillips! At this rate we won't get there 'til Christmas."

"Right...could be better, Sir"

I nodded over my shoulder and shook my head as Phillips returned to his instruments and drawing the course information on his little desk beneath the red glow of his lamp. Though I couldn't see him, I knew what he was doing...flight path, wind—airspeed, compass deviation for wind angle, all calculated to derive our true course.

Nothing we could do about headwinds but hold the course...be a much faster ride home with that wind behind us then...if we got through the run alive. Command had advised in the briefing, we were the biggest flotilla yet to bomb Germany. And the slowest, I thought, now. It was important to begin the bomb-run on time, maintain our position and then to turn out quickly after letting go our load and resuming the proper bearing homeward. They'd emphasized that again and again.

"If you slow down in the darkness," the Op officer had said in the briefing, "you'll get over-flown by your own mates, behind you. Or worse, you'll get a load of bombs dropped on top of you, from one of ours, releasing their load from above you. If you have any problems, try not to lose altitude. Try to make it home via the shortest landfall point, maintaining as much flight time over land as possible in case you have to bail out, or crash land. We will be nearly a thousand ships," he'd said. "There will be some casualties."

I got on the interphone again: "Hanson in the tail...'n mid-upper and lower...you guys watching out for intruders?"

The phones crackled: "Yes Sir...I'm watchin'. Nothin' yet, Sir."

"Same here, Sir...nothing to report," came Upton's reply from the mid-upper turret. I waited a moment, waiting to hear from Elson in the lower turret.

"Elson...you there?"

Nothing.

"Elson...hey! Elson!"

Still nothing.

"Upton...go see what' the hells up with Elson...can you see him?"

"Yessir...he's moving his head, so he ain't froze. Just a sec Sir...I'll check."

I waited a few moments before the interphone crackled again.

"Sir...Ajax—he tripped on Elson's phone cord somehow, came unplugged when he came on the catwalk."

"Can you hear me now Elson?"

"Yeah, I can hear...I thought you guys were being awfully quiet."

"OK," I said, "thanks Upton...stay alert fellows...all of you...you know how *Jerry* can sneak into the formation. Anything suspicious...let's hear about it."

"Right Sir."

Our lumbering flight, with our decreased airspeed, made us very easy prey for fighters and flak. The earlier briefing had reported: "We are aware that *Jerry's* developed some sort of night-seeing radio beam or something. Command is still unsure of exactly what it can be. Previously, unless we were over the target, the Germans had a harder time finding us in their night fighters, until...this new thing. It's now as if they can see us at night."

I glanced around, remembering the warning. The hair on the back of my neck rose in anticipation.

"Anyway," the briefer continued, "their fighters will get right up under the squadron formation, no matter the darkness of the night, so they must have something. They've blown hell out of a few bombers before the flash of their guns gave them away. But by then, they'd already peeled off and disappeared into the darkness."

My quick scan didn't reveal anything. We were fortunate in that our *Lanc* hadn't yet had the lower gun turret removed, as had most of the other ships in Bomber Command and because of that we'd been charged with keeping special watch for anything suspicious, coming from below.

"Elson…you keeping at least one eye open down there for any night fighters sneaking in?"

"Absolutely, Sir," came his reply, "both of 'em, Sir."

"Can't ask for anything more, Elson. *Anything*? Just shout it out. OK?"

"Yessir."

"How's the heat in your suit?"

"Little problem getting the plug to work…but it seems OK now, Sir."

"Good—good Elson. Have the electrical guys take a gander at it when we get home."

"*Gander*…Sir?"

My Missouri dialect had thrown him. "Uh…when we get back…have the fitters check it—electrically…find the problem—the open circuit."

"Right, Sir. Will do."

Ten minutes later Ajax was back in the jump seat squirming anxiously as I concentrated to hold the course to target. I think the buffeting had grown worse, possibly the wind was changing. It had been forty minutes since Phillips had tapped me on the shoulder, indicating we were crossing into Germany.

Our fighter cover had left us, to return to station. German fighters would refrain from following us into the coming flak over the target, preferring to hang around the back edge, waiting for us on the other side, ready to meet us when and if we came out of the flak, preparing to turn for home.

Ahead of us the antiaircraft fire suddenly began. Intermittent at first, it grew heavier as we moved toward the target. Here and there we'd encounter a searchlight. Fortunately, they never seemed to stay on our ship. We were more than enough ships to go around and so far, they'd seemed to triangulate on someone else, thank God, pinning them in a triangle of light so the antiaircraft could train their guns on them. It was usually a deadly hold.

As the second wave of bombers, we would get some of the first heavy stuff. Over target, eventually at 19,000 feet the 105s and the 88s would also be able to reach up to us. But for now, only the 155s could get flak this high and so far, we'd not passed over any of the larger caliber batteries. Flak had been bursting harmlessly beneath us for a quite a while, contributing heavily to Ajax's anxiety.

Another five minutes and the 155s were beginning to lob shells. To the gunners on the ground we must have appeared like a wallpapered dome of wings and fuselages—Lancasters, Manchesters, Halifaxes...wherever they pointed their searchlight beams, they could have any one of us in the circle of light. As a result, they were also making the mistake of not concentrating their AA fire on any individual ship, but seemed to be sweeping the length of the formation, at random.

Long before we reached the target area we saw ahead of us a confusing maze of these searchlights stabbing the sky. Some appeared in small groups. Others were grouped together forming cones of five or more beams. We watched as one of these formed a cone of light on a luckless ship ahead of us. Caught and transfixed in their apex, as if pinned to the sky by the power of the lights, the point of the apex glowed with flickering, red bursts of concentrated flak detonations on and around the victim ship, doomed in the concentrated fire.

Even that was enough to pepper us constantly with shrapnel. It rattled against and through the ship from time to time, scaring the hell out of us to a man. Looking at the ground below, we could see little flashes of light, like firecrackers, coming from the emplacements of AA guns. And in just about twenty-nine seconds, the shell would get up to us and explode somewhere among the string formation of bombers, flinging bits of red-hot shrapnel tearing through our aircraft, clothing and flesh.

In preparation for our arrival, the Germans had started decoy fires on the ground in the outlying areas of the city, using dummy incendiaries and imitation fire blocks. These were placed far from the important targets, hoping to decoy a share of the bombers to disregard their bombsights and instead, bomb the already-burning fires of a more or less harmless, open area in the countryside.

Lights on the ground, previously lit with lines of our own reconnaissance flares, strung out like Christmas tree lights and now began to take on hot spots of glowing red buds ahead of us, from the first bomb explosions of the lead aircraft.

The raid soon developed well, with random sticks of incendiaries, which were beginning to zigzag across the terrain of the city below and ahead of us. The red glow began sparkling in incandescent white, until a solid red glow showed the beginnings of a tremendous fire somewhere in the city.

The looming dread surged up in me again, like nausea: Greta, was she was below us in the beginning maelstrom. And if she was, was she was safe, injured or even…already dead. Here and there the sky would suddenly light up in front of us when an aircraft exploded from the nearly impenetrable flak. The ground batteries must surely exhaust their ammunition soon…but still, the bombers continued to come.

From our vantage point there was much confusion from the gun flashes of the squadrons ahead of us, like photoflashes, bomb bursts and streams of tracer of all colors—all coming from the AA and the damn searchlights below. It was very troublesome to Ajax. And even more so, when our own air gunners were directing us to avoid a particularly heavy flak area ahead, or a group of specific searchlights, suggestions coming in all directions—all at the same time.

Phillips called out the remaining distance as we approached the target, maintaining our airspeed so as not to run atop another ship ahead of us. Forbes had now abandoned the front gun turret, sliding back and down to his bombsight. Earlier, I'd seen the first flares go into the targets—RAF Mosquito fighters had gone in advance to mark the target. Now, as we drew closer to the city we could see the individual explosions of the bombs from the first wave. They'd have dropped their bombs and already begun their outbound turn for home. God, I prayed, don't let Greta be down there.

Ajax'd returned the moment the AA started and now appeared to be almost too scared to speak, fumbling and fidgeting in the right seat. He'd also begun shaking noticeably. I could see his jaw quivering. I knew the feeling but could do nothing beyond quickly reaching across to pat his knee. Visibly, he was trying to gain control of himself. I was sure Phillips would be able to see him from his table behind me. I don't know whether he'd noticed and couldn't turn around to see. At any rate he'd be far too occupied at the moment with our course.

The bomb-aimer Forbes, literally had the ship now: we were flying it, following his guidance on course to the target.

"Stay with me Ajax—I'll keep her on course; you just watch the controls and the wing mates. Don't change the mixture or throttles and don't try to do anything unless something happens to me. If it does, Phillips can help you get what's left of me out of the seat. Then the ship's all yours and good luck to you. You know what to do...*from the briefing*? If we haven't unloaded yet, follow Forbes's lead until the bombs are gone...OK?"

He nodded without turning, tense as a kite string. Intermittent with the bursts of flak, which illuminated the sky around us, I could see more of the incendiaries begin to go up on the ground ahead. The leading ships had loosed most of their loads, now. Our group was next, with the majority of the bomb load still yet to come behind us. God, I thought, glancing at the fires below. How was anyone going to live through that onslaught? Why me, on the Köln run.

"Two minutes-ten, Sir." Phillips interrupted my thoughts, not even looking up from his instrument. I watched the directional gyro to confirm our heading and to follow Forbes's bomb-aiming. I glanced around just as the silhouette of a struggling Halifax moved out of the line ahead, dropping back and soon to pass off our port wing. They must have picked up some flak, or were having mechanical problems. As I looked a second time, the ship suddenly took a near direct burst of flak. Pieces of shrapnel sprang through our own fuselage, zinging, twanging and rattling against and through the hull. The Perspex window by my left shoulder, shattered into a spider web of plastic and the shrapnel piece just missed me and the instrument panel, passing harmlessly out the ship's ceiling, above. Somehow, Forbes maintained his concentration, or trance, unaware of the gaping hole above him and the flaming ship to our left.

The Halifax was now on fire. The ship was easily seen in the bright, trailing flame from her port side. She illuminated the whole line of the squadron, well forward.

"Fourty-five seconds Sir."

I felt a mighty strike of a concussion against the ship and instinctively bore hard to port on the yoke to counter the force as the Halifax suddenly exploded. Nearly, instantly, it disintegrated in a ball of trailing, tumbling flame. Her fuel tanks had gone. She and all within her, disappeared to the left and below us. Even with my counter maneuver our ship sheared violently with the explosion and I counter controlled her for a few seconds, struggling to retain our place in line. After things settled down, I still had difficulty getting back on the course; but we were still flying. In front of us, Forbes lay prone in his position, cushioning his face over the bombsight as the aircraft bucked, bounced and heaved beneath him. His right hand ringed the rim of the bombsight to keep it from bruising his eye, as the ship pitched and bounced.

Still, I held the course, concentrating on the altimiter and directional gyro's needle and glancing off our sides, from time to time for any lagging aircraft while watching for someone trying to close up into position, from behind us. We had another few seconds of steady flight, before the ship suddenly leaped upward. The bombload was being freed and the ship, responding from the sudden loss of weight, began climbing as our load emptied, lightening the plane. Simultaneously, Forbes said: "Bombs gone, Sir...."

As the ship rose, I'd smoothly countered the climb with forward pressure on the yoke, attempting to maintain altitude and counteract the climb. The ship also began to gain airspeed with the downward nose angle and I countered with more yoke pressure, elevator trim and by throttling back the engines slightly. Ajax was unmoving, leaning back in his seat, arms straight out, hands on the panel frame, sitting stiffly.

"You all right, Sir?" Forbes asked. I glanced down to see he'd turned around and was staring at the shattered Perspex window beside my head. I nodded, pointing also to the hole above us.

He raised his eyebrows.

I inclined my head slightly toward Ajax, who still clung stiffly to the frame. He looked as if he was in shock. Forbes glanced inquiringly at me, but I shook my head slightly and he returned to his cubbyhole in the forward turret ready to fire against any fighters we might encounter.

With their bombs gone, our whole flight had begun a slow turn to port—off the wind and away from the target. I had to watch the *Lanc* ahead and to the right, fearful the strong crosswind we were now encountering in the turn would swerve him into us. Without the Halifax so close on our tail there should have been ample room to maneuver.

As we now broached the headwind we'd fought all the way to target, *A—for—apple* began to fall off to port, gaining airspeed as we went into our turn. I eased the yoke back, pointing somewhat into the wind again to slow the drift, maintaining altitude and the smoothness of the turn. I kept an eye on the left wing, trying to stay in formation with the other ship so close on our tail. Everyone had to coordinate the turn outs—those behind and ahead. I glanced past Ajax from time to time, all the while maintaining the slow turn to the left.

As a former attack fighter pilot, I very much respected the importance of daylight bombers maintaining close formation for the safety of their flock. When so done, machine gun turret fire control coverage was murderously impenetrable for any attacking fighters. But only if bombers remained tightly locked into in impregnable formation.

Nighttime bombing, strung out as we were, made us very vulnerable to any enemy fighter who could find us in the darkness. As I continued bringing the ship around, Phillips also turned in his seat to peer through my window, back at the continued onslaught on the target.

When we'd finally completed the turn, straight and level once again, we turned on the home course. I also took a couple of seconds to peek around the shattered plastic panel, down at the fires and the still-exploding bombs, raining down behind us from the following bombers. I could see the other bomber groups occasionally silhouetted against the glowing maelstrom, some of whom were just now also beginning their own turn out behind us, as even more were appearing above the distant glow. The ground fires were so bright, each ship was individually distinguishable against the glow of the burning city. So broad was the bomb coverage, it appeared as if the whole of the earth was afire...a continuous grass fire across the night.

Within fifteen minutes we picked up *Luftwaffe* fighters and began to catch bursts of machine gun and cannon fire. I felt the ship shudder as our guys hammered away with our twin, .303 caliber guns, returning fire at the attacking Jerrys. The Lancaster shook heavily with the recoil and as if to tear themselves free from their mounts, our four separate gun mountings blazed away at the passing fighters. In my mind I could imagine the spent brass casings clattering onto the deck, around each gunner's feet. The gunners were firing at the Jerry plane's gun flashes.

The ship directly in front and to our right of us suddenly sprouted flame from both portside engines.

"Ship afire ahead, Sir!" Phillips said in warning.

The wing on the faltering ship ahead was well ablaze. We watched as dark shadows began to drop from the bomb-bay doors, indicating that some crew members were escaping. Thank God, I thought. We watched as it climbed at a strange angle before beginning to slow, then fall off to the left, directly in our path of flight; we were going to collide if I didn't do something. I thought of throttling back, but the ship immediately behind us might strike us from behind. Turning to the right was out of the question because the majority of the formation still lay over there, coming around in their turns. So, instinctively, I put the nose down and shoved the throttles forward and began to dive—down and to the left.

The burning ship lost one tailplane and began to twist round, plunging faster, then leveling as it descend, coming ever closer—almost falling *at* us. Ajax now had one hand on his seat edge and the other braced on the flying panel. He glanced first at my right hand—on the throttles and then out the windscreen approaching *Lanc.* As we continued to gain airspeed, diving—racing to outrun the failing ship ahead of us, he leaned back, shuddered and closed his eyes.

We raced the flaming ship, the plunging fuselage threatening at any moment to disintegrate directly in front of us. Suddenly, its' port side wing fuel tank exploded, destroying the whole of the

wing, in and instant; this caused the fuselage to begin to rotate slowly. Spinning toward us like a huge, backward torpedo, it was as if we
were a magnet, no matter how I dodged it, the ship followed us.

As it revolved among a hail of tumbling, flaming engine
parts, wing panels and unidentifiable debris, the starboard wing engines, screaming in the semi-darkness at full power, pulled the frac-
tured fuselage and remaining wing, to the left, away from us. Pieces
and panels tumbled past us, missing our cockpit and mid-upper turret, as we screamed, neck and neck, beneath it, still in a steep diving
bank.

Small pieces began striking the fuselage as we entered the
debris path, pings, bangs and sounds of small objects striking the
starboard-side propellers. It was as if we were jinxed, drawing the
death ship to us no matter how we maneuvered.

I yanked the throttles back, pitched and yawed the aircraft,
totally unmindful now of whoever was behind us. If they were—they
would be performing their own avoidance measures. By the same
twist of fate that drew her to us, the ship suddenly began to tumble
to the right and in seconds, was behind us, plummeting earthward.

I began to pull our *Lanc* from her steep dive. I glanced at
the altimeter. We'd lost over three thousand feet in the race against
the burning ship. Our airspeed was off the map. The pressure on
the control was tremendous under the force of the elevator and tail-
plane and the ship shuddered as I kept steady back-pressure pulling,
attempting to slow and turn the ship before we struck land.

Bomb-aimer Forbes had been hanging on, just to remain in
one place on the deck. From time to time he'd become airborne as
the ship plunged, rending his body weightless. He was now pasted
to the floor in the nose by the g-force of my attempted pullout,
barely able to move. I couldn't see his face and could only imagined
his firm grin of resolve, half-squatting, half-lying in the nose below
us, totally surrounded by clear Perspex, fragile and vulnerable, so
visibly within death's touch. The fire of the other ship and explosion
must have seemed to him so close, he could have touched any part
of it.

After an agonizing few seconds, the larger hand on the
altimeter finally began to slow its counter clockwise race to record
our lost altitude. Then it finally stabilized and once again we were

flying straight and level in the darkness, having finally recovered at around 3400 feet. I got on the interphone immediately.

"Anyone hit or hurt...?" I spit into the mike. Forbes stuck his head around the cowling and waved up at me, indicating he was OK. One by one the other crew reported in. All were well.

"Any structural damage to the ship?" I came back.

Again, everyone reported nothing but minor shrapnel punctures...until Hanson, in the mid-upper, came back a second time.

"Uhhh...Captain...I've hydraulic fluid squirtin' out, Sir. One of the pipes is leakin'. I don't know where it goes—flaps 'er undercarriage, but there's lots of it—squirtin'.out."

"Right, Hanson, Ajax will be right back to look it over...and give you a hand."

I turned to Ajax. He had a sort of questioning look in his eyes and he just sat there. I tried to sound normal.

"Ajax...hurry back and get me a report."

He didn't respond.

"Ajax..." I pushed his shoulder, "...there's a good man...go help out Hanson, will you?"

He seemed to snap out of it then and started to stand up, but was restrained by his safety belt, which had kept him firmly in the jump seat. I ignored his confusion as he struggled to free himself.

"Don't forget to take a portable with you Ajax...and hurry, will you?"

I didn't know how effective he was going to be and thought of also sending Phillips along, but he wasn't engineer trained. Glancing over my shoulder, I saw him give a knowing look to Forbes as Ajax passed him. Then he looked at me, raised his eyebrows and shook his head slightly.

But I had other problems—above us, at altitude, the returning flotilla of bombers continued coming around from their runs. We could see them now and again in the flash of exploding flack, or if one of them suddenly sprouted flames, exploded and went down. Others were passing us somewhere overhead, spread out in line formation, some still coming and homeward bound. Did we try to inch our way up to altitude again to attempt to fit into the line, taking a chance on causing a multiple collision, or would we be better off to stay low all the way back to England. I was hoping for cloud cover in order to evade the *Luftwaffe*, but there had been none predicted. As it was, I had to decide what to do and decide rather quickly. The ship was flying straight and level in a slight climb, all the engine pressures read normal. Indications were that we were OK, except for that fluid leak. Just then Hanson came back on the intercom.

"Errr...Sir...?"

"Yeah Hanson...what's up?'

"We're not getting anywhere, Sir."

"You mean you can't stop the leak, or you can't figure out where the leak's coming from?"

"Well...neither, Sir. Actually, the leak's stopped by itself...we never did figure out where the line came from...there's so damn many of those pipes up there, Sir...'n it was just pourin' out...it's probably all run out, whatever it was."

"What does Ajax think...*he's* the engineer...you plugged in, Ajax?"

There was five seconds of silence.

"Ajax...*Hanson?*"

Then Hanson: "He hasn't a plug on his interphone cord, Sir...musta' come off...somewhere?"

"*Shit.*"

I glanced over to the radio panel where the end to Ajax headset intercom was still plugged in. Frayed pieces of wires stuck out of the end. He'd walked away with it still connected and parted the wires.

"Well, ask him if he knows what's wrong, will you Hanson...relay for him?"

"Right...just a minnit, Cap."

There was a long silence while I assumed they conversed. Finally:"Sir...?"

I waited for him to say something else. No response.

"Hanson...you there?"

"Yeah...Sir, I'm here."

I was trying to be patient. "Yes, Hanson...?"

"There's sommat' wrong wi' Ajax, Sir..."

"Something wrong? What...is he hit?"

"I don't know Sir...but—he just stands here, Sir, he doesn't say anythin'. I asked him if he knew what was broke—but he just looked at me, didn't do nothing...don't say anythin' either. I think there's sammatt wrong w'im."

"OK...please stand by Hanson."

"Right...."

"Forbes—Phillips...? Either one of you?"

"I'll go Sir—I'm closest." It was Phillips.

"Right, Phillips. Don't be long...oh, before you go, I'm going to strike a course for west-northwest. When you finish...back there, lets figure out where we are, where we're going and how high to climb...if at all. For now I'm steering west-northwest. In ten minutes, or less, with this tailwind, we'll be sitting ducks for the AA —or fighters."

"Right, Sir...be back in a jiffy."

I'd begun to climb back up to altitude.

"Cap'n...?"

"Yes Hanson."

"There's...I don't know, but I think our oxygen took it. There was an awful hissing 'n I checked the pressure. I think our supply caught it, Sir."

"Oh, great. We'er lucky the whole ship didn't go up. Anything we can do Hanson?"

"Not that I now, Sir. Just stay low enough to breathe.

"Right, Hanson. Thanks."

In a minute Phillips was back, pushing Ajax ahead of him. I glanced up at Ajax. He looked kind of dazed. I think he was in some sort of emotional trouble. Phillips met my eyes and shook his head, slightly as he pushed Ajax down onto the jump seat again and helped him buckle up.

He tried to plug in the intercom end and realized the wires were torn out. He stood there for couple seconds, holding and looking at the wires and then at me. We were now far enough out from the ground fire that I could no longer make out the expression on his face but I could pretty well judge what he was thinking by his body language. Presently he went back to his chart table and buckled into his little chair.

"Did you get that, Phillips...about the oxygen?"

"Yes Sir, I did."

"OK. How's Ajax?"

"Sir…?"

He was on the intercom again. "Yes, Phillips?"

"Sir…Ajax' has cracked or somethin'."

"Cracked, Phillips…you mean shell shock?"

"Somethin', Sir. He doesn't talk and…I sort of checked him over, 'n I couldn't find any sign he'd been hit or anythin'. I think he's crackers, Sir."

"All right, Phillips…thanks for trying."

"Right, Sir."

"Phillips, will you run us a new course back to base?"

"Right, Sir…west-northwest still our heading?"

"It is."

"Hold that while I run a plot, Sir."

"Done, Phillips. And to the rest of you…" I addressed the crew, "…we've lost the group. There's little chance we'll be able to find them, let alone get back into line because of a busted oxygen supply. We can only go up around ten-twelve thousand and still breathe, but we'll be sitting ducks for fighters or AA, so I'm going to take us down to near treetop level. There's a very bright moon now and not much chance for cloud moving in. Higher up we'd be a good target. Hopefully, flying low, only airborne fighters might see us and then, with difficulty against the ground. We're less likely to be seen at that altitude, I believe. By the time the AA guys see us, we'll be past them. Our risk will be fighters, not much altitude if we have to pick a landing spot…and fuel. We may have a problem, there. Any questions?"

I listened to the silence on the intercom. Everyone knew the plan, now, but Ajax, and I didn't know as he cared, particularly. I reached over and patted his knee. When we'd done avoidance maneuvers with that burning ship, we'd flown way south and east of the target area. Now, we had to get that ground back. It was going to cost us fuel and time. Since neither crew or the ship appeared to be in any immediate danger, time was what we had plenty of. Fuel on the other hand…that would be something we would learn shortly when Phillips completed his calculations.

Five minutes later Phillips came on.

"Sir, I have your numbers."

"All right...let's have 'em."

"We won't know for sure, Sir, until I can get something from the 'G' signals, assuming the *Jerry's* aren't jamming them...but it looks like you'd best steer two-nine-zero, for now. I'll try to get a ground fix somewhere and give you a better course from that. Maybe...when we get in range, we can get a DF steer."[11]

"Right—*when* we get in range, Phillips."

I wrote 290° on a writing pad strapped with the clipboard to my thigh and made the slight course alteration.

"Thanks...and now for the big question, Phillips: how much fuel?"

"I figure about three 'n a quarter—maybe three 'n a half, if the tailwind holds."

There was a couple of minutes silence while I did the mental calculations.

"Well, boys, looks like we can make it. The problem is, at this altitude, I've gotten the ship down to about 1100 feet, AGL. At this altitude we use more fuel. We're not getting the tailwind we had upstairs, either. But as I said, *Jerry* gunners probably won't get us. Fighters are what we're taking our chances with. I still think it's our best bet."

There was only silence on the intercom.

"Right...that's the way we'll play it, lads. Keep your eyes peeled for fighters and pray that the wind blows behind us."

I held the course, monitoring the altimeter and the ground, when we could see much of it. The tailwind we would have benefited from at altitude, was significantly diminished at our low, flying level. But we didn't encounter any effective AA, either. Several times, as we crossed smaller cities, we woke up the gunners as we passed. By the time they'd manned and pointed their guns, we were over and gone, either out of visual range, or they just couldn't see us in the darkness.

After flying the course for half an hour, we could see fires on the horizon ahead, glowing from an incendiary bombing of a large target. It lit up the sky to the west. I thought of turning to the south to avoid it, as we watched we realized the barrage was still underway, as new bombs continued to explode.

"Phillips, any idea what that city is?"

"No Sir, I can only guess at this point. But we must be getting close to the frontier—Holland, or if we're too far south, Belgium."

"Best to avoid the area, or we might get some eggs dropped right on top of us, if we fly under any incoming bombers.

Phillips...what do you think? I'm for going to the south of it. I like that northeast wind—maybe keep us from flying too far north and ending up over the North Sea, short of fuel and having to put her down in the water. This way, if we go down, we do it in occupied France. Might be some chance of getting back alive."

"I don't think we're that far off course, Sir...France—well, if we've gone that far off 'n hit the French border, we'll soon be out of fuel anyway. And we're too low to bail out, Sir...you'd have to land her...in the dark."

"Good point, Phillips. Which do you prefer?"

"Neither, Sir."

"Right...me too—let's go north, then, as you suggested."

I altered the course to take us a few miles north of the fires. As the glow passed on our port side we could see the outline of church steeples, but little else. There was AA going up and flak popping around twenty thousand, so we knew other bombers were still working over the target.

Once we cleared the burning city, I glanced at the clipboard on my thigh and brought us back onto our original compass course of 290 degrees, just north of flying due west by twenty degrees. Should the wind drift us south by about ten degrees or so, I was crabbing her a bit as a fudge factor. Flying this low had it hazards, mostly with the usual concerns of engine failure or fuel shortage. In this particular instance, neither concerned us—at least for a while yet. The solution to both problems, should they develop, was to land the aircraft, something we absolutely did not wish to do, except in England. The benefit of a runway wouldn't be available to us, either, should we have chosen that option, even if it was a viable option.

As we rolled and bounced across the skies of western Germany, or maybe Holland, in the dark of the night, I recalled the time, years earlier, when I'd landed a crop duster in a wheat field on a dark, moonless night, after losing oil pressure in the engine. A friend had asked me what I normally did in an instance like that...no lights and no runway.

"The engine stops—you're in the dark of night and you don't know where you are?" he'd asked.

I'd responded: "You glide down through the pitch-black until you think you're near the ground. Then—you turn on the airplane's landing lights, hoping you're not coming down in a forest."

"Oh?" he'd replied, "then what?"

"Well...if you don't like what you see—you turn them off again...and land the aircraft."

The other problem I was worrying over, with our low altitude, was our radio range. Without altitude we would significantly restrict the ability of the GIC signal folks to give us a DF steer, since we couldn't get up high enough to be heard, possibly until we were very near the coast of Belgium or France.

But climbing high enough to be heard would rob our marginal fuel and by then it might be too late to correct the course. If the course Phillips 'd calculated for us was wrong, we could be in central France, or worse, headed northeasterly, out into the North Sea over Holland, where we would exhaust our fuel supply before coming down in a cold, dark sea.

We finally struck a coastline.

"There's the coast...where do you think we are, Phillips?"

He'd been keeping me up to date as we progressed, as to where he thought we were, so my request didn't take him long.

"About 40 minutes in Sir."

"OK, think we're in range for a DF steer?"

"Difficult to say, Sir, but shouldn't hurt to try...not likely to pick up any fighters this close now.

Cap...If they hear us, we'll be long-gone by the time they get up and over to get us."

We prepared to begin what would be a continuous radio transmission to our GIC people. To our wireless-air gunner: "OK, Upton," "it's time to find out where we are. Let's try for station...see who you can raise."

"Right, Cap, I'm set up already."

There was perhaps twenty seconds of static and squealing in our earphones while he adjusted his equipment, before he began.

"Lefshey Station, this is A—for—apple. Do you hear me Lefshey Station...A—for—apple calling you...can you hear A—for—-apple, Lefshey Station?"

He ceased transmitting and we all listened intently for ten or so seconds until the phones crackled and squealed and then we heard a commercial signal from the BBC: "...London calling, the time is..." and then static as a broadcast program came through on our frequency.

"Dammit Upton...any way to stop the cross over? They'll never hear us over the BBC."

"I'll go to the alternate frequency, Sir. May not be so bad...'n I can alternate, too, between them."

"Right...well, don't alternate too long, Upton, we might just run out of fuel."

He began transmitting again: "Lefshey Station...this is A—for—apple...can you hear me?"

While Upton repeated the call, I turned my attention to our fuel situation.

"Phillips...what is the estimated time to fuel outage?"

He didn't respond for a moment. I waited knowing he'd be doing his calculations.

"Sir...best I can do with the information we have, it's about a break-even."

"That close is it...?" I didn't want to hear that news.

"Appears so, Sir...knowing *what* we don't know now."

"What if we're right on course...assuming this is the course to put us on top of them?"

"A quick guess Cap, is...maybe 10 minutes to spare."

"Enough to go around the patch once if we miss the first approach, right?"

"About right, Sir."

"OK...let's update it when we get a position fix."

"Will do, Sir, soon 's it comes in."

That wasn't the best news. Between maneuvering to avoid the flaming ship and the wind taking us off course, we were marginal to arrive with sufficient fuel to land at our station. There were other options, of course but I didn't look forward to any of them, particularly in the darkness, over enemy territory

"Lefshey Station...this is A—for—apple...A—for—apple...can you hear A—for—apple calling...?

For some time, Upton's voice had been droning over the interphone in the background, when we finally heard a faint reply.

"A—for—apple, this is Blackthorne Station...we can barely hear your transmission A—for—apple?"

Upton was on them hardly before the phones clicked. Blackthrone was a hundred fifty miles north of Lefshey and east, closer to the coast. Had we come too far north?

"Blackthorne Station...A—for—apple here—we're trying to raise Lefshey Station...can you provide a DF steer for A—for—apple out of Lefshey."

"A—for—apple...please stand by...your transmission is very weak..."

There was a full minute's pause before Blackthorne came back again.

"A—for—apple, please transmit continuously for thirty seconds, then break your transmission and stand by for further instruction."

Upton began the continuous radio signal transmission, counting sequentially, holding the mike button in, to keep the radio carrier modulated.

"Blackthorne Station, here is A—for—apple—1—2—3...with Little Bo Peep—and her lost sheep..."

After he gone through his sparse repertoire of nursery rhymes, Upton stopped and we all waited. Then came a reply.

"A—for—apple this is Blackthrone Station calling...we make you zed-eight-two...*repeat*, zed-eight-two, back steer two-seven-eight...*repeat*—two-seven-eight degrees."

"Thank you Blackthorn...A—for—apple understands two-seven-eight degrees. Can you remain on frequency until we can raise Lefshey?"

"We have rung Lefshey for you A—for—apple...notified them...are calling for DF steer on this frequency. We will remain on station—repeat—we...main on station and update your radial."

There was much static, but we could make out what he said

and it could only get better, assuming we remained in the air. I broke in over the interphone.

"Good job Upton—keep trying to raise Lefhsey. Phillips, let me know as soon as you can where that bearing puts us."

He knew he didn't have to reply and I knew he was already plotting our position based on a single compass radial drawn on his chart; we had flown somewhere across that line as they reported us. After another fifteen seconds, he came on.

"Cap...my guess...we're still right on break even."

Then we heard Upton: "Lefshey Station, A—for—apple...can we get a DF from you chaps? Fuel is a priority here, Lefshey Station."

I could barely hear them answering him; usually his primary radio reception, being direct, was better than ours, patched through the bomber's interphone as it was.

"Thank you Lefshey Station...A—for—apple is now commencing transmission to Lefshey Station...one—two—three—four...."

Again, Upton went up to thirty seconds of continuous radio transmission as we waited. I was unable to hear them at all when they answered, but apparently Upton could.

"Thank you Lefshey Station...we have heard...the bearing to, is two—six—six—repeat, bearing to, is two—six—six...Blackthorne Station, can you please update your bearing for A—for—-apple?"

Phillips came on the interphone: "We're awfully close to being correct, Sir...let's see what Blackthorn says and I'll let you know how far out we are and the fuel situation."

We listened as Upton worked Blackthorne Station again. They soon came back with an updated radial vector, accounting for the distance along the triangle they were cross-plotting us on and Phillips plugged it into his chart. After a moment he got out of his little desk and came around to squat between Ajax and me, holding out his clipboard with the two, diagonal lines—one drawn from Lefshey and the other, Blackthorne Stations. We were at their southeastern apex.

"'Bout twenty minutes, Sir..." he shouted above the engines, "...give or take." He looked at me, awaiting my next question.

"Fuel...?"

"'Bout the same, Sir...maybe a little more. Here's the course..." he glanced at the directional gyro on the instrument panel "...if you come south a little to here." he pointed to the number he'd written on the chart. I nodded and he climbed back behind me to his seat.

I jotted the number on my pad and corrected the course left, to 277on the directional gyro, checking it against the magnetic compass to be sure they matched, before bringing my oxygen mask up to speak into the microphone again.

"OK...thanks Upton...keep me updated on the inbound course, please." I thought for a bit as the gyro settled to the new course. "Phillips, let me know when we're five minutes out. Because of the wind resistance increasing fuel consumption, I don't want to bring the gear down until we're on top of the field."

I got acknowledgments from both crew and then called Lefshey, using their code name in order to confirm we were inbound and marginal on fuel.

"Fox 'n Hounds, this is A—for—apple calling...Apple is approaching at one thousand, emergency routing...ETA one-five, repeat Fox 'n Hounds...Apple calling, emergency routine...inbound. Our ETA is one-five, approaching at two thousand. When overhead we shall fire a red...please acknowledge, Foxtrot."

"A—for—apple... Fox 'n Hounds here...we understand fuel is priority. We will bring up emergency routing, Apple. Repeat— under emergency procedure—we will light the field Apple."

"Apple to Fox 'n Hounds...thank you. We will cross the field and make one left-hand circuit to come into the wind to land."

"Fox 'n Hounds to Apple, we understand."

Receiving that transmission, I settled deeper into my seat, maintaining the inbound course. I assumed we would land from the south and planned to drop off the bearing at the last minute in order to cross the field, turn downwind, left and then make the approach and come in on a northbound approach.

I never realized how long fifteen minutes could be as we droned on toward station. I supposed the entire crew felt the same anticipation. With each burp and hiccup of an engine I thought we might have exhausted the fuel, but then they'd steady again and continue droning smoothly on. I though of alternatives if we had to land on the sea. How many of the crew would get out if the ship remained intact and afloat after impacting? Could I keep it from flipping over...breaking into pieces? Wouldn't matter much then; no one would be conscious or able to crawl out and inflate the life-jackets. I wondered how high the swells were.

"Ten minutes out, Cap."

I heard Phillips voice and decided to try to conserve fuel. I reduced the revs on the two inboard engines, knowing she should keep flying. But we were startled by a loud alarm horn. I quickly shoved the throttles forward again.

"What the hell happened, Ajax? What'd I do wrong?"

He didn't answer for a minute. When I opened my mouth to repeat the question, he blurted a reply.

"Inboard engines power the hydraulic system...maintain pressure to the flaps and undercarriage. If you close the throttles, we won't be able to operate the undercarriage."

Well, he was the flight engineer and the alarm seemed to confirm his statement. "What can I do Ajax?"

"Don't bring them back fully, Sir."

So I slowly eased them back to not quite half-throttle, dropping the revolutions by about twenty five percent and we continued on, inbound for landing. Was Ajax back with us again, I wondered.

Another five minutes and I turned to Ajax again: "Let the gear down, will you Ajax?" I said, glancing down at the levers on my right.

He stared at me for a couple seconds without responding. I dropped my mask and turned, facing him, shouted the request again. He seemed to come out of his stupor, a little of the old eagerness returning to his face as he set himself to the task.

As he reached for the control I turned back to maintain the heading, expecting the red light which came on when he dropped the gear to gurn green, indicating the wheels were down and locked. After a few seconds, there was still no green light and I noticed Ajax working the lever again.

"What's wrong," I shouted.

He shook his head, the frantic expression returning.

"It didn't come down...Sir," he shouted, nearly in a rage, "the undercarriage won't lock. I don't think the wheels are down...you can't land, Sir."

"Didn't come down? Don't you know why?"

He glanced at me and then worked the lever again.

"Just a minute...I'll bring the revs up on the two inboards again." I shoved the throttles forward but the red light remained.

"It still won't come down, Sir. Must have been the fluid leak in back!"

"I can see that Ajax. Can you fix it—or do we put her in on her belly...hurry Ajax, we're about to turn downwind to land—I gotta know!"

He unstrapped and from a squatting position said, "Must have been the flak, Sir...when the fluid went. One side of the line is bled and a valve's stuck or something. There's the compressed air tanks...they'll push them down...should."

We both reached for the lever to release the compressed air into the hydraulic system as an emergency power to push the fluid through the cylinders, lowering the gear.

I didn't know what I should see or hear, but the lights remained red.

"There's no pressure Sir...flack must have got the tanks...if you can wait, Sir, I can operate the hand pump."

"How long, Ajax?"

"I'm not certain Sir...but we'll have to go around again...at least that long, I think."

"We can't go around again...we probably don't even have fuel to get in."

All right Sir, I'll go back 'n see what I can do..." and he tore out of his seat without the least sign of his previous condition.

I had to turn my attention to Upton so I just nodded and he disappeared aft.

"Upton—call station and tell them to light all the pots along the runway. We've no wheels—we'll be coming in on our belly—and tell 'em to get the trucks out to the middle of the runway—and some ambulances."

"Sir..." it was Ajax again, standing, slightly behind me. "I think—if I can cut the line and relieve the pressure, the gear will drop by itself"

I looked at him. "Well go do it...we're running on fumes now."

The first of the flare pots began to show up on the horizon ahead. We were too far east and north of the field.

"All right, Ajax...I'll stretch the approach as much as I can. Hurry—try 'n cut it."

He turned on his heel again and was gone. Because we were north of the field, it was just a little longer to cross north and keep going for a while before turning left to fly downwind, parallel—southbound and then do a one-eighty to the left and land, with or without gear by that time. On the interphone I broke the news to the rest of the crew..

"Chaps...we don't have any gear-down 'n locked lights, so we're going to cross north of the field, stretch it for time and come around south and land to the north. Tie everything down...Ajax's trying to fix the undercarriage."

I cut it as short as I dared, crossing the north end of the field. As soon as we swung south, I could feel the wind change, coming behind and from the left. It would be a short down-wind leg, so I might have to go further south. But...how far south? If I stretched it too long, waiting for Ajax's gear, we might suddenly exhaust the fuel and fall to earth, far short of the runway and into the sea. I waited until I thought we were where we should be and I turned left again—hard, rolling her way over in the turn and cutting power, pointing the nose down and partially dropping the flaps. They worked. I was afraid, since they were also hydraulically powered, that we'd have to come in without flaps and be unable to slow our landing speed. I could see the runway pots far ahead, two parallel lines of light...like streetlights in the blackout.

Forbes had scrambled out of the nose to go help Ajax. Above the engine's roar I could hear pounding behind me on the bulkhead; glancing around my seatback quickly, I saw Forbes holding a flash-light while Ajax swung the fire ax.

The ship was settling too quickly on final approach. I added power and full flaps; any moment I expected to hear the first of the engines begin to cough as the fuel was exhausted. I felt the ship slow and the pull of the wind resistance through my tight grip on the yoke. The red lights flickered and the green light suddenly came on for the gear. I shouted over my shoulder.

"The gear's down—gear's down...and locked!"

Forbes dove past me into his seat and Ajax scrambled into the jump seat and strapped in.

The wings passed the first of the flame pots—then the second. The ship settled—settled and then bang, we hit the ground, bounced, hit the ground again and swerved. I was on the brakes trying to control the skidding aircraft. It was a lousy landing but I didn't care. We were on the ground...on tires and it didn't matter anymore, how bad the landing was. I could hear a cheer from the crew behind me and glancing at Ajax, I saw a sense of resolve where before there had been only fear and panic.

"Damn good—Ajax...damn good," I shouted without looking at him.

After we slowed, I locked the left brake, reved the inboard starboard engine and turned the ship back down the runway, toward her nest. Just then the port engines began to backfire and sputter; then the starboard did the same. We went another hundred feet and all four stopped completely, out of fuel. For a second we sat there in the middle of the runway looking out at the flickering oil pots, our props soundlessly winding down. The sudden silence was a blessing and we all listened for a moment until the fire trucks and two ambulances roared up.

An hour later, near the end of the debriefing, the fitters came in and reported that there wasn't even enough fuel remaining in any of the ship's tanks to measure. Of course this wasn't news to us. And Ajax...at the last minute he'd somehow come up with the wherewithal to take the fire ax to the hydraulic line running to the landing gear, chop through it, permitting the vacuum pressure to bleed out that was holding up the landing gear. The gear had dropped like a stone and in the end, saved us from having to make a belly landing and probably saving our lives. All this within the last ten minutes of the mission. I commended Ajax's behavior in my report, but also recommended he be removed from any piloting opportunities until he could be reviewed for flight and command skills again. I figured this wouldn't get him sent down or court-martialed, but would possibly get him reviewed again before he killed himself and a ship's crew. After the debriefing I was offered breakfast and after that, given a private room with a bed. I awoke shortly after Noon and caught a bus into the city. I neded to get started on contacting Greta.

The next afternoon there was a note waiting for me in the ABA flight operations room. I'd been unsuccessfully attempting to contact Clyde; he was off and running somewhere, it seemed. I opened and read the single sheet before eating a late lunch. Glancing at the bottom, I saw it was from the Air Marshal himself.

"Heard about the do last evening, Johnson...Good Job," it had said, with his initials scrawled below.

I chuckled to myself. He'd forgotten and used my real surname...not my spy name.

CHAPTER
15

The Air Raid From Köln

I was awakened by the sound of running in the hotel's hall-way and I heard loud voices as people passed my door. It was still very dark and I had no idea of the time. At first I thought it was noisy partygoers returning after a night's celebration. But then the sirens in the park down the street started up. I sat in bed debating whether I should dress and go to the hotel's cellar, the air raid shelter across the street or, simply remain in my warm bed in the *Reichland* and take my chances.

I finally decided to go to the shelter. It wasn't simply my own life I was risking now, I reasoned, it was Sophia's, also. As her mother I needed to be alive if I was going to help her. Until I found her and got her safely out of Germany I shouldn't risk anything which would jeapordise her escape.

Dressing hastily, I grabbed my little satchel and a blanket from the bed and joined the parade of sleepy-eyed guests stumbling down the hallway, stairway and out through the lobby. I had no idea where the shelter was and just followed the crowd. It worked. There was a stone building—a library, kitty-cornered from the hotel. It had a tomb of a cellar, I saw, as we poured into it from the street. The authorities had installed wide sleeping platforms along the wall and also in several rows down the room's center. One could sit on them during the day, or stretch out in a lying-down position in the night.

We were far from the first shelter-seekers to arrive. Much of the area was already occupied by people fleeing the anticipated bombing. They were very noisy as they continued to file down the hallway and into the room. Parents had brought sleepy children, bundled up from the cold, their round eyes taking in the strange gathering of cranky lodgers. Parents already situated on the platforms grudgingly made more and more room for the flood of arrivals, either moving their children's things, or picking up their children to hold them so there would be room.

There was a young mother with four children on the platform I finally chose. She smiled and nodded, pulling apart enough of her children to make a space for me. "Hurry and take it before anyone else comes," she urged, kindly. I did, nodding my thanks and smiling. "Some of the drunks will soon show up. They are always the last to arrive."

I settled in beside the children. There was no sign of a father. The room finally filled and a warden shouted that it was at full capacity; Then we heard a large door slam, somewhere. At the sound of the door closing, it became very quiet, suddenly, as as if a chapter in a book had suddenly closed.

I'd lain down in the dimness beside a boy of around eight. We'd no more than told each other our names when the first bomb fell. It was so close to the building that part of our ceiling gave way in a shower of plaster and timbers. Everyone screamed in surprise. Our platform was struck by several large pieces of the plaster. As he screamed I hurried to clasp the boy to me; his mother was otherwise occupied with clutching her smaller children. I pulled him closer to the mother and we huddled in a group.

There came the sound of heavy objects striking elsewhere in the cellar, but since the lights had gone immediately, there was no way of determining where, or what had come down, or even if anyone was harmed. It sounded as if there were some persons.injured because there was much screaming punctuated by constant groaning. Someone began calling into the darkness for a doctor.

Someone else invoked the name of their mother, weeping and another, of God, asking forgiveness. I heard someone answer about the time I was considering going over and see what I could offer in the way of assistance. Flickering lights soon began casting eerie shadows around the room as several people lit candles they'd brought. There was even a lantern or two that came to life. Then, someone shouted about putting out any flames. If there were gas leaks, they said, we'd all blow up. That sounded reasonable to me, but no one paid them any heed in the midst of the screaming and whimpering adults and children; the lights continued to flicker.

The mother of the child I was comforting smiled bitterly across her three, clutching children, silently nodding her appreciation for the comfort I was offering her son. We all winced at the impact of four more concussions from closely falling bombs. The child I held was giving me something to worry about in the chaos. I discovered that by offering my comfort, I was myself, comforted.

No sooner had the cries subsided than a second wave of bombs struck. It was strange. I thought I could hear the bombs coming and feel the heavy thump—thump—thump as they struck and exploded, before the delayed sound of explosions finally caught up to us.

With this last salvo, a great deal of dust came billowing through the doors, which had been blown down by the concussion of a near miss. It didn't seem as bad as the first wave, though it made no difference to my companions; their fear was heightened from the renewed onslaught and they expected any of each of the following explosions to be as bad or worse than the previous.

The bombing seemed to last forever. I couldn't imagine how they could carry so many bombs to drop on us. How many airplanes must it take? They surely couldn't be dropping them, going back and getting more and dropping them again? It wasn't possible, but yet it seemed so. We Germans weren't winning. They couldn't be doing this to us if Germany was winning. Someone should make them stop—take the offensive...protect the German civilians from this nightmare.

But on they came, a continuous, explosive environment made just for us. In those moments, I believe everyone in the cellar became a bit insane, because it was lasting so long. It was almost as if the world of explosions became our habitat—an environment in itself and if it had grown quiet, suddenly, it would have been like a

noisless intrusion, bursting upon us. But, like birdsong, in a summer meadow, or rain on the roof on a summer night, the bombard-
ment permeated our consciousness. On it went...on and on; continuous, unrelenting—some near, some just far enough away to
frighten us anew with each successive explosion, fearing another
load could be marching toward us. We listened as the detonations,
like a giant's steps, trudged toward us and then past. Some came
evenly spaced, then the cadence would change and they would fall
rapidly, one after the other. After a while, I believe they were so
loud that I could no longer hear them...it was so deafening. I
could only *feel* the detonations.

Unbelievably, after an eternity, the child fell asleep in my
arms. But more from fright and exhaustion, I believed. Possibly, it
was from emotional shock. We'd been perspiring heavily. Eventually, I believe I also dozed. The heaviest concentration of explosions
seemed to have moved further to the northwest. We didn't hear the
siren sound all clear, when it was over. The bombs must even have
destroyed it. I'm not certain when I finally handed the sleeping child
back to his mother. It was coming daylight already I thought, when
I saw the glow of dawn coming through the empty doorway above.
Several of us stood and began gathering our things to leave.

As we emerged from the shelter, I saw that I was mistaken.
It was not the dawning of a new day, it was the dawning of a new hell
on earth. The brightness of the the city of Köln ablaze, everywhere
it was burning, giving the illusion of morning. The stark silhouettes
of building shells, with glassless windows letting the fire escape, long,
lashing tongues leaping skyward, everywhere we looked.

"We are definitely not winning the war..." I said to no one,
as I stumbled into the rubble-filled street. Pivoting around, it seemed
to me the city burned in a circle. We couldn't be winning—this, this
inferno? This is not victory, surely. Must we destroy ourselves to
win? To win what? Destruction? It made me very angry, to stand
there. I was furious with the English and Americans...*whoever—
whichever*, that bombed us to this extent. It was not fair; it was not
human-like. Certainly by now they knew we were finished? Why did
they continue then, assailing us with such destruction? As I stumbled over the rubble, back to the hotel, I was also angry with my own
people. Could *we* not see that it was time to stop...stop and talk,

seriously discuss ending this senseless devastation?

After crossing the street, I paused for a moment at the hotel entrance. I didn't know whether the onslaught was finished for the night. I waited, watching the fires, in the event I had to return to the cellar. Whatever direction I turned in the field of view I had, there were fires, but few fire trucks. The fires seemed to flare up mightily and then dye down, put themselves out, or burn until the available fuel was depleted.

To the west the twin spires of the *Döm* silhouetted against the glow. Somehow...this cathedral had survived...the largest structure in the city. With the reduced height of the other buildings the silhouette of the church's spires appeared to stand even higher, appearing larger—massively tall. Most of the nearby buildings were down and burning. Before they stumbled into the destruction, other exhausted refugees, at first stopped to stare at the inferno around us. But soon they were off. Each seemed to have their own destination and goals.

The street was obstructed by debris at each end. I decided to make my way to the end of the block to see the extent of the damage in the direction of the research center, beside the library. Walking, I was forced again and again to step around pieces of curbing and smoldering building parts, flung far from the explosions occurring in the vicinity. There would certainly be no streetcars in the morning. No doubt I'd have to walk all the way to the archive building to do my research.

Finally, I picked my way back up the street toward the hotel. Miraculously, it had somehow been spared. Stopping once, I noticed there were electric wires hanging in the street, humming and sparking, occasionally. I silently prayed the research center would also be spared, thinking of the records I hoped to locate, praying they would still be safe. I expected to have the final information before lunchtime. Oh...I was so close. Without the records there would be no Sophia.

I wondered about the scheduled trains. Would there be trains operating tomorrow? Once I found the place Sophia was living—*if* I found it...would I even be able to get out of Köln to go to her? And when I arrived there, what would her adopted parents think of me? I supposed I'd have to steal her, if they wouldn't listen to reason, after hearing any explanation I might offer, about why I'd come, especially after all these years. They probably wouldn't believe my story...extermination camps—to the east? Surely, they'd also heard the stories by now? Would Sophia be afraid of me? Certainly I'd be a complete stranger and she might be frightened, at first, especially if I took her away from the only parents she'd ever known. But it couldn't matter. She'd eventually see reason when she grew up...come to love me. I just *had* to get her and somehow, get her out of Germany, to safety.

Back in my room in the hotel and unable to sleep, I reminisced about the recent day's journey. I'd escaped sure death in Oslo; no doubt about it. I felt very badly about poisoning the young Sergeant. The other two...*pigs*. Of course there would be no chance they could recover and their bodies would not be found for days...possibly even weeks. I abandoned the car in Göthenburg after being unable to obtain diesel fuel. Using my best method of intimidation was to no avail. It had worked in Norway, where we were the victors; but the Swedes were different. They were not yet conquered and the common man took an entirely different attitude to German women waving the papers with the rank of a *Kaptain* in the civilian service. Basically, it meant nothing to them.

Getting a train from there to Stockholm had not been a problem. With my credentials I was easily able to get a flight to Köln with *ABA*. I knew this was where the documents for the *Lebensborn* project were retained and I knew the key, thanks to my work mate, to narrowing the search.

Oh...how I had prayed for Alex to be the *Kaptain* of the ABA flight that I'd taken; but he wasn't. They knew him in the terminal, when I inquired, as did the crew of the planes I'd flown in on the last leg of the flight from Stockholm, to Copenhagen, to Frankfort and finally to Köln. They didn't know where he was until I got on the final flight leg; that *Kaptain* said he'd heard Alex's airship had encountered problems on their last flight and were safely stranded in London, without an engine. I think they told me the truth, though I also believe they didn't trust me...a German asking these questions.

There were no further raids after I returned to the hotel. And I overslept the next morning, finally awakened by the noisy, crawling tractors, slowly plowing a way through the debris in the street. I hurried to prepare to leave for the archives, in order to complete my investigation and was soon stumbling through the debris-filled avenues, which the day before were untouched and immaculate.

I nearly turned my ankle on one of the many pieces of broken building stone. Whole blocks of the avenue south of the hotel were reduced to piles of smoking stones. Civilians were everywhere, crawling about the smoking piles, searching for God knew what—or who? Surviving family members? Their possessions? Hardly anyone could still be alive under those jagged mounds, I thought, deciding then it was probably both.

I could also smell gas in some of the places I walked and quickly hurried past. I met two old ambulance-men carrying the body of a young girl, around age fourteen. A weeping man, I assumed it was her father, was following them. I wondered where her mother was and decided as I walked, she had probably been killed in the building's collapse and still remained buried.

When I reached the document center, I breathed a sigh of relief; it appeared to be completely untouched, apart from broken windows on one side. I entered the building and signed my name in the book the old woman again presented to me. She made no comment about the previous evening's bombing. I climbed the four flights to the archival room. On the third floor landing there was part of the exterior wall missing and the stairs just hung there. They appeared stable, but the gaping hole gave me a feeling of dizziness from that height, especially when I leaned out and glanced down toward the rubble heaps below.

Once again in the reading room, I removed my coat and scarf and put them on the same table where I'd worked the previous day. Looking from the window, I could see even more of Köln's devastation. I stood transfixed for a moment, gazing out on what had been such a beautiful city in times past. Looking over the leveled buildings I thought I could see further toward the horizon than yesterday. In the Rhine there was a bridge lying twisted. It seemed there should be another bridge there, but I couldn't remember. Barges had floated down, probably having their moorings destroyed and had piled up against the leaning bridge girders and concrete abutments.

It was very, *very* bad, this damage. As I scanned the sky-line I wondered how they could ever repair such destruction. Certainly they couldn't use the building material again. It appeared as if every brick and stone were broken, as I'd walked this morning. Where would they put the destroyed material, in order to build new again and where would they find the new material?

Could the German people afford to do this? We were already impoverished before the war...then came the strict rationing for the war effort—the soldiers. We'd already gone without for too long. How could they expect us to sacrifice more? We had little more to give but our bodies. One couldn't rebuild a destroyed country with mere bodies. We will need much spirit and other help, too, I'd surmised. And who would even wish to help us, after what we'd done to the rest of Europe? I shook my head in frustration and sadness, turning from the scene. I had something more important to do. Once I had Sophia, I could worry about how to save what remained of my beloved Germany and return it to a time when I could again be proud of my country. With my sheaf of papers from the previous day, I began selecting the folders bearing the dates I thought I'd need.

A half-hour later, I returned from the archives's shelves, having selected enough documents to get a good start, planning to spread out again at my table and peruse the folders, one-by-one. When I emerged from the corridor of tall shelves, my arms completely full, there was an army officer, an aged lieutenant, sitting at the long table where I had been working. As I approached I thought it curious he had no documents of his own to study; he sat, slowly turning his hat over and over in his hands in boredom. I immediately bacame cautious; it appeared he was waiting for someone. *Me,* I wondered? He slid back from the table as I approached, standing and bowing politely in the old fashion.

"Good morning, *Fräulein*...my name is Lieutenant Breunig."

His forward nature surprised me. I wondered whether they had found the dead *SS* men in my house in Norway. I laid the folders on the table. Someone had been handling my coat and purse; they were in a slightly different location on the table. I assumed he had rifled them. Taking a deep breath, I decided to bluff and so put on an innocent face.

"Good morning Lieutenant," I said, cheerfully. "What brings you here to the archives on such a terrible day? Are you doing family research also?"

I arranged my folders on the table and sat down, preparing to began to work. I thought of the mixture of foreign money that was still in my purse...English, Swedish and Norwegian. Thank God I'd grown concerned and left most of the currency in a brown envelope in the hotel safe. He would have seen the large amount of money and also wondered about the different currencies.

I pretended disinterest and got right to work as if he didn't concern me. I prayed it did not.

"*Fräulein*...I must ask you to please return these items to their proper places in the archives. You may not work here today."

"Really, Lieutenant and why is that? I have much to do yet, as you can see."

"There is some concern at our headquarters with your appearance here in Köln and my superiors would like to ask you some questions about why you are in the city."

"Oh? What could your commander possibly wish to know of me, or of my work here? I assure you, I am not on official duty. I'm merely researching information about a lost child for a friend...as a courtesy."

"No matter, *Fräulein*...you must accompany me, I'm afraid." He stepped back in a gesture of finality.

I sighed, "Lieutenant, I'm simply trying to relax for a few days before returning to my assignment in Norway. I have the permission of my superiors, in Oslo, where...I'm afraid I can't reveal the nature of that work to you, or your commander, but I can offer the names of persons in Berlin with whom your commander can speak, to validate who I am. I fear he will be sorry to learn he is interfering with a project with connections at the top level of the SS." I though I might try some additional bluffing.

"No doubt, *Fräulein*, but that is for them to accomplish and to reap whatever scorn your Berlin connection cares to administer upon them. My duty however, is to transport you there—simply that. So...if you would be so kind...?" He bowed again, slightly.

He must have been someone's grandfather, and a nice one at that, I thought. To be so old and have no higher rank than Lieutenant probably indicated just that. Still, I didn't move.

"Please don't be difficult, *Fräulein*. Is there not enough trouble in our city and country this morning after the terrible night's raid? As it is we will have to walk most of the way. That is why I am so late in picking you up. I was supposed to be at your hotel in a staff vehicle, but..." he gestured toward the window and the destructive scene, "...the night's happenings prevented it...so you were not there. We are probably both fortunate to be alive this morning, unlike many other poor souls."

He seemed harmless...bored, almost. I finally stood and began to gather the folders. He stepped nearer and held out his hands.

"Let me carry them for you *Fräulein*. I can hold them while you return them to their proper places. It will be correct that way and easier, too. Then...if someone else requires them meanwhile, they will be there...or when you return, *Fräulein*."

He followed me back into the archives. I couldn't help but smile at his simple kindness and we set about returning the papers to their pigeonholes. As I slid each back in place, I wondered which of them bore the secret of Sophia's whereabouts. Had I been so close as to actually have touched the folder? I silently vowed with each folder, to return soon and conclude my work, hopefully, on the following day.

It wasn't until mid afternoon that we were able to reach his office. We stumbled over the rubble to reach the streetcar station only to learn they were not running...they could not. With the night's bombing damage, we ended up walking most of the way. We were both tired when the lieutenant brought me into an office foyer and left me with a young private, who told me to wait, the *Kaptain* had left but would return. The particular *Kaptain* I was supposed to see had been detained with the bombings and all appointments were late. Nearby, there were two civilian men sitting on a bench, fidgeting nervously.

"*Fräulein*..." the lieutenant was back, "...I hope you have a pleasant and safe stay in Berlin; thank you again for your cooperation in making my duty easier today." Before I could reply, he bowed and left the room.

After waiting an hour and a half, an officer finally strode

into the room, noisily removing his overcoat as he came. The private leaped to his feet and saluted. The officer, a *Kaptain*, stopped at the reception desk and asked the private to follow him into another office. They closed the door after them. Fifteen minutes later the private emerged and told me to go in.

The inner office was also shabby and in disarray. There was a piece of canvas tacked over a window, the panes must have been broken out during the night's bombing. The *Kaptain* didn't even bother to introduce himself.

"Well *Fräulein*...," he glanced at an open folder on his desktop, "...you have been asked here to answer some questions about your activities since reaching *Köln*. The previous night's events have caused such turmoil," he waved a hand at the canvas covered window without glancing around, "...such that the *SS* officer who was supposed to interview you, was unable to reach the office. Fortunately, by telephone he told me you were to be detained until his arrival."

I hadn't even removed my coat yet, or been invited to sit down. He gestured toward the door and stood, indicating the interview with him had come to an abrupt end. I turned toward the door with him following me back into the anteroom.

"Escort *Fräulein*..." he fumbled with the closed folder for a name before giving up. "...take her to the interview holding room to wait for *Kaptain*...," he mumbled a name I couldn't understand.

Two hours later, still without having seen anyone, I'd become both hungry and upset. I could hardly believe I was being detained. They wouldn't even look at my papers. And the room *the cell*, which was what it actually was...was despicably dirty. It hadn't been painted for years and smelled strongly of urine, especially near the corner where the stained chamber pot sat. It was so cold I had to keep my coat buttoned and scarf tied tightly. I'd assumed I wouldn't be there but a few moments, but after thirty minutes, I still huddled on the edge of the cot. I had my knees-together with my arms hugging myself to retain the warmth. Finally, after waiting over an hour I stretched out on the wooden bed-slats and covered myself with the only filthy blanket. I'd thrown the mattress on the floor earlier. It was also filthy and I suspected was probably infected with vermin.

For some reason, they'd taken my watch and now I couldn't estimate how long I'd been detained. I suspected it was getting toward nine in the evening when the lights went completely out, without any warning. I started with surprise, then grew angry, fighting back tears. I yelled for a guard two or three times but there wasn't any sound. I think I was totally alone.

After another half-hour, I sighed, got up, drying my tears on my sleeve and stumbled around in the darkness until I found the mattress. I put it back on the bed. I drew my coat tightly around me, lay down and pulled the blanket over my head. In the darkness, lying there thinking, the blanket smelled like the cell and despite the fact I'd already huddled beneath it for several hours, it still it made my nostrils flare, it stank so.

The *detention* lasted over a week, before I finally saw the *SS Kaptain*. I told him everything I dared, without revealing my true duties in Norway, which were not permitted. I gave him the name of my superior in Berlin. He apologized for the inconvenience caused by my detention, but said there were many spies about now that the war was becoming more intense, as Germany began the final march toward triumph.

I looked closely at him, wondering if he was actually that stupid or merely pretending to believe it; but I dared not say anything, not wishing to infuriate him and reduce my chances for an immediate release.

As in the previous week I was fed only twice daily. The food—if it could be called that, was disgusting. I vowed that when (and if...) I returned to Norway, I would write headquarters in Berlin, complaining, after such treatment. *When* I returned to Norway...and if?

They detained me for nearly two more weeks. It was another three days before they even questioned me again, after this second time. They'd not heard from my commander in Berlin, they said; that was the reason for the delay. This particular inquest was performed by a colonel who just happened to be in Köln at the time and had heard about my acquisition. It interested him, he'd told me. I appealed to him to release me, but he merely smiled and mumbled something about, "…we shall see where this leads…" as if this was supposed to mean something to me.

By the time I met the colonel I had had enough time to become very angry, cool down and then calmly plan what I would say, when I was next asked. I decided to hint that I was posted in Norway and Sweden with occasional trips to England and that it was of a secret nature involving the recruitment of *operatives*. They seemed to be more interested in my duties then.

"Why," I asked them, were they so preoccupied with *our* work in Norway? It was none of their business and I had probably violated the rules of convention by even telling them as much as I had (I'd really said little for which I could be admonished by my own superiors). Why did they not contact my superiors in Berlin, I recounted, there in Berlin…there must be someone in the office who can answer their inquiries…where the project was coordinated. There was nothing in Norway that should interest them. As far as I knew, it was not even that secret. Did they know I was an agent, I wondered?

"Your superiors in Berlin died in the bombing," the colonel finally replied one day. "The whole building was taken down and everyone buried…including the personnel records, which were consumed in the ensuing fire. Your Berlin contact was all that remained," he said and now that had vanished in the bombing there.

The news was devastating to me, but at least they would now have to do something, I thought, now that all avenues of inquire were severed. I wasn't now so concerned about saying *anything* to help myself, though I was still somewhat torn between responsibility and my desire to return to the archives and Sophia's whereabouts.

But the SS colonel persisted. It seemed they were interested in everything…everyone in Norway. Nothing was considered too trivial for the SS, he said. Anything he could glean, I surmised and later, use against anyone else was considered valuable information. I didn't know with whom they would use whatever they learned. I told them they were wasting everyone's time when they should be preparing for the time after the war, for it was certain we must be losing. As soon as the words were out of my mouth, I regretted it. A younger *Kaptain* who had accompanied the colonel to Köln, became immediately aroused. Up until that time, he'd remained seated at a desk, apparently going through dispatches as the Colonel questioned me. Now, at my obvious misstatement about our losing the war, he leaped to his feet and began shouting and pounding the table with his left hand.

"We are *not* losing the war, *Fräulein* Stopff. Do not *speak* such nonsense…you can be jailed for the rest of the war for that sort of…of insubordination, or even shot—that talk is…it is treasonous!"

Hoping to save myself, I seemed to only dig my grave deeper. "But *Kaptain*—just look around you," I said, cowering somewhat, but continuing, "and it is the same throughout the north of the *Deutschland*—I've only just come from there. Bombing? Everywhere—destruction, hunger, fear? And boys—ill-equipped boys and old men in new uniforms…now filling the trains, being taken to the front. Many do not even have any weapons, they told me, going off to war as if it were perfectly normal. Going to school—*to work…that* is normal?"

The colonel cleared his throat and the *Kaptain* took a deep breath, trying to regain his composure.

"You should not speak of such things, *Fräulein*," the *Kaptain* repeated this time, more sedately. "Spreading rumors which are untrue. They will cause confusion among the people," he smiled condescendingly, "possibly even unduly effecting the war effort. The *Kaptain* is correct."

The *Kaptain's* face was still red and a vein pulsed in his neck to show his underlying anger.

"What is the difference? When the war is over…at *this* rate of destruction, there will be nothing remaining to save…for the people. Have you opened your eyes to this city recently, *Kaptain*? Were you in a cellar as I recently was…the night long, smelling the feces of fear? Hearing the children crying? Holding them…the old people weeping?"

I thought the *Kaptain* was going to strike me then. His gesture was more a threat as he raised his only arm, his fist clenched. But he lowered it carefully to the table again, as if to place it nearby, should he require it again. And looking up at me through gritted teeth, he spoke, leaning very close, so no one outside the room could hear him.

"Yes...*I* was in *my* cellar...in *my* house...with my wife, hearing her and *my* children crying in fear—so do not tell me what *you* heard *Fräulein* Stopff."

He took a couple of deep breaths. I said nothing for a moment before muttering: "I'm sorry."

He ignored me. "It is for the *Fatherland*...we must endure it—to the end...*whatever* that may be...*whenever* it may come." This time he struck the table hard enough to make his pencil jump. The colonel intervened.

"Please...*Kaptain*...we accomplish nothing by this. Please control yourself."

With that the younger man rose and strode across the room, taking a seat on the leather divan where he grabbed his shoulder with his good arm, a gesture simulating crossing one's arms, I thought and then sat scowling at me, as the colonel continued.

"Köln has not yet indicated why *they* were detaining you," he'd stated. "Do you have any idea why, *Fräulein?*"

I shook my head, not trusting my voice. I'd originally assumed it was because of my prying into the *Lebensborn* records, but that question hadn't even come up. Simply the fact that I was there seemed to trouble them.

"You were in the research center: why?"

"I was seeking the whereabouts of a child of a friend in Norway...but I didn't...hadn't found anything when they came and took me away."

"Were you aware there were also *SS* records maintained on the same floor where you were conducting your research...possibly in the same area?"

"I had no idea...and as far as I know I gathered no information related to any...those records."

"We have found that out by searching your papers, *Fräulein.*"

"Do you know anything about a recent plot to assassinate the *Fuhrer?*"

"No, nothing. I heard about it before leaving Norway, but I know nothing of those things."

"Supposedly, there was a woman involved, whom we have not yet found."

"I am sorry, I can tell you absolutely nothing."

The colonel returned to his desk and shuffled some papers. Throughout the colonel's questioning the *Kaptain* didn't address me further. Finally the Colonel, who seemed to have exhausted his line of questioning, suspended the interview; thanked me and said they should learn something, soon and would let me know.

As the *Kaptain* summoned someone to return me to my cell, I renewed my protestations about the conditions of the cell and the fact that they were harming the war effort further by continuing to hold me. He made a promise that he would see that a request was made to urge Berlin to provide clear instructions for my handling. I would like to have had them contact someone in Norway but I knew for certain they would then learn about the dead men in my house.

Another day, a different officer questioned me, another *Kaptain*, this one was missing his right eye. They'd bored into the same line of questioning, some sort of odd curiosity—about Norway and my mission. I told each one the same story, fearful, each time that the bodies would suddenly turn up.

When this officer too began to speak the propagandistic rhetoric, I told him that it was just not true and that it was important that Germany begin to make plans for repatriation to the German people—to provide food—essentials of living, to her people. I didn't care anymore, I'd been in that little cell for so long.

But he merely shrugged off my suggestion, claiming it was only Köln which was this badly damaged and that Germany had nearly destroyed, or still controlled most of Europe's capitals and would soon do the same in North America. I reiterated that this was absolutely not true…that even London—as close as it was to our bombers, had suffered little damage from the *Luftwaffe*, after the first year. The other cities in England and the countryside—they did not look like Germany.

"It is a terrible shame, what we have brought upon ourselves, I said, shaking my head philosophically.

The officer said nothing for a moment, faltering, I thought. A sense of curiosity seemed to come over him then.

"Have you been in the west—to France, to England *Fräulein?*" I suspected that he was concerned about the fighting there, since the reports of the Americans coming into France and finally, that Paris had fallen.

"I have not been in France. But I was in London and I had just come down through Denmark—Luxembourg, Belgium where there is destruction, mostly from our *efforts*. But northern Germany is the worst."

"Yes...it's all nearly the same here. We seem unable to prevent the Allies from attacking by air. It first began as day and night bombing of the industrial places in the cities and sometimes, the bombs would fall astray and kill the ordinary people...women—children. But now—now they bomb the whole city, with no regard for civilian life."

He looked at the floor for a while before looking up at me again as if he would speak again, but he didn't and finally, he dismissed me, too, as had all the rest. In the ensuing days, the questioning continued, but never the same interrogator. They all treated me with respect, however. After all, I *was* a German citizen with the rank of *Kaptain*. They must.

I told them the truth—about the Allies, however...what I had seen. They'd seemed to have rolled across that country, like a *blitzkrieg* in reverse, as we had begun. I was sick of war I'd told them. One of them, I even told that I wanted Germany to lose—and soon...anything to hasten the finish of this devastation and get me out of this awful place.

The raids continued weekly on the city. During the day, if we had the electricity, the lights would flicker and sometimes go out altogether. At night it seemed worse, in the blackout. I couldn't see anything, but I could feel the bombs marching toward the building where I was held and of course, hear them; it was the same sound as the first night, when I clasped the small boy in my arms. However, now, I was alone and very afraid of being buried alive.

I had seen hardly any bomb desolation in Norway—no fighting, little destruction. It was well over by the time I arrived. Later, in the rural areas, there were small attacks from the Norwegian Resistance, who quickly went away again to hide in the mountains. One never knew when or where they would strike, but I never saw or heard them.

There was none of this widespread destruction, as we were experiencing in Germany: churches, beautiful, old public buildings, homes, farms. It was everywhere in Germany; the Germany I loved. No one person or place escaped it, it seemed.

I had ample time to consider my few options. I kept turning over various considerations in my head; things that just might have occurred. I hoped, somewhere, my Sophia had been spared the suffering. I didn't know what they did…how they brought about the finish of those they sent east and could hardly bear to let it creep into my thoughts. There were rumors they shot them: the Jews. Would they shoot the children, also? I tried to stop thinking about it. To take my mind off depressing subjects, I thought a good deal about Alex and what kind of life we could possibly have together. I fantasized about us, in future situations after the war…a future together, if there was to be one. That wasn't depressing; that was pleasant. It gave me hope. Someone loved me and I loved someone. I wanted us both alive, to love in return.

Then, without warning, after nearly another week, I was on my way again. They made no excuses, offered no resistance, just took me from my confinement one day, returned my things and let me out onto the street. I felt it was all down-hill for me from then onward; I didn't intend to look back, just do the remaining research and get my daughter.

I returned to the same hotel and immediately had to listen to the complaints of the management about my absence.and the unpaid bill. Withdrawing the parcel from the safe containing my assorted currency I paid the assistant manager enough to remain silent and give me another room, a meal and a hot bath. I felt no qualms about spending that much of the money.

The following morning I was back in the archives building practically running to complete my research. And in that single day, buried in folders, I was able to obtain exactly what I needed, despite glancing over my shoulder at every sound from the stairway, below. Around three in the afternoon I traced the final clue to a document that listed the names of my child's adoptive parents and the town where they lived. Thank God the archives had remained untouched by the bombs. My writing pad now detailed that the adopted parents of Sophia actually lived on a farm, the local town, the parent's names, birthdates…places, all the typically German details that I would not need.

I returned piles of folders to the archives room and taking the stairs two at a time, said goodby to the attendant and was soon into the street, I stumbled through the remaining rubble back to my hotel. Immediately upon arriving, I telephoned the local constable in the town nearest my Sophia's parents, a certain *Herr* Becker. Lying to him about myself and my connection to the child, I told him I was part of an *SS* attachment on special mission.

"And who are you again... *Fräulein...?*"

"Stopff... *Fräulein* Stopff. I'm with the local *SS* office in Köln, as I said *Herr* Becker."

"What was your reason for calling me, *Fräulein* Stopff? I have nothing to do with the Franks, or the *SS.*"

He was very illusive for some reason and only gave me vague answers to my questions about the parents. Probably, the rural mistrust for those from the city, I reasoned.

"We have reconsidered some of the placements from... our program, *Herr* Becker. We will be moving the child we provided the Franks... moving her Eastward where she will be... safer."

"The child has already been moved to live with her grandparents, *Fräulein* Stopff. After the parents—the Franks perished in one of the local bombing sorties on the factory where they worked; the community felt it better that the grandparents care for her... in the event that she already knew them well."

"I see, *Herr* Becker, I was unaware of the parent's deaths." As I considered my good fortune, he went on.

"There is little enough to eat for the community's families, let alone for orphans, *Fräulein* Stopff."

"I understand, *Herr* Becker and sympathize. At any rate, please inform the grandparents that I will arrive tomorrow to transport the child. Have them pack her clothing and be prepared to send her with me. Of course, your office will cooperate with the *SS* in order to make this task as easy as possible, so that I might be in and out without incident, *Herr* Becker." I was ecstatic... hardly knowing what to ask him for next. "You will provide me with directions, *Herr* Becker, to this... farm where the child now resides?"

"I... I wonder if you will wish to come, *Fräulein* Stopff... you see, someone from your office... we presumed they were from *your* office, they arrived earlier last week and *already* transported the child."

The silence after his last statement was deafening. I didn't know what to say.

"Taken? Transported...you say?"

"Transported, to be sure, *Fräulein* Stopff, to the east."

I was so confused, now, after my false triumph.

"*Fräulein* Stopff...?"

"Yes—I am here. I am trying to decide what to do now...*Herr* Becker...this was not—should not have happened. By what authority did they do this, *Herr* Becker and did you assist them in this?"

"They showed me the appropriate paperwork, *Fräulein*, I— we could do nothing but help them."

"Who were these people, *Herr* Becker...did they leave any paperwork explaining their section...division?"

"They did not give us anything, *Fräulein*, we...we were afraid to object to them...their orders...from Berlin."

I didn't know what to do. *Herr* Becker cleared his throat, breaking the silence.

"Then...there would really be little need for you to make such a long journey, *Fräulein* Stopff. Besides, the old people have since been moved to the elder house; the community considered them too frail to continue to care of themselves. Now that the child has been taken from them, there is little need for them to live alone, so far from the village and help."

I wondered whether he was lying to me. Could they have found Sophia already and gotten there ahead of me—while they had me in that infernal prison? Something about this seemed strange. Surely they wouldn't have held me while they took the child?

"Nevertheless, *Herr* Becker, I must fulfill my assignment and come to the farmhouse...make my investigation. How do I get there from the village?"

After a short silence and a deep sigh, he gave me sketchy verbal instructions about the train to the village. He said he would be certain to meet my train and drive me to the farm, so there would be no need. "Only the authorities have sufficient spare benzene to go on these...required missions," he said. I thought he was going to say: "wild goose chases."

But I had trouble getting a seat on the train. "There are many troop movements to the eastern front, *Fräulein*," the agent recounted, bored. "The Russians are coming," a statement that seemed to be on everyone's lips that day.

After flashing my identification papers, I managed to bully a seat from the agent. As an average citizen, he didn't really know how fast they were probably coming and it was not only the Russians. They had only to look to the west, soon.

I glanced at the male faces crowding into the car. The age of the soldiers was either extremely young, or far too old. There was mostly inexperience in the eyes of the young...and fear. In the older men I saw resignation...premature defeat...possibly a defeat by loneliness. Were they already missing home and the hearth fire, the family member? Possibly they, also, were fearing death, knowing in their hearts that they should not have to be serving their country at their ages...possibly for a second time, after the Great War.

I took an aisle seat beside a nursing mother. Both she and her child appeared to be asleep so I made myself comfortable. Sometime later I fell sound asleep waiting for the train to depart. I was exhausted from the emotion of the last couple days. I awoke later when the train stopped to let another group of soldiers came aboard. All the seats were already taken and they'd had to stand in the aisle, which didn't make them very happy. Soon the train started again and I expected to go to sleep again.

Many of the younger soldiers were loud and boisterous. I noticed that whenever a woman got up to go to the toilet, she was groped and jostled as she passed among them. These surely were the trash of our society. I wondered whether we were releasing prisoners...to fight.

When my turn came to use the toilet, I ignored their verbalizations, enduring each *accidental* tug, push and grasp. Once I reached the toilet I found it filthy and I didn't dare sit down on the seat. I had to straddle the reeking mass and empty my bladder.

And it was the same treatment as I wended my way back to my seat, during which I again kept my temper. But when I reached the rear of the car I found my seat now occupied and the nursing mother and child were gone, replaced instead by two soldiers. I stood in the aisle and looked down on the two, sneering young men who dared to meet my eyes and offer me an obscene gesture. I immediately lost my temper, but before I could speak:

"We have commandeered your seat *Fräulein*, in the name of the war effort." He elbowed his quieter companion and snickered.

I threatened them in my most official voice. "Get up, one of you." But neither moved. "Where is your commandant? I have a notion to have the pair of you shot for they way you're behaving."

The reply was an obscenity.

"Where is the young mother that was sitting there?" I pointed to the second soldier sitting next to my seat.

Neither replied, but an older soldier standing in the aisle stepped aside and the woman leaned into the aisle. "I am here."

I turned back to the seated soldiers. "Listen you pieces of trash..." I removed my papers from my pocket, still handy from buying my ticket. "...this...if you can read...will confirm my rank, *Kaptain* in the SS..." I thrust the black, I.D. packet in their faces, "...so I encourage both of you to get up, now!"

For a few seconds I stared at them before they finally dropped their eyes. It worked, though I'd had to turn and walk toward the front of the train before one of them shouted for me to come back. I watched as they gathered their packs sheepishly. With no further protest we were given our seats.

"Thank you, *Fräulein*," the young mother moved back into her seat.

I smiled and nodded. I would like to have inquired about the infant, but I thought it might make me cry, for thinking of Sophie. And I was so exhausted. Preparing to sleep once more, I closed my eyes and smiled to myself, on my way at last to learn the truth about Sophia. Nothing could keep me from knowing, now. I realized as I drifted off, that I had neglected to inquire of *Herr* Becker about the name her grandparents had called the child. No matter, I would find out when I meet him at last.

CHAPTER

CHAPTER

16

The Search

As soon after the bombing run as I could, I arranged a leave through my ABA contact, claiming personal family emergency. Unlike the military, had I officially been still in the RAF, this wouldn't have been possible. But ABA was a commercial company and I was *officially* a civilian, so it was possible. Besides, the ABA shops in London weren't expected to get the engine in the *Junkers*, for at least another week...probably longer. ABA Helsinki suggested waiting for another commercial flight of theirs and returning to duty, although, they said, they hadn't a free ship to give me for another week. Six of one—half dozen of the other, I told the dispatcher.

After the Köln attack and my previous months in ABA, I thought I'd earned a couple days furlough again, anyway. I called *the office*, confirming that I was going to be out of contact with Clyde's for a few days. I didn't tell either where I was going. I didn't want to have to make further excuses.

Two days later I was still frantic, remaining totally in the dark about Greta. I tried everything possible through ABA's commercial contacts in Norway and Germany...the people who dealt with the German military for air transport. I finally had word that

293

Clyde was *available* so I waited for the official call via ABA's office.

When Clyde finally called I told him the truth, expecting and receiving in impromptu lecture about the wisdom of this snap decision to visit wartime Germany, looking for a female, enemy agent with whom I'd fallen in love. And furthermore, he'd added, violating all the spy rules in the process. He resisted in the beginning, but saw that I was committed…he couldn't really do anything about it anyway, given my *employment*. In the end he relented and offered me some contact instructions for one of his people in Germany. I told him I owed him one, for that. In turn, though I wanted to hang up and continue my inquiries after Greta, he told me "a two-beer story," about a woman he'd fallen for right after he was recruited.

"So…what happened," I queried, surprised and very much interested.

He didn't respond for a moment but then he finally chuckled: "I'll tell you the remainder of that story when we next meet for the two beers," he said. "Good luck Old Boy, call me when you get back."

Looking at the odds, the little voice of conscience inside my head kept whispering to me that Greta was probably dead. I had to face it somehow but I couldn't discard the idea that she might somehow have escaped the holocaust of raining bombs in Köln. I'd also had the impression that Clyde thought the same. Something I didn't wish to face the thought of.

I considered it for a whole day and still felt I had no choice— I had to go and look for her and if not her, the child. Clyde had cautioned me about the contact person in Germany. I would be risking both the contact's and my life by attempting to make the contact. "Bear that in mind," he emphasized during our call, "you could be responsible for both your death's."

In civilian clothes again, I hitched with *ABA*, using my crew pass. I changed planes three times before I finally connected to Düsseldorf. From there I had to go by train up to Köln and at one point we'd had to stop because of an air raid. We all got out of the coaches and watched the American B-17 formation bombing the city from high above. I'd never seen anything like it. In formation flight, the American Flying Fortresses looked impregnable. We watched a small flight of Luftwaffe fighters working around the edge of the bombers. In no time, there was smoke and first one then another German fighter came spiraling down in smoke and flame. The remaining fighters soon disappeared, out of ammo or fuel, I thought. Having been there I pitied the fighters having to deal with the firing power of a B-17 and I was pleased that no bombers fell. My companions from the train had cheered when the fighters approached but groaned when each one fell. After it appeared the raid was over, we all got back on the train and managed somehow to get to Köln without being attacked.

On the ground, the devastation wrought by the bombers was unimaginable. I had no idea of what to expect but the destruction was so thorough that it looked as if the same places had been bombed again and again. The fires had long ago burned anything that would burn. Leaving Köln station I had great difficulty getting around in the city. Few streetcars were operating because of their destroyed rail-bed, or rubble from a collapsed building still obstructing the tracks that had escaped. I began to worry I might not get out of Köln unscathed, myself, before I was able to find clues as to what might have happened to Greta, or the exact location of her child.

I immediately began a two-pronged search for her: first, I left a coded message in the drop for Clyde's local contact person. Then I began searching the local *burgomaster* offices and morgues for lists of the dead for the last two weeks. I started checking hospital patient (and death) lists to see whether she might be lingering somewhere, from injuries received in the bombing, or had been killed. Each day I also checked a reply drop, where the contact was to place a reply to my initial contact, assuming he, or she, was still alive. This task turned out to be very difficult because of my restrictions on transportation. Telephone service was nearly non-existent.

After two days, the good news I gathered was that none of the government's or hospital's death lists turned up anyone resembling Greta. I even inquired of a couple of hospitals with female patients who'd had been unconscious, or in shock and were unable to reveal their identity. It took nearly a day to visit both and look at the women. One statistic remained in the back of my mind: over 378 unidentifiable female bodies had been recovered from the rubble and given anonymous burials. I tried to put those statistics behind me.

I checked the drop again on the fifth day and there was a message. Late that evening I made another written connection with Clyde's very nervous, local operative. He took all of the following day to run me on a wild goose chase, giving me the wrong information while shadowing me, I assumed. The following evening *she* came out of hiding.

She was an older woman, or sounded so from her voice. We met in a dark alleyway, at a specific hour and I never did see her face out of the shadow. She worked somewhere in the government and didn't want to get caught, she said, or she and her family would certainly be killed.

After I told her why I'd come, she didn't believe me. I became angry and either she thought I was a good actor, or she finally believed me...about Greta, because she said she would reconsider it and meet me again, soon and we would fix the time and place.

"When," I asked...she'd already begun to slip down the alley.

She answered over her shoulder. "Continue to visit the drop."

I did and after another day, had another rendezvous; this time, a different alley—different time, even later at night.

"Who would be fool enough to fall in love with an enemy agent," were the first words out of her mouth.

I couldn't believe her outburst and immediately grew angry, though I held my tongue for fear she'd flee. I hadn't time to tell her about the child during our last meeting and now blurted that out, too.

"A child? You've come down here for a child—a child you've never even seen? Your enemy's child?" she laughed sarcastically.

"If I can't find the woman, the least I can do is look in on her child...somehow. That's why she came down, in the first place, to Germany."

"How do you expect to do that? You don't even know where she lives...adopted parents you say...and, of course, no names, either."

Her sarcasm wasn't easy to bear. I could see the war had

had a significant effect of her charity.

"Listen..." I didn't' know her name, "...whoever you are, my contact said you were the best and that if anyone could locate her, you could."

"Locate who? The child or the mother?"

"Either—*both*...well, yes, both, but start with one...the mother and then try the child."

"Certainly...stop the war and find your whore."

"You..." before she could back away I stepped up, caught her by the front of her raincoat and half lifted her from her feet. Woman, or no woman, I was angry now. "She isn't a whore...she dropped everything to come get her daughter because she knew she'd be sent to the camps in...the east, or where ever they are. She's a contryman of yours...who's *also* seen the error of her ways for supporting your German madman and she's trying to do the right thing."

I'd been too fast when I grabbed her. I'd scared her and I realized I'd probably ruined my chances. I let go of her coat.

"I'm sorry...it's just...well, she isn't a whore. She's being a mother...with a child that's about to die and I respect that."

"Why didn't you say that in the first place?"

"What?"

"The truth...a mother come to rescue her child. I can help you...but only with the child."

"You can?"

"Most certainly, it is easy to find a child in this instance."

"It is?"

"Tell me Swede, who is looking for a child during war," she asked, snapping her fingers abruptly. "The SS, of course. How many children do you suppose the *SS* are looking for? Probably not very many. So I look for the child the *SS* are looking for. I'll see what I can do. Keep checking the drop." She began to walk away, straightening her coat.

"Wait!"

She turned and I took three steps to reach her again. This time she put one hand in her overcoat pocket. I backed away holding up my hands.

"One last question, please."

"Come no closer...I warn you."

I froze afraid to speak.

"Yes—yes...what about her...your Greta?"

"Try to find her first, please."

"How many women do you think are searching for children in Germany?" she waved a hand at the bombed out skyline, "...in this rubble? Keep checking the drop. I will try to find the child for you. Possibly then you will also find the mother, if she is ahead of you, is smarter than you and hasn't yet been killed—or caught." She turned on her heel and was gone.

I hadn't yet tried working my way through the official channels of the Swedish Embassy in Köln, because I knew how difficult diplomatic staff could be. They were little more than politicians in a foreign country. But I decided to try, first, asking them to probe the German authorities, unanimously, of course, in my behalf. But they were reluctant to get much started for fear of arousing suspicions. After all, they said, they didn't know me and I was an American, by rights, or at least, half American. There could be problems, they said but they would see what they could do. I left without much hope from that quarter.

In order to grease the bureaucratic skids, I'd brought a couple bottles of Cognac, more than ten, one pound tins of coffee beans, several cartons of chocolate bars and some packets of American cigarettes, all filling a single suitcase. There were also three bottles of Danish *aquavit*. I'd had to *borrow* much of the stuff from some of the other pilot's stash, promising to pay them back on my next run to Sweden and the black market, there. I also inquired one last time with ABA, asking them to query her office daily for news. No one in her Norwegian office had heard from Greta, but...ABA had said, they wanted to know who was asking and why. Apparently they were also looking for her now. I wondered whether it was because she hadn't shown up for her job, or what.

Still in Köln and checking my drops, daily, I'd tried telephoning another acquaintance of Clyde's at the Swedish Embassy. Clyde just happened to know someone in the German social services. When I identified myself as an ABA pilot looking for relatives, the guy said he'd check around.

On the third day there was a note in the drop. I could hardly keep from standing right there and reading it. But I walked the prescribed route, dodging and delaying until I was relatively certain I wasn't being followed. There was but one sentence telling me to return to the first drop…no description. I did. Another note and delay while I did the required promenade to shake off a would-be pursuer. This time the note contained a name and address…just like that, I had everything I needed: a name, a village and a family where the child had been sent. Fritz and Fredrika Franks…farmers, living outside a small village an hour's train ride northeast of Köln. The child's name was Katrina. I wondered what Greta would think of Katrina, a name that wasn't Sophia? Though I was excited by the news of the child, I remained disappointed. I'd hoped for something about Greta's well-being or whereabouts. The note contained not even the hint that they were still looking for her. I didn't really know for certain that she'd even been in the city in the first place.

The hotel—the *Reichland* where Greta'd stayed, according to her note, wouldn't give me any information about previous or existing registered guests. It would have taken months to check the other hotels, without the proper authority and resources of someone like the *Gestapo.*

And the Swedish Embassy's social services contact hadn't turned up anything as to Greta's whereabouts, either, when I checked back. So, after two more days of waiting, checking the drop one last time, I finally took the train to the little town mentioned in the note, hoping Greta had found the same information before me and was ahead of me in the search. When I get there, I thought, maybe they'll say that she's come and gone already, with the child. I thought I could always return to Köln, if the Franks proved to be a dead end and continue the search. My spirits weren't at all lifted by that thought, as I figured I'd just about run out of angles.

When the train arrived at the station there were no taxis. The town was very small. I went inside the station house. It was old, run down and a bit dark. There was a light coming through the frosted ticket window, but it was closed. Reaching nimbly through the iron bars, I rapped on the glass and waited. After a minute a shadow moved:

"The station is closed," it said from behind the glass.

"Hello…yes, thank you, I can see that. I wonder…I am Swedish…can you help me with some information?"

The shadow moved closer. There was some rattling and the frame slid up noisily by a skinny old man wearing a green visor on his forehead.

"Yes…what do you want?"

"A taxi…or, a bus. I need to go…" I held up the note so he could see the name.

"Ah…yes, the Franks. There was a taxi, once…but there is now no *bensin* to fuel it. Now? You could hope for a horse cart," he said.

After some questioning, he didn't offer much hope for that, either.

"You can walk. From here it will take possibly one…," he leaned over and glanced at my two valises, "…maybe two hours," he said, "carrying those."

Before he closed the window, I got rough directions to the Frank's farm. Outside, I took a firm grip on my bags and set about walking, not knowing what else to do. After ten minutes I really regretted bringing the larger case containing the black market items. But because hope springs eternal, I hoped for the passage of a horse and cart, but found a bicycle shop, instead.

I turned into the walkway and approached the door. I set one of my bags on the stoop, opened the door and holding it open with my knee, picked up the other and struggled inside. The jingling bell startled me. As I set the cases down it also brought an old man from the back of the shop. He was smoking a pipe and carrying a steaming cup. Like the station agent, a small capless visor ringed his partially balding head. He actually resembled someone in a poker game in a western movie. I found it amusing, in the middle of Northern Germany.

"Good afternoon, Sir," he said, bowing slightly, something obviously reserved for strangers. I had the feeling he didn't see too many people he didn't know. He set his cup on the counter. How to approach this, I thought, dusting off my German again?

"Good afternoon to you, Sir," I answered, drawing a deep

breath.

"How may I help you *Herr...*?"

"*Herr* Andersson," I replied. "I have only just arrived on the train. I wished to inquire whether it would be possible to hire a bicycle?"

"*Hire* a bicycle...hire one?" he replied, chuckling, obviously surprised by a question he'd probably never been asked. He removed the pipe from between his teeth and stood for a moment contemplating the question. His reply confirmed my suspicion.

"I have never hired out any of my bicycles before, *Herr* Andersson. I sell them."

"I can understand that...." I glanced above the counter at a sign that read: *Herr Adolph Henkel - Proprietor.* "...*Herr* Henkel...no doubt you have far too fine of specimens to hire them out...especially to strangers." I should have known better. "May I inquire if you have some good, used bicycles for sale?"

"I...of course, I have new bicycles, but this weather...there's snow on the ground. You should wait for it to melt. You will...you might have an accident, *Herr* Andersson...and the machine...would become very dirty with the ice and sand from the road. Oh...it is not a good time of year to travel by bicycle. Better to walk..." he glanced down at my two valises, "...or take the train, I think?"

"Thank you for your concern, *Herr* Henkel. Of course, you are absolutely correct. But, you see..." I lowered my voice in confidence; he leaned closer then, attentive. "I find myself in a most unusual situation. I have an important message for a family residing in the country...perhaps you know them: *The Franks?*"

"Yes—yes, I know them...they are farmers—were farmers. They live a good distance from here. Over an hour on a bicycle...even more, in this weather."

"That's correct. As I was saying, I have an important message and some items I must deliver to them..." I gestured toward the large valises. "I don't believe I can obtain transport to their farm in the absence of *bensin* and I am afraid it is too much and too far to carry...in this weather. There are no taxis, as you are probably aware...so I thought—when I passed your shop, *a bicycle?*"

"Yes a bicycle would be just the ticket *Herr* Andersson. However, you wouldn't wish to take a *new* bicycle that you purchased, onto these snowy roads? Oh that would be terrible for the paint—the metal. It would be new no longer, after you reached the Franks…no, it would be old and possibly damaged, if you had an accident in the snow, God forbid. And to answer your question, no, I have no used bicycles to sell you."

I could see I was up against a very practical man, who would save me from myself if he could. If I purchased a bicycle, he couldn't condone using it in this weather, so he probably wasn't going to sell one to me. I'd confronted the German sense of sensibility and it appeared to be unmoving at this point.

I was at wits end when I spotted an advertisement showing a depiction of Father Christmas pedaling a three wheeler with a bundle of Christmas presents stuffed in the carrier behind the seat. One of those tricycles would be perfect.

"There, *Herr* Henkel. That is what I need…with my valises. Have you any of those…*new*, of course?"

"Oh no—no I don't have any of those any more, *Herr* Andersson."

My hopes were dashed at last.

"*Frau* Applebalm purchased the last one."

"*Frau* Applebalm? Do you think she would sell it?"

"Oh…I doubt it…, she can not, actually, she died last summer."

My patience wasn't built for these simply-complicated rural ways.

"What did *Frau* Applebalm do with it, *Herr* Henkel?"

"Nothing, now, of course. She's dead—dead, these past six months? Her only daughter lives in the house, alone and she does not use the tricycle. She has her own—a two-wheeler. She is young and has no need for an old person's bicycle."

I brightened, persevering.

"*Herr* Henkel, do you suppose her daughter would be interested in selling the bicycle—just to help me out—to help out the Franks?" He took out his pipe again and stared at the cup, now no longer steaming, before picking it up anyway.

"She might…you could certainly ask her." He sipped from the cup, then frowning, put it down again. I stood, frustrated. I almost shook my head in wonderment, but caught myself.

"*Herr* Henkel, I don't know her daughter and…and be-sides, would it be proper to approach her now, barely six months after her mother's demise. She doesn't know me. I'm a perfect stranger?"

He put his pipe down with some air of finality, beside the cup.

"How considerate, *Herr* Andersson. Of course, you're right. It would not be."

I had an idea. "*Herr* Henkel—let me make you a proposi-tion. Considering the situation…." I went on to offer him a ten percent commission of the selling price and then to sell the bicycle back to him for ten percent of what it cost me, after I was finished with it. If it wasn't too badly damaged from the journey and if he didn't wish to purchase it, then, he wouldn't be obligated to; I would understand.

He didn't say anything for a moment. I could see I'd found a man who understood opportunity—for profit. He looked at me for a few seconds, considering what I had said. Then he removed a pencil from his vest and a piece of paper and began to write some figures on the counter.

After a bit, he showed me the pad, clamping his pipe firmly in his mouth in expectation of having to dicker with me. I disap-pointed him, nodding, agreeing to his price before he could change his mind. He nodded back.

"I agree to try, *Herr* Andersson; come…back to my office to take a seat. Here, let me take your coat and hat. Taking my coat, he disappeared but returned from the rear of the establishment and offered me some steaming liquid from a kettle. Once I was seated, cup in hand, he went over to a telephone on the wall behind the counter. He began a long discussion with someone whom I pre-sumed was the local operator. Then there was a silence, during which he glanced in my direction and nodded, smiling encouraging-ly, holding up his pipe to indicate things were progressing.

Then he began speaking again…pleasantries, at first, though I didn't catch everything he said. But after a while he got around to the business side and within ten minutes, I was ready to pay him the price.

"No, no, *Herr* Andersson…you should not do that now.

You have not yet seen the machine. It is *possible*...you see, that I have made a mistake. We must examine it first—the tricycle might not be worth what I have arranged. I have already cautioned *Fräulein* Applebalm we might not take it after seeing it.."

He'd began donning his coat and pulling his hat from beneath the counter. Stopping by the door, he said: "Please wait for me here, *Herr* Andersson...*Fräulein* Applebaum will unlock the shed and let me bring the machine back here, first—for the inspection. Once I have gone through that, we can speak of money, if it proves satisfactory." His hand was on the door: "And I must give it a going over, you know...before you set out...oil, tightening the chain..." the door slammed and the bell jingled and I was on my own. I could feel my patience strained, but knew I'd be little further along the gravel road, and sweaty and tired by now, had I chosen to try to walk. And then there would be the journey all the way back to town to catch the train again.

An hour and a half later, *Herr* Henkel held his shop door for me as I pushed out my newly-purchased, well-oiled tricycle, fully loaded with my luggage, tied down with straps he loaned me. He followed me out into the snowy street. I had my directions refreshed and was soon pedaling slowly along the narrow road, over the thin coating of snow. Turning once to wave at the pipe smoking figure staring after me, I wondered how crazy he thought I was?

Another hour and a quarter, having worked up a good sweat, I saw some activity beside the road ahead as I approached the area where the Franks were supposed to be living. A small girl was playing with two cats in the front yard of a small farmhouse. She was about the correct age for Greta's Sophia...maybe three years—nearing four. If it was the child she wouldn't be called Sophia, here I thought. Could it be Katrina as they had said?

I wasn't sure I had the correct farmstead but the house/barn combination fit the description, both in color and placement. Then an old woman came walking up the driveway from the house, stopping beside the child. She was stooped and wore several sweaters over her house dress and apron.

The child was occupied with something on the driveway,

out of my line of vision. The old woman stood now with her arms crossed in a posture of patient boredom, occasionally glancing down toward the child, finally reaching with one arm and speaking words beyond my hearing.

As I drew closer, I saw that she was patiently watching the little girl alternately pick up and drop a pair of of yellow and brown, marbled kittens, in turn. It appeared she was trying to place the cats in one spot and make them stay where she put them.

Turning from the road, I started down the drive toward them, wobbling in the heavier going where the snow hadn't been plowed or packed down by traffic. From the road, I'd mistakenly shouted good afternoon, in Swedish, to the old woman. They both looked up. The child only glancing, returning immediately to herding her kittens on the edge of the drive. But the old woman walked around in front of the child, placing herself between us, in a protective gesture. She put her fists on her hips as I continued to approach.

I hadn't spoken so much German since college, as I'd talked with *Herr* Henkel, but I felt my skill in that language was good enough for this woman to understand me. I greeted them again, this time in German, as I came closer. Then I dismounted and began pushing the unwieldy tricycle. I must have presented a curious sight to her.

I think the old woman recognized *foreign* in my accent and took a more relaxed stance, probably thinking at first that I was a thief, or something. She'd taken hold of the child's shoulders and pulled her around in front of her, leaving her hands resting on each side to the pretty, child's face, as if to warm the girl's cheeks. I tried to keep my brightest smile for them.

"You are Swedish?" the old woman asked, matter-of-factly as I pulled up and stopped beside them. She wasn't exactly smiling, but she'd let her arms relax at her sides and seemed more inquisitive. "I thought you were a Gypsy peddler at first."

"*Nein*...but I'm a Swede alright."

"What's a Swede doing way out here in the countryside?" she said, a little more friendly, "and I see you have *Frau* Applebaum's tricycle, too. You haven't stolen it, have you?"

"*Nein*...I have bought it from *Herr* Henkel," I replied smiling and reaching across, patted the beautiful little blond head on the child. I didn't want to get into the complication of the tricycle.

She seemed satisfied with my answer and nodded, accepting it as logical fact.

"It was a good tricycle. *Frau* Applebaum rode it everywhere."

Ja...so *Herr* Henkel told me as he was repairing it...before selling it to me." I wanted to get off this subject and learn their identity, or how far I was from the Frank's farm.

"You have pretty cats, I said to the child."

She seemed puzzled, then looked up at the old woman, her face a question.

"You have fine cats...*leibschen*..." the woman repeated in better German. Whereas the child nodded, grinned and chattering to herself, picked one up and then held it up closer for me to better see.

"*Ja—ja*," I said, imitating the woman's course dialect: "...fine cats."

I tried to pet the squirming animal without getting clawed.

"What is the child's name?" I asked still smiling at her antics with controlling the cats.

"She is called Katrina," the woman said, not supplying a surname as I'd hoped. I didn't press her further, thinking I'd probably found them. There's time, yet, I thought.

"Where are you going...walking with a tricycle?" the woman asked, a kind expression on her face. "Have you lost your way?"

"I certainly hope not," I said. "I'm seeking the Franks—Fritz and Fredericka Frank's farm. Is it near?" I had a pretty good idea this place was it—their farmstead.

"Why do you want them," she asked, suddenly on guard again. Do you have money—or food for them?" Glancing at my suitcases, she added, "...or, are you a distant relative from the city, come to live with them to get away from the bombing?"

"No—none of those, but I have some information for them...about their *adopted* daughter...from the authorities in Berlin."

The old woman's face turned into a mask of fear at the emphasis I'd put on the word "adopted" and she clutched the child to her once again.

I continued: "I learned there is to be trouble and I have journeyed from Köln—I wanted to warn them."

"You have come for nothing," she said with an air of finality. "They are both dead," she added matter-of-factly. "They died when a bomb...in the town...a factory where.they were both working...I was caring for the...." she stopped just short of saying she was caring for Katrina. I wondered if this was a grandparent, or maybe a neighbor. So, they'd died in an air raid. I don't know if this complicated matters or not.

"And why are you taking all of this trouble, anyway, to come all the way out here looking for them...and their daughter? Are you with the government?"

"The child is in danger," I said, without smiling. "Something was wrong with her...her *parentage*." I looked down at the little girl, stopping just short of saying she was Jewish.

"They will soon come to take the Frank's child away, I am told," I intoned the words, simply—quietly. I made no disguise I thought this was the child and she was possibly a relation.

"Why would they wish to take the Frank's child," the woman said, following my glance. "She is but a little girl. What use could she be to them in Berlin?" She was going to force the issue. I certainly hoped she was not anti-Semitic.

"Because the child is...is not as pure as they once thought," I said. "The father, though an officer in the *SS*, was also a Jew."

"*Juden?*" she said with a sudden intake of breath. She drew the little girl closer, telling me I'd made my point.

"The mother is a civilian official in the *Nazi* party, now living in...in Scandinavia. She learned of this information through a friend in the government and has returned to Germany...seeking the child. She was...trying to come here to warn the Franks, or take this child away before the authorities did."

"There has been no woman here...no one, wanting...seeking a child."

"She arrived in Köln two weeks ago, the same night of the last heavy bombing. She should have been here before now and...and I am...I am afraid she may have been killed in the bombing...before she could learn where they had adopted her daughter to...which family."

She looked down at the little girl, placing her palm on top of Katrina's wool scarf.

"Yes, Köln…it must have been terrible there. It looked like hell on earth we were told—even from this far away we heard about it. Was there much damage? Have you been there?"

"I have been there, inquiring at the Köln hospitals—the bombing casualties, seeking news of the woman…" glancing at the child, "…her mother."

She ignored the acquisition.

"There was no…news—of this woman?"

"No, no one has seen or heard of her. She has not been killed, or injured…*officially.*"

"In that fire, they would not have found anything left of her," the woman said matter-of-factly, hardened already by the cruelty of the war and unaware of the pain the remark caused me. I shrugged off the thought as she spoke again, regarding me very seriously.

"What were you going to do…with the Franks, when you found them…and the child? Since you did not find the woman, what would you do? You did not answer my question before; *are* you from the government?"

"No…I'm Swedish…a friend of her mother's. I've come only to look for the woman…whom I have…some affection for and failing that, to…I don't know…to *warn* them…the Franks, let them know the child will definitely be taken soon. Tell them that they should find somewhere to hide her—get her away from this place where the *Gestapo* people will soon come, seeking her. I guess I hoped they could somehow save her. Hide her, until after the war, possibly. Somewhere she would be safe. Somewhere the war would not affect her. Somewhere…somewhere her birth mother could find her after the war, if she is still alive."

"Like Sweden…" the woman said, looking me directly in the eyes.

"Sweden? Oh—no, that's not what I meant. Just somewhere in Germany where she could be well hidden. I only came to give them the information—so they would have time, so they could prepare…and I thought—I hoped I might also find the woman…possibly."

"Time for what?" She had suddenly grown quite animated. "Prepare for what? What could they do, so far out here in the country? Where could they take her...the child you speak of? There is no where we can go...at our age—in these times. They would find us and still take Katrina. They have ways—those people. She would never be safe in Germany, today, as long as she lives."

The look of alarm on my face must have shown because she stopped and smiled a wry smile then. She looked at the house at the end of the driveway and then glanced up the road.

"Must you go on tonight—*Herr*...Andersson? It will soon be dark and it is going to be very cold upon the road—even danger-ous, tonight. Why do you not stay with my husband and me. You can make further inquiries tomorrow. Possibly we can even assist you. Your German, you know? It could confuse some around here."

I considered her offer too long and she began to fidget. "I must take the child back now. My husband is ill and I dare not remain away from him for too long. We only came down here for...for the cats," she said, "so she could see her cats. They are all she has now. This was the house where my son-in-law and his wife lived, before. They had other cats, but only these survived."

The significance of that remark didn't escape me.

"I suppose I can accept your offer. I don't know what else to do. You're right, *Frău*, it's getting late, but I can't remain too long here, though. I'd hoped to find the mother...and the Franks before now. I must be getting back to Sweden tomorrow, for sure."

We had began to walk toward the road. The child ran ahead and then fell behind again, attempting to herd her cats, which was an impossible task.

"To Sweden?" the old woman asked after a moment.

"Yes...well, actually to England," I said, "then Sweden and finally, Norway, where I work, when I'm at home."

"You will go *to England*," she said, seeming astonished. "But then you are Swedish, a neutral. So I guess you can go any-where you wish."

"Yes, almost anywhere, in my job."

"Come then..." her enthusiasm was something to see as she hastened her step, "...you must share our meal tonight and talk. You have come so far and on such a kind errand. We may be able to help you. I will ask my husband."

I thought I might be making progress with her. "Do you

think he knows where the mother can be found?"

"No...as I said, he is old...and ill. He knows nothing of the mother. No one here did...until you came, now."

I was concerned about taking their food. I assumed rationing was rampant in war-time Germany. "*Fräu*...I do not wish to deprive you of your food by staying?"

"We have little, like everyone with this war, but I can fill you up with some hot food, at least. Come...hurry, please. My old husband and I live down the road...that way," she indicated a grove of bare trees in the distance. "There in that small cottage. I have something to...there is something you must consider...you...*Herr* Andersson. Oh...I...!"

She'd become frustrated and had suddenly stopped walking, putting her hand to her eyes. I reached across and took her arm, steadying her.

"Please, *Fräu*...don't cry. Come—I'll follow you home...but you must realize, I can't take the child back with me."

The child was looking up at us curiously, not knowing what to make of her suddenly weeping grandmother and the strange man.

"I—I am all right now," she said, taking up the pace again. As we began to trudge back through the snowy, weed-grown driveway, the woman finally admitted the truth. "How did you know what I was thinking?"

I didn't have time to frame an answer before her next question.

"But...we have no one else to turn to, you see. Your coming is a Godsend. This child..." she indicated the little girl, who was now running ahead of us in the road, "...this is the child you speak of. My husband and I are the grandparents. Fritz Franks...he was my man's son from his first wife. We have had no children from our marriage. When our son and his wife were killed, we were desperate to know what to do with this child. Now you have come with this news—I now know what is the answer: You...*you* must take her out of the country with you—to England, or to Sweden—anywhere she will be safe. You *must* consider it *Herr* Andersson. You must! Return her to her mother."

"But...I have no wife—no one to care for a child," I blurted in desperation at her outrageous suggestion. My God, I thought,

I didn't think it would come to this. I looked at the playful little girl. At worst, I'd hoped to take her to an orphanage, or something, where she'd be safe until the end of the war.

"Katrina's birth mother is probably dead and I know of no living relatives...anywhere. I don't even know where she came from in Germany—the birth mother. I only *know* her in Norway. I know nothing about caring for children and I am never at home—my job. I do not even *have* a home...I travel constantly. So...who would take care of Katrina if I were to take her away?"

"Who will take care of Katrina in the east, for as long as she lives?"

I didn't meet her gaze and of course, I didn't have an answer.

She stopped, turning toward me agressively: "You *know* about the east, *Herr* Andersson? You have heard the rumors of the camps—what goes on there? Yes? So...is that what you would have come of this beautiful little human being?" She wiped her eyes with the edge of her apron. "Better she wanders the streets, homeless in Sweden, than remain here in Germany after the awful news you bring. At least she would be alive there."

Katrina staggered up to us, having successfully caught up a cat awkwardly in each arm. "*Nein Leibschen...*" she told Katrina to put down the cats. "We will come again," she said, possibly tomorrow." She glanced up at me as if the answer lay in me. "Come, let us go home for something to eat. I grow cold with this conversation here on the road." We hurried along the drive I'd just come down.

"It is not far...just there," she said pointing across a small field toward the grove. I could see a house set back in the edge of the forest. The little girl ran ahead of us again, stepping deliberately in my bicycle track with each foot. When we came to the wider, main road, we turned toward the house.

"Go ahead Katrina...see what grandfather is doing with himself, *Leibschen*. See that he has awakened from his nap. Tell him that we have a visitor...a special visitor from Sweden...say the word all the way home so you do not forget it—Sweden—Sweden," she said, smiling up at me and taking my arm.

Katrina began to chant: "Sweden—Sweden..." running ahead until she was out of our hearing.

He had awakened, it seemed, *Herr* Franks. Although he appeared frail in body, his spirit was not. His mind was sharp and he was eager to speak with me, once his wife introduced me as a visiting Swede. Apparently he'd been once to Sweden, on a farmer's sojourn of some sort, years ago. Now he wished to tell me all about the country. But not before *Frau* Franks was finished with me.

"*Ja—ja*...you can talk again after I show him his room," she said and took me upstairs and installed me in a room along the long, central hallway, instructing me to come down when I was ready.

I looked around the dim surroundings of the room as I listened to her footsteps disappearing down the hallway, muttering to herself as she went. All I caught was part of a phrase: "Praise God...."

There was still a little daylight coming in from the single window. I'd been cautioned by *Frau* Franks about using the single candle on the bedside table after darkness and to draw the blind. Glancing around the chamber, I was unable to identify who might have previously occupied the room. There were a couple of copies of engravings on the wall, of people in hundred-year old costume, but no evidence of their deceased child, or his wife.

I opened the smaller suitcase and began laying out some of my things, rearranging them absently and thinking about what the woman had asked me. It was cold in the room, I realized, after spending a rather unproductive quarter hour, trying to sort out the day's events and discover a solution to questions I knew would come again from the couple, below. I finally stood up, entered the hallway and closed the door behind me, but opened it again, thinking it might warm up faster before bedtime. In pitch black I felt my way along the hallway, down to the stairway and joined my hosts again.

While his wife busied herself preparing our evening meal, I listened to *Herr* Franks tedious narration of his adventures in Stockholm and a bus tour of some of the farms in the southern Swedish provinces.

"I even have photographs..." he said, glancing toward the kitchen and speaking loudly enough for his wife to hear the hint, "...upstairs somewhere."

But she wasn't to be bothered. "There's food to prepare for our guest," she said, poking her head around the doorway and waving a paring knife over her shoulder in our direction.

Herr Franks shook his head and made a futile gesture, before grinning at me and launching into another story.

Later, as we ate the simple meal of meat-flavored potatoes, turnips and onions, he maintained an animated conversation, "about the good years...," as he called them, "...before the war."

He spoke about his son and his own first wife, smiling across the table at his *new* mate, informing me how fortunate he was to find a second spouse, equally as nice...someone to take over the role of mother to his son and wife to himself.

As he said, "...it is the most important role in the family, the mother's...." *Frau* Franks made clucking noises as he expounded further on their inability to have children of their own. "It was not for lack of trying," he repeated, with a cautious wink in my direction. "And then this little one came along...for my son's childless marriage. When the opportunity came to adopt the little girl, we urged them to take her quickly in. More children may still come naturally, later, we told them, but in the meantime, we said, they would have a daughter and we would have a granddaughter to love and spoil."

Between them, they continued the story, chatting affably, back and fourth, taking turns as if my appearance at the farmstead helped them to remember the good times. They told of happy years they'd had with Katrina. Hearing it all I began to feel a sense of conscience; guilt, actually. Occasionally, I could see Greta staring at me with her beautiful eyes, entreating me silently to take Katrina—save the child. The thought of the camps to the east for an adult was bad enough; but for a child of Katrina's age? I didn't permit my subconscious dwell on the thought. I doubted she probably wouldn't survive the journey back with me anyway, unless another woman willingly took her in hand to share her mother's love and somehow assisted me. What did I know about caring for a child of her age? Where would I put her?

As we chewed in silence I suddenly had the sense of something missing from the meal. Though the food was abundant, it lacked the usually substantial meat course, though the quantity of the vegetables more than made up for it in bulk. I didn't dare to ask what the meat flavoring was that made up the gravy. I finally realized what it was that was nagging me...after supper coffee and dessert.

Knowing they'd none of these luxuries, I excused myself after we finished and went upstairs to my room and rummaged through the large valise of contraband treasures. I unwrapped one of the cans of coffee and took three chocolate bars from their carton. As I turned to leave, I had a second thought and returned, grabbing one of the bottles of *aquavit* and tucking it under my arm; I left the room.

Picking my way down the darkened stairway again, I hoped I wouldn't need these commodities somewhere else before I reached home again. I still hadn't found Greta. Now, after what I'd seen of the Köln devastation I thought I probably wouldn't.

The old woman had cleared the table and was just pulling a nightgown over Katrina's uplifted arms as I entered the dining room.

"You are just in time to say goodnight to our little darling, *Herr* Andersson."

I held out the chocolate bar to Katrina. "Is it alright if she has a small sweet before she goes to sleep."

Frau Franks face froze. "Chocolate, *Herr* Andersson? Where ever did you manage to get chocolate?"

"Will she still be able to sleep if she shares a chocolate bar with us before bed…and I have some coffee, too. Would it be too much trouble to boil a cup for us while we talk?"

The old man sat up straighter at the word coffee.

"Oh—*Herr* Andersson…we could not think of drinking your coffee. It is so precious…and chocolate, oh…I am not certain whether Katrina has even tasted chocolate… but certainly…yes, she may have it."

I knelt down on one knee and continued holding the bar toward the child.

"It is all right, *Leibschen.* You may take the candy." To me she said: "She does not know what it is."

Katrina took a step toward me and took the bar carefully, then stepped back and leaned against her grandmother.

"Give *Herr* Andersson a hug and a good night kiss *Leibschen*…he has given you a special present, too…just like at Christmas time."

I received my wet kiss. The coffee tin and the other two bars, I gave to the old woman. She beamed, holding them up for her husband to see. Then she turned toward the kitchen. I stood up and returned to the table, sitting down beside the old man.

"Come..." I told Katrina, who still hadn't opened the candy wrapper. "Come and sit here. I will help you."

Patting my lap, I didn't know whether she'd understood my German. But she did, ran over and climbed up as if she'd known me all her life. Sitting sideways facing her grandfather, she put her arms in her lap in anticipation. I circled her with my arms and began to tear one end of the wax paper wrapping. Katrina glanced back over her shoulder and smiled up at me.

"See...." I showed her how to slide off the colorful wrapper. Then we gently peeled back the paper, turned over the bar and placed it intact on the wrapper on the tabletop for inspection.

Eight little rectangles of chocolate held together by a runner on the bottom of the bar. Each square bore the chocolate maker's name and logo face up. I picked up one end; the bar was cold from being in my room. I broke off one section first and then divided one of the little rectangles. I offered it up to Katrina. The old man watched our every move, swallowing soundlessly and smiling broadly.

Katrina took the piece and then glanced over her shoulder at me with a questioning look.

"You may eat it," I said, indicating my mouth with a gesture. She held the piece toward me, smiling.

"*Nay...nein*—for *you*...," I said, laughing along with the old man.

"She is generous now," he said, "let us see if it continues once she has had a taste of it."

As he spoke the little girl gingerly bit off half the section and began to chew it. She stopped momentarily and we watched the expression on her face. She smiled brightly and began to chew again, even more vigorously barely stopping to put the second square in her mouth.

"Ho—ho," the man said, "she likes it—and should she not."

As he spoke Katrina glanced at him mischievously, as if she'd been caught enjoying something forbidden. We both chuckled to watch her expressions. She twisted around in my lap and looked at me over her shoulder. There was a questioning in her hesitancy, but when I smiled, she returned it with a smile that was so much like Greta's, it startled me. I could hardly believe the similarity; there was no question of the child's parentage. She suddenly twisted around in my lap and gave me a mighty hug and sticky kiss.

"*Danka Papa...*" she said brightly before returning with vigor to her chocolate.

"Haaa..." she has adopted you, *Herr* Andersson," the old woman brushed a tear, shaking her head.

I knew then...I was lost to this cause of theirs. I could never abandon this child, even if I never found Greta, this was definitely her little girl. The thought of what would probably happen to her was unbearable to me at that moment...that smile haunted me.

The old man and I sat silently, enjoying the sight of her savoring piece after piece of the candy. She still had half the bar remaining when the old woman reappeared, carrying a tray with steaming pot and cups. On the tray was one of the two chocolate bars, broken apart onto a small silver saucer.

"I just fetched some milk this morning from the neighbor who still has a cow, thank God...so we have milk with your coffee *Herr* Andersson. I apologize that we have no sugar. This will have to do and I can not tell you how grateful we are for your generosity."

"You're very welcome *Frau* Franks, it is you and *Herr* Franks who are generrours, inviting me in...this fine meal...the coffee will be fine without sugar—and please, I will have none of the chocolate. I can get chocolate at home, so please...enjoy it yourselves." Who knew how long since they'd tasted chocolate, I thought...or coffee.

The woman poured the steaming liquid into small, flowered, china cups for each of us. Watching them I could see the old couple could hardly wait for the brew to cool. Both were holding up the cups, their noses nearly touching the liquid, as they inhaled the long-forgotten aroma. The old man lifted his cup toward me and then the old woman as we shared a silent toast.

Each gingerly tipped their cup carefully, deliberately spilling a small amount of coffee into the saucer, then sipped from the edge. But it was still too hot. They glanced at each other and smiled; they could wait. *Herr* Franks nodded his appreciation once more and made small noises of approval as he held the cup beneath his nose, savoring the wonderful aroma so long absent from their table. I almost forgot the *aquavit*, which I had placed on the floor beside my chair.

"*Herr* Franks, would I insult you if I offered a toast to your family?"

I reached beside my chair, groping for the neck of the liquor bottle. Finding it, I held out the nearly full bottle of liquor toward them.

From the look on his face I thought the old guy might drop his coffee.

"Oh—*Mein Gott...*" he exclaimed in surprised look of pleasure sweeping his countenance. He stared at clear liquid in the bottle and then glanced at his wife.

"*Herr* Andersson..." she said, smiling and shaking her head as she put down her saucer and stood up.

"You work miracles tonight. I will get the glasses. Oh—this is too much...coffee, first—and now *schnapps* in the same evening. It is almost too much to bear. It has been so long."

Waving her apron in pleasure, she muttered to herself as she disappeared around the corner into the kitchen. I moved the bottle across the table.

"Would you care to pour for us, *Herr* Franks, as the head of the house?"

"*Nein*," he said, "my hand will shake and I may spill it, sir. Please, it is your bottle—you must pour it.

Frau Franks returned carrying three, small crystal glasses on a little tray. Before she placed them in front of each of us, she carefully gave each one a quick polish with the hem of her apron. "I regret they are a little dusty, *Herr* Andersson, but it has been so long since they have been used you see."

I'm sure they're fine, *Frau* Franks," I intoned, carefully drawing the short cork from the bottle; I began pouring into the glass nearest her. She held up a hand in protest when I reached the half-way level.

"Please—that is enough. I shall fall asleep at the table."

I continued to pour a little more and then nodding at her murmur of appreciation did the same for her husband before filling my own glass. I returned the cork to the bottle but didn't seat it. The old man noticed this gesture which of course meant, we were not finished with the bottle. I grasped the tiny stem of the crystal and held it up toward the light. The decorative incisions in the body of the glass cast sparkling beams across the faces of my hosts as I slowly turned the stem between my fingers, admiring the clarity of the liquid.

They smiled waiting for me to finish. Looking both of them in the eye, I thrust my glass toward them.

"To my hosts and new friends, the Franks family."

They nodded their appreciation without speaking and we all took a sip from our glasses, then smiled all-round, the Franks murmuring their appreciation for the fineness of the strong drink. *Herr* Franks coughed and took up his coffee saucer again and was able to take a larger sip.

"Oh— *wundebar!*" he exclaimed.

We soon finished our first cup of coffee and had another all round. I noticed *Herr* Frank's *aquavit* glass was soon empty, so I drained mine in a gulp and picked up the bottle, drew the cork and offered to pour another for his wife.

Frau Franks refused a second glass. "It makes me silly, you see..." she said, "...and these are serious times. We have yet to discuss serious matters," she said, indicating with a smile and nod Katrina, who still sat in my lap. I hadn't noticed, but when *Frau* Franks nodded toward her, I saw Katrina'd fallen asleep, her head leaned back against my chest and both arms on the table; the ends of her fingers were slightly smeared with chocolate.

"There is a happy child...here, let me take her to bed so you can enjoy yourself," *Frau* Franks stood up.

I leaned forward slightly and gently kissed the top of the child's blond head before handing her off to her grandmother. She smelled like a mixture of perspiration, wool, cat and chocolate. Handing her up to the waiting arms, I could smell the sweet child smell of her as *Frau* Franks took the limp form and turned toward the stairway, disappearing into the darkened hallway.

"As you were upstairs earlier," the old man indicated with an inclination of his gray head, "...my wife told me about why you have come here."

He sat for a moment staring at his big hands, turning them over, trying to rub the pain from the swollen, rheumatic fingers.

"Of course we knew the child was an orphan, but we were unaware she was a product of the *Lebensborn* effort…something we do not agree with, of course. Country people like us are…conservative, you see."

He turned his half-full glass around a little, staring at the slivers of light the facets cast on the tabletop. "Possibly, it is because we are old fashioned…having children without the church and then abandoning them to the government, like puppies…it just does not seem right for many German people. But we welcomed the child, nonetheless, when she was offered to my son. Both families hungered for a grandchild, so it was truly a blessing when my son and his wife…."

I nodded, preparing myself to hear the sadness he and his wife had borne since the death of his son and his wife. He didn't speak for a moment, taking another sip of the *aquavit* and then sitting in silence, rubbing his hands slowly before he cleared his throat and looked up at me, as if he'd changed his mind.

"May I ask what you hear of the Russians, *Herr* Andersson? Do you know how far away the front is now? We are told officially, you see, that The *Fatherland* has made tremendous progress on the Eastern Front. But, unofficially, rumors are that it is not so…that we are losing the war on all fronts…something I find hard to believe, having been in the last one, but please, can you tell me what you know?"

I hated to dispel his hopes. But as I began to recount what I knew, it became obvious that he was prepared, anyway, to learn that Germany had suffered tremendous losses by this point of the war. The fact that we were selectively bombing such cities as Köln and others came as no surprise to him.

"All Germans," he said, "have seen the Allied bombers."

I didn't elaborate on most of the significant battles. He was curious that the battle for Britain hadn't lasted any longer than it did and that the *Luftwaffe* had failed so miserably. I'd told him the *Luftwaffe* was more or less, a thing of the past as they had previously known it and that the Allies, for the most part, owned the skies over Europe.

"I shall not wish to tell my wife all you have recounted, *Herr* Andersson. She will only worry more, not for us, but for Katrina."

Here he looked very knowingly into my eyes. "Should you not be able to help…it is best she should not worry more than she must." He sat back, quickly and smiled as *Frau* Franks returned, rubbing her hands and smiling.

"That is the first time she's had such a contented evening in a long time. She is usually not so agreeable about going to bed, *Herr* Andersson. It must have been your kindness and a comfortable lap to fall asleep upon," she said.

I knew she was buttering me up. "More likely it was the chocolate," I said. I looked at my own hands for a moment before glancing around the table at their faces. They didn't say a word but their eyes plead with me.

"Yes…I will be willing to take her away with me," I said, simply, "but I do not know how it can be accomplished."

"Oh—*danka Gott!..*" *Frau* Franks said, reaching across the table to clasp my hand. "You are so kind, *Herr* Andersson. How will we ever be able to thank you?"

"There is no need, *Frau* Franks…please…" I said as she continued to wring my hand.

"This calls for another toast!" her husband exclaimed enthusiastically.

"Hans!" *Frau* Franks said, sternly, "It is not *yours* to…to propose toasts to," she admonished her husband, nodding toward the bottle.

"That's all right, *Frau* Franks. It does call for a toast…one more and then…then you must tell me how I am to accomplish all of this with the child and what I am to do with Katrina if I ever get her to Scandinavia." I poured the bottle all round and as we again lifted our glasses.

"To a safe journey," the old man said.

"And to peace…" the old woman offered, glancing at her husband and me; we both echoed it, raising our glasses in silence.

For over an hour we discussed the several escape options they felt were open to me. *Frau* Franks was a very resourceful lady. Her keen mind had certainly not dimmed with age and at times I was surprised by the devious nature of her thoughts. She barraged me with question after question about my relations, my employment, how long I was away from home, if I had money for food and clothing...bribes. When she learned my father was an American I thought she would faint with excitement at the chance Katrina could possibly someday become an American.

I quickly steered her back on the course we were pursuing of getting Katrina out of Europe and back to Norway or Sweden...where, I didn't know for sure, I told her, now that I was unsure of her mother's location...or existence.

After further inquiry about my Swedish mother's relations in Sweden, *Frau* Franks decided it was best that I attempt to take Katrina there, to someone—anyone, if I could.

"Sweden is still neutral and will best be able to keep our darling safest," she said, "if only you could find a loving relative to care for her—even adopt her there."

It was decided, then—that was the course to follow. I was still not sure how I would be able to get out, traveling with a small child who had no traveling papers—no identity. I couldn't smuggle her out on an ABA flight; the *Nazis* checked every manifest and passenger.

I noticed *Herr* Franks had been quiet for a while; finally he spoke.

"There is a printer in the town," he muttered.

"Yes," his wife said expectantly, "*Herr* Schmidt is the printer in town. The same *Herr* Schmidt who still owes us for the pig we sold him—our *last* pig it was—for which he has not paid us...still, after more than a year."

"*Ja—ja*—he has no money and a very hungry family to feed. He will pay...he will pay, wife...and he knows that we know he will pay...but meanwhile, he owes us and feeds his family."

We both waited expectantly as it was obvious that he wasn't finished.

"But, if you can arrange to have him come tomorrow..." he began to outline his plan.

And so it went. After breakfast the next day, *Frau* Franks walked to a neighboring farm. Katrina and I accompanied her, stopping to pick up the only one of the kittens that came out to greet us as we walked past the farm. We walked another mile down the road to a farm house that I'd passed with the tricycle on the trip out. Katrina and I remained out in the road while the old woman went up to the door and spoke to the farmer's wife. She was requesting that the woman send her son, who also had a bicycle, to town, to ask the printer *Herr* Schmidt to come to their house as soon as he could.

Later, walking back to the Frank's farmstead, I asked the old woman why she was so certain the printer would come.

"He will come because we have never asked him for payment for the pig. He is proud and does not like owing us, but he has no choice...and no money. He may think we are requesting him to visit because of the payment, but he probably understands we would never insult him like that. He will assume we need something else. Money? He has none, but he may have what we ask of him. He will not know unless he comes and we ask it. Business is not good for him anyway, since the war. The other kitten still hadn't appeared when we passed the farm of their son to return the cat Katrina'd carried much of the way.

Sure enough, later that afternoon, around three, there came a knock at the door. *Frau* Franks signaled to me before she went to the door. By pre-arrangement, I'd been secreted in the parlor during the day with orders to keep the curtains drawn and then to go immediately upstairs to my room at any knock on the door.

After an hour, I heard the muffled sound of voices in the hallway below. Moments later the boards creaked in the hallway outside my room and then a knock at my bedroom door.

"*Herr* Andersson...it is I..." the old woman said. "You may come down now. I have begun our supper and we have some good news to tell you about." I opened the door and followed her downstairs. Her husband was sitting at the small kitchen table and indicated with a wave that I should take a seat.

"It is settled then," he said, a great look of satisfaction on his face.

"Yes? What is settled, *Herr* Franks?" I asked.

"The printer, *Herr* Schmidt. He needed food for his family last summer. We had a pig you see...."

"For God's sake, Hans...he knows that. Get on with it."

322

The old man glanced at his spouse in annoyance, as if she had spoiled his story.

"*As* I was saying…we had a pig…" he glanced at his wife, "…which we sold him. But he did not pay because he could not. Today, I have settled the cost of the whole pig."

"*All* of it?" his wife interrupted.

"All of it. I began by offering only half, but he insisted after learning the seriousness of the matter and wanted all of it."

"He drove a good bargain…simply for a little printing," the woman said regretfully.

"There is more to it than a little printing," he replied, annoyed at her doubting his bargaining prowess. "There is much at stake," he countered, "the authorities…they will know just where to look if something is wrong with the papers: the closest printer, *Herr* Schmidt. They will know we do not keep a printing press in our pigsty."

"That is true," she said, nodding patiently, waiting for him to continue. When he did not, she frowned: "Well—*go on.*"

"After I showed him the child's papers and told him what I wanted, he asked why I wanted it.

"These papers look perfectly all right to me," he told me as he examined them with a practiced eye.

"They are originals, too," he told me.

"Of course…I know that," I told him, "I am not a fool just because I am a farmer and have not been to printing school…he always boasts about his student years in…"

"Hans!" His wife brought him back to the subject again.

"*Ja—ja*…so I like to talk," he scratched his head. "Anyway, I finally had to tell him the truth about the child. He is an honest man—a good man—I know that," he said to me as if I doubted the credentials of the printer.

"Our families have known each other for many, many generations. I believe we can trust him. I did not tell him you were here, however," he said, inclining his head toward the door. "I told him a relative was going to come and take Katrina to the south to live, where she would be safe. He understood our concern for the child and felt sorry for us. Our children, dying from the bomb, leaving us to take care of Katrina…he has a family of his own, mouths to feed…"

he frowned at the warning look from his wife.

"His oldest daughter gave them a grandchild last year—so they know. After I told him about the child and *Lebensborn*, he took out his glasses and looked at her documents a second time. He looked them over very carefully and even held them up to the light to see the watermark on the paper. And at last, he frowned knowingly at me and then he pointed to the registration number.

"There was an "L" in it—the forth digit from the last [13].

He was suspicious of that, he told me. Then he took out his *own* papers…and asked me to bring out ours. There was no "L" on our numbers or his. He said he would go to the town and examine some of the papers of other, local children. He thinks, he told me, that the "L" is significant…possibly to identify where she came from.

Frau Franks and I nodded our understanding as we considered what he'd learned

"In the end, *Herr* Schmidt agreed to make new papers for the child. Her name will be Katrina Wilhamena Franks Andersson, daughter to you…he nodded toward me, looking over his glasses, "…and Wilhamena Franks. If you tell anyone who asks, your story will be that you have returned, distraught, to fetch your daughter. Your wife was killed in the recent bombing in Köln. She was German—you are Swedish. You married, had a child and she did not wish to leave Germany and her parents during the time of the war…she—her parents were old…and ill. Now—she is dead and you come to take the child back to Sweden to live with you." He sat back, satisfied, seeming to ponder and examine the plausibility of his own story.

"But what if they investigate, *Herr* Franks? They will find no record of the marriage—or the birth of a child of that name. Was there really ever such a person?"

His wife answered before her husband could. "No—only in our dreams. Wilhamena was the name we were going to use for our own daughter, had we been fortunate enough to have one."

Herr Franks didn't comment, but nodded. We all three sat in silence for a few moments. No doubt, like myself, they were thinking through the subterfuge. Would I be stopped? Questioned? Would it work? Was the story believable? I thought it seemed so, but doubted we would survive if they held us long enough to investigate.

Frankly, I was more worried about Katrina…and myself. I'd never taken care of children and had no real opinion about them, one way or the other. But I knew I was already growing to love this little girl. I still had concerns about the parenting skills I'd have to acquire, on the fly, so to speak. How would Katrina react to leaving her grand parents? Would she accept me? She couldn't even understand my poor German half the time. At least I would have the excuse, if we were stopped—my Swedish—her German. A plausible explanation: parents of different nationalities. At least that fit the story. But was it enough?

The new papers only took two days to prepare. True to his word the printer returned with news that the suspicious "L" was absent from every set of papers he dared examine in the community.

"On the children's papers I saw, there was no "L" on any of them," *Herr* Franks recounted the conversation, gravely.

That evening we began preparing for the eventual departure. During the days that we'd waited for the printer to complete his work, we practiced many things, in order to make Katrina more accepting of me. I'd already experienced her pleasant disposition and seen what an accepting child she was. Her grandparents told her a story about a wonderful journey she and I would soon take…to the place where the chocolate came from. She might even expect to find another *moder* there, eventually to go with her new *papa*. And there are many cats there. This was the only truthful thing we told her. My cousin's farm's cat population rivaled that of the cows.

These promises, only half true, excited Katrina and she spoke of it constantly in seeming expectation. I involved myself in everything to do with her day; helping her with her meals, putting her to bed, helping her with the toilet when she needed help—a new experience for me. But it didn't seem to bother her in the least. *Frau* Franks even suggested I get up with her when she cried out in the night and the old woman had asked me to help her move Katrina's bed from her room, to mine, placing it close to my bed.

Despite the pain it must have caused her grandmother to lose her, we did everything possible to push her away from her grandparents and into my role as mother and father. Unfortunately, during the night, unaccustomed as I was to children, I heard Katrina's every whimper as she slept. She usually fell asleep again, immediately after, but the interrupted sleep left me struggling in my disturbed slumber, trying to get back to sleep.

We took daily walks to the deserted farm to see her kittens, despite the foul weather. It was during one of these that I encountered my first hurdle. Every day she wanted to visit the kittens and bring food scraps for them. We were bound to continue feeding them at that farmstead, since *Frau* Franks didn't want the kittens hanging around her own house and getting underfoot. She knew Katrina would eventually want them in the house if we brought them home. *Frau* Franks hoped they might soon go their own way, half-starved as they were. She told me that once Katrina was gone and no longer paying attention to them, she intended to discontinue their daily feeding to further encourage their departure for better fare, elsewhere.

When Katrina and I arrived at the other farm the second kitten, absent for two days now, still hadn't appeared with its companion. The previous day the old woman had suggested it may have chosen an early departure from the nest.

"Out catching birds..." the old man put it. As it turned out, it was neither. As Katrina and I wandered along the main road, a bird's feather blew diagonally across the road in front of us, settling slowly on the snow. Katrina's sharp eyes caught sight of it as it passed and she'd immediately begun running—chasing it along the road as it settled toward the snow. I yelled to her in German; "Be careful...Katrina." I glanced quickly along the road behind me; there was seldom any vehicle traffic.

Katrina ran closer and closer along the edge of the ditch that paralleled the road. The feather was out of sight in the ditch.

"Katrina...be careful of the water, dear," I cautioned, hurrying to catch up to her, in case she waded into the shallow water and wet her little shoes with the thin, paper soles.

When I caught up she'd stopped short of the ditch and was bent forward staring down, her arms thrust out behind her. As I came up beside her she turned, very seriously and pointed to the ditch.

"*Katt...*" she said "...*katt* sleeping?" she repeated, alternately turning to me and back to the little wet form lying beside the road, obviously a traffic fatality.

I came closer. I couldn't tell if it was the missing cat, or not. I'd not paid them enough attention when they were both together, but it did resemble the other one. They'd both been black, yellow and white spotted; that was all I remembered about them. Calico, we called them back home. This one was most certainly dead and had been for some time, by the look of it

"Yes—yes Katrina, the cat is sleeping...." I bent and picked up the stiff form and put it in the cloth bag that contained the bowl of food.

"We'll take him home with us so he can get warm." I took her hand. "Allright?."

That seemed to satisfy her as we continued toward the farm-stead. Walking by my side, she muttered something in her childish German that I couldn't catch. Now and then I caught the word "katt." I fully expected when we arrived at the house not to find the other one waiting for us. And we didn't, either, even after poking around the buildings for a quarter hour, calling into the shed and the barn: "katt—katt, where are you cat...come...."

But it was no use. I believed we'd found our remaining cat and it was lying dead in the sack, beside the chipped bowl of food I'd taken out and put on the porch step.

"Let's go back to grandmother's, Katrina. We can take the cat and the food back with us...he can eat it when he wakes up."

That was apparently OK with her, because she turned on her heel and started off again, leaving me to gather up the uneaten food and sack containing the dead cat. I pondered leaving the food bowl on the steps, just in case the little damp form in the sack was not the only remaining kitten, but on second thought, I decided against it. All the way back home, Katrina sang her katt song.

Knowing she'd track up the kitchen floor the old woman worked so hard to maintain, I took Katrina's hand before she could run inside to tell her grandparents the news. After kicking off my own boots, I sat her on my lap and took off her shoes. The pressed-paper soles were soaking. I wished I had some rubber boots for her. Her stockings were soaked, so I took them off too. Freed at last of the wetness, she scampered through the kitchen, the little red toes flying as she hurried to squeal the news to the Franks.

I'd left the dead cat in the bag on the back stoop. Removing the bowl from the sack, I put it on the counter. Unbuttoning my coat, I walked toward the sound of voices. As I turned the corner my eyes met with a questioning glance from *Frau* Franks.

"So the little cat was sleeping on the snow?" She spoke to Katrina, while looking at me, nodding her head and frowning.

"Well—it has awakened now. Go in to see grandfather. He has a surprise for you." Katrina disappeared into the adjoining room *Frau* Franks shuffled over to me, a confidant look on her face and whispered loudly.

"The other cat came meowing at the back door—just after you left. It was so wet...cold and hungry, we brought it in. Grandfather has it sleeping on his lap now, beside the fire. How did Katrina know?"

I told her the story of the feather and the burden I'd carried back in the sack and left on the stoop.

"Ah...so that's what happened to it. A vehicle must have struck it. I wondered...possibly it was coming here for something to eat...I feel so guilty now, depriving them of their food. And the poor child...how was she when she found it?"

"She seems to believe it is sleeping. I don't think she recognizes the difference...that one of them is missing, especially when they're not together to compare."

"Let's keep it that way *Herr* Andersson. Would you mind burying the dead one? Out behind the barn, anywhere. There's a spade just inside the barn door...to the right. Open the door wide and you will have enough light...you will find it. We will keep her occupied while you do it...and thank you *Herr* Andersson for your continued kindness."

"Don't worry, I'll do it while she is...with *Herr* Franks."

I returned to the entryway and sat down to put on my boots. Then I went back out into the drizzle again and after stumbling around for a moment in the dimness of the barn, I remembered and swung the door wider and waited a moment to let my eyes grow accustomed to the darkness. Then...there it was, an old, rusty spade with a T-handle, leaning against the wall.

Back outside, I examined it as I walked around the back of the barn, wondering whether the spade's weathered and already

string-wrapped handle would hold up. There wasn't a problem finding a place to dig. The barnyard appeared to have been unused for
some time and was now completely grown up in weeds, heavy with
seed heads and brown with winter. Not even bothering to scrape
away the snow, I planted the tip of the rusty blade in a likely place
and pushed with my foot. It didn't go all the way down, because I
hadn't pushed hard enough, I was afraid of cracking the handle. But
after a couple more tries, removing a bit of sodden earth each time,
I was finally deep enough to conceal the furry little form. I placed
the dead cat in the damp earth and began to cover it. Finishing
quickly, I headed around the barn again. On the way I tried to pound
off some of the caked mud from the shovel's blade on a wooden
corner post and the handle snapped with the first swing. Picking up
the rusty blade, I returned to the barn.

After I went to bed that evening, Katrina woke me several
times, whimpering about her cat. I didn't understand her words but
she was definitely troubled by the animal; whether, it was the live
one, or dead one, I couldn't discern.

The following day I again spent as much time with her as I
could. Unfortunately, since the cat had come to the grandparent's
place, this also meant we had company and I had competition. Furthermore, she insisted upon dragging it everywhere we went and
involving it in every game we played, or tried to play. We played
horsey...on the thin carpet in the parlor which did little to protect my
tender kneecaps. We had *pretend* tea together at a little table with an
embroidered cloth, thoughtfully furnished by *Frau* Franks, who seemed
to enjoy my discomfort at playing the role of child. Somewhere she'd
even come up with some miniature plates...cups and saucers, beauti
fully decorated children's china. I worried about the china's safety,
but the old woman dismissed my concern, shrugging.

"They will only go to the soldiers when we are gone. Best
use them for some pleasure while we can. They were my great-
grandmother's when she was small and as a child I treasured them.
But now, I will gladly sacrifice a few chips , or a broken cup, for this
little one's happiness and safety."

That evening we discussed plans for our departure again.
Unfortunately, there was no word about the war's progress in the
week-old newspaper, that could be believed. Based upon what I was

329

able to glean from the paper, it was mostly lies anyway, from what I knew to be the truth. I wanted to try to get out of Germany by the quickest way possible, which would mean going north...possibly trying for *Hamburg, Bremen*—maybe even *Kiel*. Then, across the border to Denmark and over the water to Sweden. My other option was northwest, into Flanders, and Holland and somehow, across to England that way. If I could somehow get in communication with *ABA*...I knew they didn't fly into Hamburg, but if I could reach the office, or somehow get word to Clyde, he might get a military ship to swing by a yet to be determined beach, on the way to somewhere else. That seemed unlikely, considering the reward for the Brits. I didn't want the Franks asking too many questions, or learning that I was a pilot. That information would surely generate endless questions and further delays. I preferred to stay as anonymous as possible. I didn't know how the couple might be questioned by the *Gestapo* after I left, either.

To help accomplish our mutual anonymity, *Frau* Franks prepared some of her stepson's clothing for me to wear.

"It looks more German and everyday," she said. "You will be less likely to call attention to yourself."

As she talked, she'd also been packing enough of the child's clothing to fill a paper carton, so I would be sure to have enough when we reached...wherever we eventually reached. For all her other practical ways, this was one extravagance of *Frau* Franks I would be unable to satisfy: "I am afraid it is simply too large to carry, along with my own suitcase," I said matter-of-factly.

I didn't know how to tell her without hurting her feelings. I'd planned to wait until nearly the last minute but realized I had to stop her before she had me lugging a steamer trunk. We'd also planned to exchange addresses. They had no other living relations, after the death of their son and daughter-in-law, so it was imperative we somehow be able to contact one another after the war.

"It is only here you will find us after the war," *Frau* Franks said, sadly shaking her head. "We have no where else. If we live, we will be here," she said, handing me a piece of paper with their names and address carefully written in pencil.

I reached for my *ABA* notebook, patting my shirt pocket but finding only my fountain pen. I began patting my other pockets and then remembered my notebook was in my jacket pocket, upstairs.

"I don't have any paper, *Frau* Franks, to write my own address...have you something?"

Frau Franks started to answer me, but suddenly glanced toward the window. We both leaned across the kitchen table, watching as an automobile moved slowly along the graveled road, slowed as it turned from the road and began driving up the long, snow-covered drive toward the house.

She dropped the curtain, exclaiming, "*Mein Gott,*" who would waste *bensin* to drive here this time of the night."

We watched the headlights, our breaths soon obscuring the glow on the frosty windowpane.

"It can only be the police! Here," she said, tearing a piece of newsprint from that she'd been using to wrap and box Katrina's clothing, "...write your address on this...then, quickly—go hide in your room. I will go out and see what they want...delay them if I can.."

She began to button her sweater. "It may be nothing...but hurry," she said gesturing toward the paper scrap. As she turned back toward the door, I bent over the table, already nearly finished with the address.

"I will attempt to delay them...whoever they are," she said again, disappearing.

Without looking up I finished writing my Norway address and folded the scrap of newspaper. I thought for a moment about also supplying some address in England—or at my cousin's in Dalarna, but reconsidered, thinking that if the Nazis found it, it could be incriminating to the Franks.

"What do you wish to do with this...?" I said, toward the doorway...but she'd already vanished. Someone begun pounding on the back door. I leaped up glancing around, desperately searching for a place to hide the paper. The back door opened and I turned toward the pantry where she'd gone. They couldn't see me from the doorway. Then I heard men's voices mixed with *Frau* Frank's and the door slammed, muffling the sound. I knew then, she'd gone outside.

Frantically, I reached deeply into the clothing-filled box, lifting some of Katrina's clothes and buried the address between the items, before dashing up the stairway and into my room. I heard the back door close with a slam, for my benefit, probably and then the sound of loud, male voices. After a few moments it grew quieter, but I still occasionally heard the murmur of conversation and *Frau* Frank's laughter. If it was the police, I wondered, I should think they would come searching the rest of the house by now, or they would have left. What was taking so long?

Standing there in the room darkened by the blackout curtains, I began experiencing vertigo, having nothing to stabilize myself, no visible object to see and concentrate upon; I could feel myself teetering. I listened to the steady sound of Katrina's breathing in the crib somewhere beside me. Did I dare reach out for it or would I knock some brick-a-brac from the dresser top that I knew was nearby. I stood swaying in the absolute void of darkness, thinking for a moment I would go toward the crib, but the floorboards creaked with my very first step and I froze again, totally disoriented in the darkness, wavering wildly in mid-stride. I thought certainly I'd pitch headlong onto the floor, but by flailing my arms wildly, I was able to stabilize myself somewhat and reach backward to the bed and steady myself. Sitting back slowly, I began to take the pressure from my legs and feet, ever so carefully. After what seemed like minutes, I sank onto the bolster, where, aside from a slight trembling, I remained unmoving.

After what seemedl like hours I realized I'd nearly fallen asleep, listening to the rhythmic breathing of the child. Then I heard a light tread on the stairway. My heart sprang into my throat. Were they coming for me...sneaking, hoping to catch me unawares? I had no weapon...I couldn't fight them anyway. With the child sleeping in the room, I didn't want to fight, or resist. It would only make matters worse for the Franks.and the child...what would happen to her in a scuffle in her room? What if there was shooting?

I turned on the bed, facing the door in the darkness and carefully stood up, just as there was the sound of a squeaking board in the hallway.

With heart in throat, I waited for the tall *SS* soldier I imagined would crash into the room with pistol drawn. The footsteps had stopped and a flickering light now shown dimly beneath the crack of the door and a dim shadow moved quietly ever closer. Then it became totally still. No one spoke downstairs. I imagined the Franks, huddled together with guns put to their heads, frightened by their captors. Any moment my door would burst open revealing uniformed figures silhouetted against the light of an oil lamp? Would the piercing beam of a flashlight suddenly blind me? I waited, but the light beneath the door didn't move. I couldn't recall whether there was some item nearby that I could use as a weapon, thinking again of putting up a fight.

Then, *Frau* Franks quietly called my name from the hallway and gently tapped upon the door. I nearly wept with relief as the door opened slowly.

"*Herr* Andersson...are you here...are you awake," she whispered?

"Yes..." I whispered back, my voice croaking and quavering with fright. "...I am awake—who...who is it *Frau* Franks? *Soldiers...?*"

"No...not soldiers. There is nothing to be afraid of, *Herr* Andersson, please hurry, we must prepare to leave—*now!*" She said it with such urgency of command and tone that I had not heard from her and it startled me. "I must open your door and waken the child."

"Leave...why? Tonight? I said as she entered the room.

"Yes, tonight. It is someone from the town...friends downstairs Please go down right away. Pack and bring your luggage. You must leave with them—immediately." She strode past me. "I will dress Katrina and pack a small bag for her." She peered over the crib bars and then turned back to me as I stood up. She thrust the lamp abruptly to me and returned to Katrina's bed, bending low she urgently began whispering her name. "Katrina...*kinder*...wake up...you must get up *Leibschen*." Over her shoulder she urged me: "Go down to the kitchen—my husband and the men who have come, they will explain what has happened. Go—now! I will follow with the child after I have dressed her."

As her words died I was already in the hallway holding my two pieces of luggage closed, but unlatched, beneath each arm. I'd left the lamp on the nightstand and in my stocking feet, negotiated the slippery stairs in the darkness. The last thing I needed was to pitch headlong and break my neck, leaving Katrina to the mercy of the authorities.

I walked into the kitchen clutching my suitcases. Two men stood beside the door in a puddle of snow-melt. They were both large men, older than I by twenty or more years and looking very stern and wary as I struggled to put one of my cases on the table without it coming open. They were civilians and I could see beneath a wool overcoat that the older of the two wore a necktie. The other's coat was slightly open in the front revealing a uniform of some sort, but it didn't look military.

My heart had begun to beat in my throat at seeing the pair and it continued to pound against my Adams apple so I couldn't swallow to relieve my dry mouth. Was I betrayed? Had the Franks somehow notified the *SS*, or…had the printer? It had to be. That was why it had taken them this long to arrive, from wherever they were stationed. I stood there, unmoving, one hand on the table, the other holding one case closed. Would I have to fight them? Were they armed? My thoughts raced.

I must have looked rather helpless because the younger, uniformed man mumbled something and strode over and took one of my suitcases, smiling slightly and bowing a little. I was ready to resist, but was taken aback by his friendly gesture. Relieving me of my case, he now stood dumb with a burden he didn't know what to do with.

"Put them here," *Herr* Franks said, pushing himself away from the kitchen table. "You can close them up if you are ready."

To me he said, gesturing at the other man remaining standing: "*Herr* Andersson…this man is *Herr* Schriner, the *burgomaster* of our community."

The man stiffened, straightening and introduced himself in a rapid dialect I was unable to understand. Then he bowed and clicked his heels slightly, nodding to me as he did so, smiling again.

"And this other man, who has stolen your valise, is Constable Becker, our local policeman."

Constable Becker, still holding my valise closed, also smiled as he extended a free hand to be shaken. After that, he placed my suitcase on the table. I was speechless. Constable Becker returned to the side of his companion beside the back door. *Herr* Franks spoke again.

"*Herr* Andersson, let me explain…all this suddenness. It seems there has been a telephone call made to Constable Becker's office from the officials. The call's originator was probably a clerical underling of the *SS* in Berlin."

He turned to *Herr* Becker: "You do not know where they were calling from?" *Herr* Becker shook his head, frowning. Turning to me: "They were asking about the residency of my son and his wife, verifying that they still lived in the community. When he…," he indicated the other man with a nod, "…he told them they had both been killed, the person then asked if the child was also killed. Constable Becker, being a rather thorough policeman, curious and suspicious, thought this was strange that a clerk so far away was interested in whether a small child lived or died in this little, rural community, given the number of civilian children who had already been killed in the city bombings. He asked the clerk what difference it made whether Katrina died or not, there was no longer anyone to care for her. You see Constable Becker knew Katrina was adopted, but he did not know the particular facts of her origin. Being an excellent policeman, *Herr* Becker always suspected something different in the arrival of our little grand daughter," he smiled at the policeman who grinned in modesty at the praise.

"Anyway, the clerk said over the telephone that in this case, it did not matter because they were already coming to take her back if she was still alive. So, would he please confirm it or not, they said, since they were in Köln and would be there in the morning if she were still alive. This one, she told *Herr* Becker, has a flaw and is rejected and must be returned to the orphanage…in the East. She would not be re-adopted anyway, even if the parents were still living. A mistake had been made, they told Constable Becker and Katrina would be transported soon…they would be coming to fetch her, possibly as soon as tomorrow."

I looked from the Constable to *Herr* Franks and to the Mayor. I was confused, but I was no longer frightened. These were friendly—even sympathetic glances I was getting from these men.

Herr Franks went on. "This aroused Constable Becker's curiosity and concern; you see, he knew how much we loved…." Just then, *Frau* Franks entered the room with Katrina in one arm and a bundle of clothing in the other.

"You will not have enough room to take another valise *Herr* Andersson. With your own two…what must I have been thinking with this box so large. You must make some space in your own grips for her things—can you do it?"

"Yes, *Frau* Franks. Put whatever you want in them. We will make room. I have not yet closed them."

Her husband reached up and gently stroked the sleepy Katrina's arm as the woman stood talking beside him. Katrina smiled sleepily down, wiggling her fingers at his touch, snuggling into the comfort of her grandmother's bosom.

"As I was saying," *Herr* Franks began again, returning the child's smile, "it was not unknown in the community, how pleased we were when the orphan child was offered to my son. Constable Becker remembered hearing the printer had visited our farm earlier and he thought about that for a while and then began to wonder why the printer would come here. We had no more pigs. He knew the printer had no money to pay us for the last one. Why had he come? So he went to visit the printer during lunchtime when he knew there would be no customers. Is *Herr* Franks having difficult times on the farm these days, he asked of the printer? No replied he…not that I am aware of. Now the printer, too, was curious and on guard. I was wondering if *Herr* Franks was planning to sell out the farm, the Constable asked him, persisting? No, was the reply again, I have not heard that of him. Then why would he have you print sale bills advertising the farm for sale, he asked the printer, not being entirely honest with him?

He chuckled then at his own story, laying his finger beside his nose and wagging his head at Constable Becker who leaned back, beaming. He even glanced over and nodded to me as if I, too, was some sort of fellow conspirator.

"Then," *Herr* Franks went on, why did you visit the farm of *Herr* Franks and why were you asking to see children's identification papers in the community? Have you heard Katrina will be taken? At that statement, Constable Becker told me, the printer's composure fell away. He of course knew the Constable since they were boys and knew deep down that he could trust him. "What do you know about Katrina being taken he asked the Constable—who told you."

Frau Franks had finished filling the suitcases with clothes by now.

Impatiently, she said: "I do not believe you will be able to carry more *Herr* Andersson. You shall have to leave the rest." She gestured toward the large box on the table she had earlier gotten ready. Katrina was now on the floor chasing the kitten beneath the table. *Frau* Franks glanced nervously around the room, waving her apron. To her husband, she said: "You had better let them go Hans, this is no time for more of your stories."

"Yes, *Leibschen*, I am just finished anyway." Turning to me, he went on: "So the printer and the Constable each gave to the other a little of their own stories, until they both had the whole and that made them go to the Mayor in concern and for advice. They could not officially act anyway, without him. After hearing the tale he and the Constable came here tonight, wishing to tell us the *SS* were on their way. So you must leave, *Herr* Andersson."

He struggled to his feet. "You must leave now with God's speed and take all we have left to love in life with you," he began to cry then. "But we are happy to see her go, thought we already weep with sadness." He took out a dirty handkerchief and blew his nose. "If she remains with us she will surely not see her next birthday. Such, has our *Deutschland* come to…gentlemen," he said looking at the two men standing shifting from foot to foot in both pride and embarrassment at the situation they found themselves in. Both appeared near tears themselves, as was I.

"It is finished—come *Herr* Andersson. These are not men of action," the old woman said, weeping openly. "Get out— go…go…all of you!"

The two officials began buttoning their coats. I yanked my own from the hook behind the door and bent to put on my rubber overshoes. The Franks were hugging Katrina and crying. She appeared confused. The Mayor took one of my bags announcing that he would go start his automobile which had a full tank of fuel. He said he didn't know where we were going but he would go out and start it so it would be warm for Katrina. The Constable crossed to the table and took the remaining suit-case beneath his long arm. He nodded to me that he was ready, stepped toward the door and stood one hand on the knob looking knowingly at the old couple who now seemed unable, now that it had begun, to relin-quish Katrina.

I walked across the room as *Herr* Franks struggled to come around the table. Holding out my hand, "*Herr* Franks…let me help you."

He looked up, nodding as tears streamed down his face and

clasped my hand in both of his. He pulled and I helped him around. He put both arms around me and hugged me close, mumbling incoherently against my chest. I patted him on the back with one hand while thanking him for his hospitality. Finally, he pushed me away and turned toward the stairway, shoulders shaking, but he didn't leave.

"*Frau* Franks..." I said, gently, knowing how difficult it was for her above all.

She stood up standing Katrina on the tabletop: "*Danka Herr* Andersson...*Danka.*" Katrina was surprised by the sudden action and and looked bewildered as her coat was buttoned. Then *Frau* Franks snatched the kitten from her hands and dropped it on the floor. She wiped her nose and brusquely began to stuff the tails of a woolen scarf between Katrina's neck and coat collar. Katrina began to bellow before the kitten hit the floor.

"Katt! Katt," she screamed, struggling against her grandmother's efforts, trying to reach toward the floor and the unconcerned kitten, which was rubbing against the old woman's feet.

I looked at the old man for help, but he still didn't turn around. He appeared to be weeping. Beside the open door, with a long face the Constable twitched his head toward the doorway, gesturing brusquely with one hand for me not to prolong the parting...to gather the child and come. I glanced back to the old woman just as she picked up Katrina and thrust the screaming child in my arms. But Katrina began squirming and pushing against me with both hands.

"Grandmother! Grandmother—*katt...Katt!*"

Shaking her head, the old woman stepped away in a gesture of parting and as she did, stepped on the kitten's tail, which immediately let out a loud "...meeooow!" A pained expression crossed the old woman's face and she bent to pick up and comfort the cat. As I struggled to restrain Katrina's renewed protests, her grandmother stood watching me helplessly, gesturing and uttering little sounds of comfort. Finally, she reached over and stroked Katrina's cheek as she held the cat to her breast. When Katrina strained to reach for the kitten she stepped farther back in a gesture of desperation. Shaking her head slowly she yearningly stroked the cat as she stared at the whimpering child. Katrina continued reaching toward the furry ball and screaming with renewed vigor: "*katt—katt!*"

This was not going well. I'd figured it would be a traumatic parting, but I thought the departure would be more protracted, more drawn out…a long good by. But the urgency of this situation—these men waiting—the screaming child…it was all nearly too much for me. I was suddenly very sorry I'd come and gotten involved. I now wished I could just leave without the child.

I took a couple of steps toward the door which the Constable promptly opened. Katrina kicked and squirmed in my right arm as I struggled to pull my knit cap from my coat pocket. The old woman's face, as she watched the torment of her loved-one, was a mask of torture. She continued clutching the kitten to her breast in an inadvertent gesture to retain something of Katrina she was losing. I glanced down at the cat, which had thrust its head from between her hands and poked out one tiny paw between the captive fingers, reaching toward the wailing Katrina in a gesture of play. The old woman looked at me, a pleading entreaty.

"All right," I said, "give her the cat. Maybe it will quiet her."

She thrust the cat into Katrina's waiting hands and sobbed: "Go—go now Swede…go with God." She took a step toward her husband, but then hesitated. "*Herr* Andersson…" she struggled to retrieve something from her apron pocket, finally pulling out the chocolate bar I had given them. They had saved it for Katrina.

"For her…in the automobile," she said, tears running down her cheeks.

Then she turned her back to us and put her arms around her husband, leaning her head on his back. Together they stood, close to one another. I hitched up Katrina who was awkwardly clutching the kitten for dear life and finished pulling on my stocking cap with my left hand as I walked toward the door.

"I'll write to you…" I shouted over my shoulder as I was pushed forward by the Constable, "…and as soon as this is over, I'll send for you to come—or come here myself. You *will* see her again…I promise," I said as the door slammed behind me.

The snow crunched and squeaked beneath our feet and the cackling of the Mercedes' idling engine grew louder as we walked around the house. As I climbed in the back seat the car's lights suddenly stabbed through the exhaust cloud, pointing toward the road we would take. The Constable slammed my door and tumbled into the front seat with a grunt. The Mayor released the clutch and with a lurch we were off, bumping down the driveway. I glanced back toward the house as we turned onto the main road and dimly made out two dark forms in the glow of the lamp-lit window.

"Grandmother…come?" Katrina said.

"Yes…she will come. After we go to the chocolate place, she will come to see you…and katt."

CHAPTER

17

The Sweater

The stationmaster was pleasant enough, though he was rather vague in answering my questions about how I might possibly reach the Frank's farmhouse this time of year. It was a great distance, he'd said through his wire cage. He could offer me no hope for a taxi to the countryside as there had been none for over three years because of the fuel rationing.

"A horse and cart, possibly..." he'd finally said sympathetically, looking at my street shoes and stockingless legs "...or maybe a passing farmer..." he added as I picked up my knapsack and walked out into the snow. He was picking up the telephone when I turned and closed the door behind me.

A passing farmer, I wondered, in this weather? They certainly were not out in their fields, farming, I thought. I walked toward the small main street. I needed an inn first, a meal second and transportation last. I ended up going into a shabby little hotel that reminded me of an English pub. Within a moment I learned they had only two rooms to let and one was already taken by an itinerate physician. He also practiced medicine from there and was behind on his rent.

"Did I wish both rooms?" she asked. I shook my head and

thanked the woman, telling her one would be sufficient. I asked if I could have something to eat. At her grimace I added, "anything...I'm very hungry and have not eaten since yesterday, noon. The train was late and there was no time in Köln before I departed."

"*Ja—Ja*," she finally said, "we have bread and milk and cheese you can have, until the evening meal, but you must pay extra." I nodded, not caring. Would I be staying for breakfast, she asked. I said I didn't know, but to plan on me, just in case.

"That will cost extra, too," she said. I only nodded and walked toward the stairway.

An hour later, after the meager meal, she let me use her telephone to call the Constable that I'd spoken from Köln, more than two week previously. I didn't want to have to rely on him, but it now seemed my only opton. He agreed to pick me up the following morning at nine o'clock.

The Constable arrived early, but I was ready. The night had passed in a wink of the eye. I was so tired from the train ride. He introduced himself and smiled at my curious landlady who had come from her kitchen to see whom I was speaking with. She smiled in return but when she saw me staring at her, she frowned and disappeared back through the doorway. After I showed him my credentials, as he requested, he seemed satisfied. We went outside and he even opened the door to an ancient Mercedes sedan for me.

The stationmaster was right, it was a long way. And when we reached the farmhouse, there was absolutely no one there, just as he had been telling me on the ride out. Somehow, I couldn't believe it. All this way to find...nothing. I got out of the car when *Herr* Becker opened it for me and then walked a couple of meters up the narrow drive leading to the outbuildings and house. The house and yard were quite clean—barren was possibly a better description. There was little to see that wasn't covered by the snow. As if to defy my doubt, there were no footprints, nor vehicle tracks in the driveway leading to the house. And no smoke came from the chimney. By now, I no longer expected any, after what I had seen and been told about the child's parent's home. I glance around nodded at my chauffeur and then walked back and climbed into the Mercedes.

Herr Becker backed out into the main road again and turned toward the next farm: the grandparent's. "Less than a kilometer further down the road," he said pleasantly. I could just see it through the dimness of fog and falling snow, where he pointed.

"The grandparents lived there until a little while ago. After they took away the child, there was no longer anything to cheer them and they have gone to stay with friends for the winter. They are both aged and *Herr* Franks is himself quite ill," he said repeating himself from our conversation on the telephone.

As we turned, I noticed this driveway had been plowed out recently. Only a day or two of snow lay in it now and there were also some recent vehicle tracks. I glanced at *Herr* Becker and he spoke, anticipating my question.

"They come to see to the plumbing from time to time. Only that. They have both gone and there are no longer any animals since the printer bought their last pig." He drove slowly up the driveway, glancing from side to side as if to show me truly, there was no one there. "This child of the Franks'—the late Franks," he corrected himself, "what would you have done with her had she still been here?"

I repeated my lie without looking at him: "My orders are to take her away. There has been an...an error in the adoption...process and she must be returned to...to her parents; her natural parents."

"I see. That is unfortunate; I am certain they would have desired that, were she still here...that the child be reunited with her own flesh and blood. That is important in matters like these, I suppose?" he said. He was curious, but not forceful. I said nothing.

"And where is that," he finally asked.

"What...?"

I hadn't been paying attention. We'd stopped beside the back entrance of the farmhouse. There were plenty of tracks in the snow and the steps and landing had been swept clean, a sign of occupancy.

"I'm sorry...what did you ask...where is what?"

"Where is it where her natural parents live? The place you would have taken her?"

"Oh—to the east," I said, absently as I glanced around. "I would have taken her east to a small place east of here; that is where they live." There was a little sort of knowing intake of breath on his part and he nodded knowingly. What was he about, anyway.

But he said nothing further except, "I see...to the east. Can we get out...go inside?"

He looked worried. "Is it locked?"

"Oh that would be most unusual, would it not? After all, the old ones are not here." I gave him a look of resolve. "And we do not have their permission."

"Please," I said, desperate for any connection with the child. I wanted to be where she had been, if even for a moment. Maybe there would be something: a toy, stocking, a photograph, an address—anything.

"Please, it is important. Just for a moment...then we can leave and I'll return to Köln where I will make my report, telling my superiors I've tried my best...and that the local authorities have been very accommodating" He thought for a moment before reaching for the door handle; he understood about reports.

"Only for a moment. I have permission to check the plumbing, from time to time...but only for a moment. Then we must go...it is not right—their home."

"Yes, you are absolutely correct, we must respect personal property...if it were not so important." I'd already opened my door before he could change his mind and was waiting beside the back door in the little entry-way, as he climbed the stoop. With a last glance at me he grasped the handle and opened the door, pushing it open. I was surprised.

"I thought it would be locked?"

He looked at me queerly. "Why? Who, here would steal from old people?" he said, gesturing for me to go in ahead of him. I entered to get in from the cold and he closed the door behind us. The small, entry-foyer was little more than a crude porch and led directly into the kitchen, which was quite plain, clean but cold. There was a empty coal bin beside the door with some sticks of firewood.

In the kitchen, several small cupboards lined one wall. A bare table and four, equally-spaced chairs stood symmetrically, in one corner. There were curtains on the windows and over the glass of the back door. The countertops were bare. The table had a large, pressed paper box sitting on one end, as if someone had just come in and put it there...moving, packing and finally, abandoned it.

Somehow though, the place still had the appearance of being occupied. Though there were obviously no inhabitants, it was so cold, there was something about it. I felt the occupants had just left ahead of us.

"How long did you say, *Herr* Becker, since they were taken away?"

Herr Becker had moved across the kitchen and now stood in the doorway leading to the rest of the house.

"Oh—not long...not so long, at all...a week, maybe two."

Leaning sideways, I could see behind him into what appeared to be a dining room. There was a hutch of some sort with plates standing upright in the dimness. I couldn't see beyond and didn't want to appear too curious.

"As you can see, *Fräulein*, there is no one living here any longer, let alone a small child."

"Yes...it's certainly quiet, *Herr* Becker...would it be...inopportune, to examine other areas of the home?"

Standing a little straighter in the doorway, barring the way, he interjected "It would be...inappropriate, *Fräulein* and probably illegal, since this is hardly a matter of national security...endangering to the *Reich*."

I walked toward him then, as if I would walk through him. Watching me approach, he looked rather sternly at me as if I was about to touch him. I had not been unaware, from our first meeting, the effect my...my *femininity* had had upon him. I'd seen it before, of course, in other men. Stopping just short of, but directly in front of him, I smiled broadly, if not somewhat wickedly, stood on my toes and glanced over his shoulder, into the adjacent room.

He turned slightly, stepping aside but not completely out of the doorway. "Excuse me *Fräulein*...certainly no harm can come from a quick peek," he said and glanced over his own shoulder into the darkness.

I saw nothing in the interior, reminiscent of a child; I'd hoped for something. But there was no sign at all that a child had ever lived in this home: no scrawled pictures in the kitchen, no toys, clothing, nothing. I nodded, satisfied at last and turned away from him, not wishing him to see my disappointment. It was almost as if someone had deliberately scrubbed away the vestiges of any childhood occupation.

I walked to the wooden table and placed my purse atop the battered cardboard box, removed my handkerchief and blew my nose. It seemed there was little hope.

I glanced at my reflection in the window pane. Behind me, he had not moved. During the automobile ride, he'd refused my request to speak with the grandparents.

"Too traumatic. They are quote old, you know..." he intoned, shaking his head sadly.

Cold and depressed, I could think of no reason for remaining. I folded my handkerchief and returned it to my purse. I was getting a bad headache. Pinching the bridge of my nose with a gloved hand, I bent my head and closed my eyes, uttering a silent prayer that guidance would come my way now that all finally seemed lost once again.

Then, I thought, how silly. I must be strong and force myself to give up the hopeless pursuit. Grabbing the purse's strap, I pushed myself away from the table emphatically, but as I did, the top of the paper carton collapsed inward and my purse with it. I pulled on the strap while pushing down on the carton, but it didn't come free. It was angering. The carton's flaps had caught the top of the purse's hasp, between the strap ends.

I gave a grunt and pulled open the carton's flaps, tipping over the box. *Herr* Becker had approached and stood waiting beside me as I retrieved my handbag.

"Shall we return to the village, *Fräulein?*" he asked patiently.

"Yes...I am ready, just..." I reached around and pulled the remaining flap open and as I pulled the bag free, I was surprised to see a blue, child's sweater caught in the hasp on my purse. It had little colored flowers embroidered beneath each shoulder. Without thinking I removed it from the purse's catch and held it to my cheek, closing my eyes, my companion completely forgotten in the ecstasy of my precious find.

After a moment the Constable said, "Soft, is it not *Fräulein,*" he chuckled to himself, "Yes, *Herr* Frank's wife was good to knit the wool." He turned over the box so he could view the contents. Opening the other flaps wide he lifted the box.

"Hah—here is your proof for your superiors, *Fräulein*. Why not take the box of clothing back to Köln? Show them? You have the clothes—but not the child...these were all that remained when you arrive to take her back with you?"

I didn't know whether he was joking, mocking me, or entirely serious about the offer. I'd desperately wished to have something of Sophia's—anything that had come in contact with her, been close to her skin, sheltered her from the cold...been dear to her. Now...this box? It was such a surprise...so unexpected after the initial disappointment. I didn't wish to appear too eager. I picked up another sweater, glancing at it before tipping up the carton and tossing the items back inside.

"Thank you *Herr* Becker for thinking of such a logical solution; I shall do exactly that. Possibly, it will help to quell their frustration at having lost the child." With that I closed the carton, picked it up and addressed my companion. "Shall we go?"

CHAPTER
18

On the Road, Coming Home

I awoke with a start when the Mercedes swerved and hit a hole in the highway. Katrina stirred in my arms, but didn't wake up. I couldn't see the kitten but I assumed it was somewhere in the back seat with us. I'd been concerned about it's behavior when the automobile first started moving away from the Frank's, but Katrina held it tightly and it finally calmed down, probably thinking it better to relax, than be squeezed to death.

I glanced over the front seat back at the dim glow of the clock in the middle of the dashboard, but couldn't make out the hands. I didn't know how long we'd been riding. The two men had discussed the best route for us to follow, consulting with me. I didn't know any of the highways or the best and safest way, so told them we were in their hands, since they had knowledge of the countryside. We were still in Germany, surely, but driving north, somewhere toward Denmark, as they had told me before I dozed. It would be much easier to find passage across to Sweden from there…and closer.

I could see the silhouette of the policeman's head lolling with each sway of the car, in front of me. The Mayor seemed to be staying awake all right, at least well enough to continue to drive. Over his shoulder, I could only see the poorly lit highway ahead, flanked on each side by dense forest where the Mercedes' head-lights couldn't reach. Watching our progress for a while, I eventually glimpsed a numbered highway sign indicating our current route; but it meant nothing to me.

Leaning forward again, "Where are we now?" I asked, as quietly as I could. The Constable stirred, straightened and leaned toward the other side of the car.

"We have just gone through Bielefeld," the Mayor droned over his shoulder.

"I am sorry...where is that...still in Germany?"

"Oh yes, it is. About another hour or so until Hanover," he replied, rubbing his hand across his eyes in fatigue. "Beyond that we must find diesel fuel. My companion believes he can persuade some of his policemen associates to part with some of their hoarded stock," he said in a conspiratory manner. We will need several of these *associates* before we reach the north coast of Denmark and return again."

I nodded, leaned back and nearly immediately went back to sleep.

But I didn't sleep for long, or so it seemed. The motion of the automobile, starting and stopping, finally drove me to sit up again. I was also getting chilled. The cat suddenly attacked my fingers on the seat. I flinched at the tiny prickling of its claws and teeth. It was just coming daylight outside. As I straightened, Katrina sat up sleepily and smiled that Greta-smile up at me, stretching her little arms and yawning. God, I thought. I'll never be without her—ever.

"*God morgon...*" I said to no one in particular and in a somewhat cracked voice. The companions in the front seat turned half way and returned my greeting.

"Where are we now?" I asked, handing the kitten to Katrina and leaning forward between the two men.

"We are now on the road to Bremen...maybe two hours away," the Constable answered. "We are going to the house of an associate of mine. He will help us with the diesel for the automobile."

I scraped some frost from inside the window and saw that we were in a residential area from the look of it.

"I think Katrina and I must stop soon. I am not certain about the cat," I said, chuckling and looking at Katrina, clutching the furry ball. I didn't know how to tell her not to squeeze the animal too hard. I was uncertain as to whether it was house-trained, or even when it had last had anything to drink.

"*Ja*...we will," the driver replied with a backward wave of his hand. "We shall also have some breakfast...I telephoned ahead...back the road a way. They are expecting us. It will be good, I think."

"You stopped—telephoned?"

"*Ja*—we stop, back there. You and the *kinder* did not wake. That is good, for later when maybe you can drive an automobile?"

"He is a grown man, my friend...of course he can drive an auto," the Mayor put in, hitting his comrade lightly on the shoulder, then turning to me, "...can you?"

"Yes...yes, I can drive if I know where we are going."

"*Ja*, we know. The burgomaster is nearly *kaput* and so am I, so tired. After we get the diesel and some food, we will drive, you and I. I, too, have slept a little. It is still a long way to the north coast. Now, here is the story we must tell my associate when we stop, so there is no suspicion from them..."

We synchronized our stories then. I was a distant cousin to the burgomaster, from Sweden. My wife was killed in the bombing. I had come down to fetch our child from the grandparents, but was fearful of traveling on the trains with so much bombing and strafing by aircraft going on. The Mayor volunteered to drive me and the Constable went along for the ride...and to arrange fuel for the old Mercedes.

Another half-hour and we turned into a narrow driveway, between stone gateposts. There was a thick hedge surrounding the house, a mansard-roofed affair in stucco, with darkly-painted boards jutting in every direction. It was very neat around the yard, nothing out of place and nothing showed to reveal the occupation of the associate. A large man stepped from the back door of the house, smiling broadly. He was wearing only a cardigan as he trotted down the stone steps, not a particularly graceful procedure given his size.

Up close he was a giant and the type of *associate* I would not wish to be on the wrong side of. I guessed he was around sixty five or seventy years of age. He continued his lope around the passenger side of the Mercedes and yanked open the door, greeting his fellow policeman heartily, speaking in rapid German to him, gesturing toward the back seat. I smiled up at him when he bent and glanced down at us. He returned the wave, friendly and give a little four-fingered wag at Katrina who beamed and held up her kitten, thwarting my attempt to get her hands in the sleeves of the coat. She wanted to get out.

"Chocolate place...?" she asked.

"Chocolate...oh, no, not yet. It is further along the road."

"Grandmother?"

"No...well, maybe, but I do not think so...so soon."

After some twisting, I finally finished buttoning her coat. When the man saw we had finally gotten our coats on, he opened our door and we got stiffly out and were formally introduced. The man's name turned out to be *Max,* rather apt I thought, short for Maxamillian. He told us to precede him into the house. I held up one finger and muttered something about "*minuten...*" and grabbed the kitten from Katrina and tossed it onto the ground. She protested loudly, probably thinking we were trying to get rid of the kitten. I tried to tell her it had to go the toilet before we took it into the house. The Mayor intervened and explained it to her and then it was OK.

We stood around foolishly for a few moments as the cat minced around the edge of the drive, sniffing the edge of the rear garden area, freed of snow by diligent shoveling on Max's part, no doubt. The two Germans began chatting rapidly, ignoring us; I started swinging my arms and flexing my legs in an effort to get the circulation going. To my surprise, the cat began slowly circling in one spot beside the car. Then it began pawing at an area in the snow. I bent, quickly picking up Katrina, least she interrupt it. I held mybreath, watching and finally the cat turned around and squatted on the snowy ground.

A murmur of appreciation escaped all but Katrina who was too young to appreciate our relief that the cat had finally produced. After a half minute more the cat stood and began trying to paw some snow over the dark area in the snow. I waited another minute, then bent over, setting Katrina down again so she could pick up the kitten. Max laughed loudly and told us to hurry inside, so we could do the same.

Katrina and I were first in the toilet, since I'd not been since the previous evening, when, by mutual agreement, we'd pulled the car to the side of the road and all but the sleeping Katrina had tumbled out. I couldn't remember when she'd last gone. I helped her with her two pair of long stockings and the wool dress and went out into the hallway. She'd already shed a coat and two sweaters in the kitchen.

She opened the door when she finished and I let her into the hallway; she immediately rushed over to pick up the cat again. Just as I closed the bathroom door I heard an adult female outcry of astonishment: "Kinder... *Leibschen*...you dear child you are so pretty. Are you hungry little one?"

I knew Katrina was in good hands, then. I glanced in the mirror above the basin as I washed my hands; it was not a pretty face that stared back. I soaped up again and gave my face a good scrub. I badly needed to shave and wondered if there would be time, later. I supposed a bath was out of the question. I didn't look too bad, considering the bed I'd had last night. I wasn't nearly as haggard looking as the Mayor after his grueling, all-night drive. Standing out in the yard beside the cat, I'd noticed his eyes were red and very tired-looking.

When I opened the toilet door, the Constable was waiting to take my place. As we edged past each other, Max came around the corner nearly colliding with me in the hallway. Courteously and with a little bow, he backed up and escorted me into the kitchen ahead of him and introduced me to his wife Freda. With a wink he disappeared around the corner.

Freda was the opposite of Max: small and diminutive, but also easy going from the sound of her, giving me a great smile as she shook my hand. She waved at Katrina, already seated and chewing on a piece of bread and jam, pleased that the child had taken to her attentions. Who wouldn't with that much jam and bread, I thought?

To me, she said, "*Bitta...*" indicating a chair beside Katrina. The Mayor was already sprawled in a wooden chair on the end; he was exhausted from the look of him. Freda began making fussing noises, placing assorted dishes on the table and adjusting a small, decorative arrangement of pine boughs and cones, in the table's center. Max returned with a bottle of *Schnapps* and four glasses.

"For warming up," he said, "with the weather and to new friends," and began pouring the clear liquid with the care of a chemist, filling the glasses so I doubted I could lift my own to my lips without spilling it. The Constable returned and, at the sight of Max bent over the table, began rubbing his hands and smiling broadly.

"Ahh—*schnapps*," he chuckled. "And I thought you were going to be stingy, old friend." He lifted his glass from the table without first sitting down. Everyone followed his example then and as was the custom: "Prost," he said, glancing around the table at each of us before turning up his little glass. I followed suit and the fiery liquid scalded my throat all the way down and hit my stomach with a bang. Max was filling the glasses again, working his way around the table, and serving himself last. Freda stood nearby, but without a glass, watching from her command of the pot-covered stove.

"To our guest's appetite..." Max offered, this time and we glanced round once more before downing our glasses. Max picked up the bottle and began offering more...me first. I held up my hand.

"Oh...*nay tack...nein*, I will be driving on the next leg and do not wish to get arrested for intoxication."

Both policemen laughed at that. The others had one more drink, this time to a reunion of old friends and a quick and untroubled journey.

As they put down their glasses, Freda put a heaping platter on the table. We took our places and Max sat down beside the Mayor and picked up the massive dish heaped with steaming, raw-fried potatoes, stippled with pieces of bacon. There was also a pool of white cheese, still melting on the top. As the dish began circulating from hand to hand, it brought murmurs of appreciation, punctuated again and again as Freda set dish after dish of food before us.

There were boiled eggs and thinly-sliced ham—God knows where she got all the food. A basket was heaped with several kinds of fresh, hard-crusted bread. I picked up a thick slice and without thinking, inadvertently glanced around for some butter. Ever vigilant to her guests, Freda caught my glance:

"Please excuse us in these times but we can not get any butter. There is just none to be had at any price."

"I'm sorry *Frau*..." I began to apologize for my rudeness, but she interrupted me, waving a hand at my apology.

"My brother is a farmer, living just outside the town from us; he makes butter from the cream. But he has to send it to the city...to Berlin it goes. It is commanded. If it is too little, the local *Gestapo* people will come to see if a cow has died or something...to create the shortage. It is...it must be sold in Berlin by the higher-ups."

The Constable took up the conversation: "Yes, things are not always as we would have them, but we are far better here in the countryside than those in the cities. We are fortunate to have such a feast..." he waved his hand over the table, "...and someone so beautiful to prepare it so well."

Everyone raised his glass and toasted *Frau* Freda, which reaped a shy grin of appreciation.

As I ate, helping Katrina with her own food, as the others spoke in rapid German, I did a rough calculation in my head. Considering that we might spend one more night in Germany, I assumed we could get transport across to Denmark the following day. I judged we...I was already thinking of Katrina and I as a pair...could spare some of the coffee from one of the tins. I'd left one tin at the Frank's, still leaving us five yet unopened. I didn't know if I should offer Freda a whole one. I didn't know about trying to divide one in front of them, which seemed rather selfish, but considering the conditions I made a mental note to fetch a tin as soon as I could get out to the car.

Katrina'd polished off her bread and jam immediately. I finished peeling a boiled egg I thought we would share. She set upon that with relish I'd not yet seen. As she worked on the second half, I placed a little more ham on her plate and began cutting it into smaller pieces. She didn't wait for me to finish, reaching over and picking up a piece in her other hand.

"This was a hungry child," Freda exclaimed with a smile and put another spoon of potatoes on her plate, beside the ham.

After the initial rush of conversation as the food was passed, we'd pretty much eaten in silence from then on, partly from the urgency to depart but also because we were all famished. After I had cleared my plate, I excused myself, saying I must bring something from the auto. Everyone looked surprised; but Freda nodded and smiled, putting an arm around Katrina to indicate she would watch out for her.

Outside in the cold, I opened the trunk and then my larger valise. Beneath the layer of children's clothes and my own, I fished out one of the precious red and black tins, closed my valise, the trunk lid and hurried back to the kitchen.

Everyone glanced up as I entered and went around the table where I bowed slightly to Freda and asked her if she would mind making us some coffee. Everyone's mouth dropped open and every eye but Katrina's was on the coffee can. Then, because no one said anything, I wondered whether I'd offended my hosts.

"Is there not enough time?" I asked, afraid it would interfere with the urgency of the schedule.

"Yes, no—I mean...that—coffee, it is worth its weight...in gold," Freda protested, standing up and taking it tentatively in one hand.

"*Ja*," I said, "exactly like this delicious breakfast...a meal in a thousand. Please *Frau*, I believe everyone would enjoy some."

"Would we ever *Herr* Andersson," Max burst out then and took my hand. "*Dankashein—danka...!*"

Grinning broadly, Freda wiped her mouth hastily with her apron and shaking her head in wonder, went across to the cupboard and from one of the cabinets, removed a coffeepot from the back where it had no doubt remained unused for some time. At the sink, she drew water and took it to the stove. Back at the cupboard, she began rattling cups and saucers, softly singing to herself.

Conversation had resumed at the table, the discussion centering about where diesel fuel would most likely be obtained on the next leg of our journey, how much it would cost, how far we were likely to get on a full tank and the small can in the trunk. Following the rapid German was difficult and I was also lazy and full from the great breakfast. I gazed around as I continued to assisted Katrina from time to time with another bread and jam she'd been given for dessert. The men were discussing the likely route to most quickly get us to another associate, before we would run out of fuel in the Mercedes. Max stood up.

"I will telephone ahead while you drink your coffee," he said. "Hopefully, I can set up one or two rendezvous points for the diesel. This next fill of diesel should take you all the way to the coast of Denmark by my calculations. You should be all right to retrace your route back, obtaining fuel again along the same way for the return."

As Max left the room the Mayor leaned toward me and whispered: "If we are not caught," he said, rolling his eyes.

Freda had begun to set some china cups on the table.

"We have a little milk for the coffee," she said, "but, regrettably, no sugar. There will be extra milk for Katrina to take with you. I will put some in a vacuum bottle and the gentlemen can return it when they pass back through. I will also pack a lunch of some sandwiches."

Max had retreated to the interior of the house; I could hear his voice, somewhere, no doubt securing our safe passage. Still humming, Freda set about slicing from the remaining ham and hiding the pieces between thick slices of bread. When she finished, she placed them in a basket, adding a small sack of hard boiled eggs. Finally, she added a jar of pickles that had been standing on the countertop.

"You men can find some water along the way, I think...or some beer, maybe. There is milk enough, but only for the little one." The Constable and Mayor thanked her profusely and I added my own appreciation. Max returned then, smiling broadly.

"You can see my associate north of Kiel, just before Kolding at Flensburg. He will be expecting you. You shall have more diesel for the auto, food and a bed for the night should you choose. It will be an easy drive to the coast from there. I inquired, but he knew of no one who might know of someone...a boat? But he will investigate a little in the meantime and may have more to tell you when you arrive this evening.

While the men wound up the arrangements, Freda played with Katrina until we were ready to leave.

As we were putting on coats, I took out my wallet, attempting to pay Freda for the meal; the only currency I had was Swedish Kronor. She would have none of it, though, waving her hands and shaking her head adamantly. Max, too, protested, holding up both hands palm-outward. I thanked her again and she accepted a hug.

Freda then gave Katrina a big hug and kiss, both of which were returned in kind. She handed Katrina the kitten, telling her to take good care of it. She had given it a little of the ham and some milk as we were eating and it appeared content now, full of mischief and ready to play.

Max handed me the tin of remaining coffee as I finished buttoning my coat.

"Thank you so very much," he said. "It was such an unexpected and pleasant surprise."

"No…please, it is a gift," I protested, pushing it away. "Keep it for yourself and Freda. Enjoy it."

"No…thank you just the same. It is more useful to you. Give some to my friend tonight, where you will stay, as you have here. It will be payment enough for him, believe me. And you may need it yet again on this journey, before you are back safely in Sweden. Use it wisely and it will take you far."

We piled into the car and swung out onto the street, on the way to the police garage for fueling. This time I took the wheel and the Constable navigated, holding a sketch from Max in his gloved hand.

They were waiting for us at the garage. The door swung open as we approached. Someone stepped forward and waved us to drive inside, directing me toward the far end of a large space, where another man waited with a fueling hose in one hand. I waved back as we drove through the doors and stopped when the man held up his hand. I remained inside the car as I'd been advised, staying with Katrina. Best not give anyone anything to talk about, our host had cautioned. I'd hoped she didn't begin asking for her grandmother.

The Constable and the Mayor got out and I heard my companions introduce themselves and begin chatting with their comrades as the diesel hose was inserted and I heard the rush of fuel begin flowing into the tank. As their friendly monotones came through the closed windows of the Mercedes, I thought that this must have been what it was like in pre-war Germany, before the *Nazi* Party dominated the country. Just like any other place in the civilized world: helpful, friendly people, willing to come to the assistance of someone in need—loving little children. Laughing, happy…damn the war for taking Greta I thought.

Katrina was giving one of the garage attendants a big smile through the glass. In turn, he was making silly faces at her to make her laugh, which she did. How silly he looked. His actions were so uninhibited when it was for the innocent child. Children did things like that to adults. I tried to envision the man in a soldier's uniform, holding a rifle, facing an Allied soldier. Or, possibly, in the cockpit of an ME109, drawing down on me, a grim smile of earnest concentration behind his goggles just as he squeezed the firing trigger.

Soon they were filling the extra can and then another that we'd brought along from Max. He'd insisted we bring it…just in case. My thoughts continued to wander as I sat, half dozing behind the wheel. Germans were the same people as we, so why couldn't we both take control from our politicians and governments in times like these—before things began to go wrong? Could no one have foreseen what Hitler would do to Europe and this beautiful country and her people, the birthplaces of Bach, Beethoven, and Mozart?

They were finished in no time. Again, no money was exchanged. The Constable had said none was needed, when he got back into the back seat.

"This is too important for money," he said, gesturing for me to start the car. "We navigate," he said to Katrina after taking her onto his lap.

"Grandmother?"

"*Nein*…I will be your Grandmother. You do not need another, with one as big as me." He tickled her until she was weak with giggles.

Holding out Max's map with his free hand, he stared over the little blond head, his chin resting squarely on the top of hers. Katrina's eyes looked straight up, smiling at the secure comfort she had from all her new uncles. The cat was somewhere in the back.

"We should try to make some quick time. We have spent too much time with your coffee, I think," he said, chuckling.

"The s*chnapps* is what slowed you down—not the coffee," the Mayor retorted from the back seat.

"*Ja*, that is so, but it had been so long…and it was sooooo-good—the coffee. Already, I am looking forward to tonight. As we drive, I will think of an apple tort for dessert with it…or strudel, maybe? *Ja*, strudel, I shall dream of…with cream."

It took a while for me to get accustomed to the Mercedes' steering and clutch, but by the time we were a half-hour out of the city, we were fairly flying along a very deserted highway. The automobile drove nicely even though it was obviously an older model. No wonder the Germans could build such great airplanes, I thought to myself, thinking of the *Foch Wulf* and *Messerschmitts* I'd encountered.

I drove for a couple of hours. Katrina was beginning to grow bored with her new friend and the cat was forgotten for a while, asleep somewhere on the floor. It had been roaming around beneath our seat, or climbing on the Mayor, who was sleeping soundly in the back.

After another hour I suggested to the Constable that we pull over for a moment to relieve ourselves. I had a little problem with Katrina since she was accustomed to her potty. She asked for it when I told her to go to the toilet. She wanted Grandmother to help her. I tried my best to appease her and she finally gave up on my poor German and went by herself.

After the breakfast and two cups of coffee, the Constable and I had no problem. The Mayor spoke to her until finally Katrina seemed to understand. We had also let the cat out and it was crawling around, rubbing on everyone's legs, but it didn't stray too far from us, or the car, since there was no clearly-plowed area and the snow was deep off the road.

We finally crawled back into the Mercedes and prepared to start off again, this time with the Constable at the wheel. We'd discussed it and thought Katrina might have a little nap if I wasn't driving and could hold her. The Mayor stirred in the seat behind us as we settled into our seats again, sorted out Katrina and then started off with a jerk. The day was December 22. Another Christmas had nearly come, I thought. Where was the time going?

CHAPTER
19

The Long Ride Home

Finding that the child had already been taken away from the Frank's home left me psychologically devastated. I'd lived all the years since her birth in a safe form of self-contented deception, knowing that, though I'd given her away, she'd be happy and well-cared for. Now, I was a very disappointed person as I returned to Köln. Depression consumed me duringthe train journey. The vision of my failure in the ineffective quest to find Sophia recurred throughout the journey. I believe I began to conjure some sort of fantasy of somehow possibly stumbling upon news that my daughter remained alive. That thought kept me breathing.

In Köln, I took a room in the *Reichland* again. The following day I went to the *SS* administrative office and sent a telegram ahead to Berlin, requesting a few days to visit my ailing mother. But only my mother's sister lived in Berlin. I lied to them, saying my mother was dying, thinking I would not be allowed the time away from my work in Norway. My mother had died when I was only a child, but they would not know that. With nothing else to do until an answer arrived, hopefully, that afternoon, I strolled around the city, despite the bitter cold, trying to come to grips with, first, having found the location of my daughter at last, only to lose her in the end, anyway. Thinking of my recruiting work in Norway began also to haunt my thoughts, creeping into the already depressed feelings about

Sophia.

There were some signs in the city of Christmas being celebrated, despite the wartime destruction. Several children's choirs
were singing in some of the city squares, in anticipation of the Holy
Day, now only a few days away. At the *Dom*, in the center of the old
city, I read from a placard posted outside the massive doors that
there were to be several masses celebrated. They were to conclude
with a midnight mass on Christmas Eve and another, Christmas morning. I'd never been to Köln before this; the massive church, the
Dom, was every bit as large as they always said it was. Inside, like all
cathedrals, it was very cold. One could hardly see to the other end
of it, large as it was—nearly a village in itself…an unheated, unwel-
coming village. The tombs and statues of famous and rich Germans
stood everywhere, most depressing in the near darkness of the
church's interior. I found no solace in being in God's church. I
wondered why I thought I might find peace in the house of the God
of my childhood?

I couldn't take my mind away from the child. Passing a
choir in practice, each upturned little face I walked past made me
stop and ponder every female child. Faceless, I imagined my daughter there among them. Innocent, bright, red cheeks, tightly-scarfed
with a wisp of blonde hair creeping out at the edges. I'd chosen
some characteristic from each child, turning them into a composite
of one, melding them into my visage of my little Sophia.

The man that drove me out to Frank's farmstead had told
me they'd named her Katrina—Katrina Franks. I found it difficult to
think of her other than as my Sophia. It mattered little now…no one
would even mark her burial place. I wondered where it was, her final
resting-place: eastern Germany… somewhere? Possibly, Czecho-
slovakia—Poland? Poland, I finally decided, it must be Poland.
Maybe I will go there, someday…after the war…just, as a memo-
rial.

I sat alone in the pew, dwarfed in the nearly deserted church,
pondering that thought, listening to the echoes of slammed doors,
footsteps and people talking. Somewhere I could faintly hear another choir in the church…possibly practicing for the coming day. I'd
come to other cathedrals to pray as a child; now I found I couldn't
pray for my own child. I couldn't concentrate on God…only my

own, selfish self, mattered. I hurt...sorrowfully, I hurt so, my heart ached.

"Ironic." I said out loud. "Ironic...we in the *SS* take the Polish children from their parents—many of whom probably have Jewish blood, considering the Pole's past sympathy to Jews. And now, we bring them to Germany, solely because of their *Aryan* features. We send *Aryan* featured children to Poland...to die, because they have a known Jewish parent."

I debated that dichotomy within myself for a while, but could find no reason in it. Then my thoughts turned to Johan. I wondered what he would have said. Had he been completely indoctrinated yet, by the *SS?* Had they completed the work they were only just beginning when we were together? Probably, I surmised. He was a beautiful young man—a kind man—then. But now, now their hatred doctrine would rule, I thought. It would have closed his eyes...closed his heart. And it was once such a big and generous heart...to the blamelessness of even his own child—our child—dying, because she was not good enough for *The Fatherland.* The good heart no longer beat so it didn't matter, either.

"Hah!" I spoke aloud again, without regard for anyone who might overhear. I'd almost forgotten. He was Jewish—Johan. It was actually *his* fault. Would they have sent him east? Surely he couldn't have been permitted to remain alive, let alone remain in the *SS.* How had they done it? Did they search for and find him battling the enemy for them, at the front? Did they summon him to command headquarters? Had someone casually touched him on the shoulder and said: 'Excuse me *Herr* Lieutenant...your services in the *Waffen SS* are no longer required—were never required, because you are a Jew? For your information, we will erase every mark that you were ever here. Your child, first...then your parents and then...?

I considered the thought that he was long dead...I'd considered it before...his death. Not for being Jewish, would he die. I'd thought...he'd probably be killed because of his zeal—by placing himself in harm's way. He was a brave man and brave men often do stupid things. I wonder if it came as a surprise to him, his death? Hopefully, he'd not had sufficient notice to think about it. It was then I noticed I had been sitting there crying quietly. The tears were freezing on my scarf. I got up and left the cathedral, turning back toward the hotel.

There I had a small supper available, mostly potatoes and turnips in a sort of broth...from something that tasted like meat. It was light brown in color, anyway. I thought it might be horse. After that I could eat no more. I choked down the remaining potatoes and turnips. There was a small piece of bread, but of course, no butter. I went to bed early and had bad dreams.

The next day, I telephoned the local authorities from the lobby, but they wouldn't supply me any information coming from Berlin. I finally spoke to a *Kaptain* who told me I had better come down in person and pick up the message—yes, there was a reply. He did not wish to speak of anything over the telephone.

So I went to the command center, to see exactly why my simple request for some time off could be such a secret. After identifying myself, a clerk retrieved my request application from one of several paper piles and handed it to me, totally unconcerned. She could have read it to me over the telephone. There were certainly no secrets in that pile that I saw.

The reply was from a lieutenant in the Berlin office for civilian control. It said I could have the leave I requested, but first, upon entering Berlin, I must report to a *Kaptain* Schotte, in that office; for reassignment, it said. Reassignment? Why would they reassign me—and to what? My specific skills were such that they were sorely needed only in Scandinavia. In fact, the skills could only be used in Scandinavia. I considered the quandary for a while and then felt stupid. Of course I would be reassigned...no doubt somewhere in Scandinavia; probably just a different sort of posting. Maybe I could be closer to Alex, I thought and felt good for it.

The message said to take the document to the lieutenant's counterpart in Köln, a *Kaptain* Klapp and he would see that the proper travel vouchers were made out. I was to be provided a train pass. He also said I must provide the name and address of my father's sister in Berlin, where I'd said that I would be staying. I was a little frightened about providing that information, because of the lie, but I did, anyway. What if they went there and found out my mother was already dead and then questioned my aunt in advance of my arrival? Possibly, they already had. No, there could be no way they knew her name, or her whereabouts. I was worrying about nothing, I thought. They have other things on their minds...more important than to worry about me.

To the clerk I asked: "Where is the office of..." I consulted the telegram again, "...*Kaptain* Klapp?"

"I do not know *Fräulein*. He does not work in this directive," she responded curtly, without even glancing up.

"Is there a directory then...somewhere I can look...ask?" I inquired of the girl, trying to be patient. We must take the youth, too, in these times, I thought, even the stupid ones.

But the girl didn't even bother to look up at me, let alone answer me. I took one step closer to the counter and before I even thought about it, slammed my hand palm downward beside her bowed head. The slap was so loud it made the girl jump and her paper-punch machine leaped up slightly and fell on its side. She looked up in alarm.

"Listen, I shouted..." caring little now for control, "...little *Leibchen*...I hold the civilian rank of *Kaptain* in the *SS*...do you understand?"

She only sat looking at me, astonishment showing in her face.

"And I will not tolerate this sort of treatment from a petty clerk like you!" Several other clerks had stopped typing and were watching us curiously. After some hesitation the girl stood up.

"I'm sorry...*Kaptain*." She crossed to the counter where I stood. Without lowering my voice, I continued.

"I can have your fat ass in a field hospital by daylight tomorrow, little one...wiping shitty asses between dodging incoming artillery shells." She barely nodded as she began to tremble. "Now..." I said emphatically, laying the telegram on the counter, facing her "...find out where this *Kaptain* Klapp is located. When you know, telephone my hotel—The *Reichland* and let me know. And do it now! Do you understand?"

The girl had taken out a fountain pen as she listened and was writing down the information from the document. She glanced up quickly and meekly replied: "Yes *Fräulein—Kaptain*, I will see to it immediately...and I am sorry *Kaptain*." She stood up.

I didn't acknowledge her belated apology.

"See to it," I said, staring at the quivering girl until her gaze dropped. Then I turned on my heel and left the room.

Walking the two blocks back to the hotel, I was feeling little better. It was as if I'd finally pushed back, just as hard—and won, at least temporarily. I would rather wait in my room, or read the paper in the small foyer of the hotel, than stand around those offices waiting on a clerk to act. I hoped I hadn't overplayed my hand; I entered the lobby and took a seat in one of the cracked, leather chairs. The mid-day sun was streaming in. I leaned forward and removed one of the papers from the table beneath the window and began to read it. The headlines announced victories on both fronts. They lie, I thought, tossing the paper back onto the table in disgust and leaning my head back.

They lie, so we don't know how terrible things actually are. The deception printed in the paper disgusted me. I'll write Alex, I thought. I'll tell him where I am and what has happened to Sophia...to Katrina. He will be frantic...wondering. I got up and approached the front desk. I asked the clerk for a post-letter to Copenhagen and paid her for it. I decided to try to write the Denmark office of his airline. Surely they will forward it on to Helsinki or Norway, somehow, I hoped? Returning to one of the writing desks, I took out my fountain pen, unscrewed the cap and poised it over the paper.

"*Kära du*...dear friend Alex..." I wrote and then paused thinking, composing my thoughts.

I am in Köln awaiting travel orders to Berlin where I will visit my mothers sister. I miss you very much and wish we were to—gether. I plan to visit with my aunt for a few days to try to put off this terrible feeling of depres—sion which has overcome me since I at last, visited the parents of

Sophia. Her real name was Kat—rina. I will not write the last name although I doubt it will really matter any longer. I fear for the worst, my dearest friend. Someone from the authorities had already reached her before me and had taken her away to the east. I do not believe I have to tell you what that means, Kära. All seems lost for the pitiful little thing. And now all I have left is the terrible longing for that which I never had and a discarded box of her clothing. I can hardly even bear to look inside and touch the precious things that once surrounded the little body. Many of the items appear to have been made by her adopted grandmother and also, I presume, her stepmother.

It is not that I never had her, is it? She was lost long before...when I agreed to let them have her after her birth. I have now learned her parents are dead. They worked in a factory near the farm where they lived...just a single bomb. She also had grandparents who, I was told, loved her very much and cared for her after her parents deaths and up until the

authorities took her. Then, neigh—
bors have had to take them in, as
they became ill also, in their grief

I do not know how long I
shall remain in Berlin. I have
been told to report to the Kom—
mandant there, for reassignment,
perhaps somewhere else in Nor—
way. I presume I shall return
with somewhat different duties, at
a different location, so please await
me with patience and love, my dear
friend. I certainly long to see
you once again and despite the lack
of shared intimacy you might wish
for, I do truly love you as a
good and loyal friend.

Until this affair is finished,
I will also be patient. As the song
says about bluebirds, Alex…blue
sky also awaits us one day. Even
without the Sophie I never had, we
can both go forward Kära. I
must have faith dear friend, in
your love.

With Love,
G

I read the letter through, once, folded it, turned in the edges and licked the top flap. I took it up to the desk and struck the counter bell just as the telephone jangled in the back room. I heard the muffled tone of the desk clerk speaking, pausing and speaking again before hanging up.

The clerk emerged folding a piece of paper. "Yes, can I help you...oh, *Fräulein* Stopff...someone just called for your. I have here a message. I was just about to bring it up to you."

"Thank you. I'll take it. May I also post this letter, please?"

"Certainly, *Fräulein*...I will be happy to take it...however, should you care to walk to the city center and leave it with the main post office, there is a chance it will be sent yet today. It is only a few blocks walk."

"Yes, I know where it is. Thank you for the suggestion...and the message. I will take it now."

Stepping away from the front desk, I opened the folded sheet. I noted the office address of *Kaptain* Klapp. It was in the same building I'd just left, only one floor above the indolent clerk's office. I put on my coat, wrapped my wool scarf close and walked to the post office where they assured me my letter would leave some-time before morning, all things considered and normal, which meant that if there was not too much bombing by the RAF that evening. I left the post office, crossed the street and walked back toward the government office and ten minutes later climbed the stairs to the *kommandant's* office. I found another clerk on duty, this one male. He smiled when I stated my business, then immediately began search-ing among some papers in a basket on his crowded desk.

"Yes, *Fräulein* Stopff, there was a telegram from Berlin con-cerning your travel and change of assignment. Sorry—let me just look in another pile. I have processed several travel requests today and the clerk who brought yours up insisted yours be taken immedi ately," he chuckled, "...a good friend, is she *Fräulein*?"

"Nobody I knew before today but someone who now un-derstands duty a little better, I think...and will remember me."

"I see," he said clearing his throat as if to rid himself of any planned sarcasm. He rose and was rummaging in one of four wire baskets on the table behind him. I noted the name on the closed office door, to his left: *Kaptain* Klapp, SS.

"Will I not be seeing the *Kaptain*, corporal?"

"No...*Fräulein*, he left orders to carry out Berlin's request, if I remember correctly...ah-ha...I have it now." He walked back over with a sheath of papers. "Travel permit...train pass...yes—they are all here and in order, *Fräulein*," he smiled, bowing slightly and handing them over with a slight flourish.

"Anything else, *Fräulein* Stopff?"

I was taken off guard by his efficiendcy. "No...I believe that is everything I was expecting."

"Good...have a pleasant journey, *Fräulein* and please say hello to my home town when you reach Berlin. I miss everyone there so much."

"Thank you corporal, I will," I returned his smile.

That is how people are supposed to treat each other, I thought, leaving the office. Outside the door I turned down the corridor and then stepped aside, stopping to read the paperwork to Berlin. Strangely, there was no mention at all of any specific reas-signment, or destination, beyond Berlin. The name of the *Kaptain* I was to report to was plainly listed. Why...I thought, was *Kaptain* Klapp in the *SS*? It seemed a strange occupation for an *SS* officer, I thought as I resumed walking down the hall to the stairway and out of the building. Rather too...too clerical a duty, I mused.

That evening was my last in Köln. There was also another air raid—worse, even, than the previous one, if that was possible. I emerged from the shelter at daylight with barely enough time to return to the still intact hotel, wash and change before I rushed to board a train to Düsseldorf. There I would change trains again for the east and Berlin. At the station, I learned there had been two direct hits on the Köln post office. I didn't doubt the fate of my letter. Now, Alex will not know anything of my well-being. I will have to write him again when I reach Berlin, I thought, hastening to board the train.

I needn't have hurried; after reaching the station, the train hadn't yet departed and the ticket counter had no idea when it would.

"The bombing, *Fräulein*," she said.

After an hour's wait, they did call for boarding and I was happily on my way. But the ride from Köln to Düsseldorf was slow and with numerous stops. One of the stops was not without inci-dent, as our train was strafed by the Allies' fighter planes as it stood still on the tracks. Later, we learned the engine's fireman had been killed up in the locomotive. I overheard a returning soldier telling this to his companion. Two soldiers had been temporarily assigned to assist the engineer in running the locomotive. There was no re-occurrence of the incident although we did stop again one more time before Düsseldorf. But as I awaited my Berlin-bound train there, there was another raid. It seemed the raids came now twice daily.

"Late-morning and very late night..." I'd been told by a hurrying mother, on the way down the stairs to the shelter, "...will it never end?" she said pulling along her two children as we half walked-half ran.

It was nearly noon now, so they must be late in getting started, I thought. The station held together, though one bomb fell quite close by. It was not so severe as the morning in Köln. Dust and little pieces of cement fell from the ceiling. There were many arches over our heads, holding up the heavy, stone building. Every-one, I'm sure, prayed as did I for them to continue to stand up. I hope they are strong enough I prayed, after the loudest and closest detonation rained pieces of plaster and dust on us. How can anyone believe we are winning this war...with this bombing getting worse? They are damn fools, the propagandists, to keep putting out the same lies and deception.

After the all-clear sirens, I returned to my same place on the long, wooden bench in the station area. Another two more hours of waiting and they called our train. It was three and one half-hours late by this time. A well-dressed, elderly man helped me put the crumpled box of child's clothing and my suitcase into the bin over the seat. Though he look askance at my souvenir from Sophia's farm, he said nothing about it's shabbiness

"No doubt there will be debris to be cleared from the tracks near the station, or worse, having to replace the rail-bed," he said smiling at me as he sat back down. "If that happens, we will spend tonight in a station." He went on to inform me that he traveled to Berlin every couple of weeks: "It is normally a fast train—once we leave the station," he said, "but in these times, the German people must be patient until our advantage begins to swing the war."

I smiled and thanked him before taking my seat, directly across the aisle from him. Fortunately, the damage around the sta-tion was slight. He was correct in that we were soon moving slowly out from the station platform. We began winding our way through the destruction of the factories lining the rail bed. The tracks curved this way and that, probably branching off to various factories and towns. Some of the lines vanished into a mighty heap of the rubble of a destroyed building. From within the coach I could see work lights here and there and the flickering of welding, flashing like lightning through some of the building's windows, absent most of their panes. Those bright arcs must make a perfect target for the British bombers, I thought. But we surely must continue the war work around the clock. Lacking roofs, windows and in some instances, even walls, there was no way to shield the brightly-flashing lights, open to the sky at night, where there were once buildings.

"We begin to move more quickly now," the man said, leaning across the narrow aisle. "It will soon end as we leave the city and we can go faster."

True to his supposition the dismal scene of destruction quickly began to thin as we gathered speed and soon entered the countryside. The snowy landscape outside the coach window was less dirty with the broader expanses of white fields. One could almost imagine this a normal December, I thought. Leaning across the aisle, I interrupted the man's reading.

"How long does it take...Berlin...to reach there?"

"Difficult to determine these days." He let his paper fall into his lap and removed his glasses. "It takes longer each time I make the journey, nowadays," he removed a folded handkerchief from his breast pocket and began polishing one of the lenses. "I do not know if our train will be stopped," he blinked sightlessly and selected the other lens. "Other, more important trains take priority, or possibly some sort of attacks along the way will slow us down. That danger will be minimized, once it is so dark fighter airplane pilots can no longer see us from the air, unless it is a moonlight evening," he said.

I thought about what he'd said and tried to remember whether there'd been a moon the previous evening.

We were rounding a sharp curve. Pointing out the window toward the view of the train we could now see ahead of us, he went on: "We have war materials on this train, also," indicating the flat cars with armored tanks and artillery pieces, covered with camouflage nets and rigged to appear like passenger coaches. "Those will not fool the young eyes of a fighter pilot. They do not attack passenger trains, normally, but those carrying munitions, we are fair game."

"Will we likely be attacked, do you think?" I wasn't particularly worried.

"Yes, it is possible I believe." With his matter of fact response he offered a wry smile of apology for his frankness and returned to his reading.

But we were not, for the rest of the day as the train sped eastward. By the time it was early evening everyone had finished eating what they'd brought along. Before leaving for the station, I'd gotten a bit of sausage from the hotel cook...some bread and even a little lard to spread between the slices in order to give the mouth feel of butter. With salt added, it made the bread more palatable. There was a powdered concoction which could be purchased on the train that simulated tea. The water that came with it looked very hot so I bought it for the warmth, if nothing else.

I noticed the old man had unwrapped a sandwich. He'd also purchased hot water from the girl walking through the coach and had just removed a silver pocket flask from his overcoat and was pouring over his cup. He noticed my glance and smiled.

"Would you like something to add warmth to the...tea?" He held up the flask enough that I could see it, but it was not obvious to the other passengers.

"I'm sorry, I did not mean to be staring at you"

"Do not worry...I have plenty if you would like a little?"

"I...yes, thank you, I would," I suddenly savored the thought of any sort of alcohol.

"Here...," he reached toward me, "...please hand me over your cup then...but we must not be too obvious," he glanced down the aisle.

I extended my arm with the heavy cup and he held my hand and the cup to steady it as he tipped the flask for a time.

"There, my dear...," he said, refitting and screwing the bottle's cap with a shaky hand, "...that will give the tea some body."

"Thank you, *Herr*...I am sorry, I do not know your name."

"My name is unimportant, my dear, as is yours...certainly no offense intended...these times, you know. But you may call me

Herr Rudolph...that is my business name. And you...you are...?"

"*Herr* Rudolph, you may call me *Fräulein* Sophia," I offered, testing the strength of the tea. It was greatly improved.

"It is a pleasure to make your acquaintance, *Fräulein* Sophia."

"What is your business, *Herr* Rudolph, if I may ask? I believe I notice your German has a slight Scandinavian accent?"

"Very good...yes, I am Swedish; you are very observant," he sipped his tea. "My business...well, let us just say my business is war—not making war, mind you...making business from war." Nodding toward my cup, he asked: "how do you find the tea now?"

I raised my eyebrows and held up my cup to indicate my pleasure with his generosity.

"It warms it up, as you say *Herr* Rudolph, it warms it up. Thank you again."

"You are welcome, *Fräulein*. We can have another cup later if you choose. Yes...buying and selling...*merchandise*. War is good business, *Fräulein*...good business indeed. As the Englishman play writer once said: 'war is good business—invest your sons'."

I didn't now whether I liked the bluntness of that remark so I passed over his comment.

"Will we reach Berlin before daylight, *Herr* Rudolph?"

"Probably, *Fräulein*, why do you ask?"

"The air raids you mentioned earlier—moonlight? They will be able to see us again...in this light."

He glanced out on the dimming snow-covered fields and forest, speeding past. "I fear it will be a moonlit night, later, *Fräulein*. The hunters will be out, I am sorry to say," he added with another wry smile, turning back again to his reading. "Perhaps we will be too fast for them tonight, who knows."

I sipped my tea in silence; its warmth slowly spreading over my body. It felt very good, making me forget about night fighters. I hadn't anything to read or occupy myself, so I leaned back in my seat. From the warmth of the liquor laced tea, I eventually dozed, hypnotized by the rhythmic clack-clack of the undercarriage wheels striking the rail seams. Their cadence and the alcohol were a wonderful sleeping potion.

I awoke later with the hammering shock of: "Thum—thum—thum—thum..." my head came up with a jerk as the quick rhythm tore through the car. In slow motion on the far end of the car, dark holes began appearing in the ceiling . They walked their way toward me blasting insulation and metal from the ceiling and wood splinters from the floor. As passengers screamed the bullets marched forward; 50 caliber projectiles slammed the seatbacks and floorboards as a passing fighter aircraft flung tracer fire into our coach. In the bright moonlight, it was strafing us as we sped along, progressing the length of the train. Already there were cries of pain from passengers.

"Oh…" I exclaimed, finally realizing what was happening. The train seemed to be speeding up, the engineer probably feeling it was safer to race over an unsure road-bed than languish in the sights of a known enemy in the air above.

I turned to my companion across the aisle: "*Herr* Rudolph, do you think they will make another pass…?" But I stopped…*Herr* Rudolph was slumped sideways in his seat toward me, leaning into the aisle. His head lolled from side to side. His journals, open before him on his lap, were splattered with his blood.

"Oh…!" I exclaimed…"*Herr* Rudolph, *help*!"

The whole car had become a turmoil of wailing women and children; someone began yelling for a physician. One woman repeatedly screamed a child's name. I stepped into the aisle and gently pushed my companion back into his seat, leaning over the still figure.

"*Herr* Rudolph…? The old man's eyes were half-open and I saw a large circle of blood in the front of his shirt, right beneath his throat. The silver flask lay on the adjacent seat. He would never move again, I thought as I hurried back across the aisle again, collapsing in my seat.

The firing had stopped and after a moment the conductor came rushing up the aisle, stopping to speak with each passenger. Finally, he bent over the prostrate figure across the aisle before turning to me, laying a hand on the seatback behind me. "I am sorry for…your companion, *Fräulein*…there is nothing to be done. We must remove the bodies, you understand. Please remain seated. Some soldiers will soon pass through and collect all the dead and injured. You may claim the…deceased, in Berlin when we arrive."

I nodded not knowing what to say at first.

"I am sorry..." he repeated nervously again, touching my shoulder tenderly. He staggered up the aisle, reaching hand-over-hand on the seatbacks to steady himself as he moved to the next casualty.

I sat totally stunned, expecting to hear the tearing sound of bullets ripping through the car again at any moment. I cupped my hands to my eyes and peered out the window. There was indeed a moon, so bright, I could identify individual trees and structures as they flitted past the window. We must be an easy target for the fighters, I thought, ashamed of my earlier confidence. I alternately glanced at the ceiling, expecting more bullet holes to suddenly appear at any moment and peered out into the passing landscape, looking for the unseen enemy.

But the airplanes didn't return, at least to our car. Soon a contingent of four young soldiers appeared in the rear of the car. One of the men worked his way forward to assess the work that lay ahead for them. He stopped beside me.

"We will be here soon, *Fräulein*...is it all right...all right to take the gentleman?"

"Yes...yes it's all right," I said, nodding vigorously, nearly bursting into tears at the kindness I heard in his voice.

He paused for a moment as if to say something else, nodded finally and passed further up the car. I watched his three companions lift the body of a young woman and struggle back toward the rear of the train, vanishing through the door at the end of the car. I glanced again at *Herr* Rudolph's body. The silver flask still lay in the seat beside him. I looked at the doorway where the soldiers had gone.

I quickly stood up and stepped across the aisle. Leaning over the body, I deftly snatched the silver flask tucking it into my coat. Overcome by shame and cowardice, I returned to my seat, unscrewed the cap and took a long drink. The Cognac scoarched my throat, giving me the false courage I wanted. I sat for a moment, thinking the unthinkable, trying to muster the courage for what I planned next.

I saw there was a smear of blood on my hand. I stared at it for a second before wiping it on the adjacent seatback. Swiveling in my seat I glanced around the car. Everyone seemed to be waiting, though I could hears sounds of grief.. I glanced once again at the body I had pillaged and then back to the rear of the car where the door still remained closed. Determined now, I stood, crossed the aisle again, stepping past *Herr* Rudolph and collapsed in the seat beside him. I glanced at the closed door again before leaning over *Herr* Rudolph. I rummaged through his jacket pockets.

And there it was, just as I expected, a leather wallet. A businessman's wallet, I thought, as it went swiftly into my coat pocket. I felt all the remaining jacket pockets but found nothing of consequence.

Forgive me God…and *Herr* Rudolph, I thought as I crossed back to my own seat. Yes forgive me, but I may need all your money and your *cognac* before this journey is finished. The soldiers who take you away will only get drunk and spend your money on women and more liquor. I slid sideways into the seat closer to the window and sat back, closing my eyes against the pounding of my heart in my throat.

After a while the soldiers reappeared and carried away *Herr* Rudolph. I didn't open my eyes to watch, pretending to sleep.

After another half hour, when the soldiers didn't return, I began to worry, wondering if they will be surprised when they discover the body has no wallet, papers or money. They probably will not have time to think about it, there are so many bodies to take away, I thought, trying to reassure myself. But I couldn't stop worrying about the stolen wallet in my pocket.

I finally got up and walked down the aisle to the toilet. The full stench of the little compartment struck me as I opened the door. I found I had to pause to compose myself, taking a deep breath before going in and shutting the door. I struggled to latch and lock it while slowly letting out the deep breath I'd been holding. It had been at least three-quarters of an hour before the soldiers had appeared the second time to fetch *Herr* Rudolph's body. I reasoned they would be pilfering the pockets of the victims in between carrying the bodies to the rear car. Sitting there in my seat I'd worked myself up to think they might return to search a likely passengerf— me, for the wallet *Herr* Rudolph should have been carrying.

I pulled the silver flask from my pocket and shook it; finding it was still nearly full I unscrewed the engraved cap and tipped it up again, taking a smaller swallow this time, savoring the burning liquid before letting out the rest of my breath. The swallow momentarily blocked the stench of the tiny room and made my eyes water. I took another sip before replacing the cap and returning the flask to my pocket.

I removed the bulky wallet and began rifling its contents. I first glanced through the documents. A Swedish passport stated that *Herr* Rudolph was really Magnus Carlsson, of Stockholm. There was a photo of an older woman and another of the same woman, though younger, with four small children. I turned next to the cash. There was a small packet of French *Francs*, a thick bundle of Swiss *Francs* and Swedish *Kronor* and yet another bundle of thousand *Reichmark* notes, too many to count. The notes felt very good between my fingers, like security. I stood thinking and feeling very much as a thief must; partial ecstacy, partial fear.

There wasn't time to count any of it. I opened my purse, separated the *Reichmarks* and placed them in an interior, leather pocket and closed the purse again. I started to put my purse on the wash basin, but it was wet and sticky-appearing from someone's blood. I considered the floor, but it too was filthy. So I put my arm through the strap, lifted my dress and dropped my underwear. Half standing, half squatting straddle-legged over the evil smelling toilet, I stood there for a moment, hardly daring to move as I relieved myself of the two cups of tea. This stirred up an even more evil stench. Panic-stricken passengers must have rushed directly into the toilet after the attack. Now vomit was mixed with the rancid feces spattering the toilet's interior, mixing with the urine smell.

I pulled up my underpants and began stuffing the Francs inside just beneath the waistband, spreading them round my abdomen, back and hips, smoothing them to remove the most obvious lumps. Finished, I dropped my slip and then my wool skirt, smoothing it out before I dropped my coat back down.

I didn't know what to do with the wallet and its contents. There is no way I can notify his—was she his wife, I thought? I didn't dare to carry the empty wallet with me in case I could be searched. It hadn't happened yet...but these times, I thought. Finally, I threw it into the wastebasket and using my shoe, I pushing it deep in the vomit-soaked mess. Surely no one will brave that abomination with their hands, to search, I thought as I buttoned my coat again and unlocked the toilet door. I drew several welcome breaths as I strode down the aisle and returned to my seat. I immediately leaned my head back, closed my eyes and within five minutes I was sleeping the fitful sleep of fear and utter exhaustion.

CHAPTER
20

The North Coast

Katrina didn't nap, though and even whined once or twice for her grandmother. The Constable drove until well past noon before the Mayor finally stirred, sat up sleepily and looked around. After a moment he asked if we could stop for a pee. We did, changed drivers, with the Mayor getting back into the back seat, where he immediately curled up, groaned once and went back to sleep.

I drove another couple of hours until we approached an inn. The Constable suggested we pull in and drive around to the back. Drawing up beside the back porch, the Constable got out, closed the door as quietly as he could and went in. There were beer kegs and wood bottle cases stacked high behind the porch rail, probably waiting the beer distributor. Five minutes later, the Constable reappeared, carrying a box which clanked as he walked. The Mayor awakened when he put the box into the back seat; we asked him if he wanted some lunch.

"Nooo...but save a beer for me." He rolled over and was asleep again. Katrina had a good appetite. We sat undisturbed in the parking area and ate one of the sandwiches and drank a bottle of beer apiece. It seemed to me we were making good time, though I didn't really know how far we had yet to go. At my question, my companion shrugged.

"We should be there before it is too late tonight." He refolded the small map we'd used from time to time. We put away our picnic things, set the empty bottles on the back step of the inn and headed toward the Mercedes. The Mayor didn't wake up when we closed the doors and we were off again after only a half hour lunch, driving back out and onto the highway. Katrina went to sleep nearly right away and after two more hours we changed off driving again. I'd taken the back seat this time and soon was having a nap of my own.

When I awoke it was to the giggling sound of Katrina playing with the Mayor. It was dark and we were coming into a small town. As we slowed, I could see candles and oil lamps here and there in some of the windows. I thought, it must be too small a place to worry about aerial bombing; I didn't even know if you could see a candle from 15,000 feet.

Where are we now?" I asked, sleepily from the back seat. Katrina turned and smiled, reaching back playfully for me with one hand. I took her under the arms and pulled her, giggling, over into the back with me.

"We come soon to Flensburg. We have just passed through Tarp a little way back. This is near where we spend the night again—Kolding; I think we can try to arrange passage to Sweden from here...in the morning, we shall see."

"Good. It has been a long trip," I said hugging Katrina. "Are you hungry?" She nodded eagerly, "*Ja—Ja.*"

I watched the lights become fewer as we passed through the small town and then it was only dim, orange windows glowing from time to time, as we passed farmhouses. After another hour we approached Kolding. It was getting late by this time and everyone was hungry.

The Constable got out after we'd stopped in the middle of the town. His inquiries proved valuable since we then drove directly to the police office. However, there was no one there; it was shut up tight. The Constable had been rattling the latch and walking around the building. He turned back to us after peering into a couple of the darkened windows and held up both hands, palms upward to indicate what do we do now.

The Mayor rolled down his window and shouted to him to

knock at the house next door. He did and then turned toward us and waved both arms beckoning us to come also. A man emerged from the doorway and came down the steps, stopping beside a fence. He proceeded to unlatch and then swing wide an iron gate blocking a narrow drive. The Mayor nudged the Mercedes into gear and we drove up the short lane to the back door of the house. The Constable shut the gate behind us, somewhat shielding the strange car from passers by. We all got out and Katrina ran to the Constable and began chattering away, tugging his hand.

The man's silhouette was replaced by a stocky woman. Silhouetted in the orange light from the kitchen doorway, she appeared to be nervously wiping her hands on her apron in anticipation. As we came a little closer she took one good look and threw back her head in laughter, shaking her head, probably at the wonder of us all—so many to feed. Then she disappeared back inside.

Our new host and the Constable approached and the Mayor and I were introduced. Katrina took care of herself by saying "hej;" she was alternating into Swedish a little by this time, stepping forward and curtsying. That made everyone laugh and broke the ice.

"Wait until Hilda meets her," the man chuckled. "Come now...bring your things into the house and have something to eat before you retire. I go help Hilda now," and he bounded up the path to the house.

As we removed our bags, the Constable told us this was the local policeman we were looking for. He'd known, of course that we were coming from the call from our last host. After carrying in one load, the Mayor came around to the rear of the car and helped us gather the balance of our things. Behind me, I heard the woman shout happily from the doorway for Katrina to come to wash her hands for something good to eat.

Katrina was off in a flash. She'd seemed to take to traveling and meeting strangers quite readily. The Mayor took up his own bag and then the box containing the remaining beer we hadn't drunk with our lunch. I made sure I had the open coffee tin.

"I've told her what to expect from the little girl and she's excited," the policeman said from the doorway as he took one of my cases.

The woman was chatting with Katrina when we walked into

the warm kitchen. Katrina, it seemed, was our ombudsman. We were introduced to our hostess, Hilda, who immediately invited us to take a chair at the table.

"You must be hungry after driving all day. The food is ready…I just have to put it in bowls. Here…" she said to me, smiling, "…sit beside the little girl; I imagine she still needs a little help at table."

Katrina was already busy with a piece of bread. Good smells wafted across from the wood stove in the corner where the woman began lifting first one pot lid and then the other. She turned now and then to toss a comment over her shoulder toward us. Her husband and our host—a *Herr* Albert Möeller, was pouring the beer into glasses as quickly as the Mayor could open the bottles. He handed one tall glass to *Frau* Möeller first, who accepted it gratefully as she stood, spoon and towel in hand, waiting for us to all have a glass for the welcoming toast. When we were finally ready *Herr* Möeller held up his glass and offered a welcome to the travelers.

"*Prost*," he said and began to drink.

Frau Möeller took a long drink with the rest of us before setting her glass aside. An older child appeared from the next room and she began filling large, crockery bowls handed her by her mother.

"This is our only child, Inga," *Herr* Möeller said. The girl smiled and bowed her head and passed two bowls to her mother. Inga appeared to be about thirteen years. Hilda was taking the bowls as they were offered and placing them around the table before each of us. Soon she seemed satisfied and picking up her beer glass joined us at the table. We fidgeted, arranging ourselves until *Herr* Möeller gave a sign and bowed his head and said a short prayer, during which I had to shush Katrina. She was so excited by the appearance of Inga.

When he was finished, *Herr* Möeller raised his head and smiled at Katrina.

"Now—you can talk all you want, *Leibchen*—and eat too," he said handing a bowl of steaming meat and dumplings in both directions. Helga started a basket of bread around the table while Inga coordinated other, moving dishes, smiling as if she were having the time of her life. I barely had time to take the passing bowls and serve Katrina and myself before the large bowl would be on its way again.

At last there seemed to be no more to pass and a near silence settled around the table as everyone applied themselves to the food. After the initial rush of eating, the Mayor leaned back, smacked his lips and apologized to *Herr* Möeller for keeping their meal waiting, who replied that it was not any trouble for them, though it was nearly eight in the evening and no doubt the family were as hungry as we were.

Soon the bowls went around again. The daughter Inga'd finished first and it was obvious that Katrina had too. Inga volunteered to take Katrina into the other room so the rest of us could talk. I got up with them and going into my bag, retrieved a bar of chocolate for the two of them to share. Inga's eyes grew very large and I got a curtsey and several *danka*'s. I also took out the tin of coffee. I was concerned there wouldn't be enough, still not knowing how far our journey would carry us. But, if the Mayor's hunch proved right, we could be on a boat tomorrow, bound for Sweden.

When I handed *Frau* Möeller the coffee she reacted nearly the same as her daughter had. Soon we were sipping coffee with the apple cobbler she'd made for us. Its tartness didn't go unnoticed and the usual comments about the absence of sugar went round the table.

The Constable and his counterpart were in deep discussion on their end of the table. They were referencing an open map, from time to time. *Frau* Möeller, who had disappeared for a bit, returned carrying a silver tray and handed us all a glass of *Schnapps* to drink with the coffee. It contributed a welcome mellowness to the simple but sumptuous meal.

From his end of the table the Mayor joined them in the discussion, contributing his own comments toward the map. I sat trying to fathom what they were saying. Now and then I got the gist of the discussion. I decided to check on Katrina again. I found her and Inga in one of the large chairs in the parlor. Katrina was curled up in Inga's lap and they were reading a child's picture book together. The cat was amusing itself on the floor beneath the chair's skirt, an inquisitive paw thrust out at my shoe lace as I stopped. I smiled, not wanting to disturb them and tiptoed back to the kitchen.

The Constable motioned me over to the table; the others sat looking rather morose and were silent. "We are having problems," he said, "*Herr* Möeller has been unable to set up anything across the border in Denmark that will offer passage to Sweden from Kolding. He is unsure what to do at this point and I thought we should explore some ideas together."

I asked for options. They discussed it for a moment and the Mayor smiled humbly and finally said:

"At this point *Herr* Andersson, there appear to be no easy ones."

There were, it seemed, a different group of German soldiers occupying Denmark. The local police—*Herr* Möeller's constabulary, had no real contacts that far up into Denmark. All at the table agreed, they were unsure of what might happen if we were stopped and questioned in Denmark.

"My papers," the Constable said, "are valid in Germany, but I have no authority in Denmark. Who knows what the authorities will do if they become curious, because we have no reason to be in Denmark? Denmark has been a problem...you know...for The *Reich*." He said this almost as an apology.

"I don't see that we have any choice," I said.

"*Ja*...we have decided the same and will try anyway," the Mayor remarked, smiling. "So do not lose hope; you are not yet rid of us. I think we must think of an excuse why we are in Denmark...two *Deutchland* bureaucrats, a Swede and a child. give me a minute and I will think of something."

Everyone glanced around and nodded agreement and the Constable continued.

"Very well...it is agreed then. Meanwhile, we will sleep now—here and leave early in the morning. Our host, *Herr* Möeller has told us the guard is changed at 07:00. In that instance, I think we want to arrive at the frontier around 06:30...when the on-duty guards are tired and anxious to go home to bed, or to the inn for some beer. They will be eager to be done with anyone coming through the frontier at that time. I believe they should move us through with a minimum of questioning. After all, what harm is in two old fat men with a Swedish prisoner and a beautiful child?"

"Oh? That is the story then?" I asked.

"*Ja*—you are a kidnapper and we are returning you to Denmark...*Herr* Möeller will explain," he said.

"OK, you are in charge," I nodded. "We are in your capable hands, but, I will be happy enough if you simply drop us off at the border and let us take our chances."

"*Ja*—*Ja*—that will not work. You do not speak Danish? No? And excuse me saying so, your German is also quite awful. You would probably not get very far without some intensive questioning. Besides," he winked at the host, "*Herr* Möeller has this good plan and has already prepared some papers which might help us if we get in trouble and are questioned too closely by the guards. Tell him *Herr* Möeller...your plan."

The Constable interrupted: "He has prepared a document which appears to be Danish. He has a cousin in a minor government clerk's office. If it is examined too closely, or if they telephone Copenhagen, we are in trouble because it will most certainly be discovered as a forgery."

"What does the document say?"

"It explains—oh, I do not know the word—it tells that we are returning you to Copenhagen—you and Katrina, who has been stolen by you. You are to go to jail and we should return Katrina to her parents—from whom you stole her."

I had to think about that for a bit. I didn't know if I liked being the bad guy. "Well, if you think it will work," I said, unsure whether I wouldn't simply prefer to light out cross country toward the coast somewhere and try on my own to hire someone to take us across the Baltic to Sweden. They must have sensed my concern because the Mayor put his hand on my shoulder.

"You do not have to agree, *Herr* Andersson. We can leave the paper behind. But, what will we tell them if they stop us and begin to question? What if they wish to know why such a strange mixture of nationalities is entering Denmark without Danish passports and in the time of war? There is much suspicion, *Herr* Möeller tells me, of anyone coming into Denmark, now, because it is a sort of bridge between Norway and Sweden. It seems the Danes are already hiding so many people, escaping Germany and the rest of Europe."

I considered the quandary for a moment. They were right, I didn't speak Danish, but I could understand it because of its similarity to Swedish. Katrina barely spoke German, or any other language for that matter, so she shouldn't be a problem. I had no papers other than my Swedish passport and some documents identifying me as an ABA employee and pilot. Nothing there to help us, in fact, possibly the contrary. I considered it again before deciding these people had the only chance to offer us. They had the car, which, if we could get through the border without being detained, would get us north and to the Danish east coast, the soonest. Regardless, we would be on our own from that point on, assuming we got that far. I got up and turned to the group.

"Yes, I agree. We will use your plan, *Herr* Möeller, it is a good one I think."

"Wonderful...we are all in agreement. Let us go to bed now...it will be an early morning."

And it was. There was someone shaking me in the darkness. The room was very cold and I remembered being cold during the night. It wasn't until I heard Katrina whimper beside me that I remembered where I was. I'd been dreaming.

"It is time *Herr* Andersson. Please dress yourselves and let us quickly eat and go." I swung my legs from beneath the covers and began to sort through Katrina's things in the half-light of the oil lamp he'd left on the table. The floor was very cold the moment I stepped off the small rug, onto the floorboards. I felt a chill. I got Katrina onto the pot, during which she also whined and complained about being cold and sleepy. I soon had her into some warm clothes, but she was still tired and a little cranky.

Fortunately, she was such an agreeable child that it didn't last long. We were soon sitting at the kitchen table eating *Frau* Möeller's sausages and eggs. God only knew where she got the food, again, but it was delicious. I sipped the precious coffee and refused a second cup when offered it. I could drink coffee later, if we made it, I thought. In another ten minutes we were saying thank you and goodbye and climbing into the Mercedes.

The Mayor and *Herr* Möeller had already refueled the car and loaded full cans of extra diesel fuel from the police station's

supply. I offered Swedish *Kronor* to my host, but as with his prede-
cessor, he refused payment. I pressed a twenty *Kronar* bank note
into the hands of Inga and told her it was for her to buy herself
something nice, after the war. She smiled, said a quick *danka*, giving
me a curtsey and then for Katrina, a hug and kiss, which were eagerly
returned. Steam was coming from the exhaust as they slammed the
car doors after us and off we went again, on possibly what would be
the biggest adventure of all. Little did I know then what awaited us.

This day was different from the previous ones. We were
nearer our journey's end and also, probably the most dangerous part
of it. I could sense the tension in my comrades after only a few
minutes ride; I realized the border would really not be that very far
away. My heart began to beat at a quicker pace. At that moment I
would have preferred the cockpit of a Hurricane to the confines of a
backseat in a car, I thought, feeling very much at the mercy of chance
and the control of other people. After a few more blocks the Constable turned around in the seat and motioned me to lean forward.
He was holding handcuffs in one hand, I noticed, as I peered over
the seat. My heart went into overdrive at the sight of them. He
sensed my reluctance and possibly the fear that I hadn't ever completely been able to rid myself of: was the whole scheme a ploy to
take us into custody and get the child and a spy in the same net. I
believe the Constable also sensed my reluctance. He smiled and
lowered the cuffs, speaking gently.

"It will be more convincing if they look too closely, *Herr*
Andersson. I am sorry, but I believe you should let me put them on.
I realize, it is much to trust us for."

The Mayor glanced at his watch. Knowing time was everything, I only hesitated for a moment, but they must have seen the
look on my face. I'd come this far trusting them and I didn't believe
they would take me all this way to the Danish border just to turn me
in to the *Gestapo*—or would they, I'd wondered? Finally, I extended
my hands over the seat back toward him. But the Constable gestured.

"I am sorry *Herr* Andersson, it must be from behind…please
turn in the seat and hold your hands out behind you."

I did. "It is always the hands behind—*Herr* Andersson.
You could harm someone if they were in front—if you were really a

dangerous person. These policemen would wonder if it was any other way; they would question whether I actually was a policeman, in Germany, to put the manacles in the front."

When I felt the final click and the tightness of the cold steel bands, I turned back around and leaned back on my arms. I was feeling pretty helpless...more so than I can ever remember feeling in my life. Katrina had been watching and was now curious about what I was wearing and kept trying to see what the Constable had done, looking at my hands, now behind me.

It was just as well we hadn't waited, because the Mayor put the car in gear, shifted a couple times and turned a corner. Immediately I saw the the border fence approaching, which separated the two countries. There was a pair of tall iron gates with some concrete bunkers on either side of the road. Several soldiers stood among some other men, with different uniforms. I took the second group to be the Danish police.

The Mayor cursed beneath his breath. "The change of the guard is there already...they have come early. We are too late." He hesitated and began braking the Mercedes.

"*Nein—Nein*! Do not slow! They will suspect something if you hesitate in the least. Hurry, keep going and slide a little at the gate when you stop. Be aggressive. We are committed now," the Constable said, "We must now act the part."

We did, rushing right up to the tall gate where the Mayor locked the wheels. Everyone had turned toward us already as if we were going to crash through the gate.

"Let me do the talking unless they ask you anything. *Herr* Andersson—try to behave like a child stealer and guilty criminal," the Constable winked at me as he opened his door.

He got out in a no nonsense manner and strode right up the to one of the Danes and begin talking and waving with one hand toward us. The guard he'd addressed waved him away disinterestedly, pointing to the other group who were still talking in a somewhat separate group. The Constable uttered an oath and strode boldly across to them and rudely interrupted them, talking and waving his arms for warmth and jumping slightly also.

One of the men responded and began walking toward us, speaking with the Constable as they came. After a few strides our partner nodded and reached inside his coat and withdrew the papers, among them, I assumed, was the false extradition order.

I was praying. One of the younger German soldiers sauntered after them. I looked straight ahead again as he peered into the frosty windows on the driver's side, bending so he could see me better. Katrina leaned across to the glass on her side and began smearing the frosty window. I noticed from the corner of my eye that she'd also waved and smiled, holding her lips and nose against the glass and peering at the soldier through the newly-cleared opening in the side window. I glanced over as he knocked lightly on his side of the glass and smiled at the happy child in return, as she continued to make faces at him.

Finally, he stood up straight again, re-slung his rifle and strolled back to the group gathered around the Constable. The other man turned to face the Mercedes and the Constable, a frustrated look on his face and stamped toward the car, shaking his head and waving his papers with an air of feigned impatience. Two Danish policemen, a German Sergeant and the young German soldier who had been looking in the window, followed him around to my side of the car. The Constable stopped outside my door, yanked it open with an air of authority and said in a loud voice: "You...get out, *now!*"

I began to wiggle my way toward the open door, surprised and frightened at the quick turn the situation was taking. The other soldiers and policemen arrived and were spreading out around behind the Constable to get a better look at me. Impatient, the Constable didn't wait for me and grabbed me by the collar of my coat, half yanking—half dragging me out of the seat, onto the road where I fell on my knees with a grunt. Surprised, I struggled to rise just as he slammed the car door and pushed me to the ground again. I was glad Katrina would be kept somewhat away from the event.

One of the Danes asked me in Danish if I was Alex Andersson, the man in the papers. Before I could respond the Constable quipped over his shoulder in German.

"He doesn't speak Danish, officer..." and turning to me, said in very plain German: "Are you the bastard child thief he is talking about?"

I glanced at the expectant faces, trying to put a bored expression on my face, rising to my knees.. The young soldier had un-slung his rifle again, I noticed. His look of curiosity had now turned to a frown of anger, or disgust, I couldn't be certain which. Finally, I nodded to indicate that I was and looked away, trying to look guilty and disinterested.

"Speak up!" the Constable said giving me a hard shove against the door of the car, causing it to rock gently. I could hear Katrina talking inside the car, but I couldn't catch what it was she was saying. The group of men fairly circled the two of us now. One of the Danish officers said to the Constable:

"Why did you not shoot him in Germany? You bring this shit back to us to deal with. It would have been easier if you had only brought the child."

Just then the young German with the rifle stepped forward, leaned over and punched me hard, a glancing blow to my right cheek and ear. It took me so much by surprise I was unable to recover in time and fell sideways, hitting my head against the Mercedes' tire. Someone kicked me in the thigh as I tried to rise.

The Mayor suddenly appeared around the front of the car: "Don't kill him for god's sake," laughing, "we must have something left to turn over to the judge in Copenhagen. If we do not, they will keep us and make us eat lots of those awful fish you Danes eat at every meal—*ugh*!" he joked, gripping his huge belly.

"There is not enough to feed us Danes, let alone to waste good fish on you unappreciative Germans," one of the Danish guards quipped sarcastically toward the German soldiers and us.

"*Ugh*...fish...," the Mayor echoed.

"We can hardly feed the *guests* we have now," another of the Danes retorted, smiling sardonically, offering another jab at their German invaders. Evidently, though enemies and occupiers, they somehow managed to get along. But I was keeping my eye on the young German guard's boot in case it came toward my face. The Constable reached across and snatched the papers from the one Dane and before they could say anything more, took me by the collar again and waved to the Mayor to opened the door.

"Back in the car, Swede. I don't want to miss my supper again because of you." As soon as the door was open far enough he shoved me in and slammed it again. The Mayor quickly retreated around the front, opening his own door.

"Thank you all—we will see you again on the way back through. I do not want to miss my supper either," he shouted as he slammed his door. The Constable started and then jerked the Mercedes in gear, edging up right against the gate and roaring the engine. After a couple seconds hesitation, one of the Danes nodded toward the soldier who had struck me and he walked over and lifted the latch on one of the large gates, giving it a shove to get it started.

Racing the engine as he urged the Mercedes forward, following the gate's slow swing, the Mayor kept creeping ahead, the bumper nearly pushing on the metal gate rail, until finally we were clear. He sounded the horn a couple of times and we sped away. I'd slid down in my seat and leaned my aching head back on the seatback; my ear was still ringing from the blow the soldier had handed out, but I could easily hear my every pounding heartbeat.

No one said anything for ten minutes. Finally, I leaned forward and opened my eyes. The Constable saw me and turned around in the seat and got out his handkerchief.

"Lean forward...please, *Herr* Andersson. I am sorry that the soldier struck you. At least he did not shoot you and it was probably for the best because it relieved the tension and helped the others to decide and accept our story. It was a good story too. If you will now sit forward and turn a little I can remove one of the handcuffs. I believe we should leave the other one in place, just in case we are stopped again for some reason. If we are, quickly turn so I can put it back on," he said as he unlocked my right hand.

I slid back into the seat. He turned around again and wiped my cheek, turning my head to inspect my ear, which still rang from the blow.

"It is nothing that appears very serious. Does it hurt?"

I shook my head. Katrina had been playing quietly, looking at a book given her from Inga as a going away present. She smiled gently at me and reached up almost touching the cut on my cheek. She said something in German I didn't understand and then pointed out her window, shaking her finger and saying something else to herself.

From the front seat the Mayor and Constable began laughing.

"Well, you have one protector it seems, *Herr* Andersson. She is saying the man was a bad boy because he gave you…gave you such a hurt." the Mayor turned back, facing the windshield, shaking his head and chuckling to himself.

"*Danka* Katrina," I said reaching over and patting her knee. She took note of my bracelet and picked up the loose end and put her own hand through it. She began talking to herself and turning her hand from side to side within the ring of the handcuff. We both sat back as I began to relax somewhat, finally on the road to Kolding, where God only knew what lay ahead. And the Constable fulfilled his promise to free me of the cuffs.

Two hours later we entered the outskirts of the city; my head had quit hurting for the most part. Kolding was larger than I'd thought it would be as we slowly worked our way through the light traffic in the general direction of the harbor area. There whould be a long inland bay, according to my guides. Suddenly the Mayor turned the Mercedes hastily to the left, accelerated and drove down the street and turned left again, abruptly.

Over his shoulder he said: "There was a barricade ahead, back there. We almost drove into it. Soldiers were stopping traffic from coming too close to the docks. And I believe I saw a machine gun emplacement on each side."

He stopped at the street we had come in on and turned right again heading back the same direction we'd just come.

"There must be something important going on over there— we'd better stay away."

"We must look at the map again," the Constable said, rummaging around in the seat between them, "and ask someone about boats."

"But who?" I queried.

We'd made a couple more turns and were headed back the way we'd come.

"I'll stop up here," the Mayor said. I saw what looked like a restaurant. We can perhaps have tea and something."

The Constable dropped the map and turned back to me. "Here, let me take away your bracelet, *Herr* Andersson."

He removed the remaining cuff and put them in his pocket

as the Mayor eased the car up beside the timber-framed inn. We all got out. Stiff from spending so many tension filled miles confined, it really felt good to stretch and wave my arms. The movement made my cut hurt again and my ear still continued to ring from the blow.

Inside, Katrina skipped ahead of the hostess, climbing up into a chair beside the first table she came to. She was beginning to discover the restaurant routine. I noticed that the woman had stared at the cut on my face when we entered and again, after we sat down, I indicated it with a questioning look to the Mayor. He glanced at it and shook his head, waving with one hand that it was nothing and to pay it no attention. There were no other customers so I let Katrina have her freedom after the confinement of the car. The waitress let us know what we could have to eat. They had homemade tea, the bread was fresh and there would be some baked fish in another half hour if we cared to wait for lunch. We ordered tea all around, milk for Katrina and a basket of bread. After it arrived my companions quietly discussed strategy. I listened while helping Katrina with a bite of the bread the waitress had brought and a sip or two of the milk.

"I believe we should proceed immediately to Vejle...that you should not try leaving for Sweden from here. Vejle is a larger city, but the harbor may be less protected," the Mayor said. "There are just too many soldiers here by the border. I am afraid, sooner or later, someone will choose a reason to stop us and look closer."

"I do not believe it will be any better in Vejle," his companion offered, taking a sip of tea and shaking his head. "The situation might become even worse...but he is probably correct, we have no choice," he said smiling. "Best we have some of that fish Then we will be ready for whatever comes. Always easier to make wise decisions on a full stomach." We called the waitress over and requested three plates of the fish and asked for more bread while we waited.

On the road again after an hour and a half, we all felt better after the good meal. Katrina went to sleep right away. As we drove, we reasoned from the amount of German military traffic we were encountering, that the harbor would not have been very easy to get close to—possibly impossible.

It proved to be the latter. In fact, as we skirted the harbor district, there were cautionary warnings posted on signs anytime we came near to the dock area. As soon as he would see one of these signs, the Mayor would turn the car aside again, choosing another street. After skirting the secure area for a half hour, we gave up, turning northbound, out of the city. And we were soon on our way again, this time toward the community of Horsens and the great Horsens Fjord.

"It may be no better," the Constable mumbled, looking at the map. It is still across the sea from the land mass of Zeland and the city Copenhagen. The military are very worried about this area of Denmark; probably concerned about sabotage by the Allies."

He couldn't have been more correct. It was the same all over again when we got there; guards were everywhere to be seen and soldiers randomly patrolled on foot. Finally, we stopped at another pub-like hotel-restaurant for supper. There were a lot of guests in the restaurant. Many of them were sailors from ships, probably off-loading in the harbor.

"We had better stay the night here if we can," the Constable said. "I will get out and ask the landlord if there is room." We waited ten minutes for him, looking at the Danish menus. They reminded me of Sweden. For a change, I could read them easier than the Mayor. There were lots of dairy products shown and of course, fish was plentiful.

The Constable returned in five minutes: "There were just two rooms remaining and we now have them. *Herr* Andersson, have you some of those Swedish *Kronor* now? They will take them here."

I stood up and took out my wallet.

"Yes...how much do you need...?" I gave him a fistful of bills. He nodded when he thought there was enough.

The Mayor and I played with Katrina until he returned with the change.

"I learned there are very many people from the ships in the city. I think I will go to the pubs tonight, to see what I can learn...possibly find passage for you two."

The Mayor's eyebrows raised at that remark. "Lucky you...an evening *working* in the pubs. Be certain to keep your mind on your work my friend."

"*Ja—Ja*," the Constable retorted, smiling, "possibly I can find a local criminal who knows the best way to get *official* passage to Sweden." Holding up the extra *Kronor*, he said: "If you do not mind, I will hold onto these—possibly make an investment in your future by purchasing some drinks tonight, in exchange for information. We shall see."

"Fine. Would you like more money?" I offered, knowing that any bribe, if it was to come about, would not be cheap.

"No, I have enough for now. If I need more, I will ask. We will most likely need the Crowns at the boat and again, when you reach Sweden. Not before."

We ordered our fish and sat sipping Danish beer as we waited, hungry again. The beer seemed thin after some of the heavy English and Irish beers I'd grown accustomed to in the RAF.

As we begin to dive into the dinners, I decided to let them in on my secret, so I told them then about something I had been considering all along but had hesitated to mention, knowing there were no identification papers for the child.

"There is something I want to ask...and tell you. I have an idea?"

They nodded, though continuing to ply knife and fork.

In my job in Scandinavia, I am a commercial airline pilot," I said. They both raised their eyebrows and the Constable smiled, nodding. "The airline that employs me—ABA—has an office in Copenhagen. I have flown there many times from all around Europe and Scandinavia. They know me there and would probably be willing to help me, if they thought they could. If we could get to the island and then to the airport, I might be able to get Katrina hidden in an airplane, somehow and ride out on a flight to Göthenburg or Stockholm."

They thought about it for a moment, while I helped Katrina manipulate the heavy glass of milk and then wiped her mouth. Finally, the Mayor spoke first.

"There would be no problem in Sweden—with the authorities...bringing in a child from Germany?"

"I doubt it." Sweden is quite liberal about refugees, now...I think."

The Constable spoke then: "Your fellow employees in Copenhagen, they are—they would need to be trusted. And Katrina has no papers so she could not depart in the normal fashion. It would be illegal—they would be breaking the law?"

"Yes, that's true. But I'm sure I could trust them not to say anything. Not that many would have to know anyway. I'm certain they would be discreet and we could probably figure out something for papers, or simply sneak her into the aircraft."

"Yes—I'm certain they would be discreet," the Constable muttered, as if he didn't believe me.

The Mayor interrupted: "I believe what my good friend wishes to say is that your associates would have to be discreet for a good long while…'til the end of the war and even longer—when…*if,* Germany triumphs in the war. Otherwise…they would always be in grave danger of suffering retribution from the *Nazis.*"

I had to ponder what he'd said, especially since I didn't want to say that Germany was obviously losing the war.

"You see," he continued, "should the government—the occupying forces, learn of the deed and the role any of your associates played in assisting the smuggling of a child—a German citizen, whom they are probably already at this time seeking…I feel certain the *SS* would shoot any and all of them, without question, or trial."

I opened my mouth and then closed it again; there was no argument. He was right.

"Never mind they're Danish citizens, *Herr* Andersson. Are you aware of that and do you wish to risk the lives of your friends and associates in Denmark, to do this for yourself and the child?"

I hadn't considered that side of the coin. I was a little ashamed for not thinking it further through. Risking myself was one thing, but I was unwilling to put anyone else in harm's way, let alone Katrina. There must be other ways, I thought and told them so.

"Your argument brings to bear another way of looking at it that I…in my eagerness to…bring out the child, hadn't given adequate consideration to. Now, I think it would be foolhardy, considering the risks you point out…if it were only me…but not others."

They both nodded, turning back to their plates.

"Yes, it is best to wait—exhaust all the other avenues first, before we begin to act desperately. We still have a little time. So far as we have seen, there has been no one yet searching for Katrina, or you."

The Constable chimed in. "I'll purchase some well-placed

cognacs tonight among the dockside crowd…see what I can learn about alternatives. Surely, among *that* crowd, there must be an active, though somewhat subdued, smuggling and black market operation or two, currently going on, despite the *Nazis*. I'll report my findings tomorrow morning over a late breakfast…shall we say 08:00?"

"Why so late?" The Mayor asked his companion, a smile playing about the corners of his mouth.

"Late…I will probably just have come home. Those smuggler characters do not even come out until after midnight and I will have to butter them up with snaps and…and I am not as young as I once was, to party the night through."

He leaned over and hit his companion on the shoulder roughly and we all had a good laugh. Then we agreed to meet no earlier than eight, letting him sleep a little later after his late night, or early morning's carousing on the shady side of justice, in the Danish pubs.

CHAPTER
21

On To Berlin

After the frightening experience of the night fighter's strafing the train, I found sound sleep difficult. The motion during rail
travel usually helped me fall asleep but tonight, I'd awakened again
nearly immediately; the image of the now deceased *Herr* Rudolph
and the photo of his spouse and children haunted my dreams. With
the disposal of his personal items in the toilet wastebasket, there
would never be any evidence to indicate what had happened to *Herr*
Rudolph...Carlsson—that he had been killed somewhere in central
Germany, on a train. Lacking this information, his relatives would be
forever tortured with the question of what had really happened to
him. I toyed with the idea of going back into the toilet and retrieving
his wallet and trying to go to the car where they had taken the bodies
and maybe plant it on the corpse. I assumed they weren't guarding
the dead too closely. Even if they were, I might feign grief, or pretend I wanted to fetch my...friend's identification so I could return it
to his family and then sneak the papers back into his pocket. But
consider it was all I had the nerve to do. I was unable to summon
enough courage as I sat there thinking and knowing it remained a
cowardly thing, not to do it.

I was not alone in my restlessness; the other passengers
were also fitful. I could hear muffled conversations in the coach
from time to time; the anxiety in their voices, apparent. The seri-

ously wounded passengers had been concentrated into the next coach forward, to be looked after. It had begun to rain and the bullet holes in the roof steadily dripped water into the car. I'd moved further forward in the coach, twice, seeking a dry seat.

The first seat I'd tried was where a passenger had died; there was blood on the arm of the seat when I sat down and the floor was slippery. In disgust I hastily wiped off the sticky wetness on the adjacent seat back and moved just across the aisle. No more had I sat down when I began to be dripped on. By my third move I was so tired and so frustrated, I no longer cared what I sat in. Fortunately, this time my chosen seat was and remained, dry. I curled up and lay with my eyes closed listening to the rumbling sounds of the train, punctuated by the clacking of the wheels on the track joints and now and then, a passing passenger in the aisle, bumping my feet in the darkness. Finally, I fell into a fitful slumber again.

Around dawn, the train began slowing and finally stopped altogether. No one knew why. The breaking of dawn began to illuminate the horrid details within the coach, which quickly became a horrible reminder of the previous night's attack. Blood had been spilled on the seats, seat arms, windows and the floor and with the hasty movement of the bodies and the panicked passengers in the dark of night, the blood had been further smeared by the foot traffic in the aisle, to and from the filthy toilet. The early morning sight soon set the victim's surviving family members to renewed weeping

The conductor passed through the train informing everyone that the railway would soon exchange our damaged car for a clean one and leave the coach containing the bodies to be taken away. This news caused much disturbance from the living family members and some chose to remain with their loved ones. The conductor said he would speak with them after those who wished to go on, were transferred.

It appeared to be very wet along the right-of-way, but it had finally stopped raining and blue sky and sunshine hinted at a fine morning. Some of us lined up in the aisle and began filing outside and down the track to the new car, standing alone on the siding. Some of the men began reliving themselves against the train car's wheels, as we walked toward the new carriage. During the night, I'd heard several women talking of having gone out onto the coach platform, between the cars, where they'd no doubt done the same…and more. Immediately after climbing up and into the new car, a line of women formed at the toilet door. I felt like it now, myself when we entered the car. The only liquid I had had since the shooting was from *Herr* Carlsson's flask, still safely in my coat pocket…and only sips of that.

It was wonderful to have a dry and blood-free accommodation again. The fact that no one had been killed in the new railway car and the bright sunny day, made a noticable difference in everyone's mood, especially after seeing the horrible state of our previous car, in the full light of day. By the time the engine performed all the switching of cars, finally connected to our coach and started moving again, the water closet line had diminished.

Our journey lasted a little less than an hour before we arrived in Hanover, where there were tea and cakes available in the restaurant. After eating and drinking two cups of tea, I went for a short walk along the platform. Hanover was no different from the other German cities I'd seen, with bombing destruction visible everywhere one chanced to glance. I didn't even bother to read the newspapers that were available in the station. I knew the lies would depress me further. Instead, as I strolled, I thought of what Alex and I would do when next we met; where and when we would meet again was a question. I would completely miss Christmas and now I very much looked forward to summer and seeing Alex as soon as I could. I knew he would listen to my disappointment of having missed my child. And he would comfort me again. He would understand my grief and hold me. Oh…how I longed for his arms.

I was on my second round trip around the station platform when I noticed the passengers moving back into the cars. I turned back myself. Alex would make a good husband. I wondered whether he liked children. I wanted very much to have a child, I thought. Very much…another child, I corrected myself, wondering again what Alex would be like, caring for a child.

CHAPTER
22

Narrow Escape

After breakfasting on porridge, the Mayor and I were sipping the remainder of our tea, and Katrina was halfheartedly nursing her glass of milk. Earlier, I'd considered taking out part of a chocolate bar for her, but thought better of it after telling the Mayor. He advised against it saying it would undoubtedly draw attention to us, rare as chocolate was.

I glanced at my watch and the Mayor saw me, nodding.

"The Constable came in quite late," he said, "he will be doing little driving today," chuckling. "I hope he was able to learn something. He snored even louder than usual."

"He must have had some beer."

"Oh yes—count on it and *schnapps*, too."

When the Constable did finally appear, he was an hour beyond the time he'd suggested we meet. Stumbling across the dining room, he collapsed in the chair at our table, groaning. He hadn't shaved yet and as he leaned back in the heavy chair, he sighed.

"Oh...what a night—what a *morning*...I am afraid this has cost you dearly *Herr* Andersson—your Swedish Crowns...but I believe it will pay you back." He dropped the chair back on all four legs. "In the end I believe I have made the proper connection. If only my superiors do not learn of it back in Germany. I spent the evening seeking out the most despicable characters I could find. They did not trust me at first but finally I told enough lies that they

399

believed me. They think I am being paid handsomely for this deed. They believe it is diamonds and gold I am smuggling. I told them it was something beautiful and sparkling..." he glanced over at Katrina "...they will know soon enough, it is something even more precious."

"We should eat...at least place our request, while you tell us of it,' the Mayor said, "so we can get started."

"There is no hurry, now...it is arranged.

"Really?" I said. "That easy."

Rubbing his eyes, the Constable groaned: "Oh...it was not easy, but it is done I think."

"What is the plan?" the Mayor queried.

"The plan is something I will enjoy, after the night I just had. First, we must stay here today, trying to get some sleep—which will not be a problem for me," he said rubbing his hair, "sleep all day, or as much as we can. Then, tonight we will all be up very late," he said looking at the Mayor. The Constable beckoned our waitress, heard the breakfast offering and nodded conceding to her suggestion of oatmeal porridge with milk, bread and cheese.

Later, we watched him noisily slurp his milk-flooded oatmeal. After putting some cheese on a thick slice of bread, the Constable finally got around to telling us why there was no urgency.

"I have arranged your departure in his boat, late this afternoon—around 17:00."

"He...?" I asked.

"Yes...I met this man—a terrible Norwegian...a smuggler, who agreed, last night, to do it. After many drinks and some money to prove my sincerity, he has agreed to take the "precious cargo" and a passenger on his boat to Sweden. I did not tell him this precious cargo was a small child, escaping." He paused for effect, glancing from one to the other of us. The Mayor made a gesture of frustration for him to get on with it.

"I promised him he would be paid more Kronor when you departed today and the balance on the shore in Sweden, when you are safe. If you did not pay, he said he would retain the precious cargo until you did. We drank many glasses of *aquavit*. He is a very bad man, *Herr* Andersson, I believe—but a good drinker. Because of his character I believe you can rely on his ability; whether you can trust him to carry you safely to Sweden, or not, I do not know. He may just try to take you out into the sea and throw you overboard. This is a the only chance we have, you see, at this point. You do not have to take it. We can continue to search for other transport, but I do not believe you will find anyone more *unreliable*...honest people are too afraid of the *Gestapo* or the Danish police," he paused, considering what he'd said.

I swallowed after such a description. "So, the question is, can I trust him...will we be in danger during the voyage?"

"I wish that I had a pistol to give to you, *Herr* Andersson, I certainly do, for I fear he plans to keep the *precious cargo* and your money, but not you. He is that evil. But I do not believe he will kill the child, so that might change how he would treat you. He will be very angry though, I think, when he learns there are no diamonds. You must not reveal to him the fact that there are none...or gold, either. Keep this knowledge from him until you reach Sweden."

"A pistol might get me into more trouble than I need. What do you think he will say when he learns the precious item is a small child?

"As I said, that is something we do not reveal until we have to; hopefully, he will not realize it after you board the ship." He thought for a moment. "How many more of those Kronor do you have, *Herr* Andersson?"

I opened my wallet and we quickly counted the Swedish bills.

"It is not enough but it will have to do until you reach your country. Are you certain you can arrange more in Sweden?"

"Absolutely."

"Good. If he keeps his part of the bargain, you must be prepared to keep yours, that is, if you don't have to kill him, yourself, before."

I swallowed at his remark but didn't comment. "When does his ship depart?"

"He will leave with the evening tide, when it is well dark. We will drive earlier in the day to a place of rendezvous, far up the coast."

He stood up and patted his pockets until he found and withdrew a folded paper, sitting down again. He moved aside some dishes before reversing the paper in order that we could make out the map's outline as he spread it before us.

"Here is about where we are now...on the east coast. And here—here is where we are to drive, just past Grenå, on the seashore. The *Kaptain* told me the bay there is very deep and if we arrive early and wait in the darkness until around 17:00, he will show two lights from the sea. We should then flash three lights, two times each—short then long, holding the flashlights on for about two seconds, so he can not miss seeing them. He said if we do not see a light at 17:00, he has had weather problems, or gotten drunk and isn't coming," the Constable chuckled.

"We should continue to wait, signal and watch for his reply at each half hour, until he finally shows a light. Then and only then should we respond."

"What about the flashlights," I asked.

"We brought three with us...all new batteries, too," the Mayor replied.

That satisfied that curiosity, but I had more questioons: "It sounds dangerous to me," I said, in the darkness—boats, water...what about *Nazi* patrol boats?"

The Mayor nodded, "I agree with *Herr* Andersson...do you feel he can be trusted, my friend?

"No, not at all; so you must plan accordingly...what other choice have we found? And we have something he wants—something he thinks he wants, anyway. He will not betray us to the soldiers as long as he continues to believe he will get something. He will try to get his payment, or get what he believes are riches from you—or both. After that—he might give you away. But not before he has given up all hope of getting something for himself and hopefully, you will by then be in Sweden. And I really do not believe you have much of a choice *Herr* Andersson...this is the end of the line as they say. The longer we linger here, trying to find passage—making inquiries for a boat, no matter how discrete, we stand a greater chance of being stopped, questioned and apprehended."

"My friend is probably correct, *Herr* Andersson. I believe it is the best option available if you are willing to take the risk. We have come this far without knowing that we would make it even to this place. And now the chance you wished for...the chance to go across to Sweden with Katrina, it has come.

"How long will it take—did he say...to cross over?"

"Yes. He said he could not be certain, since it depended upon the weather at the time; but he felt you should be there in two long days, or possibly part of a third. He said it made a difference if he had to avoid patrol boats and it could be more, or less, days, based on where you make landfall on the Swedish coast."

"Seems like a long time to me. What do you think, *Herr* Mayor?"

"I am sure I do not know. I have no idea about matters of the sea. Do either of you know the distance across and how quickly does a ship go...do you even know the speed his boat travels?"

The Constable shook his head. "No, I did not think to ask him what kind of boat he was *Kaptain* of, or how fast it went. So, he didn't tell me that...and I didn't think to ask, either, I must say, re- grettably, I was quite drunk by the time we finally struck the bargain and did not have all my wits. It can not be too large, I shouldn't think, if he is able to bring it that close to shore to pick you up."

I nodded, agreeing. "I've flown across the Baltic there...many times," I said. "It took only minutes in an aeroplane. But that is different, of course." I must be about a hundred—hun- dred fifty miles...that is around three hundred kilometers, give or take. It seems too long a time to take, to cross such a short dis- tance."

"Does it—yes, I suppose it does...but then, we don't know the speed of the boat, as we said?"

I left them to their discussion in order to take Katrina back upstairs to the toilet in the hallway and then back to the room to see whether she would be able to nap before we left.

While she played on the bed, pretending now and then to be trying to nap, I sorted out our meager belongings and consoli- dated everything as best I could. I still had three, full tins of coffee remaining and half a dozen chocolate bars. There were also two packages of cigarettes, which I'd forgotten about; I hoped I'd have no further adventures to bring out the need for any of them.

After a few moments my companions knocked on the door

and asked me if I still wanted to try to make the rendezvous. I told them I didn't think we had any better options. We agreed to meet in the Mercedes in an hour, hopefully giving Katrina some time to rest.

We left our lodging with take-away lunch for three. The server in the inn, whom we'd gotten to know a little during our stay, told the Mayor about a local farmstead known to sell cheeses, when they had them; it was on the way of our northward route to Grenå. We should stop and ask, she'd said.

My companions assured me we would probably find a second source for lunch in the town and that I was to take both of their lunches and anything else we could purchase, for the boat ride.

"What if you get lost?" the Mayor had said. "You will need extra food. We do not know what provisions the Norwegian has lain in, if any."

"I don't want to even think about that," I said, shaking my head as the Constable rolled his eyes.

Throughout the trip I'd been contemplating abandoning the kitten at some convenient location, but thought better of it each time as it seemed to occupy Katrina's attention when I wasn't able to. If we were going to be aboard ship, I thought it might be best to take it with us because of the calming effect it had for her. I'd discussed this with my companions and they agreed. At the breakfast the Mayor had suggested we obtain a traveling basket for the cat before departing and offered to ask our landlady about it. He turned up with a burlap sack, apologizing for his lack of resourcefulness.

"If you must contain it for some reason, this will work, though it isn't the best way to transport an animal." I packed it in my smallest suitcase.

We realized this was to be our last day together, so there was a little celebratory spirit in the Mercedes as we wound our way northward. Though the sun had been shining brightly when we started, it became cloudy and the wind changed to the northeast, pushing gray-striped clouds ahead of it.

"We are in for some snow from the look of it," the Constable said, bending to peer beneath the windshield visor.

We soon found the farmhouse, but were able to buy only a single, small cheese. When we reached Grenå, though, we found a fine pub in the town; the owner had just baked rye bread. He served a good lunch of fish soup to us, too—thick and creamy with the fresh bread.

"…with cheese in the soup," she told us with pride as she placed large glasses of pale beer on our table.

The meal seemed uncharacteristically Danish to me. We three, in our leisure, pondered the nationality of the cook, whom we never saw. They also agreed to pack three more large lunches…for eating the next day, she was told. We would not all stay the night. Only two would return. I would have liked a second beer but I wanted to keep a clear head in preparation for meeting the Norwegian *Kaptain* and boarding his ship later in the day. We lingered as long as we dared and then piled back into the Mercedes for the final drive to the coastal rendezvous.

It had begun to snow and blow heavily. By the time we drew near the rendezvous point we were a quarter of an hour late because of the slippery roads; it was 17:15 when we turned off onto a side-road. Even at that, the Constable had to locate it with his flashlight, getting out and shining it along the highway shoulder. The Mayor was concerned about using the flashlight and said so when the Constable returned to tell us he had verified that it appeared to lead down to the bay's shore. At this point we were supposed to turn off the headlights. After another ten minutes of driving in the dark we skidded at a sharp curve where there was a fork to the left. The Mayor stopped the car and they both got out to choose one or the other.

"The way to the left leads inland again," the Constable said, slamming his door. We backed the car and then bore to the right.

It had begun to snow just after we left the restaurant and had grown worse as we drove. The distance the Constable had written down when he'd met the Norwegian—east of Grenå, was nearly exact. The road continued on the way we had been driving, but the map indicated this was our spot to stop and signal.

"The *Kaptain* said three lights…and at 17:00," the Mayor snapped with the precision of the German mind. "Not one light shining and wobbling about in the snow."

"Who is not to think it a passing motorist? It is past that

time anyway," the Constable said, hoping to get moving again.

Of course he was correct after we thought about it, but the nagging thought of something having happened to the boat haunted me as the car crawled forward. When I'd peered out my open window, trying to make out the way, the sleety snow stung my face. The road had become little more than a track as we approached nearer the shore.

The Constable was driving now. Because we had our windows rolled down, looking out past the clogging windshield wipers, we eventually got so close to the surf, we could hear the sound of waves. The sea was fairly quiet I thought, surprised; I laid it down to the tide. By the time we finally stopped the car, it was even past 17:30. We quickly discussed whether to show the lights.

"It is too late," the Mayor said, adamantly.

"It is only barely too late," responded his companion. "The *Kaptain* is probably still watching—such a short time has passed."

"I agree..." I butted in "...let's show the lights—hurry!"

We three got out of the car quickly, each carrying one of the flashlights and turned to face northeast, into the blowing snow.

"Ready..." the Constable said "...on three we will do the first flash...ready? "One—two—three!"

We flicked on our flashlights nearly simultaneously and held them, counting aloud: "One...two...three..."

But suddenly the Mayor's light careened onto the rock we were standing on, bounced and went out. The Constable's foot quickly slammed on it, keeping it from rolling into the sea. He bent quickly and retrieved it, flicked it on—then off, banged it on his knee until it came on. He didn't return it to the Mayor.

"Again—one—two—three...."

Again, with him turning on and off two switches and I one, we were nearly in unison with our signal before we switched off again. We stood staring at the blackness, enduring the biting sting of the flying ice pellets. From the car behind us, I heard Katrina shout something, but it was lost in the wind. She must have opened a window. I turned around, thinking I should go back least she open the door, or fall from the open window and somehow, end up in the sea.

"No!" the Constable put out an arm. You must use the

flashlight...Mayor, go to the child and see she is kept safe."

He hardly left off staring toward the sea. We watched, eyes watering, waiting for almost five minutes. We were getting very cold and wet.

"Let us return to the car," the Constable finally conceded. "We can watch from there and then return again when it is time for the second signal."

We quickly got back in the car with the Mayor and Katrina, who tumbled happily into his lap in the front seat.

Start the car...I am freezing," the Constable said.

The Mayor complied. "She thought we had left her and could not see us in the darkness," he hugged her to him. "She was afraid of the bogey man getting her."

"Do not start frightening her," the Constable remonstrated, "she may be frightened enough, later."

The Mayor released her and Katrina climbed over the seat to hug me and then, with a squeal, she scrambled back over into his arms. I felt warm despite the wetness and cold. I believe the child had caught the mood of our own excitement.

"Speed up the engine so it will warm up," the Constable admonished the Mayor..

"You must go out again soon and we should control our fuel."

"To hell with the fuel; we are cold and it is not yet time," the Constable retorted, sharply. "He will not signal until the time. It is still another quarter hour to go."

I was worried that we hadn't yet seen any return lights and that my normally-jovial companions were beginning to bicker. Then the Mayor spoke my concern aloud.

"Do you believe he had trouble..." the Mayor fished for some sympathetic excuse to bolster his hope. "The weather...or has he gotten drunk and forgotten his promise?"

The Constable didn't answer immediately. I worried about their morale and jumped in, myself.

"Certainly—no doubt he has had some small trouble...I would have too—in my aeroplane; this storm. He must be steering by purely dead reckoning...the compass and a clock to time his runs. My concern would be running onto the shore in the darkness and destroying the ship. And there are no shore lights to help him navigate by."

I'd done a fair amount of sailing, myself and although it was only inland lake racing—no tides—I understand the effect a flowing tidal current had on a moving ship, pushing it in the direction—leeway—the way the current was flowing. It was no different from a crosswind in flying an aeroplane. One compensated by steering more into the wind to offset and compensate for how much it slowed you down.

"I'm certain the *Kaptain* and his crew know what they are doing," I tried to be reassuring.

The fifteen minutes seemed to drag into an hour, but we were finally outside again, this time, leaving the Mayor in the car to watch Katrina. We were prepared in advance for the signal, this time, peering blindly into the windy darkness inhaling the smell of the sea.

The Constable and I stood waiting, flashlights in hand, thumbs on the slider buttons, waiting. But the two lights from the sea never came. We even waited an extra five minutes. Nothing showed. We returned to the car again and only shook our heads at the Mayor's questioning look, not wishing to discuss our disappointment. The action we were taking was our only choice

"Nothing?" he asked, not really expecting an answer.

And again, endless waiting. I went over the contents of the suitcases in my head, what we had to carry aboard. Would they be too large to struggle into a ship's boat, the boat he'd send to shore for us? Would it be a launch, or a dinghy? Would we have to wade out carrying Katrina and the luggage. Possibly he would make two trips. If he refused, I could tell him the diamonds were in the second suitcase. Would we be able to keep an eye on our cases after we'd gone aboard the boat? That reminded me of the cat and I opened the smaller case and took out the burlap sack in case I needed it for the kitten.

Then the Constable was nodding to me again. "There are only a few more minutes…I will go out."

Just as he opened his door, he shouted, "There! Look— two lights!"

And there were…and they were close in, too, from the looks

of them. Without warning me, the Constable turned on his two flashlights. I quickly flashed mine…late, but I caught up to him on the second flash. Immediately the lights went out in the dark and there was only the sound of the waves again, as if the boat had never been there. The Constable turned to me.

"Come, let us carry down the cases. Be careful with the slippery rocks. The ship must be very close. We must not keep him waiting."

We hustled around to open the Mercedes' trunk and take out the other case. I was sorry I'd had to leave that box of Katrina's clothing with her grandmother. But now—in this weather and a boat to catch, I was happy for the lighter load, as we stumbled over the rocks in the darkness, struggling with the bags I did bring.

We stopped near the water, where the rock outcropping formed a natural dock beside the sea. I'd only just set the bags down and straightened up when the Mayor elbowed me. He and the Constable were directing their flashlight beams seaward, into the blowing snow.

There he was…standing straddle-legged in a small boat—a dinghy, from the look of it, both his hands full with the oars as he deftly stood the bouncing little craft away from the rocks. He had a rope line, ready in his teeth, which he suddenly flung in our direction, as we watched, before continuing to row frantically again. Then he shouted in booming Norwegian to take the line and stand the boat off the rocks as he approached closer.

I caught the line and wrapped it around my left arm and braced my legs. Spread-legged as I was I didn't dare move to help them. The Mayor was occupied with Katrina and the Constable was leaning forward over the edge of the rocks trying to catch the boat's bounding prow with one hand while holding on with the other. But it was no good, the bow bobbed and danced beneath him. Giving up in frustration, he finally stepped boldly into the water and took control of the craft with both hands. I held steady pressure on the rope so the boat wasn't bouncing so wildly. Nevertheless, I stood straddle-legged, keeping the line taught while he held the small dinghy away from being battered on the rocks. The Norwegian turned the oars in and came forward gingerly, balancing with both arms held out-stretched until he could safely step over the side beside the Constable. Together they pulled the wooden hull onto the rocks with a single haul from each side.

The Mayor handed Katrina to me. I stepped aside quickly to get out of harm's way and at the same time, holding her close. Seeing my movement the Norwegian hesitated, glaring first at Katrina and then at me. Then he leaped away from the outcropping as a small surf came ashore; all this in the intermittent bobbing of the two flashlights.

"Bring the boat up farther," the *Kaptain* shouted in the wind, grasping the taught line and walking backward. The pair followed his instructions, and dragged the tiny dinghy up the rocks, away from the rushing surf. They secured it from the buffeting wind by sitting on each gunwale. I slowly edged closer, with Katrina hugging me tightly, while still trying to see what was going on. The *Kaptain* extracted his own flashlight, switched it on pointing first at me, where he held it momentarily. Then he leaned over and shined it first at the Mayor's face and then the Constable's. Seeing him, he stepped back, raising one arm and began shouting.

"Which one is the passenger?" he asked, gesturing the light in our direction.

"The man...with the child," the Constable replied, "they are your cargo."

He glared at me. "You said nothing about a child! What the hell...I can not take a child, tonight of all nights! This is dangerous! This storm...and it is getting worse. I do not even know if I can make it across safely."

A man with a conscience, I thought, listening to his harangue. I expected a dirty, bad character-type; maybe he was trying to raise the price. He was about sixty or sixty-five, as best I could judge, tall with a neatly-trimmed, gray beard. He had a tight, wool-knit cap pulled low and wore dark, sailor's garb with oilskin trousers and boots, which he now began to draw off and empty of cold seawater. He wasn't wearing socks. I stepped forward before the others could answer, feeling it was my responsibility.

"The child makes no difference," I shouted in Swedish, speaking to him for the first time, she weighs almost nothing and she is very small." He looked me up and down for the first time as if to weigh me as cargo.

"Her size makes no damn difference to you or to me, Swede…if she is dead. The sea cares little for her size—or her life. The sea is…is, unforgiving!" he spat. "One does not carry out children on the sea on nights such as this, especially if she is—kidnapped."

"She is not kidnapped, she is…she is my—my daughter. We lied to you so you would take us to safety."

"Daughter! Then you, better than anyone should know, it is dangerous—very dangerous—for your child. And safety you say…I would be carrying you away from safety, right into the lion's mouth. She and you may drown." He looked down as if to gather strength. "And there are German patrol boats everywhere. Just tonight, I saw…" he stopped suddenly, in mid-sentence, then he raised his arm and pointed up the track we had just driven down.

"Are they with you?"

We all three turned around simultaneously when he pointed. There were as many as a dozen flashlights bobbing their way down the hill toward us. They were moving fast and were very near. Involuntarily, I drew Katrina close.

"Damn…somehow, they have followed us," the Mayor yelled. "What now?"

The Constable took charge immediately. "*Kaptain*, you have no choice now. Take them…or they will both be killed."

"Killed—why would they kill them…the child?"

"He is an American…" the Constable shouted, gesturing in my direction. My head jerked up at this…how did he know that? "And the child—the child is a Jew; they will not imprison her, like him—they will simply kill her."

The sailor looked first at me and then at the bundle I now held in my arms.

Possibly to reassure the *Kaptain*, the Constable continued: "We will take care of ourselves," he nodded toward the Mayor, who bobbed his agreement.

The sailor appeared as if he would ignore the Constable and launch his boat.

"If you leave them here I will reveal all your illicit smuggling operations to the *Nazis*. You will be safe in no port again while the Third *Reich* rules the land and the seas. But if you take them away immediately, tonight...who is to say you were ever here? I do not know your name, so if they should torture me, I can tell them nothing The patrol boats will not be searching for you—if you take them—they will only know when and if they discover you at sea."

Glancing up the hillside we noted the flashlights had come nearer; the Norwegian hesitated no further. Turning to me he shouted against the wind:

"Hurry then—we have already wasted too much time! Give me the child," he said, holding out his arms, preparing to put her in the dinghy.

"No!" I yelled, emphatically. "You get in first—then they will hand the child to me."

The pair had begun to drag the boat toward the sea.

"All right—have it your way but make haste—lest they see the dinghy and start shooting."

I turned and gave Katrina to the Mayor. "Thank you both for everything...both of you."

"*Ja—Ja*—get in—*hurry...go*!"

I took the cat from Katrina and unceremoniously stuffed it into the burlap bag I pulled from my pocket and tied the ends shut. If it protested I didn't hear it, for the crash of the waves and the howling wind. I handed the bundle back to Katrina.

"Don't let the cat out Katrina. Keep the sack closed!"

The *Kaptain* had already slid the dinghy into the water and the Constable was steadying it for me as I clambered in and turned, taking Katrina from the Mayor's arms as she clutched her burlap bundle tightly.

"Boat..." I heard her say, beneath the muffled wool scarf that covered most of her face. I placed her in the bottom of the boat in front of me, between my feet.

"Wet...Papa...!" she said sharply "...cold!"

The *Kaptain* stood over us and dropped a piece of my luggage into the middle, between the seats.

"Here..." the Constable handed the second piece over and I dumped it between the *Kaptain* and Katrina. As the third piece came, the Constable pushed the boat away from the rocks.

"Grandmother...?" Katrina whined, wrapping her arms around my leg.

Just a minute, Katrina." I nearly tipped backwards as the *Kaptain* pulled strongly on the oars, giving such a pull to keep us off the rocks, that I wasn't prepared for the sudden movement and nearly dropped the heavy valise over the side. I steadied myself and stood the case upright on the narrow seat beside me; Katrina snuggled backward again, against my legs. I sensed, rather than saw, the broad back of the *Kaptain* arch and roll toward me in the dimness of my friend's flashlights as he pulled hard on the oars. I could hardly make out his form. Then their flashlights went out.

As the little boat turned away from the shore, we struck the first swell and the Norwegian pulled hard again, grunting loudly in the darkness with each stroke. Sitting in the stern, I was facing the open sea. When I glanced over my shoulder, I could occasionally see the bobbing and weaving of the approaching flashlights, through the snow. I knew my companions were there but I dared not shout my thanks.

Within seconds the flashlights converged into a close group and stopped moving, no doubt surrounding our faithful escorts. Now and then a couple of the beams appeared brighter as they flashed out toward the sea, unable to penetrate the driving snow, though we could see them. I didn't think they could see us. They were seeking what might have been coming, I hoped, not what had come already and departed and I'm sure my companions had come up with a believable story to that effect. Then, I could see nothing but blackness.

Would the searchers follow up with a patrol boat to learn the truth, or was one already on the way? And would our friends give their lives for us this night, I wondered, saying a silent prayer for two more of my enemies.

CHAPTER
23

Berlin, Almost

The train took all of the day getting to Berlin, mostly because there were two daylight raids, from the air. I didn't even know about the first one until the train stopped. Something had gone wrong with the locomotive, possibly from the strafing airplanes. We had to stop to let them make repairs. It didn't take more than an hour and we were on our way again.

But not long after, there was another raid—not on the train this time, but on a city we were about to pass through; there were factories there and we could see the bombs coming down and the explosions as the train approached. It was like watching a cinema.

The engine driver, seeing the bombs exploding on the factories, stopped the train outside the town to wait for the bombing to stop. Most all the passengers got out to watch the formations of passing bombers. I was the youngest adult among them.

"We are easy targets, standing here," someone commented. "What if a *Engländer* fighter comes along?"

"I will jump under the train car," another responded, "if that should happen."

"The planes...," an old farmer said, "...they are like the geese in the spring. See how they fly together. They are interesting to watch."

"But deadly geese...to those below," his wife added, giving him a knowing look.

"Yes, but like the geese, they just keep coming. Look..." he pointed to the northwest "...they don't fly from the south...still, the flocks are stretched out so far as I can see. I like to watch them, especially when our fighters shoot at them."

Someone else complained about our vulnerability standing there and returned to the rail car for what protection it offered. It seemed everyone was an expert about the airplanes and the bombing.

"What if those *English* in their bombers see us standing here?" another asked. Will they not come over here and drop some bombs on us?"

"They are not coming here," someone said, "they save their bombs for the factories."

"Yes...and also, they are not *English*, either," someone else said. "They are *Amerikanisch*."

"Oh, really...just think, they fly so far...all that way, across the ocean," the farmer added. Kindly enough, no one corrected his wanting geography.

"Look!" a woman shouted. "Up there. An airplane is attacking them It must be one of our fighters."

Shading our eyes, we watched as a single German fighter approached the endless formation from the east, flying directly over our heads. We couldn't see or hear the firing of their guns because of the noise of the engines, but we assumed they were fighting each other. The pilot of the fighter didn't swoop, or dive as I'd seen others do. He continued on, straight at the middle of the formation. They were so high, it was difficult to see them but on and on he went. I felt proud of his daring foolishness.

After a minute, we saw smoke coming from the fighter. Yet, it continued. Closer and closer it went, the smoke growing darker. Then it disappeared for a second within their midst. There was a flash, a cloud of smoke and a flicker of fire, high in the sky. Everyone was leaning back, craning our necks, with both hands shading our eyes.

"They have got him," someone said sadly. "See, he is coming down...there."

We watched, as a smoking object fell from the formation.

"No...one of them is coming down! It is too big for the fighter."

A man with a crutch spoke up then: "Our pilot has crashed into them to destroy one of them. It is the *Amerikanisch* bomber that we can see which is falling. The one he hit before being exploded into pieces."

Sure enough, we stood transfixed for a moment absorbing the import of his comments. Without a word we'd resumed our heads-back, leaning stance as the bomber's fuselage spiraled downward before us, trailing white smoke. As it came closer, we saw it was missing half of its back end and part of a wing. Down and down it came, turning very slowly and spinning as it came, but remaining upright all the while. The engines even seemed to be running, still. It truly was a marvel to see—like a child's broken toy.

It struck the earth somewhere between the city and us, behind a grove of trees separating us from the city. We at first didn't see hear anything but then there came a dull thud of an explosion, different sounding from the bombs which had been exploding intermittently. A blackish-white cloud of smoke rose over the trees and began slanting away downwind.

We stood around mumbling to ourselves like a crowd that has accumulated in the lobby outside a moving picture theatre, talking about the feature that we have just seen played. Just then someone else shouted, pointing skyward again.

"Look...parachutes!"

All our heads went back up again. There was one, two...then three parachutes blooming against the bright blue sky. They slowly drifted toward our little party. Two were further away from us, but one was coming quite close. Everyone seemed surprised and silently watched, curious.

The bombers had passed over now, so the train crew began trying to get the passengers back on the train. But when they saw the parachutists, too, that effort was abandoned. All of us were occupied with the falling Americans who'd escaped the airplane.

We could see the men's bodies suspended from the little mushrooms as they came closer. Their bodies were swaying back and forth in the wind as they drifted. Down—down they came, wagging like clock's pendulums. Someone pointed at the single parachute, closer than the other two. "That one will fall on us. Maybe we had better get back on the train? He may shoot when he lands?"

And after some moments it appeared he was correct; it became evident the airman would be landing very near. Now we could even see the color of his uniform: dark brown with a white collar on his jacket. It was astonishing, the wind continued to carry the man right into our midst and we began spreading out to avoid having the swaying body land on one of us. No one seemed to fear being shot; everyone was curious, wanting to see the enemy. His two companions were farther away, quite close to each other.

Then our airman landed. Surprisingly, the old men and some of the women rushed right over and jumped on him, before he could draw his gun. I thought they were brave for this, remaining where I was watching his companions. They were less than a half a kilometer away when they struck. Immediately, one after the other leaped up, struggled from their own parachute lashings and began running toward each other. They stood in the middle of a field staring in our direction, watching as our little group surrounded their companion, beside the train. I was afraid they might come running over, with their guns and try to harm us, too, or take over the train.

"They had better look out," someone said about our brave comrades who stood around the airman, "he will shoot them all and take over the train. I looked over to where the crowd surrounded the lone airman. They were beginning to step back to let him get up. Strange they weren't more afraid of him. He wouldn't have enough bullets, I thought—there were too many of us for that.

Seeing their comrade land in our midst, all but captured, his companions began to run in the other direction toward a nearby forest. Evidently giving him up for lost, I guessed: they were going to hide and try to get back to England, or wherever they could. Strange, I felt sympathy for them, too. It must have been the hunted animal instinct we all have within us. Though they'd just been devastating our factory, killing my countrymen and shooting at us. I think I knew that they were only hastening the end of this madness...and that action was welcome. The sooner the better, I thought...no matter who.

The small crowd returned carrying the airman up to the

coach's entrance. He must have been injured. The old men had made a cradle by linking their hands and had borne him, sitting with his arms around their necks. As they drew up, staggering under the bulk of the young man, they set him down, panting from their effort.

I walked closer, wanting to see the enemy up close. He'd been crying; I was unsure whether it was fear or the pain of his injury. He was definitely frightened as he glanced from side to side like a cornered, wild animal, afraid of what we might do to him. He's so very young, I thought, gussing his age at about nineteen or twenty years.

"He is hurt," the farmer's wife said, a look of sympathy on her face as she stepped up beside me. "His leg is broken, there—below the knee…and only a boy, too. Pitiful…they will shoot him…the *Gestapo?* He may as well die here—now. I am going into the train…I can not watch that."

The train's engine driver must have wondered why he hadn't yet received the signal to start the train and had walked back along the length of cars. Someone told him what happened and he joined the crowd around the fallen airman. I followed him closer to the young man, now leaning back, leaning on his elbows. The passengers, bored, now that the excitement was over, began boarding the train. Near where they'd put the flyer down, the engine driver and the train conductor seemed to be trying to make a decision. I listened to them debating the options available for a moment, all the while, watching the American flyer.

I thought of Alex, for some reason, when I looked at him. He looked tall lying down, but very thin and now in quite obvious pain. His leather flying suit was torn away over his right shin and blood covered the white wool under-fleece lining that bloomed around the hole in the brown leather trousers. As if to prove it was broken, his leg was turned at a strange angle. He must have somehow broken it during the attack on the bomber, or when he'd leapt from the falling airplane, or possibly the fall itself. I doubted the boy was even twenty years old.

Even in his pain, he had that look of him…like Alex…the American openness. His eyes met mine when I looked at him, holding his glance for a second. He was definitely afraid, but still, there was openness in the face. I walked closer to the debating train crew. They seemed little nearer a decision about what they should do with the flyer.

Though I was anxious to leave, I'd now become somewhat concerned about the boy's well being. Enemy or not, we couldn't just abandon him there beside the track, as I could hear the trainmen were now contemplating among themselves. I wondered whether they planned to tend to his leg first. No one was even looking at him any longer, secure in the knowledge he could not escape or harm them in his condition. I decided to try to help. I put on my most official voice and stepped up to them.

"How much longer to Berlin?" The men stopped speaking and turned to look at me, glancing up and down, deciding whether I was as official as I sounded.

"If there are no further delays...another two hours and a half," the conductor finally responded. There may be rubble on the tracks ahead," he indicated with a wave the smoke rising from the direction of the city.

"Then why not put him on the train now. Let him ride with us and leave him with the authorities in Berlin. They might wish to question him. And we can finally get going again—before something else happens."

I glanced significantly up at the sky to add emphasis. Their eyes followed my gaze.

"There will be police in Berlin. They will take care of him...probably turn him in to a military hospital. We can get going."

As if I were not standing there, the engine driver spoke to the conductor.

"I agree. I for one do not wish to remain standing here like a sitting duck, waiting for another fighter to find us. The repair we made on the engine the first time, back there...it will not hold forever. Why not do as she suggests?"

They both looked at me again, gauging the wisdom of my suggestion, then glanced at the young man. He'd been listening without apparent comprehension, watching us decide his fate. There was a look of hesitant expectation about him. No doubt he felt better that a woman was involved.

"It will take too long to fetch someone from the town and get them over here...they may not even have a policeman there...*Ja*...let us get him on the train."

Turning toward me the conductor asked: "Are you willing to watch him...in the coach, until we get to Berlin?"

"Certainly. I have nothing else to do."

Without waiting further for the others to decide, the engine driver walked over to the flyer and bent over him.

"*Se Deutch sprachen...?*" he asked.

Obviously confused, the airman stared back at the train-man, then toward me and said something in English as he also shook his head.

"I don't believe he can speak German," the conductor said to me.

"Pity, what do they teach them there in America?" the engine driver said.

Ignoring him and turning to me, the conductor asked: "if we put him in the car you can have some of the others help you watch him until we get to Berlin? I will telephone the authorities when we arrive?"

I glanced at the man-boy, lying propped up on his elbows, tentatively glancing from one to the other of us.

"Yes," I said, turning to the farm-woman who was now smiling kindly at the flyer, "yes, but first let's fix a splint for his bleeding leg, or he will not live to go to prison."

The engine driver nodded. "I will go back to watch my engine." He turned to the conductor: "Signal me when we are ready to start." He turned around and started walking toward the engine.

The conductor touched my arm to get my attention. "Please wait here; I will look for...splints." He left us, walking back to the end train car. In a minute he was walking back, having found some old signal flags from his compartment. He pulled the rectangular cloth from the heavy, round sticks and we three began ripping the faded flags into strips to make a cloth-rope. After knotting several strips together we began to bind the sticks to the airman's leg, as a makeshift splint. After fifteen minutes work and some pain for the young man, we were fairly certain the break wouldn't shift much, during the remainder of his transport.

In the absence of the engine driver, the conductor and I made a cradle with our hands and arms and bent near the airman. Several passengers tipped the young man into a semi-standing position on his good leg. We crept a little closer and tried to lift him. He was very heavy. I knew immediately that we would have a problem with the high, coach steps. He cried out in pain as he sank back into our arms, nearly taking us down with him. I could smell the leather of his flying suit and a light odor of perspiration. Our three faces were very close as we struggled to hold on and keep our balance. I could see how clean his face was. He'd barely begun to shave. The conductor and I looked at one another, both probably wondering whether the other would be the first to drop our cargo. Our three noses were only a couple of centimeters apart as we grunted to lift him from his good foot; he yelped in pain again when the weight went on his leg again. But we didn't drop him. As we staggered toward the train car, it was obvious the steps up to the platform wouldn't let three of us pass abreast, even if we were able to hoist him up. Lifting side-by-side as we were, we stopped and I began to wish we had first removed his heavy jacket. He was so bulky in it and had now also begun to sweat with the effort and pain from our rough transport.

The conductor wasn't a youngster. Only inches from my own, I saw how red his face had gotten and he was breathless by the time we stopped at the bottom of the stairs. Some of the people in the coach had come out to stand on the platform and watch. One woman said to put him down and let him hop; that was how her husband had gotten around on one leg, before he died from the gangrene in the other one.

I looked at the conductor and nodded, as together, we lowered the airman to a standing position at the foot of the platform step. He still had one arm around each of us. He looked at the steps and then glanced at me. I nodded and inclined my head that he should get himself on the train. I stepped beside and a little behind him, taking his elbow in one hand and the other I put beneath his armpit. The conductor watched and then did the same on his side.

The American bent forward slightly and took a small, tentative hop. A grimace of pain showed what it cost him. He glanced

421

again at me and I smiled, nodding assurance again, lifting a little as he hopped. The conductor finally stepped completely aside since there was now no room for him and given that I was the younger and probably, stronger of the two of us. The American hopped again, groaned, hopped and groaned again. When he reached the first coach step there wasn't enough space that I could assist him much. Boldly he grasped one the round railing bars in each hand, stooped low and leaped with his good leg. He cried out louder this time and stood trembling, his head lowered in pain, his eyes shut.

Then, once more he stooped and leaped—crying out again. I thought he was going to fall backward and I jumped up to the steps to stand just below him, gripping the railings in case I had to hold him up, myself.

But it was unnecessary; he lunged once more, finally making it up to the platform. I noticed that only the front half of his boot was on the step, looking as if it might slip off. I was kneeling on the stair treads right behind him. I quickly bent, putting my shoulder beneath his rump and grasping his boot at the ankle, lifted with all my mite to push it up and forward. He cried out again and nearly toppled backward over me, but somehow, was able to maintain his hold. Then, since I had my shoulder under his rump, I told him I would help lift him up. Of course he didn't understand me. I gently stiffened my legs and lifted his ankle at the same time I straightened my shoulder against his rump. He must have figured out what I was doing, because he pulled up the remaining length on the handrails with his arms, half-sitting on my shoulder and let me pick up his good foot to the final platform level. Two of the passengers on the platform had also taken him by his arms by this time.

By then we were both sweating profusely from the effort. It had cost him his composure. He was crying from the pain in his leg and smiled at me through his tears for my effort. I climbed the rest of the steps and we stood together on the platform, panting and perspiring, looking at one another. I couldn't help but reach out a hand and pat his arm and smile back in encouragement. He looked as if he might be about to break down completely, so I stepped back, nodded, smiled again and got behind him to put an arm around his waist and start him forward when he was ready to hop.

After a moment's rest he hopped into the car and pulled

himself to the first free seat, easing himself into it and collapsing in a lump of brown sheepskin. I asked the surprised woman, sitting in the facing seat, whether she would mind changing seats with me so I could tend to the American airman. She appeared relieved by my request, no doubt already trying to decide how to escape having to sit next to an enemy.

As soon as the train began to move I went forward in the car to my previous seat, grabbed my luggage and moved back to slide in opposite the American. After putting my paper box and bag in the overhead rack, I collapsed beside him. He was lying with his head back and eyes closed. His good leg appeared to be undergoing some sort of spasm. The heavy sheepskin breeches offered some support for his injured leg, but disguised the wound, which I suspected was still bleeding underneath. The possibility of severe blood loss concerned me and I thought about cutting around the torn area to see how much he had already bled.

I moved to the edge of my seat and leaning over, examined the area on his leg as best I could. There was little to see because of the heavy flying suit. The conductor stopped on his way up the aisle, still carrying a rolled-up signal flag.

"How is he?" he asked leaning close to peer at the blood with me.

"Resting…but I'm worried about the leg. The bleeding doesn't seem so bad, but I'm afraid of an infection and I can't see how bad the tear is, under all this. Do you suppose we could cut the trouser leg to see under it better? We probably should have done that before we put him through the misery of the splints. But I don't think we want to take them off, do you?"

"No, it will hurt him again if we do…let me see."

He laid the flag on the floor and took out his pocket knife and bent over the airman's leg. The lad had opened his eyes as I was examining his leg and now looked a little stressed in anticipation as the conductor unfolded the knife. I reached across and patted his hand and smiled at him in reassurance.

The conductor bent to the task, carefully unzipping the boy's flying boot and doing his best to ease it off. Twice the young man cried out in pain, gripping the seat arms. Next, the conductor unzipped the bottom of the flying trouser and inserted the blade point in the sheepskin, just below the knee. As he worked it downward toward the injury area the leather appeared tough and his hands trembled, despite what appeared to be a very sharp blade.

Very carefully, the old man withdrew the blade and inserted it again lower down, slowly working the knife up through the leather. His tongue protruded between his lips in concentration as he cut. The trouser fleece rolled away as it parted on either side of the blade and, near the wound, began to ooze bright red blood, which run down the knife and onto the conductor's hand. A couple of times, the young man flinched and cried out as the conductor slowly worked the knife through the leather and fleece. With each outcry the old man glanced up in sympathy, but continued cutting.

"Cutting the leather lets some of the strain off his leg; but it also lets it shift and move more freely within the splint structure," he said, technically, his voice trembling like his hand. "The tight leather was acting somewhat like a plaster cast. I am afraid to cut too far up, or it will remove the helpful effect it is having to keep the leg stationary."

As if to reinforce his statement, the airman cried out, grasping his leg, above the knee, holding it as if to still the pain.

"I think I may have struck the bone with the knife," the conductor said, leaning back against the seat cushion and looking guiltily up at me.

"Maybe you should stop," I said, putting a restraining hand on his shoulder.

"Yes…probably…will you take a closer look?"

I bent over the seeping mess of bloody wool. There didn't appear to be any excess bleeding.

"Why not cut his trouser leg completely open. If there isn't a lot of blood in his boot, it means the bleeding isn't that serious. We can leave him to rest and let the doctors take care of it in Berlin."

He did and when he finished, he handed me the boot and we both looked inside. There was very little blood…mostly at the top.

"Good, he has not lost that much, then. He should be fine."

"The sheepskin lining could not have absorbed that much," I told the conductor, "I believe it's all right…we can leave him be then."

"Yes," he said, standing again with effort. "Let them deal with him in Berlin."

He seemed relieved not to have to do any more cutting. He started to fold his knife but noticed his bloody hand and blade. He wiped it on the airman's leather trousers, smiling an apology as he folded the blade, stood up and put the knife in his pocket again, took up his flag and walked up the aisle.

I sat down opposite the young man who'd closed his eyes again. We rode in silence; after a while he opened his eyes and we exchanged wordless smiles. Mine, sympathetic, his, thankful, or so it appeared. Once, the airman surprised me by chuckling out loud to himself. As I looked up to see what was so funny, he gestured, smiling and pointing to the right leg, turning, gesturing with his hand far to the right, demonstrating the exaggerated angle of his foot. His broken leg was jutting out to the side as if some joker had taken off his leg and put it back on again, crooked...as a child might, in play. We smiled over that for a while and I thought he was doing all right.

We both slept for a while, but as the afternoon progressed he seemed to be perspiring more, despite that he'd loosened his flight jacket. And later that afternoon as the ride progressed, he became somewhat delirious. I was able to get some of my cognac into him after the conductor and I finished with him, but what he probably needed more was water.

By the time the train pulled into Berlin, he was quite fever-ish and even more delirious. I couldn't get him to understand my gestures. He was speaking English to us, but no one could under-stand him. I stayed with him for about an hour after the train arrived at the station, until the police came with a military doctor in an ambulance. The doctor spoke some English.

After examining the American, the doctor told me the young airman was fortunate in that there had been a lull in the bombing in the city. Otherwise, as a prisoner of war, he would have been taken directly to prison without any medical attention. He dismissed the bored policemen, who drove away. We returned our attention to the American.

"This way, I will see he goes to hospital first, to have his leg tended to; then off to prison, or a prisoner of war camp as soon as he is able to travel."

In short order the attendants had the airman loaded onto a litter and strapped down and it was easy for the white coated drivers to carry him from the train, with the physician and I in tow. I felt pleased when the litter slid safely into the back of the ambulance and the rear doors were slammed shut.

But just then, the sirens went, announcing a raid. The physician frowned. "It is going to get dangerous around here rather quickly. Is there somewhere we can drop you *Fräulein?*. We must hurry or we will get stuck down in a shelter somewhere around here and have to wait.

"No, I have come to see my aunt who lives in the outskirts…to the north…but thank you, just the same. I can get there on my own. I should be safe enough."

"All right. Get into the shelter though and—good luck to you, *Fräulein.*"

"Thanks for your kindness—same to you."

I gathered my suitcase and the box containing Sophia's clothing and walked out to the street entrance to wait for a streetcar that could take me to the main exchange terminal, where I hoped to catch another car out to the suburbs. I decided not to enter the shelter in order to save time. The first of the bombs began hitting, far across the city from the terminal. I couldn't see the aircraft, but the spotlights were up and sweeping the twilight, though it wasn't yet completely dark.

I began to plan ahead as I walked. Tomorrow, I'll find out what this reassignment means. I looked forward to getting through the clerical mire, which was bound to be a part of it and get back to Norway…and to Alex.

Their sirens honking, a group of fire engines roared past, headed toward the area where I could hear the bombs exploding. There was a contingent of police guards stationed at the station entrance, manning a movable, iron gate. One of them had stepped into the street, blocking the exit in order to let the fire engines have a clear run past the station.

There was a young officer in obvious charge of the guard unit. By the way he shouted at everyone it was apparent he also wanted to be known as the person in charge, bossing them around as he did. He was missing his left arm and carried a riding crop in his right hand, which he used to point with from time to time, or to strike at the taxis when they didn't move past as quickly as he would have have them. From my position on the street corner I watched his antics without emotion. He reminded me of Herman, my dance companion. I was very tired. The officer represented what we have become—we Germans, I thought. One arm remaining—striking at taxis. As the rolling thunder of another salvo of bombs burst, this time closer, he flinched and shook his crop at the direction of the explosions, cursing the invisible airplanes, above.

The soldiers in his charge were briefly searching every vehicle that emerged from the tunnel, coming out of the platform area. As I waited for my streetcar, the ambulance van containing the American rolled up to the gate. The officer was soon arguing with the driver about not letting them pass directly through to the hospital. I could hear everything. It was silly bureaucracy. The attendant was waving one arm out the window and arguing with the officer.

"We have only just gone into the station on an ambulance call. Why can we not leave again without this silly nuisance of a search?"

"There is nothing silly about it...there are spies in the city and we must check all vehicles."

"But...we have a wounded man inside and we must get the doctor back to the hospital to be prepared for the bombing victims who will be coming after the bombing." He pointed toward the direction of the explosions.

"You must get out of the ambulance and open the doors. We are searching all vehicles, as I said. If you do not wish to .." he put the quirt in his left armpit and drew his pistol with his good arm, waving it at the driver motioning him to get out. "There have been many spies traveling the trains...and I, for one, will take no chances on anyone getting past my squad." Another volley of explosions fell, drowning him out for a moment. "Bastards...god damn bastards..." he said, gesturing with his drawn pistol, "...going to get my other arm, are you?" He turned toward the driver again. "If only...."

The frightened driver interrupted him: "Lieutenant—please, we need to get going. They will need the ambulance van and the doctor back at the hospital...after this..." he gestured toward the sound of more bombs falling.

"I decide who comes and goes here, driver. Get out—at once!" He motioned again, stepping away from the ambulance. The back door of the ambulance finally swung opened then and the physician emerged, no doubt curious about the delay. He came striding around the ambulance, frowning.

"Lieutenant, why can the driver not depart? I have an injured man back there?"

"You have nothing to say, here, doctor. Here I am in charge. We search all vehicles and I decide when you stop and when you go."

"Yes…I understand that, but…" the doctor saw what he was dealing with and tried to humor the power mad officer.

But the officer had already begun walking around to the rear of the ambulance. The physician saw me standing there watching and raised his eyebrows in frustration, gesturing with both hands at the futility of small-minded soldiers.

The driver and other attendant had gotten out of the front and walked around the back of the ambulance and opened the doors. One of the attendants and the officer disappeared inside. The physician smiled wryly, raised one hand in another gesture of farewell and turned to question the officer, still inside the van.

Suddenly, I heard the sound of a muffled gunshot. The attendant, a frightened look on his face, leaped from the rear of the ambulance and the driver jumped away from the open doors. The police guards hurried over.

I thought…no, he couldn't have…and began running to the rear of the van, abandoning my luggage on the curb. As I crossed the street, both ambulance doors were flung wide and the officer emerged, his pistol still smoking in his hand. The doctor had rushed up before me and began screaming at the officer.

"Did you shoot my patient!"

"Of course…because he was dangerous…he tried to attack me when I came into the vehicle to search him for a weapon."

"Attack you?" He wasn't even conscious. He couldn't have!"

"There was nothing wrong with him except that he was a dangerous enemy. What did we need with another prisoner to use our precious medicines and eat food meant for the German people?"

The physician seemed speechless with anger; he stepped around the stretcher as the cocky officer jumped to the street.

"Get the doors closed and leave. You are interfering with our duties and blocking traffic." He turned, holstering his pistol and exchanging it for the riding crop again.

"Let this vehicle through," he shouted to the man at the gate, again, waving his riding crop before slapping the side of this boot with it. He glanced back at me.

"One less prisoner to feed, *Fräulein*...eh?"

I'd been standing behind the open doors of the ambulance and couldn't take my eyes off the image of the American airman's boot and foot. They faced toward me from the stretcher where he lay dead. The stocking foot was turned so far askew it appeared he was doing it as a child might, in a game. I could only think of him in the train, making fun of how his crooked leg looked...chuckling to himself at the sight, despite his suffering at the time. I looked at this image for a second and spun round, directly into the arms of the physician, opening my mouth to scream at the back of the departing officer. I must have staggered, because soon the doctor was helping me around to the passenger door of the van. He yanked open the door and motioned the attendant out.

"Get her baggage from the sidewalk..." he gestured across the street, "...and put it in the back and ride back there, yourself. When the man hesitated, he said: "Move—we must get to the...morgue now and then to the hospital."

The attendant scrambled for my luggage as the doctor gently pushed me in the into the middle seat of the ambulance before getting in himself and slamming the door. I sat in a daze with my head in my hands. I heard the back doors slam after a moment and the driver climbed in beside me, started the ambulance and drove through the gate. The German officer waved us forward with his whip and yelled at the driver to move faster. As we passed I heard the *slap* of his riding crop against the side of te ambulance.

"Are you all right, *Fräulein?*"

I nodded, without glancing at the doctor, trying to smile. I felt as if I grimaced instead. My facial muscles didn't seem to want to obey my will.

We began to wind through the streets of Berlin. After a

while I wished one of my companions would say something; I was afraid I was going to scream and to stifle the urge, I held my head down and stared hard at my hands, held tightly together, fingers interlocked and clamped between my knees. I squeezed my fingers together, digging my nails into the flesh of my hands, hurting myself...but not caring, trying to feel some pain, somewhere else besides in my mind. We swung in and out of the light traffic. The sound and flashes of the falling bombs now appeared farther away. After a moment the doctor leaned across me to speak to the driver, placing one hand gently on my arm.

"Drive to the central streetcar hub station...then to the morgue." He leaned back, placed his arm around my shoulder and hugged me. I couldn't help myself, finally, turning toward him, I buried my face in his chest and holding my mouth against his coat, I screamed silently. All the while he held me tightly without speaking as I sobbed.

By the time we reached the terminal, I'd regained my composure somewhat. The ambulance stopped, the doctor got out and helped me from the step and around the rear, taking my baggage from the attendant as he handed it out.

Through the open rear door of the ambulance I could see the stretcher. The airman's body was totally covered. But beneath the sheet, his right leg laughingly jutted out to the right. Even in death, the American flyer and I could share a final joke.

The door slammed shut. The doctor smiled sympathetically. "Will you be all right now?"

"Yes, I believe so." I tried to return his smile, but failed.

He held open his arms in one, last, welcome embrace of love, sympathy and understanding. I stepped into them and let him hold me for another moment before I pushed away reluctantly, picked up my bags and walked into the terminal. I didn't look back at the ambulance, though I heard the door slam before the vehicle drove away. Two of the three people who'd had a significant role in my life in the last twenty-four hours were dead. And I didn't even know the airman's, or the doctor's names.

When I finally reached her in the outlying area of the city around nine thirty, my mother's sister was surprised to see me when she opened her door. She put on the kettle and we stayed up a while drinking homemade tea and discussing the war. She, too, believed Germany was going to triumph. When I questioned her about all the damage to her city, she couldn't answer, but later did ask: "...but at what a cost?"

"Germany has already lost this war, Aunt Fredia."

The look of shock on her face told me she found the comment difficult to believe. Before we finally retired for the night, after several cups of tea, I told her about Scandinavia, England and elsewhere in Europe where the Allies were advancing at a steady rate. I was unsure then, whether she really believed me.

And the next morning, drinking tea again after a long bath and some clean clothes, I felt much improved. My spirits were uplifted from visiting with a familiar person again. I set out by streetcar for the government offices I'd been told in Köln to report to. I believed I had turned a corner with the needless death of the American airman and that I would soon be again in Norway, if not at my old job, at least doing something where I would be able to see Alex again, a thought I very much looked forward to.

CHAPTER
24

The Passage Begins

Despite the tossing seas we somehow got settled in the smuggler's wooden dinghy. I'd quickly gotten Katrina situated on the seat with me. One of the bags lay behind the Norwegian *Kaptain*, who'd taken the oars, sitting in the middle seat, facing me. When he'd first begun pulling on the oars, I'd grabbed both sides of the dinghy and placed my legs on either side of Katrina, wedging my toes beneath the seat edge in front of me, thinking as much to hold her in the wildly-pitching boat, as to also shield her from any breaking swells. On the seat in front of me the *Kaptain* continued to grunt loudly with each pull, occasionally cursing loudly as he leaned far forward to take yet another bite in the pitching seas.

I guessed we were moving away from the shore, although I had no way of knowing, other than by the direction of the wind and swells, which continued to strike me squarely in the back of my head. Bending over Katrina I shouted words I hoped would comfort her. I thought she'd possibly been crying, though I couldn't hear her. Everywhere, it was wet. She remained hunkered in front of me without raising her head. Whether her passiveness was from fear, or simply to shield herself further from the tempest's blast, I didn't know. I held my arms around her, both hands on her shoulders.

As he continued rowing in the darkness, seemingly without making any progress in the absence of landmarks, my fears mounted.

Would the man be unable to keep the pitching little shell of a dinghy upright long enough to find his ship. As if to answer my concern my shins were suddenly struck by something solid and my toes curled in pain.

"*Bail!*" the Norwegian shouted, swinging a wooden bucket against my knees.

Leaning forward, I splashed it onto the boat-bottom, already well-awash and began to scoop and dump. He plied the oars again hardly missing a stroke as they creaked and clunked rhythmically. Leaning forward to do his bidding, I knew Katrina was wet with the cold water nearly covering her legs up to her knees. She half sat, half leaned sideways in the crook of my knees .

After fifteen minutes my back began to ache and my fingers were numb with the cold. I couldn't see whether or not I was keeping ahead of the washing sea. But I continued dipping and flinging the bucket's contents sideways to the wind.

After what seem like half an hour, I paused to get my breath and mumble some comforting words to Katrina. With my hand into the bottom of the boat, I felt to see whether my bailing was making much difference. It was. I tried to take a good look around, pivoting to each side and ahead, hoping for any sign of the ship, but in the darkness, I saw nothing. I leaned forward tapping the *Kaptain* on the knee; but got no response. I leaned closer and shouted above the roar of the wind:

"*Till båt…hur långt bort…?*"

Silence. He wasn't going to respond, probably because he couldn't tell me how far to his boat. I just knew it. But then, he did pause, seeming to hold the oars, steadying the boat for a moment. In the darkness I imagined he'd cocked his ear…turning his head to one side, listening, even peering into the blackness. Finally, he roared some incomprehensible oath into the wind and went back to rowing. Whatever he'd said, it was my answer.

Bailing only occasionally, Katrina and I shivered for another quarter hour before he seemed to slack up again, though we still faced into the wind. He'd stopped rowing completely, but kept pulling the oars as if to steady the boat. I, too, leaned closer sensing that we must be close to his boat now. Did he hear the shout of a crewman? Why hadn't he brought a larger boat to fetch us? I wanted to ask these questions, but didn't dare, as he'd turned his head slightly back toward us in the bow, as if about to speak. When he didn't, I laid a hand on his knee. He held up an arm. I realized he meant that I was to listen. Why, I wondered, was he listening behind us instead in the direction we were going. When I leaned forward to ask that question, we both heard waves crashing on a rocky shore, very close behind us.

With an oath he began pulling hard on the oars again. Grunt—sigh—grunt—sigh, he pulled steadily for several moments. I felt helpless, hunkered in the stern. By this time we were quartering the wind that was now coming over the portside. I believe then that I knew that he'd lost his ship. A deep dread swept over me. Oh, God, I thought, putting both my hands on Katrina. We were about to disappear in the North Atlantic, never to be heard of again.

But I'll give him this, I thought in my misery, he continues pulling and pulling, like a machine. On and on we went into the darkness, seeming to get us nowhere in a sea absent all landmarks to gauge our progress. By now I'd given up totally. Numb and shaking, I leaned over the child, holding her as close as I could and talking, trying to comfort her with my body's heat and kind words, while trying to keep both of us in the boat as we rolled over wave after wave.

Why hadn't I taken the *Kaptain*'s advice about the danger of carrying a child out to sea? My belated concern about her exposure to the cold seawater and possible drowning did neither of us any good. Katrina was well-clothed in layers of wool, which, when wet, would continue to keep her somewhat warm; but she couldn't go on for much longer, I knew. My own hands were numb and I was barely able to bail whenever part of a wave washed over the bow. I wished I could row for a while. Exercise, I thought, would make me warmer. But I knew I wouldn't know in what direction to turn the boat and I didn't trust the smuggler with the child.

After another half hour passed. I was about to request that the *Kaptain* take us ashore and let us take our chances on dry land, a prospect which seemed more promising than drowning. I thought all of us were surely going to perish of exposure first and then crash onto the rocks, after. Better to do it while I still had some life and could hold onto the child, I thought, than wash helplessly ashore, unable to help Katrina or, myself.

Then it happened. We ran into something hard with the dingy—a glancing blow, nearly tipping me sideways into the sea. It was solid. As the Norwegian bellowed, he turned, leaping into the bow and snatching up a line. I realized then it was the side of his ship. At last, I nearly sobbed, my heart leaped with gratitude. The *Kaptain* scrambled round in the small space of the front of the dinghy, shuffling the oars while shouting for me to take the rope and climb aboard when he got the dingy positioned just right.

He carefully stood up and, hand-over-hand, began pulling the hull with the dinghy scraping the side of the boat. It was so dark I knew we would lose sight of the dark hull if we drifted even two feet away. There was no ship's light showing and as he pulled us around the stern to her leeward side, I began to realize what a small ship it was. Boat was a better word. But it was still afloat, bobbing and bouncing in the windblown, running sea. I could hear tackle rattling above us as if something on the deck had broken loose. I suspected there was no crew to come to our assistance. Likely, there was no one aboard who'd heard the impact of the dingy striking the hull.

As we came around the stern along her downwind side, I realized it wasn't a ship at all. It was a sailboat—a sloop, or ketch at best and not very long…possibly forty—maybe fifty feet.

"There…" he shouted, waving at a cable-rope ladder hanging over the leeward stern quarter, "…up now!"

Making certain he had hold of Katrina, I grabbed one of the wooden ladder rungs and crammed the rope through, clumsily pulling it tight and wrapping it, trying to tie a knot with cold-numbed fingers. This I did on the high side of a swell. When the dinghy fell into the trough as the swell receded, for a moment the dinghy's bow came out of the water, nearly standing it on its stern transom. I quickly yanked the knot loose and let go the rope, grabbing for Katrina, as the rope spun through the rung and the bow dropped.

"Not so short!" the Norwegian shouted. "Tie it off with some slack—then pull on the line to get the dinghy close and then climb aboard. I will hand up the child to you once you are aboard."

He'd turned around, standing just behind where I hoped Katrina still sat. I saw he had a gunwale in each hand, as if to steady and balance the dinghy. I had to trust him now with the child as I turned back, rearranging the line again, finally managing half the knot. Testing the line's slack, I hesitated as the wave swelled once more and fell again, before finally tying it securely. This process seemed to take hours but finally I turned and shouted:

"I'm going up now."

I made the first attempt to scramble up the ladder, but I found I was barely able to crawl. I hadn't realized how cold I'd become and nothing, no part of my body seemed to work when I willed it to. But somehow I made it to the deck, lay down on my stomach and squirmed around. I reached toward the dinghy, one arm around one of the wire ship' rail's short posts. I extended my arms down into the darkness where I hoped to soon feel Katrina.

"Ok...hand her up!"

I didn't have to wait long. The soggy little bundle of the child was thrust into my hands. I dug in my numbed fingers, closing them around and arm and then a leg. Then I pulled her up, simultaneously rolling onto my side to pivot her up and over and onto the deck beside me, not trusting my hands to grip her.

I slid away from the ladder and hugged her tightly. She was crying weakly and I could feel her hot breath. I heard a thump and pushed us further away from the railing to make way for the second of the valises that the seaman seemed to be flinging aboard. Still lying on my back on the deck I hooked it with one leg, sliding it safely away from the rail. It had bounced off the first, nearly careening back into the sea.

"Is the cat still there?" I shouted.

"What? Cat...what cat?"

"There is a cloth sack...somewhere in the boat—with the child's kitten inside...if it did not fall out."

I waited several seconds, listening to the seaman's curses. Suddenly the wet bag hit me in the face and I snatched at it before it could tumble into the sea.

Then, the *Kaptain* came up the ladder, appearing quickly. He immediately began pushing the luggage away from the edge, grumbling.

"Who in hell would ever bring a cat onboard...but a Swede."

He untied the dinghy and disappeared toward the stern,

pulling it along by the line, where I assumed he'd tie it off. In a moment, he returned and drew up the rope ladder, which he rolled up and quickly clinched with some rope ties. He bent toward us.

"Come—bring the child and come below."

I gathered up Katrina and the wet cat sack. I could feel movement from inside and a loud mewing, so I knew there was life there, yet. The *Kaptain* dragged the bags along the space between the rail and the short superstructure, toward the stern, where I imagined a small companionway must lie, offering access to the internal hull and cabin.

I found I was unable to stand on the pitching deck with the weight of the child, so on hands and knees, I pushed my burdens to the rear. I found the side of the companion cuddy and finally, the hatch itself. Clumsily, I worked my way around and then went down the short companionway, feet-first, holding Katrina and the cat in one, numb arm as I hung on with the other. Below, I couldn't stand upright for the low deck over my head. From the darkness came the *Kaptain*'s voice, deep and hollow in the confines of the small space.

"Get your wet clothes off and wrap up in some blankets. I will get the boat underway before a German patrol boat finds us."

I'd recovered enough that I felt like I wanted some explanation. "But..." I stammered, taking the second case from him, "...it is only a sailboat."

A single candle flickered alive just then and I saw his huge silhouette, bearded and swathed in wool beneath his oilskins.

"What the hell did you expect Swede—a yacht? After rowing that long in the dark, I would have welcomed a floating shingle, myself. We were lost! Did you not know that?" With that he stomped past us toward the companionway. "If we do not move from this place, a German patrol boat will soon cut us in two in the darkness. If it was not for the storm, they would probably already have done so."

We both glanced at the floor at the sound of a meow from the crumpled bag. He looked at me, stepped over the bundle and with one foot slid it over the deck toward me, turned and vanished in the dimness. Then I heard him scrambling up the companionway ladder into the darkness above.

"Can we not have another candle?" I shouted after him.

His silence was my answer. Then I realized, even the one might be beacon for a passing patrol boat.

I began to attend to Katrina who'd been whimpering all the while. As I struggled to get a valise onto the bunk, she'd begun to cry, quietly. I hoped our things hadn't gotten too wet, but was thankful to have them at all, along with our lives.

"*Kat...*" she intoned as the creature continued it's plea for freedom. I bent and loosened the sack's opening, reached in and pulled out the lump and wet fir. Seeing the candlelight, the cat renewed it's plea. I tossed it onto the bed beside Katrina, before I hurriedly tore open the larger case containing Katrina's few remaining items of clothing. In another moment I had her wet things off and a wool nightgown over her head. I paused momentarily as the *Kaptain*'s feet slammed above my head on the deck. Katrina was shaking hard as I pulled dry stockings on her cold feet, before wrapping her in a blanket the seaman had flung from the end of the bed. Like the whole cabin interior, the fabric smelled of mildew, sea-salt and wet wool, but it was relatively dry.

After I pulled on a dry pair of my own wool trousers and a sweater, I put Katrina on my lap. I'd found another blanket and covered us both with it and lay back on the bunk with her and stared at the candle. I had the child completely covered, but she continued to shiver.

Occasionally, I heard the *Kaptain* clumping about the deck above us...walking toward the stern, then back to the bow, as I rocked the little girl, whispering quietly in her ear, trying to get her warm again. Having drawn both blankets over us, I hoped our combined body heat would warm her faster.

After several moments and the intermitent sound of clumping and scraping, I felt the boat heel slightly to starboard. Then , the sound of water rushing along the hull, as we finally began to make way. The boat's heel increased so much, I had to twist round on the bunk, propping my bare foot against the opposite bunk railing to keep from slipping into the narrow walkway. I was relaxing at last, thinking we're finally at the point when I should worry about something else. After what we'd undergone in the dinghy I didn't care about much else. Katrina had ceased her trembling and relaxed in my arms and soon, her steady breathing hinted that she'd probably fallen asleep. She finally felt warm, too, beneath the blankets and eventually I dozed, myself.

When I later awoke with a start, we were changing course—tacking. With my joints aching, I carefully tipped myself into the walkway, laying Katrina carefully onto the bunk, covering her. I bent, pulling up the board along the bunk's side to prevent the boat's pitch and roll from dumping her out, onto the floor. To be extra safe, I piled one of our bags on her other side least she hit the hull side. Then I held onto the bunk sides and worked my way aft and up the companionway ladder where I partially stepped out of the opening after lifting the storm hatch.

"*Hej...*" I shouted into the darkness, "do you have any more wet gear?"

"Below...under the bunks...a locker slides out," came the answer.

As I crept back down the ladder, he shouted: "Put out the candle when you finally come on deck."

I continued down the ladder and stumbled my way over to the bunks where I groped around until I felt a slotted handle. I yanked one of the wooden drawers open and rummaged among the crackling oilskin garb, until I'd found trousers, coat and hat.

Back on the bunk opposite Katrina, I decided to put on another sweater before dragging on the stinky oilskins. My brief exposure to the night had immediately chilled me. I didn't bother with the rubber boots, thinking they were probably too small anyway. My shoes were wet, but I put them on again anyway, thinking they'd be better traction on the wet deck. Before I turned for the gangway again I leaned over the bed, checking on Katrina once more. Satisfied with her steady breathing, I pinched out the flame on the short candle, climbed the ladder, unlatched the hatch cover and stepped onto the deck, turning and in the darkness of the slanted deck, reversed the procedure immediately to secure the hatch cover.

Taking no chances I went down on my hands and knees and crawled backwards into the darkness until I felt the oilskin of the seaman's trouser leg. I swung in against the transom and sat beside him on the opposite side of the boat's tiller. At knee-level, there was a small, lighted binnacle between us, with a compass card dancing slowly in the orange glow. I wondered whether there was a candle or an oil lamp hidden beneath the glass cover, wondering how the Norwegian could ever have gotten it lighted in the near gale wind. I noticed we were steering just east of northeast on the present tack. Watching the dim glow of the little binnacle I sat without speaking for a while. Finally the *Kaptain* leaned over and shouted in my ear.

"Can you sail a boat?"

I nodded before thinking and then added aloud: "Yes...I think so...if you tell me the course."

"Can you hold a course—have you sailed a boat before?"

"Yes, I can hold a course—tack. Do you have a jib up?"

"No, only the mainsail. I did not dare to try to do it alone since I could not tack in this...I think he waved an arm in the darkness, without someone to help work the sheets. We run under the main only now—and it is reefed, also. I too must go below and get dry clothing; can you hold this course while I go below to do that thing?"

"Yes," I said, grasping for the tiller.

"Wait—first let us tack; then we are sure to be away from the shoals. Bring it over and steer west of north and then after half an hour, come about to this course again...alright?"

"Yes."

Watching the compass card and noting the course against the lubber line I pulled the tiller to me and felt the ship come around, righting and tilting once again. The tackle slid and scraped along the track and the block rattlled and squeaked above our heads as the boom slowly traversed to the other side. I glanced at the compass rose and realizing I'd come over too far, I over-corrected, causing the boat to heel way over to port and momentarily lose much of our headway. As the bows slammed into the running sea, I brought it over again quickly. The *Kaptain* said nothing, remaining seated for a while and monitoring my attempts to accustom myself to the feel of handling his boat, running off the wind.

At last I had the line pegged to the card in the binnacle. The *Kaptain* still didn't speak but watched as I minutely adjusted the rudder position until I'd pretty much locked the compass card to the lubber line in the little binnacle. After a few moments, I was still holding it steady.

Apparently satisfied with my limited sailing skill, the *Kaptain* got up and leaned forward near my ear.

"If you have a problem, stamp your foot on the deck."

"Yes—I will."

He disappeared in front of me while I watched the card carefully. I didn't want to endanger any of our lives, or cause him to have to rush to the deck half dressed to try to get us out of trouble. It was hard to keep watching the compass, so I glanced away from time to time. The boat held fairly steadily and after what I thought was a half hour, plus a few minutes, I tacked the boat, this time a lot more smoothly. Another quarter hour or so passed before I felt him approaching again before he slumped along side me, opposite the tiller. Silently, we watched the card for a while.

I leaned across: "Was the child still sleeping?"

"Yes and still covered...I checked."

We sat in silence for a while longer.

"How long before we tack again," I finally asked.

"Another hour, at least...we want to get north—away from the usual patrol routes. The smaller boats, they do not go so far north, away from Zealand. Only the big boats...the heavy cruisers. They do not run with lights, so you must listen for them in the night. If you hear one, you must turn away quickly, if you can find from which way it is coming. You must be very quick, or it will break the boat in pieces."

I nodded in the darkness. He still didn't take the tiller from me, but finally, he leaned close once again.

"I think I could get the jib up, if you can hold the course, I believe the boat will take the jib in this sea...can you work the sheets as well as the helm, if I try?"

"Yes...but first, show me where the cleats are for the jib-sheets?"

"Let me take the tiller—there...now, work your way up along the side of the deck companionway—just lean forward and reach out...you can feel the starboard cleat...use your hands—feel for the second cleat. It is larger than the first one. There is a round eye just ahead of it for the jib-sheet cleat. The line will pass through the eye, then back, under and around the cleat."

I did as he said and located the rigging of rope and pulleys. I didn't bother with the other, mirror-image side, knowing the port side cleat was in the same location as the starboard.

I leaned close to him again. "I found it all right. If you get the halyard and sheets on the jib, maybe I can help get it up, or work the sheets back through the eyes for you."

"No...remain at the tiller. That will be too much for you to do and steer at the same time in the dark. I will go set the sail now...try to keep it pointed close to the wind, when I shout to you...but be careful not to come too far and jibe her."

He disappeared before I could protest, crawling forward; he must have had second thoughts after a moment and crawled right back.

Leaning down, he said: "If the sea takes me over, it is three days sailing to Sweden, against this wind...but when and if the storm clears, the wind will go northwest...with a fine day to follow. Head to eastward. Good luck," he seemed to add this comment as a Norwegian jibe toward a Swede. Then he was gone again.

I pushed the tiller over slightly to bring her bow into the wind and immediately felt we were losing way. For a while the bow rose and slammed back into the sea. I continued to hold the same course, locked in a position that kept the wind's pressure off the mainsail and would allow him to fix and haul up the jib. After a while I thought I'd lost him overboard. But then I felt the jib-sheet being pulled back on the windward side, sliding through the eye; after a few moments the leeward sheet slid. I continued pointing into the wind to take the pressure off the jib. It was difficult in the dark to gauge the way she went against the wind.

As he drew each of the lines through, he would shout for me to take up the slack. With one hand I pulled each when instructed, cinching the tail around the cleat with the other hand, one leg hooked over the tiller and the other braced against the cuddy. Then it was time for the jib to go up. Hand-over-hand, on his command, I hauled the jib sheet, as he took the halyard up higher on the mast and set the sail.

Before I could sit down again I heard the wind flapping the jib as it started filling, with him on the halyard. I could feel the boat take on a bit of sluggishness. I waited, watching the dark for him to appear, after I cleated the windward sheet loosely, knowing he would have to re-cleat the leeward line for better trim, when he returned. The boat kept wanting to point into the wind and flounder. I inched the tiller toward me a little more to make it up, watching the compass card to insure I didn't go off course too far. It took him a long time, setting the jib. But then he was back, appearing suddenly out of the darkness.

"I will trim the sheet tight now," he grunted. "Prepare to bring the tiller off the wind if you must because the boat will probably try to point even more."

"Ok," I said and made the necessary corrections as he hauled the line tighter and re-cleated the sheet, before he slid in across from me again. We sat in the silence of the roaring sea as she picked up momentum. With the jib set and drawing, the boat was now more active on the swells and I found her easier to correct.

After a few minutes he leaned across the tiller and I tipped an ear close.

"You did that very well, Swede. We were still on course. Why not join me in the smuggling business. It is more profitable than being a...a parent."

I shouted back, "*nay...tack,*" and left my thanks at that.

We carried on like that for another half-hour. Now and again the bows came up and slammed down in the depth of a trough. We would momentarily lose way as she dug into the oncoming swell and the little boat floundered momentarily, but then gained way again, heeling to leeward as I alternately hauled her off and pointed her into the wind to give her the help she needed. A couple of times the deck would go awash all the way back to our little cockpit and I was thankful for the oilskins, then. Finally, the Norwegian roused himself.

"Can you hold the course yet? I will make tea for us if you can."

"Yes, I can hold it—it will be all right. If I have a problem— I will stamp my foot if I must. Please look at the child."

"Aye...."

He disappeared for nearly half an hour. A couple of times I found my attention straying while staring at the compass rose and alternately glancing around in the darkness. I was holding the course satisfactorily, but suddenly realized I hadn't bothtered to listen and was neglecting the possible appearance of a patrol craft.

"Look into the darkness at all times," he'd stressed, "and listen..."concerning a possible encounter with an unlit warship. I doubted I could hear, let alone see an approaching destroyer, unless it was showing some lights. It would have to miss us from the start, I thought and went back to staring at the feeble binnacle light.

Finally, I felt a hand creeping up the tiller, touch mine, then a large tin cup was pushed against my hand. I grasped it, hanging my left arm and elbow over the tiller, I held the cup in one hand, steadying it with the other until my companion had brought his own tea and taken his seat in the darkness.

"The child sleeps."

"Thanks...*tack*."

When I took the first sip, I was surprised to find that my cup contained real tea. I suppose there was little out of the reach of a good smuggler. I wondered what he would think of my several tins of coffee below the deck. I wondered whether he had even more, himself, hidden in a warehouse, somewhere. Maybe he'd already searched my cases while waiting for the tea water to boil.

Probably, he'd been looking for the diamonds the Constable had alluded to, which, of course, weren't in my gear, below since they didn't exist. That meant he thought I had them hidden on my person. I wondered what he intended doing with us when he learned there were no jewels. If he thought I was carrying the diamonds, he certainly wasn't likely to push me overboard.

He interrupted my thoughts, leaning across the tiller.

"Good tea...yes Swede?"

"Yeah, very good. Thanks...it's good and hot," I shouted as the bow slammed and went under again and I braced for the small flood to come over the deck.

Once the sea's wash passed, the *Kaptain* said.

"I will take her a while...you can have your tea."

I leaned back and braced my legs, no longer having the tiller under my arm to steady myself. We continued like that, both lost in our individual thoughts. I'd finished my tea, which had quickly grown cold. Finally, I leaned across the tiller.

"Here...I will go below," I shouted, "I want to look at the

child."

I'd wanted to check on Katrina again for some time. Though she should be dry and warm, I'd already developed that motherly instinct, worrying about a child that was out of sight. Carrying my cup, I crawled through the hatch and into the dark below, feeling claustrophobic the moment I had to feel my way along the beds to the little galley area. There I left the cup. I could smell the dampness of the sea...of old, stale meals long eaten and of wet wool from our earlier adventure in the dinghy. I felt my way back along the slanted deck until I came to the bunk and then touched the lump of blankets with Katrina beneath. She seemed to be asleep. I leaned my forearms on the hard mattress and reached around carefully until I touched her cheek. It was warm. I leaned close and low, my own cheek touching hers and felt her hot breath. I remained there as she breathed steadily, reassuring myself she was all right and somehow drawing courage and strength from the innocent responsibility she posed for me. She seemed to be sleeping soundly enough, so I plumped the blankets around her, tucking in the edges.

Then...it happened so suddenly, I was slammed against the bed rail. Instinctively I made a fence of my arms on each side of Katrina, bending low over her to keep her from being pitched from the bunk, or against the bulkhead. On the rebound, I hit my head on the deck above as we both came up and off the bunk for a second.

The boat was struck, or had struck something very hard and had lain way over to leeward so far, I thought we were going to turn turtle. But the sloop righted itself before the mast went under, so suddenly, that it flung me back against the bed rail and nearly on top of Katrina again. We nearly rolled over, I thought as I hung there by my thighs, one arm over Katrina and the other pressed against the side of the hull.

With my arms still spread, I held Katrina against the bed covers. I guessed we could both be upside down at any moment and I would have to keep both of us from crashing onto the ceiling, or the deck. My next thought was how we were ever going to get up and out of the cabin and into the safety of the dinghy before the boat sank. Did we still have a dinghy? What had the Norwegian done? Had we run aground, unknowingly, or had we hit something, or been hit? I recalled his ominous warning again about darkened ships running in the night seas.

It couldn't have been more than a few seconds when we were hit again. The first collision had lasted such a short time, but this one felt like we were being carried along—dragged. The boat was being flung back up and sideways, with such force I was flipped over on top of the bunk with the now, well awake Katrina. She had cried out in alarm when we were first struck and now began to scream in earnest. As I struggled to gain a hand-hold in the wildly careening boat, there was a terrible roar and scraping sound, then bumping and bouncing as the boat seemed to spin round, laying way over again, this time in the other direction.

Finally, we seemed to settle. We were not upside down after all and there was no inrush of water in the companionway, that I could tell.

I shouted, "I will be right back, Katrina. Don't move—stay there on the bed."

I wanted to see if the Norwegian needed some help. Were we aground...sinking?

In the darkness on deck, I glanced around.

"*Kaptain*...what happened?"

The boat wasn't bouncing on rocks or any sort of shore, though we didn't seem to be making any forward way, either as she seemed to be just wallowing between the waves. The sails had to be slack as I heard them flapping and the halyards slapping the mast. Listening, I thought I could hear the dull sound of an engine, somewhere and the churn of a propeller in a wake.

"*Kaptain*..." I shouted, turning forward into the darkness. "*Kaptain*...!"

I crawled free of the hatch. Standing on deck I sensed we weren't taking on any water. I could hear the sails flapping harder with the force of the wind, confirming the boat was luffed—pointing directly into the wind and wallowing between the waves. Something terrible had happened. Maybe it was the rigging—there'd been damage somewhere. If there was a collision, there was bound to be. We were rocking and pitching at the will of the sea.

"*Kaptain*...!" I felt my way back to the stern well, in the rear of the boat and with my outstretched hand, found the tiller idly swinging with the motion of the ship, completely free. Reaching into the darkness I extended and waved my hand wildly about, but touched nothing but the side of the boat and the decking ahead the transom, where the Norwegian should be sitting.

"*Kaptain..*!" I sat down and took the tiller, swinging it from side to side. There was resistance. We'd not lost the rudder. I felt for the jib-sheet cleats and yanked on each sheet in turn. Again, there was resistance as they tugged back from the force of the wind. Apparently we were still carrying the jib. I thought for a moment; the Norwegian might have gone forward the moment we had struck the...whatever we had struck. And now? Was he taking down the main, or repairing something? If he were, he'd need my help.

"*Kaptain—Kaptain—*heyaaaa!" I yelled. Again, with my hands cupped I shouted forward toward in the bow. I wondered whether I dare lash the tiller, not knowing yet how the boat sailed. What if we'd been damaged? Finally, I inched forward to the hatch and shouted some words down to Katrina...words I hoped would sound like reassurance, telling her to stay there until I came down again. Then I secured the cover again so she couldn't get out. She had to be deathly afraid there in the dark and damp.

Slowly, feeling my way forward, I got down on my knees and edged along the deck between the cabin roof and the rail, hanging on with both hands wherever there was a hand-hold. Now and then I waved one hand in front of me to feel for the Norwegian, hoping he would be there, attending to something or other. Then I felt my way along the boom, working my way forward along the foot of the sail until I reached the masthead itself, then past the clew of the jib. The mainsail seemed intact and in place and didn't appear to be in the process of being reefed, as if the *Kaptain* had abandoned a task half done, or something. The jib seemed secure also.

"*Kaptain...?*"

A wave suddenly crashed head-on, over the bows and I hung on for my life as it swept the length of the sloop, nearly taking me off the port side with it. I came out the end of it still holding on, but choking with the cold shock of sea water in my mouth that made my nose and lungs burn. As the little boat came around again, settling in a trough, I coughed and held on for dear life.

"*Kaptaim*nn...." I yelled again, turning back toward the stern, this time, on the starboard side, hoping now to find the unconscious body of the Norwegain as I was making my way back to the hatch. But I didn't, so I hurriedly unlatched the cover and made my way back down to Katrina.

Feeling along the bunk, as I approached, I heard her whimpering that she was cold. I quickly shucked my oilskins and climbed onto the bunk beside her. She'd been sitting on the bed with the blankets loose around her. I quickly wrapped us again and sat hugging her.

After five minutes she was quiet, but I could tell she wasn't asleep. I felt she was at least warm again. I knew she must be terribly frightened, not understanding anything that was happening.

"Papa has to go outside again and sail the ship, darling."

She began to cry. "*Grandmother...?*"

"I know you want me to stay, but I must...so go back to sleep in our bed and don't get out of it...because the floor is wet and you will get cold again. All right?"

"Papa?"

She seemed to snuggle up against me, reluctant for me to leave. I held her as long as I dared, worredly listening to the boat shudder and pound around us. I also listened for the rush of any water that could be seeping through a damaged hull. And I listened again for footsteps on the deck, steps that never came. I was afraid the boat might broach in the heavy sea, or turn over completely. I had to decide whether to sail her, or take in sail and let her drift helplessly. I didn't know what to do. Then I thought about the real possibility of blowing back ashore somewhere on the Danish coast— the ship breaking up and us drowning. Finally, I laid Katrina back down, with a verbal admonition to stay in the bed and go to sleep.

Outside again, after latching the hatch door, I hurried to the tiller.

"*Kaptai*mn...!" I shouted into the wind...no longer expecting a response. I took a seat again and looked at the binnacle expecting to see the compass card rocking in the dim glow. But the light had been extinguished. This was terrible. Now, I wouldn't be able see the compass to know what direction we were going. I couldn't steer a course in the dark. I pondered—what to do, trying not to panic. We'd been blown around—or knocked around and were now heading back the way we'd come...southwesterly, assuming the wind was behind us. How long before we struck the coast of Denmark…I tried to reason? We'd been traveling downwind much faster than we'd been sailing against the wind, that was for sure. I had to turn her back into the wind, if for nothing else but to hold our own until daylight.

I could think of no solution to the *Kaptain*'s disappearance. Only that the Norwegian had been knocked overboard in the collision; nothing else could explain it and I reasoned that…if the wind hadn't changed—still blew from the northeast, I could bring her about and steer roughly as close as I could into the wind, tacking when I thought I needed to. It wouldn't be very accurate but at least we wouldn't drift back to the eastern shore of Denmark.

Without another thought I pushed the rudder hard over and waited, holding my face forward to sense the wind direction—feel it. The boat came around slowly on a beam reach, healing heavily to starboard. I kept the rudder over until I felt the wind full on my face before I eased the rudder back amidships, but too late. Hearing the flapping of canvas, I jerked the tiller back toward me and felt her sails flap as she pounded in irons, sitting straight into the wind. Finally the sails filled again as she fell off the wind and began making a little forward way. I held the tiller a little longer until I felt the boat begin to heel to starboard. When she was fairly well over, I brought the tiller back little-by-little until I thought the boat was pointing as close as I dared to the wind without anything visual to steer by. I thought again…got to get her back on course—but how? What was the course.

This might not be too bad, I thought; she was fairly forgiving to sail. I settled back then, bracing myself with both feet. How much darkness remained? I didn't have a watch. I couldn't even guess. Right now, we were undoubtedly south of where we should be—or from where we'd started. If I held this course we'd be going roughly northeast, where the *Kaptain* said we should be. Large ships—cruisers, he'd said, didn't hang around in the north.

Continuing to steer blindly, I considered that it must have been a ship like he described…we'd struck a ship of some sort, or glanced off one. Lucky, it hadn't caught us square. Even the *Kaptain* didn't hear it coming. Strange it didn't put on a light to find out what they'd struck in the darkness. Maybe they didn't even realize they'd hit anything.

If I sailed as we were, holding the eastward tack half as long as the northward tack, sailing approximately northeast into the wind, we should end up further north of east, somewhere where the Norwegian said we should be. That was discounting any flow of the sea...currents, about which I knew nothing, in this area of the world. I'd have to totally disregard them. Then, if that worked, once we had daylight and could see the compass, we could turn due east—toward the west coast of Sweden?

But that would have to wait until daylight. I'd assumed the compass hadn't been damaged, so we would be able to see the course to steer. The sun would help, too, at first. Could I stay awake? For the most part, I was dry; relatively warm. Damn right, I'd stay awake—I had to, I thought, settling into a hunkered-down position and taking a new hold on the tiller. I'll stay awake to save us.

CHAPTER
25

Another Interrogation

The streetcar ride to *SS* headquarters was a far cry from the Berlin streets I remembered before the war. I had to change cars twice because the tracks had been covered by rubble from newly bombed buildings.

"Lieutenant Klapp does not wish to see you," a corporal with a typewriter said, "but a leutenant will."

I waited an hour before he arrived. He was young and newly wounded. "He walks with a severe limp from having both legs broken...," the corporal had informed me earlier, in a hushed voice, "...he must also be in a lot of pain...because of his mood." But then he said no more.

I muttered expressed sympathy for his wounds when I was finally brought before him. But he waved it aside, as he began. It turned out to be an interrogation. I'd learned earlier that his name was Lieutenant Kutzik.

After half an hour of rather mild, one-sided questioning, I interrupted him respectfully and asked about my reassignment. He replied rather that it hadn't come up yet so he could tell me nothing. Someone else handled reassignments, he said, I could ask the corporal when he was finished questioning me. The questions were much the same as in Köln. I interrupted him nearly immediately.

"Excuse me Lieutenant Kutzik, but I've answered all these questions before, in Köln. Do you not have the papers from my questioning which they executed there? I know they wrote down my answers because there was a stenographer in..."

"We have nothing from Köln but the telephone transcription done after you were told to come here and...anyway, we have our own questions for you. That is why you are here at the *SS* and not...wherever you think you should be, *Fräulein.*"

His interruption hinted at his growing frustration with me; I was growing angry myself, by this bureaucracy and finally threw caution to the wind. I decided to tell them everything I'd been doing in Norway on my assignment there, prior to the visit the last night by the *SS* interrogators. Berlin had no papers, my supervisor's offices had been bombed and the personnel were all either severely wounded or killed. So there was no one to explain, or to accuse me of anything. As I related to the Lieutenant what I did in Norway, he sat open mouthed. He stopped me and brought in a stenographer, telling me to continue. He made notes from time to time himself, as he questioned me.

After a half hour he went out to summon his superior, while I went to the toilet. Were they...everyone in the *SS,* trying to gather information about the other. For what purpose, I wondered. The Allies...maybe to trade "dirt" to the Allies, once they became victorious? To buy leniency, or clemency?

When I returned a *Kaptain* Schmidtt was seated behind the Lieutenant's desk. He introduced himself and asked me to have a chair again, stating that he only had a few questions himself, for me. He nodded to the lieutenant, who'd just returned, accompanied by another man, dressed in civilian clothes. They introduced him to me as *Herr* Kline.

Without preamble *Herr* Kline began to interrogate me in earnest, his questions seeming more pointed and intuitive. He appeared to have a good deal of experience in questioning people, but toward what end I couldn't fathom, for the life of me. I had a sudden feeling they'd found out about the *SS* who visited my home and died, or the dead Swedish businessman on the train, *Herr* Carlsson. I began worrying about the money I was carrying. I'd left more than half of it, along with the box of Sophia's—Katrina's clothing, with my Aunt Fredia, but there was still a sizable sum of mixed currencies in my purse.

Confused, I interrupted, questioning my interrogator: "Why are you now asking these sorts of questions?

But the reply came from *Herr* Kline. "Your activities in Norway have been associated with some rumors about out dispatch pouches being opened, *Fräulein* Stopff."

"Dispatch pouches? I have no dispatch pouches—never have had any. We did not receive things in dispatch pouches in Norway...or, at least I did not in my duties as cultural director for the project there.

"Tell me again, *Fräulein*, about this project," this came from *Herr* Klein again.

As I did, recounting the history of my stay in Norway and the other countries I'd traveled in, performing and coordinating performances, the *Kaptain* glanced from time to time at the Lieutenant, who nodded knowingly, as if to say: I told you so.

After several interruptions for further questions and my answers, the interview seemed to wind down. The *Kaptain* thanked me for my forthrightness and departed.

They—the military, suspected I was a spy for the Allies, the remaining interrogator, *Herr* Kline, informed me once the *Kaptain* left the room.

"But...how..." I sputtered, I didn't even...have never seen the enemy," I lied.

"There has been a...a breach of security in the Norwegian or Swedish operations, we are informed. And you just happen to be in Norway, *Fräulein.* And now, here you are, traveling to Germany without formal authorization and you travel so freely, during these times—I am surprised you have not been arrested...before now?

"Before now? Am I arrested? Why? Because you suspect that I have somehow been reading your dispatches in Norway. I told you, I know nothing of any dispatches, there or here."

Kaptain Schmitt entered the room again. "*Fräulein*...may I please examine your handbag? He held his hand outstretched.

"Why? It contains nothing that would concern you." I tried to be nonchalant, not even glancing at my purse on the floor.

He bent his head and frowned. *"Fräulein...?"*

Reluctantly I bent and picked it up from beneath my chair, handing it to him. I could think of nothing among its contents that they could possibly have any interest in...except the money. As I watched, he removed the purse's contents, placing them on the desk blotter. My mind raced for an explanation for having so much money, but I could think of nothing. There were several small sheets with addresses: the Franks village, my aunt's, Johan's mother, assorted offices I had been researching in Köln. From these depositories, I had obtained receipts for the items I had checked out, daily and taken back to my hotel at night, when I was searching for the Franks. These seemed to interest him at first, but when I explained, so readily, the logic of them, he lost interest. Then he discovered the brown package containing the remainder of the bank notes I took from *Herr* Carlsson.

"Why do you carry so much cash, *Fräulein?* And from so many countries...were you thinking of running away, to...France...Switzerland...Sweden?" he said as he identified each separate bundle of banknotes. One by one he placed the little bundles on the desk as he recited the currency origins.

"You have notes from several countries. Surely, you did not mean to use this..." he gestured toward me with a fist-full of notes, "...money, here in Germany. Unless, of course, you were paying off one or more of your spy friends." He smiled.

"I have no spy friends, *Kaptain.* It is cash I obtained...in Norway, before I came to Germany to search for my daughter." My mind was working so fast. "I—I didn't know where I would have to go looking for her and it was all that was available to me from my local savings."

"Curious, *Fräulein* Stopff...but you have hardly any *Reichmarks*...in comparison, that is. Why is that, please tell us?"

"It's because I spent it on bribes," I lied.

"Bribes? Who would you have to bribe?"

"No one important, you know, trains, taxis, policemen and other—and for lodging...during my search. No one wanted the other countries' money...that's why those notes still remain."

He was examining several of the bills minutely, holding each of them up to the light.

"Lieutenant, do you have a magnifier glass, by chance?"

The Lieutenant leaned over and opened one of his desk drawers, removing a round magnifier by the handle. The *Kaptain* passed the bills to *Herr* Kline who held out his hand for the glass. He examined the bills closely. He'd opened a folder, earlier in the meeting and was now referring to some notes from time to time, but said not a word. Finally he looked up, took off his glasses and began polishing the lenses.

"*Fräulein...*" he glanced down at the papers on the table, "...Stopff. Would you like to tell us where you *really* obtained this money? I am asking this question only one time. I know you are lying about its origin and if I do not receive a satisfactory answer, I will send you immediately to prison to await trial as a spy. The ultimate outcome resulting in your being shot as a spy."

He paused to let the announcement take its toll on my nerves.

"Where did all this..." he gestured to the notes, "...come from?"

I didn't know what to say and stumbled for some answer that might be more believable.

"Did you actually acquire the notes in Norway, as you said, before beginning this journey?"

I drew a breath and was about to launch on another lie, when he held up a hand.

"Before you answer, possibly I should tell you that these notes...they are not money at all—well, it is currency, certainly, but it is currency disguised to be something else."

I stalled, waiting for him to go on, gauging what my answer should be...how much truth and how many falsehoods.

"It is very serious— you're having these...so I urge you...tell me the truth this time."

I'd been watching them examining and passing the glass and bills back and forth. The *Kaptain* and Lieutenant were quietly mumbling as they scrutinized. I knew now, there must be something to do with the money...something wrong...possibly with the serial numbers. Maybe they were counterfeit, or they bore secret code markings. It wasn't just that it was so much money, or even of different denominations. There was some reason they had so much in-

terest in the individual bills. They were examining them too closely—looking for something. What career did the dead Swede on
the train really have? Could he have been a spy, himself and were
there codes on the bills?

"Certainly," I finally replied without hesitation, deciding to
tell the truth.

"I lied to you about bringing the money from Norway. I
have not enough of my own money to trade for that much foreign
currency. I took it from a dead man on the train from Dusseldorf to
Berlin, the one I came on."

Herr Kline raised his eyes curiously. "A dead man...on a
train. In Germany? How did you come to make the acquaintance of
a dead man, *Fräulein?*"

"I didn't really make his acquaintance—we were fellow passengers. He sat across the aisle from me and he gave me a drink for
my tea."

"I see, another passenger on the train. Did you know this
passenger before...had you met?"

"Oh, no. I'd never laid eyes on him before this. He was
just a friendly man—a Swede, I think."

"Interesting...well, go on. How did he come to be dead,
dear lady?"

"We were fired on by a night fighter after we went to sleep.
He was killed instantly by the bullets coming through the roof."

"Oh—well, that certainly makes sense. What train number
was it...do you remember? And when did it leave Frankfurt?"

I told him, as best I could remember. He nodded to the
Lieutenant who took note of the information.

I corrected him: "And it was from Dusseldorf—not Frankfurt."

"Oh, yes, you did say that," he mumbled, glancing at the
Lieutenant.

"About where did the train get attacked? Do you have any
idea...a town—city, nearby?"

"No. It was night—dark, of course. And we were
awakened...surprised. No one except possibly the conductor would
know that."

"When—what time during the night?"

"Maybe 3:00 a.m., my guess."

"And the cash, *Fräulein*...how did it come into your possession...around 3:00 a.m.?"

"No, I waited to take it."

"Waited—waited for what?"

"Until I got enough courage...in between the soldiers collecting the bodies of the people who had been killed."

"And...?"

"I just got up went over to him, reached inside his coat and took his wallet...oh, and—yes, his liquor flask, too."

"I see. Was this all the money he had?" he said, holding up some of the bills.

I thought a moment before I answered.

"No, it wasn't. I gave some of it away."

"Ah, so benevolent, *Fräulein*...to whom, *Fräulein*, did you give it?" he raised his pencil and looked at me over his glasses.

I hesitated a moment but decided I'd best tell all the truth.

"I gave some of it to an American aviator."

He nearly dropped his pencil. "You gave...where did you encounter an American aviator?"

I told him the story quickly. Speaking of the bombers, the parachutes and the rest of the train ride when I'd cared for the prisoner. I recounted how I'd put some of the Swiss Francs in his flight suit, hoping he might get better treatment and possibly be able to obtain better food and living conditions if he had some money. I felt the Swiss currency would have the highest value and would be the easiest to exchange.

Herr Kline was also writing, catching up on the details of the story.

"That was just before the officer shot him," I added, almost as an afterthought.

"Who shot him?" he said looking up in mid sentence.

"A German officer...a lieutenant, directing traffic outside the train station—here, in Berlin. He shot him in the back of the ambulance."

"What did the aviator do that the officer shot him?"

"Nothing."

"Well, that hardly seems likely, *Fräulein*, did he not attack the officer...attempt an escape...something to justify being shot, right inside the city like that?"

"No, he could do nothing. His leg was badly broken. He was delirious with fever. He could not have done anything. The bombs were falling, the officer had been injured himself...sometime during the war. He was missing his right arm...and he was very angry at the time."

I glanced at the Lieutenant, having forgotten for a moment that he, too, had been recently wounded. He was staring at the floor.

Herr Kline followed my glance. "I see...was that all the money you gave away?"

Again, I hesitated before incriminating my Aunt Fredia.

"No, I also gave some to my aunt here in Berlin...the sister to my mother with whom I stayed last evening. She is poor, has no husband and is caring for her many grandchildren."

"As are many German widows, *Fräulein*...many."

He wrote something down and then addressed the Lieutenant, who'd spoken not a word during the civilian's questioning.

"Do you have the aunt's address, Lieutenant?"

"Yes, *Herr* Kline, we do."

"Good. Please go and tell the corporal to send someone to the aunt's for the remaining banknotes...immediately, tell him to question her as to whether she has yet spent any of them and then follow any trail to retrieve any and all of the money."

The Lieutenant rose and hurried from the room. *Herr* Kline...was obviously a man to be reckoned with. Turning to me again, he consulted his notes once more, tapping the pad with the pencil eraser as he read.

"Ah...*fräulein*, such an adventurous journey you have had since leaving Norway. It is almost..." he glanced at me over the top of his glasses, "...too bizarre to believe...like a storybook journey."

I didn't reply and he continued to tap the tablet on his lap.

"However...tell me, where is the wallet of the dead man...the one on the train? Do you still have it somewhere...your aunt's house, possibly?"

"I pushed it deep into the vomit in the waste-bin on the

train, thinking no one would willingly search there."

"Probably a valid decision at the time, but why did you do that...why did you not wish for anyone to find it? Couldn't you have just...thrown it away?"

I repeated my fears of the soldiers, taking the body to the car with the other corpses, searching the body for valuables, missing *Herr* Carlsson's wallet and coming back to question me about it.

"Humm..." he thought for a moment, "you do not have a lot of respect or trust for the *infantry*, do you, *Fräulein*?"

I didn't reply.

"So...did you happen to look at the dead man's papers, *Fräulein*? Read them...at all, by chance?"

The Lieutenant entered the room again and nodded to *Herr* Kline.

Again, I thought quickly. *Herr* Carlsson is long dead. He couldn't be harmed by anything here. What of those working with him? If my interrogators learned his true name, or name he gave me? What about his family...could any harm come to them through my answers?

Oh...I thought, it is so complicated. They were the enemy of the *Reich*...what concern should I have for them? But what if the truth proved me innocent of anything worse than robbing a corpse? They were all staring at me, waiting for my answer

Fräulein...we are waiting?

"Yes, I looked at the papers...in the toilet of the train-car; he'd told me his name was *Herr* Rudolph...but his name on his papers was *Herr* Carlsson...from Sweden. He was Swedish and he had a Swedish passport there, too...that said the same thing."

"And where have you...these papers?"

"I was afraid to keep them, as I said, so I put them also into the dust-bin in the toilet."

"What a disappointment. Why would you wish to retain his papers, anyway, *Fräulein*?"

"So I could let his family know that he had been killed...there were some photos in the wallet—a wife, children, maybe grandchildren and I thought—because of what I'd done, stolen his wallet. There was no way they could ever learn the truth of what happened to him, how he died...after the war, if I took his papers. But I was also afraid, as I said…if the soldiers returned, they might search me and find the documents."

"Humm…I see," he said without glancing at me, "how benovelent…how *bizarre.*"

He seemed occupied with his notes. Looking up he turned to the other man

"Have you any further questions of *Fräulein* Stopff?"

"No, *Herr* Kline, none."

"Well then…," he smiled cheerfully in my direction, "…*Fräulein,* you may go then. I must say, you have been most coop-erative. Your tale…although quite fantastic, just could be true—enough of it, anyway. You certainly tell it well and without too much hesitation, either. You must remain our guest yet tonight, though, unfortunately. We will obtain the other currency from your aunt, if she still has it and you may likely be questioned again tomorrow as a result of it. But until then…please reconsider what you have told us. If there were anything you have omitted, I would suggest you pass over any additional information to your questioner tomorrow and make any alterations to your statement at the same time."

That was the conclusion of the interview and I was put in another detention area. The bed was clean this time and the food edible, a tribute to Berlin restaurants, I imagined.

The next morning I was given breakfast of bread, cheese and something hot, representing tea. I wasn't taken to the interro-gation room until mid-afternoon. *Herr* Kline wasn't there when I was let in the room again by the corporal, but after ten minutes, he en-tered brusquely, carrying his long overcoat and smiling at me as he began to open his leather satchel.

"So…*Fräulein* Stopff, hello again…you've rested well, I trust?"

"Considering I am a prisoner of my own division of the *Re-ich,* yes, well enough."

He ignored my jibe as he removed documents from his leath-er *attaché* and began laying them along the end of the table.

"If it is any consolation to your…confinement inside, it is not at all a nice day outside…raining, as you can see and the British kept us awake with their aeroplanes all night," he said. Finishing the papers, he had picked up the coat to move it and was shaking the droplets of water onto the floor before draping it over a hook on the stand beside the door. He returned to the desk and sitting down, began straightening his stacks of documents.

I thought I would further clarify my remark since he had not chastized me for it: "As well as one can when one is not in their own home, *Herr* Klein...and against their own will." I answered his question so he would know my feelings, though he might not care.

He glanced up at me above his glasses, seeming confused for a moment; then:

"Oh—yes...I know what you mean, *Fräulein.*"

He'd withdrawn a brown portfolio and was unfolding it as we conversed. He consulted a sheet on one of the piles he'd placed on the desk.

"Well...it seems they have discovered several things since we last spoke, yesterday, *Fräulein* Stopff. They located your aunt and were able to obtain all the monetary notes you gave her. It seems she was saving them for a rainy day," he glanced up at me again, chuckling. "Good German thrift, eh *Fräulein?*"

I didn't answer and he didn't notice.

"They were unable to recover any of the money you gave the American airman at the train station. We have interviewed the attending ambulance physician...who seemed quite concerned with your well-being, by the way, when he learned we were detaining you."

He laid down the papers and stared seriously at me for a moment.

"Your concern for this American is somewhat suspect, *Fräulein.* Had he not—dropped from the sky, so to speak, we would be quite suspicious of the seeming intimacy of the connection. However, one assumes you were not previously acquainted, though, as it is, your behavior toward him seems rather unusual...for a German woman of your political standing in the *Reich*...toward the enemy. Do you have sympathy with our enemies, *Fräulein?*"

I glanced down at my folded hands and said nothing. Undeterred, he went on, shuffling through his papers:

"The physician in attendance...a *Doktor* Klausen, has stated that you were quite disturbed by the entire incident—'rightfully-so' he states, 'with the death of the flyer'. He said you had a sort of 'breakdown' there in the street." He glanced up. "Why is that *Fräulein?*"

"*Herr* Kline, I have seen much in this war—from both sides— Allies, Neutrals and German. I...I am tired, that's all. Simply tired of it. Having sought, found and lost my daughter again, after so many years of longing for her, has taken a great deal from me, emotionally. And this constant bombing of Germany—everywhere destruction—every city I pass through...and that we do not give up, give in, let them conquer Germany and be finished with this horror...it is just too much to endure at times. I know—I feel that it is inevitable and I do not understand why the rest of Germany does not, also."

Without anger he seemed to consider my outburst.

"You speak like a traitor, *Fräulein*...do you realize that? You should be careful of expressing your misguided opinions—how and to whom you express them."

He didn't say this unkindly...more a statement of fact.

"But isn't it being a traitor to *my* Germany, which I love dearly, to continue upon a course which is destroying Her and many of her people—innocent people, in the end?"

"The cost of modern warfare, *Fräulein*. As for the rest, that is not for me to say; I am merely a minor bureaucrat in the civil service, not a philosopher, or a historian. As I said, I would urge caution in the expression of your views. You are in no condition, civilly, or politically to be given consideration for...feelings about the lack of progress of the *Reich's* war."

I nodded without replying. He stared at me for a moment in thought, then smiled:

"Apparently..." he went on, taking up another paper "...the ambulance drivers took the money from your dead American flyer's body, although they deny ever having seen any money. They suggested we investigate the hospital personnel instead. But no matter, we believe we have enough of the currency to learn what we must of this..." he glanced over his glasses again, "...this organization."

He said nothing further for a while, giving the appearance of reading and sorting his documents.

"Well, *Fräulein* Stopff, I believe I am finished with you in this matter. It will be up to the higher civil authority to determine your fate now. I do not believe it is a military matter, or that you were involved in the espionage of the dead man in the train, or his coded currency, so in the meantime..."

I breathed a sigh of relief. "In the meantime *Herr* Kline?"

"In the meantime you will remain in custody of the civil government—not the military, at least, until after your trial."

"*Trial?* But what have I done that I am to be tried for, *Herr* Kline?"

"The money—the assorted currencies you allegedly removed from the dead man on the train were coded, as I said. They and your *Herr* Carlsson were part of a network of Allied spies we have been monitoring for some months, *Fräulein*. How much, if any, your involvement played in this...the court will decide, though I happen to believe your fantastic story, myself. But...later evidence often appears, so we will detain you until the trial, at least."

He chuckled to himself, which angered me, but I kept my mouth shut. He had not been unkind.

"It is too bizarre a story not to have some shred of truth. So, first, the military justice will review your case. If they feel your involvement in the matter constitutes espionage...they will act accordingly. If they feel your part was minimal, as do I, or not participatory, you will be given over to the civil government for judgement. There will be a trial. Meanwhile, you will remain incarcerated...until that time. After all *Fräulein*, stealing from a dead body is robbery, even if it is the body of a spy."

I didn't know what to say.

"Again, *Fraulein* Stopff...if I were you I would keep my political views to myself...do not repeat what you said to me, to anyone you encounter before, or during your trial. It will not serve you well to speak of these things...in these times."

CHAPTER

26

Finally, The Dawn

As hard as I tried I couldn't stay awake at the boat's helm. Several times throughout the night I fell asleep, steering blindly into the darkness, only to awaken with a start, cold and fearful I'd gotten too far off course. I'd continued to get wet; each time the boat fell off the wind, we were broached by a wave.

With nothing to do but the activity of steering, I was freezing cold. I didn't dare go below, as much as I worried about Katrina. Each time I awoke, I was afraid she'd somehow gotten out of bed, come on deck and manipulated the latch open and then fallen overboard. I knew the cat would have followed her if this had happened and would now be wandering the deck looking for her...meowing.

I had to remain at the tiller as long as the storm raged, despite the fact she might be frantic with fear, down below, never knowing if I was still on the boat. I'd been shaking with cold but concentrated on staying on the correct course, as best I could judge it. Once, during my wakeful periods I thought I could see the sun beginning to come up. But I waited and watched, finally realizing that it was a spotlight from another ship, somewhere out at sea. Dangerous business in these waters—showing a light like that, I thought. It wasn't close, but I was sailing directly toward it at the time, on a starboard tack. I quickly pulled the tiller to me to come further off the wind, hoping to skirt the source of the light even further.

The boat heeled at a greater angle by heading more easterly and began to pound heavily between the swells, diving and sliding on and sometimes beneath the waves, the rigging complaining loudly all the while. We had to stay beyond the range of the spotlight, I knew. It could only have been illuminated for a couple of minutes when it suddenly went out. I assumed they feared detection by another ship or a submarine, or possibly, that they'd gotten what they were spotting in the first place. They must have thought they'd heard or seen something in the darkness and turned on the light to investigate. Thank God they hadn't found us in their wide sweep.

I thought about the missing Norwegian, but decided, no...it couldn't have been him they'd seen. If he'd gone overboard when we were struck, he was now miles behind us and his body would still be drifting deep in the ocean depths. He'd risked his life for us and I'd begun feeling guilty. There were the diamonds too, of course and he'd probably have gone to no end to secure them...hopefully, stopping short of murder. Nevertheless, I felt badly, deceiving him to carry us, the way we had.

Surely, he wouldn't have come had he known the truth. It was greed that enticed him, not the will to rescue a child from certain death, as with the Constable and the Mayor. I changed my train of thought, not wishing to dwell on his death.

I held the sloop on the reach for what I thought to be about a half hour, before gradually easing her back into the wind, after which she ran easier, cleaner again, with less pounding. Finally, after another hour, I tacked once, heading more easterly, holding the course, the wind in my face on the port tack.

Tacking thereafter each half-hour, this continued until I was finally able to see the beginnings of dawn over my right shoulder. I thought my tacking seemed to be taking me further north than east but I couldn't be certain. Another hour and the sun was up sufficiently, though still behind cloud, to make out the digits on the compass card. I thought about the *Kaptain*'s admonition to go well north to avoid the patrol boats, before heading across and easterly to the west coast of Sweden. I checked my facial-wind steering against the compass. I had been sailing more northerly and decided, that was probably good.

With the dawn I seemed to become even colder—so cold by this time I didn't know whether I could make it down below, when I finally decided I must check on the child. I knew I should examine the sloop for damage, too. But first I had to check Katrina and somehow, get something hot to eat and drink for both of us.

The sea's run seemed to have abated somewhat. It had nearly stopped snowing. The sloop was running well on her starboard tack...nearly a reach, we were so far off the wind. I brought her around one last time and realized I had difficulty crossing to the other, higher side of the boat, as the boom came around. Once I had the course square on the lubber line of the compass, I tried to stand upright, but realized I couldn't. I tried again and then once, rocking forward and backward before finally succeeding in half-standing—half-leaning against the low bulwark, holding onto the boom. Shakily, I was barely unable to maintain that position for very long and gradually and helplessly, slipped back onto the seat beside the tiller. The pain in my legs was devistating. But I thought I felt a little warmer with the exertion, though my feet now also began to ache. I rested for a bit, trying to wiggle my toes, but I couldn't tell whether they were moving, my legs were shaking spasmodically from the effort.

If she hadn't already, Katrina would soon be awake and needing my attention. And I wouldn't even be able to walk, let alone prepare food for us. Thinking of warm food and drink, I made another effort to rise. I was more successful this time, but I nearly pitched forward onto the other side when a sudden swell came across the bows. Because I was unprepared, the boat came pointing into the wind and seemed to hang there in irons, the jib and main flapping. The movement wasn't so violent as earlier in the night when she came off on a port tack again and was bowled way over on her side, before gradually picking up enough way to come up again.

I corrected the course and she resumed cutting through the swells. I stood again and tried to look over the condition of the boat. I was still concerned about any possible damage, after the collision. The short fore-stay appeared to be intact but the tack of the jib was discolored part-way up—blackish, as if it had rubbed against something dirty. I'd never seen the sails in daylight, so the discoloration could have already been there. I couldn't see far enough along the bow to determine whether there was structural damage.

Glancing about her deck, I took in the fact she wasn't very well painted. She did have quite a bit of weathered teak and though she was gray and mottled, she didn't seem the worse for wear for it, for she was sharp, crisp and clean about her construction.

She was a cat-rigged boat, running both triangular main and jib sails—no mizzenmast, or gaffs, something I'd already learned from my earlier crawl-about. She seemed about fourty-five or fifty feet in length, but not so broad in the beam as I expected so she probably was faster than most boats her size.

I pondered her lines, wondering what she'd been built for in the first place. How old was she? Maybe she'd been constructed for smuggling from the start. With her rig and narrow beam, she didn't seem like a fisher; there were no nets in evidence and no place to store ice or a catch of fish. Glancing forward over the low cabin I noted the main was reefed possibly two points, something I'd not discovered the previous evening. That explained her slow response to the tiller now in the lighter sea. I pondered her rig as I exercised my legs, alternately rising, standing for a while and collapsing to a sitting position, trying all the while to maintain the course. I could feel my legs gaining strength with each renewed effort and the improvement in circulation, though I was still cold to the bone and my feet were all pins and needles.

Would she run well under jib alone, I wondered? Somehow I had to get below and get into some warm clothes and prepare food for the pair of us. I thought about dropping both sails or throwing over a long length of rope, secured to her stern rail...to act as a sea anchor; maybe the *Kaptain* even had something like a sea anchor down below? Or, a canvas bucket—anything which would create drag in the water when thrown over the rail and the ship left to blow downwind with a bare mast slowed by the drag.

Unsure of how she handled without hands on the tiller, I wondered whether the wind might spin us around if I abandoned the tiller and probably blow us back the way we'd come. I dreaded the though of losing all the headway I had struggled so hard to make in the dark of night. But I had to do something. Finally, I decided, first, to try to drop the main. Gauging by where the mast was placed, I expected she might run well under jib alone. I might be able to lash the tiller and keep her headed somewhat into the wind, at least long enough to do what I had to do. There might be enough superstructure above the water to catch the wind and bring her around, with the jib acting as center-pivot. It was worth a try. I knew I could probably get the main up again with the calmer seas that had come now, after the storm.

I exercised steadily for another five minutes until I was sure I would be nimble enough to move about the deck without tumbling overboard. Then I pointed her into the wind, let go the tiller and made a wobbly-run forward toward the mast-head. Once there I began sorting out the confusion of lines, bobbing and dangling among the cleats, glancing upward and down again, until I finally located the main halyard, wound double round a cleat, its tail surplus done up neatly to prevent fouling.

Unwrapping the free tail, I yanked the coarse hemp from the cleat, bracing myself for the weight of the sail. By then, the mainsail was flapping loudly and the boom swinging erratically, slamming from side to side against its cleating in the main sheet. As I freed the halyard and began slacking it off, with the tension released, the mainsail began sliding down the mast, the boom landing on top of the deck of the cabin, just missing the cradle. I'd been unable to get the boom cradle tipped up. I moved back, holding onto the boom. Digging into the pile of the mainsail, I located the boom cradle and tipped it up, struggling to position the heavily-shaking boom into it while keeping from being enveloped in the flapping mainsail. Succeding at last, I used the main halyard to loosely wrap and bunch the balooning mainsail around the boom and mast to keep it from blowing overboard and dragging in the sea.

I rushed back to the tiller and gauging from the boat's position, slackened both jib sheets, slightly. I sat down and hauled the tiller toward me, trying to catch the jib-full for a port tack. Nothing happened for an agonizing ten or so seconds. Finally the front of the sail began to bow out, the leech straightened and then grew taunt as it spilled wind and the boat held her own in the running sea.

It was slow going, but I believed we were just possibly holding our own, if not making some way north-easterly. I glanced over the side at the passing water. Yes, we were definitely not going backward...well, very fast, anyway. I looked at the course on the card and then hauled the tiller all the way into my stomach. She hardly heeled at all and we didn't seem to be floundering, either. I continued to hold her over, waiting to see if anything adverse would happen. But it didn't. I waited a little longer and satisfied she would do little more than wallow, I lashed the tiller tight, slipped around it and rushed as fast as I could, to loosen the cabin hatch.

My fingers were still numb and I fumbled with the latch before I was finally able to slide it back. I eased my way down the short ladder and into the cabin.

The first thing I heard was the sound of the kitten's meowing. After the brightness of the deck, it was dimly lit inside the space from the small portholes running along either side of the cabin. As my eyes grew accustomed to the light, I made out the huddled form of Katrina on the bunk. I stepped off the ladder toward her and into ankle-deep water. A saucepan was bobbing and banging the side of the bulkhead. I picked it up and tossed it on the opposite bunk. The cat was on the high side on the opposite bunk and jumped when the pot hit the mattress. Katrina whimpered and sniffed but didn't cry as I sloshed my way over to her and folded her into my arms.

"It's all right now Katrina. I can hold you for a minute. Are you cold?"

I could feel that she wasn't, but soon would be if I didn't shed my oilskins and soggy trousers. After holding her and saying some reassuring words, I peeled off the oilskins. Thankfully, all our luggage had remained safely behind the rail of the top bunk. I grabbed the large valise and flung open the lid. Katrina had resumed her whimpering but seemed more alert. I found one of the chocolate bars and broke it in half.

"Here...take this Katrina...I'll get us something warm to eat in a minute. Are you hungry...?"

She nodded slowly, preoccupied with a mouthful of chocolate. The cat leaped onto my shoulder as I poked through the case for a sweater. I grabbed it, tossing it on the bed beside her. She began talking comfortingly to it as if it were as destitute as she must have felt herself; the mother instinct was definately born into females, I thought.

The water on the cabin floor presented a quandary. I hadn't realized we were taking on water; that explained the sluggish handling of the sloop. I didn't believe we were taking on that much, that quickly, but it was something new and somewhat urgent that had to be dealt with soon, or we'd soon flounder with the added weight. The bilge pump must be topside, forward of the cabin; I vowed to investigate and set right the water as soon as I could.

I found a pair of trousers. Climbing on the bunk opposite Katrina, I swung my dripping feet onto the end of the bed and slid down the wet trousers. Then, drawing my knees up to my chin again, I leaned back and pulled on dry pants and buttoned them with numb fingers. About to climb back down, I thought twice and rolled up both trowser legs to just below my knees. I decided, to be safe, I'd better go back topside and check the way of the boat again.

"I'll be right back, Katrina...I'm just going to look out to see if everything's all right."

"Hungry..." she said, looking sadly out from her tent of blankets and probably thinking I was going to abandon her again. She shivered. "Cold..." she added snuggling deeper.

"I'll make something to eat in a minute—just let me look...," I pointed up, "...first."

I climbed the ladder again, slid the hatch cover open and stuck out my head and shoulders. We appeared to be skidding somewhat sideways; I couldn't tell whether we were making much headway and didn't care as long as we weren't about to swamp. The seas seemed to have moderated even further, I noted and slipped the hatch back. Thank God, I thought, neither of us had gotten seasick. We hadn't time to even think about the possibility of that.

Back below, I patted Katrina on the head as I waded past: "Something to eat—now, little one."

The small galley was part of the forward cabin with a two-burner gas stove suspended in gumball mounting to the wall. I twisted both knobs in turn and there was a hiss of pressure, but it seemed low. I unscrewed the knob on the pump and pumped it for ten seconds, which would have brought the unit back up to operating pressure. I didn't know how much gas there was in the tank, but assumed the *Kaptain* had laid in sufficient stock to hold the whole voyage. It should heat up the cabin, too, I thought in warm anticipation of a fire on both burners.

Looking for matches, I rummaged in a couple of the latched drawers. On the second try I found a capped tin that rattled when I shook it. I pulled the lid off and took out a match. It broke in my first attempt to strike it. I picked up the stub-end and had success the second time. As the match flared I opened both gas valves on the burner and the flame caught, blue and bright.

"Wonderful, I said, rubbing my hands together above the flames. I glanced over at Katrina who was watching me.

"We'll soon be eating Katrina," I said, wishing I'd remembered the three brown bags of sandwiches we'd forgotten in the Mercedes.

I rummaged in the other drawers. I saw two loaves of bread in the first drawer I opened and grabbed one. Below, there were enameled pans. I'd put one of them on the little table and began looking for the fresh water source, finding it in one of two barrels suspended above the bunks. I opened the spigot and trickled some into a tin cup and sniffed the contents in case it was kerosene...no odor. Turning off the spigot when the pan was a little over half full, I dipped in a finger, smelled it again, then tasted it. Definitely water; I put the pan on one of the burners and secured it with the wire bales to hold it in place. Next, we needed something to go with the bread.

Lard, or salted fat—something was in a tin beneath the stove. Whatever it was, it smelled delicious. I didn't realize how hungry I was. I tore off a piece from one of the loaves and with a spoon smeared on what appeared to be lard. I handed it to Katrina. She smiled wanly at me and took a bite as I pasted up another for myself.

"There'll be more in a minute, darling and some hot chocolate."

Turning back to the cupboard I found a tin of evaporated milk with two holes already piercing the top and located another pan, adding water and an equal amount of the milk. I set it on the other burner, securing it. From my valise I retrieved a chocolate bar and a tin of coffee. I broke the bar into the heating milk.

I searched for two cups, but found only one, remembering then, that we'd just finished our tea when the Norwegian came below. Maybe his cup was somewhere on the deck beside the tiller. I'd have a look later, I thought, wanting to check the progress of the unattended tiller, anyway. Either the seas were abating, or the rig was serving better than I'd thought it would.

I rummaged further, finding dried herring, cheese and what looked and tasted like dried, salt beef. I pondered the mixture of foods, trying to conjure an appetizing meal from the conglomeration. At last, I settled on a gruel, made with some of the beef juice, crumbled bread and a few pieces of fish in water, thickened with evaporated milk. There was a small, sealed container of salt, but I didn't use any, figuring the fish and meat already had plenty.

Coffee can in hand, I couldn't find a tin opener. I finally settled on a dull splicing knife I found in the drawer. It appeared to be the tool used to pierce the top of the milk tin. The hot chocolate pan was emitting a steamy vapor. I removed it and set it aside; I left the burner on to continue warming the cabin.

After it had cooled a little I poured some of the chocolate in the single cup and handed it to Katrina.

"Careful—it is very hot. Sip it...."

There wasn't enough of the steaming liquid to harm her much if she did spill it.

Back at the water barrel, I filled the coffeepot and put it on the blazing burner, then gave the stove's fuel tank a few pumps for good measure and the gas flame hissed cheerfully higher.

"I have to look up there again...darling," I said gesturing toward the hatch. "I'll be right back, so don't get off the bed."

She only looked over the cup's lip, watching me with little interest now she had her chocolate. Up the ladder I went again, feeling far stronger than when I'd descended, moments earlier.

The stove was warming the cabin quickly. I could really feel the difference topside. I glanced forward at the full jib. It seemed to be pulling steadily and was not distressed. We weren't heeled as much, either and the seas were definitely abating, or at least holding steady. I calculated that putting up the main would be easier than I thought, especially on a full stomach.

I turned my attention to the missing cup and found it immediately, lodged beside one of the scuppers in the well beneath the rear cockpit. There was no sign of the other cup. It must have gone over with the *Kaptain*. We were expecting no guests, I thought, as I turned for the hatch again to go below. Glancing around before ducking inside, I noticed a brightening in the northwest. There was a thin, blue line on the horizon; a cold front would bring sunshine soon and possibly higher seas, with an increasing northwest wind, ideal for reaching and running toward the east. Before going below I scanned the foredeck, wondering about bilge pumps, thinking about having a look around; but I was barefoot and there wasn't a good deal to hang onto on deck. I decided to wait until I had something more inside me before attempting anything like that. The water hadn't seemed to be rising in the cabin. Cup in hand I went below again to the welcome warmth and a smile from Katrina.

The concoction I'd mixed up on the stove was near burning. I yanked it off the burner. My coffee water had just about boiled over, too. I decided to leave both burners hissing away. Placing the pot on the table, I shook in a healthy helping of the coffee through the jagged opening in the can and stirred it. Plates or bowls were next. They took a while to locate in a compartment on the end, with a bottle of *aquavit*—a very pleasant surprise.

The plates were pretty disgusting, both had some dried crust of food adhering to them. I guessed then, the *Kaptain* probably ate directly from the pan he cooked in. Given the circumstances, I decided to do the same and soak the pans later, somehow. Fetching another spoon for Katrina, before I sat down on the opposite bunk, I pulled the cork on the bottle and had a short swig of the fiery *aquavit*.

"We're going to have our breakfast, dear," I said, shuddering slightly from the cold water on my feet and the gulp of aquavit.

Wrapping a discarded sweater round the handle, I carried the pot over to the bed and put it on the sweater. I dipped in and tasted a bit of the thick mixture. It was wonderful.

"Careful now—it's hot," I put the spoon to Katrina's lips. She gingerly tasted it, promptly made a wry face, but swallowed anyway. She was hungry, too. I'd joined her, sitting on the edge of the bed, the pan on the blanket between us. She was holding the now-empty cup in both hands.

"Here...let me get you some more chocolate." I handed her the spoon, taking the cup. Returning to the stove, the coffee grounds had just begun to settle, so I gave them a stir and poured a little more chocolate for Katrina. As I sat back down, she was happily chewing away on another mouthful.

"When you want a drink, just tell me ...I'll hold the cup."

I sat there, the cup in one hand, the spoon in the other wolfing down a couple of mouthfuls, before Katrina held out her hand for the chocolate. I put a spoon of our food on the sweater for the cat; it didn't hesitate to eat it.

Everyone was very hungry; we ate eagerly but quietly. Finally Katrina's apetite began to wane and finally, she seemed satisfied. I pressed a couple more bites on her before she turned her face away, wanting no more. I finished what was left of it. She'd done well, considering the ingredients and the chef's limited supplies, imagination and skill. I got up and took the pan back to the stove, setting the chocolate aside while I poured myself a half cup of coffee, adding a little of the canned milk. Sitting on the bed, I gave her another drink of chocolate and began to sip my coffee. This was quite comfortable, I thought, so long as we didn't run into any battleships, or submarines. I gave a little start at the thought. The odds...certainly not twice in the same trip, but I silently vowed not to linger too long over my newly-gained comfort. I knew if I became cofortable too long, I'd become sleepy.

There was work yet to be done topside to get going again and I hadn't yet decided how to do it with Katrina along. She could hardly be expected to remain below deck all day. If the seas continued mild, she could come topside, but not until I'd set the mainsail again. Maybe I should bring her above deck first, lash her to the taff-rail and then set the main? What if she got cold and wanted to go below? What would I do? I'd have to reverse the whole procedure again to take her below. Would the boat hold a course long enough to get the hatch cover open and take her safely below...and me back topside, again?

I finished my coffee and took a refill from the pan, adding a little more milk. It was the best coffee I ever tasted. Our stomachs full again, we played with the kitten together. It was ready to entertain itself and us. Its belly was a little rounder. It leapt from one bunk, across the narrow aisle, onto the other bed, then ran around, poking into all the corners—generally being a kitten. Katrina giggled and chased it as far as she could from the confines of the bunk, nearly tumbling onto the deck, once. It was still awash with water. I caught her in time and gently admonished her to be careful. Rolling up my sleeves, I searched around in the water with my hands and located her soggy clothes. Only her coat had remained dry, on the bed. The long, wool stockings were soaked. I wrung them out and draped them over the edge of the upper bunk.

I'd not had time to explore the remainder of the boat below deck, so while Katrina played with the kitten, I went forward. There was some sort of stateroom—smallish, with a table and chair. I noticed rolled charts in a rack screwed onto the starboard hull. Removing one, I rolled it out on the table and found the west coast of Sweden. Great, I thought, if we only knew where we were—we'd know where we were. I returned the chart to its rack and opened a tall closet door. There was a set of town clothes hanging there: the *Kaptain*'s, no doubt. Feeling guilty, I closed it and opened an identical cupboard across the aisle. It contained some sort of apparatus for the plumbing, or so I assumed. I nearly closed the door again before I thought twice and examined the affair more closely.

There was a shaft-like rod going all the way through the upper deck, through a brass bushing with a rubber-grommet. Near the lower deck level, there was a pedal, resembling the brake or clutch on an automobile, with a rubber pad covering, apparently for traction. But why? This was folded up against the rod. It was attached to a slotted outer tube, which covered another tube. I wondered...could it be a foot-operated pump?

Folding down the pedal lever, which extended outward and locked parallel to the lower deck, about a foot from the flooring, I lifted one leg, placed my bare foot on the pedal and pushed. There was a squirting sucking sound. It *was* a pump. I lifted my foot and the spring-loaded pedal returned to its previous position. I pushed again, there was a little more resistance this time and the sucking sound turned to a gush. I repeated the movement, again and again. I'd found a bilge pump which was accessible from topside or from there within the cabin. I shouted over my shoulder to Katrina that I had to do a little work and would be back to play with her and the cat again, soon.

After ten minutes pumping, changing legs twice, there was no longer any water visible on the floor. I stuck my head around the corner, checking on Katrina. She still seemed content to play with the cat, so I returned to my pump.

Another ten minutes and I felt it suck dry, so I folded up the pedal and closed the door, smiling to myself. Now, dry socks, rubber boots and what to do with Katrina. I returned to poking around in my valise to see what clothing the old woman had given me. There were long stockings and dresses but no trousers. She still had her boots, but they were wet.

I decided I'd take her topside to sit beside me; I intended to tie her to the rail with a quick-release slip knot in case I had to move her fast. Going forward again, I retrieved one of the oilskins from the closet, intending to wrap it around her, more or less as a windbreak-tent affair, once I had her tied in place. I put on all her tights and stockings and added her coat and scarf. I'd taken a length of line from the closet where the pump was lodged, to use to secure her to the rail. Finally, I added a knit stocking cap from the *Kaptain*'s closet.

Katrina was enduring my rough dressing of her, all the while chattering away to the cat and me.

Finally I asked: "Want to go outside and sit with Papa while I work?" She nodded vigorously, obviously understanding only that we were going to be leaving the confines of the cabin.

"Papa—kitty—kitty come...?" she queried, waving at the marauding cat.

I thought for a moment; surely the cat could easily remain on the deck with its sharp claws, though what it would think of the open air and spray I didn't know.

"Yes, kitty can come," I finally conceded, standing her up and putting on my own oilskin. I glanced around our little home to insure all was well, put the cat in her arms and then picked up Katrina, before starting up the ladder.

Her head came through the hatch first and she blinked at the brightness, shading her eyes with one hand. The cat immediately took advantage of her momentarily inattention and leapt to freedom on the slanted deck.

"Katt?" she exclaimed, reaching toward the marbled fur ball. It was clinging, spraddle-legged to the teak deck, with a surprised look, as the deck pitched and rolled.

"Katt's allright," I reassured her, not really knowing whether it would slip overboard any second. But it didn't slip, slide or leap. After a few seconds, it jumped over to the scupper near the rail and began pawing at a trailing rope tail.

I knew we didn't have to worry about the cat, at that point and climbed onto the deck, latching the cover behind me. The sun was bright. In the northwest, big patches of blue sky showed between the clouds, which were scuttling southeastward. The front was finally moving through and the wind was swinging northwest, I guessed, glancing at the compass card as I sat Katrina down and began tying and then wrapping her up.

Once I finished figuring out the best way to lash her to the tiller area and finally secured the knots, I turned face into the wind to gauge its direction. North-northwest—it was definitely shifting. It would be getting colder too and I was glad I'd bundled Katrina with the extra clothes. If we changed course after I had the mainsail up I calculated we could do a near beam reach all the way across to Sweden. That track would also be the fastest for the boat. It will also be a very cold night, I thought, not wanting to think about how I would remain awake to steer, at this point. We are in luck for a favorable wind, anyway and we were free of the *Reich's* threat, out of Germany with Sweden only a little more than a day's sail eastward, to freedom.

"You have to stay here, Katrina. That's why I've tied you up—so you don't fall in the water." I knew she couldn't undo the knot. "Will you do that? Yes...?"

"Kitty...?"

The cat had disappeared somewhere forward, to explore, I figured.

"Kitty's fine. Just leave it alone. "I'm going forward now Katrina...stay there so you don't fall in the water. You'll be able to see me while I work...all right?"

"Water..." she said, leaning back and pointing over the side. "Katrina fall in water..." she said with a serious expression, all the while shaking her head no.

"That's right. Stay there. I'll not be very long."

Unlashing the tiller, I waited for the boat to come back into the wind before I inched my way forward along the port side and tried to pull up the mainsail again. I didn't know what would happen during this process, but I hoped the boat would continue to point. I loosened the mainsheet to free the boom's swing and glanced around the deck once more to insure no ropes could whip about and strike the child, if what I was trying to do went wrong somehow. I shaded my eyes and looked up at the leech of the jib, trying to gauge the force of the wind. Should I reef the main, or not? I didn't want to have to drop reef points again in the mainsail, once I'd gotten it up and we were running before the wind. If I reefed it a point we'd go slower; if I used two points, our progress would be significantly slowed, but safer yet. I decided to try for one point, given the clearing skies and freshening breeze. We had daylight, and if it went OK, I could always reef in or let out again before nightfall. The weather wasn't likely to change before the following day, anyway, I thought.

Taking a deep breath I prepared to haul up the main, but on second thought, decided to make my way on up to the bow, to look closer for any damage from the collision. I carefully hand-over-handed my way forward along the cabin deck. There was a nasty dent in the wood trim on the port side bow and the brass fore-stay deck cleat was bent at a wicked angle. I watched as water washed over the bow. I couldn't be sure, but it looked safe enough. If the cleat had held this long it should continue to. That could also be were we were taking the water into the cabin, below. There was nothing I could do about it so I worked my way aft again and began to set the reef points along the main.

We were still pointing when I began pulling down on the main halyard. I reached as high as I could and let my weight drop, my body's heft helping draw the line through the pulley at the top of the mast. This had to be done quickly as with that much canvas up and exposed to the brisk wind, anything might happen.

Up went the triangle of grey-brown canvas. It began to catch the wind and flap madly, the higher it went. The boom careened to right and left wildly. Getting the last yard or so up was a real tug. But I managed. The boom was out of the cradle and the mainsail all the way up and tight, lifting the boom. Almost surprised at how easy it had been, I didn't dally, quickly wrapping the halyard round a cleat on the mast and doing up the end of the line to minimize fowling. I took a quick glance up the mast again and hurredly worked my way back to the tiller.

Katrina was sitting quietly with the cat in her lap. She'd been watching me. She now pointed at the sail as if she was about to say sail, but looked at me emphatically, lowered her arm and closed her mouth, not having the word for it.

"*Segla*," I said in Swedish as I slid back into my seat, taking up the jib-sheet again and hauling it tight again before cleating it. Then I did the same for the main sheet.

"Say—ge-la," she repeated. She may as well learn the language she'd be speaking soon, I thought, hauling the tiller over and watching the bow as the sloop slowly came off the wind again and filled her sails. We heeled way over at first, frightening me for an instant with her power. God, maybe two reef points would have been better. The wind was really getting up.

Katrina's eyes also became large and she grasped at me as the windward side of the sloop came out of the water.

"It's OK," I said, holding her from sliding with my free arm, wondering if I was telling her a lie to reassure myself.

Slowly the boat began to make way forward and as the bow cut through the waves, the tilt of the mast lessened and she came up on her ear and really began to move faster through the foam. The jib was hauled a bit close and was back-winding the mainsail so I eased off the sheet and the dimple disappeared from the front of the mainsail. I glanced at the compass and eased her further off the wind onto the broad, beam reach that would take her up to her top speed and all the way to Sweden.

Alternately watching the rig and the compass, I held the sloop close to the wind for over an hour. I didn't want to put too much strain on her mast and rigging until I could better judge her behavior in what would be a very strenuous reach, keeping her heeled over to starboard and completely burying the bottom of her stubby rail. I felt pretty good about her behavior, feeling for the first time we were really on our way home.

I noticed a small tip-open compartment in the transom seat. I open it and discovered a small coil of tangled line and several brightly-colored flags. Sorting them, I found every Nordic country represented and even one from Great Britain. I selected the blue and yellow of Sweden and looked around for the halyard to fly it from. I decided the best place was on the port side back-stay, so I pulled the tiller in a little and loosely lashed it, then dashed over, unsnapped the snaffle on the line, quickly fitted the corners of the flag and hauled the little flag aloft about three quarters of the way up the stay. The wind made it behave like a tell-tale, flapping briskly in the direction the wind blew toward.

It looked fine, I thought, as I took my seat again. Katrina had been watching me and she pointed at the colorful rectangle, silently mouthing the nameless object.

"*Flagga*" I said. "*Svenska flagga….*"

She smiled, nodded and went back to talking to the kitten, not even trying to repeat the word. I eased the sloop further off the wind, alternately monitoring her behavior in the water and glancing down at the compass card.

Remembering that the binnacle light had gone out during the storm, I bent over it, found the catch and releasing one side, tipped it open. I explored the operation of the compass housing and discovered a wick and oil resevoir, the latter nearly full of oil. Everything appeared intact. I screwed the resevoir cover back on. More than enough to get us to Sweden, I though, but vowing to light it again while it was still early enough to do any repairs I might discover should it not maintain a flame. I squeezed the wick's end and sniffed my fingers. Oil. There should be enough there to catch a flame from a match and burn away any water that had accumulated. I closed it up again and glanced around at the horizon. When we were cutting due east, I glanced up again, taking in the canvas, the mast and the windward stays, looking for anything amiss.

"God—I hope it stays together long enough to get us across," I said looking down at Katrina.

"For your sake little one."

27

Surprise Encounter

After another hour of reaching we continued making excellent time. I was fairly certain the wind would remain steady—northwesterly, for twenty-four hours, anyway. The sky was deep blue with no sign of cloud. The sun was warm, but because of the wind, the December morning was brisk and cold. So far Katrina'd shown no sign of being cold or tired. Nearly every article of clothing the old woman had sent, I probably had put on her and I held her next to me most of the time, shielded in her little oilskin tent and safely secured to the deck.

I glanced at the compass intermittently. After another hour, I made another minor course adjustment, laying the lubber line just east of northeast. Leeway should put us roughly on a directly easterly course. The boat remained heeled well over, making it difficult for Katrina to maintain her seat without clinging to me. She occasionally pushed herself back uphill as she played and talked to her dolly. She had her feet up and at times even tucked up beneath her, but I could tell she was uncomfortable from the way she continued to shift position. Still, she didn't complain.

I think it was the kitten, which continued to offer diversion for us both. It would be up on the bench beside her, then on her lap,

481

finally squeezed too hard, it would bound back down on the deck. It had easily mastered the slatted, teak floor and would leap from place to place around the cockpit, entertaining us both such that I didn't see the warship steaming up behind us, approaching from the southwest, off our port aft quarter. Katrina saw it first and pointed.

" *Hus...!*" she said, thinking it was a house.

I looked at her and then in the direction of her extended arm. It was even bigger than a house. The bow of a German, cruiser-class battleship was closing steadily and would soon be nearly even with us. Because of the blowing wind, our pounding bow and rattling rigging, she'd approached in silence, her bow slicing the water cleanly, rock-steady in the sea's heavy swell. As she drew closer I could hear her humming engines.

Surprised and not knowing what else to do, I continued to hold our course. I tried to think of what to tell the Germans if they decided to overhaul us. She was still three or four hundred yards to the southwest. Her course was slightly diagonal to ours and would soon force one of us to turn away to avoid a collision. We would ordinarily have the right-of-way, in civilian times. Chuckling to myself, but mad with fear of what they would do to us, or specifically, Katrina I wasn't going to argue about right-of-way. They had guns and to prove it, sailors were scrambling around topside like ants. I could see two, twin cannons with a firing crew, manned and already, pointing directly at us.

Frantic, I tried to think up a plausible story if we were stopped. After considering it, I decided I would tell them Katrina was my daughter and that we were returning from visiting Danish relatives and that my Danish wife had remained to care for her ailing mother, who was German. Where? I wondered—where was my wife doing this? I chose Grenå, the city we'd just departed from in Denmark. At least I had some idea where it was, the local geography and how to get there, after the experience of the ride with my German companions. I went through the story in my head a couple times for possible flaws and decided, without the ability to query authorities, it should hold water. If, that is, the Germans even cared.

The warship continued to close fast, though she'd definitely cut her speed. The hull that soon loomed over us, seemed monstrous. It began to rise and fall slightly with the swell and her slow headway. Katrina was all eyes. We could hear hissing and clanking, coming from inside the metal structure and we could see blue-coated seamen gathering beside one of the closest guns as they leaned over and stared down upon us, casually considering their potential prize. One of them raised a pair of field glasses and was looking us over closely.

Fearing they might do something foolish, I pivoted toward the group at the rail, high above as the towering bow drew near, then slowly moved past. I hooked one leg over the tiller to hold our course and held up both arms, palms upward to indicate I had no weapon. They still made no move nor did they acknowledge me. Realizing they probably couldn't see Katrina in her oilskin tent, I gestured toward the wiggling bundle beside me. Covered, as she was they might think I'd hidden a weapon in the pile of canvas. I stood up and unfolded the oilskin, untying the lashing around her waist at the same time. She blinked and smiled at the bright sunlight.

"Ohuuuu—*hus*...!" she exclaimed again, pointing toward the looming shadow. Picking her up, I faced the ship and held her high in the air, so they could see I had a child aboard. My leg still straddled the tiller in an attempt to maintain a course parallel to the cruiser. She'd come so close she'd begun to shield the wind from our sail. Still, no one onboard acknowledged us.

Another minute and she'd completely stolen our wind and we began to wallow in the doldrums of her shadow. A man with field glasses was scanning the sloop. After a moment he turned to his companion, said something and handed the glasses over, stepping away from the rail and disappeared from view.

I realized it must have been her intention to stop us and stealing our wind was the easiest way. Someone aboard the German ship knew sailboats. We were rendered entirely helpless in her wind shadow and we lost completely, all our headway and steering control. The sloop began to pitch and roll erratically with the swells, wallowing in the water, rattling her rigging and flapping her sails. I felt helpless as the slowly rotating sloop wallowed in the shadow. For the sake of safety I finally sat down and re-tied Katrina.

Two officers leaned over the rail. One raised a megaphone

and began shouting at us. I turned to face him, but for the life of me, I couldn't understand what he was saying. After a few seconds, he began shouting again and then I realized he was trying to speak Swedish. I still hadn't any idea what he was saying and shouted back in my poor German.

"My child and I are Swedish—we are alone and going home...to Sweden," I cupped my hands to make myself heard over the throb and splash of the monstrous ship.

The officer nodded turning to his companion—either the Mate or the *Kaptain*. The two of them conferred while the other seamen continued to stare down at us. I was reassured to see the gun crew had left their positions and come to the rail to watch. Their weapons were helpless, anyway, at this range, unable to be pointed downward enough to place us in covering fire. Several armed seamen lounged beside the railing, staring at us, rifles and sub-machine guns carelessly slung across their forearms. The officer returned to the rail and pointed a megaphone again.

"I am boarding you, *Kaptain*. Please stand by," he said in German.

Katrina was squirming, wanting to see more of where the voice came from.

"Stay where you are Katrina. The men will come aboard and search."

I couldn't understand the rest of what he'd said, but before long we heard the sound of winches above the dull throbbing of a donkey engine. A boat was being lowered along her hull, behind us. Katrina saw it, too.

"Boat...Papa," she said, pointing backward over our stern.

"Yes, dear...boat. The men are coming to talk to us."

We were still clear of the ship's hull, so I relaxed and waited. I didn't know if there was a gaff aboard our sloop. It'd be somewhere forward I reasoned, deciding to let them worry about keeping us from any possible collisions as they drew alongside.

"Let's watch them come in their boat, Katrina." I untied her again and picked her up. We watched together as their boat was lowered and freed from the gantry's cables; then the engines started. There were six passengers aboard in addition to the coxswain as they came alongside. Three seamen had rifles held waist-level at us. The other two held long gaffs, ready to grapple us. They steered between the cruiser, which now stood about 200 feet away and slowly came alongside. Of the six sailors, one was an officer, possibly the one I spoke to earlier. Two of the sailors leaped aboard under small arms cover from the others and made fast a couple of lines as the officer watched.

"Are there others aboard?" he shouted.

"None," I replied, shaking my head, "only us."

The officer leaped aboard near our bow, followed immediately by another armed seaman. They approached along the rolling deck, between the rail and the cabin. The seaman struggled to remain upright while continuing to point the rifle at me. The officer gestured for me to raise my hands. I was holding Katrina with one but elevated the other. The seaman stopped a rifle length away, looked me over and then came closer and with one hand, began searching me for a weapon.

He was very young. I could see his short, red hair beneath his sailors cap. As he bent closer to pat my pockets, leaning forward, Katrina suddenly grabbed the top of his hat and picked it right off his head. I heard a murmur from the boat's crew, above.

"Hat..." she said cheerfully, holding it high with both hands while trying to put it on top of her own head.

"No...Katrina." I started to lower my raised hand.

"Stop!" the sailor said, stepping back and brandishing the rifle. I did and he straightened. He put one hand to his bright stubble and glancing at the hat now on Katrina's head. Then he glanced at the officer, as if for instruction. He looked confused, realizing that Katrina, not I, had taken his cap from his head. After his initial surprise, he seemed embarrassed.

From the deck above, a murmur of laughter rained down. The sailor smiled, still confused, but making no move to take back his hat. He seemed to be awaiting instruction, but from what I could see, the officer in charge was doing everything in his power to control himself. I finally spoke first.

"*Nay*—Katrina, you can not have the sailor man's hat...sorry," I said it as much to him, cradling her in my right arm with my left still up in the air.

Still confused as to what to do, the youth glanced at me, Katrina and the officer and his face melted into a boyish grin. He stepped closer and as he reached for his hat, Katrina twisted away and held the hat behind her head.

"*My* hat..." she exclaimed in German, smiling at him coyly and cocking her head in a feminine gesture, her face turned slightly to the side. This brought a couple guffaws from the boat crew and a roar from the deck above.

One of the sailors shouted down: "Stop charming the young lady Heinz and get your hat back...you're out of uniform...can you not see it. The *Kaptain* is watching from the conning tower and you will be in trouble."

They all laughed again. By now the word aboard ship must have gotten out and the rail of the ship had begun to fill with spectators. There were hoots and catcalls. Young Heinz, who's face was now redder than his hair, turned and grinned upward.

"Katrina, that is not nice," I said, gingerly lowering my arm and retrieving the hat from her.

"Sorry...Heinz." I said to him, smiling and handing back his hat.

He nodded, bowed slightly and stepped back, turned to the officer.

"They have no weapons, Sir."

The officer, himself still suppressing a smile, nodded.

"Do not be so certain Heinz, the young lady rather disarmed you I think...you had best keep an eye on her.. Nevertheless, go below and be sure there are no others aboard," he commanded, inclining his head toward the hatch cover. Glancing sideways, he addressed the other seaman standing behind him.

"Schott—you had best accompany Heinz—in case he loses his trousers this time."

Schott drew his pistol, sprang forward and gave Heinz a little nudge in the back to torment him. They fumbled with the hatch cover for a second, finally slid it open and disappeared below. The officer gestured for two other seamen to stand in front of the opening. They leveled machine guns at the dark opening from each rail.

The officer approached me, bowed slightly and offering me a casual salute.

"*Kaptain*... I am *Kaptainleutnant* Rudolph Alfronzi from the ship *Klastenaut.* What is your name and why are you sailing in the middle of the Kattegat on Christmas Eve Day?"

"I..." Just then Katrina's kitten leaped from the corner where it had been hiding and attacked the officer's boot. He glanced down, confused for a moment and stepped slightly backward. Then he bent, picking up the kitten.

"Please go on, *Kaptain*, I did not wish to trod upon this little thing," he said, smiling and petting the cat with his other hand. "Continue please."

I'd completely forgotten about it being Christmas tomorrow. "I—my name is Alex Andersson, I am a Swedish citizen and we...my daughter Katrina and I, are returning after spending a week with my wife at her parents in...Grenå, in Denmark. Her parents are old and she will remain to care for them, for the remainder of the winter."

"Kitty..." Katrina pointed to the cat, frowning slightly and extending an arm toward the cat.

The *Kaptainleutenant* glanced at her, smiling, but continued to rub the cat's ears.

"Yes, I suspected you were Swedish," he inclined his head toward our little flag.

"Where do you berth you sloop, *Kaptain* and what is her name?"

"Uh—in...Halmstad—the western coast, *Kaptainleutnant,* her name—it is...*Lisskulla.*"

"*Liskulla...*?" He appeared to hesitate, stiffening slightly and glanced toward the others. "Why then *Kaptain* Andersson, does the name painted on the bow say Poseidon?

My heart raced. Before he'd even asked, I knew I was trapped. I didn't even know the name of the ship I'd been sailing.

"Oh—I've not changed it yet...I only purchased her in the fall and with the cold winter...I didn't wish to make a mess of painting her name. I will change it in the spring." He seemed to relax a little.

"You are quite a way south of Halmstad, *Kaptain.* Are you having trouble sailing this boat?"

"No...not at all...you see, we departed late because of the

storm yesterday. And then the wind came around so strong, with the child aboard I decided to try to make the most direct course for a landfall…directly for the west coast and then work my way back up in case there was trouble with weather, or with the sloop. We would not have far to go to shore if anything happened."

He pondered my answer for a moment. I wondered whether it satisfied him. Seaman Schott came up the companionway followed by Heinz, striding briskly behind; he reported to my interrogator.

"No one else down there, *Kaptainleutnant*…the quarters are…" he glance at me "…are quite a mess. Things lying on the deck—wet clothes, dirty cooking pans. It looks like they took on some water in the storm, yesterday."

I spoke up then. "Yes—we had a time of it last evening in the weather—I had to remain on deck. I've had no time to clean up since I pumped her bilge this morning."

"Has anyone been ill down there," the officer asked me?

"No…we're seasoned sailors. We got wet in the storm and had to…just leave everything. This morning, I wanted to take advantage of the good wind…strike a landfall as soon as possible, as I said."

"Yes, that is understandable."

"Hungry Poppa," Katrina said interrupting him.

"Yes Katrina…" I soothed her, "…we'll eat soon. Just wait a little while." To the officer I said: "We've not yet had our lunch."

He smiled, "*Lisskulla*…that is the child's name, is it *Kaptain?*"

He was still trying to trap me.

"Katrina is her name."

"What is the meaning of this…this Liss—kulla then?"

"It is Swedish…it means little girl."

"Ah…I see," he said smiling broadly. "This little girl, no doubt?"

"Yes sir, to be sure." I was relieved. I seemed to have squeaked by another.

"Well, we were patrolling in the North Sea *Kaptain* Andersson and are now inbound for Kobenhavin, hopefully so the crew can spend the day ashore."

He seemed to pause for a moment in thought.

"Excuse me *Kaptain*. I will be only a moment...I must report—my *Kaptain*," he said, indicating the rail of the ship. He strode two steps toward the rail and then turned and absently walked back. He smiled and handed the cat to Katrina, smiled again and turned again for the rail. A seaman passed him a megaphone which he pointed toward the cruiser's deck and he began speaking rapid German, most of which I couldn't catch. Schott and Katrina's new friend Heinz were smiling broadly at the wriggling child and cat I struggled to hold in my arms.

"Please Katrina, be still. We will be leaving soon. Then we can have something to eat."

There followed a response from above, a pause and then another speech from our end, again. The *Kapitanleutnant* finally returned, smiling.

"I noticed that you speak German to the child, *Kaptain*...what is the reason for that, if you are Swedish?"

"Her mother is German, *Kapitanleutnant* and it seemed natural to teach her German first since she was with her mother most of the time...before her grandparents became old, that is."

"Hummm...I see. Well, I have made my report, *Kaptain*, favorably I might add. You may be on your way immediately." He hesitated, seemingly to see my reaction.

I smiled and nodded, trying not to seem too eager.

"Thank you, *Kapitanleutnant*."

"However...our *Kaptain* wishes to make an offer to you and hopes you will accept it."

My alert went up.

"Understand, please, it is merely an...*invitation*, one which you can accept, otherwise, refuse and be on your way immediately."

I think my surprise showed: "Yes...the invitation?"

"You see, he wishes you and your daughter to be his guest aboard *Klastenaut*, for a Christmas Eve lunch. I have taken the liberty to pass along the...the plight of your stormy passage to him and he is feeling most hospitable. We were about to take our own lunch, you see, as we came upon you...and the fair Katrina." He smiled and touched her cheek.

"There is warm food...a celebration of sorts, warm clothes

and we can see that your things are also dried for you while you eat. My *Kaptain* wishes me to assure you, he will only delay you for an hour or so, at most?"

He paused, monitoring my reaction. I must not be too quick to decline, I thought.

"My crew will remain with your sloop to see nothing happens to her. Please, do not think you must accept, *Kaptain*. We...the officers and crew, are all anxious to see the child eat a good meal. You need not worry about your things below; German sailors are not thieves, despite what you may have heard from our enemies."

I still hesitated. Could I survive further interrogation, even in the casual sense they might be meant? It would be good for Katrina...a warm meal and possibly to get her other clothing dried. I was in no hurry to do anything—other than escape and besides, I might learn something useful to report back to Clyde. The immediate threat of detection seemed past, anyway, so I decided to accept his offer; it would certainly show that we had nothing to hide.

"Yes *Kapitanleutnant*, we would be pleased to accept your *Kaptain*'s thoughtful invitation...so long as there is not too much delay.

"Very good!" he exclaimed, "then let us get started. Do you need to take anything with you...for yourself or the child?"

I thought for a moment. "Only the wet things, below."

"Do not bother with them. My men will collect them all. Come..." he said, gesturing toward the launch with a flourish, "let us make haste. The meal awaits...and who is to tell, *Lisskulla* may even encounter Father Christmas."

"What about the sails—I should take down the sails?"

"No need. My men will tend to those also. Are there any special instructions for your boat?"

"No, none." I suspected he'd given orders to search the sailboat more closely.

"Good...please..." he gestured that I should precede him to the rail. I handed Katrina down to the waiting arms of the crewmen in the launch. I was handed over also, followed by the officer who gestured for me to take the child forward, behind the small windscreen. The journey was brief. As the launch swung out and around our bow I noticed the front of the sloop had been stove in somewhat from the collision. It also had a swipe of gray paint along the port side. I averted my eyes and prayed no one else noticed. Fortunately, Katrina had let out a squeal of excitement when the launch stared and all eyes were temporarily on her.

We swung on around the sloop's starboard side and stern and picked up speed for a moment before we maneuvered alongside the giant hull. There, we were duly hooked up, fore and aft and hauled up by the winches on twin cranes. By the time we were pivoted aboard at deck-level, our little sloop had grown quite small, below. I followed the young officer from the launch. We no more than stepped on deck and there was another, older officer waiting for us.

"Good day *Kaptain*. My name is *Kaptain* Mueller..." he extended his hand. "May I welcome you aboard the Klaustenat...both of you." We shook hands and he gave a slight bow.

"How do you do, *Kaptain*, I am Alex Andersson."

He nodded, continuing to shake my hand: "And this is...?"

"This is Katrina...my daughter."

"Hello *Leibchen*, welcome to my ship..." He took her hand and gave it a little mock handshake. She smiled the perfect smile that would endear any budding grandparent and he patted the kitten's head.

"Well, come this way; you must be cold and we have told you we would not delay you unnecessarily. Let us go directly to the dining room. A hot meal is awaiting us...but first, did anyone become wet in the crossing?"

"No, *Kaptain* Mueller, we are quite dry."

"Good, well...come along then...please."

We followed, leaving the *Kapitanlutnant* to move the gawking crew into action to secure the ship's boat. The *Kaptain* apologized for the shape of the ship as I followed him down a corridor and stairway.

"Wartime, *Kaptain* Andersson, does not leave one with the best ability to keep the ship as she should be kept. In peacetime, well...that is another story."

We reached his quarters and were gracefully ushered into a formal anteroom by a seaman steward. "*Kaptain*," my host inquired, "if I may be personal for a moment, would you like some dry stockings. The men are gathering the remainder of your and your daughter's clothing, which I understand you have not had time to put right...the storm the previous evening?"

When I put Katrina down on the deck I realized then our sorry state. The kitten leaped from her arms and began running around the room investigating the strange surroundings.

"What is the name of your kitten, my dear...little...oh—does she understand German? I completely forgot, you are Swedish."

"Uh...her mother is German, I'm Swedish and she understands German if...."

"Kitty..." Katrina said, pointing to the cat who was not squatting in the corner on the spotless floor.

"Kitty—*poop*! *Bad* kitty!"

I started to apologize, but the *Kaptain* held up a finger, chuckling. "My wife has two cats, *Kaptain*...you need not say another word. My steward will see to it. After all, there is hardly a back garden flower bedding for this cat to take advantage of, is there? Excuse me, please."

He disappeared to summon the steward while I surveyed the salon. It was immaculate, very military in décor including several framed pictures of old, non-military, square-masted sailing ships, a dented, old brass sextant, telescope—all the trappings of a man's room, one who has long followed the sea. Glancing in a wall mirror, I had to say, Katrina and I were definitely in a sorry state. At least she was dry, though absent shoes or boots. I still wore my rubber deck boots with wet stockings inside. The *Kaptain* returned, followed by a crewman with pail and cloth.

"He will attend to it shortly," he said, "...now, how can we make you more comfortable as the table is being set. Some dry shoes for you, possibly, *Kaptain*...and for the child?"

"Yes, it would be nice, thank you, *Kaptain*. I believe Katrina is fine, but I am in a rather sorry state."

"Certainly, *Kaptain* Andersson..." he nodded to the steward, then held up one finger halting him in mid-step and turning back to me: "Are your clothes dry?

"Yes...only my boots and stockings, Sir; they're wet."

"Excellent. If you would be so kind as to remove them, I believe—yes, here they are."

Another seaman knocked and at a word from our host, entered with a pair of gray stockings and some large shoes.

"These should serve in the meanwhile. Now…" he glanced around and finally indicated a small chair. "Sit here…"

I stepped out of my boots and peeled off the dripping socks. I draped them inside the boot-tops and handed them over, nodding my thanks. The *Kaptain* watched as I slipped on the heavy, wool stockings and shoes.

"There…are you sure you are dry? Warm…we have ample supplies?" But he went right on talking. "It must have been terrible, the night—the storm? But I must say, I envy you, *Kaptain*…small craft—braving the elements, nearly single-handedly. Reminds me of my own years before—ah, but I am about to lament these times and this war. Forgive the ramblings of an old seaman, *Kaptain*. These times, they take one so by surprise, trying to change—to keep up with the politics. It is often a trial for an old sailor, even at sea."

He'd taken our coats and piled them over another steward's arm and having removed his own, handed the bundle of garments over.

"I have a little chocolate coming for the child, *Kaptain*…Andersson. Would you care for something yourself—to…warm you up, considering it is Christmas Eve?"

"I would very much like something, *Kaptain* Mueller…anything, if you are having something also."

"But of course…please, have a seat here on the divan while the stewards prepare. I promise you *Kaptain* Andersson, it will not take but a moment and you will be on your way again, well-fed and warm. It is the least we can do for our allies, considering the times…and the weather."

I wondered why he thought Sweden was a German ally, but decided not to broach the subject. The other steward arrived with a silver tray, handed each of us a linen napkin and offered the tray containing a cup and two glasses. I took the little porcelain cup with milky-colored chocolate for Katrina; feeling its outside and deciding it wasn't too warm for her, I gave her a sip and put it on the coffee table, before I picked up one of the two glasses. The steward repeated the gesture, serving his Master, while I offered Katrina a sip of her chocolate.

"Good... good chocolate," she exclaimed, smiling at the older man.

Another point in our favor I thought, suppressing a smile. The *Kaptain* grinned, nodded and proffering his glass to me said, in Swedish: "*skål...Kaptain.*"

"Yes—*prost...*" I countered and we raised our glasses.

It was good *Schnapps* and it felt very good, once it had gone down. The *Kaptain* sighed and took a seat opposite me.

"You know, I am an old sailor, or should I say I have sailed many boats—ships, including sloops like yours. Tell me about your sloop, *Kaptain* Andersson...how does she reach on a day like today?"

"She's a little sluggish, Sir, in heavy weather, especially with water up to your ankles below decks."

He nodded enthusiastically, shifting in his seat in excitement. "You have been able to rid her of it—the water?"

"Oh yes, this morning as soon as I could. I've not had any real experience with her in high seas, before—I only purchased her in the fall, but she went well, this trip...going and coming," I hastily decided to add: "I had to do some experimenting, running under a reefed mainsail during the night and with only the jib for a while this morning, in order to take care of our needs—Katrina's and mine. She went fine in both instances"

"No doubt...no doubt. How many knots do you think you were making...just now as we came upon you?"

"I wasn't towing a log, Sir, but I would estimate ten—maybe twelve." I took another cautious sip of the *Schnapps,* worried that I'd slip up on one of his questions. They seemed innocent enough.

"Was she reefed at all?"

"Yes, one point this morning and last evening, in the storm she was also—I dared not take any risk you see—Katrina..." I said, inclining my head toward the child "...we were down to two reef points during the storm."

"Of course, of course...yes, absolutely. What kind of seas were you encountering...how did they run?"

"This morning, after the front moved through, they seemed to follow the northwesterly flow of the winds. Last evening, though,

I am unable to say…during the storm."

"What do you mean?"

"Well…" here I almost slipped up and said we'd had a collision with a ship, but instead: "…we took a broadside wave and I lost the light in the binnacle early on. I had no idea of our heading. The seas were so treacherous—the wind, snow…I had to steer purely by dead reckoning…the northeasterly wind in my face until daylight, assuming for that time that it truly was northeasterly."

"My God! What an adventure that must have been! Talk about resourcefulness—seamanship! Congratulations *Kaptain*, that is a splendid tale. I wish it could have been me. I must tell the officer's mess about it this evening. Superb…absolutely superb."

"Thank you *Kaptain* Mueller, but it was merely what one does in situations of that sort, I am sure you know that. I knew we were unlikely to strike the coast on that course. So the only real concern, other than keeping from capsizing, was striking another vessel in the darkness. Fortunately, neither occurred."

"Yes…little chance though, these times. There are few enough craft upon the sea, especially in a winter gale of that proportion. But you could have been knocked over, you know." He wagged a finger at me. "Cross-running seas—wind wrong, too much canvas carried…yes, many things could have gone badly for you *Kaptain*."

"No doubt, but fortunately, nothing did."

"Well…something apparently did," he said, turning suddenly serious. I sensed his mood had changed.

"Something, Sir…serious? I am sorry, what do you mean? Nothing serious has happened today." My heart had leaped into my throat; I was suddenly so frightened.

"Apparently something went wrong—sometime. We were glassing your sloop as we approached and notice she had taken quite a blow to her bows—banged her in rather smartly, someone did…left their mark, too. Gray paint—like…*military*, in color."

"Oh…" I hung my head smiling and feigning a sheepish smile. "Now Sir…I am afraid you must learn the truth about my seamanship."

"And that is, *Kaptain* Andersson?"

"Yes…" I tried to look embarrassed, "I ran her into a freighter…just after I bought her."

"No?"

"Unfortunately...yes Sir—I did...and in daylight, too, though it was in a fog, but that is the embarrassing part to admit."

He chuckled, the serious mood immediately erased and he was back to his doting, grandfatherly self. I silently breathed a sigh of relief.

"Really, you did not?"

"Oh yes. No question of it...and it was so humiliating...let me tell you, I will never live that down in Halmstad."

"I can understand how embarrassing it must have been for you..." he chuckled. "The pride that comes before the...you know, the collision?"

He laughed at his own pun. We were interrupted by two stewards who set about tipping the leaf up from the side of a stationary table that was bolted to the floor on one end of the salon. One steward unfolded and flung a white linen table covering and the other helped straighten it. While we watched they quickly set plates, glasses and silver on the cloth and it shortly resembled a setting in the finest restaurant.

"Would you care for another *apéritif, Kaptain?* I must be fair to warn you, we will have wine with the meal and *cognac* later, if you choose. I know you must sail your vessel, after, so you decide."

"No thank you for now...but I will certainly sample the wine and just maybe a little of the *cognac.*"

"Good." He stood with a slight groan. "We may as well be seated...ah, they have found taller seating for little Katrina...good. Please, *Kaptain*...sit here—and Katrina there, of course," he made generous gestures.

One of the stewards slipped a long-legged stool between the *Kaptain*'s and my place at the table and held it steady while I put Katrina down. He unfolded a napkin and handed it to her, grinning.

"Here, little one...thank you...I'll deal with that," I said, folding the starched white square into a triangle and putting it around her neck like a kerchief, triangle forward for a bib.

"That should keep the food off you."

Katrina picked up one of her forks. "Hungry..." she prompted, making the old *Kaptain* laugh again.

"Oh what a pleasure to have children about again. One

forgets…you know, *Kaptain* one forgets so soon in these times. And for the Holiday, too, how special."

"Yes, children certainly are a pleasure and especially this one."

The stewards returned: one guided a small trolley up beside our table. The other uncovered various dishes and handed them to his companion, quickly stowed them beneath the cart.

"I am afraid the faire is rather lowly this early in the day, *Kaptain* Andersson. The grand meal is not until tonight. Too bad you can not remain and enjoy it, but I imagine you would prefer to return to you family in Sweden. You do have family there?"

I sensed the need for caution. Was he fishing, or merely making polite conversation? "I am not certain whether the *Kapitan-leutnant* told you, but we were visiting my wife's family in Denmark. She is remaining there for the holidays to care for her old parents. They live on the east coast in Grenå?"

"How kind of her. Yes, I know Grenå…sailed past it many times, going up the estuary; quite a ways inland but nice, deep harbor."

Fear flashed a warning. I decided the truth was best. "Excuse me Sir, we must be thinking of two different towns in Denmark of the same name."

"Oh, how so?" he asked innocently as he took his napkin and spread it in his lap. "I am unaware of two."

"The Grenå, where my wife's parents live, is right on the sea, not inland, or on an estuary, at all."

"Oh…yes, so it is…so it is. I do recall now. Getting my ports confused, *Kaptain.*"

He nodded jovially as the stewards began serving us what appeared to be warmed over roast beef. I carefully breathed a sigh of relief. Seems the questions just didn't stop. I guessed then that I still had a lot more to learn about this game of espionage.

Katrina was served the beef first, then some whole potatoes followed with a brown sauce over them. She dived right in, even before I could cut it for her. There were canned vegetables, too, peas and beans. The other steward placed a glass of milk beside her plate, which she went for immediately.

"Milk!" And she was gulping and smiling at the same time.

I was served next, more than twice the portion size of Katrina's; then followed the *Kaptain*, receiving somewhat less.

Although Katrina had already begun, the *Kaptain* turned to me as the steward started to serve him. "Please *Kaptain*, do not stand upon formality…begin, by all means, begin, waste no time."

I needed no second encouragement and set about devouring the plateful. As I did, I noted the stateroom clock above the *Kaptain*'s head; the time was a little after noon. We'd been aboard the warship less than half an hour.

The *Kaptain* didn't question me any more during the meal. After Katrina had eaten what she wanted the steward returned with a small bowl of milk for the kitten. Katrina wanted to get down from her stool to help it with its milk, until the other steward appeared with a steaming Christmas pudding, changing her mind.

"Had to rush the pudding a bit," did you, the *Kaptain* chuckled? "I trust it will be up to what's left of her appetite."

The steward cut a slice that was far too large for her and the other began to spoon a thick, fruit-laden sauce on top.

"Now for the fireworks," the *Kaptain* chuckled, nodding, as the stewards trickled a little *Schnapps* on the saucer and the other man set it alight.

Katrina squealed in delight and clapped her hands as the blue flames danced around the mound of cake and fruit, much to the delight of our hosts. I had to watch her for fear she'd stick her hand in the flame. But the flame only flickered for a moment and died.

"All right, Katrina, you can eat it now, but be careful—it is hot."

As everyone watched, Katrina tasted the sauce, expectantly and smiled brightly.

"Ho-ho…it is up to her discriminating tastes," the *Kaptain* quipped.

As we watched her devour most of her serving, we had our own dished up, accompanied by coffee and *cognac*. I didn't inquire how the *Kaptain* happened to have coffee, given these times. It made me wonder whether they may have searched my bags on the sloop. There was really nothing there to incriminate us.

The *Kaptain* could have been receiving updated reports on

the sloop's contents and passengers whenever he'd ducked out earlier. At least we were being well-fed, if this was our last meal, which I strongly doubted it was. I wondered whether I should make a fuss over the pleasure of having it, but decided not to, unless he asked.

Without warning a fat man in a red and white coat strolled into the room, laughing and dancing to the sound of a button accordion and penny whistle, which also started up, around the corner. Katrina screamed in surprise, nearly falling from her stool, clapping her hands and giggling. I grabbed her arm to steady her; she wasn't a bit afraid as Father Christmas performed his antics, singing and dancing beside her. The *Kaptain* watched her with all the delight of a doting grandparent.

The crew was apparently going to give us a treat. The *Kaptain* was beaming, having stood up, snifter in hand to make more space in the stateroom. He was nodding and smiling, first at the wriggling little girl and then at me as he tipped his head from side to side in time with the music. There was hardly room in the stateroom by the time the whole assemblage of entertainers squeezed into the salon. After Father Christmas finished his dancing and song, the group stood silently for a moment and then quietly beginning to sing Silent Night. Numerous sailors, out of sight in the companionway, accompanied them with deep, rich voices and the whole warship seemed to ring with this song of peace.

I picked up Katrina and held her high, so she could see and be seen. She wiggled, kicked and clapped her hands as each song was finished and the *Kaptain* and I applauded. Finally the program came to an end and we thanked each of them profusely. Each entertainer filed past shaking my hand and then Katrina's. She treated it as a game, loving the attention even shaking some of the seamen's hands two times.

As the last crewman filed out, the *Kaptain* said:

"Still time for one more coffee, *Kaptain*? Possibly and another *cognac*?"

"As much as I would enjoy it, Sir, I believe we must be leaving, if you don't mind."

"Perfectly understandable, young man…just wish I was going with you—that I do—half a mind to go, too. However…" he smiled seriously stood up and put on his hat "…duty calls…heh—

heh...duty calls."

He strode over to the door, swung it wide and stepped aside. I gathered Katrina in my arms.

"Please..." he said waving us through, then taking the lead again in the companionway, guiding us back up through the labarynth to the topside deck. Before we went through the door and out onto the deck, I was given my boots, and a seaman's bag, which seemed extraordinarily heavy. I leaned against the companionway wall to remove my borrowed footwear. They must have cleaned house in the sloop.

"Your other things are in there, *Kaptain*," indicating the bag, "all the wet items from your boat, washed and dried. Should find them all in order, I believe." I could feel the cold of the companionway, standing just inside the outer bulkhead door. I didn't relish another night on the sloop after such a pleasant interlude. Before a seaman opened the door the *Kaptain* spoke once more.

"You will find a few extras inside the bag also, *Kaptain*. I hope you enjoy them, with our compliments."

"Thank you Sir; your hospitality is...extraordinary. Thank you again for your attention to Katrina. I certainly could not have.given her a Christmans to equal this."

"Not at all. You are very, very welcome, *Kaptain* Andersson...shall we...?" He stepped aside as the seaman opened the heavy door.

A blast of reality struck us from the northwest. Katrina ducked her head and squinted at the bright sunlight and biting wind. We followed the German through the portal and along the deck to where the ship's boat slung in readiness. I could see our little sloop tucked under the bows of the battleship. It seemed safe enough though it continued to roll with the swells, the tall mast waving.

An officer stepped up and spoke quietly in the *Kaptain*'s ear.

"Ah...*Kaptain*...one moment, please," the old man said, putting a hand on my forearm. A pang of fear rose in me again.

"The crew have been busy it seems and Seaman Heinz would like to present something to the child...a little Father Christmas spirit, it seems, from all of the men."

"Why...yes, certainly, *Kaptain*." I turned to the waiting seaman, Katrina slung in the crook of my arm. I was so relieved I could have kissed him.

"Seaman Heinz?"

He stepped forward, the same smiling youth, red in face now from embarrassment, pride and the minor gale which was blowing from the northwest.

"*Bitta...*" he said, clicking his heels and holding out a homemade rag doll to Katrina. Someone had sacrificed a new pair of stockings for its construction, adding buttons for the eyes, nose and mouth.. She looked at it and then at the seaman, wonder on her face. I stepped closer.

"Take it Katrina; it is for you. It is a doll....and say *danka*, Seaman Heinz, for the present."

She gingerly took the doll, turned it around and held it out in front of her, examining it closely. Then she kissed it on the face, roughly and clasped it to her chest smiling beautifully all around— Greta's smile. The whole ship's company roared their appreciation and applauded enthusiastically. The *Kaptain*, obviously proud of their improvised spontaneity, beamed his delight at his crew's innovation. I stepped closer to the young seaman, who was now about to burst with pride.

"Seaman Heinz...*Danka*. Katrina...please give Seaman Heinz a kiss."

She leaned way over and kissed him wetly on the cheek.

The crew roared again as the seaman Heinz pivoted around and grinned proudly at them all, pointing with one finger to the spot on his cheek where she had kissed him, turning his head from side to side so all could see, his hand still pointing.

He started to step back in ranks but then, seeming to have second thoughts, turned and yanked off his cap and handed it to Katrina.

"From Heinz...*danka*...*danka*," he said and stepped back.

"Well, the *Kaptain* said, quite a send off you are receiving *Kaptain* Andersson, quite the sendoff. It makes the official ones I receive from them rather...inconsequential, does it not?" he said smiling and extending his hand. "But never mind. Have a good journey, Sir."

"Thank you for taking an hour's interlude to brighten our

Christmas Eve, *Kaptain*. And *bon voyage*." I shook his hand and thanked him once again. I followed the *Kapitanleutnant* along the deck and we were helped into the ship's boat again for the short ride to our sloop. In five minutes we were being towed safely away from the battle cruiser by the ship's boat. I'd dashed below quickly to return our clothes and found the cabin had been done up and was far cleaner than when we'd left. They'd certainly been busy...the seamen. My luggage still lay on the top berth as I'd left it, apparently unopened.

Back on the deck again, I was soon hauling up the jib and then the mainsail, as we slowly moved away, still in tow. I'd tied Katrina to the transom seat again. In just a few minutes, I had the sails up, but not sheeted securely. Standing by the tow line on the bow, when we were well out of the wind's shadow from the warship, I waved to the boat crew who then slacked their speed. I cast off their tow line, our last link to comfort, friendliness and the potential to be captured by the enemy, from a mere slip of the tongue. I was relieved to have my tongue back aboard our sloop, still in my mouth.

Back in the stern, in the cockpit, I drew the jib and mainsheets taut, cleated them and hauled the tiller to me. After a moment, we quickly fell off the wind heeling steeply as we side-slipped. I reached across and took Katrina's arm for safety sake. Soon we were making way and gaining speed. I pointed her closer to the wind again to straighten her up, glancing at the compass occasionally. Once I looked over my shoulder toward the warship. I knew the *Kaptain's* field glasses were probably on us at that moment; he was probably filled with envy at our resuming adventure on the high seas. He would have been welcome company and an able steersman during the long night that I knew lay ahead of me.

We heard the engines of the warship pick up their deep throbbing. Her bow began to cut the water briskly. They gave us a long blast from her whistle and the crew cheered faintly, waving as they steamed away southward to a Danish capital city for a festive Christmas Day ashore.

Within half an hour it was as if they had never been, except for the food in our stomachs and the glad feeling in our hearts. Tonight was Christmas Eve and I'd forgotten. My enemy, unknowingly, had shown me he had not and for part of a day, anyway, we were simply people again, sharing an ocean and the joy of gathering together to make a child happy.

As I stared at the binnacle, watching the card rock gently on our coarse, Katrina talked to her *Jul* gift from the crew; the kitten looked neglected. She would smile at the nearly shapeless form, speak to it seriously, then smile and hug it to her and rock slightly on the seat. I daydreamed as I stared at the card, keeping the course and thinking of Greta, wondering whether she was alive and if she was, where she was? Would she find someone else? As much as it pained me to think her in another's arms, it was better that she be alive to love someone, than to have perished in the maelstrom of a burning Köln.

After an hour's steady sailing, Katrina finally grew quiet and snuggling close to me, began to nod off. I worried about her getting cold and decided to heave to for a while and see if I could find something in the way of a snack for us, before giving her a mid-day nap. By now, I was wishing I could have napped myself, while the German *Kaptain* fed Katrina and the cat. But then, I'd have missed that little celebration. Nevertheless, I was exhausted and didn't know how I would make it through a night's sailing, again. I planned to tie myself to the deck. Though she didn't complain of it, I wondered whether Katrina wasn't also rather chilly.

So I pointed the sloop, let go the tiller, undid the mainsail sleet and let her come into the wind where she remained, the main flapping, the boom rattling and the mast pitching as she dipped and dived in the swell. After a minute of observation, I decided there was no need to even drop the main. She seemed to lie well enough with just the sheet slackened. Whoever designed this craft knew their business, I thought; she had near perfect balance.

I carried Katrina below, having had to awaken her. I lay her on the bed.

"Stay awake Katrina...I'm fixing something to eat."

I began heating water for chocolate. Then I remembered the seaman's bag the *Kaptain* had given us and opened it. It was heavy as I picked up the bottom and gently tipped the contents onto the mattress.

"Look, Katrina, what the *Kaptain* gave us."

She wasn't very interested. There were tins of assorted

fish—Norwegian, something that appeared to be various kinds of tinned meats from Denmark, and a tinned Christmas pudding—English! Where did they get that, I wondered, but preferred not to think about it? But it did make my mouth water.

Three loaves of fresh-baked bread were wrapped in waxed paper bags and there was another waxed parcel containing some holiday buns with a fruit filling of some sort. There was also a bottle of *cognac* and a small box of mixed chocolates, probably intended for Katrina. I set aside the *cognac*, one of the loaves of bread, tinned sardines and a couple of the Christmas buns. I opened my own valise, extracted part of a chocolate bar to make the hot drink for Katrina and one of the coffee tins for myself, which I planned to leave out for the night. I would be making several cups well in advance to help keep me awake.

Within minutes after eating Katrina and her doll fell asleep, bun in hand. I was enjoying my third cup of coffee and the second of the rolls. The cat had knocked off even before Katrina, right after enjoying its very own, half-tin of sardines, probably its first ever taste of fish. It lay curled up on the foot of the bed, twitching in its kitten dreams. Finishing my coffee, I tucked both Katrina and the kitten in, before returning to the deck with another, large coffee, laced with some of the *cognac*. I'd wrapped it in a small towel to keep it warm, longer.

Topside and underway again, even before I glanced at the compass' card, I knew the wind hadn't changed, either in velocity, or direction. The sky was dark blue and the sun had already crossed the mid-quarter point of the horizon over my back and was well on its way to setting. I'd donned an extra sweater and half way through the coffee and cognac, unbuttoned the heavy, wool navy jacket I'd been wearing, already too warm from the effort of steering...and the *cognac*, probably.

Ater opening the binnacle and lighting and adjusting the lamp's wick, I made certain it was firmly closed before turning slowly around in my seat, scanning completely the horizon; there was no sign of life in any quarter. I settled back, put one boot up on the board brace and tucking the tiller in my arm-pit, daydreamed again, warmed by the coffee, pastry and liquor.

The past week's events flooded past. I'd had little opportunity to seriously consider them over the last few days…the coincidences of the foster grandparents, the Franks—meeting them, then the mayor and constable. I felt a twinge of guilt, wondering what had finally happened to that pair. Their kindness would never be forgotten; I wondered whether I would be able to contact any of them after the war. Probably the only way would be to return to the village; see whether they'd made it back.

Considering our brush with the *Nazi* warship, I shook my head, still in disbelief that, not only had we come through the encounter, but we'd come away with a very unlikely amount of kindness *and* some great provisions for the remainder of the trip. I supposed, in considering the events, they'd gotten more from the encounter than we—being able to demonstrate their pent-up kindness and generosity for the holiday season, on Katrina. But it was still special and something to remember with lasting gratitude.

Still…I wondered…what had happened to Greta? Certainly she was killed. How had it happened…had she suffered? Could, somehow, she still be alive? I suppressed the false hope…hope springs eternal, my grandmother always said and I'd proven that to myself more than once before I jerked myself back to reality.

Would I ever love again? Was there someone else, somewhere? Someone I could come to love as much as Greta—in that short time we'd been friends—or even longer? And would my love be returned? The heart doesn't pick and choose I reminisced, watching the white tops of the waves rolling past. Whom the heart chooses to love doesn't always reciprocate; I'd definitely control my heart with my head the next time.

"Yeah," I said aloud. "Yeah—you will, Alex. You're really strong that way."

We ran that way until after dark—tacking occasionally, generally due eastward with a little favoring of northeast to counter the sea's current. In order to check on Katrina, I slacked the tiller and main sheet twice. The second time I let the cat come back on deck, as Katrina slept on, no doubt bushed from the day in the fresh air and the party event. I was afraid the cat would awaken her if it remained below. Best if she sleeps it off, I thought, scratching the cat's fuzzy ears. It was a playful devil and didn't bite that hard as it rolled on its back kicking at me with both hind feet, trying to hold my fingers with its front paws and teeth.

It turned out to a pretty good pass-time for me. After another hour, I slacked the rig again and slid through the companionway to find Katrina sitting up on the bed, looking rather confused and crying. I knew something was wrong when she began whimpering when she saw me at first. I thought she might have had a nightmare, but when I crossed to the bed I saw how blotchy her face was. I took her in my arms, I felt her fever burning against my cheek. I held her away and looked in her eyes, bright now and slightly teary and her face was flushed. I didn't need a thermometer to reason that I had a new problem. How would I be able to care for her while steering and navigating in the dark? She should be down here, warm in bed, not bundled in the darkness with a cold wind blowing occasional spray on us.

An hour later we still weren't underway. I'd remained on the bed, after trying some hot chocolate, holding her and comforting her with what seem worthless words. Then she suddenly vomited and began chilling. I pulled on a couple of her sweaters and part of a ragged wool blanket, torn down to size for her and carried her around the cabin as I worked over the stove, heating water and some of the sausage from our German hosts. I'd started it in a little water, which boiled away quickly and the sausage had begun to fry. In a hurry, I didn't take too much care and it splattered on the little stove. I'd added water to the other burner for tea. Finally the food was done. I sliced some bread and a little cheese for us both. I'd snatched seconds while cooking to wipe up the vomit.

Katrina wasn't very hungry. She did finally drink a little of the tea. I had some, too, but it wasn't as enjoyable without sugar and anyway, I preferred coffee. Once I finished the food and tea, I added coffee water to the pan and set it to boil again. Fatigue was beginning to make my movements sluggish and I was having trouble concentrating. I would still be spending a sleepless night at the tiller, simultaneous with my child-care.

Having thought it through, I'd decided I had no other choice but to take Katrina on deck. I planned to make up a makeshift bed with some of the tarps and a torn jib-sail and wrap her in one of the oilskins packed full of blankets. She'd be warm and I could vent her when and if she became too warm. I only hoped she didn't become sick and vomit again. The seas hadn't been breaking over the cockpit area since earlier in the day, but it was now much colder.

Another half hour and I'd finished arranging the nest. I carried Katrina up quickly, well wrapped in the layers of wool and oilskins. I stowed her inside the canvas bundle; then I tied her life-line to the taff-rail behind me. The cat leaped up on the mound and Katrina pulled it inside with her. It was quite dark now.

"Stay in there *Kinder*...Papa must check the sails. I'll be right back."

I went forward where all seemed well as I felt my way along the assorted attachment points on the sails and lines. With both hands, I *looked* the jib up and down as far as I could reach, pulling and tugging on both the sheets. I moved to the main, were it attached to the mast. Each stitched canvas area appeared sound and intact.

The jib and main halyards were cleated tightly along the side of the mast and both seemed fine. Finally assured that all was well, I moved Katrina slightly, pulled the mainsheet taunt and with the tiller, hauled the sloop back on course.

From the darkness of the cockpit I talked to Katrina and the cat, trying to play with them to keep her occupied. The light from the binnacle didn't reach far enough to even illuminate my face for her and there was no gift of a flashlight in the seaman's bag from our German hosts. I wished I'd thought enough to ask them for one, thinking of the three we'd carried in the Mercedes for signaling. I considered going below instead and lighting one of the lanterns to bring topside, but decided, on second thought, that I didn't dare. We might not be so lucky the second time, if we were spotted.

Finally, around midnight, as I could best estimate, Katrina dozed off. I slacked the mainsheet, pointed the boat into the wind, picked up Katrina and the cat and went below. As the water heated on the stove, I tore a piece from the bread loaf and dipped it in the warmed-over sausage fat, remaining from our dinner. I opened a tin of beans and wolfed them down without heating them. I was hoping a full stomach would help me maintain some wakefulness for the remainder of the hours of darkness. I thought the water would never boil and with each lurch of the sloop, I suspected we were going to broach, she was wallowing so much in the darkness. The previous collision with another vessel kept me on pins and needles. We might not be so fortunate the second time. I was exhausted; the thought of having to remain awake for the rest of the night loomed. I watched the sputtering blue and yellow flame beneath the pot, aching for sleep.

Back above deck I carried my food and drink to the cockpit, checking the way the boat went, before returning below for Katrina. I was tempted to leave her sleeping on the bunk, but I didn't want her to awaken in the darkness, feverish and unable to see or hear anyone. For the first time since I'd made her acquaintance, Katrina had been really fussy. I suspected she was normally a rather placid, well-behaved and intelligent child. She simply had a pleasant disposition. I believed her curiosity contributed a great deal to that pleasant bent.

I fetched Katrina and got us both settled in the cockpit. It took a while for her to quiet down. Since she'd awakened, she moaned and cried for a few minutes before she eventually dozed again. The cat was somewhere on the deck. As the night passed, from time to time it would return to the cockpit, from who knew where, leap upon my lap for a bit of petting and scratching and then hop off, disappearing for another hour. It seemed to have completely gained its sea legs and had never had a fear of sailing.

I believed that I slept much of the long night. With daylight came a tremendous effort to remain awake, a battle I eventually lost. Each time I dozed I would be awakened when the sloop pointed into the wind, shaking and rattling the boom and mast, while I slumbered, losing the course. I would be awakened by the slamming noise of the boom and slapping mainsail. I'd yank the tiller back against me and promptly fall asleep. This process seemed to go on for days, instead of hours, as I dozed and awakened, corrected the course and then slipped off again, only to have the boat come back into the wind once again.

Finally, sometime in the gray dawn, I heard Katrina moaning inside her canvas cocoon. I leaned over and parted the layers of canvas, oilcloth and wool to find the two bright eyes peering sleepily out at me smiling the Greta smile, weak as it was. I let go the tiller, quickly bent over and picked her up, blankets and all.

"You're awake my little Greta. How beautiful you smile at me. I hope I never lose you my little darling. As long as I have your smile, I will have some of your mother."

"Kat..." she asked, looking around for the kitten. And as if on cue, the cat appeared out of nowhere, leaping onto to my lap at the sound of her voice. "*Katt—hej katt,*" she said again, giggling weakly.

"Shall we have some breakfast, Katrina...and *katt?*" I turned loose the tiller, loosened the sheets again and we were soon below with the water merrily boiling and more of the sausage frying noisily. Though I'd not had a good night's sleep, somehow, I'd slept enough that I felt refreshed in spite of the long, wakeful periods.

"Do you want some chocolate, Katrina?"

The smile was my answer. She was hungry—a good sign. Her face wasn't quite so blotchy and her fever seemed to have dropped. Sitting on the bunk, with the blanket over her like a tent, she and the cat would disappear and reappear beneath it as they played noisily, while I manned the stove. I was rushing, anxious to get back up on deck and underway again, in order to make every moment of daylight count, now that we'd gotten through the night.

I presumed we should make landfall somewhere along the Swedish coast before darkness, this day. We wouldn't know where we were but I'd hoped we might strike land where there was a port, or even encounter another vessel—preferably a friendly one—and find out where the nearest port was. From there, I'd locate a telephone and some form of transportation. I prayed we'd make landfall before dark; I didn't relish the thought of a night approach to a rocky, unlit Swedish shore.

I crumbled part of one of the chocolate bars into the cup as I thought about the best course of action, once we were ashore. In order to get back to ABA, I would have to arrange a caretaker for Katrina. I'd thought the best course still to pursue. That was where I planned to leave her until I could return, or the war ended. The latter, I knew would go on for a while yet, but I knew we were probably past the worst of it, in Europe.

And now, there was the complication of the sloop. What

was to become of it? From what I could determine by my limited exploration of her she was very sound, not that old, though left to run somewhat into neglect. The latter I thought may have been deliberate, a disguise for the smuggler to appear as unimpressive as possible to any authorities. I'd have to arrange berth space for her wherever we landed and then maybe, investigate her possible ownership. Would the sloop's registration papers indicate any information? Were there even any papers?

And did her skipper have family? Could they be found? I wanted to relinquish control of her if possible, preferably back to his family. But in the absence of family, who then, owned her...the government? Or, did I have some international right of salvage ownership, since we struck the other vessel in the night and the rightful owner was apparently lost overboard? I pondered that thought. What would I do with a forty foot sailing sloop, berthed on the west coast of Sweden, especially when I returned to North America. I really had no plans of what to do after the war. Before Greta's death...I hated to think that way, but I knew I must. I'd occasionally fantasized about marriage to Greta and living...somewhere, America or Europe, maybe Sweden?

If I moved back near my Dalarna cousins, I couldn't very well sail the sloop up the river, the Västerdalsälven. There were no lakes nearby, of sufficient size to really let her stretch out, though Lake Siljan did come to mind. But, transporting a craft of that size inland, just to putter around a lake in an ocean-going sloop, seemed silly, especially for three to four months a year before ice-up. I decided not to worry about it. I could easily sell her, I figured, if she didn't go back to any of the remaining family of the dead Norwegian *Kaptain*.

If I went back to the states, that would be the logical course of action. Funny, I hadn't thought about that subject—the states, for...how long? I had no idea. I'd come to look on the North Atlantic—*Scandinavia*, as home, for so long now. My mother was still living in America. Would she want to move? Would I? If so, where would I...*we* live? I certainly hoped to keep Katrina now that I'd had her this long. But she could have other close relatives, too— female relatives, far more able to care for her than I. Did Greta have a sister? I couldn't remember. Thinking of having to give her up later, was troubling to me.

Otherwise, I'd have to adopt her and if so, from where? What would be left of the *Third Reich* after the war? Would she be a refugee and qualify for some sort of displaced persons status. It sounded as if I'd need a little help from Clyde and his connections. Certainly he'd help us sort out our little family.

Shortly after noon it suddenly dawned on me—today was Christmas Day! In the excitement and then the fatigue, I'd completely forgotten. I didn't know what to do to celebrate, I thought, watching Katrina playing with the cat. She and I already had our presents: she, her doll from the ship's crew and me—my *cognac* from the *Kaptain*. I wondered what they were doing now, in Denmark. I guessed what the crew's celebration was probably like. And the *Kaptain*? Probably spending a quiet afternoon in his cabin, or maybe a fine hotel in downtown Copenhagen...writing letters home and enjoying a good meal.

I began singing Christmas carols to Katrina as she and the cat played together. At first she sang along with me, mimicking my words and sound, her little voice rising and falling, though she knew neither the words or the tunes. Eventually she became bored with that and later still, fell completely asleep . I drew the canvas layers tight around her. Her fever seemed to have declined, though she appeared more tired than usual. Possibly it was the sea air. I wasn't certain, though I didn't believe she was in any immediate danger.

Around two in the afternoon, I sighted what appeared to be a fishing trawler, coming downwind, directly toward us, her smoke stack was belching a long column which was being blown ahead of her. We were fortunate that she was approaching from that general direction. Had it been further west we could have missed her. Instead, it continued to steam toward us. I changed course, steering a little more into the wind, tacking toward it. Then I turned off the wind again on the tack; the setting sun should have flashed off the side of the sail. I'd hoped to attract their attention...and I did. I saw her change course. She flashed a spotlight at us a couple of times. I had no light with which to return the signal.

As she approached, I welcomed the sight of a Swedish flag

flying off her bridge; the blue field with a yellow cross blazed in the afternoon sun. I hove to, pointing the boat and slacking the main-sheet as she came around into the wind to stand off beside us. They'd came on downwind and then turned upwind to swing within hailing distance and hold position near us, out of collision range. She would also somewhat shade our wind, by her size, similar to what the battle cruiser had done and there then would be less slamming about of the rigging as we nestled in her diminished swells.

"*Hayyyy...*" a tall, bearded man in oilskins shouted through a megaphone. "Do you have trouble," he asked me in Swedish?

"*Nayyyy...*" I yelled back, through my cupped hands. "I am headed to any port in Sweden. I do not know exactly where we are. I have a small child aboard and she has been sick." I gestured to the bundle of tarpaulin and oilskins, which now began to wriggle. There was silence for a moment while they considered my message, staring down at the blond head which suddenly popped out of the oilskins.

"Where—what is our position?"

"You are about fifty kilometers south of Göteberg. Our home port is Varberg. How ill is your child?"

"She seems better today but she was feverish all night and I have not slept much for two days."

Neither of us spoke as they considered the situation. Final-ly, I asked: "How long to sail to the closest berthing?" I waited while he conversed with another man who had now joined him. This fel-low was dressed the same but appeared older. He had raised a hand and waved a greeting. Finally the first man spoke again.

"This is our *Kaptain*. He has offered to take you and the child aboard and lay out a long line to tow your sloop to our port. Do you believe she will tow safely and do you wish us to do this thing?"

I thought for a moment. That would get us safeely aboard a friendly ship, even in the event something happened to the sloop, we'd be OK. I cupped my hands again: "*Jaaaa...*" I shouted, re-lieved at the offer of assistance. "She should tow well with a long line. How long to port?"

"After we start..." he turned to the *Kaptain* again and they talked, then back to me, "...*Kaptain* says four—maybe five hours to port."

"Is there berthing space for the sloop in..." I'd forgotten the name of their home port, "...in your port?"

"*Ja...i Varberg*...have we much space for your *sagelbåt*. You can speak to the harbor master about it tomorrow if you come with us."

I looked around the sloop, happy to take them up on their offer. I needed sleep badly and might make a fatal mistake if I tried to finish the voyage by myself.

"We will come aboard, then...throw the line to me when I reach the bow and I will make it secure."

I waited as they made ready, first a thick hawser and then seeming to have second thoughts, exchanged it for a smaller line. I peeked in on Katrina. She'd nearly fallen asleep again.

"Stay here, dear. Papa will be right back. Then we will have a surprise." I went forward and a crewman dangled the line down and began to swing it so the end came within reach. After a couple of tries I caught it and pulled the slack as he let it out. I knelt on the bow and within a couple of minutes had the line secure.

I waved them away, gesturing with one hand: "Take up the slack and then I will lash the tiller." They waved and slowly began reversing against the running sea from the northwest. Hurrying to the stern, I double lashed the tiller to the rail on both sides, assured it was centered amidships, in order to steer straight and neutral. I hoped there'd be no need to come back aboard and physically steer her as she was being towed. I seriously doubted that I could be trusted to do it without falling asleep. Finally, I went below and secured the cabin area. As I was about to leave, I turned back, opened my valise and put the cognac bottle back inside and removed a partially used tin of coffee. I closed the companionway cover, went over and untied Katrina and sat her up for a moment.

"Sit here, *Kära*...for just a minute while Papa folds the tarpaulin." I rolled up her canvas tent and stuffed it in the compartment beneath the seat. The crew was suspending bumpers along side, from their deck, so as the two boats came together, there was no clash of hulls to damage either ship's sides, as they moved together to transfer us.

I thrust the kitten in her arms and picking up Katrina again, I crossed to the port side in time to catch hold of a steel ladder they had secured over their side. I just caught the bottom rung with my left foot and had a one-handed hold on an eye-level rung, when the deck of the sloop dropped away immediately and I was two feet off her deck as the two vessels rose and fell in and out of unison in the swell of the seas. Now what should I do, I thought as I held on for a moment. Finally, with my only hand on a ladder rung I turned loose and grabbed for the next rung, got it—took another step up and repeated the move three more times until someone was able to bend low enough over the ladder to take Katrina from me.

My legs were shaking as I climbed the remaining distance and swung a leg over the side. I was steadied by a mate's strong hands. The *Kaptain* was holding Katrina in one arm and talking to her while he petted the kitten. She was holding it out to him, all the while jabbering away in German.

"*Papa,*" she exclaimed as I came up to them after thanking the mate for the hand up. "*Papa...*" she said again, holding out her arms to be held.

I smiled at the *Kaptain* and took her from him. "Yes...Katrina, I am here now. Hello *Kaptain,*" I said, offering my free hand. "My name is Alex Andersson and am I pleased to see a Swedish vessel at this time of day. I didn't know if we would make it to the coast before dark, let alone find a berth for the night."

"Hello *Herr* Andersson—*Kaptain* Gustafsson at your service...welcome aboard."

"Thank you for inviting us, Sir...and for the tow." I was gently prompted as the trawler took up the slack on the tow line and gave a little sideways jerk to the trawler. They increased the revolutions on her engines and we turned and watched as the bow of our sloop came around obediently, as the cable tightened again, lifting completely from the water as the slack was taken away. More power was added and the sloop began to cut through the waves. We stood watching for a moment as a little more power was put on and again, the sloop obediently followed..

The *Kaptain* turned to me again. "I believe she will tow well, from the looks of it, *Kaptain* Andersson. You said you were in doubt of making landfall before darkness; how long have you been at sea?"

"We left the east coast of Danmark—the night before Christmas Eve...I believe."

"And you have been the sole crew for that time...?" he asked with raised eyebrows.

"Yes...the cat, the child and I."

"No wonder you are tired. The cat is a little young to be of much help, but I am not so sure about this little girl...she certainly is friendly. Was her mother not able to come along...?"

I sensed he was fishing for information—suspicious now that he'd heard her speaking German.

"Her mother was...killed in the bombing in Köln a few weeks ago. That is why I had come, first to Germany to fetch her, then escaping with her, through Danmark."

"I am sorry to learn of that *Kaptain*, please accept my condolences."

"Thank you *Kaptain*. She was Danish/German," I lied. "She had been caring for her old parents in Köln and...well, the English were bombing the city one night...need I say more?"

"Yes...it is terrible, this war. But soon it will come to an end...yes?"

"I certainly hope so, *Kaptain*."

"Please," he said bowing slightly and indicating with a flourish of his arm the door to the quarters, "Come inside now for something warm and then you both can have some sleep if you want. The crew will watch your sloop, *Kaptain* Andersson."

"Thank you *Kaptain* Gustafsson," I said and proceeded through the door. He passed me in the companionway and led the way to an assembly room that doubled as kitchen, containing a small table with four chairs.

"Please sit down. I will see what we have to eat. Will the child have something to drink...Swedish tea, possibly?" I knew he had no real tea.

"I think you will find she will eat or drink most anything, *Kaptain*, as will I. You might want to make up some of this for yourself and your crew." I handed him the opened can of coffee, still over half full.

"It is small down-payment for the tow and the food. I will not take any for fear it could keep me awake...and I very much wish to sleep."

"*Kaffe?*" he exclaimed raising his eyebrows. I hardly know what to say, *Kaptain*...where did you ever...?"

I raised one hand wearily, "Do not even ask, *Kaptain* Gustafsson...it is a long story."

"Thank you...I will see we have some of it immediately if you do not mind. Are you certain you would not like some?"

"Not at all, *Kaptain*. I will eat whatever you offer and then I must sleep quickly."

"Yes, I completely understand." He started to descend the narrow stairway but stopped, his empty hand on the rail. "You did not happen to see any debris floating...or any survivors—from a shipwreck?

"Shipwreck? *Battle*...where?"

"We are not certain...somewhere near where you must have come from. East...off Danmark. We heard about it on the wireless from another fishermen. We actually wondered, at first, whether you were carrying survivors from the battle. It took place, yesterday sometime. A large German warship was apparently bombed by the English. It went down with almost all hands, I am led to believe. Apparently the bombs hit directly on the gun powder storage. Of course there is no real news—only what we hear from other ships...fishermen's talk, mostly."

I was stunned. I wondered whether it was the Klastenaut?

"Did anyone happen to mention the name of the ship...the one that went down...the Klastenaut, possibly?"

"I do not know...it sounds familiar, but I know only that she was a very large German warship. I think it must have happened very quickly," he said and turned down the stairway.

The rhythmic throb of the engines was so soothing that I fell asleep several times while we awaited our food. Ten minutes later the mate carried up two plates of creamed potatoes and herring with thick slices of bread. Katrina and I set about devouring them. I had mine down in less than five minutes and was offered more, but my appetite wasn't what it had been when we were rescued. News of the sinking of a German ship also bothered me. So, it seemed I had developed an affinity for the enemy after seeing him up close. So often I'd wondered whether this ever happened with foot soldiers, grappling with each other from foxhole to foxhole?

Pardon me…but would you like to sit down for a moment…you see, I have this pack of cigarettes…and I'm due for a rest…I'm so tired of fighting you.

I snapped out of my reverie; I was getting tired.

"No…thank you *Kaptain*. I am too tired to eat any more. Have your coffee and do not bother any more about us."

"We have already started it boiling, thank you. We will care for Katrina, *Kaptain* Andersson, if you wish to sleep. I have a spare bed in my quarters. Come, I will show you. Do not worry about little Katrina. There are more than enough grandfathers and uncles aboard who will keep her occupied."

I followed him down the stairway to an even smaller room with a bed and a desk. As everywhere else on board, it smelled of coal smoke and fish.

What seemed like only five minutes later, I was awakened by someone repeatedly shaking my shoulder. I couldn't understand what they wanted and wished they would go away. But finally I opened my eyes and saw again the dimly lit cabin of the fishing trawler and realized where I was. The *Kaptain* was standing beside the bed with Katrina, who was holding the kitten.

"*Papa—Papa*—get up—get up. We are home," she entreated.

"Sorry to disturb you *Kaptain* Andersson. We will be in our berth in fifteen minutes. I will have the crew go aboard your sloop, if you wish, to help you with the berthing. With us, having power, it is quite easy for us."

I was dazed, my head thick with sleep and could hardly comprehend what he said to me. We must have been steaming for several hours, but it seemed only minutes.

"Yes…thank you *Kaptain*…I will go aboard—possibly, someone could watch Katrina here, until I am finished?"

"Oh, yes. I will take her until you finish tying up. I believe you can take one of the buoys just east of our moorings. If the harbor master says you must move her, it can be done tomorrow, when you can see better. We will question the harbor master and wait for you to secure her and your things Will you honor my wife and me by staying the night at our house? We have plenty of room and our house is nearly empty now with our children gone."

I accepted his offer, gratefully, still thinking of sleep. As I came on deck, he introduced me to a crewman who would be helping me with the buoy. With mostly his help, half an hour later, he and I pulled the sloop to an inboard buoy as the *Kaptain* recommended. They'd quickly secured the trawler dockside and waited while the youngest crewman and I made the sloop fast to a bouy with a chain.

Down below, as I gathered our few belongings, I noticed the sloop had taken on a little more water, undoubtedly from the water pressure against the bow while she was being towed. I reasoned that it could wait until the next day to pump out, so I secured the hatch, handed down our stuff and slipped over the side into the waiting dinghy. Then young Swedish seaman rowed us back to the trawler, already secure at her own mooring. We stowed the dinghy as they tidied the trawler in preparation to leave.

Finally, we waved goodby to the crew and in moments Katrina and I were sitting in *Kaptain* Gustafsson's ancient Volvo. In another fifteen minutes we were introduced to his wife, who noticed that I nearly fell asleep standing in the hallway. As she showed us our accommodation, she made a fuss over the child and Katrina loved having the female attention again. The *Kaptain* suggested I go immediately to bed. When Katrina felt sleepy, they said, they would put her to bed in the same room with me. Sometime later, they did just that, though I never heard a thing until the following morning.

Because the *Kaptain* and his crew had spent Christmas Day at sea, returning to their home port, their holiday celebration was a day late. As a result, Katrina and I became very fortunate guests at a sumptuous family Christmas meal, prepared by *Kaptain* Gustafsson's wife. The Gustafsson's parents and older children came home for the holiday and there was plenty of young and old family about. It also provided a day's welcome rest for me, some entertainment for Katrina and, despite the cluster of children and grandchildren, the *Kaptain* and I were able to talk a little about the Norwegian sloop and how to best deal with it. He told me he doubted it was even registered legally and any papers we might find aboard her would probably prove to be false.

"Smugglers?" He conjectured when I told him the whole

truth. "They are very elusive. You probably could own the boat simply by filing the appropriate salvage papers with the Swedish government. If no one makes a counter claim after a certain time— they publish it in the shipping papers you see...then, it is yours, after the tax of course—they must always have their tax."

I asked him about storage costs while I took Katrina to Dalarna and later when I returned to work. He assured me they would be minimal and ever the businessman, offered to arrange it himself, for a small fee, or at least go with me to assist, which of course would bring about an unwanted delay on my part. I decided to pay him the few hundred *krona* he asked to arrange it, until I could speak with my business associate (Clyde) to further establish my claim with the Swedish government.

I didn't know who to contact if the sloop's registration proved false. The Norwegian smuggler *Kaptain*'s wallet, if he'd had one, had gone over the side with him; though I'd not done a search of the sloop, there didn't apper to be any ship's papers aboard. My host promised to obtain the proper papers for my later signature. Thus, the arrangements were made with *Kaptain* Gustafsson to deal with the sloop.

The following day, Katrina and I were to board a train for Stockholm and then on to Dalarna. The *Kaptain*'s wife and daughters had come up with some surplus clothing, which fit Katrina: there was a heavy sweater, stockings, underwear, two blouses and a dressy-dress. Along with a thick winter coat, they also had packed several snacks for the day-long train ride. I could see Katrina was unhappy about leaving, so I reassured her again about all the children there would be to play with at my cousin's farm. We talked about the cows, horses and other animals she would have, too...and of course, hundreds of cats to carry around. She smiled at that thought and seemed satisfied again.

Kaptain Gustafsson drove past the harbor where *Lisskulla* was moored, on the way to the railway station, in order to take a souvenir photograph. As we drove, his wife wrote down my ABA mailing address. Down at the pier she had everyone get out of the car so she could use her camera; first, a photo of everyone huddled together and then a single shot of Katrina and me, standing with the little sloop in the background. How small it looked as it bobbed about it's buoy. It was a gray and windy day and we didn't linger after the photos. She promised to mail us a photo, once they were developed. From there we proceeded directly to the station, where I bought two tickets, hugged and kissed our hosts and straggled onto the train like a couple of derelict hobos.

Katrina showed them a long face through the train window. They stood in a long row, everyone waving and smiling brightly. The entire family came along to the station, as if we were part of their family; I felt very happy about that, for Katrina's sake. She didn't want to leave the fun children. It was bittersweet. We'd certainly come to feel like family in the short time we'd spent with them. I had also to confess to a feeling of reticence, watching the group grow smaller as the train picked up speed, carrying us home to Central Sweden.

I looked across at Katrina seated opposite me. After the overland voyage and being tossed about in the sloop, her clothing had suffered. I was sorry I hadn't taken the time to put on some of the newer clothes we'd been given by the *Kaptain*'s family. She was wearing a sort of woolen snowsuit coat with matching heavy pants that buttoned up the side of each leg. I'd struggled to get her into them, but now wondered if changing into something more feminine might improve her mood. What woman didn't like to try on clothes, I thought. There wasn't anyone seated near us on the train so I stood up and took down the little bundle they were wrapped up in brown paper tied with heavy string.

"Do you want to put on this nice dress, Katrina?"

She hadn't seen the gift items and brightened at the thought. We worked off the heavy wool coat. Five minutes later, after adding the sweater, we'd greatly improved her appearance *and* her disposition. Playing in the seat, her stocking doll continued to occupy her and she seemed already to have forgotten about her newfound friends and was enjoying her new clothes and her very first train ride.

While Katrina played with her doll and her cat, I took to making written notes about the voyage and particularly, the armament of the German warship, as I'd observed it. After half an hour, I noticed Katrina had slipped out of her sweater, warm from the train's heating and her activity in the seat. It was a pleasure to see her healthy, red face and her happy countenance once more, as she talked with her doll before explaining something in great detail to the kitten. The cat wasn't paying her enough attention so she pulled it closer—by the tail.

Staring idly at the passing countryside, I decided I should check in with ABA's office in Stockholm as quickly as I could so as to get back on the flight roster within a week's time. That was one reason for going to Stockholm before taking Katrina to Dalarna and my cousin's. I also hoped, on the off chance, there might be something in my drop from Greta, or hoping against hope that something might have been sent again via ABA. No one had known where I was off to, beyond my note telling them I'd gone. Escaping with Katrina, our extended voyage and all the circumstances surrounding our eventual arrival in Sweden hadn't gone unnoticed. I was certain they must have the ears for my whereabouts and activities up to the point of looking for the Frank's farm.

Since my duties as an unofficial employee of both the Norwegian and British government hadn't ended with this interlude to Germany and the North Atlantic, I'd have to do something with Katrina insofar as arranging a place for her. I suppose, officially, she was a war orphan. If I left it to the hands of either government, I was certain they would relinquish her to the impersonality of an orphanage for the duration of the war, or until she was adopted, by someone through their channels. That wouldn't do, of course. She was Greta's and...I almost said, *my* child. Early in our escape attempt across the water, I decided to attempt to hide her on the farm, hopefully to vanish. I planned to say nothing to *any* government about her. I knew she'd be safe enough there, happy and loved and would remain isolated from any risk or misery related to the continuing world war. These were my thoughts as I watched the Swedish countryside passing the train window.

The train arrived late in the afternoon. I questioned a cab driver about the name of a decent hotel somewhere near ABA's offices. It turned out to be a very nice hotel called the Black Crow and after we completed the check in, the desk summoned a bellman to take our luggage to the room. The aged bellman struggled with our luggage, in and out of the room, finally placing it all up on the stand beside the window. I tipped him to show our appreciation, which I think, surprised him, as tipping was not yet the custom in

Sweden.

I brushed my teeth while keeping an eye on Katrina, who was having a quick bath before we went down to supper. Stockholm had changed little with the war. There remained some Christmas window dressings to show the *Jul* season was still going. There'd been a light snowfall during the day. Out on the street we made our way to a nearby restaurant, recommended by the desk attendant.

I ordered our meal and as I enjoyed a glass of beer, Katrina had some *saft*, a refreshing Nordic drink made from *rödvinbar*—red currants, probably her first. She liked it and gave her dolly several sample sips, adding the first color to the crudely drawn face, sketched by an unknown sailor. We ate in near silence once the meal arrived and saved some of our portions for the cat. We were both tired from the journey.

Then it was back to our room, brushing our teeth and Katrina went to bed...but not before asking again about her grandmother. I don't believe she really believed the excuses I was offering by this time...she'd heard so many. But she finally snuggled into her pillow with a thoughtful look on her face. I remained sitting on her bed for a while until, after tossing and turning for a bit, her breathing became even. I moved to the desk, enjoying the freedom from responsibility at last. I made a few more notes on my recollections of the countryside in Germany, Denmark and again, of the German warship, noting the rumor the Norwegian fishing boat captain had related.

We were up early—Katrina played in the room's cavernous bathtub while I shaved. Then we dressed and went downstairs, Katrina again enjoying the ride in the elevator. After we'd finished our breakfast of croissants and currant jelly, I took the opportunity, in the lobby, to telephone the Dalarna exchange. It was at a time of day when the cousin's farm chores would likely be finished for the morning. I suspected they would be in the house lingering over their own breakfast. My cousin's wife answered on the third ring, sounding a little disinterested. She perked up when she heard my voice.

"Where have you been...Robert? We have been so worried about you? We wondered whether you had gone back to *Amerika* without telling us, for some reason." She went on for a moment or two. My contact with them had been somewhat sporadic since I'd

taken the position with ABA, so they were accustomed to my infrequent telephone calls from some distant place. Of course they had
no knowledge of my extra-curricular activities at ABA, or the Norwegian government and they simply put my extended silences down
to the erratic flight command in the RAF, unaware of the change in
employment. I'd always marveled at how this ordinary small rural
community in Sweden could be so impervious to the world war raging around them.

When she finally stopped for breath, I asked to speak with
my cousin if he wasn't in the barn. We exchanged pleasantries and I
asked about the farm's operation. Finally I broached my question.
When he learned I was coming up directly for a visit, he welcomed
me, as usual. Then I told him I would be bringing a small, female
child with me. I could tell by his voice that he was surprised, though
he asked no further questions, as was their manner. I told him I
would speak more of it when I arrived and that I knew I was asking a
very large favor of them. Furthermore, I wished to leave the child
with them, I unfolded...for a yet, unspecified length of time. He
asked to take a half-minute to tell his wife. There was only static and
the muffled sound of voices, before he came back on the line. He
said to come as soon as I could and the child was, of course, welcome, too—there was plenty to eat and enough chores to go around.

"Is she old enough to milk cows, he asked joking.

I said, "No, only old enough to get in the way."

"All right..." he laughed, "...then she will have time to grow."
He also wondered whether there was anything they should do in
preparation for Katrina, ever concerned for a guest at their home.

"No...nothing, thank you. Just treat her like your own; you
won't be sorry."

"Of course, we would do that, anyway." Then, hesitatingly,
he asked whether she was my child.

"No," I replied, "but I wish she was."

He grunted his comprehension, if not his understanding.

"She will be my daughter, if I can make her so," I added,
"after the war."

"Fine, she is welcome...come as soon as you can. We can
speak more of it then."

We chatted a minute more before I hung up, reassured that

the stage was now set, thanks to the understanding and generosity of my distant Swedish family.

Then I called the ABA office and without being specific, told them I was dropping by and arranged a time of 15:30 that afternoon. Katrina had been playing quietly with her doll in the center of the lobby while I made my calls. When I'd finished, I strolled back to the front desk, passing her and patting her head as I did.

"Is the manager in?" I asked the clerk on duty. She'd glanced up from her ledger, surprised.

"Yes Sir...he is in his office," she nervously pulled a long strand of blond hair back behind her ear.

"Would you kindly ask him if he has a moment to speak with me?"

Laying down the pen, she appeared a little startled and concerned.

"Yes...I can do that Sir, but...is there something the matter—your room...our accommodation? I can remedy any problem you may have."

"Oh—no, there is nothing wrong with the accommodations...they are fine. It is about another matter I wish to speak with him...no complaints."

She nodded and passed around behind the wall of pigeon hole boxes blooming white guest correspondence, bills and keys.

After a moment, an elderly man, slightly balding, with thin black rimed glasses, came out from a door on the side of the desk cubicle, buttoning his dark jacket as he came.

"How do you do, *Herr* Andersson...*Herr* Nilsson is my name. I am the hotel manager. How can I help you?"

We shook hands and with a wave of my arm, indicated I wished him to join me beside Katrina on one of the divans in the center of the lobby area.

After we were seated and he had chucked Katrina beneath the chin, I told *Herr* Nilsson the circumstances I found myself in...traveling alone with our child, her mother remaining in Germany with an ailing parent, I needed to conduct some business in the city. Did he know of a nursery nearby...a safe place that he could recommend, where I might leave her, without worry for a few hours...somewhere where there would be other children to occupy her.

Of course he did—a facility, he said, which came most highly recommended. He told me he would personally make the arrangements...if I would only give him the time I wished to deposit and pick up the child. I thought for a second and then gave him the times, allowing a few minutes for complications at ABA.

With a nod, he stood, motioning that I should bring Katrina and accompany him to his office. We followed him through the doorway, into the small cubicle. He indicated the only chair beside his desk before sitting down himself.

Drawing up each coat sleeve slightly, he exposed starched French cuffs with blue, stone cuff links. They didn't go unnoticed by Katrina who was now safely on my lap. She pointed to them boldly and said something I didn't catch. He smiled at her while opening one of the drawers in the desk. He removed a clean sheet of paper bearing the hotel's crest and placed it on the large blotter, nearly covering his desk. He removed a fountain pen from his breast pocket, unscrewed the cap, reversed it and poised his hand over the bare sheet in thought before looking up.

"Uhhhh...*Herr* Anderssson? A rather delicate matter, first, possibly?"

"Yes?"

"The nursery...it is operated by the Catholic Church."

"Yes?"

"This will not be a problem?"

"No...certainly not. should it be?"

"No, certainly, though some...but good,,,the Sisters, they are kind with the children, strict, but loving."

"That will be fine. It is only for a couple of hours, *Herr* Nilsson. I merely wish her to be safe and happy in my short absence."

"Yes, of course."

He slid open another drawer with his left hand and peered inside, referencing some unseen address source. Then he began to write slowly. After each sentence, he paused, examining what he'd written. Finally, he seemed satisfied and removed an envelope from one of the small, pigeonholes beside his head and addressed that, too, before screwing the cap back on the pen and returning it to his pocket. Methodically, he closed the drawer, lifted the paper by one corner and flourished it in the air above the blotter, to insure the ink had dried, smiling at Katrina as her eyes followed every movement of the paper. He folded it twice.and inserted it in the envelope. During this entire process Katrina watched his fastidious movements, fascinated. We stood up and he handed the envelope to me with a broad smile of self-satisfaction.

"Here you are *Herr* Andersson; the nursery's address is on the envelope. I will telephone the Sisters to advise them, so you may arrive at your discretion within the next hour. You will find them expecting you when you do. Please give them this envelope; it will assure them you are who you say you are. Is there anything else we can help you with?"

I said no, thanked him and shook his hand while holding Katrina's. We left the lobby, had another exciting elevator ride to our room where we prepared to leave for the school. I asked Katrina if she would like to go to play with some other children. She asked whether it was the Norwegian children we'd just left, but I told her they were new children. She thought for a minute and asked whether she could take the cat. I told her no, that it didn't want to go, but that she could take her doll. That seemed to satisfy her.

We took a taxi to the address on the envelope, which turned out to be a very impressive day nursery. The Sisters answered on my first knock, inviting us inside and taking Katrina's coat. At first Katrina was a little shy with the Sisters. I think their dark dresses impressed her as well as frightened her a little. But her fears disappeared when she saw the children. I took off my coat and sat with them while chatting with the Sister in charge, as Katrina grew a little more accustomed to the strange children. After fifteen minutes of watching them at play, I finally had to interrupt them to tell Katrina I had to leave and that I'd pick her up again, soon. She hardly glanced up from the play...just nodded and went on serving make believe tea to her new friend and their dolls. I asked the Sister at the reception desk if she could call a cab for me.

As we waited for the cab, I could hardly wait to get to the airdrome. The airline maintained a large facility at the airport, located in the north suburbs. As the cab approached the aerodrome I noticed several *swastikas* on some of the airplanes parked on the apron around the buildings. I assumed they were probably on official government missions of some sort, especially since I hadn't arrived in my usual flight schedule.

ABA's staff were very surprised to see me. I visited with the office personnel for a while before checking in with my contact. After the door was firmly shut to his office, I was told that it had been slow. We chatted for a while before I nonchalantly brought up the subject of mail. No, there was no mail for me. After I asked him whether he wouldn't mind checking again, He didn't and left the office but then returned nearly immediately, having found nothing. Though I really hadn't expected any, I was let down, nonetheless, by the absence of any communication from Greta. Why couldn't I visualize her as gone? Possibly, it was the presence of the child, bringing her mother to life in my memory, again and again each day. Each spontaneous smile and that same intent manner of staring so directly into my soul, were such strong reminders. Knowing there was still hope remaining that the letter drop down by the harbor might hold something, I finished my business and had them telephone for a taxi.

At the nursery I held the cab as I went inside to collect Katrina and settle the bill with the sisters. Twenty minutes later within three blocks of the drop location I had the cab leave us at the curb. After paying the driver I took Katrina's hand and we walked the three remaining blocks. But there was nothing there, either. Hope still springs eternal, I thought. The drop appeared totally undisturbed since the last time I'd visited it, three months previously, before going to Germany.

I was once again left completely without anything but hope and very little of that remained. Disappointed and depressed, I took Katrina's hand and we walked toward the harbor and for a while, looked at the sailboats and motor launches. But it was bitter cold and quite windy, reminding me of our recent North Sea crossing, somewhat like a bus driver's holiday—a journey I'd taken little pleasure from and now that it was over, I found little solace in staring once again at the grey seascape.

Before Katrina became chilled, I raised a passing cab and we returned to the hotel and the lonesome kitten. I'd ordered sandwiches at the desk before going up: milk and tea, sent up to the room for our late lunch, sounded good to me. Besides, I wasn't in much of a mood to be sociable at a restaurant.

After Katrina had eaten her fill, I put her down for a nap. I pulled the large chair up before the tall window facing the buildings across the avenue and sat, alternately reading and staring out on the gray, December day. It was almost the new year. I've definitely lost the one I love, I mused, letting self-pity settle into my bones. I watched the light vehicle and pedestrian traffic moving slowly along the canal and crossing the many bridges. I could see one edge of a commercial business district. The gray-green, copper roofs on many of the old buildings had lain undisturbed for years. Stockholm had not seen war for centuries. I could see a portion of *Gammalstad*...the old district.

In pre-war times restaurants and bars in this area catered to tourists and summer visitors from the north of Sweden and elsewhere in Scandinavia. But now, I imagined, international visitors were more likely to meet with bowed heads in the dark corners of back-street cafes, discussing secrets over pickled herring and *knäckebröd* as they sipped small glasses of ice-cold *aquavit*. Instead of the sights, sounds and merchandise of Stockholm, I imagined they bartered the secrets of European espionage.

Soldiers and sailors coming and going into the narrow streets were eagerly spending their meager pay on *Schnapps* and girls; or, they would be returning to their vessels with no regrets of what the leave had cost them, but dreading the duties of war that lay ahead.

After breakfast, I telephoned to reserved two seats in a compartment on Swedish Railways as far as Borlänge, in Dalarna. We returned to our room, finished packing and rode down to the lobby again where I checked us out and ordered a taxi. The train would go direct to Uppsala, change cars to Borlänge; there we would change again, taking a standard, single car for the remainder of the journey to Järna.

For some reason there was a good bit of traffic congestion and we barely made the train. The cab driver didn't seem to be in any hurry and belligerently refused to hasten his pace, even after I told him we had a train to catch. He received no tip for his absence of effort, nor did he expect one. He had his pace and was willing to pay for it.

With our tattered luggage, I was in a rush to get to our compartment. I was unaccustomed to caring for baggage and a curiously-wandering child. After we finally settled ourselves in the plain cubicle and the train began to move, Katrina went to sleep again. Something about motion and her body, I suspected. She slept well, stretched along the seat across from me, the early morning sun shining in the window. Soon, the cat was dozing beside her. The pair presented a very peaceful scene and I marveled at her child-like beauty, softly lit by the frost-shaded window. She so resembled her mother. Sitting there, staring at her soft features set me off again into my revelry of longing for what I could not have.

My daydreams were interrupted by the conductor's knock as he slid open the compartment door. As he entered, he noticed Katrina asleep, smiled putting a finger to his lips. I nodded, handing him the tickets. He made a show of punching them quietly before returning them. Nearly standing on tiptoe, he backed from the compartment with a wry smile and slid the door carefully shut. We weren't disturbed again as the train rolled smoothly along until we arrived in the station at Uppsala, where we had an hour's wait for the northbound train.

Aboard again, as it pulled out of the terminal, I watched the brown brick towers of the *Dom* slowly recede as we turned north and west. The train picked up speed and before long a different snow-covered landscape moved past the window as more and more red and white houses and outbuildings lent validation that we were traveling deeper into the land of agriculture. My thoughts turned again to Greta, wondering under what circumstances she might still live, but not be able to communicate with me. She still could be in a hospital, hurt...possibly suffering from memory loss. She could be in a coma, unconscious and unable to speak...to call to us for help...or, she could simply be dead. Why did I resist this again and again? I tried to read the paper I'd brought from the hotel, in hopes of improving my disposition, but the news was boring, mostly internal politicts.

We changed trains in Borlänge, as expected, this time riding coach. Katrina had awakened much earlier and had been playing. It was a struggle to gather our luggage, climb up the stairs, cross over the track platform and go back down again to catch the small train waiting to take us northwest. We stopped at Avesta and the other towns along the way which I remembered from driving. Soon, the track criss-crossed and passed along side the Västerdalsälven, toward the little community of Järna. Fortunately for Katrina, she'd found another child to play with and they occupied themselves in the aisle, while I read and day dreamed out the window. They seemed to be discussing the merits of her dolly.

We arrived after midday to the excited smiles of the whole family of cousins, despite that it was near milking time. It was already growing dark by this time, it being still so near the winter solstice. They sang us a Christmas carol right there on the station platform, much to Katrina's giggling delight and presented her with a red, wooden sled, with a rope handle. All of the children were still out of school for the holidays. They quickly took charge of her, absorbing her within their ranks as if she had always been there. She beamed at the attention, while I greeted my cousin and his family, receiving generous hugs from everyone.

They used Katrina's new sled to collect the luggage, along with Katrina, who was set on top for a ride to the parking lot where it all went into the car's trunk.

The car windows steamed up as we drove through the outskirts of the western Dalarna countryside, toward the farmhouse. We passed many disused hay racks, their long poles stacked neatly for the winter. Each end of the six or so long, wooden poles pointed diagonally into the sky with the other against the ground. They awaited the next hay cutting the following July, when they would be draped full to dry. I commented about what a lonely sight they made in the depth of winter. A Swede had once bragged that, since there were so many of them stacked in the fields, throughout Sweden, the *Nazis*, while flying over, mistook them for Swedish antiaircraft batteries. And that, he said, smiling, was why they never attempted an invasion of Sweden. I didn't point out the sad fact that, after all, Norway and Denmark had just as many of the "hay cannons" and their countries went down to a surprise Nazi invasion, before most of Europe.

At the farmhouse, the elderly *Farmor*—father's mother, as

she was called, was waiting with a late lunch of festive holiday food. I broke out the two remaining tins of coffee beans and the last bottle of *cognac* and the little chocolate that remained for the children. The coffee was soon steaming stoutly in the little cups and we all enjoyed the thick farm cream and a dried, fruit-filled *tårta*...layered cake, which looked so festive after our trip.

As the adults enjoyed coffee and cognac, I told them as much as I dared about Katrina, explaining about her mother and my concern that she'd probably been killed in the bombing of Köln, though without explaining my part in it. I explained that if it was discovered who Katrina really was, she would most certainly be killed if she returned to Germany. They'd not heard of the *Lebensborn* program and shook their heads in disbelief that their cousins to the south could be so cruel as to foster that sort of behavior. But they were aware of the *Nazi's* treatment of the Jews and for that reason alone, readily agreed that Katrina should remain with them for as long as necessary.

They grew fascinated with the story as I recounted our frantic race with our two companions, up through Germany and into Denmark, against the unknown authorities who were surely in close pursuit of the jovial Constable and Mayor. I was interrupted as one of the older, female cousins inquired after the fate of Katrina's foster grandparents. I told them what little I knew, I mentioned my hope against hope that the old couple would live through the war and contact me, in order to receive news of Katrina...possibly even come visit her in Sweden, if that was all right?

Every listener ringing the table nodded their approval and welcome, they said, though *Farmor* shook her head indicating in a couple words, her disbelief that they would survive.

"I have not lived to be over eighty years not to know better about men...who make war on innocents and children." There was half a moment's silence after her comment.

But as I continued with my tale of the sailing journey, their coffee grew cold in the cups as my story unfolded and I describing the feisty, Norwegian smuggler *Kaptain*. I revealed my uncertainty as to his unexpected fate in the stormy darkness. As they wondered in awe, I described the condition of the sloop, which we'd found ourselves in command of. Their eyes were wide and their mouths the shape of "O's," they were so taken by the adventure.

My cousin interrupted, saying we could go to look at the sloop, in the spring, before the planting of the crops. And *Farfar*—the old grandfather—stopped me once again to ask questions about the armaments aboard the German battle cruiser, until his wife shushed him.

"Let him tell the story," she said. "How are we to get anything out of it if you are constantly interrupting and changing the subject, speaking about weapons?"

Her husband shrugged off her criticism with a wave of his hand. But his wife soon followed suit, herself interrupting me with a question of her own, breaking in to ask about the food we were served and the type of china and silver the *Kaptain* of the German cruiser ate from.

That evening my cousin and his wife sat up with me, later than their usual bedtime, going over the journey again with me, discussing what might eventually become of the child. They were concerned that if Germany won the war, the authorities might come looking for her. I assured them on both counts that the Germans would not be victorious, so they needn't worry about their second point. Besides, we'd left absolutely no trail to follow, I said.

Time, in the pastoral environment of the farm, just seemed to fly past. My plans were initially to remain with my cousins only four days, planning on spending less and less time with Katrina, as she grew accustomed to her new family and home. However, I continued to find her personality so infectious, especially as it began to expand in her new environment at the farm with the wealth of children and boundless cats. And I too, soon settled into the routine of the farm life and ended up spending over two weeks relaxing with the family, between daily chores. Every gesture—every look of Katrina's and the increasing frequency of the sound of her laughter—everything reminded me of Greta. Katrina would come searching for me to show me some wonder she had just discovered on the farm, wanting to share her joy with her Papa. The birth of a calf was a crowning joy for her and afterward, she was permitted to give it a name. She chose *choklad* to match the little heifer's color. We all agreed, it was the perfect name.

Her little cousins, though not at all related, took her into their hearts, completely, embracing her as if she'd been born into the family. And she willingly accepted the role and was soon crawling around the haymow, between the cow's legs and trying her hand at getting in the way of the adults. Everyone worked together to get the twice-daily milkings completed in time to outdo each other at the thrice-daily meal offerings and an equal number of *fika*—coffee servings, myself in the forefront. For a few days, I nearly forgot that there was a war on outside Sweden and the part I was supposed to play in it.

Because it was midwinter, there were only the repetitive milking and cattle-related jobs to attend. But pitching the manure, cleaning the floor beneath each of the 22 brown and white cows also gave me some needed exercise. The cows were permanently confined by their neck chains in the barn with each animal secure in a stanchion of her own, until the coming spring, when they would be freed to pasture the whole night and day long, among the lush Dalarna grasses and wild flowers.

So my cousins and I had ample time to take coffee, as they were so wont to do. I attempted to discourage them from drinking the precious commodity while I was there. But they said—and truthfully so, that I liked it as much as they did, so we all may as well enjoy it until it was gone. There will be plenty more after the war is over.

With Katrina and the other children, we all took *spark* to town. *Sparkstottingar*, or *sparkar* as they were called, were kick-sleds—spark meant kick in Swedish. These long-runnered, stand-up sleds had a small, armless chair situated on the front of the runners and were propelled along the ice-packed byways by the kicker, who stood directly behind the chair, kicking the sled along with one leg. Wooden handlebars, situated atop the chair, were positioned for the kicker to hold onto. He or she stood on one of the two, long steel runners, kicking the sled along with the other leg.

My cousin, kicking with his youngest in the seat in front of him and I, with Katrina in mine, raced his two older children on their own sleds. We kicked along the narrow, snow-packed roads, around the little lake and back into the little village of Skålö, only to start all over again once we'd caught our breath, or reinforced ourselves with refreshments.

Red faced, Katrina squealed and giggled as we maintained a deliberate, side-by-side position with my cousin, carefully challenging each other from time to time, pushing ahead, only to drop back, deliberately testing each other's strength, much to the delight of the young passengers. The younger kicksledders were soon well ahead of us and would probably have lapped us had not my cousin's wife stopped them for a snack before the evening's milking.

It was with a heavy heart that I finally packed my valise, hugged everyone good bye and took the train to Stockholm. I knew Katrina was safe and at home. I longed that her mother could have been, also. She gave me a long hug and a brief kiss when I left, but she didn't cry, though I thought she might be about to.

CHAPTER
28

Freedom

I don't know how all that Allied bombing missed the prison. At first the bombers had come late—every night and then returned and bombed again each day The guards said it was Americans flying in daytime and English by night. The section of city I was able to see from my prison window, was growing more devastated with each dawning day and setting sun. I imagined, after this long duration, it must be even worse than I'd seen, earlier in the larger cities.

Lately, though, the airplanes came less and less and finally, not at all. The guards said it was because we Germans were winning. I recalled the streets of Köln and Berlin before I was imprisoned and wondered how we could be winning with so much devastation to our courntry. Then I learned the truth when, suddenly, we were freed. We weren't *officially* discharged. Early one morning a fellow prisoner from one of the floors below came strolling down the hall. She was unlocking the doors to each cell, smiling at each of us in turn, pleased by our surprise and happy to be our deliverer.

"Surely you are joking...there is hunger everywhere," she said when I asked if we were going to be fed anything that day. "There is little chance of food, since the guards and administration have taken everything of any value and fled with the impending arrival of the Allies."

Our rations in the cells had been barely adequate for the

last two months. Looking into a mirror beside the guard station, the first glimpse I'd seen of myself since my admission; I thought I must have lost nearly ten kilos. I stood staring at my visage, hardly believing the person staring back was really me. My hair had grown longer than I'd had it since I was a child and its greater length only exaggerated my now, emaciated face. I was dirty, skinny and my eyes had sunken to two, dark shadows.

Twisting from side to side, I looked sideways at myself, thinking I should smile—we were free, but I was afraid to smile. I was afraid of what I would look like in the glass, so I walked away and smiled at the blank wall to see how it felt; it felt strange.

Outside, on the street, it was early summer. I was unsure of the month but assumed it must be April, or more probably, early May. It was a beautifully sunny day. I felt the sun on my back, my arms and my face. It felt wonderful, but a bit overpowering. I thought to myself, I must find something to drink…and eat. After three or more hours of slow going along the road, I began to think I might be sick from the strength of the beautiful day.

I'd set out, attempting to walk to my Aunt Fredia's apartment. But I'd had to sit down after walking only ten minutes. It was that way all day—walk, sit and rest. Fortunately I finally caught a ride in a truck that got me quite close to her house. After I was dropped off, I struggled to walk through the remainder of the suburbs. Berlin was in a shambles around me. How would they ever repair it, I wondered. It was even worse than I expected and it seemed to grow more desolate as I walked toward my aunt's apartment.

I was unable to walk along any specific street for very long. The streets just disappeared into a gigantic heap of rubble. Most of the streets were filled with the rubble—mountains of broken bricks—the mortar still attached—stone, wire and splintered timbers and boards. Rats were everywhere, creeping on their little legs, in and out of collapsed buildings. The ruination went on—block after block…rubble heap after rubble heap. I eventually decided the avenues were better to walk along, but I had to be careful of the army trucks that sped past. Being wider, the fallen buildings had not obstructed so much of the avenues. Would it not be easier, in the end, to simply move the city, I thought and build another, rather than trying to clear the rubble heaps?

Here and there, people would suddenly emerge from a dark opening, beneath a leaning beam, surprisingly, dressed neatly and sometimes...carrying cloth bags, or business briefcases. Elsewhere, people walked among the ruination, carrying bits of odds and ends. I began to suspect all this was in order to salvage anything which could be useful, or could be sold for food and that they were probably, themselves, without homes. I began to watch for any item of value, myself, fearing soon enough that I would become one of them.

Among the broken blocks and stones, adventurous urchins played like children of the past, but now...they leaped from timber to timber, swinging, laughing, instead of frolicking on monkeybars, in neatly-manicured playgrounds. They can adjust, I thought, passing them as they shouted and laughed; they are pliable...so long as we can feed them a little. No one paid me any attention as I picked my way through the street rubble. My appearance was worse than most of them, anyway, so there was little danger of them trying to rob me of what I didn't have. What could they take, anyway?

How old would she have been? I wondered as I walked around a crushed automobile, mostly buried under the building it had been parked beside. Around four years, I guessed, not knowing what day of the month it was. She would be four and a half, if it were May.

I passed on through the destruction until I came to an avenue I thought I recognized. I wouldn't have known it, though, but for the church, still standing. Every familiar landmark around the spires was leveled. The main thoroughfares were cleared, here. It appeared the rubble had been cleared with crawler tractors with wide blades. The tumble-down destruction of buildings, which had previously lined the thoroughfare, had been pushed aside, as if by a winter snow plow. The smaller rubble pieces were neatly windrowed, right and left, with a larger pile running continuously down the center of the avenue, which had grown wider, absent the sidewalks.

Here and there a snag of a tree tried its best to welcome summer, jutting from the concrete piles and sprouting fresh green leaves from broken and twisted branches. The darkened buildings, where they still stood, lined the avenues like a jagged fence of hollow castles, here and there a turret, a buttress, or a tower. Where before there were commercial buildings, offices, brightly lit parlors with delicately-curtained bedrooms, now there stood only empty, paneless windows and walls. I couldn't bear to look at them, except to attempt to maintain the occasional landmark. Where had all the people gone, I wondered? It finally occurred to me there was nowhere for them to live. Many of them must also be dead from the bombing, or had moved away.

I was careful to avoid the traffic, growing heavier now with the morning. Most of the vehicles were American military...trucks and jeeps with a white star on the side. As a truck had stopped to wait its turn to enter the street, I heard the sound of several men laughing in the back and the sound of English being spoken. I wondered how this victor would treat those of us who had driven vehicles bearing the *swastika?*

At last, I came to an area of the city which seemed to be somewhat an island of preservation, in the melee of the bombing destruction surrounding it. My aunt Fredia's apartment lay in the middle of this block. Thank God, I thought, as I turned off the smooth pavement and began climbing over the rubble again, slipping several times. I'd already skinned my shins and ankles.

But I had to sit down once more, the third time since getting my ride. It had been six or seven hours since I'd left the prison; I'd had little water to drink and nothing to eat, but I didn't mind. I was free and it was summer...I was feeling rather reckless and carefree; unfortunately my body's stamana didn't match my mood.

When I arrived at last, I knew I wouldn't have been able to walk much further. My aunt's building was damaged, but only on one end. I walked up the three flights of stairs too tired to care now, whether she was even home. I planned to lie down in the hallway if she wasn't there and rest until she returned. I dared not even consider that she'd possibly moved away.

But she was home, though she didn't recognize me when she opened the door to my knock. She was thinner, too and I might even have had trouble recognizing her on the street, had it not been for her familiar voice. She sounded tired and the sound of children playing came from inside. They must be grandchildren, I thought, as my cousins were all grown. I could smell something cooking. It was so strong I almost vomited from the strength of the odor: cabbage and...something.

"We have no use for anything you are selling..." she said, not meeting my gaze "...and we have no money to pay you...if we did want something."

When I didn't respond at first, still choking back the nausea, she said:

"Go away...please."

I interrupted her, raising a hand, intending to speak; but I still couldn't. I tried again and uttered only a squeak, staggering as I did and grasping the door frame to steady myself. I needed to rest again.

"Here..." she said, alarmed, "come in a moment and have some water. You don't look very well...but you can not stay. We are already overfull."

She'd looked directly at me for the first time, though I could still tell that she didn't recognize me as her niece; more as a person in need. She helped me into what had been the living room. I remembered it somewhat, though there were now two beds and no sofa. The old wood sideboard was missing; probably sold for food, I thought. She guided me onto one of the beds and gently lowered me to a sitting position.

"I'll get you a drink...some water. Don't move, now...will you be all right?" she queried. I had only the strength to halfheartedly raise one hand and wave away her concern, nodding my head as she turned and left the room in the direction of the sound of children.

She returned after a moment with a chipped glass jar, which looked as if it had once held mustard. Two children poked their heads around the corner to see the thin stranger.

"Here..." she sat beside me and offering the water. I took it and with shaking hands raised it to my lips, dribbling as I drank. She raised a hand and steadied mine.

"Let me help you," she said, then hesitated. "You do not have lice, do you?"

"Gret..." I finally managed to stammer.

"What?" she replied, still somewhat disinterested.

"Greta...my name is Greta...your niece." She looked away, having misunderstood me again. "Greta...your sister's daughter...Greta...that is me, Aunt Fredia. I am Greta," I managed to say with a little more insistence.

She seemed to come awake then. "What...my sister...what did you say your name was?"

"I am Greta, your niece. Can you not remember me—your sister's daughter? I have been locked in prison by the *Nazis*, for...for a long time."

"Greta!" Obviously astonished, she raised one hand to help me with the glass again circling my waist with her other hand.

"Greta...daughter to my sister Helga...we wondered...how are you? We had not heard...so long. Oh....you know—they came—the SS men and took back all the money you gave us? We were so afraid...they said...they told us you were in trouble for the money and afterwards...we heard nothing further...nothing at all. We feared you dead from that, or, maybe from the bombing. You have been in prison, you said...whatever for...why would they put you in prison, of all people?"

I was too tired to reply and merely waved my hand wearily. Now that she recognized me, she couldn't get enough of looking at me. She sat beside me, hip to hip staring, bending at the waist and leaning round to look in my face.

"What have you done, child? Why would they put you in prison?" I saw she was weeping.

I began to cry then, too, somewhere finding the strength to utter one sob, before I could no longer summon any sound. The tears came freely, but I didn't have the energy to really weep. We just sat there with her uttering comforting words until a last I was able to speak again.

"I must lie down aunt Fredia. If I do not, I will become sick...please?"

"Of course Greta..." she stood up, concerned for my well being.

"Here Greta, let me help you. How long since you have eaten?" Taking me by the shoulders, she gently tipped me back onto the bed and then went around and lifted my legs, taking off the remnants of the shoes I'd worn from Norway, so long ago. I'd no stockings since…I could no longer even remember. I'm certain my aunt would normally have been shocked by the shoddiness of my footwear, but unknown to me, conditions in Germany had worsened to such a sorry state that ordinary citizens were no longer surprised by another's appearance, many were worse off than they were. They merely counted themselves more fortunate. I closed my eyes and though she was saying something to me, I was far too weary to expend the effort it took to concentrate enough to understand. I closed my eyes and fell immediately asleep.

I awoke early in the morning, thinking for a moment that I was still in prison. I'd remembered hearing voices from time to time during the previous evening. It must have been the rest of the family who lived with her, possibly coming home from work. She must have grandchildren in school—if they were attending school. I raised myself up on one elbow. The room was just as I remembered it. It was filled with beds—beds occupied by sleeping persons. Additionally, there were children sleeping on pallets, scattered on the floor.

I lay back, languishing in the glory of freedom in early morning light. How far down Germany had come that we are reduced to this…and conquered, besides. What shame…far better it was over, though. Now we can get on, get back to what we were before the war. However, this time, without the false dream of a Third *Reich* and all who fostered that idiotic nonsense. I thought about that as I lay there and slowly realized I was one of the idiots—one who should also be damned along with the SS…all of us who furthered that cause. Was I also responsible for the death of my daughter and her father Johan? I pondered that thought before I finally fell asleep again.

I convalesced at my Aunt Fredia's for three weeks. It was very crowded, but she had no choice. There was so much destruction to the city—everywhere. So many family, friends—neighbors, who now had no homes or apartments. My aunt was a kind person. She could turn no one out. I was too ill to be moved, even if they'd had anywhere to put me. The hospitals, the ones which remained intact, were working short staffed and tended to cater to those who could afford to pay for their care.

I slept in the same bed in the room with her youngest child,

Hylde, a girl of thirteen. She didn't mind me in her bed, she said later, smiling shyly, especially once I'd stopped crying out in the night. I wanted to get out of the apartment as soon as possible since there simply wasn't enough space for three families, her children who'd been forced to move back home to mother. That was not to mention former neighbors who'd also lost their homes. And there was little to eat. I was another mouth among many.

But I was fortunate, for one day my aunt's son-in-law told me he'd heard the Allies' occupying government were seeking Germans who could speak other languages, particularly those from eastern Europe, Polish and so forth. I also knew some English, by this time after being imprisoned with several political prisoners from various countries; English had become our universally language of communication.

I borrowed a dress and some better shoes from a cousin. The shoes were too tight. As soon as I was able, I went to the place where my aunt's son-in-law said the Allied Command had their headquarters and made an application to work. There were many other applicants, most of whom looked about as ill-dressed as I. After inching forward in the line (we started outside the office building) my turn came at last. Most of those ahead of me had been turned away, saying they would be contacted if there was interest. Listening to the exchange of conversation, I was unable to understand what they wanted from those of us in the line. The interviewer spoke excellent German as well as several other languages. It seemed the applicants in the line in front of me were encouraged to speak freely about their previous applications and tell why they thought they could qualify to work in the job which no one knew the qualifications of. There were many cubicles created by waist-high partitions in the room and each had someone in them working away at something...typing, speaking into the phone, or writing.

As I stood in the front of the line, after giving them my name and contact information, I was asked about the work I'd done prior to the war. Of course, I was a student and told them that. They wished to know what I did during the war. I was afraid to say I'd been a member of the *Nazi* political party, or employed directly by the *SS* in the Norway *Lebensborn* recruiting effort. So instead, I told the man that I worked in Norway with the occupying Norwegian

Nazi government, in the cultural division; this was the truth, at least. During this exchange an American Army officer, who'd been working in one of the cubicles nearby, apparently overheard my answers and came out to ask some questions. After a moment he invited me to come into his office, which turned out to be a real office down a hallway, filled with pictures of his family. He introduced himself as Major Osborne; I was afraid at first that they were going to arrest me and I would soon find myself in a cell again. But as soon as we were seated and he closed the door, he began asking detailed questions about my past.

I suddenly realized I was being interviewed about my role in the war, especially in Norway and not about the job application. But Major Osborn was a nice, kindly man and I felt comfortable with him. I was also very tired from the long walk and sitting down felt so good to me. The more we spoke, the more comfortable I felt and before long I'd told him a good deal about what I'd done for the *Lebensborn* project.

He was very interested and after we'd talked for fifteen minutes, he stopped me, asking whether I minded if another person joined us. I saw no reason to object and he left the room. In a moment a young woman knocked and opened the door. She smiled and placed a tray on the table beside his desk. I could smell tea and coffee and there appeared to be sugar and milk containers beside the napkins. My stomach immediately began making hunger sounds as I waited for him to return with this other person, who turned out to be another officer: a man named Colonel Anderson. I thought of Alex and wondered whether they could be related. Together, they questioned me for another hour and a half, during which we shared the contents of the tray. I couldn't decide which to have and my stomach growled so, I finally said I'd take tea, please. It was delicious.

After another two hours I was showing signs of fatigue, which Colonel Anderson noticed. He suggested we stop and have lunch and resume the interview after.

"Is that allright with you, *Fraulein* Stopff?"

"I…I did not bring…it is a long walk back to my aunt's for lunch." I was so embarrassed about lunch that I didn't know what to tell them. Of course I had no money to purchase a meal at a restaurant and we did not eat lunch at my aunt's, because there wasn't enough for anyone but the children.

"Oh...don't worry, you can eat here in the canteen. We'll get you a chit to use and it won't cost anything. Then we can continue talking after we've all had something to eat."

We went out to the lady at the reception desk, a German girl named Erika, who had obviously learned to type somewhere. The Major introduced us.

"See you back here again at 13:00, *Fräulein* Stopff."

Erika smiled at the Major and reached in a drawer, handing me a piece of paper, saying it was a free meal ticket to use to eat today with the staff in their restaurant. She said if I would wait a moment, she would go down with me, so I wouldn't have to eat with strangers. The Major smiled and left.

I hung around a few minutes before Erika finally took me downstairs where there was a sort of cafeteria set up, with a long, noisy line. She showed me where to gather a tray and eating utensils and we got in line. There was meat, bread, milk, gravy and onions. I felt surely everyone in the line could hear my stomach.

I had a very large plate and it was delicious. I could have eaten two more, easily, but would have been ashamed of the bad manners hunger had brought. Erika and I talked a little bit about how hard the times were in Berlin. She said she really enjoyed working in the office and that everybody was very kind to her, though they expected her to work very hard, since she'd come nearly three months ago.

After lunch I waited in the reception room until the Major returned and we went directly to his office. The same girl brought in coffee after a while, again with sugar. I couldn't recall how long it had been since I'd had sugar. Coffee, tea and sugar in the same day; I was in heaven. I put two spoons of it in my coffee when no one was looking, though I never took it with coffee, before...only cream.

Colonel Anderson joined us again and we talked for two more hours. Finally Colonel Anderson thanked me and left, saying he hoped he'd see me again. I didn't know what he meant and dared not ask the Major. I really wanted to ask him about Alex, but I didn't dare. Major Osborne said he thought sure I was going to get the job, but that I should come back in two days to see. He was very honest, telling me that they were going to try to check up on my story to see whether I had told them the truth, about the war and my part in it. He asked me whether I wished to change any part of my story. I told him that I did not.

I was so excited by the time I got back to my aunt's; as she prepared the evening meal, I kept chattering and getting in her way. Then, her son-in-law came home with his own great news. He told us he knew where we could get an apartment together—his family and I, if I got the job. He felt he was only a week away from a job of his own and if we moved together to this flat, we could share the rent, making it affordable and relieving Aunt Fredia of several of her unneeded tenants. She welcomed that, she said, but would regret losing the grandchildren.

The following day we both went to speak to the landlord and he promised us the flat, if we both got a job. The old man who occupied the rooms had moved to a nursing home that previous week, so we were happy. Certainly not about the old man, but we were both rather callous by that time about old age and death and felt an old man taking up that much space was redundant, terrible as it seemed.

True to my promise, two days after the the interview, I showed up at the reception area at eight in the morning. Erika, smiled a greeting.

"Hi...we're having creamed codfish for lunch today...I hope that you like it."

I thought that news was a good sign since I hadn't heard whether I was going to get the job, or another ticket for lunch. I would be very disappointed if I didn't get the job, but not getting the lunch sounded worse, somehow. I sat in the waiting room for over an hour watching the girl typing and sorting papers. From time to time Erika, smiled and nodded reassuringly toward me. Her telephone rang intermittently and when she wasn't scribbling upon a piece of paper while speaking, she was clattering away at her typewriter. I tried to take my mind off my excitement for another interview, but there wasn't much to look at in the office. Surely, I thought they wouldn't keep me here so long, only to tell me I would not be getting the job.

Yet, when the door opened and Major Osborne suddenly

breezed into the lobby, he stopped at Erika's desk to speak a few words, glancing in my direction, but otherwise totally ignored me as he continued to speak to her in hushed tones. Without giving me a second glance, let alone a smile of recognition, he turned and walked down the hallway to his office. I knew then I wouldn't get the job; why didn't he just tell me...and I would leave? I considered it and nearly stood up.

After a moment of shuffling papers on her desk and mumbling to herself, Erika leaned forward and whispered: "He's had a bad morning...I thought I should let you know," she nodded.

What should I make of that? He hadn't even acknowleged me.

Major Osborne came back down the hallway, but went through a closed door which lead to the office area where they had taken me two days previously for the interview. I was feeling very anxious; I also had to go to the toilet rather badly, by this time. I just knew the job had gone to someone else—someone more qualified and I wished they'd tell me so I could go. When I stood up Erika smiled sympathetically. I could tolerate it no longer and asked her where I might find a toilet. She pointed to an unmarked door on the opposite side of the room.

"Be certain to lock it behind you. Everyone uses it and the officers don't always knock first, hoping to catch we girls, with our dresses up and our pants down."

I smiled despite myself as I turned the long key on the inside of the door and heard the bolt roll over securely. Indeed, I will wager they probably did, too and my guess was that she teased them as much as propriety permitted, to encourage it.

I exited five minutes later, drying my hands. Erika beckoned me.

"The Major wishes to see you now. Please go right in—but knock loudly first. Remember...down the hall—last door on the right?"

I couldn't hide my nerviousness walking down the hall. I was certain now, he would tell me in his own words why I had not fit the qualifications. I stopped in front of the door that had "Maj. Osborne" painted in gold letters. I took a deep breath and knocked loudly.

I was wrong; five minutes later, I was standing before Erika, with the job. I was so excited I couldn't contain myself.

"The Major has given me the job and asked me to give you this paper." I handed her a folded piece of paper, filled in by the Major himself, as he told me the good news. It contained my salary information and other things I didn't understand.

"Wonderful…" she said, studying the list. "I knew you'd get the job. Pull over that chair and sit down while I study this."

I did and listened as she mumbled over the paper. "I'll get busy and see that we get you some of the items you will need for your office."

"My office?"

"Yes," she glanced up. "You will need a place to conduct your interviews…in private. Somewhere you can close your door and not be heard, when you choose to.

"Oh…yes, I suppose." I was a little overwhelmed by my swing of good fortune. Major Osborne had told me I would be interviewing displaced people, others…from the war. He called them DPs and I'd be questioning them about their personal experiences in the war.

"You will have a list of areas to question them about, at first, Greta," he'd said, "but eventually you'll know what to ask each person as their story comes out and you won't need to follow the list precisely."

After a week at my job my cousin's family and I were able to move out of my aunt's and into the flat. The landlord required a reference letter from our employers, mostly to prove we both had steady work. I was afraid to ask such a favor so soon after getting work and was uncertain what to do. So I asked Erika, who asked the Major, who complied without even telling me. He gave me a letter later in the day with a glowing reference, even though I'd only been in their service one week. He had Erika type it on US Occupying Force's stationary, but written in German for the landlord's sake.

"There are many families eagerly waiting to take the flat if you do not," the landlord said, when I gave him my letter. He wanted some security that we would be paying the rent, for which I couldn't blame him.

The days turned into weeks, then a month and before I knew it I'd worked nearly a year. I very much enjoyed my duties and just as I thought I might become a little bored, the Major would invite me into his office and discuss some new task that he had in mind, wondering whether I felt capable to take it on. Of course I was eager, leaping into every opportunity.

Over two years passed. All the while, I remained enthused about my position. The Major had promised an increase in salary at the end of the first year's term. We—our group, had really gotten organized and we were accomplishing a good many post war investigations. I did interviews and coordinated the information in order to make it more logical for the investigators. The Major and other officers handled these investigations, though I often sat in on some of the interrogations. Major Osborne had come to trust me and my judgement in interpreting some of the "clients" responses and would sometimes consult me about other projects he was working on...relate some incident to me and get my opinion. I always felt flattered for that. He seemed to respect me...and I, he.

As time passed, I liked the job even more. The people I interviewed varied, from common soldiers, farmers and laborers, to wealthy citizens, military officers and sometimes, government officials. There was even a bank official, once. The Americans were very interested in what he had to say about where a good deal of money and gold had disappeared to. It was in his bank for safe keeping at the end of the war, but now, wasn't. But, more and more, I dealt with the funding of Germany's portion of the war reconstruction, fostered by the Marshal Plan, something that was becoming a lifesaver for my countrymen, I soon learned. I could hardly believe what a generous enemy America had become and the part they played in encouraging other countries to help us recover our economy.

At other times, I worked with helping to discover the depth of *Nazi* Germany's moral destruction and decay, during and even before the war had begun. Major Osborne was interested in how I thought the Allies could improve the German people, psychologically and help them "...get back on their feet," as he put it.

By the beginning of my second year, around 1947, we were coordinating our offices, mostly from the point of improving the lot of the common German, getting every industry running again, continuing to provide loans, rebuilding the commercial sector…things like that. Sort of the reverse of what I had done in Norway, during the war. I still felt ashamed for my part in that. The Russians had cordoned off the East and were causing us no end of problems. Worst of all, that part of Germany was standing still, while our western sector was racing along the road to recovery with the help of the Allies.

Major Osborne was very considerate of his staff and prior to assisting him with this particular area of questioning, the Major had asked me if I had any qualms about probing my country's immediate moral past, given the circumstances of the examination and subject matter. I replied that I had none; in fact, I said, I felt it my duty. He seemed to like that answer and smiled, thanking me and saying we would soon be interviewing a different "…kettle of fish," as he'd put it But it did cause me a chill; how deep and where would they be probing?

And it wasn't long before the change-over took place. We began to question people who were involved in the concentration camps. I immediately thought of Sophia, my daughter. As the interviews progressed, I began to hear many horrible things from some of the interviewees and the written records that passed through my hands; things far worse, even, than the recruiting I'd been responsible for in Norway. This was mostly to do with life in the camps and sometimes, with the whole population of small villages in countries like Poland. I read much testimony about these atrocities and each time, after hearing some poor creature's tale of misery, I couldn't help but think of Johan's father and of course of my Sophia, who had perished in one of those places.

At one such session I was so horrified by the revelations of the candidate being interviewed that I was having difficulty translating for the others present, who included Major Osborne. The Major had been leading the questioning, through me. The candidate was a female and had been an *SS* warder in one of the camps…Poland I thought.

She'd begun telling a most horrible story about some of the experimentation conducted on the inmates, which included the children housed there, some still together with parents. The particular experiments had to do with nutrition and health studies. The woman told the tale as if she were itemizing her shopping list, telling it without a sign of remorse, or regret. She described in detail how the doctors and staff gradually reduced the diets of the children, while increasingly placing them out of doors and exposed during cold winter days. What she eventually related revealed how the children were being slowly starved and frozen to death, to study the effect of various diets on their ability to recover after a documented time of exposure. She termed it scientific study.

"When a child became too weak to be of any further use..." I related to the American participants, in translation, "...in the experiment, the child was given over to the ovens to be disposed of and another would come from the ready supply we accumulated, weekly."

"What determined their failure in the...scientific studies," one of the other officers asked me to query to her.

Her reply was immediate: "Once they could not gather the strength to walk out each morning to take their place in the laboratory line up. If they were just a little weak and had to be carried, that was usually an indication they would be replaced the following morning, so we could prepare another child in advance. We became quite efficient at it," she recounted, "the physiques of children are quite predictable, we learned." She related this accomplishment almost proudly.

"And how long did that usually take...how many hours, days—weeks?"

"Oh, every individual varied in that capacity...it might not be for several days. Sometimes, of course, they were carried out because they died first, in the middle of the experiment, often during the cold nights in the unheated barracks. The other children did the carrying then. If we happened to have siblings—you know, brothers, sisters, or one of each, they usually lasted longer, we learned. We thought that was one of the most valuable things we gained from our statistics...they seemed to make each other stronger—the pair were stronger than as individuals."

"And then?"

"Well, one or the other would die first...of course it was inevitable. If the female died first, the male would carry her out and Sophia would be given over to the ovens."

"Excuse me, Greta," the Major interrupted. "You said *Sophia* was given over to the ovens...what does she mean, *Sophia*? Is that the name of the camp section, or something—someone in the experiment, what?"

I hadn't realized what I'd been translating. My voice was beginning to crack with the stress of this particular interview and I was having difficulty with the assortment of papers I'd used for notes to write the questions and translations. My hands were trembling. I sat looking at the Major, unable to answer his question. I know my mouth was open but, for the moment, I could no longer speak.

He looked at me curiously for a few seconds, nodded and said: "Never mind...carry on, Greta, I'm sorry I interrupted."

I nodded, took a handkerchief from my case, blew my nose and continued, or tried to. I'd accidentally repeated one of the previous questions on the list I held, asking the woman what they were doing to the children.

"We were conducting empirical, scientific experiments," she replied rather irritably, "I've just told you that."

Looking over at the staff, the only thing I was able to utter back was "...they were being starved to death...the children." I was trying to say more than this—but I kept saying these same words to the Major. I found I could not stop—again, repeating the phrase to the woman, that, "...you starved them to death?" I asked this over and over again to the camp matron, the interview candidate. I couldn't stop asking her—no matter what the Major said to me, as if I was feeding from the pain her answers caused me.

Finally, Major Osborne got up from the table and walked over to where I sat beside the witness, who now sat calmly looking at *me*—staring, as if there was something wrong. By then I was crying openly and mumbling something totally incomprehensible. Gently, Major Osborne took me by the arm and said we should go out of the room for a while. To the others, he announced that they could take an extra hour for lunch. The Major walked with me into the foyer, past my office, where he had me retrieve my coat while he grabbed his own. I couldn't stop the weeping that had started. My friend Erika looked strangely at me as we passed through the foyer. Sophia's fate was all I could think of, starving, alone in the camp. That cruel woman's description had been so matter-of-fact—so lacking of any sensitivity. The little girl, without her mother, or her father...no one to offer comforting words, or sheltering arms...it was so terribly sad, what we had done in the name of *Nazism*.

Outside, the Major told me we would go to a real restaurant, newly-opened a few blocks away in the basement of a bank. We walked there in silence with the Major taking my arm now and again to guide me through the throng of office workers, out for their own lunch breaks.

Inside the restaurant after we'd removed our coats and put them on the backs of our chairs, he ordered the meal they'd prepared for that day and we chatted a little about nothing, before the woman brought two plates.

The Major ate heartily, while I picked at my food and he made small talk to keep me from being embarrassed. Finally, they brought us some tea and the Major began to question me through a smoky veil of his after-lunch pipe.

"Do you feel like telling me what happened in that interview, Greta...why you were behaving that way? Surely, we've heard enough of these atrocities that people have suffered...some, even worse, as I recall."

I considered his question for a few seconds, wanting to explain about Sophia but not knowing where to start. He waited on my words, patiently smiling. Finally I said: "I was sad."

"That's an understatement, Greta...we could see that. Was it that we have given you too much work?"

I feared for my job then and burst out. "Oh—no, please, no...it—it was not that. I like my job very much."

"OK, then, was it the woman—the subject matter...what? You've been interrogating and translating for us now for a long time. I've never seen you behave like this before."

"It was the children...the hungry, suffering, crying and—dead children...she spoke like they were...sticks or something, unfeeling." Probably because I looked and felt as if I would burst out again, he put his hand on my forearm.

"OK—please, take hold of yourself, Greta." After a moment, as I blew my nose, he asked: "Are you all right now?"

I nodded, his face a blur through a fresh flood of tears.

"I believe you should tell me a little about this, Greta. Perhaps I have misplaced you…your position…you are unhappy?"

"Oh—no! I am very happy."

"Then, for the good of our department and for your own well-being, too…" he glanced at his watch "…we have a little over an hour. Do you care to talk a little about what's bothering you?"

I blew my nose and blurted out through the wet handkerchief, shaking my head. "I couldn't help but think of my own child, Sophia, lying dead, with the other children she described, somewhere in a camp just like that one. Lying in a pile of adult bodies…we've all seen the photos…," I sobbed, "…the arms, the legs that lay over her naked little form couldn't comfort her, for all their closeness."

I saw through my tears that the Major had looked up with a slight start, leaning back in his chair. His eyes widened a little. I should have known, but I couldn't stop. I babbled on: "Did they comfort her when she was hungry? No! Was there any comfort for any of them? I am certain there was not. They…."

"You have a daughter—a daughter in the camps, Greta?" the Major patted my arm. "…had…a daughter?" he corrected himself.

I took a breath and began blurting out the story of my life with Johan. I hadn't even told my aunt this…I don't know why but it all just came out. I felt comfortable when I was around Major Osborne. I began to speak, for the first time feeling I could talk directly to him like an equal, like someone who really cared.

After an hour I'd finished my story and we sat with a third cup of tea. He'd smoked continuously and occasionally interjected a question for clarity, or to keep me on the point I was making. Then we went back to the office and he gave me the rest of the day off. He said he though I should take the time and do something to relax. And besides, he said, I'd earned it by putting so much of myself into my work and doing such a good job for the department. That made me feel a little better.

CHAPTER
29

Home Again...Almost

It was a great relief in 1945, over a year after I'd put Katrina in hiding in Dalarna, to learn the war in Europe was finally over. Of course we'd already seen it coming after we'd gone in at Normandy. Certainly, there was still the Pacific Campaign to complete, but we all knew it was just a matter of time, once the European Theater wound down and began to free up men, equipment and management resources, we would devote them to the final campaign on the other side of the world. I knew I was soon to be surplus material from that point onward.

ABA/Finnair were going to be getting into business and wanted me to stay on, with business expected to be expanding significantly. I figured there'd soon be an awful bunch of surplus pilots who'd been trained in the military, looking for work in the civilian sector, once they were mustered out. So I declined the offer, at least for the time being.

I told them I wanted some time off to sort things out for my niece in Sweden. I contacted Clyde's group and without even having to speak to him, I immediately had two months leave, with the promise to check back every fortnight or so, after that, until they got around to deciding what to do with me. ABA didn't need me yet, since there weren't enough serviceable aircraft to serve the already mounting, passenger need. I seriously suspected that I'd never return.

Scandinavia—Europe in general, held far too many sad memories for me, for the time being, anyway. I really wanted to get Katrina adopted, legally and get out of there, back to America—back home; get her safe and away from the chance of anyone ever coming back for her.

All thoughts, sounds and smells of this terrible war, I wanted far removed from us. I'd hoped to eventually forget about Greta, too and figured being back home with family and in familiar countryside—away from all the reminders, might help. I hoped to Americanize Katrina and the sooner the better. I couldn't wait to see how much Katrina'd grown.

But nearly a week later I still hadn't left Norway. Since returning from Germany, Norway was where I had mostly been based. The Germans had capitulated in Norway in May. I planned to vacate my quarters in a few days' time, heading for Sweden and Dalarna. I wanted to visit my cousin's farm for a while, let Katrina get accustomed to me once again and then head back to The States as soon as I could. I knew there'd be problems getting transport. I'd already checked in with ABA Stockholm. I thought I might be able to pilot one of the many transports heading back to The States in exchange for our rides…and my freedom, but that didn't appear too likely.

And there was no need to return to England, for that matter. When I cabled London, planning to ask Clyde about my impending discharge, I had a reply from someone else in the department. They were vaguely familiar with our operation. I was informed Clyde was on extended leave, whatever that meant. They cabled that I would only plug up the discharge procedure if I returned to London now and they didn't really want to deal with me. The processing-out of servicemen was already flooded and my discharge, or re-discharge, would be special anyway since I'd technically already been discharged before I'd taken on ABA employment. Nonetheless, I wasn't really discharged, they didn't think. They had to add this to my service record and there were more urgent matters taking precedence. So they gave me extended furlough with two week follow-ups by coded cable.

"Remain where you are, or, if you must, come here." I

could do pretty much as I pleased as long as I kept them apprised of my whereabouts on a regular basis. Possibly, I thought, Lord Whittwell would contact me, meantime.

When I'd checked with the Americans about transport back to The States, it sounded like a real hassle. Because I wasn't a British citizen, or officially in military service for the USA, I was a special problem and they had no idea what to do with me. As far as flying something back to America, they said, not in my fondest dreams. I didn't even mention Katrina. I inquired about one of the returning troop transports the Americans were sending out as fast as they could process the long-timers. He said they'd see what they could do, but not to hold my breath, if I was RAF. I might wish to consider something Canadian; otherwise, private transport, they suggested…an ocean liner or even the newly-resumed Pan Atlantic flights.

I hung around Oslo for another two weeks; I even did a couple of passenger runs for ABA out of boredom. Then, just like that, I receive pseudo-muster-out orders by cable, confirmed a few days later direct from London via airmail courier parcel. I say pseudo, since I was no longer officially in the RAF. And it wasn't Clyde who'd written the cover letter. For lack of that, I was disappointed. Why wasn't I hearing from him?

When I tried again later, this time by telephone, I was told Clyde hadn't returned from his last mission behind German lines, some time ago. He'd gone in just before the armistice was signed, it seemed and hadn't come out and no word on what'd happened. At least, they weren't telling.

"There was still a chance…" they told me, "…the prison camp occupant's listing was still very sketchy, especially for anyone taken late in the war. The Germans weren't up to their usual snuff with documenting the late internees to the camps."

That news really put a damper on the week for me. Later, the evening of my last ABA flight to Bergen, in a hotel bar, I heard a jovial Englishman talking and laughing with his friends. For some reason, that guy reminded me of Clyde. The fellow, somewhat in his cups, was joking with some Norwegian women. I thought of Clyde's easy manner with the ladies.

"Somewhere…" I'd said aloud, "…you're being a pain in

the butt for somebody...." raising my glass to my image in the bar's back-mirror, I muttered, "coward...are you ...*buddy?*" I drained my glass "...not likely." Then I went up to bed.

That same week I bought a car, an old Volvo, from a departing Swiss diplomat. The price was right, though I considered the earlier trek across Denmark and northern Germany with the Mayor and the Constable—with no small amount of affection...my last overland driving expedition. I planned to drive the Volvo back to Dalarna.

Though it was no longer wartime in Europe. I figured I'd better prepare well, not knowing the car's mechanical condition. Rationing of gasoline was still a problem. I'd *confiscated* a couple of used tins to fill and carry along for hording extra gas, when and where I could find it. I'd conned some oil from one of the ABA mechanics and one evening, beside the curb, I changed the oil in the little Volvo's engine. I replaced the water and alcohol in the radiator and, when I couldn't find anything else on it to tinker with, I set about planning my departure on paper...for the coming weekend. At my little table on a Friday evening I began laying out my course on an old roadmap the diplomat had left in the car's glove box.

I decided to head more due east into the southern third of Sweden, thinking the likelihood of obtaining gas would be higher. I considered I'd get farther toward my goal by remaining in the more populated area of the country, as long as I could, eventually swinging further northward, then back northwesterly, into the more central province of Dalarna. There were more arterial highways along this route, than driving directly across the mountains from Oslo. And I planned to stick to these routes leading to major cities, in the event of purchasing fuel and in the (hopefully) unlikely instance the Volvo decided to develop a mechanical problem. Being a Swedish car, I figured repairs could be more easily arranged and there was the availability of spare parts to consider.

Looking at the map I thought things might become pretty thin, population-wise, above the city of Borlänge, though I wasn't planning on going that far easterly. Finally, I folded the map, satisfied with the rough outline. By that evening my kit was packed and placed neatly on the floor beside the door. Nothing remained to do in the morning but lock the door and drive away. I was ready to leave Norway and my part in the war, hopefully, forever. Brushing my teeth, I got undressed and climbed into bed.

But I couldn't sleep. So I lay there, my head pillowed on interlaced fingers behind my head. thinking too much...worrying, waiting for sleep to come, but unable to stop going over the day's and week's events. I probably should've tried to fly back, somehow, but I wanted the mobility of a car after I got to the farm. I didn't know what sort of transport resources there would be, there. I'd considered hitching an airplane ride as far as Borlänge, but that might've taken a few days to get set up. I wasn't really in a hurry and I knew I'd enjoy seeing the sights from ground-level again by driving. And of course, I still thought about Greta possibly alive, somewhwere, as I did nearly every night before drifting off.

CHAPTER
30

A Note from The Past

Though I enjoyed my expanded employment position with the Allies, I continued to avoid opportunities to mix socially outside my immediate family. Erika finally gave up asking me to go out with her friends. I didn't really know why, though I wondered whether it was some sort of depression. I was also afraid someone would find out what I'd been doing during the war. Then, maybe we all feared that question. I'd gone to visit Aunt Fredia and gave her some money to help her out. I was earning far better wages than anyone in the family and all I did was save it. I didn't like hanging around my apartment on weekends with nothing much to do; a couple hours there with my aunt would do me good, since I'd not seen her for over two weeks. I'd long since moved out of that first apartment I'd shared with my cousin and his family, to one of the many new buildings going up, now that I could afford it. I found her at home, caring for three of her grandchildren, as usual. Their parents were either at their work or out seeking work. Despite our office's effort to improve employment, quite a few Germans still lacked many of the skills needed for the new jobs being created with the continued recovery, even three years after the armistice was declared.

My aunt and I spent over an hour visiting, discussing my work and the varied endeavors of her children and their families. I'd given her the envelope of *Deutchmrks* and I was growing hungry. I got up to leave, knowing she also had things to do and I didn't want her to think she had to feed me lunch.

"Greta, thanks again for the money...which reminded me...before you go...do you remember when you returned from Köln and gave us that money...before they...they kept you in that place...prison? You also carried home a box of children's clothing and left it with me. Anna found it in the attic yesterday, where I had put it away for you then."

"Oh...yes, I remember." I'd completely forgotten about that brown box on the kitchen table at the Frank's farmhouse that cold, winter day.

"Anna asked if you would mind if her daughter wore some of the dresses that did fit, until they are too small again?

"Oh...why I hadn't thought about that box...for I don't know how long." Now that she'd reminded me of the parcel, I didn't want to give it up.

"That was a long time ago. Her children's clothes are badly worn and those in the carton...they are almost new. I said I would ask you. Do you mind?"

I thought for a moment, remember again the afternoon in the Frank's kitchen. The memory and disappointment over missing Sophia came flooding back; the large, brown carton with little Sophia's sweaters and other clothing, but no child. I'd come so close to having her. My heart ached again at the memory and the thought of giving her clothes away was too much. A sudden longing overcame me. I wanted to see the clothes again, smell and touch them. Could there possibly still be a scent of Katrina remaining? Or maybe a spill from a meal long since eaten? I'd never really investigated the contents of the box, thoroughly. By chance would there be a stray hair from the darling little head? I knew I couldn't bear to part with them yet.

"Let me go through them first, Aunt Fredia—sort them out...I...I have told someone else—someone at work about them and promised them some...before you asked." After all my aunt had done for me, I felt very guilty for lying. "I should have though of

Anna's children first. How stupid of me. Let me go through them
Aunt Fredia and I'll bring some for Anna...do you think that will that
be all right?"

"Of course," she answered, absently, seeming not to give
the subject any consideration. "Just let me know, will you?"

"Yes...in fact, I could go through them tonight...may I take
them with me now, Aunt Fredia?"

"Certainly—yes, of course," she said, "I will get it down
now if you will help me. The stair to the attic is steep." We got up
and walked to the hallway between the bedrooms. "Where did you
get those clothes anyway, Greta?"

I helped her pull down the little trap door that extended
folding stairs leading up to the roof. "They belonged to a little
girl—the daughter of a very dear friend of mine, someone who died
in the camps. She was very special to me."

"Oh...how sad. I understand, Greta. But...why did you
wish to keep them, then?"

"Just...fond memories, I guess. I'll sort through them,
though and Anna won't be disappointed."

"Good. I'll tell Anna. Come...help me with the ladder and
let us get you your box. They will be home for supper soon and I
have not yet started."

I carried the box all the way home without stopping, though
I was tempted to sit down at a bench and open it on the street, take
out some of the clothes and see if there was anything remaining of
the child I never knew. But I didn't. I'd learned patience at my job
and self control.

When I got home, I took it to my room immediately, planning to open it after I'd eaten. I tried to fit it beneath my bed, but it
was too large, so I finally put it on my closet shelf and closed the
door.

I prepared my dinner as usual, knowing I had a special treat
to look forward to after I ate my bread and soup. Half an hour later,
after doing my few dishes I dried my hands, put away my apron and
went into my bedroom. I retrieved the box with Sophia's clothes. I
must stop calling her Sophia, I thought...*Katrina*. But as I placed the
fragile container on my bedspread, I rationalized, why not? She no
longer lives on this earth; I may call her anything I please. Especially,

since I never knew her as Katrina.

Opening the box after so many years in storage, made the paper crackle. It crumbled somewhat on the spread. The smell of old clothes and my aunt's attic was strong. The box had been lined with sheets of old newsprint. As if in defiance of the name Sophia, the letter "K" was embroidered into the breast of the top item, a little pink sweater. Picking it up, the odor of old wool greeted me. "K" for Katrina," I thought, unfolding the little garment and holding it up to the light. I turned it round, attempting to visualize the size of my daughter when she'd worn it.

It had been put away, unbuttoned; maybe it had just been removed by the child, folded and placed in the box by the grand-mother, that man had mentioned. I brought it slowly to my face, smothering myself with its soft, woolly feel and breathed deeply the life-before-death of my little daughter. Oh, how could I give these clothes to someone else, just when I have found them again? I knew Anna truly needed them, but my heart—it needed something too, just now...and I could buy her some new ones. I had the money...now.

Was there any scent remaining, I wondered, sniffing the sweater gingerly, some odor of a child? But I couldn't tell. I held up the sweater again examining it carefully for anything, a strand of hair, food stain...something in a pocket. Seeing nothing after a moment, I gently folded it and laid it beside the box.

A dress was the next item...linen. It had a stain in the front, but I couldn't tell from what. Someone had tried to remove it as the fabric was a little lighter in color around the stain. And it had been washed several times and now was very faded. It was a child's sum-mer jumper. There were blue and red flowers worked around the edges of the pinafore front and along the two, button-down shoul-der straps, faded, green leaves wove their course down to the button holes. Again, I examined the garment carefully, sniffed it, I thought; but I found nothing in the way of odor, different from the previous one. They all probably smelled of my aunt's attic and general age.

I removed two more items, another couple of sweaters, one red and the other, dark blue. The blue one had several short, white hairs adhering to it. Looking closely, I wondered: rabbit, I thought...maybe a cat? She'd had a pet. That meant she'd probably been happy. I smiled to myself in satisfaction and resumed my search. Out came a cream-colored, wool skirt which looked far too large for her, based on the size of the other items. This must have been a hand-me-down from someone older, accepted by the grandmother in anticipation of when Katrina would grow into it. Since she'd probably not ever worn it, I only gave it a glance before placing it on the growing pile, another candidate for my cousin's daughter. I felt somewhat guilty, coveting all the clothing.

I worked my way to the bottom of the box without finding a single sign of the child who'd worn the clothing. Only the light stain on the linen jumper indicated the clothing had ever been used. I carefully returned the garments to the box in the same order I'd removed them and closed the box, keeping the skirt aside to pass on to my aunt.

I held the skirt up once more and turned it around—examining it more closely. As I did a small piece of folded newspaper fell from within the pleats, onto the bed. I thought I saw something else—yes, it was…a strand of hair! I laid the skirt on the bed and deftly plucked the strand from within the pleats.

"Yes!" I said aloud, unable to contain my excitement. "It's a hair! Maybe it's Katrina's." I hurried over to my dressing stand and turned on the lamp, but in its feeble glow my disappointment grew. The hair was coal black and quite curly. It couldn't have been from my little daughter, blond haired like her father and me. There was little chance it could be hers. I stood there nearly crying with disappointment.

I returned to the bed and stretched out beside the pile, the disappointment of discovering nothing in the box had drained me. It could be hair from a neighbor's child—a child who played with my daughter, I thought, grasping for anything. I lay thinking about this for a bit and finally decided I would keep the strand. I wondered what to do with it. How does one keep a single strand of hair? I had no box that small; a locket would have been ideal, but I didn't have one of those, either. Then my eyes fell on the small piece of folded paper, forgotten for the moment on the bedspread.

"Yes," I said, "folded within paper the hair couldn't become lost that way. I can keep it in my bureau drawer for a while."

Gingerly I picked up the paper and went back to the dressing table. I could fold it up in the paper and press it in a book for safe-keeping. Carefully, I laid the strand onto the white, dressing table covering and began unfolding the paper and smoothing it out. There was something written on one side, but it was upside down. I reached for the hair and started to lay it in the paper. The writing appeared to be an address. With the flat of my palm I smoothed out the creases, careful not to drop the strand of hair. The handwriting appeared vaguely familiar as I stared at it, upside-down. There was a name—and an address. I carefully rotated the paper and held it toward the little bulb and read the neat old-fashioned writing. It was...in Swedish:

> *After 1 January, 1943, my address will be:*
> *Kapt. Alex Andersson & Katrina Stopff*
> *(Franks)*
> *c/o ABA Aerotransport*
> *21 Kungsvagan No. 3*
> *Bergen Norge*

Bewildered, I stared at the torn scrap.

"Now...when, or where did I write this," I said aloud. That date...January—1943? It's November of '47...I'd been out of prison since 1945—May; so that paper would be nearly four years old. No...I couldn't have written this. The A's—they were the old fashioned A's of my grandfather's time. Where had I seen this handwriting before...it is very familiar?

Then, my heart leaped! It was Alex's handwriting! This was Alex address—when he was going to be working from the Bergen office, the new flat he'd casually mentioned that time before he left. I pondered the script, holding it closer to the light. His moving to Bergen wasn't supposed to happen until after the first of the year—that last year we were together...1942—1943, was it? Oh, I can't remember anymore. It was just before I went to Köln to search for Sophia? He'd told me...when we were together the last time in Oslo in early December. Bergen, he'd said, I could reach him in the Bergen ABA office.

Then I said aloud: "Why am I getting so excited? I've merely found a piece of paper with Alex's address—so what? I've just forgotten that he gave it to me…or…?" I sat and looked at it for several minutes, still puzzled. But…where did I get it and when did I put it in the box with the clothes? I thought and thought, but I couldn't remember when he might have given me it. It had to be from Alex because of the A's. No one made A's like that anymore and I recalled remarking to him about it, once. And he was the *Kaptain* Andersson. I desperately tried to remember where I'd put the note he'd given me that night in my hotel room, after the dance demonstration, the night we'd eaten dinner together. Was it Alex's writing? That note had to have been left back in my house in Oslo, before I went to search in Germany. I wonder if someone cleaned out my things? The authorities probably found it if they searched my flat. This…it must have been sometime before he left my house in Oslo…in the fall? But it just didn't make sense. Oh…the dates…I'm very confused.

"Think…you stupid woman!" I said aloud, so frustrated that my memory was so slow. He'd also written Katrina's name? Yes—that was Katrina Franks Stopff…*my name*? Curious? I could remember nothing, sitting there. My head was so muddled. I sat on the bed for three quarters of an hour attempting in vain to fathom where I could have gotten the paper and when I could have put it in the box. The strand of hair was now forgotten, taken by the note as I was. I went into the kitchen, took some paper and a pencil and sat at the table writing down years and months during that time in Norway, trying to work out a chronology of when and where I could have obtained that note. Finally, around midnight I went to bed, agitated and confused. It seemed a long time before I finally fell asleep.

The following morning, Friday, I refolded the newspaper and put it in my purse, along with my confused chronology, before I went to work. All day I had difficulty concentrating because of it. Several times I removed the paper and examined it, hoping to inspire a lost memory. Where had I gotten it? When? Had Alex really written it? Where had he done it. The newspaper was a German paper. Was he on a flight somewhere and then had he given it to me on purpose? By accident? How had he known her real name: Katrina? Not Sophia, as I had called her at birth and told him, also. And the name, Franks; could he have known all along? Was there some sort of deception in this—which he'd known about the child from the beginning? But why—for what purpose? What was to be gained by it—how could it benefit anyone? It could only cause harm and only the child would suffer—and perish as a result of it. No—Alex wouldn't do something like that...not the Alex I'd come to know...come to love.

The next day, Saturday, I gathered up the skirt and went to visit Aunt Fredia. The walk took me nearly an hour. I could afford to take the streetcar, now, but preferred to walk, hoping the fresh air would clear my muddled thoughts and possibly bring to light some new revelation about the note.

After supper, in my aunt's sitting room, I examined the note again before showing it to her.

"Have you ever seen this before, Aunt Fredia, and if so, did you put it in the box of children's clothing I picked up last week?

She gave it only a glance. "No...I've never seen this before, Greta. I don't know these people, either."

"Please listen, Aunt Fredia, this is very important to me." She sat up straighter and raised her eyebrows, looking at me a little annoyed, as I went on, my voice shaking.

"The man...he wrote the address on the newspaper—he did not know her—Katrina—the child. *I* knew him—so I know he did not know her, at least he didn't know her real name."

"Hmmm," she mused. "You said this..." she waved the scrap of newspaper at me, "...was in the box of clothing?"

"Yes, it fell out when I was going through the box."

"That box has been here all along, since you got out...in the attic all the time. Nearly as soon as you disappeared, after...the money—I put it up there because the family began to arrive from the bombings. I had to make every inch of room available."

"Yes, I understand."

"And when Anna brought it down last week, we looked through it rather quickly and that is when she asked to borrow some of the clothes for the little ones. It could not have left this flat...honest Greta, all these years. And I certainly don't believe your cousin would put anything in the box to try to trick you."

"Oh, I believe you Aunt Fredia...but I am so confused. It

should not be. I can not imagine how he could have known the name or when he wrote it."

She was idly looking at the note, rotating it between both hands. She turned over the scrap; leaning back and holding the paper to one side so the window's light could shine on it, she squinted under her glasses.

"Well, it was after 3 December, 1943, anyway...that's what it says here, over the headline...the day the paper was printed."

"What? Here, Aunt Fredia, let me look at it!" I nearly leaped across the divan toward her. She smiled and held it out toward me, almost like a shield.

"Goodness, Greta, take the thing...you become so excited! You must learn to be calmer...you young people today."

Ignoring her, I read the newspaper's print date. I worked the mathematics out in my head. There was no mistaking it. The paper was printed on the third of December. That was three weeks before I was to go to the Frank's farm. How had a paper, printed on that date, been written on by Alex? And with my daughter's real name and his new address in Norway...in a box which I picked up and carried from the Frank's kitchen, when I left their farm, empty-handed, escorted by the village Constable.

I inhaled deeply. Could that man...the Constable, have put it in the box? Why would he? To deceive me? He couldn't also have known Alex...to come up with an address where Alex was supposed to be. I was becoming very perplexed and my aunt was looking at me strangely. I decided it would be best to leave. I could think better in my room.

"I must go home now, aunt Fredia. I must go home and think," I said. "Good bye...." And I hurried out of her little apartment leaving her sitting on her divan with her mouth open in surprise.

CHAPTER

31

The Journey, Part Way Home

Lying in my bed, about the time I was musing over the sights I expected to see on the drive to Dalarna in my new, used Volvo, I fell asleep and the next thing I knew, it was another beautiful morning, a Saturday and my last day in Oslo, at least for quite a while, I suspected. My decision to return to America with Katrina had weighed heavily, but I was resolved to break the hold the loss of her mother still had upon me. The disassociation of all that reminded me of her would help, I thought.

The Norwegian cities and the countryside we'd both come to know...the people—the overall situation of the war—all were a constant reminder of the tragic past, while I remained there. But the single association with Greta that I knew I would never be able to escape, was Katrina's smile: the image of her mother's. The month of June, 1945 was only two days away. I thought we'd remain in Dalarna for *Midsommar* and then head home to The States, as soon as we were able. I didn't care whether it was by ocean liner, passenger aircraft, or military aircraft...though there, I expected I would encounter problems if I tried to take Katrina. Probably stupid to even consider it.

After a cold breakfast, I left my keys beneath the door mat, loaded the Volvo's trunk with my few possessions and steered into the quiet street. Oslo was still sleeping, probably nursing another hang over from the continued celebration of the German capitulation.

After a couple hours on the road, the old Volvo continued to hum along for me. Each time I shifted down, negotiating turns, intersections, or sharp curves in the narrow highways, it had a snappy recovery. I had the fresh air ventilator open and the windows rolled down. I'd just begun to enjoy the southern Dalarna scenery after working my way across western and then central Sweden.

The hardwoods, covering the foothills of southern Sweden, began to turn to *tull* and *grän*, the dense, green pine and fir trees. Mostly, the large field edges were interspersed with patchy conifer forest, with birch and popular along the lakes and rivers, between the mountains.

The drive from Oslo was taking longer than I'd expected. The roads were in terrible condition. I'd spent the first night in a *stugu*, rented from a farmer. For a few more crowns, his wife had thrown in a breakfast of coarse bread, sour milk and cheese. Plain, but fresh and filling, it had left me full and satisfied the next morning, as I slid behind the wheel and fired up the Volvo. There'd been no coffee or tea and I'd considered getting a little from my stash, but decided against it. I'd save it for my cousins. I was thinking nice thoughts as the tires droned along the highway. I wondered what Katrina would look like; how much had she grown?

CHAPTER
32

More Questions Than Answers

The following Monday I went to work at the Allies Center, as usual, but my mind was trapped by the contents of the note and my wits still weren't with me. I had several interviews scheduled which I was to conduct alone, or with Erika now helping me take notes. I found myself sitting in silences more than once during the morning. I'd suddenly realized the candidate had long since answered my question and Erika was waiting for my dictation, which she'd eventually type during the coming week.

At lunchtime, I knocked on Major Osborne's office door. The absent sounding "come" told me he was busy as usual and I felt guilty about bringing him my personal problems. That he didn't even look up after I had entered and closed the door, confirmed his preoccupation with his work. I was already feeling guilty. What did Major Osborne care for my trivial problem, I thought, nearly ready to turn and leave the room.

Without even glancing in my direction, he waved a hand toward the rightmost chair, indicating I should take a seat. I paused then, ready to retreat. He must have sensed my hesitation, because he glanced up from the document we was working on. "Greta..." he smiled broadly "...hang on just a minute will you...I'm nearly finished. Sit..." he again indicated the chair with a flutter of fingers while continuing to write.

I watched him read and write notes in the margin of the document. I tried to compose what I should say about what I'd found in the box of clothing. Would he think it a waste of his time? I wished already that I'd never bothered him. Finally, he looked up again.

"There," he closed the folder and placed it in one of the wooden baskets stacked on his desk. I knew Erika picked up a pile of these and put new ones in another box each time she entered his office. It seemed his work was never ending. I felt tongue-tied sitting there, both unwilling and unable to frame my request.

"I was about to go to lunch, Greta...want to come along?" He capped his fountain pen, placed it in his uniform pocket and leaned back in his chair, smiling and waiting for me to answer.

"Oh—no...you took me to lunch last time." I stood up, flustered, ready to let him go to his meal.

"Sit down—sit down...nothing to get excited about." He looked me over, curiously. Not in a sexual way—like some of the men in the office did; but casual, intelligent. "What's going on Greta? You're not the type to come in here without a good reason. The conversation—the interviews...something troubling you?"

"No Sir, it's not that, it's...."

He looked steadily at me, waiting for me to speak. Oh, I was so frustrated with myself. I'd lost so much of my command, my presence and self-confidence in prison. Why couldn't I speak up for myself?

"Major Osborne...I wouldn't trouble you with my personal problems, but...."

He watched me and when I didn't continue, he said: "But you're about to...otherwise you wouldn't have preambled your comments that way...come on, what is it Greta? Come, out with it. Surely you can ask me. Just because I'm the boss doesn't mean you can't talk to me...are you pregnant?"

"Oh—no! Certainly not! Why...I don't even have a boyfriend."

"Ok, sorry...though I'm surprised—about no boyfriend, I mean. So...what gives...out with it?"

"Do you remember, I told you about a daughter I once had?"

"Sure I remember."

"Major, I have reason to believe my daughter may still be alive, Sir. Just the slightest hope."

"That's great news, Greta."

"I've recently learned something to give me that hope, but I don't know how to learn more from…from the lead I received. I thought, possibly you could advise me?"

Drawing up his shirt cuff he glanced at his watch, he waved toward the door. "OK, but not on an empty stomach…go get your hat…you're going to have to come to lunch with me, or I won't be able to hear your news for a couple of weeks. I have to leave in an hour for Hamburg, so we have to talk now, or not at all…ok?"

When I just stood looking at him, he waved one hand impatiently, indicating the door and began putting folders in drawers. I nodded and hurried from his office, hearing the jingle of keys as he locked his desk.

We nearly ran to the restaurant. He was carrying a briefcase, a small suitcase and his raincoat. He repeated again that he had to leave as soon as lunch was finished. Ten minutes later, sitting at a table, the Major knew everything I knew about the box of Katrina's clothing, the note, plus the story of Alex and my relationship. Major Osborne took notes in a little book as we ate our roast pork and potatoes. I'd totally lost my shyness. Major Osborne had seen to that. He managed to convey his complete concentration on my story and seemed genuinely concerned.

"If I weren't a married man, Greta, I'd be a very disappointed man right now, learning you had another boyfriend—and an American at that."

I smiled, embarrassed by the compliment.

"You know you are a very attractive woman and could easily have any number of dates with any officer in Berlin. *But…?*" he smiled, leaning back and putting out his pipe and filled it.

"I have chosen no one, Major, because of…the past."

He was quiet for a little while, sketching some invisible design on the tablecloth with the end of his pipe stem.

"I think I often guessed about your love life, Greta, but no one in the office ever mentioned a suitor and you never did, either. You aren't exactly the most informative person in the office, but now…I understand why, somewhat."

He pulled up his sleeve again, glancing at his wristwatch he continued on a serious note:

"This is important to you and I think we can help...try, at least."

"Thank you, Major Osborne."

"I'll get started making inquiries, Greta, in some of the foreign services as well as our own people. I have enough from the information you gave me...let's start there.

I was nearly crying again, but this time, for joy.

"Thank you again, Major; I'm...I don't know how to thank you."

"Don't worry about it...sorry to leave you here, but I must run. They won't hold the plane for a mere major. Can you find your own way back to the office, all right?"

"Certainly...thank you so much for hearing me out. I didn't know who else to turn to again."

"You did exactly right, Greta." He patted his breast pocket containing the little book. "Let me call some people—see what I can learn. I should know something in a couple weeks. I'll be back in the office mid-next week. If I hear anything meanwhile, I'll shout. Ok?"

With that, he grabbed his valise and giving me a snappy little one-fingered salute, turned on his heel and was gone. As I picked up my purse I saw that he'd left two banknotes on the table; he'd paid again. I'd try to figure out some way to repay him. Maybe I could somehow get some meat from someone in a rural area. I could have him home for dinner...no, better as a guest with my aunt or cousin's family. He was a married man. As I walked back to the office, I thought about how lonely the Major must be with his family still in America.

Major Osborne got back when he said he would, but I still didn't hear anything from him for over a week; I'd begun to wonder whether he'd forgotten. I was mistaken. After another week passed, on a Friday, just before the staff left to go home, Major Osborne stuck his head in my office:

"Hi Greta. How have you been?"

I glanced up, startled. The Major never came to me; he usually sent any correspondence or requests through Erika.

"Oh...hello Major." I answered, surprised. "I'm well, thank you."

"I have some news for you...from our discussion. Can you stop in my office before you go home?"

"Oh...yes, definitely!" I stammered, still half standing from when he'd surprised me.

"Good...see you after a while then," he said, as if what he had to tell me was just another routine piece of news about the office. I could hardly stand it, but I waited until I thought most of the other staff had left for the day. Picking up my coat and purse I walked to his office and knocked at the door.

"Come in...."

I opened the door. He was as always, working over the inevitable pile of brown paper folders. I was reminded of the first time I'd gone in, nervous, concerned that he was going to tell me that I wasn't going to get the job. I was about to sit down when he stood up.

"Hi Greta."

I opened the door, thinking we were leaving his office.

"No—no...please sit down...I'm just coming around to your side. It's easier from the other chair," he said, picking up a stack of folders and taking the chair beside me. From the first folder he pulled out several papers and placed them on the desktop. He opened the first document, sat down, hitched his chair closer and bending over the paper, began reading, following the paragraph with one finger.

"Hummm...let's see now...several items have come up from our inquiry, Greta..." he paged through a few sheets "...where to start? For one thing, let me tell you up front that we have found absolutely no evidence of your daughter yet, I'm sorry to say."

I know that," I shuddered visibly, "I don't know that I really expected you would, Major."

"Don't yet despair, we've found your American-Swede, whatever he is—well, we've found evidence of him, anyway."

"Alex...oh that's good news. Where is he, Major?"

"Well, that's what we still don't know. We've only found

where he's been."

He watched me for a moment. I was pensive, digesting what he had just said. Two blows at once. After I'd lost all hope, he'd given me hope by inviting me to his office only to dash the hope again.

I bravely smiled to let him know the disappointment wasn't too bad, though a tear trickled from one eye.

"You OK, Greta? Don't be too disappointed, yet...but don't get your hopes too high, either. We're just beginning this...and who knows what will turn up...could be good, or it could be bad."

I nodded and sat up straighter. "I understand, Sir."

"Listen..." He opened another paper and explained what and who he had asked information of and what he had learned, little as it was.

"We sent an inquiry to our service officer in Bergen...the last known address...the one you'd shown me on the newspaper."

I nodded, waiting.

"There was a record that he'd lived there for a while, then Oslo...there, for the duration of the war in Europe. He bought a car from a vacating diplomat and left for points unknown, just after the armistice. The landlord remembered him, because your Alex used to give the guy black market stuff from time to time...coffee, chocolate, you know?"

"Yes Sir, that sounds like Alex...he's—he was, very generous."

"This says..." he turned over the typewritten document "...that your Alex lived alone, no children...not even a girlfriend."

He glanced up at me again. "There's no sign of any children before, during, or after his stay in Norway. Sorry, Greta."

"Did they have any idea where he'd gone...in the automobile, train...?"

"No...no one knew."

I sat watching him shuffle yet another document from the pile. It was like a card game of chance. He was dealing my hand, card-by-card. But my hand didn't look too promising. I remained silent, knowing he had more to tell.

"Then we checked the Finnish airline ABB Aerotransport, they also call it ABA."

"Yes, that's what Alex called it. He was a pilot for them, flying all over northern Europe."

"Right…that's what we learned. But we also ran him through American Intelligence people. They turned up an RAF connection…Royal Air Force…British?" Did you know he'd been in the RAF, Greta?"

"The Royal Air Force…no…not at all. He never said anything about that and he didn't have a military uniform that I ever saw…only the one for the airline—ABA. How could he have been? Was it after I left him?"

"We don't know for sure. The RAF is keeping the lid on that pot. We only know he'd been in the British Armed Forces and most probably the RAF, as a fighter pilot."

I didn't give that strange revelation much thought, instead, wanting him to get to the place that had some good news—something I could base some hope on. Then it dawned on me and with dread, I asked my question, thinking the Major might be trying to protect me.

"Was he killed in the RAF, Major…in a fighter airplane?"

"No…no, nothing like that—at least not that we know of. There's no record and that's what is making this so damn difficult. We also suspect there's some of the spooks involved here…military intelligence, secrets, spys and all that. But they're not talkin'. Do you know anything about that, Greta—anything that could shed some light on this new knowledge?"

"No Sir, nothing."

He commenced to shuffling the folders again.

"When did he leave Bergen, Major..or Oslo? Do you know what time period…month? Year?" He returned to a previous paper. I shook my head in disbelief. "Yeah…looks like…more than four years ago…nearly five, best I can figure out from this."

We sat in silence as he read and re-read some of the documents.

Major Osborne glanced up, sympathetic: "We're not finished with this yet, Greta. There're still a couple of things to poke into here. We checked ABA Aerotransport's office in Helsinki and Stockholm. Seems he did a lot of correspondence with their Swedish office, though we didn't learn what it was about. Do you have any idea why there...some Swedish connection, somehow?"

"Yes!" I suddenly remembered. "He had relatives in Sweden from...one of his parents, I can't remember which side. He visited them occasionally I think and could speak Swedish well, though in an old fashioned dialect."

The Major made some notes.

"That's something new, at least; so we might follow that lead...see where it goes, the Sweden one." He made a note in the margin. "They offered him a job—ABA, to work for them, flying, after the war when things got back to normal. First news they had was he said OK, but wanted some time off. Later...don't know for sure when, he told them no dice. He was leaving the country."

My disappointment was plain; I was slumping again. "The country...Norway."

"Right. Not a good deal to go on, you know, Greta? Still—it's something."

Major Osborne thought for a little while longer; I squirmed anxiously. "We could try to connect him back from our end...take some time? Do you happen to know where he came from in The States...what state...area of the country?"

"No, I'm sorry. I doubt he ever told me that and I don't know enough about America to have picked up on anything either."

"Do you happen to know if Alex Andersson was his real name?"

"Real...name...how—why...I never had any reason to doubt it wasn't? Why would he have a different name...just, being a pilot?"

"Our folks seem to think there's more of a connection to MI5, or something of that ilk,, the spooks...as I said...intelligence sector,"

"I...I don't know. It never entered my mind to think he might be a spy. Does this mean we'll probably never locate him...or my daughter?"

"No...not necessarily Greta—don't jump to conclusions. It's not over yet. Just a cold trail. We'll pick it up again."

"Oh...I'm so frightened of what you will find now, Major?"

Staring at the paper in his hand, with the other hand, the Major rolled his pen around between his fingers like some people did cigars.

"We haven't hit bottom, yet. We still have the ABA thing. Seems to be the closest thing we have." Looking up and grinning at me, he added. "We'll stay with it, Greta. For a while, yet, we'll hang in there."

He stood up then, stuffing the papers back into the folder. "On the Sweden connecton...I'll keep you informed, when and if anything else comes back...Ok?"

"Yes...thank you, Sir." I stood, turning toward the door. As I turned to close the door to his office, Major Osborne was returning to his side of the desk, still reading from the sheath of papers he was carrying.

I walked out of the office feeling very let down, but still, thinking about this strange new news about Alex: a spy...I never suspected a thing. He must have been very good at it...a professional, I thought, admiring his skill but feeling a little hurt for his deception. But it wouldn't make a difference to me, if they were to find him again.

CHAPTER
33

The News Grows Worse

It wasn't Alex's real name. A month later the Major stopped by my office and asked me to stop in after work. They'd gotten new information about Alex.

"I don't have time to go into it right now, Greta, but stop by after everyone's left; I'll have more time then and we'll have privacy. I can tell you this though; I think it's good news, but still not all the news you're waiting for."

I hardly knew what to expect after the first, seeming failure the Major had reported. I'd not given the first meeting much further thought, trying not to get my hopes up. As my duties had increased with the occupation work, the Major's and my interaction had increased in proportion. I felt the Major had come to depend on me more, also, as he now brought me in on more and more special client interviews. We'd developed a good, professional working relationship. I both liked and trusted him and I believe he felt the same about me. There was none of the sexual harassment I experienced from some of the other men, married and otherwise, in the office. We would sometimes speak of his family back home in America when a new letter or photo arrived and he always spoke kindly of his wife. He would show me the new photographs of her with the family, when the letters from home came. He was very proud of them and I usually listened to some story for several moments about them, before going back to work.

After he stopped by I couldn't keep my mind on my work. I certainly didn't earn all my wages the rest of the day. I was in a trance until, shortly after five, I crept into the hallway and peeked into the foyer. Erika's desk was neat, the chair pushed up against the front and her typewriter wore a green oilcloth covering. I could hear voices in the hallway, but they disappeared at the sound of the entrance door closing. It appeared that nearly everyone had left for the day. Though the Major's door was closed when I tip-toed down the hallway I could hear him speaking on the telephone with someone. I waited in the foyer for a few moments and then went back down the hall again. All was quiet within and after listening for a moment I gingerly knocked on the closed door.

At the muffled, "Come..." I turned the knob and walked in. I had my tablet and pen, as was my habit. I didn't know what the Major would have to say, but wished to be prepared, in any event.

"Hi Greta...everyone gone?"

"Yes, Sir, it appears so; nearly everyone anyway. I listened and it's pretty quiet."

"Good....have a chair will you. I've got only one more letter to read and sign and then we can talk."

He turned his attention back to the document he was holding. He'd turned his chair slightly and it squeaked as he leaned back, crossing one ankle over the other knee. He idly scanned the document, fiddling with his pen and occasionally tapping his teeth. I studied his profile. He wasn't a handsome man. I'd noticed this before, but he had a pleasant face. His hair wasn't graying yet but some color change was appearing in his moustache, which was thin and close-cropped. He was a young major...probably in his late thirties, or early forties...older than Alex, I reasoned. The photograph of his wife was sitting in a frame on the table behind his desk; I could only see the side of it. I envied him his family, even though they were a great distance away and he didn't get to see them as much as he wanted. At least they were there—waiting for him when he finished his business with the postwar work and the processing of information he had to deal with. And he did go home twice a year for visits.

There was a recent rumor our office could be taking on new duties and growing significantly in size. Major Osborne had held a meeting of all the staff and informed us there would be more responsibility and additional staff to train and supervise. I would have been excited by the news but for the other news I so anxiously awaited.

Major Osborne finally sat up abruptly, leaned over his blotter and signed the letter. He slid it into one of the boxes, separating us.

"Erika can handle this now," he said, "so..." he unlocked the top right desk door and removed a small, brown portfolio "...let's see what they have for us, shall we?"

He'd smiled broadly at me as he stood and came around to my side of the desk again. He took the other chair and sat down, placing the white papers on the desk in front of us. My hands were trembling when I opened my notebook and removed the cover from my pen.

"Hmmm..." the Major made noise and muttered as he read. He turned the first page, scanned the second, turned to the third, his lips moving.

"Well, Greta, it appears we have come to the end."

I sat looking at him, waiting for him to go on—explain further. I couldn't believe he would call me in, make me wait all day and then tell me this.

He glanced up and his expression changed when he saw the disappointment in my face. I looked down, knowing now it wasn't good news. I replaced the pen's cap and sat back, calmly expectant.

"Yes, Major, you were saying?"

"We've gone about as far as we can go, Greta. The story goes on, of course, but its classified information. Even Colonel Martin can't get at it...I asked him to try, as a personal favor, but it didn't work."

He paused and looked at me as if to see how I was taking the unpleasant news.

"Yes, Major?"

I thought he might say something else, but he went on: "It's the *Brits*—they've got a lid on it—hocus-pocus stuff—he was a spy, Greta...your Alex, but for the *Brits*. Regular RAF in the

early part of the war, I understand, but later on undercover assignment for espionage in Scandinavia."

"I understand, but what does it mean, Sir...is it final?"

"Basically, it means the files are sealed—that we can't get a
look at them, they won't give us anything more. We're not gonna'
find him, Greta, if he's still alive and it sounds like he was at the end
of the war. Only way now would be if he looked you up, now the
war's over. Or, if the Brits someday declassify the information."

"Is there no one...anyone who can look in the records and
just find the information we need...not tell us the secrets?"

"Afraid not, Greta...I'm sorry."

I left his office with a heavy heart that day and my depression returned.

Less than a year after his final attempt to help me find my
daughter and Alex, Major Osborne was transferred...up the ladder,
as the Americans say, promoted to colonel, not long after our disap-
pointing conversation. He moved somewhere else in Germany. He
was able to go home, first, for which I told him I was happy for him.

His replacement joined the operation within the month, but
we were never as close as I was with Major Osborne, probably because he'd hired me from the start. And after a year, I didn't know
where *Colonel* Osborne had gone; he was transferred once again.

I soon received a good promotion, myself and was kept
very busy, having several staff of my own. And eventually, I just gave
up on the search for my child, believing I'd never get the answers. I
did fanaticize for many years after, of special ways I would someday
encounter Alex, or Alex and Katrina. Of course, I never did and as
the years went by, I was pretty certain I never would.

CHAPTER

34

Dalarna Again and Home

A couple of hours after crossing the Norwegian border, I was driving into Dalarna; I paralleled the Daläven...the river made up of the eastern and western forks of the Dalälven. At the community of Floda I crossed the river and began following the north shore of that branch, the Västerdalsälven, the western fork. The highway paralleling the river would take me all the way to my cousin's farm. His land straddled the clear-flowing, rock-stream stream where our ancestors had floated boats and timber for centuries.

Farther up stream at Vansbro, beyond my cousin's, the Vanån river struck the Västerdalsälven. And upstream from there, where the Van widened, becoming slow-flowing and flat for several miles, its western bank sheltered *Vansberget*, the *fäbod*—animal place—of my ancestors. My grandmother had been conceived there. Pristine and isolated, the tiny log houses and outbuildings sheltered the women, children and grandmothers, every summer, as they exercised the timeless job of caring for the cattle and goats. Each spring, migrating to this wonderland, they grazed animals on birch leaves, marsh and meadow hay—any bit of nourishment which might produce butter and cheese from the milk.

Several hours walk north of the farm,.I knew Katrina might

be there, with the women, now. I could hardly wait to see it all again. I very much needed the pastoral lifestyle, I'd seen too much war...too much destruction. The humdrum routine of the twice-daily milking, with time in between for a cup of coffee and a snack, sounded wonderful to me. Katrina would already have experienced at least one summer in the *fäbod* and this summer would be her second, if they were there. They were probably filling her head with fairy tales...ancient folklore stories of *troll* and invisible *vitra*-people and *Rånda* and *Näken*—all the imaginary forest spirits. I imagined her eyes growing wide as she heard the folklore images come to life before an open fireplace. The old women would take such pleasure in painting a picture for her of how the long-gowned *Rånda*, the mysterious woman of the forest, with the tail of a fox, would suddenly appear and steal a young girl's cows, when she wasn't watching them. Or of *Näken*, the beautiful, young man who played his fiddle, standing naked, in the middle of the stream...playing it so well, it was said, once you heard his music, you could never stop dancing.

These musings made the miles pass quickly, at least until the last hour. By then I was very anxious to see my adopted daughter. All during the drive I regretted only one thing and I couldn't get the smile of her mother, out of my mind.

I finally made the turn onto the winding, gravel drive, up to the farmhouse. It was late in the afternoon. They were already in the barn doing the evening's milking and didn't hear me drive up. I was obliged to close the car door carefully least I pinch any one of curious cats and kittens in the car door that greeted me. Their tail's, like tall flagstaffs, waved and twitched as they wound their way around my ankles, rubbing and meowing to be petted. I wondered whether Katrina's cat was somewhere around, as I walked over to the open barn door and stepped into the dim interior.

The midsummer sun remained high, but inside the barn I had difficulty seeing what I could only hear around me. There came the lowing of a cow, calling for her wayward calf. Here and there a cow shook her head, rattling the neck-stanchion's chains. A nearby cow blew loudly through her nostrils, probably having just caught my strange scent. I could hear children yelling somewhere, above the sound of running water. Someone shouted a question from the other end of the barn, asking for instruction about how many pails of water to put...somewhere. And nearby I heard my cousin Lisa answer, hidden from sight, probably sandwiched between two cows as she sat on a wooden milk stool. Outside, a team of horses passed the barnyard, pulling some wheeled vehicle with iron rims on the gravel drive. I glanced around as a wagon rattled and grated across the road, the horse's trace chains jingled in time to the clip-clop of hooves.

I leaned against the cool fieldstone wall, mindless of my city clothes, letting my eyes grow accustomed to the dimness. I heard a milk stool scrape on the floor, the clank of the heavy lid being removed from a milk can and the sound of a full pail being emptied. Someone began whistling a tuneless *schottische* and a milk can lid clunked down, the bail-handle on a pail rattled again and someone spoke kindly to a cow named Cherry. There was the scrape of the milk stool again and the process continued, on to the next cow in line. A door further down the barn alley from where I stood, groaned open. In the rectangle of bright sunlight I saw the silhouette of a cat run in, followed quickly by a young girl trotting behind. She bent toward the cat, holding out her hand.

"*Katt...katt! Kom nu lilla kattor,*" I heard her calling as the kitten ran along the aisle ahead of her. She chased it farther into the barn, talking all the while. Behind her four or five more cats, tails in the air, followed within easy reach. Katrina was taller than I'd expected she'd be and her dress hardly met her knees. Her legs were thin as pipe stems and her bare feet slapped the cement as she pursued the cat. Her arms were lanky as she bent to tease the cat with a piece of straw, trying to tempt it nearer. Finally, she seemed to lose interest, straightening and turning my way. Seeing me leaning against the wall she stopped abruptly and stared for a moment before she suddenly leaped down the aisle toward me.

"*Papa!*" she screamed, "*...Papa—Papa...*you've come, you've come home...you've come *home...!*"

Her skinny arms and legs pumped like pistons, her body barely contained by the faded dress. Cats scattered like ten-pins as she came, full speed down the aisle, mindless of the fresh manure littering the cement walkway. When she was fifty feet away I stepped away from the wall and bent to face her, arms outstretched. She leaped into my waiting arms.

"*Papa*—oh...*Papa*...you have come to see me at last," she said in Swedish, throwing her lanky arms around my neck and kissing me squarely on the cheek. I crushed her bony body to me, already blinded by tears. Two years hadn't dampened her ardor. She smelled like hay and milk and her breath was fresh and child like...sweet against my neck.

At last I held her out to have a closer look. She brushed her nose with the back of a dirty hand. Her blond hair was straggly and appeared not to have been combed that day. Here and there a wisp of hay bristled from it. But she was clean—except for her feet, though I barely noticed when I turned her around, still without putting her down. Her eyes sparkled blue with yellow highlights as she took in my features. Her little teeth were even, white and shiney.

"Why are you crying, Papa?" she asked.

Before I could answer, a milk stool had scraped farther along the aisle and Lisa stepped from between two cows peering down the aisle toward us, no doubt wondering what the excitement was about.

"Oh...*you* are here—today...already." She put a steadying hand on the nearest cow's hip and stepped over the manure gutter, weighed down by a bucket of milk in her other hand. "We did not hear you come...*Välkomna...har*! It is so good to see you again," she laughed jovially.

I walked over and attempted to put my free arm around her to hug and kiss her in greeting.

"*Nay*...I am dirty—wait—wait!..." she said, laughing and giggling, "...you will make me spill the milk!"

"You are not that dirty," I said, managing a lop-sided hug as she twisted away shyly.

"Have you seen Olle yet, or did you just come in? He is with the horses...somewhere."

My daughter answered for me. "*Farbro* was in the field, plowing...I know, I just saw him come past with the horses."

She'd called my cousin Olle, *Farbro*, father's brother—uncle, in deference to me, her Papa.

"Uncle...you call Olle uncle, *Liskulla?*

"*Jå*..." Lisa answered, "...we thought it...appropriate."

I nodded. "Thank you, Lisa. I think she's right...somebody

did just came past with a team and wagon."

Giving Katrina another squeeze, I said, "You have grown so much Katrina...I can hardly believe it."

"Yes and I can run fast, too...so fast the calves can not keep up—watch!" She squirmed to be put down and as I complied, Lisa chuckled.

"I do not believe they want to keep up with you, Katrina, you torment them so much."

Already tired of the adult conversation and so excited, Katrina was off like a shot along the aisle, excited and eager to prove how fast she could run, screaming all the way, scattering cats in every direction and frightening the cows in their stanchions. Here and there a cow turned her head nervously, wondering what was happening.

"Most of the cows are now accustomed to that little blond head speeding behind them...you see her go?" Lisa said. "The cows hardly glance at her...they are now so used to this whirlwind you have brought us."

We both watched Katrina's antics for a while. "Ah...we love her so...it will be like losing one of my own, when you take her to *Amerika*."

Katrina disappeared between two cows who continued leisurely chewing their hay, hardly giving her a glance as she squeezed between their bulging midsections.

"The animals love her and she loves them...well, when she is not teasing them. She seems to be afraid of nothing. The moose and fox do not come around as much now, since she has come. And the bears...we have not seen one in years. They are afraid of this one, I think."

We laughed to watch her as she emerged from between another pair of cows, further down the aisle, beginning her antics again to show off for me.

And so it went. My early summer return let me settle slowly into life at the farm. Thinking we might leave a couple of weeks after my arrival, summer somehow turned into fall. There'd been the first haying and an extra field hand was always welcome to hang the hay on the *häsja*...the horizontal drying poles. There was no shortage of food at the farm. Most everything they needed, they supplied themselves. We still found coffee difficult to obtain. Our sugar had to come from the several bee hives, scattered around the pasture edges, along the river and beside the apple orchard. When I wasn't helping with the farm work Katrina and I went everywhere together, exploring the surrounding mountains, lakes, forests and the streams. We fished a good deal at first, until mid-July, when the blueberries ripened. Then our fingers were blue-stained for weeks, picking pail-after-pail for Lisa, who canned them for the winter. Later came the oat harvest, followed by a second haying, followed by the large, barleykorn harvest in mid-August. As fall approached, *lingon*, the tart look-alike and taste-alike of our American cranberry turned the forest floor bright red and we picked these by the box-full for Lisa to preserve in jars, to be eaten all year long on our morning porridge, beef, or moose meat roasts and even on homemade ice cream.

Before leaving Norway to come to the farm, one of the decisions I'd made, in an attempt to learn what had happened to Katrina's mother, was a vow to begin a letter-writing campaign to the German government, which was mostly American military personnel overseeing the bureaucrats. Shortly after settling in at the farm I took a trip to the Mora library and the local hospital to acquire the addresses of health facilities in Germany. There turned out to be a lot of them, so I carefully composed a form letter and had several hundred copies of it printed so that I would only have to sign it, address envelopes, stuff and stamp them. Even then, it was a monumental task. My cousin's family helped me in the evenings and each morning the postman would find a small bundle waiting in the farm's mailbox for him to send on their journey.

I also wrote every sanatorium and mental hospital whose address I could find, asking after her. I presumed she might have suffered any sort of injury causing memory loss. I described her in detail and what she'd been doing, during the war in Norway, in the event they might have someone as a patient about whom they knew nothing. I wrote the occupying American authorities in Berlin and asked them if they had a missing persons department established and received a letter back from a lieutenant saying that there were so many thousands missing, civilian and military, that they still had no means of coping with it. He suggested I contact a newly-formed

Jewish organization that was in the early stages of attempting to build a go-between organization to identify the dead and connect the survivors of the terrible holocaust inflicted on Europe's Jewish population by the *Nazi* regime. I didn't think this organization could offer any help with a non-Jew seeking a non-Jew, though I sympathized with their monumental undertaking.

Over the months of the summer, every week a letter or two would trickle in. At first I was excited to get them, thinking each one would surely bear the news we so much anticipated. I would race the children to be first to get to the mailbox, but the letters either advised me that they had no one fitting the description of Greta, or my own letters simply came back, unopened, undeliverable. Often, someone in the postal service had written "hospital destroyed in the bombing," on the face of the envelope. Only a small proportion of replies returned, in ratio the inquiries I'd sent. Eventually, no more were delivered and I realized I must find another way.

I was getting restless by fall. Like my relatives who'd left Sweden for *Amerika*, a hundred years earlier, seeking some new promise to take them away from their misery in Sweden, America began to look good to me again. I wanted to go home and take Katrina with me to begin life anew. So, before the first snowfall, Katrina and I had a tearful farewell at Frömansgården, leaving *det gamla landet*—the old country, in the early fall.

Everyone assembled in the front yard on the morning of our departure. We'd been milling around all morning since finishing the milking and had eaten a big breakfast. It was a difficult time for everyone. In my cousin's family, no one could begin their normal work routine because we were leaving and they felt they must say a proper goodbye; the cows waited for their feed. We had our lunch packed in advance by Lisa. It was so heavy I could hardly carry it with one hand, to put it in the back of the car.

When the time finally arrived to drive to the railway station to catch the mid-morning train to Borlänge, my cousin's children had started and stopped crying several times as we made promises of how we would write, send photos from America and even visit, maybe, someday. Then the hugs came and the farewell kisses and more tears, as we climbed into the car and my cousin drove us to the station. Katrina was in the back seat sobbing and waving out the back as she watched the only family she could remember, growing smaller and smaller where they stood beside the withered flowerbed at the end of the gravel driveway. She'd been so excited to go, but also so very sad. When the baggage was on the train platform, I got a firm handshake from my cousin, a hug from Lisa and a hearty welcome back to Sweden, from both. We vanished into the coach and took seats just in time to watch as our cousins were going past the window of our railcar, as the train picked up speed.

I had only to decide what to do with the sloop we'd left in western Sweden...and the Volvo, which was easy: I left it at the farm as small payment for nearly two years caring for Katrina. We'd changed and taken a different train from Borlänge, westerly, across Sweden and Norway to the port city of Oslo. There we telephoned *Kaptain* Gustafsson, in the fishing village, but only reached his wife.

"The men are at sea...fishing," she said, "and not expected to return for another week. "Were you going to sell the sailboat," she asked, "or try to sail it across the Atlantic to *Amerika?*"

We told her we could write from America when we settled in, but meanwhile, the *Kaptain* should make arrangements to sell the boat and send the procedes, less a commission for himself, to my cousins in Dalarna...another small payment for the loving care they had given Katrina in my absence.

I gave her the address information and confirmed the selling commission her husband and I had previously agreed upon.

"I will tell him Herr Andersson...have a pleasant journey...you and the child."

"Thank you...we will, I'm sure."

"Oh...before you leave...did you receive the photographs we sent of you and the little one...standing beside your little sailboat, just after you crossed from Danmark?"

"Yes—we did, thank you; I forgot to write you back. They were fine and we appreciated them very much. A reminder of a not so pleasant journey."

"Good...we thought you would like to have them. As you say, something to remind you, in years to come, of your good fortune."

She rang off then and the next day we left for England. We caught a ferry to Hull and a liner across the once treacherous North

Atlantic, safe at last from the U-boats.

Landing in New York City after ten days steaming, we were a small contingent of the total passengers, mostly US servicemen, going home from the European theater. But there was nothing in New York City that interested me; I wanted to go home.

After a couple days of looking at the sights in the city, we took a train to St. Louis and then a bus, home. I didn't feel I wanted to travel again for an awfully long time. The mystery of Greta continued to haunt me. What else could I do? Why was I worrying about looking for someone who was already dead, I told myself? Again...and again...I told myself that.

CHAPTER
35

An American Wedding, 1960

Dora was a coworker from my early Marshall Plan and Berlin Airlift days, right after the war. She and I had maintained a consistent correspondence over the years. So, I was not surprised when she sent me an invitation to her son Ronnie's wedding in *Amerika*. We'd met two years after I received my assignment with the American Army in Berlin and had become fast friends immediately. We continued to work together for over five years during the new German government's implementation of the United States' aid and rehabilitation programs in my new Germany, which was then quickly becoming like a new country to me. Everywhere the evidence of the bombing, poverty and crime were fast disappearing. I was very proud of my part in helping to make this happen. Dora and I worked very hard in those days and we enjoyed every minute of it.

Like most Germans, after the war, I didn't speak much of my experiences during wartime. I never told Dora about my daughter and those early years in *Lebensborn*…or, even my brief encounter with true romance with Johan, or Alex.

I was ashamed of my part in the war, as I became even more aware of what the *Nazi* regime had done in Europe and the part I had myself, played in it: *Lebensborn* and those girls in Norway. Working as hard as I did, I felt I was doing my best to make up for what I considered *my* transgressions. I did my best to remain a loyal public servant, even after my work for the American agency ended and I took a position with the German Social Services Department.

Whenever Dora asked me about what I did in the war...I'd just smile and tell her: "You don't want to know, Dora. You would be ashamed of your friend Greta."

"Surely not, Greta. You're too nice...not at all *that* type."

I wasn't certain what she meant by *that type*. She'd once asked me, hesitantly: "...you didn't really kill any of us...did you Greta...in the war?"

I'd laughed, trying to make light of the question. "Oh no, Dora—of course not...none of the Allies."

I thought my emphasis on the word Allies troubled Dora, but she believed in letting sleeping dogs lie. She was very fond of me and thought me to be a good woman and friend. The feeling was reciprocal.

"Well...I didn't think you would have, Honey, "she'd replied. "I understand how you don't want to talk about the war. A lot of our boys are like that, too, you know. Some of 'em have to have *therapy*—even...tryin' to get over it, 'n all. It's terrible—just terrible. Land sakes...I'm so glad it's over."

We'd always left it at that, coming close—but only so close, before I would gently back away and change the subject. Eventually, it was never mentioned again. Because we worked so well together, we were transferred together, a couple of times, within the organization. First, from Berlin to Bonn, then Düsseldorf and finally, Frankfurt, as we set up new offices and got the gears of government going. Dora was a minor American Government official in the American State Department so she eventually returned to the United States in the early 1950s to marry another State Department bureaucrat she'd met in Europe. It was a second marriage for her, after her soldier-husband was killed early in the Pacific campaign, before she and I met. Dora had three small children by her first husband: Sharon, Ronald and Charles Jr.. I'd known them since they were small children, but once they moved away, I saw them only in the infrequent snapshots sent from various places around the world, as the family traveled with her new husband's, Mark's, jobs.

So, Dora's oldest son Ronnie's wedding was a perfect excuse for Dora to insist I cross the Atlantic at last and visit my old friend and America, for the first time. I reluctantly agreed and began planning for the trip. I'd hardly left Germany since the war's end. Dora and I had taken the three children to England one summer for a sort-of working vacation on the southern seashore. My English was quite good by then, but I still spoke with a slight accent. I still found the English to be a snobbish people, even in the southern, tourist areas. I'd first met Alex there and thought of telling Dora about it as we passed the old Royal Bath Hotel, where the party had been the night Alex and I met. But I decided against opening that part of my life to my friend, for once broached, the subject would never be satisfied by Dora's curious nature.

The English shopkeepers detected my German accent as soon as I opened my mouth. Memories of the war weren't quickly forgotten and they often treated me accordingly. Both Dora and I were happy to be back home after a week's time, tired and sunburned with the three children. That was the last trip we'd taken together, though I still spent a good deal of time with the fatherless family.

Curiously, before Dora met Mark, neither of us went out with men very much. Dora didn't really have the time and I didn't have the inclination, for some reason. At the office, I was asked out more often than Dora. To appease her hurt feelings I told her this was because everyone knew she was a widow with little children. My good looks had come back after the rigors of hunger from my time in prison. Somewhat to my annoyance, I attracted men and that fact seemed to annoy Dora, sometime, threatening the friendship.

I wished they'd just leave me alone. I read a good deal and had acquired a number of 78 phonograph records, both classical and popular, with the American hits being my favorites. Every once in a while I'd revive my fantasy about Alex and I, together again somewhere where they would be playing the tunes and we could dance again.

Finally the time for the wedding arrived and I began the series of airplane rides that would land me in America on the beginning of the weekend. The Atlantic crossing on SABENA went well, but I'd barely made my St. Louis flight connection from New York and was pretty rattled by the time the next aircraft departed. I'd changed to an Ozark Airlines flight which landed me late, in between June thunderstorms, at St. Louis's Lambert Field.

Dora's youngest son Charles...or, Charlie, met the plane in St. Louis, picking me up along with my luggage and a large box of wedding gifts. Together, we'd driven the nearly four hours to Charlie's parent's house, in Southern Missouri, where the wedding would take place the following day, Sunday. It was the hometown of both the bride and groom.

"Everyone always said what a beautiful bride Kate would make," young Charlie commented, after loading my baggage in the car and comfortably seating me in the wide front seat. The automobile seemed so large.

"I look forward to meeting her", I replied, as he swung the car around the parking lot and onto the highway heading south. Then Charlie showed me a photo of his sister-in-law-to-be and the bridegroom. I smiled to myself when I saw how much the groom, Ronnie, had grown and how handsome he now was, since I'd seen them as children in Germany. The bride-to-be, Kate, was truly beautiful. From the photo, she looked tall—nearly as tall as Ronnie, with long, light-brown hair. I enthusiastically agreed with Charles.

"Kate certainly is stunning," I mused aloud. "They will make a lovely couple."

"You got it in one, Aunt Greta."

"Actually...as I examine the photo more closely...she looks rather familiar...somehow."

"Oh? Well, Kate's an orphan, or something," he said, glancing across the wide seat. "Ya' know...I've heard the story a hundred times...but I can't remember the details. Her father's Robert Johnson—the guy who adopted her. Anyway—he raised her, but he wasn't her dad."

As we drove along the river road, paralleling the great Mississippi River, Charlie filled me in on the lives of himself and his siblings, going into humorous antidotes about Kate's habit of practical joking, recounting some of the pranks she was constantly playing on her friends, his brother and himself. Now and then he would point out some landmark of local, historical interest. I'm afraid I didn't know what he was talking about, most of the time. I knew very little about America.

My mind wandered as I watched the Mississippi River scenery passing. It seemed Kate liked to tease and was a regular prankster, but she also possessed a well-balanced sense of humor of her own, Charlie recounted. With his spirited description of these antics, the foursome friendship gradually came to life.

Apparently, Ronnie and Kate had only become serious about one other after college. Charles' animated conversation kept the wearisome ride to the small town from becoming too boring. The scenery along the mighty river reminded me of my own River Rhine, though on a far larger scale. It was dark when we arrived at Mark and Dora's house.

"You're just in time for a midnight snack..." Dora said through tears of joy as she hugged me several times in the foyer. Charlie filled his mom in on the arrival in St. Louis and the drive home, as we carried the luggage up to my room, formerly occupied by one of the children.

"Mark's not home yet...Honey; he's haulin' stuff back from the party at the restaurant. It was an after rehearsal dinner, but it was almost too much for me," she added, stepping back and holding her stomach with one hand, the other on my shoulder.

"I'm sorry your flight came so late that you had to miss the shindig tonight. I couldn't do any more than nibble, though...I was so frazzled—between thinkin' about you comin' in, 'n wonderin' how everything was goin',' to thinkin' about tomorrow. Oh...! But, I'm hungry now, Honey. I'm so happy your plane landed all right. Now, it's just like all the family's here now, 'n so good to see you," she said turning me toward the kitchen and pushing from behind as we descended the stairway.

Dora saw me seated at the plastic-topped table in her American kitchen: "I'm so happy you decided to come over for the wedding, Honey...I know Ronnie and Kate...they feel real honored that you did."

"Thanks, Dora." I was wiping away my own tears. "It is so good to see you, too...and the children. Charlie...oh how he has changed...a young man now."

Dora pulled a chair away from the table but then changed her mind and opened a monstrous refrigerator. "Let's see...."

I glanced around the neat kitchen. There were assorted items hanging from the walls, an embroidered work of an old kitchen stove, with a tea pot steaming and the words "home-sweet-home" embroidered in cross-stitch. A white plastic clock, shaped like a sitting cat hung beside it. An electrical cord hung precariously close to the cat's tail, which wagged slowly as the second hand went around.

"Will it be a large wedding, Dora?"

"Hundred 'n fifty—at least...makes me wish I'd had more girls, dear...but, I may change my mind after tomorrow. Now..." she turned from the open refrigerator doorway, "...just sit there while I get us a snack. Then you can hit the hay...bet you're tired, aren't 'cha Hon?"

"That bed will feel very good to me, Dora."

"I'll bet."

"Charlie is such a dear young man. His chatter kept me awake...such stories. I was entertained the whole way and he is so interesting and chatty...I know you're proud of them all."

"Oh Charlie's somethin', he is."

I chuckled, remembering. "He told me stories about his brother and his future in-laws. You've done such a good job with him, Dora."

She took a seat beside me and exhaled loudly. We finished our snack, chatting and laughing until I finally begged to go to my room. I unpacked my nightgown and carried it into the large bathroom, where I showered and then collapsed onto the firm bed. There were colorful posters taped to the wall and statues on the shelves, probably collected by one of the children from the various countries they'd grown up in. There were also tarnished trophies awarded for American sports I was unfamiliar with: basketball and football. A photograph of Mark and Dora, taken early in their marriage, stared back at me from the bedside table. That was the last thing I saw before turning off the table lamp. I drew up the bed linen beneath my chin and thought to myself. How quiet it is, I thought, other than that constant humming buzz that Dora said was caused by thousands of insects, outside. There was no traffic to disturb my thoughts. Well…here I am in Amerika, at last,,,the place and the people who have meant so much in my life, since the war. Who would have guessed how much an enemy would influence my life in the positive.

The bird's chatter was so loud the next morning, it must have wakened me. I got out of bed and drew aside the curtain, wondering whether Mark and Dora kept exotic birds in their back garden. It would be a fine wedding day, I thought, yawning and looking down on the neatly-trimmed grass. Unfamiliar birds hopped and scratched in the closely-cropped grass. The sun was bright, splashing through the large trees surrounding the house. The trees harbored more of the whistling, chirping and chattering birds. The garden was just like a park, everything was so neat.

"America is naturally a land of music," I muttered to myself—how do they ever sleep late here with that much bird noise?"

After I'd had a wake-up shower, I sat on the bed looking out the window and enjoying the bird calls, still in full force. Eventually the quiet was interrupted by the sound of a motor. I presumed it was a grass cutter, but finally decided it was a noisy airplane and finally saw it, high overhead, looping, diving and spinning around. It was an old fashioned biplane and that made me think of Alex, so I sighed and got up and began dressing.

It wasn't long before I heard stirrings elsewhere in the house. The rest of the family were also up early. After all, I thought, happily, it's somebody's wedding day.

Downstairs, I met Dora's husband Mark, again, after more than fifteen years. He was still a jolly man whose personality now nearly equaled that of his wife, though he wasn't the one in the family in charge and he didn't talk as much; I think Dora had worn him down.

After breakfast I helped Mark, Sharon and Charlie fill Charlie's car with gaily-wrapped gifts, delivered earlier to their home by friends who wouldn't be attending the service. Afterward, we lingered for a while over breakfast coffee, as a family, skipping church in order to catch up on the old days and new happenings in our lives. Before I knew it Dora signaled that we'd better retire to our rooms to begin dressing for the wedding, which we did, eventually, assembling again, this time in the "front room," as Dora called it. When everyone was there, Dora decided we should go.

It was as we were going out the door, the telephone began ringing.

"Oh, Mark...will you get it. I'm too warm to run back in. We'll wait here on the porch. Tell ém we're on our way to a wedding; goodness."

Mark smiled and did as he was told.

"People just don't think, you know, Greta? Everybody in this whole town knows we've got a wedding in the family today...and they call now. What do they expect?

We strolled down the sidewalk and got inside the warm automobile, leaving the doors open, but staring at the door. No one spoke, watching for Mark who eventually appeared, locking the door before loping over to the car and poking his head through the driving-side door.

"Well...?" Dora probed annoyance in her voice that he didn't report immediately, "...what did they want?"

"It was Kate, Dora...Robert...they just found Robert over in the cemetery. He...they took him to the hospital in Cape...he's had a heart attack, according to Doc Woolsey. It's...Kate said it was pretty bad. He couldn't talk...he wasn't conscious."

"Oh, God! What're we gonna do now, Mark? Everything's ready! The guests will all be here...Greta's come from Germany...the food, gifts...oh, Mark...do they think he'll be all right?

"Kate was crying pretty hard and...she didn't say. I don't suppose they know, yet."

"What should we do?"

Kate suggested we go to the church as planned. It's still another...nearly two hours until the wedding. She said she may have some news before then. If there's no change in his condition, she said she would hurry back, quickly go through with the ceremony and then return to the hospital, skipping the reception to be with Robert, when he regains consciousness. She said, that way, everyone wouldn't have come in vain."

Mark drove us to the church with Charlie and Sharon following in their car. Mark and Dora quietly discussed potential changes to the day, while I looked at the different houses we were passing in the small town. Though we were a little early, Dora said it was the proper thing to do..."to help out where we can," she'd said, leaning over the front seat. Mark promptly disappeared with his arms loaded, as did Charlie and Sharon.

Carrying as many gifts as I could, I was soon installed in the church basement at a table beside a very flustered Dora, opening and arranging the accumulated cards and gifts. I was already feeling tired and wondered whether I was beginning to experience a little flying lag from the previous day's flight. What a thing to happen. I felt so sorry for the bride...Kate. Her father, Robert, seemed to be so well respected by everyone and to have this happen less than two hours before his daughter would marry.

The ceremony would be followed by a reception and meal in the basement, catered by a church women's organization. I'd been introduced to the chairwoman of this group, whose name I'd forgotten shortly after she'd bustled off on an unknown errand of her own. Behind a counter that resembled a cafeteria, several of these ladies were busy with the reception food preparation. Some worked in the kitchen and others at the many tables spaced around the basement. They chattered and gossiped as they worked, arranging plates and cutlery. Of course the topic of Robert's condition was the subject. Dora and I worked at our own table, receiving and arranging the incoming wedding presents as neatly as we could.

"I'm surprised I'm feeling tired already, Dora. Could it be the time difference?"

Dora was mumbling to herself as she shuffled among the gifts, arranging them on the other side of a large table, for later display to the guests, during he reception.

"Could be Greta...look, this is Kate when she was a child."

Dora waved a framed photograph in my direction. A gangly, eleven or twelve year old Kate stared out of the enlarged studio photograph, smiling brightly at the camera, for what appeared to be an old school photograph. She looks familiar, I thought and very gangly. But there's a certain energy there, too. I laid the photo on the table as Dora walked to the other end of the table.

"Oh—it's here somewhere. There...look at this one...this was taken in Europe—somewhere, during the war. Robert—he's her dad...he told us that last night at dinner.

Dora had picked up another, smaller photograph that was still partially wrapped.

"He gave her this, sort of as a rehearsal gift, I guess. We asked him if we could bring it today—keep it unwrapped...so the wedding guests could look at it during the reception. Robert—he's so easy goin'—he said it was OK with him. Imagine, finding it after all these years in an ol' foot locker, he said.."

She finished unwrapping the photograph and held it up briefly. I couldn't see it from my side of the table and she wasn't holding it still, anyway.

"He had it done up—enlarged...as one of those memory wedding presents for them; sort of unique, isn't it?"

She waved it in my direction again before turning it over and polishing the glass against her hip.

"He said it was one of the only mementos he had from her early childhood, outside of her baby clothes."

She stared at the photo for a moment and then turned back toward me.

"She was a *DP* [12]...during the war you know Greta? Robert...he adopted her—brought her back. Imagine, him without a wife, too. He said he'd known her family over there and he was the only one still alive who did, so he felt it was up to him to bring her back to America with him and be his little girl. Wasn't that special of him? He's like that, you know...you'll like him *Hon*. Here...look—Greta."

I'd been unwrapping another gift, which I then put down among the jumble of paper steadily filling the table. I glanced across where Dora was holding the photo out for me, but she turned it around again and pointed to the man I cold barely make out.

"That's her dad...Robert? Wasn't he handsome? He told us this was taken right after he rescued her from the *Nazis*. They sailed across the ocean to get away from them...imagine. Wouldn't it have been frightening, Greta—taking a small child alone in only a little, bitty sailboat?

I'd nearly winced at the word *Nazi*, cringing inwardly, but smiled outwardly. "It certainly was, Dora." I'd gotten accustomed to hearing the word used, again and again, over the years and hearing Dora use it now didn't bother me that much.

"*Dora*...telephone...."

We glanced up; one of the ladies in the kitchen was holding up a telephone and pointing, beckoning to Dora.

"Here, Hon...take this," she told me. "I've gotta take a call. Might be something about Robert."

Dora stepped further along the table toward me, holding the picture out as she passed.

I stepped around and took it as she rushed past. The photo wasn't much bigger than a wallet snapshot. There was something about the man's posture that immediately caught my eye. I cocked my head, bending closer, squinting at the photo and recognized Alex Andersson holding a child.

I gave a sudden exclamation. Putting one hand up to my mouth I stared at the man in the photo, my total attention captured by the male figure and the small child he held cradled in his right arm. Blond hair peeked around the child's winter cap. The enlarged, monochrome photo was old but still quite clear, though a bit out of place in the modern frame. It was wintertime in the photo. The man—Alex, was holding a child wrapped in old-fashioned, heavy wool clothing, common in the '40s. The man wore a dark sailor jacket and bulky pants. They were standing on a dock somewhere, in front of a sailboat. The scene behind them was a typical harbor, somewhere I didn't recognize. Oh...could it be...I wondered? Can it truly be them? After all these years?

I realized I'd staggered a little and grasped at the table's edge for support. I could feel the blood draining from my head. It must be the time difference I'd heard someone in the airport talking about. I glanced around the room, looking for somewhere to sit down. Dropping the photo atop the wrapping paper, I stumbled toward a row of folding chairs that lined the nearby basement wall. The photo was definitely Alex and taken around the same age as when I'd known him. And Katrina...it had to be my daughter Sophia—Katrina—Kate, now, they called her...that made sense. I sat there, breathing deeply, watching Dora in the kitchen. She was holding the phone to one ear and was covering her other ear against the clink of cutlery, china and women's conversation.

No question, it was Alex in the photo. Where would he have been sailing? That's what Dora had said, earlier, escaping the Nazis? The harbor didn't look familiar. Of course it could be anywhere. He was still young in the photo. Oh, it had been so long. Could I be mistaken? There were no harbors near where the old couple had lived with the child. None near Köln, either; Denmark, that was the closest. That farm where I'd gone was kilometers inland from the sea.

I stood up and walked back around the table and peered down at the photograph without picking it up. Alex was smiling slightly at the camera, but not the child. Both looked the worse for wear, either because they were tired, or because it was very cold and they wished to get out of the weather. The pair had a huddled look about them. Alex had the start of a beard and the little girl looked thin and hollow-eyed—not very well-fed. Or, she'd been ill, possibly. But the way the two fit together...there was something. Like they belonged, they were related...a pair. So much acceptance was reflected in their stature, especially the way the child clung to Alex.

So what should I make of this? So many scenarios have I put through my mind in the years past, to add yet another. The only conclusion I had before was that, somehow—Alex had gotten the true, adopted name of my daughter. Could he also have gotten my daughter...taken her out of Germany? If so, how did he snatch her from the hungry mouth of the camps? The photo...I leaned closer, looking again at the little girl. This child would be about the correct age for Katrina. It is also likely that she would be blond, coming as she did from blond German parents...if it was Katrina?

Where was Alex from, in America? How old would Katrina be now? Was she of marriageable age? Yes, certainly...by now. The newspaper date...Alex had written December, 1943...she would now be...oh, I can not think—in her twenties, possibly. I've gone over this so many times. She was born in.... I closed my eyes and tried to think.

I can see the frame of the photo—how important an item it has become, innocently lying there on the table, now nearly hidden by the raft of gifts. What would he look like today...Alex? Is his family here—the family of the bride? Certainly, they would be hosting the wedding...that was the custom. I haven't met either parent of the bride, or, even the bride yet, so I can still not be certain. What will I do...or say, when I see him? Or, to his wife, the mother who raised my daughter...if she is my daughter...if he has a wife, now? And if she isn't mine...I thought for a moment: what will I do? I don't want more disappointment. How could it ever be...this coincidence...so long in coming, so far away? I remember now...didn't Dora say he did not have a wife? Or, was that only when he found the child—Kate? Could he have a wife now, twenty-something years later?

I watched the coming and going of the guests, guessing at their ages and occupations. It was all still so new...Americans—*Amerika*...their manner of dress and the American sound of their voices. I feel like I am back in the old office in Berlin, working with Major Osborne.

I closed my eyes. I'd so enjoyed my position there, especially in the beginning. It was a time for joy and for great disappointment, too, later. When the Major finally informed me that it appeared they would never be able to locate my pilot friend and learn whether he had, in fact, actually found my little daughter, I thought I'd die. The depression lasted for years, knowing I'd lost both of them.

I put my head back and let the sound of the guest's voices blend together, lulling me, leaving me with my own thoughts. I'd arranged a holiday shortly after the Major's depressing news about not finding Alex. The Major was very understanding and urged me to try to put the matter to rest so I could get on with my life. I didn't tell him, but I took my holiday at the old places...the places where I was a *Nazi*, hoping something would jog my memory. It wasn't the same, though, visiting again—Norway and then Sweden. Returning to Bergen, Oslo and to Stockholm, not so much on the off chance I would encounter him, but to again see the places we'd been...places where we had interacted together as a couple.

The Norwegians were very anti-German after the war. And because of the large number of children with Norwegian mothers and German soldier fathers, they treated these mothers very badly, considering them traitors to their country and to Norwegian men.

All sorts of bad things were done to them, I heard. Their offspring are now maturing all over Norway—Europe, for that matter. Feelings against me would have been very, very adverse, had anyone known what I'd done. The *Lebensborn* affair was best left unmentioned—best forgotten. But I couldn't, completely, as it had occupied most of my early years.

And who could blame them…the young, German soldiers were mostly kind and lonely themselves? I know the girls weren't all persuaded to go with a German man…by *my program*. Many simply went because they wished to have a man…sex. So many of their own men were away, hiding from us, in the north, or elsewhere. Many were fighting from the mountains. And of course, many were also dead. Nevertheless, it was a very sensitive subject. I knew enough to avoid any government offices, or other areas where I might encounter anyone who could possibly recognize and remember me and my part in the earlier *Nazi* occupation.

Getting off the streetcar in Oslo, I was surprised to find my little house gone and the whole block replaced by a large apartment complex. Whether destroyed by bombs or simply demolished to accommodate the growing population, I didn't know. Nothing remained to remind me of the little rear garden where we had shared Alex's coffee and talked that special spring day, growing to know and understand one another. I'd planned to visit the old message drop sites, too. Already, I'd learned one that was in Stockholm had disappeared, an old mailbox, located in an alley and unused by the building. And all of the others, both in Stockholm and Oslo, were also empty. Of course there was no sign they'd been used for anything in years.

By the time I'd drawn a fifth blank in Oslo, I'd grown so emotionally overwrought. I simply couldn't remember where the last drop was located and I eventually gave up, as I was becoming too depressed. And that was the way the whole excursion ended. I was definitely not uplifted, or put at peace about the whole affair…not at all; but then I guess I never expected to be. It had been my own fault for ever opening those old wounds by revisiting old places, old memories. The wounds had only been blunted with time, not erased.

If I persisted by thinking too long about Katrina and Alex, the pain would return, fresh and sharp.

But now that I think I've found him again...and possibly her, too, what should I do. Am I too late? If I am, can I get myself through the wedding without breaking down? I sat down again for a few moments, trying to quiet my heart. The coolness of the wall returned each time I moved my head even slightly and it felt good.

"Oh...the organ..." I said aloud, opening my eyes. The sound of playing vibrated the church floor above my head. Footsteps overhead hinted that the guests were beginning to assemble and take their seats. Sure enough, Dora is walking my way with a tall, young man carrying a tuxedo jacket. I got up slowly as they approached. I suspected it was Ronnie. I could tell from the photos she'd sent over the years; he was smiling broadly, freshly scrubbed with a red carnation boutonniere in his jacket lapel.

"Well Ronnie, here she is. All that way after all this time. Greta, do you remember this guy?"

"Ronnie..." I smiled at him as he grinned down at me. He seemed slightly embarrassed to be wearing formal clothing. He certainly didn't look like the same child I'd known in Germany.

"Hello Aunt Greta." His voice was deep and very manly, belying his impish countenance. I held up my arms to be hugged. After a bear hug I seemed to relax.

"I remember a little guy—not this fabulous example of a man. My, how you have grown, Ronnie."

"*Gutentag*, Aunt Greta..." Ronnie clumsily tried his childhood German.

"Hah...you remember! How hard I worked with you to learn some German. I'm so pleased you've kept it."

I gave him another hug, patting his broad back. "I am sorry to hear about your father-in-law, Ronnie. This is going to be a wedding day to remember, for both of us."

"Yes, thank you Aunt Greta. Kate's fit to be tied with..."

"That was the hospital on the telephone, Hon; Kate's on her way over. There was no change in Robert's condition, so she decided to hurry over and get the ceremony over with...what an awful way to think about your wedding." Dora nervously glanced around the room, taking in the final preparations, looking toward the stairway and glancing at her wristwatch.

"And to think, I was so worried about keeping him away from Kate...the big fool. He knows he's not supposed to see the bride on her wedding day...until the ceremony, but that's all changed, now."

Smiling, Ronnie ignored his mother as he put on his jacket with her help. Over his shoulder, Dora frowned: "He has some joke or other he wanted to play on Kate...honestly...and to think you're getting married in a few minutes...oh, so...*juvenile.*"

"I really look forward to meeting your *fiancé,* Ronnie," I said, winking at him to cushion his mother's remark, "she looks..."

Dora interrupted me. "Ronnie...it's time, Hon. Sorry, Greta...you'll have to save it for the reception. There'll be plenty of time to catch up." Turning to her son, she pushed him forward. "Greta will be here for a while and you two can talk later."

"OK Mom. See you later, Aunt Greta...thanks for coming. You're gonna love Kate...just wait."

"I'm certain I will, Ronnie."

"OK, Greta...lets..."

The woman from the kitchen interrupted her again.

"It's the hospital on the phone again, Dora...?"

"Oh...I hope nothing's happened, 'n Kate's probably almost here. Hang on Greta...let me take the call. Then we'll go upstairs."

I went back to the gift table to wait, once again, picking up the little framed photo of the man and child. I tried to read the expressions of the pair, once more. Alex looked steadfast, decisive and committed...a man to be reckoned with. If in fact it was Alex (I knew it was), he was all of those things, at least as I knew him. But the child, she was too young to read much other than the way she held onto Alex, like she'd made a decision that this was someone she wanted to be with, be a part of.

"Greta..." Dora had come up behind me and I turned to face her, the photo in one hand. There were tears in her eyes.

"That was the hospital. Robert has just died."

"I'm sorry, Dora."

He didn't even wake up first, Greata. Doc Woolsey called to say someone here should meet Kate...a friend, someone who loves her, to make it...easier."

I stood looking calmly at Dora, as I had stood so many times in my life: stoic, hard, steadfast...unmoved by the news my friend imparted. Like when Major Osborne told me there would be no Alex in my life. I didn't weep in front of the Major. All these years...I'd convinced myself, long ago and I knew it could never be; that's why I lived the fantasies...Alex and I...dancing, meeting, talking...in my daydreams, going to the movies. I'd never been without him.

"Oh...Greta...Robert was *such* a nice, nice man. You would have loved him. I know you would have."

I took my friend by the hand. "Dora...I think I already have. Can we sit down for a moment? There is something I need to tell you. Something you need to know...before Kate arrives.

-- The End --

Afterword:

My Enemies Child

It is mid-March 2003 as I labor to edit this volume for the second time (of an eventual six times). Much of my research materials for WWII in Europe surround my work station. Depicting parts of Scandinavia, Central Europe and England, they also include descriptions of bombing destruction and photographs, both from the air and the ground. At ready-reference, even taped on my wall, these graphic reminders of the horrors that transpired from the round the clock Allied bombing in Germany, are stark and graphic. Photographs of this particular war's aftermath include bombed-out, burned-out shells of the once-beautiful German cities of Köln, Berlin and Dresden. Some of the illustrations depict body-strewn streets with civilian corpses lying akimbo in the aftermath of the fire storms created by the indifferent Allied bombs. The American's by day and the British by night, meticulous in the end, executing a plan, doing a thorough job of war.

From numerous television documentaries, vivid, visual memories of concentration camp dead already lingered in my consciousness, and were unnecessary now, to complete the mental image of this piece of work, wrought by the once-popular *Nazis* political regime in Germany.

I make no particular judgements about either *side*, for the folly is *man's* folly. Stupidity knows neither nationality nor frontier. Many Germans committed atrocities at the time in the name of *Nazism*, but all German people were not evil. Like us, most were mere human beings, on the *other side* and also subject to the human frailties of persuasion, self-deception and cowardice, especially, given the distressing times.

As I write this after word, four of the world's *powers* are struggling with the United Nations for a final resolution for the once-great Saddam Hussein, before unleashing a concentrated (hopefully) version of something far worse upon the country of Iraq. I suspect that country will be struck before the week is out, possibly before tomorrow's nightfall over the Middle East and the playground bully *will finally be taken to the office*. May Allah and God and all other Deities, forgive we meager men our mutual stupidities.

For, when we *succeed* in liberating and democratizing the Middle East, they can then join us in the over-consumption of *their* petroleum resources, assist us in further savaging our respective environments and encouraging cultural emphasis on and toward fostering even more consumer-orientated societies, in their neighbors around the *Gulf.*

Surely, it would have been far easier and less bloody, to issue each and every Iraqi a credit card with a $10,000 credit to spend, then recruit them to labor in constructing a few thousand department stores across the Middle East, paying them a good wage all the while. There would be little time to fight and little will...as they got on with it. Time will tell.

I doubt a book of any size or historical accuracy comes about without help from many quadrants and this work is no exception. The espionage theme from this work was born during an interview I once did for the director of Radio Sweden's English Programming Service, the details, though, are all mine and are pure fiction, including, of course, the characters.

The story structure is the same, fabricated from a seed story idea: a neutral aviator with access to the whole of Scandinavia and much of Europe and a tragic but beautiful, female, Nazi agent. But it is certainly a fact that many Americans, eager to get into the fighting before America came into the war, joined the Royal Air Force (RAF) in Canada and eventually became part of the American Eagle Squadron, fighting and beating back the German *Luftwaffe*, before America finally came into the war, after the attack on Pearl Harbor.

The protagonist in this work, however, predated that period, as I'd not yet encountered that particular piece of American bravery and history. Though, I did draw upon the knowledge of a member of that daring group of early American combatants, as I credit earlier in the acknowledgments.

Footnotes -- Footnotes

[1] *GIC* – Ground Intercept Control. The ground-based control room which tracked all incoming enemy bomber flights and coordinated RAF fighters to intercept them, usually over southern England.

[2] *TR9D* – The rather unreliable radios often picked up commercial BBC radio broadcast signals intermixed with fighter and enemy pilot conversations.

[3] *Mil Org* - Military Organization; the Norwegian resistance organization, re-supplied by airdrops from England.

[4] *Major Vidkum Abraham Lauritz Quisling* (July 18 1887, died by firing squad October 24, 1945), organized founder of the Norwegian Nazi Party in 1933 as well as his *Regiment Nordland.* He was never fully trusted by the Germans to govern Norway during occupation and was branded "traitor" after the war.

[5] The *New Forest* — a tract of land comprising some 45,000 acres (150 sq. miles) located in southern England. It was set aside over nine centuries ago by William The Conqueror as a private hunting preserve for himself and his followers.

[6] *Fäbod* — a secluded, rural location in Scandinavia, consisting of a collection of one or more small houses and farm buildings, usually located in the forest, often mountainous. Livestock were driven there to summer pasture by the families where old women, or young girls who would remain, cared for the animals through the summer and processed the resulting animals milk into cheese and butter from the twice daily milking.

[7] Many Norwegians never forgave Sweden for occupying their country for several hundred years and a *friendly* rivalry yet remains (also with the Danes), some of which may be left over from W.W. II when Norway and not Sweden, was invaded and occupied by the Nazis. Strangely (to the Norway Norwegians), today, this angst is even stronger, among remaining descendents of Norwegians in America today.

[8] *Ninety Day Wonder* — Early pilots had a mere 90 days of flight training before being sent into combat.

[9] *Bunad* - Colorful, Norwegian folk costume-replicas of clothes worn in the 18th and 19th centuries.

[10] *Røros pols* — is a dance from the area around *Røros*, in east central Norway, which has three basic steps.

[11] German military had by this time developed a "secret weapon," a form of tracking radar with antennae attached to the nose of their fighters. This permitted the fighters to maneuver in closely at night, completely undetected by the RAF bombers. Once they were in position beneath the bomber group, they would use another new weapon, upward-firing guns called *schrage musica*...meaning, slanting music. It was very effective against RAF Bomber Command who sustained heavy losses from this stealthy tactic.

[12] *DF Steer* (direction fix steering) — The process whereby one or two radio control centers located in England would monitor the strength of an incoming bomber's radio transmission signal and triangulate the source. They would then report to the bomber pilot the angular degree(s) from north, from which they received the radio transmission signal. This information would tell the bomber's navigator the following: if only one station reported the signal, only the angular direction could be offered, but if two or more stations reported to him, the inbound course to fly and the known distance from the transmission point could be determined.

[13] "L" — The mention of an "L" in the identity papers for children of the Lebensborn Project is pure fiction on the author's part

[14] DP — "Displaced Person," slang expression given many European refugees from US government personnel.